THE LEGEND MAKERS

Kate Cameron

BALLANTINE BOOKS • NEW YORK

Copyright © 1995 by Beverly McGlamry

All rights reserved under International and Pan-American Copyright Conventions. Published in the United States by Ballantine Books, a division of Random House, Inc., New York, and simultaneously in Canada by Random House of Canada Limited, Toronto.

Library of Congress Catalog Card Number: 95-94541

ISBN 0-345-38058-4

Manufactured in the United States of America

First Edition: December 1995

10 9 8 7 6 5 4 3 2 1

Congratulations to my adopted state
FLORIDA
On the occasion of its Sesquicentennial
(1845–1995)

It isn't truly Paradise; Eden never offered the contrast and controversy, the drama and diversity, that are as much a part of Florida today as they were in the sixteenth century. Nor did Eden have within its borders a unique wilderness called the Everglades.

There is still a parallel to be drawn, however, and it is not a pretty one: Ignorance and greed led to the loss of Eden; and now that same ignorance and greed are persuading us to destroy a magnificent river of grass that has no counterpart anywhere in the world. If action is not taken to prevent it, then Florida—like Eden—may soon find itself without an Everglades.

Once again, man will have deprived himself of something irreplaceable.

—Kate Cameron

Acknowledgments

For their help, advice or support during the writing of this novel, I would like to thank:

Becky Smith, Research Section, Historical Museum of Southern Florida.

The staff of the Miami Lakes/Palm Springs North Branch, Dade County Library System.

Theresa and Paul Rousseau, my hosts on Florida's west coast (and special thanks to Theresa for acting as guide while I explored what used to be Calusa territory).

Donald and Pat Randell of Pineland, Florida, for allowing me to investigate the Calusa Indian mound that makes an exciting place of their backyard.

Marjory Stoneman Douglas, Grande Dame of Conservation, whose book, *The Everglades: River of Grass*, was both inspiration and challenge to me.

Gigi Rounds of Hayward, California, for letting me use her daughter's lovely name for Kwambu's daughter.

The members of the Writers Group for their perceptive critiquing.

And, of course, my family, for their patience and understanding.

—Kate Cameron

La Florida

NOTE: The experts disagree on whether Narvaez and De Soto came ashore at Charlotte Harbor or at Tampa Bay. For the purposes of this novel, I have used the Charlotte Harbor site favored by Henry E. Dobyns and David O. True. I have placed Calusa's town on the small island in Estero Bay described by Rolfe Schell in his book *1000 Years on Mound Key* (Island Press, Florida, 1962).

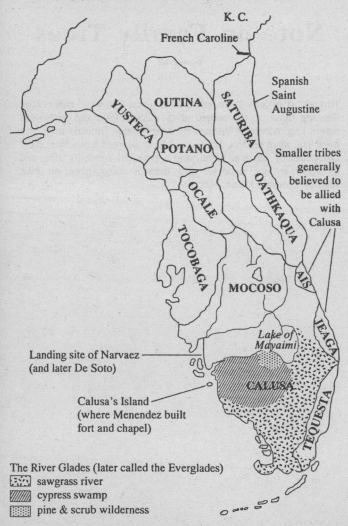

Note on Family Trees

⬤— —⬤

To make it easier for readers, I have given two-word names (e.g. Dancing Egret) to the people of the Calusa tribe and three-word names (e.g. Moon of Winter) to those of the Timucua tribe. For tribal and town leaders, however, I have adopted a practice of the Europeans of that era: identifying a principal town, its tribe, and its leader, by one name (or title; there is disagreement on this), such as Calusa, Outina, Mocoso.

CALUSA

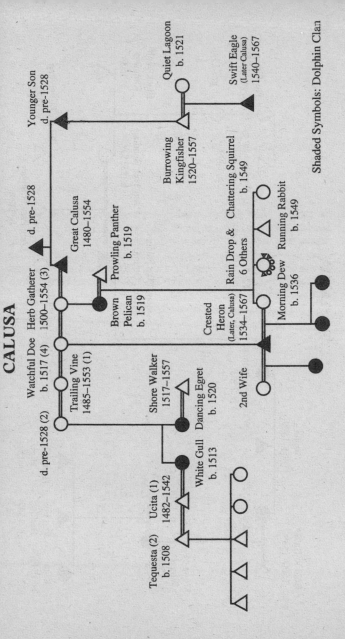

Shaded Symbols: Dolphin Clan

TIMUCUA

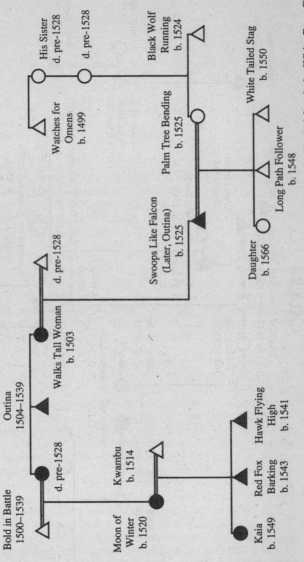

Shaded Symbols: White Deer Clan

Prologue

⬗ ⬗

The beach glittered in the midday sun. Yesterday's thunderstorm had swept it clean of all but finely fragmented shells and a ribbon of brown seaweed that showed how far the wind-driven water had encroached upon this section of Calusa's island. Five men, moving with the easy gait of people accustomed to walking great distances without tiring, stepped onto the gulf-facing crescent at a point midway between its sandy cusps. The tallest, a lean yet substantial man whose long black hair was embroidered with gray, looked to the right to inspect the conch-shell rampart standing between town and sea, then turned to scan the opposite end of the cove. He was already striding toward the figures sprawled on the farther shore before his companions even realized that the beach was not as empty as it had seemed.

By the time they caught up with him, he was crouching over the nearer figure, that of a lanky boy whose face was partially turned into the sand. Clearly, the waves had swallowed him up, then spat him out among the waving sea oats.

"A boat," the tall one muttered. "They must have come from a boat." Standing up, he shielded his black eyes with one hand and peered out over the water. "There is no debris floating out there, however, and we saw no wreckage on any of the other beaches." He looked again at the youth, nudged him with one bare foot. "Can it be that the fools tried to swim ashore from some sailing vessel?"

The eyelid on the exposed side of the youth's face fluttered, lifted, drooped once more. The tall man glanced over at the second boy. Quicker to regain consciousness, he had been hauled to his feet by the two men sent to see to him. The tall man grunted at the sight of immature features skewed by a

1

mixture of alarm and exhaustion. "Take that one to the Arawak village," he called. "He will lose the fear that shames him when he is among others from his home island."

As he spoke, the boy he stood over opened his eyes again, grimaced, and lifted his head out of the sand. His gaze touched on oversized callused toes, then traveled slowly up a remarkable length of legs and torso. It came to rest on a chiseled face in which a jutting nose cast ominous shadow over a slitted mouth.

Unlike the Arawak youngster, this boy's features did not twist with apprehension when he understood that he was at the mercy of possibly hostile near-giants. Instead, the youth coughed to reclaim the man's attention, then gathered in his gangly arms and legs and attempted to jump to his feet.

The tall man made no effort to help him when he stumbled, and showed no flicker of emotion when he succeeded in righting himself. He remained impassive as the youth spread trembling legs and—making valiant effort to show contempt for the pair of spear bearers who had come to flank the older man—spoke in a voice that had not yet achieved depth.

"You may stick me with your blades," he said fiercely, "yet however much I bleed, I will not cower before you. I have had enough of groveling."

He used the language of the Arawak people, used it perfectly; yet something in the inflection he gave to certain words told his listeners that this was not his native tongue. And he certainly did not look Arawak.

After a long silence, during which the boy clung to his defiance despite the tightening of warrior fingers around efficient-looking weapons, the tall man threw back his head and roared with laughter. "The cub that snarls when he is cornered," he said when his mirth subsided, "will be a wolf to be wary of when he is grown. Besides"—he stretched out one huge hand and poked at the youth's narrow chest—"I have never seen flesh so dark. It is black as a moonless night, this flesh."

He turned and began to walk away. "Bring the boy to my house," he said over his shoulder to the warriors still standing guard. "I have decided that such a bold-spirited lad should serve no one but Headchief Calusa."

PART I

1528–1541

Chapter 1

⬛ ⬛

A panther's scream shattered the golden afternoon.

The sound might have been taken for the shriek of a woman in agony; predator cats often fooled the ignorant with their oddly human yowling. But this cry had been made by neither woman nor beast; it had come from the warrior patrolling the sea-pointing causeway bordering the canal. When it was repeated, the people of the village reacted immediately.

White Gull, newest of Chief Ucita's four wives, erupted from the house perched upon the taller of the village's two mounds. She leaped down the shell pyramid's stepped ramp, scanning the plaza below as she descended. Women were catching up small children and summoning older ones to their sides. Warriors, with spears, bows, and death hurlers at the ready, shouted questions to the sentry who had given the alarm. Elders cradled infant grandchildren as they gently but efficiently herded the rest of the villagers in the direction of the dense mangrove thickets that marked the eastern limits of Ucita's town.

Where oh where was Dancing Egret? White Gull's heart pounded as her eyes continued to search the rapidly emptying square. Her sister was scarcely eight years old, and the two of them had come here only six short months ago. But, White Gull reminded herself, the signal to flee at once was the same in Ucita's town as it had been on their father's island, and she had made certain that Dancing Egret understood what she must do the moment she heard the distinctive sound.

A taggle of ruddy-skinned youngsters raced up from the beach, sped across the open space between the mounds and caught up with the mothers who had deliberately kept to the rear of the decamping crowd. Soon the boys and their mothers

5

had disappeared from view, and only warriors remained in the plaza.

Dancing Egret was too much inclined to go off on her own, and White Gull the matron could not watch over her as closely as White Gull the maiden had. The young woman tensed her muscles, prepared to sprint toward the causeway. From its summit she might be able to spot the child she'd taken care of ever since their mother had died in the season following Egret's birth. Fear filled White Gull's stomach with wriggling eels.

Then she heard her name called out and spun around to see Kneeling Cypress, Ucita's fifteen-year-old daughter, approaching on the run. Holding tight to Cypress's hand was Dancing Egret.

White Gull grabbed the little girl's free hand and tugged the pair toward the plaza. "Hurry!" she said sharply. "The rest have already gone to the mangroves."

Cypress nodded toward the top of the mound. "My father's other wives," she said. "Has he sent them away as well?"

White Gull neither knew nor cared about the three women who had lately begun making mock of her because she had not yet conceived a baby. White Gull cared even less about Ucita, who, if he came at all to her bed, never went beyond fumbling caresses. As though fondling a woman's breasts was enough to beget a child! But she could not say this to the man's own daughter, even though she and Kneeling Cypress were nearly the same age. And there was no time for explanations anyway.

"*Must* we go to the thicket?" Dancing Egret gasped as they put the town behind them. "That tree"—she wrenched one hand free and pointed at a solitary oak whose canopy of leathery leaves was enormous—"is a wonderful hiding place."

"Nonsense," White Gull snapped. "If you try to climb so tall a tree, you will fall and break your neck." She recaptured her sister's hand and urged her onward.

But Cypress had halted abruptly. "Dancing Egret can climb as easily as a squirrel, and as quickly," she told White Gull. "If we leave her here, she'll be as safe as if we take her to the mangroves. You and I should go back to my father. His other women have remained with him. Even my grandmother has. Should his youngest daughter and his newest wife shame themselves by deserting him?"

Dancing Egret looked from her beloved sister to the girl

who had recently become both friend and mentor. "If you go back," she said firmly, "I go, too."

The young women's expressions registered identical dismay as they gazed at her. Egret's square chin, prominent nose, and wide mouth would have looked more appropriate on a boy's face. Her thickly lashed eyes, the only feminine feature she owned, were at the moment narrowed unbecomingly, emphasizing her determination.

"Can you climb this tree?" White Gull asked Kneeling Cypress. Desperation roughened her voice.

Cypress nodded.

"Then hide yourself among its branches with my sister, and see that she keeps quiet. I will go back to Ucita and explain that I told you to stay with her."

Egret shook her head before Cypress could speak. "No," she said. "*Both* of you must be safe from the awful men who travel in ships with wings. Or I do not choose to be."

Kneeling Cypress's voice was as ragged as White Gull's had been. "Leave us, and go to the thicket with the others," she said to her father's wife. "Egret and I will conceal ourselves in the tree. Ucita will understand."

As she dashed away, White Gull wondered if he would—Ucita was frequently annoyed by things that White Gull's father would have paid less heed to than sand flies on a summer evening. But at least she no longer feared for Dancing Egret; Cypress, who knew what it was like to have been motherless since infancy, would protect her fiercely.

Egret, snuggling into a crotch near the top of her favorite tree, looked down at Kneeling Cypress, who clung to the trunk just below her own perching place. "I was only a baby when the winged ships last came to Calusa country," she said. "Do you remember what the people they brought here were like?"

"Be still," Cypress hissed.

"Don't worry," Egret said. "One of the reasons I like this tree is because, from where I'm sitting, I can see the whole village and part of the shore. I will tell you if any strangers come, and then I'll be as quiet as . . . as that tiny yellow-eyed snake crawling along the branch next to your left arm."

Cypress ignored the hastily departing reptile. "Can you see my father?" she asked. "Or my grandmother and the other women?"

Dancing Egret parted the gray-green spikes of an air plant. "Chief Ucita is standing with the warriors," she said, "and

Clattering Tongue is by his side." She realized at once that she ought not to have used the village children's secret name for the chief's elderly mother, and added quickly, "I mean, Star Watcher is."

Despite the tenseness of the situation, Kneeling Cypress grinned. She knew full well what the youngsters called her grandmother, and knew that the old woman had earned the unflattering name.

"You haven't answered my question about the strangers who came before," Egret reminded her.

What did it matter what happened last time the big ships came? Cypress thought hysterically. Only *this* time was important! For the child's sake, however, she knew she must calm herself. "I will answer it now," she said, and was amazed at the evenness of her voice. "Although I'm surprised White Gull has not already told you the story; after all, the ships came into the part of the bay that lies closer to Calusa's island than to our village. Ucita's warriors were with your father's only because the sails were spotted while the vessels were still a long way off and Headchief Calusa had time to send a courier here."

As she spoke, Cypress tried to peer between branches and leaves to see what Egret was seeing. It was no use; she simply was not high enough. Nervousness goaded her into continuing a tale she hadn't the slightest interest in relating. "The island warriors brought along a Christian slave, who recognized the leader of the pale-fleshed strangers who came ashore that day. It seems that the slave had been a soldier with this man, this Ponce de León—" She halted abruptly as Egret tensed. "What is it?" she asked urgently.

"Your father and grandmother have gone back to your house," Egret said, "and the warriors are leaving the plaza. They don't look happy to be going, and I cannot tell where they are headed ... somewhere beyond the burial mound."

"Perhaps my father has sent them to the bay," Kneeling Cypress said hopefully, "to welcome the hairy men the same way Calusa's did Ponce de León." But she suspected he had probably sent them to the mangroves instead, to guard the women and children. Ucita always put his people's safety ahead of his own. To dilute her anxiety, she forced herself to recall what she'd been telling the child. "Calusa's warriors were determined to avenge the comrades they had lost during their first battle with Ponce de León," she went on. "And this time the Spanish leader wasn't given a chance to run away, as he'd done seven years before. When one of the warriors gave him a mortal wound, his soldiers picked him up and raced for their boats, leaving our people with a victory to celebrate." She peered up at the younger girl, and found her looking around. "Egret, please keep your eyes on the village. Is anything else happening?"

Egret focused her attention obediently. "The plaza is still empty," she reported. Then, "Why did you call the soldiers hairy?" she asked.

"Because, unlike our people, they have hair on their *faces*."

"Like animals do?"

Although it seemed incongruous to be having such a conversation, Cypress made herself go on talking. Silence would have made the waiting worse for both of them. "Not exactly like animals," she said. "These men have hair that sprouts from their chins and grows above their mouths."

"Some of my father's slaves have hair like that. They are funny-looking, but they still look like men. Even if they do have skin the color of a sun-bleached dead crab." Dancing Egret sounded disappointed.

"Well, they *are* men," Cypress said. "They are not as handsome as your father and mine, of course. Which is doubtless the reason they cover themselves from neck to knee with what they call *armor*, instead of wearing only loincloths."

"They try to hide their ugliness," Egret agreed. "But what exactly is *armor*, Cypress?"

"It's a kind of clothing made out of pieces of metal joined together. The pale-fleshes wear metal on their heads, too, or so I've—"

Egret had inhaled suddenly and noisily, and Cypress froze.

"They are coming," the little girl whispered excitedly. "Men with hairy faces. And they have on the armor you described, Cypress! Sunshine is bouncing off their chests. One of them has on only a long black robe, though, and he isn't carrying a sword, as most of the others are." She was silent for a moment as she took in as much as she could. "Some are carrying strange-looking bows instead of swords," she announced. "And . . . and there are dogs running along beside them. Not little dogs, like we have in the village, but dogs as big as wolves, with very long bodies."

"Can you see my father?" Anguish wrung out Cypress's voice.

"No. Yes! Yes, I can. He is coming down the ramp from

your house, and one of the strangers is going to meet him. Oh! The stranger has taken the metal thing off his head. Cypress, his hair is red as fire! And the hair on his face is, also." She squinted and leaned forward as the man turned a little and she saw him full-face for the first time. "Oh!" she squealed, "the man has only one eye! The other is nothing but a dark hole."

"You must be quiet," Cypress warned. But she had to know what was happening, she had to! "Tell me what you see, but keep your voice very, very low."

"The man in black is watching while two soldiers plant a wooden post with a crossbar in the middle of the plaza," Egret said, trying to speak softly. "Two others are setting up another post. This one is thinner, and has a piece of cloth tied on top. There are colors on the cloth, bright colors, and the breeze is making it dance. It looks quite pretty, Cypress."

"What is my father doing?"

"He is just standing there. But now the red-haired one is unrolling something that looks like a long piece of bark . . . bark even thinner than the kind our men use to make sails for their ocean-going canoes. Now he seems to be talking to Chief Ucita." Her forehead crinkled. "Do you suppose he knows our language? If he doesn't, your father will never understand what he's saying, will he?"

Kneeling Cypress did not answer. She had closed her eyes tight and was begging all the gods, from Sun and Moon to Dolphin the World Maker, to watch over her father, to bring his warriors to him quickly, quickly! He ought not be by himself at such a time! Briefly she considered scrambling out of the tree and rushing to stand by his side. She longed to be able to summon spirit power into herself, to become so infused with it that merely the sight of her would send the hairy men scuttling back to their ships.

But she could not. And she had given her promise to take care of Dancing Egret. She must remain where she was, no matter what happened in the village.

Chief Ucita did not look at either the banner or the cross that decorated his plaza. He kept his eyes fixed on the flaming-haired man who had stepped away from the other strangers and was now filling the air with staccato sounds. They were probably words in his own language, Ucita thought, but they meant nothing to him.

He wished the women who were surely peeking from the house on the mound had gone to the mangroves with the rest of the villagers, but he had known when Star Watcher refused to leave that his wives would do likewise. The fools would take their chances with the invaders rather than risk his mother's wrath, he reflected irritably. But at least his favorite daughter had hidden herself, as had his newest wife. He wondered if the two realized how closely they resembled one another, asked himself—as he'd often done of late—if that was why his marriage to White Gull was without passion. He had never wanted a fourth wife, anyway. What peace-loving man would? If Star Watcher had not insisted . . . He sighed; he longed for nothing but peace these days. Indeed, it was in hopes of maintaining peace that he had sent his warriors away. Perhaps, if he did not have armed men around him, the people from the winged ships would understand that he wanted no bloodshed.

The breeze coming off the bay wrenched at the feather-trimmed cloak his First Woman had laid across his shoulders. One of his younger wives had fastened around his head an embroidered band she had decorated with the wing feathers of a purple gallinule, and another had tied around his ankles bracelets made of sharks' teeth and janthina shells. But the red bearded stranger did not seem impressed; he continued to rattle off words that made no sense to the man whose town he had come into without invitation.

Perhaps that was as well. Panfilo de Narvaez, who considered himself governor of all the territory from northern Mexico to the outermost end of *la Florida*, was reading the last of the Spanish king's Requisition to the Indians:

> "*. . . understand this well which I have told you . . . Recognize the Church as Mistress and Superior of the Universe. If you do not do this, and of malice you be dilatory . . . I will enter with force, making war upon you from all directions. I will take the persons of yourselves, your wives, and your children to make slaves, doing you all the evil and injury of which I may be able . . . It will be your fault and not that of His Majesty, nor mine, nor of those cavaliers who came with me.*"

He let the tail of the parchment roll up with a snap and passed the document to his treasurer. Then he turned and nodded to the soldiers massed behind him. They broke ranks promptly, fanning out and going in pairs into the small houses on the first level of the mound capped with Ucita's own home.

"No," Ucita said firmly, his eyes indicating his displeasure.

Narvaez, who understood Ucita no better than Ucita had understood him, merely raised the brow above his good eye and shrugged. Scavenging soldiers moved on to the next level.

Ucita began to wish he'd kept at least some of his warriors with him. When they returned, his people would find their possessions in disarray and some of their belongings missing. But what worried Ucita most was what would happen when his own home was invaded and the soldiers came upon Star Watcher and three of his wives.

"No!" he said again. Stepping forward, he gripped the red-headed man's left forearm.

Narvaez's right hand went to his sword as he spun around, but he stayed the motion as a triumphant shout came from one of the soldiers on the third level of the mound. He contented himself with wresting his arm free from the savage's grasp and glaring at him.

Ucita's hand itched now to be holding his longest and sharpest knife. But he only drew himself up tall and returned the intruder's glare.

Narvaez ignored him; he was intent on the soldier who had pelted down the tiered mound and was displaying three thin golden disks.

The chief saw no reason for the excitement that suddenly lit the sallow faces of the soldier and his leader. What they looked upon were only bits of the shiny metal his people often found on the beach after a big storm. If they collected enough, Ucita did not have to send such large measures of corn and beans to Calusa when the time came to pay him tribute. The Headchief had a liking for the yellow metal; presenting him with a quantity of it meant he would demand less of the town's precious food crop, and that pleased those who worked so hard to grow it. It pleased Ucita also; those whose bellies were full rarely complained, and a chief whose people were content was known far and wide as a praiseworthy leader.

Panfilo de Narvaez turned to Ucita. "You will show me," he said harshly, "where you have put the rest of your gold."

Ucita understood nothing; Ucita said nothing.

The Spaniard's single eye became a slit. He reached for the blade he wore at his waist, slid it from its sheath, held it up so that the sun glinted off of its finely honed edge. "Show me!" he ordered.

Ucita did not need to decipher the words to recognize that he was being threatened. He stood taller still, and again met glare with glare.

"Then we will continue searching until we find it," Narvaez snarled. "But first—"

He nodded, and two of his men sprang forward and seized Ucita's arms. Then, with the deadly speed of a striking rattler, their leader's hand lifted. The knife's cutting edge found the ridge between Ucita's eyes, angled downward, sliced bone as easily as it would have a ripe avocado. The chief's nose plopped to the ground, bounced once, and came to rest against his big toe.

Blood gushed from the place where the nose had been and painted Ucita's lips crimson. The salty taste of it seeped into his mouth.

From atop the mound a screech rang out. "You will die for that," Star Watcher cried, and flew down the ramp as though her many years had been stripped away by her fury. Her big-knuckled hand held Ucita's own knife, the one he had wished for only moments ago. "You will die, die, die!" his mother shrieked as she flung herself upon Narvaez.

The other women followed her down, having armed themselves as best they could. But Ucita's wives were subdued as quickly as Star Watcher had been, and all were forced to kneel in a row in front of the angry Spanish leader.

He surveyed them coldly, but was aware that the eyes of many of his men were hot as they fastened on the youngest of the four. The girl's round face was unremarkable, but it was not her face they were looking at; it was her large, upthrusting breasts that caught and held their gaze. Narvaez beckoned to his treasurer. "Have these two females taken at once to the ship," he commanded, pointing to Ucita's first two wives. "The girl can be kept for the men to amuse themselves with tonight. Warn them to do her no permanent damage; like the others, she goes to Cuba to be sold as a slave."

The priest made a sound of protest, and Narvaez nodded. "I have not forgotten, Father. Naturally, they will receive religious instruction and be given baptism before they are sold. But that is your domain, not mine. Make what arrangements you will for it." He turned his head as Star Watcher, who had gone on ranting even while her scrawny arms were being twisted behind her back, let out a keening wail. Ucita, faint from the blood he had lost, had crumpled to the ground. "The crone," Narvaez said, "is of no use to anyone. And I am tired of the sound of her voice. Throw her to the dogs."

The priest shook his head dolefully. But he only turned his back and studied the Temple atop the village's second mound as the soldiers released a dozen huge hounds and herded them into a circle. Nor did he turn around when the screams of the Indian women, the jeers of the watching soldiers, and the menacing growls of hungry dogs fighting over brittle bones and meager flesh made obscene music in the plaza. When at last he gave up his contemplation of what could only be a structure built to honor evil heathen gods, Star Watcher's tongue had long since ceased to clatter. All that could now be heard were the sobs of Ucita's wives and the soul-wrenching groans of the helpless chief.

The treasurer gestured toward Ucita. "And the old man?" he asked.

Narvaez studied the mess of raw tissue and twisted cartilage where the savage's nose had been. "He will probably die," he said indifferently. "If he does not, he will be a reminder to others of his kind that Panfilo de Narvaez will not be thwarted in his quest for riches and slaves. Bind him while we finish searching the settlement. We will take with us any gold we find, and any people we happen upon will be sent back to Havana with the women. The rest have probably hidden themselves in that jungle we saw from the bay, however, and I have no desire to waste time hunting them down. I wish to head inland tomorrow, and the soldiers will complain less about a long march if they are going toward booty and slaves instead of away from them."

One of the hounds that had feasted on Ucita's mother came to sniff at the semiconscious chief. Narvaez whistled the dog to his side and wiped his red-stained blade against the beast's gray fur. Licking at the smears on his coat further whetted the hound's appetite, but Narvaez was impatient to set up camp. He turned the animal over to the soldiers who were leashing the rest of the pack, and shouted to the men still searching the mounds to hurry and be done.

When finally the last pair of soldiers, grumbling like their fellows because they'd found no real treasure for all their pillaging, followed Narvaez back to the shore, Chief Ucita still lay sprawled upon the ground of his deserted plaza. The sun, sliding slowly down the western sky, let fingers of light rest briefly upon him, but he did not respond to the warmth of that touch, or to the cooler caresses of the shadows that were soon his only companions.

The tears she had shed left Kneeling Cypress's cheeks as stiff as fire-baked clay, and her heart was heavy as one of the stone plummets the Lake People used to weight their fishing nets. When Egret's voice had become choked with sobs as she tried to tell how the Spaniard cut off Ucita's nose, Cypress had closed her ears to the creaking protest of thinner branches and climbed higher into the oak. Both girls had been watching when Star Watcher was stripped and thrown to the snarling and slavering dogs, had continued to watch while the man in black sent some of the soldiers into the Temple and organized the burning of the ornate wooden boxes that contained the bones of Chief Ucita's ancestors.

Only a self-discipline worthy of one twice her age had kept Cypress where she was until night brought concealing dark to the world and fires on the shore told her that the Spanish were congregated some distance from the village. Then she clambered down from the oak, monitored Dancing Egret's descent, and sent the child running to fetch the warriors from the mangroves.

"My father will have told them to wait for his signal before they return to town," she said tightly. "They have no way of knowing that he cannot—" She swallowed hard and gave the younger girl a gentle shove. "Go!" she said.

Egret went, her feet flying over uneven ground, instinct alone keeping her on a path that was ill-defined even in the daytime.

Kneeling Cypress drew a single shuddering breath, then sped toward the village, to the place where her father lay. She knew she had done the right thing by waiting until now, but she knew also that she would never forgive herself if Ucita died before she could reach him.

Chapter 2

 ⊪ ⊪

Kwambu hauled his canoe a safe distance up the shore, then took out of it the pack destined for Ucita's town. A broad smile creased his dark face as he recalled how Headchief Calusa had come near to apologizing—something he rarely did, to anyone—for asking him to attend to this errand. "Now that you have completed your training and will be recognized as a trader even by my enemies," Calusa had said, "I should not be using you as an ordinary courier. But I wish to know how matters go with my old friend, Ucita, and with my daughters. I want the truth, Kwambu, so I need someone with the eyes and the ears to discover it. It has been nearly two years since the invaders came, and if Chief Ucita continues to be less than he was before his encounter with the Spaniard, then I must accept that I can no longer depend on him. And his town is closest to the borders of Timucua territory. . . ." Kwambu had understood, and been pleased to have the Headchief's faith in him openly expressed.

He straightened, slung the small pack over his shoulder, and reached up with his free hand to be certain the black-barred blue feather in his headband was standing tall. Similar feathers were tied to the staff he took up next, for the jay's plumage signified that here came a man bound on a peaceful trading mission. So long as he displayed such feathers, Kwambu might go where he would, when he would. To someone who would never forget the day slave chains had been clamped around his wrists and ankles, such freedom seemed miraculous. Even after escaping from Cuba and finding sanctuary among the Calusa, Kwambu had never dreamed the time might come when the Headchief would trust him enough to send him alone into the north, carrying goods to Holata Outina of the Timucua.

16

Sinewy legs took him swiftly over sandy ground dotted with clumps of tough, salt-encrusted grass, let him skirt with ease the sprawling round-leafed shrubs which, in their season, bore long clusters of the grapes much relished by birds and turtles. He wove his way through the trees, sparse-growing at first but soon crowding each other enough so that he walked in near darkness. He could have climbed onto the causeway, of course, and moved without impediment. This path was more pleasant, however, and Kwambu was in no hurry. Dawn-fresh air whispered among the leaves and brought to him the scent of jasmine and pine, aromas the sun's heat would rapidly neutralize. It was his favorite time of day.

It was Dancing Egret's also. The trader approached the quiet village and found the girl perched on a limb of the huge tree she had once told him gravely was *hers*. Because it was natural to him to walk noiselessly, she was not immediately aware of him, and he paused to study her for a moment. She was a child still, despite her sturdiness, composed of angles rather than curves, but from the length of leg she was swinging back and forth, Kwambu could see that she would not be a child much longer. He wondered if becoming a maiden would change her from the plain-speaking, quick-to-laugh girl she had always been. He hoped not. Despite the difference in their ages, and the fact that they'd seen each other infrequently of late, he considered Egret his good friend and delighted in her ready wit and directness.

She did not turn her head, but: "I know you are there, Kwambu," she called. And giggled. "You thought to fool me, but you didn't."

He ambled over to her. "How did you know someone was there? And how did you know it was me?"

She smiled smugly. "I knew *someone* had come up behind me when the breeze's song took on a new rhythm. Since most of the villagers are still in their houses, and since I saw where the other early risers went, I knew it couldn't be one of them. Ucita's sentries are trained to miss nothing; they raised no alarm, so obviously it couldn't be a stranger that was coming into town."

"That still does not explain how you knew it was me," Kwambu challenged.

She shrugged. "I can't explain it. I simply knew." She slid down from the branch. "Or perhaps I only hoped it was you. It's been a very long time since I've seen you, Kwambu." She swatted lightly at the blue feathers on his staff. "Now that you've finished your apprenticeship," she teased, "I guess you're too important to bother with old friends."

"You were my first friend among the Calusa, and you will always be my best friend." He smiled, but his brown eyes were serious.

One of the things Egret liked about Kwambu was the way the steadiness of his glance proved his sincerity even when an easy grin lit his face. Kwambu would never say one thing and mean another, any more than she herself would. This straightforwardness had often gotten Dancing Egret in trouble with her elders, and had put Kwambu at risk upon occasion, too. "Do you remember," she said to him, "the day you won the footrace?"

"I do. But I find it hard to believe that you can. You were scarcely six at the time."

"Perhaps I remember it well *because* I was so young then," she said. "You beat every other boy in the village, and my father was much impressed."

Kwambu nodded, recalling when the Headchief had summoned him, and he—still panting and sweaty from his run—had crossed the plaza, knelt, and turned up his palms in the traditional gesture of respect. He'd found it hard to restrain the triumph he felt as Calusa complimented him on the victory.

"My father decided you ought to be rewarded for what you'd done," Dancing Egret was saying. "He offered to give you a new name, a Calusan name."

"Swift Flyer," Kwambu confirmed. He narrowed his eyes as the moment recreated itself in his memory. The boy he'd been had stood up then and squared his bony shoulders. *My mother was the daughter of a chief in the country of my people,* he'd said slowly, *and my father was a brave warrior there. When I was born, she gave me the name that had been my father's. I would like to keep it forever, Great Calusa.*

"I was close enough to hear what you said to him," Egret said. "I admired you for it, and at the same time wondered how you dared. I saw Calusa's face change, and I shivered. I couldn't decide whether he was going to explode with anger or burst into laughter."

"He did neither," Kwambu reminded her.

"No. He only said, very quietly, 'It shall be so.' "

"And charged me to live up to the name that I wore," Kwambu added.

Egret giggled again. "You wasted no time doing so," she

said. "You walked so tall, once he'd dismissed you, that it was a good thing nothing lay in your path. You would have tripped over it and ended up looking remarkably silly!"

"I went to the beach." Kwambu, still absorbed in reminiscence, ignored her jest. "I was in a daze, I think."

"And I followed you. You were just standing there, looking out over the water, digging into the sand with your toe. I asked what you'd have done if my father insisted you be called Swift Flyer."

"Do you remember what I said?"

"Of course. You said you would have answered to the name, but that in here"—Egret reached out and touched his forehead with her fingertips—"and in your heart"—she touched his naked chest—"you would have been Kwambu still."

"And so I would have been," he said softly.

"How is it you became a trader, Kwambu?" she said after a moment. "I would have thought the son of a warrior would want to be one also."

He laughed a little. "In this country, my black skin would make me too easy a mark for any enemy!" Then he sobered. Should he admit to Egret how often his fingers had itched to take up a death dealer and show youths being trained in the art of combat that Kwambu could throw a dart farther and more accurately than they could? Tell her how greatly he had envied all of them because he'd been so certain that blood runs true, that he had in him the makings of a fine warrior? No; Egret's own father had conferred on him the status of trader, and he would not have the girl think him unappreciative. And despite the yearnings he still had to stifle now and then, he was proud of what he had achieved. "I like traveling to new places, and meeting new people," he said instead, "and since I seem to be skilled at learning different languages, it seems only sensible to make use of such talents. But I can handle both bow and dart thrower, if need be."

"I'm sure you can," she said. Traders crossed vast stretches of wilderness, and Calusa did not send his out until he knew they were capable of fending off the predatory beasts who called such places home. "Is my father well?" she asked.

"He is. I've heard he is thinking of taking Prowling Panther's sister, Watchful Doe, for a wife, but I wonder how he will find the time for a proper marriage ceremony."

"He hopes still for a son," Dancing Egret said, "someone to be Headchief after him. For that, he'll make the time. Perhaps the sister of his War Leader will be able to give him the boy-child his other wives could not."

"They gave him many daughters, however, and admirable ones," Kwambu said quickly.

Egret smiled. "Thank you, for myself and all my sisters," she said. "But we know how Calusa longs for a son, and will be happy for him if that happens." She looked toward the pack Kwambu had set down. "Has my father sent something to me," she asked, "or only to Chief Ucita?"

Kwambu bent and opened the pack. "He sends greetings to both you and White Gull," he replied, "and sends as well a new flute to you and some shell ornaments to your sister. To Ucita, he has sent a panther pelt and a bundle of wood ibis feathers, and some of the sassafras root I hope to get more of when I reach Timucuan country. Tea made from the root's bark is tasty, and their Shamans claim it can restore good health to those who have been unwell."

But Egret was already coaxing trills of music from the flute he had handed up to her, and she continued to do so while she trailed him along the path into a village that had come bustlingly awake. She stopped playing only when she saw her sister come out of the house that topped the mound. "White Gull!" she called. "Look who has come to visit us."

Ucita's wife, the only one he had left now, peered down at her sister, then descended the ramp. "Kwambu," she said, smiling briefly, "you are welcome here."

White Gull had always been pretty, and still was. But cheeks, breasts, and buttocks were not as attractively rounded as they had been, and her eyes held little of their old sparkle. Her hair had less shine, also, but perhaps she had not yet combed it this day. And she did not smile again, even though Kwambu made a small ceremony of giving her the artfully made bracelets and anklets Headchief Calusa meant this daughter to have. "Egret, *must* you be making so much noise?" she snapped as her sister tried to call attention to her own gift.

It did not surprise Kwambu to hear Egret sigh as she lowered her flute. "I have something for your husband also," he said to White Gull.

Her mouth tightened. "I will take you to him, then," she said, and started back the way she had come. "He is in the house," she said over her shoulder. "As is usual these days."

"We will talk again when I come out," Kwambu said to Egret, then followed White Gull up the ramp.

Dancing Egret sighed again. He would have questions for her then, questions she did not look forward to answering.

Kwambu did not stay long in Ucita's house. He would have been less conscious of the man's lack of a nose if Ucita himself had not taken such pains to conceal the ridged and mottled flesh that marked the center of his haggard face, and the snarl-shaped upper lip that the painful healing had bestowed upon him. Apparently Ucita had never adjusted to the awful thing that had happened to him, and neither had his wife. White Gull kept her face averted whenever she spoke to Ucita, which was no more than was necessary, and the chief shielded his face with one hand during most of the time that Kwambu sat across from him. Calusa was right to be concerned, Kwambu thought; Ucita took no delight in the gifts the Headchief had sent him, and showed scant interest in news from the island. In truth, he responded to one thing only: the entrance of his daughter Kneeling Cypress. He spoke to her pleasantly, and pride briefly strengthened his twangy voice when he presented her to Kwambu, who noticed that Cypress—unlike White Gull—was able to look without flinching into Ucita's face.

"He is better than he was," Dancing Egret told Kwambu, once he'd found her again and waited while she dispersed the group of little girls who had been sitting in a circle around her. Egret was still holding her new flute, and Kwambu knew she had been entertaining the youngsters with a story-song based on one of the Calusan Legends that had always fascinated her.

"Cypress tries to make her father look upon the loss of his nose as a battle wound, something he should be proud of," she went on as the last of the youngsters scampered away. "And if his mother had not been killed in so horrible a way, he might be able to do that. But to watch Star Watcher be devoured by dogs . . . well, I suspect he blames himself for everything that happened when the Spanish came." Her expression, as she thought back to the day she was describing, was all at once stripped of childishness. "And to have three of his wives taken away, and the remains of his ancestors destroyed besides . . ."

"Your father worries that Ucita may not be the leader he used to be," Kwambu said bluntly. With Egret there was no need to dissemble, and he wanted to cut short her painful recollection.

Her brow puckered. "Ucita keeps his warriors always at the ready," she said hesitantly, "although he seldom goes among them himself. His War Leader speaks for him, but that's not unusual, is it? And Kneeling Cypress tells me that he is thinking of sending her to be wife to Mocoso, the Timucuan chief who lives just north of here. This is the sort of thing my father would do, I think."

Kwambu nodded. Calusa was known for encouraging his clanswomen to wed potentially hostile Townchiefs. Ucita would be carrying the policy a step further by marrying his daughter to a Timucuan chief, and this spoke well for him. "Perhaps it is only that I am neither kin nor close friend, then," he said. "I can understand how he might feel self-conscious in such circumstances."

"White Gull may be responsible for much of what ails Chief Ucita," Egret said unhappily. "She has changed, Kwambu, even more than Chief Ucita. I don't suppose she ever loved her husband, since hers was an arranged marriage, too. But even though most of us have gotten used to the way Ucita looks, White Gull has not."

Kwambu had seen that for himself. Still, perhaps he would avoid emphasizing it when he reported to Calusa. If Chief Ucita was thinking and acting like a chief—and from what Egret said, he was—that was all that truly mattered. And White Gull probably could not help the way she felt, even though Calusa would surely expect better of any daughter of his. "I must remember to tell Shore Walker that you like the flute he carved," he said.

Egret's face was a child's once more. "Shore Walker carved it? Oh, yes, Kwambu, do tell him that. Say that I said his fingers must be as talented as his grandfather's." Mask Maker, as his name implied, had long been supplying Calusa's town with both ceremonial and utilitarian objects beautifully crafted from pine or cypress.

"He will be glad you think so," Kwambu said. "But Shore Walker is a warrior now, Egret, and unlikely to surrender that status to follow in Mask Maker's footsteps. When he is older, perhaps; meanwhile, he carves only to amuse himself and to keep his fingers strong and nimble."

"I wish I could see him again," Egret said. "He was my good friend, too, and I miss him."

Kwambu laughed. "I can remember when you were something of a nuisance to him, Egret. You used to follow along whenever he went to prowl the beach after a storm."

"To find treasure," Egret said, laughing also. "But he never shooed me away, even when he had good reason to. Once, he was filling a basket with bits of blackened metal. It looked ugly, and I wanted him to dump it out and take back the pretty shells I'd found instead. I was annoyed when he wouldn't, but my father told me later that Shore Walker had brought him something called *silver*, which his traders could use to barter with."

"It did not take your people long to realize that pale-fleshes place a high value on both silver and gold," Kwambu said, "and once they understood it, they began to desire these metals also."

"I still prefer shells," Egret said firmly. "Oh, I know Calusa had ornaments made out of gold and liked them so well that he decreed only the Headchief may wear such things. And it does seem that he wears a small sun on his forehead when he ties on his ceremonial headband. But even if they do not shine as brightly as Calusa's gold disk, I think shells are prettier."

"In the uplands, where I am going now, the Timucuan chiefs also wear gold ornaments on important occasions," Kwambu said. "No doubt they, too, appreciate that this metal is the same color as the sun. Tribes everywhere see the sun as life-giver, even if they honor him in different ways. Chiefs in Timucua country call themselves and their families Children of the Sun, and believe that he and Moon made This World."

"Sun and Moon are our ancestors also," Egret said, "and *we* were the First People, Kwambu. But we know that Dolphin made the world, which is why we honor him as much as we do Sun and Moon."

Kwambu forbore to say that the Timucua believed that the First People were their own White Deer Clan. Who could say what was the truth of it? The people in Kwambu's faraway country believed that the Original People were those they were descended from. Perhaps, somehow, all of them were right. It was not for a simple trader to make sense of Legends. "I must be on my way," he said to Egret. "I have a long journey ahead of me."

She was young enough to pout. "But you've only just arrived."

"If I make good time, I will stop on my way back," he said, but a cry from the sentry drowned out his last words.

Egret clutched at Kwambu's arm. "Ships!" she said. "The Spanish have come back, Kwambu!"

He could barely make out her words. All around them peo-

ple were pouring into the squareground. Mothers called frantically for their children, and men swarmed like ants over the
mound as they raced to the houses for their weapons. Yet all
took the time to glance toward the timber and wattle house that
crowned the flat-topped pyramid. The sentry had not imitated
the cry of the big cat this time, and it remained for their chief
to say what they should do.

It seemed an age before he appeared, but he had taken only
long enough to put on his feathered cape and finest headband.
When he showed himself, when he left his house with deliber-
ate tread and spread his arms, the chorus of confused murmurs
ceased. With the rest, Dancing Egret and Kwambu turned up
their faces.

"The ship—and there is only one—keeps to the middle of
the bay," Ucita told them, and Egret realized that the chief had
been looking out over the harbor from the rear of his house.
"It sails back and forth, back and forth, as though searching for
something."

A sentry raced across the plaza and up the ramp and spoke
urgently to Ucita. "It looks like one of the ships that came here
before," the chief said next, "and I hope that it will anchor,
and that the men it carries will come ashore."

He raised his arms again to quiet the astonished villagers.
"How else," he said strongly, "can we repay the pale-fleshed
marauders for their cruelty?"

"He wants revenge," Egret whispered, and Kwambu nodded. This, Calusa would be pleased to hear.

"The old people and the women and children will remain in
the squareground," Ucita said. "The warriors will conceal
themselves along the shore and make ready to seize any Spaniard who dares set foot again in Ucita's domain."

"There is but one ship," Kwambu said slowly, "and it is
keeping a careful distance from land. The Spanish are not
fools, Egret; they will suspect that the people here hunger for
vengeance. They may decide not to come into the harbor at
all."

Egret's eyes flashed. "They must!" she said sharply. "Oh,
Kwambu, surely there is a way they can be persuaded to?"

"It is possible," he said, his brow wrinkling as he considered, "that some at least can be lured ashore." He looked
around. "Can you point out Ucita's War Leader?" he asked.

Egret went up on tiptoe, swiveled her head this way and

that. "He is there," she said finally, pointing to the causeway, "in the middle of a circle the warriors have formed."

"His name?"

"He's called Club Wielder. Come. I'll take you to him."

"No need. His body paint will identify him," Kwambu said, beginning to move in the direction she indicated. "Stay here with the rest of the women and children, Egret. If the little ones are frightened, you can sing them one of your Legends to distract them. Their mothers will be grateful, and your sister will be proud of you."

Perhaps so, Egret thought as her friend moved swiftly toward the causeway, but she'd meant to sneak closer to the shore and watch what happened there.

She grinned wryly. Kwambu had probably guessed that, which was why he had reminded her that she was old enough now to act responsibly in an emergency. So she would collect the small children and keep them occupied until Ucita's warriors had done what must be done. But, oh, she hated to miss seeing the hateful Spanish given what they so richly deserved!

Club Wielder, a wise man as well as a brave one, showed no reluctance to hear the advice of a trader, particularly when that trader had lived for some years among the Spanish. "Your idea is sound," he said when Kwambu finished speaking, "and well worth acting on. Will you go with us to the shore? I do not ask you to bear a weapon; that would violate your status. But you might like to see how your plan works. There are many places where you can stand unseen and watch."

So Kwambu had gone with the grim-faced men, had used his own blade to strip a length of bark from a cypress tree while two of the warriors pounded a post carried from town into the sand. When Kwambu had thinned the bark and shaped it into a rectangle, the War Leader made a slit in the top of the post and wedged the bark into it. Then he came back to where Kwambu waited behind a trio of twisted mangrove trees. "Will that do?"

Kwambu nodded. "It looks like the parchment the Spanish use for messages," he said. "If the ship comes only a little closer, the men it carries will think that the soldiers who went overland from your town left a message for any who might come here another time. At least, I hope they will."

Club Wielder smiled. "I have an idea that might convince them to come still closer," he said, and spoke tersely to the

warriors who had set the post. They nodded and went farther
down the shore, lifting their hands high over their heads and
making beckoning gestures as they shouted loudly and repeatedly. "Sound travels far over water," Club Wielder said to
Kwambu, "and it matters little what they say since they would
not be understood anyway. They will attract attention, though,
and their hand signals will be understood." For the men were
now alternately waving and pointing to the post.

Kwambu held his breath as he waited to see how the Spanish would respond. He expelled it in a whoosh as the pinnace
slowly turned its bow toward land. "They are coming," he
said, but Club Wielder had already slipped away to join the
warriors, whose presence would not be revealed until the last
moment.

The small ship, which surely held no more than a score of
people, approached warily. Soon Kwambu could make out individual men on its deck; could even tell, from the excited
bursts of Spanish that wafted to his ears, that there was dissension among them. The older, more experienced men were suspicious; the younger were mainly curious and eager to prove
themselves.

The captain of the pinnace barked an order, and the ship
came about until its length was parallel to the shore. This was
as close as they would come.

Kwambu felt a rush of disappointment, even shame. If he
had not interfered, the Spanish might eventually have persuaded themselves to risk landfall; Ucita's warriors would still
have been waiting. If Kwambu had learned nothing else about
these people, he knew that they were capable of infinite patience.

Suddenly he stiffened, leaned forward. A small boat was
being lowered over the side of the pinnace, and one—no,
two—men were sliding down a line into it! Should they be
named the most courageous of those on board, he wondered,
or the most foolish?

The younger of the two picked up the oars and began to
row. His strokes were powerful, and it seemed no time at all
before the boat's keel grated against sand and its occupants,
leaping out of it, raced each other to the upright post.

Club Wielder and his men swooped onto the beach, surrounded the pair and seized them. Kwambu stifled a laugh as
the younger man's jaw dropped in amazement. He was nobly
born, this one; his shirt was silk and his doublet and breeches

had been sewn from wine-colored velvet. Such luxury reminded Kwambu forcibly of the young man of the house where he and his mother had once been slaves, awakening memories better left asleep.

His fingers clenched around the haft of his knife. How he yearned to dash to the shore and let his well-honed blade avenge old wrongs! But Club Wielder had been right; for Kwambu to wield a weapon would make mock of the bluejay feathers he wore. He closed his eyes, resigned himself to his passive role, then focused once more on the scene in front of him.

Suddenly, the nobleman's companion, a common sailor from the looks of him, broke from his captors and bolted for the rowboat. Ucita's War Leader lifted his huge club and let fly with the weapon that had earned him his name. The spiny conch shell embedded in its broad end struck the sailor squarely in the back of the neck, and blood gushed from the wound it made as the man pitched forward into the damp sand just above the waterline.

Now all the warriors turned their attention to the young nobleman, who had ceased to struggle in the moment his comrade died. But before they had agreed upon whose privilege it would be to take their remaining captive to their chief, Ucita—accompanied by Tradition Keeper, the village priest—came down the causeway and onto the beach. "Bind him," Ucita said to Club Wielder, staring fiercely at the Spaniard, "and take him to one of the huts by the river. Assign men to guard him tonight. Tomorrow he will be sacrificed to the Eater of Eyes."

Chapter 3

❖ ❖

Dancing Egret, flanked by White Gull and Kneeling Cypress, stood with the rest of the villagers as the chief and his priest led the procession up from the shore. Like the others, Egret spared scarcely a glance for those in the lead, or for the warriors who followed behind. All her attention was on the dark-haired youth who stumbled along between Club Wielder and his deputy. The ballooning sleeves of the Spaniard's white shirt were torn and filthy, and he was covered with sand and matted seaweed. But despite that indignity, and despite the thongs that linked his wrists and hobbled his ankles, the young man's head was not bowed. His dark eyes darted right and left, resting with undisguised curiosity on one red-skinned face or another as he was prodded across the plaza.

What were his thoughts? Egret wondered as she watched him focus on a group of hard-eyed soon-to-be warriors, glance toward the wrinkled but remorseless faces of a trio of elders, and look with something like surprise at a pretty maiden who quickly averted her own eyes. As he approached the foot of the mound, he studied Egret, Cypress, and White Gull, and they studied him. His face was unbearded, and his features were fine-drawn rather than coarse. White Gull muttered under her breath, then turned her back as the Spaniard, yanked to a halt by his captors, continued to stare at the three. The expression on Kneeling Cypress's face was one of bemusement. Could being so close to one of the cruel Spanish have shocked her into immobility? Egret wondered. She tugged at her friend's hand, tugged a second time when Cypress's attention remained fixed on the young man. But not until Ucita and Tradition Keeper climbed to the first tier of the mound and everyone turned toward them did Cypress blink and look away from the pale-skinned youth.

"The ship that brought this Spaniard here has made haste to sail away," Ucita said contemptuously, "and the only other man to come ashore is dead. Yet even though we have but a single captive, he will pay dearly for what his fellows did in this town. A special ceremony will be held at daybreak tomorrow, and our priest will offer up our prisoner to the Buzzard God."

Egret knew she was not the only one to feel exultation. No sterner judgment could be passed among the Calusa than to consign a man's three souls to the Eater of Eyes! Whenever someone died under ordinary circumstances, one of his souls, the one contained in his shadow, went immediately to be with his ancestors; his second soul, the one associated with his image, ultimately disappeared after seeking sanctuary in smaller and ever smaller living things; but the soul that resided in the pupil of the eye lived on forever, so long as a body was properly interred. If this soul tried hard enough, it could communicate with kin who remained in the visible world. But the Buzzard God consumed every part of a man, even his third soul, until it was as if he had never lived at all. The Spaniard faced not just death, but annihilation.

Tradition Keeper was speaking now, telling the people to fast in preparation for the ceremonial feasting that would follow the Ritual of Sacrifice. "Now," he finished, "I will go and gather tobacco to sprinkle on the fire that will be lit at sunrise."

As he started down the ramp, and Ucita—with a final lifting of his arms over the heads of his people—turned and climbed to his house, Club Wielder ordered the way cleared for him to take the captive to one of the riverside huts where the women sometimes sat and chatted when they went to fish or bathe or wash clothes. They would not need to be told to avoid the river today, Egret thought; the young Spaniard and his guards would have it to themselves.

"He does not even know what has been decided!"

Startled, Egret turned toward Kneeling Cypress. Now her friend's expression was one of angry disbelief. "He does not speak our language, Egret, and has no idea what is planned for him."

Egret shrugged. "He'd be a fool to think we would spare him after what his people did to your father and your grandmother."

"He may not even know what was done here that day," Cypress rejoined.

"He is Spanish, and a noble," said Kwambu, who had come up behind them. "He cannot be ignorant of the way soldiers treat those they set out to conquer. The man is a cavalier, Kneeling Cypress; this may be his first campaign, but he knows what the Conquistadors do."

"Conquer!" Egret exclaimed. "If the Spanish believe they can conquer us, they shall soon learn differently. We Calusa will never be conquered. By anyone!"

Kwambu opened his mouth to reply, but White Gull spoke first. "You should be rejoicing," she said tightly to Cypress. "Your father will have the revenge he is entitled to. Not that revenge can undo what has been done, or make matters better for us." She took hold of her arm. "Come. We must arrange for food and drink for tomorrow. And Ucita will want his ceremonial garments put in good order."

"But he's so *young*," Cypress murmured, looking back over her shoulder as she followed White Gull toward their house.

"Cypress has a soft heart," Egret told Kwambu, "but I would never have thought it might extend to one of *them*." She nodded in the direction of the river.

"A woman's heart can be a peculiar thing," Kwambu said, and smiled. But his eyes were troubled, which puzzled his companion.

It was still dark when Tradition Keeper, blowing into a conch shell with one end lopped off, summoned the villagers from their beds. Egret, who had wakened before the signal, was one of the first to run down into the plaza, but soon night had seeped away, leaving behind a sky the color of a dove's wing, and everyone was moving toward the Temple mound. The priest, wearing a tight-fitting red cap and a mask carved into the likeness of a buzzard's face, stood at its foot. In his right hand he held a dagger fashioned from bone, its haft shaped to imitate the head of the carrion bird. Nearby, a pole grid had been set up over a heap of kindling and driftwood. The whole was ringed with shells whose pale surfaces had been splashed with red pigment to signify that here was a place designed for the letting of blood.

Tradition Keeper lifted his free hand and silence fell. He turned to the east, where streaks of coral announced the stately approach of the Sun into the world, and paid homage to the giver of life. Then he looked to the west and spoke courteously to the departed Moon. He faced the sea when he offered thanks to Dolphin for the firm ground upon which Ucita's people stood, but it was the sky he looked into when he addressed the Eater of Eyes.

"You, we are commanded to appease," he intoned, "to keep you from descending and consuming the third souls of our honored dead. We do so this day, and beg you to accept what we offer and be content until we invite you to feast again."

His assistant held the conch shell now. He raised it to his lips and blew once into it.

Before the mournful sound died away, the War Leader came from behind the mound, pushing ahead of him the Spanish nobleman. No longer did the youth's face register avid curiosity. Egret, who stood in front of the throng along with Kneeling

Cypress, White Gull, and Chief Ucita, saw that apprehension dominated now. As well it should, she told herself.

Two of Club Wielder's warriors sprang to help stretch the prisoner atop the wooden grid and lash wrists and ankles to its outlying posts. The priest and his assistant moved without haste to flank the grill-like altar, with Tradition Keeper taking up position by the Spaniard's head.

Kneeling Cypress felt for Egret's hand and squeezed it so tightly that the young girl choked back a cry and nearly missed seeing the priest's helper accept a flare brought to him by Club Wielder. As the first rays of the new-risen sun angled into the squareground, the flare was lowered to the kindling that made a bed for the driftwood. And Egret's hand, although she tried to wrench it free, remained painfully pinioned as Tradition Keeper took tobacco from his neck pouch and tossed it on the low-burning flames. As scented smoke began to rise, the priest lifted the ceremonial dagger, held it point downward just above the eyes that stared desperately from the Spaniard's fear-contorted face. And the young man began to shriek words that Egret could make no sense of, save that he repeated the same agonized sounds again and again and—

"No!" Cypress screamed. She released Egret's hand and threw herself on the ground in front of her father. "Ucita, please! Do not let this happen!"

Tradition Keeper frowned darkly and fumbled for more tobacco. It did not do, to have a ritual interrupted. This part of it must be repeated.

But Ucita, also frowning, spoke the priest's name and signed for him to wait. "Daughter," he said to Kneeling Cypress, "you bring shame on both me and yourself."

"But I asked you and asked you," she sobbed. "And you said you would consider it."

White Gull spoke up. "That is what you told her," she said to her husband. "As I recall, none of us slept until you gave your promise."

"I considered it," Ucita said sharply. "I decided against it."

Cypress lifted a tear-streaked face. "Father, if you love me, you will reconsider," she implored. "And remember what White Gull said: Headchief Calusa's status is enhanced because he owns so many Christian slaves. Surely yours would be if you kept this Christian to serve you?"

Dancing Egret had been startled before; now she was positively astounded. Her *sister* had tried to help Cypress persuade

Ucita to cancel a sacrifice that was surely called for? What could either of them be thinking of, to do such a thing?

And Ucita was being persuaded! As Egret and the rest of the confused villagers watched, he bent to help his favorite daughter to her feet, and with one finger brushed the tears from her cheeks. "It means so much to you?" he asked quietly.

Cypress nodded and swallowed a sob.

"Then so be it," he said. "But," he warned, for his people must be assured that he was chief first and father second, "he lives only so long as he is useful to me, and he has only a little time to prove that he can be. If he fails, he dies. That is understood?"

Kneeling Cypress clasped her father's hand. "It is," she said. "And I thank you. You will not be sorry that you have shown yourself to be generous, Ucita."

The young nobleman's voice rose in a spiraling scream, a scream abruptly cut off as the odor of scorched flesh filled the air and unconsciousness claimed him. Cypress spun around and began to weep despairingly.

But at the chief's signal, warriors rushed forward and kicked away the driftwood that had begun to burn, scattered the flaming kindling from under the altar. The priest, glowering, stalked away, gesturing to his assistant to follow him up to the Temple. And when the thongs that held the prisoner fast had been severed and he had been lifted from the smoldering grid, Cypress and White Gull followed the berdaches who carried the young man back to the hut by the river.

"I don't understand," Dancing Egret muttered as the crowd in the plaza slowly dispersed.

"What is it you do not understand?" Kwambu had come to stand beside her.

"Any of it," Egret told him. "Why Cypress wanted the Spaniard's life spared. Why White Gull supported such foolishness. Why Chief Ucita finally did as Cypress asked."

"Chief Ucita," Kwambu said, "loves his daughter more than he hates the Spanish. Kneeling Cypress sees something in this young man that she has not found in any other. And White Gull"—he shrugged—"perhaps she feels that one unhappy woman in Ucita's household is enough." He grinned at Egret's look of disbelief. "You are young yet," he said. "One day, you will understand what is beyond you now."

"I hate it when people say that to me," she said morosely.

"Yet you do not understand," Kwambu pointed out, "which

proves that you are too young." His grin faded. "I almost wish," he said quietly, "that you could always be so young, Egret."

"Well, I don't. I want to understand *everything*, Kwambu!"

"That is a lot to ask," he observed. "But if ever anyone manages to do so, it will probably be Dancing Egret." He smiled again, to show he meant his words as praise. "I must be leaving now," he added. "I came to find you to say good-bye."

"I wish I could go with you," she said. "I like meeting new people, too, Kwambu."

His smile vanished. "You will be needed here, I think," he said. "Cypress may need a friend to turn to if things do not go as she hopes. And she may need a friend even more if they do."

"Now it is you I do not understand," Egret said crossly.

He grinned and tousled her hair. "To find something out for yourself is the best way to learn it," he said. "Trust in that, Egret. And let your own good sense be your guide."

Her face brightened. "Do I have good sense?"

"You were born with it, I think."

She felt quite cheerful as she watched him stride away.

Juan Ortiz never remembered much about the rest of that day, or the two that followed. He was vaguely aware that several of those strange men who dressed like women took turns sitting beside him, and that they periodically spread a soothing unguent over his blistered flesh and gave him a bitter potion to drink. Mostly, he slept after they had ministered to him, and as he slept, he healed.

Only after he'd become well enough to eat a little now and then did someone other than the berdaches come to the windowless hut he lay in. The girl who silently brought bowls of tasty soup and rounds of bread to him was, he thought, about his own age. And when she smiled—as she did whenever he'd eaten all she offered—she was, in her pagan way, beautiful. But she never spoke, not even when Juan, as his health improved, began to try to coax a word or two from her. He told himself that he would not be able to understand her if she did speak, any more than he could understand the conversation of the skirted men who continued to care for him; but more and more he wanted to know if her voice was as lovely as her face and her body were.

"You are kind, senorita," he would say when she came. Or, "I am especially hungry today." But the girl only lowered her huge eyes whenever he spoke. He soon realized, however, that while his attention was fixed on the food he was eating, those same eyes considered him shyly but steadily.

But as the days and nights flowed in and out as monotonously as the tide, it was not so much the girl's silence but his inability to communicate with *anyone* that began to obsess him. That, and being confined to this fishy-smelling hut. He knew that he had, for some reason, narrowly escaped a particularly horrible death. Yet if he must spend the rest of his life in a place unfit for dogs and never again be in the company of someone he could *talk* with, then why had the Blessed Virgin granted him the life he'd pleaded for on that terrifying morning?

Escape was out of the question. The berdaches were constantly around and—although he had come to realize that they were mostly older men, or infirm in some way—they apparently wore woman's garb only to show they did not have warrior status; many looked quite capable of restraining him should he try to bolt. Also, if he somehow managed to elude them, he would still have the scowling sentries to contend with. And if he could get away, where would he go? The captain of the pinnace that had set out to find the missing Governor Narvaez had been quick to abandon Juan to these savages. And while Senora Narvaez had sufficient influence to demand that her husband be searched for, an impoverished nobleman had no one who could do the same for him.

The Indian girl who continued to bring him food began to look less pretty to him. When Juan spoke to her now, it was irritably. One day he even shouted at her, but so quickly did the warrior standing outside burst into the hut that he let a mute sullenness speak for him afterward.

This—or something—finally had an effect. One morning, the girl did not come alone. With her was someone who wore a tattered seaman's shirt over a clumsily tied loincloth, and whose feet were shod in the remnants of a pair of leather boots.

"You are Spanish!" Juan exclaimed.

"Yes," said his visitor, casting an uneasy glance over his shoulder to where a warrior stood watchful in the doorway. "They brought me here from Calusa's island. I am"—he shrugged, spread his hands—"one of the Headchief's slaves."

The Spanish he used, that of the lower classes, grated on Juan's ears, yet he was overjoyed to hear it. His joy was nullified by the man's final words, however. "A slave? You, a Spaniard, are a slave?"

The man grinned briefly. "Better a slave than a sacrifice," he said bluntly, "as you ought to appreciate, cavalier." A hint of satisfaction colored his voice; slave he might be, but didn't he have a home of sorts in what Calusa called the Christian community, and a soft-fleshed Indian woman to cook for him and warm his bed of nights? This stiff-necked noble would never unbend enough to take advantage of the situation he found himself in. He'd have to be beaten into submission, more likely. "My name, it is Alvarez. Rodrigo Alvarez. I was rescued by the Calusa when my ship was wrecked off this coast. That was"—he paused deliberately—"fourteen years ago."

Ortiz paled. Fourteen years! "You have been a slave ever since?"

Alvarez nodded. "As you are, too. Now. It is what I have been sent to tell you, cavalier." He grinned. "That you have been judged well enough to begin serving the chief of this town. And he has good reason to resent our kind, so you'll do well to obey without question. No matter what you're told to do."

Juan Ortiz was tempted to respond sharply that he and Alvarez were not of the same *kind*, but he exercised restraint. The man was clearly enjoying himself, taunting someone he would have been forced to address with the utmost respect in other circumstances. He was probably exaggerating, if he was not lying outright, Juan thought. Hadn't a blackamoor appeared on the beach he had so rashly run onto? If these savages truly kept slaves the way civilized people did, then they had somehow acquired those the Lord meant to be held in bondage. Still, caution was clearly called for here; he did not wish to find himself once again with no one to talk with. This, he could not abide. "How can they tell me what to do?" he demanded instead. "I do not understand their gabble."

Rodrigo Alvarez shrugged. "For now, I interpret. But you'll be wise, *compatriota*, to begin learning the language of your captors. It is expected." The guard, whose patience was clearly wearing thin, uttered a series of short, sharp sounds. "On your feet, cavalier," Alvarez said. "It is time. You will be taken to stand watch over the dead."

* * *

"He guards our newly dead," Kneeling Cypress said to Egret.

The two stood thigh deep in the river, waiting for fish to swim into a net they had made from the fibers of the many-spears tree. As daughters of Townchief and Headchief, such work was not required of them, but the two were alike in their scorn of idleness. And it was a beautiful morning; the sea sent a westerly breeze to temper the heat, and a lone mockingbird serenaded them sweetly from somewhere in the trees massed behind them.

"You're speaking of the Spaniard?" Not that Egret really needed to ask who *he* was.

The older girl nodded. "His name is Juan Ortiz," she said. "That Christian your father sent to us told me so." She seemed pleased to be able to make the odd sounds that said how the Spaniard was called, but Egret thought them pitifully unmusical. "It's a task that the berdache who had it before Juan is glad to be done with," Cypress went on, her brow puckering. "To be out there, all alone, with those restless second souls prowling around . . ." She shuddered. The recently dead were kept far from the town, in special log-built tombs, until their bones had been stripped of flesh. Only then could they be ceremoniously removed to the Temple and—in due time—their disarticulated bones placed reverently in burial boxes whose inner lids were elegantly carved so that the third soul forever had something beautiful to look upon. "And animals often sneak through the night and try to carry off the bodies," Cypress said. "I hope the Spaniard stays alert. A hungry beast will not care if the body it seizes is still breathing."

"Club Wielder's little son lies there still?" Egret asked. The child, who was Cypress's cousin, had died at the time of the last round moon, of some fever the priest had been unable to send away.

"He does," Kneeling Cypress confirmed, and her big eyes grew moist. "It's so sad when a child dies. And he was Club Wielder's only son."

"Perhaps the child his wife carries now will be another son," Egret said quickly. Cypress cried easily these days, and Egret felt helpless when she did. "Look!" she added, keeping her voice low. "The fish are coming, Cypress."

And so they were, a whole silvery swarm of mullet riding the current and unaware of the trap that waited downstream.

Soon both girls were laughing as they hauled in a brimming netful and carried their praiseworthy catch back to the village.

Juan Ortiz knew nothing of dispossessed second souls that hover over the newly dead during their time of exposure. He would not have believed such a thing had anyone told him about it. A man had only one soul, and when this was properly dedicated to God, its future home was assured. But Juan did not much like standing watch over dead bodies, not even dead savages. And Rodrigo Alvarez had taken considerable relish in warning him that he would be severely punished, maybe even killed, if anything happened to the corpses enclosed in the trio of log pyramids Juan had been set to guard. "That small body," he'd said, "is a nephew of the chief. Be especially protective of that one, cavalier!"

Since he'd issued his gruesome warnings, Alvarez had returned to wherever he'd come from, but before he left he'd taught Juan to understand the commands he was most likely to hear from his captors. If one of the warriors said *Come*, Juan knew to move quickly after him, and he responded with equal promptness to *Stay*, *Kneel*, and *Eat*. It became easier to distinguish the words after failing to do so earned him a series of bruising blows, and gradually others began to make sense as well.

He supposed he ought to be grateful that his duty was guarding the dead; he might have been put to degrading labor instead. He wished he'd been given some weapon other than a knife fashioned from bone, though; its blade was sharp, but a gun would have made him feel more secure after darkness fell and the bushes surrounding the clearing began their mysterious rustlings. Juan told himself his imagination was what peopled the dark with ferocious beasts, but even the hoot of an owl could make his heart leap into his throat. Occasionally, he heard a far-off growl; then the hand clenching his knife became drenched with the sweat of fear and he prayed fervently for morning to come quickly, quickly! And if the sky-shattering thunderstorms that so often visited this accursed place came during the night, the rain that sheeted down to douse his fire brought bloodthirsty mosquitoes swarming in its wake. A man's reason could be destroyed by that voracious horde, and he would no longer care what larger creatures might be waiting to pounce on him.

Juan Ortiz was no coward, he told himself over and over.

But the impenetrable dark, the loneliness, this standing night after night in an alien place among alien dead ... Mother of God! It was enough to unman even a Conquistador! Juan was left so tight-strung that he could do no more than doze when he was permitted to sleep, during the daytime. This was his undoing.

When at last his body refused to go a moment longer without proper rest, when it demanded that he lay himself down and close his eyes, it was not while the sun stood high overhead. The compulsion to sleep overtook him while blackness still shrouded the world.

He slept; but the beasts he had so often pictured creeping through the bushes did not.

Chapter 4

⇔ ⇒

In the darkest reaches of that summer night, something moved on four legs beneath branches dripping with dew. It did not hurry; the scent of man was strong in its nostrils and counseled wariness.

Belly low to the ground, it eased into the clearing and slunk past a fire which, having gone too long unfed, burned listlessly. It paused briefly beside the sleeping man, then continued on. Two-legged creatures whose breath fouled the purity of the forest came equipped with weapons, and the animal had lived many, many years by avoiding them. But age imposed limitations; the beast's hunting skills were less than they had been, and not only the fire had gone too long unfed.

The pyramids of the dead stood in triangular formation, and the starving animal made for the one farthest from where the man lay sleeping. Carrion was what the rough-hewn logs sheltered, and there was a time when the beast would have scorned that sort of thing. But no longer.

It tested the structure's lower corner, where narrow logs lay athwart one another. When they began to slip apart, its belly rumbled and the saliva of anticipation oiled its jaws. This night there would be feasting instead of fasting!

The clatter of tumbling logs penetrated Juan Ortiz's coma-like sleep. He leaped up, swung his head this way and that, tried vainly to locate the source of a sound he was too befuddled yet to put name to. Behind him leaves rustled; he spun around and peered vainly into darkness so compact his dying fire could not push it back. But as the predator abandoned caution in favor of haste, the embers were reflected briefly in a pair of slanted eyes.

The bone knife was in Juan's hand, as it had been even while he slept. He lifted it, sprinted toward the place where a sudden thrashing told him the creature must be. But he could not see it, could not distinguish so much as a stirring of shadow as it retreated into the deeper dark beyond the clearing.

He swallowed hard, sent up an urgent prayer to the Blessed Mother and all the saints, and flung the blade with every ounce of force he could summon. He threw blindly, and though he ran quickly to the fire then and coaxed a length of deadwood into a flare, although he risked he-knew-not-what by running well beyond the clearing and searching, searching, searching, he found nothing to tell him his aim had somehow been true.

Not until he gave up at last and came slowly back to his post did he spy the dismantled pyramid and understand that one of the bodies he had been commanded to guard was missing. When he realized which one it was, he sank to the ground and buried his head in his hands. As he waited for morning to come, he begged God to have mercy on him. This was his only hope; the savages, when they learned what had happened, would show him none at all.

For weeks Juan had spent every night longing for sunrise. Now he shrank from it. He saw a face haggard with fear when he splashed himself with river water, but by the time he had smoothed his hair and his clothes as best he could, he had taken control of his features. When his usual escort of warriors came for him, he made himself face them calmly, refused to flinch when they spotted the scattered logs of the miniature pyramid that had been erected over Chief Ucita's dead nephew.

He was hard put to maintain that brave front after one of

them had run back to the village and returned with the noseless man who was the chief and with the man Juan had learned was War Leader. Their eyes proclaimed their fury, warned of the awful vengeance they would claim for what Juan Ortiz had permitted to happen.

They turned away from him to speak with the warriors whose own eyes were hot with hate. Juan made himself listen, deciphered what he could of their words, then wished he had not. He had known that the dead child was part of Chief Ucita's family; he had not known until now that the boy was also the son of the War Leader. And both of these men were convinced that Juan Ortiz had stood idly by while a ravaging beast devoured the child's remains!

Suddenly he, too, was angry. Where once he had vowed never to utter a single word of the pagan language he was inadvertently learning, now he struggled to shape a few of the phrases he remembered. "Knife!" he shouted, but he could not think how to say *threw*. So he flexed his arm and hurled an invisible knife into the forest. He pointed to his dead fire and mimed the making of a torch. Recalling another word, he lifted the imaginary flare and said, "I look." He gestured to the massed trees on the far side of the clearing and stamped his feet to indicate that he had gone there to track down what he could not even see.

The War Leader only scowled more ferociously, but the older man, the one with the disfigured face, signaled the warriors and they sped away, disappearing into the trees. Sweat trickled down Juan's back and he clenched his hands to conceal their trembling. Would the warriors find anything? If they could locate the weapon he had flung, and the track of some animal clever enough to have crept into the clearing no matter who had been standing sentry, that would prove he had done what he could. It was not so much a vain hope of escaping punishment that made him pray earnestly for such a thing to happen; it was the pride of a cavalier yearning for vindication.

All at once there was a shout, and in a moment the warriors began to reappear. The first two were empty-handed, but tenderly cradled in the arms of the third was a fragile skeleton from which much of the flesh had eroded. And when the last man came back, he held aloft the carcass of a lean gray wolf. Protruding from the creature's scruffy neck was the hilt of the bone knife the War Leader himself had given to Juan Ortiz.

Incredulity and grudging respect replaced the hatred in the

eyes that surveyed Juan now, and he found himself bowing gravely to acknowledge it. He knew well they still had sufficient reason to punish him, but these savages would certainly speak with admiration of what he had accomplished last night!

After the child's body had been gently placed in its rebuilt log tomb, Juan Ortiz walked tall as he followed the chief and his War Leader back to their village.

"Next season, he is to have his own house on the lowest level of the mound," Kneeling Cypress said, "and Club Wielder himself is teaching him to use a dart thrower and a spear. When Juan Ortiz has learned enough, he will be allowed to go out with a hunting party."

"But he will not be adopted by one of our clans," Dancing Egret said. She had been listening when Cypress tried to persuade her father to that idea.

Her friend's face clouded. "No. Not yet. But he has proved himself once. If he does so again, if he manages to bring down a bear by himself, for instance, well, who can say what will happen?"

Egret thought it unlikely that the Spaniard would ever show himself as capable as the Calusa, who learned to hunt nearly as soon as they learned to walk, but she kept the thought to herself. "It doesn't upset Chief Ucita," she asked, "to have a Spaniard moving freely about the village? I should think the sight of him might remind your father of a day he would rather forget."

"That's one of the reasons I offered to be his message bearer to Juan Ortiz." Cypress's eyes smiled as she repeated a name her friend was growing tired of hearing. "At first, I had to use gestures more than words to talk to him. But by the time three round moons had come and gone, he had learned many of our words. Now, we communicate rather well." Cypress was plainly elated by this. "I have learned something from him that will interest you, Egret," she went on. "Do you recall, when we watched the cruel Spanish chief and his soldiers march away to the north, how we saw that some of them sat upon strange-looking beasts?"

Dancing Egret was indeed interested. The long-nosed, high-stepping beasts had snorted and whinnied as Narvaez's company passed perilously close to the canebrake the villagers were concealed in, and only the need to keep absolutely silent had prevented Egret from exclaiming when she saw them. "You have found out what they were?" she asked eagerly.

Cypress nodded. "They are called *horses*," she said triumphantly. "The Spanish raise them to bear men on their backs, so that soldiers can travel quickly from one place to another."

"Yet how fast can those horses go over marshy ground?" Dancing Egret wondered aloud. Surely the beasts must weigh too much to cross with ease through stretches of mire. "But I'm pleased that you learned what they are," she added quickly, "for I've never stopped being curious about them."

She was less than pleased to realize that Cypress was spending so much time with the Spaniard. Still, it was good to see her smile frequently, good to have her as ready as she herself always was to harvest shellfish from the bay, or take a canoe downriver to the planting fields to pick tender ears of young corn. "What shall we do today?" she asked. "Shall we go into the swamp and see if the wild rice is ready for harvesting?"

The older girl nodded vigorously. "That's a fine idea! Why don't you get a large basket, while I see about a canoe? Oh, and don't forget the flails."

Egret sped away, grinning. She was grinning still when she returned, the rice pickers protruding from the steep-sided basket clasped in her arms. But delight drained out of her when she saw who was standing beside the small canoe Cypress had selected.

"Juan has agreed to go with us," her friend said quickly. "If he is to be a hunter, he must learn to handle a canoe. This can be his first lesson."

"Gathering rice is women's work," Egret said slowly. But she knew it would do no good. She examined the silent young man. "He should leave his clothes behind, if he wants to go with us," she added. "It will be hot in the swamps, and wet."

The silk shirt and hose Juan Ortiz had once treasured had long since disintegrated into threads; his crimson doublet and breeches—although he cleaned them as best he could—were tattered and faded. But the Spaniard could not bring himself to put on the deer-hide vest and loincloth Kneeling Cypress had arranged to be given to him. A cavalier did not dress like a savage! Each day, he clothed himself in pitiful remnants of velvet, pulled cracked and scuffed leather boots over his bare feet, and believed that he put on dignity by doing so.

Cypress looked uncomfortable. "I tried to tell him," she

said. "But although he understands more and more of what I say to him, he did not seem to understand that."

Juan spoke for the first time. "I wear this," he said haltingly. But there was firmness in his voice.

Egret shrugged, then smiled. "My friend Kwambu says the best way to find out anything is to learn it for yourself," she said. "I believe he may be right." She knelt down and, scooping up mud from between her feet, proceeded to smear a thin layer all over herself. Since she wore only a breechclout, she had considerable flesh to cover, but Cypress, who was doing the same, helped her coat the places she could not reach. "You should do likewise," the older girl said to the Spaniard. "It makes a shield against mosquitoes."

Both girls were thoroughly daubed now, but Juan, with ill-concealed distaste, waved away the handful of mud Cypress offered him. "No," he said.

Kneeling Cypress opened her mouth to persuade him further, but Egret shook her head. "Why try to make him when he truly does not want to?" she asked.

Juan flashed her a grateful smile, which she ignored. He would not be so grateful when they had gone where the brisk bay breezes could not follow them!

She bent toward the canoe, but the Spaniard anticipated what was to be done next. He seized it, upended it, and lifted it over his head. "Thank you," Egret mumbled.

Cypress beamed. "The river we will take is this way," she said to him, pointing, and speaking distinctly.

Juan nodded, and followed the two girls to the cove. When they came to a mangrove-lined inlet, he set down the narrow craft and slid it carefully into water that flowed gently between the interwoven roots of the trees that lined either side of it.

Cypress beamed again as she stepped lightly into the canoe and laid down the double-bladed paddle and sculling pole she had brought along; then she took the basket and flails from the younger girl. "Why don't you steady the canoe while Juan gets in?" she suggested.

Egret shrugged, then complied. Even so, the dugout rocked ominously when the Spaniard tried to imitate Cypress's descent into it, and the consternation on his face did not vanish until he had managed to seat himself.

Dancing Egret said nothing; she only picked up the paddle and sent the lightweight craft smoothly into the narrow entrance of the river. A black-headed gull dipped from the clear blue sky and shouted insults at the trio, then abandoned the game to dive for an oyster he'd spotted. As they glided along, moss-hung mangroves surrounded them with welcome shade and Egret's annoyance was erased. As familiar as this river was to her, she never ceased to be enthralled with everything she saw or heard or smelled as she traveled it. A tiny green frog, sleeping contentedly on the brown tip of a slender mangrove seedling, caught her eye, and she smiled. A lizard darted across a tangle of roots, searching for a dinner he was certain to find. And when a pair of dolphin arched gracefully out of the widening water ahead of them, she laughed aloud. Without haste she steered the canoe from the maze of mangroves into more open water and admired the lush ferns surrounding the buttressed bases of the cypress trees that waded in the shallows.

Suddenly the Spaniard started. From the muddy bank, what he had assumed to be a length of deadwood animated itself and splashed into the water. All that remained above the rippled surface were the tip of a bulbous snout and two wary eyes he could have sworn were staring at him. "*Madre de Dios!* What *is* that?" he asked hoarsely.

"It is an alligator," Cypress told him.

He tested the word, repeated it. "We say, *caiman*. But *caiman*, he not so big!"

"Our men hunt them," Kneeling Cypress said, "and they will show you how. I promise to cook the first one you bring back to the village, so you will see how good a meal it makes."

"Unless it makes a meal of you instead," Egret said, smiling as a mosquito lighted on the tip of the young man's nose. She set aside her paddle as Cypress picked up the long sculling pole, which flared at the lower end into an elongated flat blade. When she had fitted it into the peg in the canoe's transom, she was able to keep them on course with a minimum of effort.

"Gators can be dangerous," she agreed, frowning as Egret smiled again to see Juan try vainly to shoo away the pesky mosquito and the whining kin it had summoned to the feast. "Among our people there is a story-song that tells how dangerous they are." Her young friend was grinning broadly now, and Cypress searched for some way to make her stop. "Egret has taken many of our longer Legends and made shorter story-songs for our small children," she said. "Why not tell us Alligator's story, Egret? If you speak slowly enough, Juan will be able to understand most of your words."

Egret knew full well what Cypress was trying to do. Well, the Spaniard was already paying for ignoring their good advice, and it made no sense to jeopardize a friendship she cherished by continuing to annoy Cypress. "It is a good story," she said, "and I enjoy telling it. So if you are sure you wish to hear . . . ?"

Kneeling Cypress, much relieved, nodded, and Juan Ortiz, furtively scratching his earlobe, nodded also.

"In the Beginning," Egret said, letting a lilt creep into her voice, "some of the Calusa laughed at Alligator. They mocked his thick-skinned body and cumbersome tail, his stubby legs and his drooping eyelids. 'It is easy to mistake him for a rotting log,' they said to one another, 'but at least a log was once a tree and remembers when it was dressed in beautiful green leaves. And Alligator knows how ugly he is,' they agreed. 'Because he saw his reflection in the river, he is forever scowling.'

"They did not fear Alligator, you see," she said, her voice somehow signaling the folly of that. "They thought a creature so heavy and low to the ground must be slow-moving and clumsy as well. But that was before a foolish young boy—who had listened to this talk and believed it—went alone to the riverbank and began to shout insults at Alligator. For a time, Alligator simply lay in the sun and listened to words he had heard all too often. But today Alligator was hungry; although he seemed as sleepy as usual, he was noticing how well-fleshed the jeering boy was.

"Suddenly, Alligator opened his huge mouth and bellowed." Egret's voice strengthened; excitement underscored her words. "His short legs carried him swiftly, swiftly, to where the startled boy stood. And he fastened his sharp teeth around one meaty ankle and yanked that boy backward into the river."

Juan had understood enough to be leaning forward in anticipation now. This young girl was an admirable storyteller! And her face, which he had earlier labeled unattractive except perhaps to savages like herself, had taken on a fascinating glow as she chanted her tale.

"When he had made a meal of the boy," Egret went on, her voice both regretting and accepting the lad's unhappy end, "Alligator surfaced. And the people who had heard screams and run to the riverbank saw that he was no longer scowling.

Alligator wore a big-toothed grin now, a grin that warned the Calusa never to laugh at him again."

Her dark eyes studied the young man, moved to gaze at Cypress. "And we never have," she finished solemnly, "nor ever will." Then she smiled modestly as her listeners praised her for the story, and there was genuine warmth in her expression as she looked again at Juan Ortiz. "You will be careful," she said in an almost teasing tone, "never to approach Alligator until you are a seasoned hunter? You do not want to give him yet more reason to grin!"

"I do not," Juan said fervently, then looked to his left as Cypress turned the canoe into a slow-moving stream angling from the river. Now, thick-trunked hardwoods intruded among the more slender trees, and on the overhanging branch of one of them sat an ungainly bird with a long, curving neck. Its broad wings were widespread, and Juan could clearly see the white feathers that contrasted with the darker plumage covering most of its body.

"That is Anhinga," Kneeling Cypress said, looking in the same direction. "He has been fishing and is drying his wings."

Egret noticed the confusion in the young man's eyes. "The anhinga swims in the water while looking for fish to eat," she explained, using her hands as well as her voice to describe what she meant. "Only his neck sticks up when he is hunting, and from a distance he looks rather like a snake."

"Your country, it has many strange things," Juan said after a moment.

"They are not strange to us," Cypress told him. "They are part of the world that was made for us to live in."

Once again the Spaniard seemed confused. "We travel far," he said, waving toward the river and the land on either side. "All this, your father owns?"

It was Cypress's turn to be perplexed. "Owns?"

"No one *owns* land," Dancing Egret said, more shocked than perplexed. "We may own clothing and trinkets and weapons and tools, and such things as baskets and pots, but never land. This land was given to the Calusa to live upon, as Cypress said, but we do not own it. It has nurtured us from the Beginning, and in return we guard it from those who would not respect it as our people do." She looked up, frowning as a distant growl of thunder brought an answering roar from a gator deep in the swamp they had not yet reached. "A storm is coming," she said.

One moment it was coming, the next it was there. A surge of cool air descended to prickle their arms and brought with it a horde of mosquitoes. After brief investigation of the mud-covered girls, the insects swarmed upon the unprotected flesh of Juan Ortiz. As he slapped at them with both hands, fretful breezes matured into gusts and rain began to spill from the sky. Lightning flared in the west, casting the wind-lashed trees into quivering silhouette. Thunder echoed and reechoed around them; the pelting rain forced its way through the branches arching overhead, threw itself upon the helpless river and ravished it gleefully. Even the vicious mosquitoes fled in the face of such brutality, but the miserable young man did not think to be thankful for this small boon.

Egret and Cypress were unperturbed; in summer such storms came regularly. "It will not last long," Cypress shouted to Juan as her long wet hair whipped around her face.

Egret nodded confirmation, then tipped up her head and opened her mouth to let the rain fill it, the precious rain that meant the survival of This World and its people.

Although the onslaught seemed interminable to Ortiz, barely a quarter of an hour passed before the rain diminished, then ceased. Thunder rumbled querulously a time or two, then fell silent. And the sun showed its golden face once more.

The laundered air was honey-sweet and refreshing. Birds of every size and color flocked to the trees and began to imitate the anhinga the trio had seen earlier. Perching on branch and twig, they fluffed their feathers and twittered and chirped with joy as they efficiently disposed of inhibiting rainwater. The sun's slanting rays transformed the drops that lingered on leaf and blade into rainbow-filled prisms. The pointed leaves of a water oak glistened as though new-made, and a red-bellied turtle prepared to bask again in the emerald froth of young ferns growing on a fallen cypress log. From the marsh that lay just beyond the river's bend, the peeps and clicks of insects rose in exultant chorus.

Egret turned herself around, took up her paddle and prepared to navigate the turn in the gradually widening river. "If you'll bail out the water, Cypress," she called over her shoulder, "the going will be easier. Or perhaps Juan will do it."

But Cypress did not reach for the hollowed-out gourd that lay at her feet. "We must go back to the village," she said quietly. "It is senseless to go farther today."

Egret was astounded. "I did not suggest that we go all the

way to the Lake of Mayaimi," she said. "This river can't take us that far, anyhow. But in no time at all we can be at the swamp where the rice grows. Which is where we were headed in the first place, if you remember. And I thought you wanted to teach Juan to paddle a canoe? Once we come to the straight part of the river, it will be a good time for him to try."

But her friend was paying her no attention; every bit of it was focused on the young man who sat between them. The mosquitoes' assault had left his face so swollen that his left eye was virtually closed; his sodden garments clung to his lean body and steamed unpleasantly as the sun strengthened. "We are going home," she said firmly, and maneuvered the sculling pole until the canoe obediently swung about.

Dancing Egret knew it would do no good to argue. With a sigh, she dipped her paddle first to one side, then the other. The dugout responded sluggishly until Cypress, after flashing an approving smile at the younger girl, began to bail. "We'll come again soon," she said consolingly.

But Egret was not appeased. The Spaniard had only himself to blame for his sorry state, and Cypress knew it. If he had come with them today in order to prepare himself for handling warriors' canoes, then it was serving him ill to cater to him. Club Wielder and the others would not hesitate to let him know that a man who cannot endure discomfort might just as well put on women's clothes and go live among the berdaches!

Not even the sight of the whiskered, wrinkled face of a manatee could coax a smile from Egret during the silent journey back to the village. If Cypress's unseemly concern for this fool of a Spaniard continued, Dancing Egret knew there would be less and less to smile about from now on. And instinct told her that something more potent than a Healing Ceremony would be needed to rid Kneeling Cypress of her obsession with Juan Ortiz.

Chapter 5

❦ ❦

Like the Calusa everywhere, Ucita's villagers gave hearty welcome to the drier and cooler half of their two-season year. It was oddly pleasant to shiver occasionally in the darkest part of the night, to slip bare feet into moccasins fashioned from alligator skin and, once in a while, to need light cloaks when they went out in the early morning.

"I enjoy this weather," Dancing Egret declared. "Sweat doesn't cling to your skin and hair or drip into your eyes whenever you bend your head. During the hot season, if you are not soaked with sweat, chances are you'll be drenched with rain at some time during the day. It's a wonder we bother going to the river then; even without bathing, we are rarely dry!"

Kneeling Cypress laughed. "I'm surprised to hear you complain about having to bathe, Egret, when I've more than once suspected that you are clan-kin to a fish."

"I'm not complaining," the younger girl said hastily. "But you must admit that even the air is different now; it smells cleaner and lighter than it does during the rainy season."

Cypress did not deny it. "It's good to know that the garments and bedding we wash will dry thoroughly," she said. "And it's certainly easier to build or repair our houses when we don't have to worry about waterlogged timbers and thatch." Her eyes moved to where the newest house, raised on stout pillars to outwit periodic flooding, presented its roof of interlocking palm fronds to the benevolent sun. "Juan's home seems so small, compared to the rest," she said.

"He has no need for a larger one," Egret said, "since he has neither wife nor children. And he certainly has no kin in this land that he might have to make room for."

"If he did," Cypress retorted, "he would be able to make

49

them comfortable. Juan has already built a bed and three stools for his home, and shelves to hold his belongings."

"I thought the wood-carver made those."

"Well, Juan helped, and he made one of the stools by himself."

Dancing Egret smoothed the soil over the seeds she was planting in a shallow, crushed-shell-lined basin below Chief Ucita's house. "I'm glad Kwambu traded for these seeds when he stopped at Guacata," she said to change the subject. "Even though we've always gotten a generous supply of gourds from there, we'll never run out once we're growing our own. No matter how many break or get holes in them."

"We get a good deal from the towns around the Lake," Cypress said, diverted, "plums and zamia flour and beans, as well as gourds. But I was especially pleased that your friend brought us dates from that Timucuan town—Canegacola, was that its name? Juan Ortiz is very fond of dates."

Egret had no intention of letting the conversation drift back to the Spaniard. "Canegacola, yes," she said. "His town is near a lake that lies north of our lake of Mayaimi. His is a smaller lake, Kwambu tells me, but the soil around it is exceptionally fertile." She shaded her eyes with one hand and peered across at the causeway. "Someone must be coming," she said. "Two of the sentries are going to the bay, and they only leave their posts when there is a visitor to be greeted."

"Perhaps it's a courier from your father," Kneeling Cypress said. She glanced toward the house whose shadow they stood in. "I ought to go and tell Ucita and White Gull to expect a guest."

"Guests," Egret informed her. "The sentries are bringing two men along the causeway." She narrowed her eyes. "I do not think they are from Calusa's island, or from any of his towns. Their hair does not hang loose, but is pulled up on top of their heads. And I think . . . yes! They are tattooed all over, Cypress, not just here and there to mark their status. Their headdresses are peculiar, too, but the white feathers in them probably mean what they mean to us: that they come in peace."

"My father has seen them," Cypress said. "He is coming out now." She cocked her head. "And from the sounds I hear, White Gull is already having her women prepare food and drink."

Hearing Cypress's voice, Ucita looked over and smiled

briefly at the two girls, then returned his attention to the squareground through which sentries and guests were now walking.

"Will you go in?" Egret asked.

Kneeling Cypress shook her head. "Not unless my father sends for me." She looked down at her dirt-streaked knees, held up a pair of equally dirty hands. "Having seen the state I'm in," she laughed, "I doubt he'll want me there."

"Then let's finish our work," Dancing Egret said. "That way, we can get a close look at the men as they come up the ramp. And maybe hear what they say to your father, too."

"It's not likely to be anything we'll be interested in," Cypress replied, picking up her hoe again. "But Ucita would have signed had he wanted us to go away, so we might as well finish our planting."

"And then haul up the water to dampen the seeds," Egret reminded her.

Cypress grinned. "If the men return from their dolphin hunt before we finish, I might be able to persuade Juan to do that."

Egret made a face; their conversation had come full circle again! But since she was busy loosening the soil in the next planting basin, Cypress was unaware of Egret's disgruntlement.

"We are emissaries of Holata Mocoso," said the stocky warrior who had identified himself as Killer of Whales. "Wind That Whistles and I have just been visiting Headchief Calusa to let him know that Mocoso has agreed to renew their trading agreement."

Ucita nodded. "That is good." It was also good that these men spoke the language of the Calusa, although how they had learned it was a different matter. Before Calusa had arranged for Ucita to defend this stretch of border, and then engineered the truce with Mocoso, Calusan women and children had been carried off during sporadic raiding. The Timucuan men the women had been given to, and the families that adopted the abducted children, had had ample opportunity to learn how the Calusa speak.

He accepted a steaming cup from White Gull, sipped from it, and passed it to Killer of Whales. "You are welcome here," he said formally.

His guest drank, then handed the cup to his comrade. "Ucita is a generous host," he said, equally formal. "But we would expect no less from a man who hopes to link his family to that of our Headchief."

Wind That Whistles nodded. He was older than his companion, and considerably thinner, and the long jagged scar that puckered his brow gave his right eye a permanent squint. In his presence, Ucita was less conscious of his own disfigurement.

"My wife and her women will bring food soon," he told the pair. "And they will arrange a place to sleep, if you would care to spend the night in my village."

Killer of Whales waved a hand dismissively. "No need. We have pledged to be home before full dark, to report to Holata Mocoso. He wishes to know"—he paused as White Gull deposited a tray of warm bread and raw oysters on the bench around which the men were sitting—"how soon the wedding is to take place."

Chief Ucita selected a plump oyster, tipped the liquid from the shell into his mouth, then dislodged the tender meat with the tip of his knife. "My daughter must be consulted, of course," he said. He popped the meat into his mouth, chewed and swallowed, then smiled to see his visitors helping themselves to the food. "Women need time to prepare," he said vaguely. "To make new garments. Kneeling Cypress will want to be properly garbed when she becomes the wife of so honored a man as Headchief Mocoso. And there is a separate treaty between your town and mine to be negotiated first." Although he said this last almost casually, the two sitting opposite him knew that unless steps were taken to stop Mocoso's younger warriors from honing their skills by occasionally harassing Ucita's town, there would be no marriage.

"We are authorized to make the treaty." Wind That Whistles spoke for the first time, his bear-sized voice hilarious contradiction to his scrawny-rabbit appearance. Ucita felt no urge to laugh, however. Wind That Whistles's eyes, even the one with the squint, were uncommonly shrewd, and Ucita did not doubt that, of the two, this was the man who truly spoke for Mocoso. The copper gorget he wore on a thong around his neck, as well as his elaborate tattooing, named him one of Mocoso's Principal Men.

"Then if we can come to terms now," Ucita said smoothly, "I can doubtless persuade my daughter to make haste with her preparations. Shall we say the ceremony will take place at the next full of the moon?"

His guests merely grunted, for their mouths were crammed with oysters. But Ucita understood that this news would please Mocoso. He smiled again. Headchief Calusa would be quick to praise a Townchief who managed to establish a permanent peace along one of his borders.

Kneeling Cypress's face wore a mask of distress as, finger to her lips, she beckoned Egret after her down the ramp. "How can he?" she sputtered as they reached the plaza. "How can my father make such a pledge without asking me first?"

Egret was puzzled. "You've known for more than a year that Ucita was considering marrying you to Headchief Mocoso. Even I knew that, Cypress."

"But it was not definite," the older girl insisted. "You know it wasn't; you were there when my father first mentioned it. All he said was that it might be a way to improve relations between our tribes."

"But you said nothing then to discourage his idea."

"I did not care then." Cypress's eyes flashed, and her slender hands clenched into fists. "I will not do it, Egret. A woman has the right to choose her own husband."

"Most women do, but a chief's daughter generally does not. When I'm old enough, my father will almost certainly arrange a marriage for me with someone he wants to bind more closely to him. And I'll be happy enough to go where Calusa sends me."

"You can afford to sound unconcerned," Cypress snapped. "You are still a child; you do not know what it is to be in love."

"I am no longer a child," Egret retorted, hurt to be suddenly called a child by the very person who had attended her during her recent initiation into womanhood. White Gull, as a matron of Egret's clan, had performed the ceremony, but since there was no other woman of the Dolphin clan living in Ucita, she had asked Kneeling Cypress to assist. At the end of the ritual, White Gull had called upon their ancestors to recognize that, through the blessing of Grandmother Moon, *Here stood Dancing Egret, who yesterday was child and today is woman.* And Cypress had solemnly added, *In every way she is a woman: in her body, in her thoughts, in her feelings, and in each of her three souls.* But apparently Cypress thought it took more than a ceremony marking the onset of monthly bleeding to confer the status of woman upon Dancing Egret!

"Then do not talk as though you were a child," Cypress said. In the next moment, her angry face crumpled. "Oh, Egret, what am I to do?"

Dancing Egret hesitated. What response would a grown-up make to that question? "You might speak with your father," she said slowly. "He loves you, and will not want you to be unhappy. But"—she paused again; should she add what common sense told her to say?—"I would not rush to talk to him, Cypress. Calm yourself first, and try to see matters from his point of view. This Canegacola we were discussing—the chief whose town the dates came from—I remember my father saying that Canegacola's warriors are among the fiercest in the land. And Canegacola is Mocoso's brother-in-law." Her brow puckered as she tried to make plain what bothered her. "If you refuse to marry Mocoso and he becomes angry enough to deny Calusan traders safe passage through his territories, Canegacola's warriors will swoop down on them the moment they set foot across the border. You know that Mocoso's provinces lay between here and all the other Timucuan provinces, so we could not even go farther north to trade unless we went by water. And Mocoso's warriors can fight nearly as well from canoes as they do on land. Almost as well as Calusa's can," she added loyally.

"But we just heard Mocoso's men say that the treaty with your father has been renewed," Cypress said.

Egret sighed; she had not made herself clear, after all. "Treaties can be broken," she murmured.

But Cypress was too caught up in her own problem to listen to any more talk of trading and treaties. "Your suggestion that I speak with Ucita is a fine one," she said. "It's true that he loves me, as dearly as I love him. He is sure to agree that we will both be happier if I remain here, in his village."

That Cypress was probably right only gave Egret something else to worry about. For she knew full well why Cypress did not want to leave Ucita's town; it had little to do with her friendship for Dancing Egret, or even with her love for her father.

Kneeling Cypress took Juan Ortiz for her husband on a day made mellow by the winter sun. Her face glowed with happiness despite the fact that—so far as Egret could tell—the Spaniard was more bewildered than delighted by the ceremony he was taking part in.

Couriers had long since been dispatched to Headchief Mocoso, to deliver an extremely tactful message. They had reported to Ucita that the Headchief had not been pleased to learn Cypress's father had found he could not bear to part with his youngest daughter, and Mocoso had refused outright the niece Ucita offered in Kneeling Cypress's place. But two moons had waxed and waned, and Mocoso continued to honor the treaty he had made with Headchief Calusa; it seemed that his displeasure would have no disastrous effect.

"He will hear about her marriage to the Spaniard, however," Kwambu, stopping briefly at Ucita's village, told Dancing Egret. "Mocoso will be even more displeased about that. He has never owned a Spanish slave, although I have heard that he wishes he did. But if he had one, he would never allow a slave to marry into his family. Any more than Headchief Calusa would." It still astounded Kwambu that the word *slave* did not stick to his tongue and refuse to be uttered. Of course, in this country, slave was merely the status assigned to enemy captives or shipwreck survivors, people having no clan-kinship within the community. Except for those unfortunates who were singled out for ceremonial sacrifice, a slave's life was not much different from a servant's. Nor was either status necessarily permanent; many respected craftsmen had once been either servants or slaves. Yet it was equally true that Juan Ortiz was the first slave Kwambu had ever known of to marry above his status, and he wondered aloud what Chief Ucita was thinking of to permit what was ordinarily forbidden.

"He truly cannot refuse Cypress anything," Egret explained. "I know you're right, Kwambu, but what has happened has happened. So long as no harm comes of it, even Calusa should not object."

"Headchief Calusa shall do as he always does, wait patiently and see what happens. He has not criticized Ucita, to my knowledge. Nor will he, unless the man's actions bring trouble that might have been averted had he chosen the wiser course."

"I felt sorry for Chief Ucita, Kwambu. He had little choice but to let Cypress marry Juan. And she's so happy that I can't help but be grateful he did."

And Cypress continued to be happy. "I can wish nothing better for you," she told Egret, "than to wed the man of your choosing." Her smile was radiant as she pounded corn into meal.

"You do not mind sharing his tiny house?"

She shook her head. "I prefer living here, where we can be alone." Her cheeks were flushed, and not from the sun. "I do not feel less like a chief's daughter because I live on the mound's lowest level. Besides, it's not whose daughter I am that matters, but whose *wife*. To be with Juan, I would be willing to live in the middle of the river glades!"

Dancing Egret doubted that her friend would be content for long if her home were on a lonely hammock surrounded by a virtual sea of sawgrass, but that her love for Juan Ortiz was as constant as the ocean's tides, Egret did not doubt. She only hoped that the Spaniard loved his new wife even half as much. Juan certainly seemed to be trying to fit in to village life. At his insistence, Cypress had taken tanned hide and sewn for him a shirt with sleeves, and straight-legged breeches. He wore these most of the time, but Egret had noticed that when it was sweat-making sultry, he would strip down to a breechclout. And he had let his hair grow, although he continued to pull it back and tie it with a fiber cord so that it hung from his nape like a misplaced tail. Still, Club Wielder and the other warriors did not object to these aberrations. Juan had shown aptitude in everything they had been teaching him, and that was enough for them. And now that his flesh had been reddened by constant exposure to the sun, Egret supposed that to the casual observer he might pass for a native of this land. Not for one of Calusa's people, of course; an eternity of sunshine would never darken his skin to that degree. But the Timucua who had come here had been more bronze than brown, and according to Kwambu, this was true of all the northern peoples.

"Will Juan be taking part in the games against the warriors of Muspa?" she asked Cypress. That chief's town lay on an island on the sunset side of the bay, and his warriors and Ucita's had a tradition of rivalry that culminated each year in an arduous three-day competition. This year, Muspa would be the host.

Cypress's smile widened. "Club Wielder has said that he may compete in the knife-throw."

Because he had never forgotten how Ortiz had slain the wolf that absconded with Club Wielder's dead son, the War Leader had chosen to tutor him further in that particular skill. "By all accounts, Club Wielder is a demanding teacher. You must be happy that he thinks so highly of your husband's ability," Egret said.

"I am happy for Juan, and proud of him, too. I only wish

the games were being held here, so I could watch him compete."

Egret added a little water to the cornmeal she was shaping into small, flat rounds. "Muspa's best warriors will come to this village next year," she said consolingly. "And Juan will probably be ready then to take part in a number of contests."

Cypress laid down her pestle and hugged her friend. "You are kind to say so," she said. "And it's true. Juan is both strong and agile. A little more practice, and he'll be adept in everything."

Egret began setting the molded bread on the upturned clamshells arranged around a low fire over which slabs of dolphin were smoking. Kneeling Cypress's praise-songs for Ortiz no longer annoyed her, but they did tend to go on and on. Since it would be discourteous not to listen, it seemed sensible to keep busy while she did.

"I had forgotten," Kwambu said, his rueful smile a flash of white in his dark face, "that this was the time Ucita and his warriors would be away at Muspa. But I have no real need to speak with him; I wanted only to ask if he would like more of the sassafras root I got from Holata Outina while I was in the north this time."

"I'm sure he would," Dancing Egret said. "He has become quite fond of tea brewed from the root's bark. Perhaps you could leave it with White Gull? And when you return, Chief Ucita will give you whatever you want in exchange."

"I want nothing in exchange; it is a gift. But I think I will give it to you instead," Kwambu said. "Share it as you will."

"You have gone to trade with this Holata Outina before," Egret said, smiling her thanks as Kwambu took the prized root from his pack. "I remember you speaking of him. What is he like?"

"He is probably as old as Ucita," Kwambu replied, "but he looks younger. That is not surprising; before he took his uncle's place as chief, Outina was one of his people's finest warriors, and he takes pride in his physical well-being. He is a man more suited to action than to words, if truth be told, being both slow-thinking and slow-talking. Unless he is describing a battle he once took part in; then his words pour out like water from a jug, and his voice—which he tries hard to keep pitched low in keeping with his status—rises with excitement until it is almost a squeak."

Egret laughed. "I recall my father having guests, and also talking about long-ago wars. But at least Calusa's voice never resembled a mouse's, no matter how thrilling the tales he told."

"Calusa would never forget himself, in any situation," Kwambu agreed. "I think there are few men in this world as single-minded, however, or who match him in any other way. And I have met many tribal leaders in the course of my trading."

"It's scarcely news to me that you admire Calusa," Dancing Egret said. "You even talk the way he does most of the time, almost as though you were making a speech."

"I learned your language from listening to him," Kwambu reminded her.

"So you did," she said. "It suits you somehow, and at least no one will ever misunderstand what you say."

"I hope they do not," he said gravely. "In my business, that could spawn problems." He looked around the plaza. "I do not see Ucita's priest, and I have brought the bundle of heron feathers he asked for when I was here last."

"Tradition Keeper is in the Temple," Egret said. "He goes there each day at this time, to ask the souls of Ucita's dead warriors to lend their spirit-support to those who have gone to Muspa. While you're waiting for him, why don't you tell me more about this Holata Outina? Has he a wife? Children? Are the Timucuan ways very different from ours?"

"Dancing Egret still wishes to know everything," Kwambu teased. "Well, Outina has no wife. He lives with his sister, Walks Tall Woman. Among the Timucua, you see, an unmarried man lives with his mother's clan, and for Outina, that is the White Deer clan, the ruling clan of his people. Walks Tall Woman is a widow, and her son Swoops Like Falcon and her niece Moon of Winter also live in her lodge. Moon of Winter is a girl about your age, a remarkably pretty girl. Outina is inclined to spoil her somewhat, partly because—like you—Moon of Winter was only an infant when her mother died. Walks Tall Woman does not approve of this; since Swoops Like Falcon will probably be the next Headchief, I imagine she thinks he should receive all of Outina's attention."

"What a great deal you discover about the people you meet as you travel!" Egret said. "I envy you."

"A trader needs to know more than how to barter," Kwambu said. "He must also be certain never to offend those he hopes

to trade with. The more I know about the person I will be dealing with, the less likely I am to offend."

"That makes sense. But if you were a woman, you would be
much in demand among the gossips." She looked down as a
pair of childish hands tugged at her moss skirt. "Do you want
something, Night Blossom?"

"Isn't it time for our story?" the little girl asked.

Dancing Egret looked up. The sun was halfway down the
western sky. "It will be, as soon as I have finished speaking
with my visitor," she told her. "Go ask White Gull for my
flute, and then fetch the other children. I'll be ready by the
time you get back."

Kwambu chuckled as the child darted away. "You have
made a ritual of your storytelling, I see."

"The little ones enjoy it, and so do I," Egret said. "And our
people have so many story-songs that I can tell a tale a day
and never run out of them."

"It is good that they learn them so young," Kwambu said.
"I wish I could remember more of the Legends my mother told
me."

Egret was instantly intrigued. "You do remember some?"
Kwambu nodded.

"Then you must tell me those you recall," she said. "I'll
make them into story-songs the children here can understand.
They'll like hearing tales from a faraway country."

"When I come again, I will tell you one," Kwambu promised.

"And you'll tell me more about Outina's village, too?"

"I will," he said, and lifted a hand in farewell as a covey of
eager children began to congregate. "For now, I will go to the
Temple mound and wait there for Tradition Keeper," he said.

Egret signaled her own good-bye and gathered the children
around her. But she had scarcely begun the day's story when
a sentry's warning howl cascaded from the causeway. As startled villagers spilled out of their houses, a score of painted
warriors rushed upon the squareground—warriors who brandished knives and spears, and whose whooping cries announced that they would not hesitate to use them.

Chapter 6

◆—— ——◆

Egret's first thought was for the children who had leaped up to cling to her hands, her skirt, each other. Their eyes were white-rimmed with fear, a fear that seemed to permeate the dust cloud raised upon the plaza by the invaders' pounding feet. The dust seeped into the children's nostrils and tempted them to retch, and Dancing Egret, gagging, realized that she was not immune to it, either. They were all half blinded, too, but underscoring a vibrating chorus of shouts and shrieks was the ominous whoosh of dart and spear, the awful thump of war club striking flesh. The cries of panicked mothers sliced through the din, but Egret was unable to restore their boys and girls to them. All she could do was slide cautiously toward the edge of the plaza, taking the little ones with her.

She did not get far. All at once six warriors surrounded them, shouting words neither she nor the children understood. But they understood well enough the blades clutched in upraised fists. Dancing Egret wrapped her arms around as many of the frightened youngsters as she could reach and felt her own fear melt away as anger raged through her. "They are children!" she screamed. "What kind of warriors kill little children?"

Even as the words left her mouth, she wanted to grab them back. These Timucua—their tribe revealed by their top-knotted hair—would not recognize her words any better than she did theirs. But her voice had been saturated with fury, and this they could not mistake. Now they would slay her first of all, for daring to scream at them. And who could offer this flock of terrified children even a semblance of protection once she had been stabbed to the heart?

Or would they punish Dancing Egret by killing a child instead? Or by killing all of them, one by one, making her un-witting accessory to a massacre of innocents? And all because she had lacked the sense to keep silent. The cold sweat of fear sheathed her flesh as she watched for the first warrior's arm to descend; would she be brave enough to fling herself in its path? Could she do so quickly enough to satisfy the warriors' lust for blood and, perhaps, save the children from a similar fate?

She was not put to the test. Although the warriors' right arms remained menacingly raised, with their left hands they began to make the sort of motions the villagers made when they wanted to shoo scavenging gulls from a clam bed. For a moment Egret was too stunned to move. Then, with stumbling steps, she urged her charges in the direction indicated by the scowling warriors. Several of the little girls were sobbing, and the smaller boys were hard put not to do the same. "It will be all right," she said to them, and prayed she did not lie. "Only stay together, and we'll be all right."

So intent was she on reassuring them that she did not real-ize, until the warriors signaled them to stop, that they were be-ing herded toward the center of the squareground, and that many of the elders, women, and older children had been brought there also. She risked a glance around; White Gull was nearby, and Cypress, and even Kwambu and Tradition Keeper were there. What did this mean? Were all of them to be taken captive? Would Chief Ucita and the warriors who had gone to Muspa return to find that everyone, even the village priest, had disappeared?

No. Some would be left. The younger, less-experienced fight-ers Ucita had not taken with him, those who had tried to defend his town, would be here still. The sentries were sprawled atop the causeway while miniature rivers of red streamed over the conch shells that formed its side. At the foot of the Temple mound were more youthful warriors, their eyes staring sight-lessly into a sky in which buzzards were already circling.

With her body, she shielded the little ones from the grisly sight. Over their heads her eyes met those of Kneeling Cy-press, moved on to exchange an equally despairing look with White Gull. What did the invaders mean to do with the people they had so efficiently rounded up?

Tradition Keeper pushed his way to the front of the now-silent group and confronted one of the warriors. "I call upon the Eater of Eyes," he intoned. "Should you harm just one of these women or children, he will destroy all of you. Not even your spirits will survive to receive honor from your families."

The alien warrior remained impassive. He'd understood nothing the priest had said, and probably the Timucua did not acknowledge the Buzzard God anyway. But even if the god's name was unfamiliar, one man who had listened to Tradition Keeper had been able to decipher his words: beside the warrior that the priest was cursing stood a man with a scar puckering his forehead and angling into a corner of his right eye. Dancing Egret had seen that face before.

She stared fixedly at him until he looked in her direction. "Will you tell us," she said loudly before he could turn his glance elsewhere, "what the warriors of Mocoso plan for us?"

She heard a pair of startled gasps; Kneeling Cypress and White Gull had also recognized the man who had called on Chief Ucita to arrange for a marriage that had never taken place.

Wind That Whistles considered for a moment, as if wondering how this young girl realized that he spoke her language; then he nodded. "You are to leave this town," he said tersely. And, as Tradition Keeper began to protest, "All of you, and at once. There will be no more killing. Mocoso's men do not slay priests or"—his hard eyes flickered toward the bluejay feather in Kwambu's headband—"traders, any more than they do the very old, the very young, or women. Unless of course"—he looked back at the priest—"you refuse to go."

"You are taking us prisoner?" Tradition Keeper, frowning at Dancing Egret, asked the question she had opened her mouth to ask.

"We take no captives this time," Wind That Whistles said. "You and your people will go to the bay. Under guard. But your guards will leave with us once we have done what we came here to do. Then"—he shrugged—"you may go, and do what you will."

For a single wild moment Egret wished that everyone, from the oldest to the youngest, would simply refuse to move. But Wind That Whistles had told them what would happen if they did, and Ucita's dead warriors testified to the fact that Mocoso's men would kill if they must. Yet even though the Timucuan had promised that no further harm would come to those who were plodding obediently to the far side of the square, dare they believe him? Egret tightened her lips so the little ones would not see them quiver.

Others were experiencing a similar dread as they were led into the prickly brush beyond the mound and over uneven ground to the shore; the set faces of Ucita's people, the involuntary trembling of the very old and the very young, the uncertain shamble of everyone's feet, told Egret that. So did the anguish on the faces of the mothers who, singly or in pairs, sidled through the crowd to reclaim their terrified children.

By the time they reached the cove, Dancing Egret walked alone, but not for long. "We will survive; the Timucua dare not kill Headchief Calusa's daughters," White Gull hissed into her right ear.

"I'm so grateful that Juan is on Muspa," Kneeling Cypress murmured into the other. "I would be a widow now had he been left behind, and I'd rather die myself than have anything happen to him." She shuddered, and Egret reached for her hand.

With gestures, their guards told them to sit, but the Timucua did not object when family members sought one another before doing so, and it was apparent that talking among themselves was to be allowed. Gradually, snippets of murmured conversation multiplied; to exchange a few words with your neighbor made the situation more bearable.

When Kwambu claimed a spot near hers, Egret was glad to see him. "What do you suppose Mocoso's warriors plan to do?" she asked him quietly.

"I think, if you look back toward the village, you will soon see for yourself."

But Tradition Keeper was the first to spy the smoke rising like a pale plume into the winter air. "They must not fire the Temple!" he exclaimed, and struggled to his feet.

From the middle of the group a woman sent up a brief keening wail; it was not the Temple she was mourning, but the home she had shared with her husband and children and with her husband's aged mother. She was shushed by friends who shared her feeling but recognized before she did that weeping would not give them back what they were losing; it would only offer amusement to the warriors who stood guard over them.

"It is unlikely that they will burn the Temple," Kwambu said, urging Tradition Keeper to sit again. "The Timucua have as healthy a fear of ghosts as the Calusa do."

The priest subsided, muttering an incantation to bring emasculation upon every able-bodied man of Mocoso. Even if they did no harm to the Temple, just their presence in the town profaned it.

"My sister believes the people here were spared because she and I are Calusa's daughters," Egret said to Kwambu, wincing as a tongue of flame spat sparks into the sky. "Do you suppose she is right?"

"Mocoso knows that the two of you live here," he said, "and that White Gull is Ucita's wife besides. His quarrel is with Chief Ucita; he will be careful not to invite Calusa's wrath."

"But surely my father won't let the burning of Ucita's town go unavenged!" Egret said.

Kwambu hesitated. "If he feels that Mocoso has just cause, then he will," he said. "And your father will be scrupulous in deciding the truth of the matter. As always."

Cypress had been listening. "Are you saying that, because I would not go and be wife to him, Mocoso has a right to leave all of us homeless?" Her voice was sharp, and the huddle of slump-shouldered people looked her way. They had suspected the reason for the raid, Egret realized; there was no surprise in their faces.

"He might have left all of you dead," Kwambu said to Cypress, "and still had a chance of proving justification. For Ucita to promise you to him, and then renege, was an assault upon Mocoso's honor."

Tears welled in Cypress's eyes. "Oh, my father! My poor father. He will never forgive me, never, if Headchief Calusa holds him to account for what is happening here. And how unfair that would be, when this woman alone is the cause of it!"

"My father will be fair," Egret said tartly. "He is likely to decide that to have his town destroyed is sufficient punishment for Chief Ucita." For the flames were leaping high now, dancing obscenely over the mound upon which so many homes were perched. And the storehouses by the river were burning, too; the odors of charred corn and smoldering animal skins were wandering from the riverside and slithering into the cove.

All eyes were fixed upon the sky-reaching flames, but they were eyes too filmed with despair to reflect the fire's hurtful glare. And no one was keening now; there was no agitated exclaiming, no bewailing of their fate. Most of the upturned faces wore masks of stoic acceptance, and the people spoke together in tones muted by resignation. As for the children, they simply sat and stared toward what had been their village; they did not talk at all.

"This is not good," Kwambu said softly. "Egret, we cannot change what is, but the children at least should have their attention diverted. Offer to tell them a story."

She was aghast. "Now is surely not the time for such a thing."

"It is if they are to be able to sleep tonight. Or for many nights to come."

"Kwambu is right," White Gull said. "Perhaps even we grownups can be spared a few bad dreams if you give us something else to think about." Her sister's voice was thick with barely restrained tears, and Egret began to understand why Kwambu had made his suggestion. But to suppose that a tale told by one so young as Dancing Egret would solve this problem . . . "I have never told stories to anyone but children," Egret said.

"You told one to Juan Ortiz once, and he was as intrigued by it as any child ever was," Cypress reminded her.

That was true, but Ortiz was only a Spaniard. Still, Cypress also seemed close to tears, so perhaps everyone in the cove really would welcome some sort of distraction. Egret sighed. "I'll try, if you think I should. If the guards will let me."

"They are permitting us to talk. Why should they care if it is one person talking, rather than many?" Kwambu turned to White Gull and Cypress. "Pass the word along, that Dancing Egret has a Legend to tell. Let us see how the people respond."

A hush fell upon the villagers, and those in a position to do so looked at Egret almost beseechingly. This made her a trifle nervous until she glanced toward Night Blossom and her brother and sister. I'll pretend I am singing only to them, she told herself, and decided to tell one of the first Legends she'd ever learned. Nervousness was less apt to interfere with the flow of her words if she sang so familiar a song. She reached for the flute tucked in the waist of her moss skirt, then stayed the motion. The men standing guard might misread her piping notes, think them an attempt at some sort of signal. Clearing her throat, she began:

"Here is how Raccoon learned a lesson," she said, then raised her voice in response to a signal from Night Blossom's mother. "Long, long ago, when the world was new-made and the Calusa and all of the animals lived on a single island, Raccoon came one day to the house of First Man. 'I have been thinking,' he told him. 'Deer runs like the wind; Panther creeps through the brush unseen and unheard; and Alligator bellows so loudly that his enemies flee from him. Man can do none of those things as well as the animals do, so he was given wisdom instead. Since I can do none of those things, either, I would like you to teach me all that Man knows. Then I, too, will have reason to be proud.' "

Everybody watched Dancing Egret now, and most seemed relieved to have reason not to look toward the burning town. Egret let the rhythm of tale-telling enrich her voice. "First Man laughed a little, but he agreed to do as Raccoon asked. 'Before I do so,' he told him, 'you must prove that you truly want to learn by meeting certain challenges I set for you.' "

The children old enough to know that something terrible had taken place, yet too young to understand why the grownups had been powerless to prevent it, were having difficulty settling down. Their small faces were still distorted by fear and bewilderment, and Egret ached for them; she looked directly at each in turn, willing them to concentrate on the story she was telling.

"Raccoon agreed to be tested, so First Man sent him alone deep into a cypress swamp. Then, without warning, he sent Wolf after him. Soon Raccoon caught the scent of his pursuer. He could never outrun Wolf, but if he did not manage to elude him, he knew well what Wolf's next meal would be." Egret paused, rolled her eyes, and patted her stomach suggestively. Here and there a child laughed.

She smiled in response, then went on. "Raccoon did the only thing he could do. He made for the nearest tree and climbed up into it. When he had done this, First Man called Wolf back and sent him to his den. Then he told Raccoon to return also.

" 'Now you must bring me some food,' he said to him. So Raccoon scampered off to the river and waited patiently on its bank until a big fish swam by. He used his paws to scoop up the fish and he carried it back to First Man."

The acrid smoke was thinning finally, Dancing Egret saw, but everyone else was looking at her and she did not interrupt the story to tell them so. Their noses would deliver the message, in any event. " 'I like fish,' First Man said. 'But I would like it better if I had some fruit to eat with it. And there are berry bushes on the far side of that stream.'

"Raccoon hurried to the narrowest part of the stream and

paddled across. He picked a basketful of ripe berries and swam back with them. But dirt and bits of leaves clung to some of the fruit. So before he took the berries to First Man, he dipped each one in the stream and washed it thoroughly."

The children Egret had been discreetly watching appeared less forlorn now, and she thanked the gods that she had chosen a Legend about the kind of furry creature that children find appealing.

"First Man was happy with the berries," she continued, "but he said to Raccoon that he had a hunger for custard apples as well. 'They grow far from here,' he said. 'It will take you many days to travel there and back. But I promise that this task will be the last I set for you.'

"Raccoon hesitated. Then he shook his head. 'I would like to do as you ask,' he said, 'so that you will teach me all that you know. But there are babies in my den; I cannot be away from them for so long. I will go on as I am, and never have reason for pride, rather than leave my children unguarded.' "

The children listening to Egret were clearly disappointed at this turn of events; Raccoon had come so close to getting what he wanted!

Egret leaned forward. "First Man nodded slowly," she told them. " 'Listen,' he said to Raccoon. 'Like me, you have sense enough to climb a tree when danger stalks you on the ground. You can fish as well as I can, and are able to swim when you need to cross water. You wash your food carefully before naming it fit to eat. But most important of all, you choose to deny yourself something you want in order to keep your children safe. You need no lessons from me, Brother Raccoon. You already know all the things that matter. You have reason enough to feel proud.' "

Now all the children were smiling. Better than that, they were cuddling against their mothers, and the mothers— although the smiles they put on competed with tear-wet eyes— looked happier also. Despite the horrors of the day, the little ones felt secure again, and those who loved them—even the women who grieved for sons and brothers slain during the raid—were heartened.

"The guards have left us," Kwambu said softly. "During the tale-telling, a warrior came for them."

It was true. But the people, when they realized that their captors had disappeared, remained hesitant to move.

"I will check the village," Kwambu said, standing up. "If no one is there, we can be certain Mocoso's men have gone home."

The priest had overheard him. "If they have not, you will be putting yourself in danger," he warned.

Kwambu grinned. "Dancing Egret kept us so engrossed with her story that I think no one but me noticed that night came while she was talking." He unfastened his breechclout, then removed it. "I can blend into the night," he said to Tradition Keeper. "Even if the warriors have not left, none will see me."

He was back before they knew it. "The town is empty," he said soberly. And from the look on his face, those who had waited anxiously for him knew that it was more than just empty.

"Everything has been destroyed," the priest said heavily.

"Except for the Temple," Kwambu said. "And the plaza is thick with embers. I suggest that you make temporary shelters and sleep in the cove tonight. Meanwhile, I will get my canoe and go to Muspa. Chief Ucita must be told what has occurred here."

"Tell him first," Tradition Keeper said, "that the elders and women and children are alive and safe." He turned to his acolyte and asked him to lead the women in a search for leafy branches thin enough to be wrenched from nearby trees, then sent the children to find clamshells with which to dig shallow pits in the sand. "Tell Chief Ucita, too, that we will sleep in reasonable comfort tonight," he said to Kwambu.

"Tradition Keeper will not sleep," Egret said softly as she followed Kwambu a little way down the shore. "Nor will I."

"But most of the children will, thanks to you. And once Ucita knows, he and his men will come home at once. Chief Muspa will give him food to bring with him. Everyone will eat, come morning."

"With the storehouses burned, we'll need a great deal of food," Egret said.

Kwambu halted. "You should turn back now," he said. "The others will worry if you are gone too long. I shall go on to your father's island as soon as I have spoken with Ucita, and of course Calusa will send more food, and blankets and clothing and the like. He will take care of the villagers until they can fend for themselves again."

"My father takes care of all his people," Dancing Egret agreed. "I thank you for your help, Kwambu."

"I have done little," he said tightly. "When Mocoso's men

came, I wished that I was a warrior. A brave warrior, like my father. Perhaps . . ."

"You would have gotten yourself killed, and accomplished nothing for the rest of us," Egret said firmly. "They were too many, Kwambu. I'm glad you're a trader and they spared you because of it. Otherwise, who would have taken a message to Ucita, and to my father?"

He managed a smile. "Very likely it would be you, Dancing Egret."

She tilted her chin up. "You're teasing me, but yes; if there was no one else to do it, I would have tried."

"And succeeded," he told her, grinning now. "But enough; I must be on my way, and you must go back to the rest. Unless—would you like to go home, Egret? To Calusa's island? I will take you with me if you do. After we go back and tell Tradition Keeper, and White Gull and Cypress, that you are leaving."

For a moment she considered it. There was no longer a home for her here, or for anyone. Her sister, barren still, did not truly need her help. And Cypress . . . she had Juan Ortiz now. But Egret had lived among these villagers for nearly six seasons. How could she bring herself to abandon them at a time when they would need every pair of hands available to re-make their lives?

She shook her head. "I will stay here," she told Kwambu. "For a little longer, anyway."

But she wondered, as she hurried back to the cove, whether she had made the right decision.

"It was fitting that the young men who died trying to defend it should have been the last to be buried within the Temple," Tradition Keeper said. "Now the Temple will be burned and the ashes of the warriors, along with the ashes of your ancestors, shall be covered over with a new layer of crushed shell and soil." Despite his regret that abandonment of the sacred mound was necessary, the priest was adamant. "It will all be done with due ceremony, and the spirits that dwell there can remain in peace. But after what happened in this village, no new Temple can be built atop the mound."

He and Chief Ucita turned to look at the mound opposite, at the few charred timbers that marked the places where—only a few weeks ago—neat homes had stood. The midday sun was strong enough to let them make out an ash-covered stone pestle here, a smashed mortar there, a tumble of conchs that had been used as cups and ladles and had somehow escaped the worst of the fire. Most of the debris was unrecognizable, however.

"You are priest; I would not presume to argue such a thing with you, even if I had wanted to rebuild my town here. Which I did not." Ucita's initial rage had subsided; now he was filled with misery. And with questions. "Why did our gods let such a dreadful thing happen? How have we offended them, that they did not protect us when we needed them? I have honored them all my life; so far as I know, my people have also. You have seen to it that each god received recognition in his season. Are the Timucuan gods stronger than ours, Tradition Keeper?"

"Man fights with man. The gods merely look on when they do. It is no concern of theirs," the priest said reprovingly.

Ucita shook his head. "That was no war," he said stubbornly. "No signal was given that Chief Mocoso had named me enemy. It was not even a proper raid. Mocoso's warriors took no captives. And instead of stealing the goods in our storehouses, they put them to the torch."

Tradition Keeper shrugged his bony shoulders. "About such matters, you know more than I," he said. "But it is possible that Mocoso felt you named him enemy when you refused to send him the daughter you promised him as wife." He had been there when Ucita assured a distraught Kneeling Cypress that she must not blame herself for the warriors who lost their lives defending their town. The priest had not agreed with him, but he had kept silent, as he would do now. Dissension between priest and Townchief upset the spirits and invited their retribution. Things were difficult enough without giving them cause to loose disease demons in Ucita's new village. "The building goes quickly, across the river," he said, glancing toward the south where the narrow river he spoke of lay sparkling in the sunlight. "The boatloads of conch shells Headchief Calusa sent will let us raise our mounds within weeks instead of months. Before the next full of the moon, the men will have built a new Temple and a house for you and your family."

"And be ready to build their own new homes," Ucita said. He was not sorry the priest had skirted a subject he himself found disquieting. "At least Calusa did not object to my moving the town to the south side of the river." His tone was morose, for the Headchief had forbidden Ucita to take retaliatory measures against Mocoso. A chief who let his town be destroyed without claiming revenge was marked with shame forever, so far as Ucita was concerned. And if the gods permitted his humiliation, surely they were saying that they had no further use for him.

"You chose a good site," the priest declared. "It is near enough to the old town for the men to walk to familiar hunting grounds, and the women to the gathering places they know best. Your people seem content, which is a promising sign."

Ucita was cheered a little by the reminder. He had spent day after day working alongside his people and made it a point to talk with as many as he could. They did not seem to bear any malice toward their chief for the misfortune that had visited them. And yet . . . and yet . . . "I must discover the reason that the gods are displeased with me," he muttered. "I must!"

But the priest, leading the way to the canoe that would take them back to Ucita's new town, did not hear him.

Dancing Egret rubbed bear grease into her sore hands and winced as she massaged the tenderest spots. She knew that once the dawn to dark labor was over and all the people's houses finished, her crop of blisters would harden. Hers, and everyone else's. For only the very youngest were not taking part in making the new town. The women and bigger children worked with the men each day, toting shells and baskets of soil, selecting and bundling fronds for thatch, even hauling some of the timbers cut by the men. But demanding though it was, the work was exhilarating, too. They had grieved for their dead following the raid by Mocoso's warriors, but after Ucita revealed his plans to build a whole new village, a sort of elation had blossomed in them. Now, people often sang as they hefted and tugged, pounded heaps of shells into fragments, scraped the tiers of the new mounds until they were properly level. Except for axes and knives and the like, they were using mostly stone, or the wonderful variety of shell available to them, for tools. Much the way their earliest ancestors had done, Egret thought.

She smiled, closed her eyes, and pretended for a moment that she was one of the First People, come to live on the island Dolphin had made, instructed by Sun and Moon to devise shelter for themselves, to hunt and gather their own food. They had managed well, the First People—so well that their descendants were too numerous to count and the land they lived upon was

vast indeed compared to the tiny island given to their fore-
bears.

She smiled again, then yawned and opened her eyes. From
where she sat, on the new-made mound capped with Chief
Ucita's fine new house, she could see the sun's face redden as
it poised over the bay before descending into the west. The sky
around it was blushing also, and its glow was reflected in the
water beneath. The world given to the First People had been
beautiful, and its expansion had not subtracted from its beauty.

She sent up a silent salute to departing Sun, watched idly as
her sister and Ucita walked together up the stepped ramp and
into their home. Even White Gull had put aside her discontent;
she was working as hard as the rest of the villagers, and she,
too, sang snatches of song upon occasion. Egret felt good
about that, and hoped this new mood would last.

Looking down, she saw the house that Kneeling Cypress
and Juan Ortiz were building. It was larger than the one they'd
had in the old town, and needed only roofing to be complete.
It seemed strange to be able to see inside of it, as Egret was
doing now, to watch Cypress setting baked conch on one of the
broad leaves everybody was using for platters until new
wooden ones could be made. Everybody was eating a great
deal of conch these days, too, for they had harvested huge piles
of them to supplement the shells Calusa had sent. Naturally,
the meat inside must not go to waste.

Reminded that it was time for the daily meal, Dancing Egret
got up and started for the chief's house. She should be helping
White Gull cook, yet she just couldn't make herself hurry; the
evening was too lovely to be abandoned in haste.

"I have been meditating, and asking the spirits to tell me
why they have turned against me, why our gods no longer favor Ucita."

The chief's words floated out of the doorway Egret was approaching and stopped her in her tracks. Ucita had been more
silent than usual these past weeks, and apparently his wife had
asked him what was wrong. Well, this was good; for a long
time, White Gull had neither known nor cared if Chief Ucita
was unhappy or out of sorts. But her solicitude might be un-
dermined if Egret went in now.

She would wait until their conversation ended, she decided,
and turned to walk away.

"It is because I denied the Eater of Eyes his sacrifice," Ucita
continued. And Egret halted again.

"When you spared Juan Ortiz?" White Gull's voice was hesitant as she asked a question Egret feared she knew the answer to.

"It does not do, to promise a sacrifice and then withhold it. And to anger one god is to anger them all. We are taught that everything happens only because something else happens first. The gods are displeased with me; therefore, I have aroused their anger. Until I make amends, there can be no harmony in my life. And because I am Townchief, there will be disharmony in my town as well. Unless I atone for my wrongdoing."

"Did Tradition Keeper tell you this?" his wife asked.

"He told me that the gods had nothing to do with Mocoso's men coming here," Ucita said. "Tradition Keeper insists that raiding and wars are the work of men, not gods. He says that is why we ask the gods for protection for our warriors when a battle is imminent. If we did not ask, they would be indifferent to the whole affair."

"He is a priest; he should know," White Gull said firmly. When it came to spirit matters, Headchief Calusa always relied on his priest. Ucita should do likewise.

"In any event, Tradition Keeper agrees that it cannot hurt to try to appease the Eater of Eyes," Ucita said. "He says that when a man believes sincerely that he has offended the gods, then he has surely done so. It is a priest's duty to help such a man restore harmony to his world, and I have a duty also. As chief, I am responsible for the welfare of my people. For their sake, as well as for my own, I must do what I can to win back the gods' benevolence."

Dancing Egret clenched her hands and waited for what she knew would be said next.

"There will be a ceremony to mark the completion of our new town," Ucita said. "On that morning, the three souls of the Spaniard will be offered to the Buzzard God. And this time, the ritual of sacrifice will not be aborted."

Chapter 7

⟸ ⟹

Kneeling Cypress looked up as Dancing Egret burst into her house. "If it were anyone but you, Egret," she said with a smile, "I would think my visitor was being pursued by ghosts." Then, when her jest did not win her the grin she'd expected, "What's wrong? Is it my father?" She jumped up, ignoring the meat that tumbled from the leaf she was holding.

"In a way," Egret said. "But he is all right, Cypress. It's only that . . . that . . ." She drew breath, tried to compose herself. "You will not like what I'm going to tell you," she warned. "I just overheard Chief Ucita and my sister talking. Well, your father was doing most of the talking, but White Gull—"

Cypress held up her hand. "Please!" she begged. "Don't ramble, Egret. Just tell me what he said."

"Your father has decided that our gods are displeased with him," Egret said in a rush, "and that this is why Mocoso's warriors came here. To get back in their favor, Ucita means to make a sacrifice to the Buzzard God." She paused, hating to say what she must. "He plans to offer him the souls that were snatched from him before—Juan's souls, Cypress."

"No!" It was an anguished cry, and Egret flinched as from a blow. "No; he would never do that! Juan is my husband now. And I'd hoped that, next season, Ucita would permit him to be adopted by one of our clans, to become Calusa in truth."

"I wish I could tell you I might have misunderstood," Egret said wretchedly. "But I know I didn't."

Kneeling Cypress had sunk to her knees, quietly sobbing. "What shall I do? Oh, what shall I do?"

"Perhaps, if we went to *my* father . . ." The younger girl said after a long moment. But Cypress did not have to shake her bowed head for Egret to realize that this would do no good. Headchief Calusa would not interfere; it was his own practice to sacrifice Spanish slaves. Yet Juan Ortiz was no longer a slave, and he was the man Cypress loved. "There must be somewhere you and Juan can go," Egret said. "Once you told me you would be happy if the two of you lived in the middle of a swamp. The river glades are still out there, Cypress, and always will be. If you go far enough into them, you and Juan, and find a hammock where you can put up a small house, it's unlikely your father will ever find you. And I think I can point out one of the waterways that, even in the dry season, leads into the heart of the glades." Her voice rose with excitement. "I've always liked listening to the boys talk about exploring the glades, you see, and once I even took a small canoe and went the way they had gone, only not so far. I truly think I can take you and Juan to a place where he will be safe."

But Cypress was shaking her head again. "Even if my father doesn't send men to search for us—which he will!—how long could we hope to remain undiscovered? Wherever we go in the glades, we risk having hunters come upon us; if not my father's, then those from Calusa's island, or bands from Chief Tequesta's village in the east. All of them camp on the hammocks you speak of, Egret. You know that." She stood up shakily. "Besides, what kind of life would we have, living all alone, spending every day watching the ocean of grass that surrounds us and hoping not to see a canoe coming our way? What will happen when my child is born, when he must grow up with never another boy or girl to play with?"

"Child!" Dancing Egret's amazement rang in her voice.

"Yes, and I've been so happy about it. I was going to tell Juan tonight that he is to be a father. Now . . ." She began to cry again.

"Perhaps," Egret said, "this will change Ucita's mind for him. If he knows he is to be a grandfather, Cypress, surely he'll let the child's father live?"

"Ucita will be a grandfather whether Juan lives or dies," Cypress said bitterly. "And that his daughter has proven herself fertile will make it all the easier for him to persuade some Townchief to have her as wife. Then Ucita will be able to forget that he was ever weak enough to let his love for me cause him to offend the gods." Her jaw set in a way that was unnatural to her. "I will kill myself before any of this happens, Egret; I swear it."

Egret was appalled, and more than a little frightened. "Do not say such a thing!" she cried. "All three of your souls will forever wander the earth if you take your own life. Besides, how can killing yourself save Juan?"

"Nothing can save Juan," her friend said. "Nothing! And without him, I do not want to live."

But Egret was recalling something Kwambu had told her. "One thing might," she said slowly. "I've heard that Chief Mocoso has no Spaniards in his town, and that he wishes he did. His must be the only coastal town that survivors of Spanish shipwrecks have not yet reached." She hesitated; it would not do to say to Cypress that it was a Spanish *slave* Mocoso yearned for. "If you and Juan went to him and asked for sanctuary, perhaps he'd grant it." Egret was proposing a daring plan, and she herself doubted the wisdom of it, but it was all that she could think of to drive thoughts of self-murder from Cypress's head.

And Kneeling Cypress was listening, listening and considering. Then, with a sigh, she shook her head a third time. "How can I throw myself upon the mercy of a man I refused to marry after my father promised me to him?" she asked. "If the chief was angry enough about that to destroy our town, he'll hardly be moved to pity by my plight. He's more likely to be delighted by it. Or else *he* will have Juan slain, and force me to wed him afterward."

"Didn't your father say that Mocoso took another bride, during the last rainy season? Had he still wanted you, his warriors would have seized you when they came to burn Ucita's village. I think he's satisfied to have taken revenge against your father, Cypress; it was the unhonored pledge that rankled, not your wanting to wed another man." Dancing Egret knew no such thing, of course, but common sense said that it was probably so. Besides, she had nothing else to suggest.

"I will go to Mocoso."

Both young women started, then spun around to see Juan Ortiz standing in the doorway, framed against the dark that had descended while they were wrestling with a seemingly unsolvable problem. "I have been listening," he said tightly, "and I tell you that I will seek sanctuary from Satan himself before I will be stretched over another fire and have my eyes gouged out! And any town would be better to live in than some miserable swamp!"

Cypress ran to him, embraced him. She was crying again.

"That will not happen!" she vowed. "But ... I don't know who this *Satan* is, Juan. Or where his village might be."

"His is not a town you would want to see," Juan said grimly. "Which is why I will go to Mocoso. I mean to cheat your father of his sacrifice, now and forever. If Mocoso's warriors slay me, it will at least be a cleaner death than Ucita plans for me." He looked toward the low fire. "I will eat before I leave, however."

"Before *we* leave," Cypress said, wiping the tears from her cheeks and hurrying to fetch him food. "Did you think I would not go with you, husband?"

"Your father has no thought to sacrifice his daughter, I am sure," Juan said. "You will be safe enough here."

"Where you go, I go," Kneeling Cypress said. And her jaw set again, which pleased Dancing Egret.

What did not please Egret was that Juan, who had obviously been listening outside the house for some time, had made no mention of the babe Cypress was carrying. His babe. She told herself that he had been too horrified by learning that Ucita meant to offer him to the Eater of Eyes to be able to think of anything else, that later he would hold his wife close and tell her how glad he was that they were to have a child. Still ...

"I am going with you to Mocoso's town," Dancing Egret said.

They waited until the village slept before meeting at the foot of the Temple mound. Each carried only a small bundle of clothing, for they needed to move swiftly, but Egret had tucked into her pack the flute that Shore Walker carved for her. This, she would not part with. Ever.

After the sentries' measured pacing took them to the far end of the town, the three flitted like shadows around the mound, making for the canoe Juan had been using earlier that day. Haste at this point would invite disclosure, and they knew it.

They had considered traveling along the coast to Mocoso, but had chosen instead to cross the two freshwater rivers that lay between Calusan and Timucuan territory, then go the rest of the way on foot. Chief Mocoso would probably have men guarding his coastal approaches, and they might have no chance to explain if they were sighted and taken to be the vanguard of a raiding party. "We cannot know what enemies Mocoso has, or how many might be given to attack in such a fashion," Juan Ortiz had said. Egret, whose father's warriors often employed such tactics, had been quick to agree.

The moon, although not quite round, provided sufficient light for them to slide the canoe into the water and step cautiously into it. Without speaking, or even whispering, Egret and Cypress each picked up one of the paddles they'd retrieved from the bushes nearby and began to take the craft across the narrow river. Although Juan handled a dugout capably now, he still could not dip paddles as noiselessly as those born in this land could. He would take them across the wider river that lay ahead, the river beyond Ucita's old village. The only sentries there would be the spirits of the warriors who were interred in the abandoned Temple mound, and Egret and Cypress had convinced one another that these would have no interest in the movements of two young women and a Spaniard.

They looked over their shoulders, however, as they carried the canoe past the old town and launched it in the second river. Night was the time for spirits to roam, and not even priests dared predict what spirits might or might not do.

"You will have more reason to be wary once we have reached the other side," Juan said impatiently when Egret and Cypress has paused to glance around them for the fourth time. But he was uneasy, too; how could he be certain the Mother of God, whom he continued to pray to devotedly, still spread her protection over a cavalier who no longer lived, dressed, or spoke like a Christian?

They had timed their traveling carefully; to arrive at Mocoso's town while it was still dark would be folly. Far better to approach it after Sun had chased Moon away and drenched the land with his stronger light.

"Anyone who spots us then will see that we are unarmed," Juan had said.

"And that two of us are only women," Egret had added dryly. Warriors everywhere saw women as prizes, not threats.

Insects and other small creatures made the night vibrate with sound. They fell silent as they sensed intruders, then resumed their pulselike rhythms as soon as the trio had passed by. This was additional cause for unease as Juan, Cypress, and Egret plodded over marshy ground, recoiled from the attack of unseen whiplike branches, or sought ways around ranks of trees that rose up to bar their passage. Those intermittent silences would be readily interpreted by any ears that might be listening. All three were grateful to see the paling of the dark and to have the night chorus stilled.

Yet they were granted no real respite from danger. Before the day was fully born, they were spied by a pair of early-rising fishermen, men old enough to have their topknots liberally streaked with white. These ancients could scarcely be blamed for mistaking Juan, who had taken the lead in the trek overland, for a Calusan warrior. His long hair had deserted the thong he usually tied it back with, and he had put on only a loincloth so that his deerhide breeches and vest would not get wet during the river crossings.

Elderly though they were, the pair from Mocoso's town met the weary travelers with sharp fishing knives clenched in their fists. And the questions they barked at the three were couched in a Timucuan dialect the runaways could not interpret.

Frustration moved the fishermen to shout the questions these suspicious strangers were failing to answer, and their raised voices brought spear-bearing warriors on the run. One of them, fortunately, was the wiry man with the scarred face. "We have come to ask Chief Mocoso for sanctuary," Egret said to him.

Wind That Whistles lowered his spear a little. His shrewd eyes studied her drawn face, moved on to Cypress's, then to Juan's. "Why?" he asked bluntly.

"That is something we shall tell only Mocoso." Juan's voice was sharp-edged, and Wind That Whistles raised his spear again.

"Chief Ucita wants to sacrifice this man to one of our gods," Dancing Egret said desperately. "We had heard that your chief would be pleased to have a Spaniard living in his town, so his wife and I urged him to run away, to come here and serve Mocoso."

Only a murmured warning from Kneeling Cypress kept Juan Ortiz from declaring that he would never again serve any heathen. Wind That Whistles frowned to see rebelliousness in the Spaniard's eyes, but what the girl said was true: Holata Mocoso had more than once offered tempting reward to any warrior who brought one of the pale-skinned Spanish to him.

He spoke briefly to his attending warriors, and they lowered their spears halfway before arranging themselves around three people who might or might not be named captives by their chief. "We will take you to Holata Mocoso," Wind That Whistles said.

They were led into a village that boasted a single tall

mound, rather than two. The homes of the people were built in its shadow, on slightly raised ground encircling an open plaza, and all of them stood on stilts to foil flood-bearing storms. This town was at least twice as large as Chief Ucita's, for Mocoso was Headchief of his tribe. And it was not hard to know which of the homes was his; it occupied a small mound of its own and was fully as spacious as the Temple that decorated the sky-reaching mound.

"Wait here," Wind That Whistles ordered as soon as Juan, Cypress, and Egret had been brought into the plaza. They stopped obediently and watched as he strode toward the home of his chief. Holata, not Chief, Egret reminded herself. She had been trying to recall anything and everything Kwambu had ever said about the Timucua. Now, although she kept her eyelids courteously lowered, she peered beneath them to study the people who were going about the day's work. Several women were laying slabs of animal flesh on a grid over a smoky fire, and Dancing Egret hoped sincerely that Juan Ortiz would not look in that direction. It might remind him rather forcibly of the fate he had twice escaped! The women did not look much different from Calusan matrons, she decided; although their skin was paler, their bodies were well formed, and they moved gracefully as they tended to their cooking. The moss skirts they had on did not simply hang from the waist, however; they covered part of the upper body as well, being draped over a single breast and fastened at the shoulder. And the exposed flesh of two of the women was either painted or tattooed. Not far from their fire, two hunters were gutting and skinning a bear. Someone would have a beautiful cloak to wear on chilly days, Egret thought, for the black fur was thick and lustrous. If these people were anything like the Calusa, it would most likely be given to their chief—to their Holata, she reminded herself again.

A group of children had ceased to stare at the strangers and gone back to kicking a ball around the plaza. Their excited shouting, and the triumphant grin of a small boy who sent the deerhide sphere arcing over all their heads, made Egret smile. She had deeply regretted leaving the children she'd become so fond of, but now she felt better about it. Children were children, no matter where they lived or what tribe they belonged to. If Mocoso allowed the runaways to remain in his town, Egret vowed that she would get to know its children first of all.

If. She looked up to see Wind That Whistles striding toward them. Well, they would soon know whether or not Mocoso would make them welcome. If he did not ...

She followed Cypress and Juan Ortiz, who trailed Wind That Whistles up the neatly kept steps and into the home of Holata Mocoso. Its main room was lined with stacked benches and, on the tier against the farthest wall, the chief sat on the highest level. The supplicants padded across the packed-earth floor, then stood side by side for Mocoso's inspection.

He took his time about it, and Egret—noticing he did not frown when she raised her eyes—inspected him just as closely. He was younger than she'd expected, and a truly handsome man. His flesh was darker than most of his people's and had a burnished look about it that elaborate tattooing could not conceal. His hair, arranged in the now-familiar topknot, also shone. Dancing Egret thought he must apply bear grease liberally each morning to attain such a gloss, but the result certainly was attractive. Kneeling Cypress could have done worse, much worse, than to marry such a fine-looking man. An older woman sitting on one of the lower benches looked to be Mocoso's mother; her face, despite its wrinkles, was similarly handsome. Still, appearance did not reveal a person's nature, and that was surely the important thing when it came to living with someone.

Cypress, her eyes downcast, tried to conceal her trembling; Juan studied their host as avidly as Egret had done.

When Mocoso finally spoke, it was to Ortiz. "You have had enough of Calusan hospitality, I see."

Dancing Egret stiffened, then made herself relax. The arrogance in the man's voice grated, but what he said was true.

"I have," Juan said. And his tone matched Mocoso's so perfectly that Cypress's trembling increased threefold.

Mocoso only laughed. He recognized in this Spaniard a fellow *ibitano*, a man of noble blood. "What has persuaded you that mine will be better?"

"I cannot know that it will be. I only hope that it may."

Mocoso nodded. "As to that, we shall see." He turned his penetrating gaze on Kneeling Cypress. "You are Chief Ucita's daughter."

She nodded.

"And Juan Ortiz's wife," Egret said quickly.

She was rewarded with a scowl. "I did not address you,"

Mocoso said coldly and turned again to Cypress. "You are the woman who would not have Mocoso for a husband?"

Again Cypress nodded. "I loved another," she said faintly.

"Yet you come to me now, and for sanctuary?"

Dancing Egret was afraid Cypress might burst into tears, which would doubtless amuse both Mocoso and the silent old woman whose mistrust of the newcomers was almost palpable. Egret reached for her friend's hand and squeezed it. "All of us do," Cypress confirmed, her voice a little stronger.

Mocoso stroked his chin with long fingers. "Will you be willing to serve my mother, and the wife I took in your stead, in order to stay here?"

Cypress hesitated, then bobbed her head.

"And you," he said, regarding Ortiz with a faint smile, "are you prepared to serve me? To be my slave, in fact, as so many of your kind are in other towns?"

"I am a cavalier. Cavaliers do not become slaves," Juan said strongly.

"In this country," Mocoso said just as strongly, "they do. And you have not answered my question."

Cypress made a small pleading noise, and Juan sighed. "I cannot go back to Ucita," he said slowly. "If, to stay here, I must serve you, then I suppose I must."

Mocoso smiled. "That is sensible of you. But I would be discontented with an unwilling slave. Make me believe that you mean what you say."

Juan bit back an angry retort. "I will serve you the best way I know how," he mumbled.

Mocoso laughed, said something in his own language to Wind That Whistles, who laughed also. "You would make a sorry slave," he said to Ortiz. "Ucita's Paracusi—his War Leader—trained you to be hunter and warrior, I understand."

"He did."

Mocoso did not speak again for a long, agonizing moment. "Such training should not go to waste," he mused. "Perhaps . . . well, we shall see."

He was playing with them, Dancing Egret realized. She fought to keep anger from her expression.

It was as well that she did, for the chief turned to her next. "You are Headchief Calusa's daughter," he said. "But you are neither old enough, nor pretty enough, to attract one of my warriors. Although you will get older, you are unlikely to become prettier. I cannot see what use you can be to me."

Kneeling Cypress was no longer trembling. She stood straight and tall and looked earnestly at Mocoso. "Dancing Egret owns a talent few may boast of. She is a fine storyteller."

"Indeed," he murmured. But his eyes showed his surprise that a woman he had labeled spineless should spring so quickly to another's defense. He faced Egret again. "You speak and understand the Timucuan language, then?"

"I do not. But I am quick to learn. And," she continued boldly—for she realized now that this man, like Calusa, had nothing but contempt for those who cringed—"all Legends fascinate me. I would be as interested in yours as I am in those of my people. I would respect them as much also."

Mocoso stood up. He was taller than the warriors they had seen thus far, yet somehow Egret was unsurprised. He was so much like her father, in many ways. "I must confer with my Principal Men," he said dismissively, and Wind That Whistles came to stand beside the three once more. "Meanwhile, my War Leader will show you to an empty storage hut so you can rest from your journey. When we have decided what to do with you, I will send word."

And he would make them wait before he did, Dancing Egret knew. Wait and wonder and worry. Well, *she* would not worry! That would please this arrogant man far too much.

But as they were taken to a small, round, tightly thatched building, windowless and with only a narrow door—to which a sentry was promptly assigned—she suspected that, for all her resolution, she would worry just as much as her companions.

"We must go to Mocoso's town and rescue them."

Headchief Calusa looked at the stern-faced young warrior who threw down his statement as though it were a challenge. Ah, the impetuosity of youth! "I think not," he said mildly.

Shore Walker was shaken. He'd been certain his offer to lead a war party north would be accepted. Kwambu, watching, hid a smile.

"My daughter and her friends went to Mocoso willingly. To attack his town would be to imply that they went under duress."

"It was duress, of a sort," Shore Walker said stubbornly. "Kwambu has told us how Chief Ucita meant to sacrifice Kneeling Cypress's husband. They were made to run away."

"But not necessarily to a Timucuan," Calusa said. "They could have come to me. Of course, I would have had to send

Kneeling Cypress and the Spaniard back to Ucita. What I expect from my Townchiefs, I give in return."

"But Dancing Egret may be in danger," Shore Walker said. "Your treaty with Mocoso does not make the Timucua our friends."

Calusa eyed him thoughtfully. He had always encouraged the people on his island to look to him for advice in matters of importance, and this was plainly a matter of considerable importance to the young man who had been a good friend to Egret when both were children. But youthful warriors did not always see clearly; they were too impatient to take action. "That is so," he said. "Yet my daughter has been able to look after herself since she was a child. She is"—he smiled—"much like her father sometimes, for all that she's only a girl. Her first words were *how, what,* and *why*. And when she had learned other words to go with them, she would pester anyone—even me—until she had answers to her questions. That is not the mark of a timid person, Shore Walker."

"She is still the same," Kwambu said quietly.

Calusa clapped the trader on the shoulder. "And we will be kept informed of how she fares," he said to Shore Walker. "Kwambu will visit Mocoso's town regularly. If I have reason, any reason, to suspect that my daughter is not being treated properly, then it shall be you who takes a band of warriors to fetch her home. This, I promise. Meanwhile, let her remain where she has chosen to go. Like you, I wish it had not been to Mocoso. I do not trust the man. But the Timucua do not mistreat women, any more than we do. She will be safe there, at least for now."

"And will have a chance to satisfy her curiosity about a people other than her own," Kwambu said. "Do not be concerned for her, Shore Walker. She is not the child you remember, but a young woman. An intelligent young woman."

"It's true that I still think of her as little," Shore Walker admitted. "I regret that I have taken so much of your time, Great Calusa," he said formally to his Headchief. "It was only that I worried when I heard the news."

Calusa smiled. "Never think that I do not worry, too," he told him. "I worry about all of my people, everywhere, when there is need for it. And Egret is my own daughter. I will be as glad as you are when she is home with us again. But the time must be right for that, or she will never forgive either of us."

Kwambu concealed another grin. This was another way in which Dancing Egret was remarkably like Headchief Calusa.

Chapter 8

⇐ ⇒

"Both Sun Spirit and his sister Moon Spirit wanted their children to have their own world to live in," Dancing Egret chanted. "But Sun wanted them to live in a warm, dry world, while Moon said they would be happier in a cool, wet one."

One of the little girls who was listening to the Timucuan creation Legend giggled. "Moon thought the People were fish," she said, and giggled again.

Egret smiled, and shifted herself so that Cypress's oldest, three-year-old Squawking Duck, would be able to curl up in her lap. He was true to his name, however; although he'd been drowsy before, now his eyes flew open and he voiced his annoyance at having been moved. "Hush," she said to him. "I am telling a story. If you don't wish to sleep, then listen."

She reminded herself to see that Cypress's children learned the Legends of the Calusa, as well as the Timucuan ones she regularly told to the children of Mocoso, then went on with her tale. "Sun and Moon quarreled about this and, because neither would give in, each went a different way. They have lived apart ever since."

She lifted her flute to her mouth and blew a series of discordant notes: music to emphasize the dissension between the ancestor-gods of the Timucua. "On the day they separated, Sun Spirit made a huge plain midway between the Upper and Under Worlds. He covered it with grass and trees and fastened it to the sky with four sturdy bowstrings. Then he went into the west, taking with him the glowing Day Fire. But because he was in a hurry, sparks flew from it and stayed behind."

"The sparks became stars!" a grinning boy shouted, and Egret nodded.

"So they did. And when Moon came into the Sky Vault, she was happy to see them. But then she looked down and saw what Sun had made for the People. She was not happy about that." Egret took up her flute again and piped a few notes to express Moon's displeasure. "Moon immediately surrounded the land with oceans and laced it with rivers great and small. But it was dark, and she could not see clearly. At the sources of certain rivers and streams she poked her finger so deep that she made passageways between This World and the Under World."

The children looked at one another and shivered; everyone knew that fearsome monsters lived in the Under World.

Squawking Duck was squirming, and Egret tightened her grip on him before she continued. "The animals were allowed to come and live here when the People did, but only a few of them made homes in the water Moon had made, and only a few took advantage of the blanket of warm air Sun had spread above This World. So Sun Spirit made winged creatures he called birds to fly though his air, and Moon Spirit—not to be outdone—made creatures with gills and fins to dive and swim through her cool waters. And most of these creatures, just like most of the four-footed animals, became food for the People and their descendants."

"Why can't we eat all of them?" a small voice asked.

"Some are forbidden," Egret answered. "Those that cross the boundaries between Worlds—like beaver and frog, who live both on land and in water, and kingfisher and gull, who belong to both water and air. But except for those that defy natural law, the Timucua may eat whatever their hunters bring home, so long as proper ritual is used during each hunt."

"I will be a hunter someday," Squawking Duck said confidently, and Egret hugged him. But instead of confirming what he'd said, she coaxed a merry trill from her flute to let her audience know that the story was over.

"I couldn't promise him that he would be a hunter," she said quietly to Cypress when she'd led Squawking Duck back to the house Mocoso had allowed Juan Ortiz to build on the outskirts of his town. The house was so close to the mangroves marching along the river that it was mosquito-ridden in nearly all seasons, but the three who had come here for sanctuary knew better than to complain about that. They simply kept smoky fires burning throughout most of the year, and coated their flesh with bear grease every morning and evening.

"All little boys long to be hunters and warriors," Cypress said, laying her infant daughter in a hanging cradle and sending her younger son to play with his brother. "What harm would it have done to encourage Squawking Duck?"

Egret took a handful of grapes from the bunch her friend offered and munched them as she pondered the tactful way to answer the question. "He is the son of a Calusan woman, Cypress; should I let him believe that he'll grow up to be a Timucuan warrior, and therefore enemy at times to our own people? And what of the tales Juan tells now and then, about the Spanish cavaliers? That's part of his heritage, too, yet my father and yours look upon the Spanish as enemies. Squawking Duck is too young to understand any of this, so I simply said nothing when he spoke of being a warrior when he's grown."

Kneeling Cypress pushed back a wayward strand of dark hair. "Juan can never return to my father's town, or to any other town in Calusa country," she said wearily. "If our sons ever become warriors, they will be Timucuan warriors, Egret. You know that as well as I do."

"But they are still half Spanish," Egret said. "And you know that Holata Mocoso told Juan, when he gave us all permission to live here, that he may return to his own people if any of them come again to these shores."

"He didn't go when the Spanish ship came," Cypress said.

"That was because he didn't believe sails had actually been sighted," Dancing Egret said softly. "Juan thought Mocoso was testing his loyalty. And he was plainly unhappy when he realized that hadn't been the case." She did not bother to add that, in any event, the ship had never entered the bay. Whether those who sailed in it had mistaken the outlying islands for coastline, or whether the Spanish had finally heard of the Apalachee tribe to the northwest and decided to seek gold and slaves there for a change, no one knew. But they had shown no interest, this time, in the southern provinces.

Cypress, for all that she wanted to, could not deny the truth of this. "But that was long ago," she said, brightening. "Our first child had not even been born then. Now we have three. Juan loves them; he will never leave them. Or me."

"Perhaps, if ships come another time, he will want them, and you, to return to Cuba with him," Egret said carefully. "Or even across the eastern sea to Spain. He might want his sons to grow up to be Spanish warriors, to become soldiers like Juan himself once was."

"Juan will never leave here," Cypress repeated stubbornly. She began to work again on the basket she'd been weaving when her hungry daughter's fretting interrupted her. "Did Wind That Whistles's son come and listen when you told your story this morning?" The teasing note she tried to inject into her voice signaled her determination to say no more on the matter they had been discussing.

Egret, unwilling to trespass further into an area Cypress was warning her away from, obliged. "He did not," she said. "He doesn't come *all* the time, Cypress!"

"He comes often enough to show that he's interested in a certain young woman I know. And lately one or two of his friends seem to have become his rivals where you are concerned."

Egret felt her cheeks grow warm. She was uncertain how to handle the young warriors who were suddenly paying attention to her, particularly since she couldn't understand why they were seeking her out. Mocoso had been right: becoming a maiden had not turned Dancing Egret into a beauty. Oh, her waist had narrowed a little when her breasts blossomed, and her hair had taken on a new thickness and sheen. But her hips, instead of rounding attractively, remained boyishly slim. And her face had not lengthened to mark her passage into womanhood—it was as square-shaped as ever—and her arms and legs, well, the best that could be said for them was that they were sturdy. And to make matters worse, she was tall enough to look down on many of the young men.

Egret had no way of knowing that the face she deplored was vividly expressive, particularly when she was singing story-songs for the children in a language she'd found remarkably simple to learn. She had never seen her own thickly lashed eyes sparkle and dance when she was excited, nor did she realize that she owned an athletic grace many young women lacked. "Perhaps they just enjoy listening to the tales I tell," she said lamely.

Cypress smiled. "And is that why they're suddenly so eager to take Juan with them when they go hunting, and to help him carry his share of the game back to our house? Nor do they hurry to leave once they have come. They sit around and boast of their skills and accomplishments, and all the time they're sneaking glances at you, Dancing Egret!"

Egret began to rock the neatly woven cradle Kneeling Cypress had made for her daughter. "I don't know why the warriors come here so often," she said at last, and somewhat irritably, "nor do I care. After all, they are Juan's guests, not mine."

But Kneeling Cypress merely smiled again, so when the baby began to fuss, Egret lifted her from the cradle to sing an ages-old sleep-song to her. And was reminded, as she frequently was these days, that it would be a fine thing to have a babe of her own. She was pleased that the village boys and girls had grown fond of her, and it was good to have Cypress's children to play with and cuddle. But it would be a wonderful thing to have a child call her Mother instead of friend. And for that to happen, Dancing Egret thought, she must first have a husband.

From the pouch hanging on a thong around his neck, Kwambu took several tally disks. He selected a painted one, the flat piece of polished tortoiseshell bearing the likeness of an alligator, and slipped it into the bundle Mocoso had given him. Now, when he reached Tocobaga, he would know which feathers were to be offered for pearls. Kwambu had pledged to do his best to make the desired exchange, but pearls were rare south of Apalachee, and shrewd bargaining would surely be required to convince Tocobaga that he ought to part with a few of the ones he had managed to accumulate.

Feathers were popular trade items, and Headchief Calusa had also entrusted Kwambu with several bundles of them. Some, like Mocoso's, contained only egret plumes, but heron, ibis, and spoonbill feathers filled other sacks. Kwambu was taking a supply of conch shells along, of course; they were always in demand inland, as were the purple-lined janthina shells and yellow cockles he had in a smaller bundle. And Vision Seeker, Calusa's priest, had come to him at the last moment with a basket of fresh-picked beach plums and sea grapes. "Trade them for rattleweed and button snakeroot and swamp cottonwood, if you can," he'd told Kwambu. "My stock of medicines is running low." Kwambu would do what he could for the priest; sick people seemed to recover faster when medicine was given immediately following a Healing Ceremony, and no one should suffer more than he must. Kwambu thought he might try to obtain some wild garlic as well. Not only did it add flavor to certain foods, the women prized the deep orange dye they made by boiling its skin.

He stepped into his canoe and picked up one of the two double-bladed paddles he always brought with him. When he must go overland with a heavy load, as he would be doing this time, he fastened a length of deerhide between the paddles to form a sort of litter. On this he stacked his wares, lashed them down, then pulled his improvised sledge along by means of a strong fiber rope attached to the paddles. He had to skirt marshy places while pulling it, and often needed to look for a sufficiently wide path between close-growing trees once he reached the hardwood forests. But the sledge allowed him to carry more goods, both going and coming, than he'd been able to do in the days when he toted everything on his back.

The idea had come to him after he'd realized that he no longer had to portage his canoe. Whenever he came to a river that would take him in the direction he wanted, he simply borrowed a small dugout from a nearby village. The people who lived in the towns he visited were happy to oblige a trader, and knew Kwambu well enough to be confident that he would return the canoe during his journey home. And Kwambu made sure to prop his feather-topped staff upright in any borrowed craft so that those who spotted him would know that a trader, and not some enemy scout, was on the way.

It was a pleasant morning, warm but not hot, and birds clustered in the trees that ranked themselves along both sides of the river. Kwambu watched a black-and-white striped woodpecker hopping up the trunk of a hardwood, spiraling around its girth in short spurts, his crimson head jerking this way and that as he hunted bark-burrowing insects. Grackles swooped down and foraged for brittle bits of a vine that had entangled itself in a spiky clump of bromeliads; they were nest-building, and would repeat this procedure from now until the setting sun marked the end of day. A host of songbirds, infected with mating fever, put passion into their lilting voices. Marsh hawks tipped their wings above a low-growing cypress, while a gray heron stood unmoving among the tree's roots and waited for dinner to swim by. A chorus of angry squawks alerted the traveler to a pair of yellow-footed egrets. Dressed in elegant mating plumage, they were disputing a nesting area; white wings menacingly raised, graceful necks arching and dipping, they stabbed at each other with long black beaks. Like warriors confronting enemies during battle, there was a distinct rhythm to the birds' movements, as though they were doing a ceremonial dance. Which, in a way, they were, Kwambu thought.

Watching them, he was reminded of the young friend he had visited that morning. How excited she had been, and how delighted for her father, when he'd told her about Watchful Doe being safely delivered of a son. They had laughed together over the babe's being given so stately a name as Crested Heron, and agreed that Calusa wanted to make sure everyone remembered that this boy would one day be Headchief.

Egret, always curious, had asked him then about the pearls she had heard Holata Mocoso mention, and he had tried hard to describe them to her. His word picture must have been an appealing one, for she'd become so excited that he had rashly promised to make her a gift of pearls on the day she wed. He would do it, too, even if he had to exchange for them the fine new staff he had commissioned from Mask Maker. On two of its narrow sides, Shore Walker's grandfather had carved an image of the bluejay's head; on the other two surfaces, detailed representations of the jay's wing. Then he had painted each carving in blue, white, and black. The staff was truly beautiful, and Kwambu would regret parting with it, but he would gladly present it to Holata Togobaga if doing so brought him enough pearls to make a suitable gift for Dancing Egret.

And if Kwambu had interpreted correctly the looks sent Egret's way by some of Mocoso's youthful warriors, he might be needing pearls for her sooner rather than later. He had teased her about her admirers, and enjoyed seeing the usually imperturbable Egret duck her head and stammer, but he had not been teasing when he told her that she deserved the best and that he hoped she would never settle for less. She had laughed again then, but he prayed she had taken him seriously. From childhood, it had been her habit to put other people's wants ahead of her own, yet there were certain occasions when to ignore your own wants and needs was to invite disaster. It was not, for instance, the way to choose a husband. He had told her that at least twice, as he recalled!

He wondered uncomfortably what had moved him to counsel Egret. He was far from an expert when it came to love and marriage, and his situation was unlikely to change. Except for Ucita's daughter, all the women Kwambu had known in this country had wed their own kind. Egret, even if she married outside her tribe, would still not be marrying outside her kind.

This was the natural and probably the wise thing for people to do. Yet there was no woman living among either Calusa or Timucua whose skin was the color of ebony, whose earliest memories might be similar to those Kwambu the trader cherished.

Yet he had meant every word he said to Dancing Egret. The advice had come from his heart, even if he had no idea what had spawned it.

The river narrowed as it entered the piney flatlands he would be traveling over next. Kwambu steered his canoe toward the bank, unloaded his cargo, and pulled the dugout onto dry land. As he stretched his length of hide between the paddles he had laid parallel to one another, he mentally mapped the rest of his journey. On to Tocobaga, then to villages in the Ocale and Potano provinces, and finally to Outina's town, where there lived another maiden who would probably also be marrying soon.

If he happened to have reason to speak with Moon of Winter, Kwambu told himself sternly, he must take care not to offer words of wisdom on a subject he knew nothing about. To make one mistake was permitted; to make the same mistake twice would be to name himself Fool.

Not that the lovely Moon of Winter had ever spared much attention for a humble trader, fool or not. It was unlikely that she ever would. This was also perfectly natural, Kwambu supposed. But his expression was bleak as he turned his concentration back to the task at hand.

Chapter 9

Moon of Winter moved without haste along the pine-needle-strewn trail leading to the river. The summer sun, filtering through the trees over her head, warmed her bare flesh and enhanced the colorful designs that wreathed wrists, ankles, and breasts and draped her shoulders and upper chest with an elegance of permanent necklaces. Now that the painful pricking was only a memory, the young woman was able to admire the results of it. At first, after Walks Tall Woman had delivered her niece to the home of Holata Outina's Shaman, his collection of gleaming garfish teeth had terrified Moon of Winter. But Watches for Omens had spoken so eloquently of the status the tattooing would represent, had explained so persuasively how the markings would emphasize her natural beauty, that she had calmed down enough to endure the torturous skin piercing.

Soon she had begun to appreciate the cleverness with which dots of red, blue, black, and yellow dyes evolved into appropriate decoration for the soon-to-be bride of Holata Potano. She'd paid little heed to the Shaman's recital of the plants that permitted him such a variety of colors. Since Moon of Winter belonged to the Original Clan of the Timucuans, the White Deer, she knew that sunflowers made possible the honey-colored ceremonial robes only members of her clan were allowed to wear. But what did she know, or care, about bloodroot or rattleweed or black cherry bark? It mattered nothing to her that the same tree whose inner bark was the source of the Shaman's yellow pigment owned leaves and seeds that were poisonous, or that certain other shrubs and vines were not as innocent as they looked. Moon of Winter admired pretty flowers, but she'd never cared enough to learn their names, and she cared even less about the names of those that fascinated Watches for Omens. She cared a great deal about how she looked, however; and this, more than the old man's attempts to distract her, had kept her from doing more than whimpering while the Shaman worked his magic.

Now all the world would recognize that Moon of Winter was wife to a Timucuan chief. Not that she was his wife yet, of course. But when the sun had traveled five times more across the blue vault of the sky, the day of her marriage would be here.

She shifted her pot of cassia-scented oil from one hand to the other. Once she had bathed, she would comb the oil through her long hair to make it shiny. On the morning of her marriage day, she would do the same. She would anoint even her body with the oil then, she told herself. Holata Potano would appreciate having a bride who smelled sweet from head to toe.

She giggled. Potano, in addition to being a man of importance, was pleasing to look upon. He was fine-featured, tall, and aristocratic of bearing. Walks Tall Woman had sniffed when Moon of Winter, after Potano delivered to Outina the huge bearskin that would line the bridal litter, said that about him. "He is an arrogant man," she'd pronounced. "That is what you see in his face, and in his bearing." Well, perhaps he was. Why not? He was lord of a province as large as Outina's, one that lay to the south and west of it. And Walks Tall Woman was certainly in favor of the marriage, despite her disparaging remark. She had most likely persuaded her brother to the idea; the marriage was, after all, what Outina's Principal Men called *political*. Once Outina's niece was Potano's wife, there would be no more warring between the two Timucuan tribes. Even Moon of Winter's father, Bold in Battle—who was Outina's Great Warrior—admitted he would be glad of that. "If there can be unity between us, then our warriors and Potano's together will be more than a match for our common enemies. If white-fleshed strangers come inland another time, we will be able to join forces to drive them away."

Moon of Winter had never seen the strangers her father referred to. She had been a little girl when last they ventured into Timucuan territories, and Outina, having been warned by a messenger from the south, traveled some distance to intercept them. He had been determined to keep from his town a horde of grotesquely garbed outlanders who had been leaving so much grief and turmoil in their wake. Succeeding in his mission had been less difficult than he had feared; their leader had sworn that they were interested solely in finding gold, and Outina had been able to convince him that they must go into Apalachee territory for that. It was unlikely that they would come this way again, Moon of Winter thought, but she was happy to be pleasing her father regardless. In truth, she would miss Bold in Battle when she went to Potano's town to live. Under ordinary circumstances, of course, Moon of Winter's husband would live with her people, but political marriages were exempt from this custom. She did not mind going away; although she hated to leave her father, the girl knew she'd get along perfectly well without Walks Tall Woman. Her aunt was an unflagging advocate of hard work, and Moon of Winter was uninspired by her lectures.

She passed by the granary positioned within easy reach of the river and entertained herself by envisioning her marriage day feast. The bear haunch Potano had presented along with the pelt would be roasted, naturally, but there could be venison as well, and possibly baked fish. Certainly they'd have acorn bread and cornflour dumplings to serve with the bearfat-seasoned hominy. Grapes and blackberries should be offered, and perhaps some of the spicy prickly pear preserve that traders brought north from the peninsula. Sassafras tea sweetened with honey would make a fine accompaniment to the meal, and it must be the grandest of grand meals that the White Deer clan spread before Holata Potano and his bride. Even Walks Tall Woman had agreed to that.

Her musings had taken her around a bend in the river and out of sight of the storehouse. Moon of Winter knelt and scooped a shallow depression in the damp soil of the bank, for she would not entrust her pot of precious oil to uneven ground. Suddenly she stiffened, straightened, backed away. From out of a mass of fern a hand's span from where she'd been digging slid a long, blotchy brown snake!

She had no idea whether the snake could harm her, but she froze in place as her father had taught her to do when she was a child. She dared not so much as tremble until it lowered its ugly head and slithered away, flicking its tapered tail almost derisively. Then she shut her eyes briefly, drew a shuddering breath, snatched up her oil and started running.

A snake was not a good omen, for snakes were closely allied with the Under World. Moon of Winter stopped short and peered up into the sky. At least there was no sign of a thunderstorm. Snakes were said to intensify such storms, and just a wisp of dark cloud would have sent her racing for home.

Perhaps she should do so anyway? But the sky continued clear, and the fragrance of sun-warmed oil teased her nostrils. No, Moon of Winter thought. I will not go back to the village until I have bathed. That is what I wanted to do; that is what I will do.

She walked a little farther, until she came to a place where only tall trees grew and the scant underbrush offered concealment to nothing bigger than an ant. She found a secure resting place for her pot, removed her plaited grass skirt, and prepared to step into the water.

She heard no sound except the twittering of birds and the lazy drone of insects. Only a vague awareness of movement made her pause with one foot extended and turn swiftly toward the right, to where a giant oak lifted densely leafed branches high above those of its kin. And even when the tawny cat completed its leap, even as the weight of it tumbled Moon of Winter to the ground, she was slow to understand what was happening.

Then the panther snarled into the face of its human prey, its fetid breath absorbing hers, leaving her panting and gasping. She wanted to scream, ached to scream, and could not. And that unborn scream seared her throat as the cat lifted one huge paw and unsheathed the awful claws that were its weapons.

Yet she never felt the rake of them, was unaware of the blood gush that marked the mutilation of her tender flesh. Terror had thrust her into sheltering darkness, a darkness briefly lit by the ghastly afterimage of slitted amber eyes.

Her face was on fire, her left cheek blazing hotter than its twin. The heat the flames gave off made the blood in her veins sizzle and roil. Moon of Winter groaned, mumbled, cried out.

"Lie still," someone said sharply. Something cool and damp was laid upon her face. Moisture, soothing moisture, trickled past Moon of Winter's left ear and slanted down her neck, puddling at her nape. In response, the fire subsided; but only briefly.

"Hurts," she mumbled as the blaze resurrected itself.

"The balm must be applied again." A different voice, male, raspy. The Shaman's?

The compress was gently removed, but the pain that flared in Moon of Winter's cheek was agonizing. And when a hand began to smooth a gelatinous substance over her flesh, she screamed.

"You must be still!" She recognized that voice now. Walks Tall Woman.

"Don't touch me," Moon of Winter sobbed.

"In time, you will be glad that we did," Watches for Omens said. And as the medicine began to penetrate, it brought a blessed numbness to the girl's torn flesh.

Moon of Winter opened her eyes. "Thirsty," she muttered.

The old man smiled. "That is good," he said, and moved aside so that Walks Tall Woman could give his patient a sip of water. "You are using the water I gave you, with the infusion of fever tree leaves mixed with it?" he asked her.

If Moon of Winter's throat had not been so sore, her tongue so swollen, and her lips so dry, she would have answered his question. Plain water was not bitter.

She drank a little more when her aunt offered the gourd again, but the contraction of facial muscles that swallowing demanded brought back the pain. "Help me," she whispered.

"We are helping you all we can," Walks Tall Woman said, "as we have been these past three days." Exasperation was in her voice, but concern softened her expression. "And you have had more help than you know. If my son and his friends had not been fishing close to the place where the panther attacked you, you would not be alive to feel pain, Moon of Winter. Fortunately, they were spearfishing, rather than using nets. Swoops Like Falcon's spear drove off the cat before they'd even beached their canoe." She was smiling now; her son was barely thirteen years old, yet he had aimed true and thrown with force. And as soon as the boys leaped ashore, Falcon had pursued the injured panther and finished him off with his knife. Never mind that he'd said frankly that it was an old cat, starving and half crippled; the whole village should be proud that so brave a boy would one day be Holata. Walks Tall Woman intended to make sure that the incident was not forgotten.

She looked down at her niece, and knew that Falcon's courage and skill would be long remembered without any help from his mother. Moon of Winter's face would be a reminder even years from now.

"She sleeps," Watches for Omens said. "And I am finally able to say that I think she will mend." His relief was patent. He had done what he could, repeated the proper incantations even as he made use of all the healing arts he knew. Yet he had been plagued with doubts, especially after the stubborn fever set in.

Walks Tall Woman nodded. Just to see her niece regain consciousness was reassuring. The skin on Moon of Winter's arms and legs was no longer so hot to the touch, either, even though her swollen face still radiated enormous heat, and yellow pus continued to ooze from the lacerations. "You have done well," she said.

"I summoned the right spirits, that is all," he responded a trifle testily. He would not risk offending those spirits by accepting credit for what they had done.

Walks Tall Woman shrugged. "I thank both you and the spirits, then," she said. But she spoke absently. Once her niece was well enough to sit up and take nourishment, she would have a talk with her. She could not let the girl go in ignorance any longer than was needful. She sighed. Moon of Winter would not be happy with what she heard, but it was Walks Tall Woman's duty to see that she heard it. And Walks Tall Woman would never let herself be accused of shirking her obligations.

Moon of Winter tipped up the bowl and drank the last of the meaty broth. "Venison stew has never tasted so good," she said.

"It is the first you've had in weeks," Walks Tall Woman pointed out. "Any food that can be chewed is bound to be more satisfying than clear soup."

The girl smiled agreement, then reached up and traced with her fingertips a trio of puckered scars that ran from temple to jaw. Her smile disappeared. "Will they always be so . . . so knobbly?" she fretted.

"They may smooth out a little, in time," her aunt said.

"But not completely?"

Walks Tall Woman shook her head. She did not believe in encouraging hope where none existed. "I remind you again that you are fortunate to be alive. What is a little scarring, when you think that you might have been killed by that panther?"

Her niece was silent for a long moment. "Do you suppose," she asked slowly, "that Holata Potano will find my scars . . . ugly?"

The moment had come. Walks Tall Woman took up her basket of beans and began sorting them, some for cooking, some to be set aside for planting. "You will not be marrying Potano," she said bluntly.

Moon of Winter stiffened. "But it is all arranged," she began.

Her aunt frowned at a shriveled bean, named it a seed, and tossed it into a smaller basket. "You know as well as I do that a tribal leader, whether he marries a daughter of one of his own Principal Men or goes farther afield for a bride, always chooses the most beautiful of the maidens available to him. The people expect this; it has been so since the Beginning. You no longer qualify to be wife to a chief, Moon of Winter."

"Perhaps Holata Potano will choose to defy that tradition," the girl ventured. She fingered the scars a second time, winced. "I guess he won't," she said miserably.

"Outina has already returned the bearskin to him and explained matters," Walks Tall Woman said. "Potano was not pleased. My brother tells me he went so far as to blame you for depriving him of the bride he had planned on."

"He blames *me*?" Shock squeezed her voice to a whisper.

Walks Tall Woman spilled a handful of plump beans into the cooking pot. "He says you should have known better than to go so far from town to bathe." She looked across at Moon of Winter. "I told you he was an arrogant man."

The girl bent her head, studied the colorful designs encircling her bare breasts. "I wear the symbols of a chief's wife, yet I will never be one," she mourned. "That doesn't seem right, Walks Tall Woman."

"It is not. Your tattoos, Moon of Winter, will have to be removed now that you are well enough to have it done."

Moon of Winter's head snapped up. "Removed? Why, that will be as painful as having them made in the first place."

"It is the rule, nonetheless," her aunt said. "Since the status is denied you, you may not display its symbols."

Tears welled in Moon of Winter's eyes, spilled over her cheeks, streaked both the unblemished one and the one that would forever bear the marks of the panther's claws. "I cannot endure it. I cannot."

"You have to, therefore you will," Walks Tall Woman said, and came to her feet, the pot cradled in her long arms. "As soon as I start these beans cooking, I will go to Watches for Omens and tell him you are ready for him. And I trust you will not disgrace our clan by acting the coward while the Shaman does what he must."

Once again Moon of Winter felt as though she were on fire. Although this time the illusion was not powerful enough to make her cry out, it was more extensive; wherever there had been decoration, there was now only raw, plum-colored flesh. The balm Watches for Omens gave her had stopped the festering that immediately followed the abrading, but it could not dim the purple blotches that bloomed on her arms, legs, breasts, and shoulders.

"They will fade eventually," the Shaman had assured her. "The day will come when you will scarcely be able to tell where the tattooing used to be. Meanwhile, however, you must avoid direct sunlight. Cover yourself whenever you go out, from head to toe, and bathe only early in the morning or late in the evening. Even then, do so quickly, for the gentlest touch of the sun will seem to you a fiery brand."

So in the heat of the summertime, Moon of Winter had to go outside swathed in a cloak. When she went out at all, which was seldom. Unfortunately, remaining in the house kept her virtually tethered to Walks Tall Woman, whose own impatience with idleness led her to devise tasks for her niece even when there was no work needing to be done. Finally, Holata Outina himself protested, after his sister pounced on Moon of Winter when she saw the girl sitting and talking with Swoops Like Falcon.

"Your son is telling her that he wants her to have the pelt from the panther he killed," Outina said. "Naturally, she is interested enough to give him her full attention."

"She can sew while she listens," Walks Tall Woman replied, and dumped into her lap the makings of a pair of winter boots. "Our niece is inclined to brood too much; busy hands go a long way toward preventing that."

But Moon of Winter never ceased to mentally bemoan her fate, whatever her hands might be doing. How could she forget her woes? Walks Tall Woman managed to look directly at her, but everyone else either refrained from looking at her or visibly recoiled when, inadvertently, they focused on her scarred cheek. That was why Moon of Winter rarely left the house, why she kept her head lowered whenever she did. It hurt, to have people shrink from her when she had once been openly admired for her beauty, and this sort of hurt was far, far worse than any wounding of the flesh could ever be.

"It is not large enough to make a bed robe, that panther skin," Falcon was saying earnestly. "But perhaps you can make a skirt or something out of it."

Even though his head was turned slightly away from her—naturally—the tension in his body told Moon of Winter he was hoping for a word or two of praise. Well, he had certainly earned as much. "I will mount it, intact, right here in the great hall," she told him, "to remind me of how you saved my life. You proved yourself both brave and resourceful that day, Falcon, and I am proud of you as well as grateful to you."

His head swiveled around then, and for a moment a grin widened his boyish mouth. But it vanished as soon as his dark eyes touched on his cousin's face, and she could not bear to see the pity that flooded into his eyes before he looked away again.

Moon of Winter stood up, flung around her the ankle-length cloak she'd fashioned from an old, thin bed robe. "I feel the

need of some fresh air," she mumbled, and made for the doorway.

She wished Outina's rectangular house did not sit directly in
the center of the compound, that it was not literally surrounded
by the palmetto-roofed, dome-shaped dwellings of the townspeople. And she wished most ardently that so many people had
not found reason to be outside this midday. Hunching her head
between her shoulders, she hurried to the tunnellike passage
that took her beyond the log palisade enclosing the village.

She would not go near the planting fields, she told herself.
Even if the men had finished the hoeing, women with digging
sticks would be seeding mounds of soil made dark and fertile
by seasonal burning. Nor did she want to chance meeting any
of the folks who lived in the homes built in clan clusters on the
adjacent lowlands. But she could surely find some isolated spot
among the trees that marched away from the base of the rise
upon which the town itself was situated. She might find shade
there as well, enough to let her shrug off the suffocating cloak
and fully enjoy the breeze that was teasing at her unbound hair.

As if this girl could truly enjoy anything ever again! The
hideousness of her scarred face made her an alien among her
own people, and it was suddenly clear to Moon of Winter that
marriage to Holata Potano was not the only thing denied her
now; no man alive would care to be husband to the repellent
creature she had become. And the children she had always
dreamed of having . . . they would remain just that, a dream.
A dream that would plague and distress her throughout the rest
of her lonely life.

Tears blurred her vision as she pushed her way deeper
among the trees she'd come to, and when her cloak snagged
on a thorny bush, she let it slip from her shoulders and went
on without it. If it was not shady enough, then let the sun's fingers reach down and scorch her. What did she care?

Sobbing, she threw herself down on a mossy patch of
ground and let her grief spill out and form a salty pool beneath
her ravaged cheek. If she could never have a man to love her,
and children around her hearth, then This World held nothing
for her. Why had the spirits Watches for Omens called upon
bothered to let her live, if she must spend the years left to her
alone?

Well, she did not choose to do so. She scrambled to her feet,
blinked the tears from her eyes, looked wildly around her. Beneath the leafy trees grew shrubs of every conceivable size and

shape. Vines clung to rough-barked trunks and twisted themselves around and through any bush sturdy enough to support
their growth, and lush flowers made splashes of color against
the green. Amid such abundant growth there was surely a solution to Moon of Winter's problem.

How she regretted her inattention when Watches for Omens
had spoken so passionately about the venoms that hid within
ordinary growing things! She tried to call back his words, but
most remained tauntingly beyond her reach. Seeds. He'd mentioned seeds. Seeds from blossoming plants. No. Vines. But
had it been their seeds or the nectar from their flowers that was
deadly? Both, perhaps. Or he might have been referring to
more than one vine.

She studied the vines growing nearby. There were so many
of them! Still, she could eliminate those that showed no signs
of flowering. Had he said anything else that might steer her in
the right direction?

Yes. Yes, he had! He'd described the vine's flowers as being
cocoon-shaped before and after they opened, and had explained that they opened fully only once a day. Morning? Evening? It had been one or the other, and since it was early
afternoon at the moment, it hardly mattered which.

Moon of Winter began to walk around the small glade she'd
come to in such despair, examining closely anything that even
remotely resembled a flowering vine. By the time she'd completed the circuit, she had identified two that met the specifi-
cations she recalled. Both had clustered blossoms which were
presently rolled lengthwise the way a bit of thin bark might be.
She could not be sure if they were the same vines the Shaman
had spoken of, but she was certain now that it was the seeds
he had said were poisonous. And both displayed capsules that
must contain the seeds of plants yet unborn.

Just as her children must remain unborn, Moon of Winter
thought, so would the progeny of the two vines. For she meant
to eat the seeds from both, rather than trust herself to choose
between them.

Nor would she let herself hesitate. Some foolish instinct for
self-preservation might stay her hand if she did. As it was, her
fingers trembled when she plucked the seed pods and twisted
them open, and her palms were perspiring so that the seeds she
tipped out clung to them.

She tried to shake the seeds into her mouth. When they refused to release their grip on her damp palm, she put out her

tongue and dislodged them, took them into her mouth and swallowed.

Then she stretched out on the mossy ground and waited to die.

Chapter 10

❦ ❦

"I would like something special, something both special and beautiful, to give to my niece." Holata Outina's eyes rejected the goods Kwambu had arranged on the blanket between them. "It should be something few women possess," he went on, careless for once of the weightless voice that had been an embarrassment to him since his warrior days. "Indeed, it must be, or she will not smile when I give it to her. And I want very much to see Moon of Winter smile again."

Kwambu had heard about the dreadful thing that had happened to Moon of Winter. Everywhere he had gone in Timucuan country, people had been speaking of it. But he had not yet seen for himself what the panther had done to the young woman's face. Nor did he expect to, even if she returned from her walk while he was still sitting in front of Outina's house.

"She wants no one, not even her family, to look at her," Outina had said sorrowfully when Kwambu asked how his niece fared.

Now Kwambu watched as Holata Outina considered the bundle of janthina shells and cockleshells, then shook his head to indicate that they were neither rare enough nor beautiful enough to serve his purpose.

The trader's hand strayed to the pouch he wore around his neck, hesitated, then clutched it firmly. Within, wrapped securely to avoid contact with his tally disks, a plum-sized crystal he had taken in trade from a chief near Lake Mayaimi, and a few other possessions he went nowhere without, lay seven perfect pearls, pearls that had cost him his distinctive new staff and more besides. He had meant to keep them until Dancing Egret married, then make a gift of them to her. As he'd promised to do.

But the thought of beauty destroyed made him ache. A lovely blossom may be torn from a bush and another will grow in its stead, but no one can grow a new face. He untied the pouch and withdrew the packet of pearls. He would get others for Dancing Egret, he told himself, even if he had to travel to Apalachee country to do so. He unfolded the moss the pearls were shrouded in and tipped the glowing globes into his palm. Silently, he held out his hand.

Outina's eyes lit up. "Ahh," he breathed. "If I can give my niece such a gift, surely she will put aside her grief, if only for a little while." He looked pensively at the trader. Outina was a slow-thinking man but he was far from stupid, and the ritual of barter brought out the best in him. "You know what it is like to be Holata," he said, automatically putting on a mask of martyrdom. "We have not only our own families to provide for, but any of our people who come to us for help. And there has been drought this year, with signs of more to come." He spread his big hands in mute appeal. "Times are hard, Kwambu. Much as I want your pearls, much as Moon of Winter needs to receive so magnificent a gift, I fear that I can offer you nothing even close to their worth."

Obligingly, Kwambu entered into the ritual. "That is sad, Holata Outina." He looked down at the pearls. "You may believe me when I say that a trader is no stranger to want and need. I gave one of my most prized possessions to get these pearls"—he shrugged to indicate his own unenviable position—"which means I have come near to impoverishing myself again."

"Perhaps," Outina said after a protracted silence, "I might be able to replace what you gave for them. If you tell me what that was."

"I would be ashamed to tell you," Kwambu said swiftly. "You would think me mush-headed to have given so much. Even for pearls." He flattened his hand, let the white spheres roll this way and that, made sure they absorbed enough sunlight to take on new lambency.

Holata Outina looked away from them, drummed blunt-tipped fingers against one angled knee, lifted his hand and scratched his jaw. "I have a bearskin robe," he said at last. "It was made from a prime skin, and is both warm and elegant. I have only had it for two seasons, and had hoped to wear it for the rest of my life. But for Moon of Winter, perhaps I will let myself shiver when the cold weather comes again."

"I am mostly in the south," Kwambu pointed out. "What use is a warm garment to me?"

"You travel in the north in every season," Outina said. "And you need not keep the robe, after all; I am sure there are many chiefs among my people who would give much to have it."

Kwambu let uncertainty rule his face, but made mental note of the fact that there ought to be tribal leaders among the Apalachee who would barter even pearls for such a robe.

"I might even," Outina said, "give a gold ornament as well. A small one, of course." He smiled. "I have heard that Headchief Calusa has a great admiration for gold. Surely he would be properly grateful if his trader brought him a gold armband, for instance, or a gold clasp for one of his feather capes?"

"It is worth considering," Kwambu said cautiously. "If—"

A keening wail from the direction of the gateway wrested the attention of both men from their negotiating. The eerie sound was attended by a hubbub of excited chatter and the shuffle and scritch of many moccasins.

Outina sprang to his feet to look, but more and more people were spilling out of the nearby houses; they swelled the throng that already obstructed his view of the palisade. And now the keening sound had become a chant of sorts, indecipherable sounds stabbing rhythmically at the summer air. "I must see what is wrong," the Holata muttered, and hurried toward the source of the disturbance.

Kwambu returned to his pouch the pearls that would soon be Holata Outina's; the interruption did not alter the fact that Outina would have them in the end. And if they brought some small joy to Moon of Winter, Kwambu thought, he would be happy for both the girl and her uncle.

He stood up and strode in the direction Outina had taken. There must, indeed, be something wrong in this town for the people to be milling about and talking so agitatedly. He eased through the crowd until he found himself at its forefront, paused between a trio of whispering matrons and a man he recognized as Outina's Shaman.

He paid no heed to any of them, for within the circle the onlookers had formed stood Moon of Winter. The girl's face was tipped up toward the sky, and her eyes were half closed. Her long hair, bristling with leaves and twigs, hung to the back of her knees, its tangled ends brushing against flesh marked with bruise-colored splotches. Similar blackish-blue marks decorated the slender arms that stretched toward the sky. She appeared to be straining for something just beyond her reach, but there was nothing, nothing at all, in the air around or above her. And her unintelligible words, a repetitive babble that raised the hairs on Kwambu's nape, were likewise directed toward no one and nothing.

Outina stood beside her, with a tall youth whose resemblance to the chief suggested to Kwambu that this must be his nephew, Swoops Like Falcon. Like his uncle, the boy was attempting to attract Moon of Winter's attention by speaking her name again and again.

The girl did not react to their urgent calling. She simply went on jabbering and reaching for the unattainable sky. The sun shone down upon her, painting her face gold and highlighting three parallel scars that extended far enough down her cheek to slightly lift a corner of her once perfectly shaped mouth. A man, the trader thought, particularly a warrior, would wear such scars proudly. But a young woman? Never mind that her nose was admirably straight, that the cast of cheek-and jawbones was appealingly gentle; whenever Moon of Winter gazed into a quiet pond or rain-spawned puddle, she was sure to see only disfigurement.

"She speaks with the spirits!"

The sentence burst from Outina's Shaman, and two long strides took him to where Outina and Swoops Like Falcon stood. "And see! See how the marks left by the panther resemble the symbol we use for our Sun God!"

Kwambu started. What Watches for Omens said was true. And the panther that had clawed Moon of Winter's face . . . why, among the Calusa, the tawny cat was regarded as Sun's earthly totem! Again he felt a stirring of the hairs on the back of his neck, and a feeling of disquiet that escalated as the Shaman went on speaking.

"Moon of Winter has been singled out by the Sun God," Watches for Omens said solemnly. The girl began to dip and sway as though moving to the tempo of music only she could hear. "Even now she is communing with him," he added, excitement ruffling his voice.

The chatter of the onlookers dropped to a murmur, a murmur infused with awe. Kwambu could feel the people in the rear pressing forward, felt their need to be able to see for themselves what the Shaman was speaking of, to hear more clearly whatever else might be said about Holata Outina's niece.

But Kwambu was already close, close enough to notice when the girl's movements began to falter, close enough to watch her head slowly droop as though it were a blossom on a broken stem. Outina and Falcon were looking at the Shaman now, Falcon's face betraying the fear Moon of Winter's peculiar behavior had aroused in him and his relief at having it explained. The chief was no doubt equally relieved to know that Moon of Winter had not been transformed into a madwoman, but he had long since trained himself to separate innermost thought from facial expression.

A woman on the far side of the circle, her belly bulging with a child she would soon be delivering, slipped away from her friends and neighbors and approached Moon of Winter. When she was near enough, she put out one hand and briefly touched Moon of Winter's dangling hair. Then, smiling ecstatically, she stepped back and rubbed her protruding stomach with her hand. "I shall bring you a gift, to say thank you," she called softly, then returned to her place in the crowd.

The Shaman nodded approvingly, and Kwambu wondered uneasily what would happen if the babe the woman carried should be stillborn, or born alive but with some deformity, and found himself praying to the gods of his childhood that neither of these things would happen.

Suddenly, Moon of Winter ceased her erratic dancing. Her voice dropped to a monotonous mumble and her slender body began to shiver. Her eyes opened briefly, tried vainly to focus, closed again. The bemused watchers sighed collectively as her shivering intensified, and Outina and Falcon swung around and made ineffectual moves toward her. But it was Kwambu the trader, alerted to what was happening sooner than the rest, who sprang forward and caught Moon of Winter as she collapsed.

Walks Tall Woman materialized beside him as he swept the girl up in his arms. She sent a venomous glance after the pregnant woman, then turned to Kwambu. "Carry my niece into the Principal House and put her onto her bed," she said sharply. "It's plain the girl is ill; she does not need fools hovering around her at such a time."

Hers was the voice of reason, and Kwambu was glad indeed to respond to it. He had no qualms about leaving Moon of Winter to her aunt's ministrations, even if these did include forcing upon the girl an apparently vile-tasting restorative just as soon as she had roused enough to swallow it.

"Even Walks Tall Woman will have to acknowledge, eventually, that this Moon of Winter is not the same Moon of Winter who left your house earlier today." Watches for Omens had followed Outina and Swoops Like Falcon inside, and it perturbed him to be shooed away from the girl's bed. He had wanted to speak with her as soon as sensibility returned, to discover what the spirits had revealed. But not even the Shaman would risk angering Walks Tall Woman, who was known to be a staunch upholder of the ancient law that decreed payment in kind for any act, especially those deemed wrongful. To be fair, Outina's sister was as quick to return generosity with generosity, but this did not make her vengeful practices any easier to deal with. Watches for Omens was not about to antagonize her, despite his eagerness to speak with her niece. "I hope Moon of Winter does not forget all that happened to her before she tells me about it," he fretted. "This is a possibility, you know." He turned at the sound of a voice, muted but recognizable. "And she is able to speak now," he said. "Holata, it is imperative that I question her while the memory is fresh!"

Outina put a calming hand on the worried man's shoulder. "Soon," he said soothingly. "I, too, am anxious to speak with Moon of Winter and assure myself that she is truly all right."

Swoops Like Falcon, the pelt he had fetched from near his bed draped over one arm, looked up at his uncle. "When you do, will you give her the panther skin that I promised to her?" He paused, looked uncertainly toward the Shaman. "Or perhaps you should be the one to give it to her, Watches for Omens. You know how to approach people who have spoken with spirits."

"There is no reason you cannot give it to her yourself," Holata Outina said gently. "She is your cousin still, no matter what happened to her today." He turned his eyes toward Moon of Winter, who, helped by Walks Tall Woman, was sitting up now. Even from across the hall he could see the haunted expression in her eyes, the way she clutched at the bed robe her aunt had draped around her. "I have a gift for her also," he said, and glanced inquiringly at Kwambu.

The trader nodded. "Agreement had been reached," he confirmed, "even if we had not said as much. I will get the robe and gold ornament from you later." He lifted the pouch from around his neck and extracted the pearls, passed them to Outina. "I hope they bring you the smile you long for," he said quietly.

But even after Walks Tall Woman had allowed the men access to Moon of Winter, neither the panther hide nor the pearls won a smile from her. She averted her head, as she always did, when her uncle and cousin neared her bed, and her acknowledgment of their gifts was muted at best.

"What is wrong with you, girl?" Walks Tall Woman demanded, incensed on her son's behalf. "You let Swoops Like Falcon believe that you dearly wanted this hide; yet you act as though he'd dumped a handful of dried grass in your lap instead of a skin he risked his life to get!" She pounced on the glistening pearls that had rolled into a crease in the bed robe. "And these . . . why, these are treasures indeed. Anyone, woman or man, would be delighted to have them. Have you no appreciation, Moon of Winter?"

The young woman put up her hand to cover her scars, turned to face Outina and Swoops Like Falcon. Despite the disappointment that painted their features, she could not summon up the elation they expected of her. "I thank you both," she faltered. Then her eyes brimmed with tears, and she covered her face with both hands.

Watches for Omens moved closer, stood between Outina and his nephew. "You will have to accustom yourself to receiving gifts," he said to Moon of Winter. "The people recognize that you have been marked by the spirits. They will be bringing offerings to you so that you will intercede for them with the gods. I know this is difficult for you to accept, so soon after your first spiritual encounter. It is natural for you to be bewildered, to be asking yourself why you were chosen. But this is a question that has no—"

"Spirits? What spirits?" Moon of Winter cried, forgetting her ravaged face and dropping her hands. "I begged for only one thing from the spirits, Watches for Omens. Their response was to ignore me."

The Shaman's face grew stern. "The spirits give what they will, and that is not necessarily what we have petitioned for. To you, they may have decided to grant the gift of healing, or of precognition, for instance. It is too soon, much too soon, to know just how they have favored you. But in time you will discover some power in yourself, Moon of Winter. Always it works this way. And you must joyously accept whatever you have received. Your uncle and your cousin may forgive you for your poor reception of what they had to offer, but no spirit will be so forgiving, I promise you."

"I want nothing from the spirits," the girl sobbed. "I want nothing from anyone. I want only to . . . to . . ."

Her wailing drowned out her final word, but Kwambu was certain that he knew what she said. It was death Moon of Winter craved, and his soul was chilled to recognize this.

He backed away from the group trying to console the anguished young woman and eased himself out of the house and into the sunlight. He could be of no further use, beyond praying earnestly that Moon of Winter might come to see that life, even a difficult life, was not something to be cast aside like a worn-out moccasin. He inhaled the mouth-watering fragrance of venison roasting over some family's cooking fire, heard the heart-swelling song of an unseen mockingbird, lifted his arms to invite the fullest caress of a passing breeze. Whether she had been endowed with spirit power or not, Moon of Winter was still able to smell, to hear, to feel. Surely she would come to realize this, and to cherish the realization? If she did not . . . Despite the sun's warmth, Kwambu was suddenly cold again.

He was grateful for the diversion when spear-bearing men, their topknots studded with arrows, came pouring into the compound. From the shape of the stalking masks a few of them still wore, Kwambu knew before he saw the scaly monster they carried so proudly that the party had been hunting alligator. Bold in Battle, Outina's Paracusi and Moon of Winter's father, was in the lead, as befitted his status, but he did not remain with his fellows to enjoy the praiseful exclamations of the elders and young boys who flocked to admire the kill. The haste with which he approached the Principal House, the anxious look on his face, told Kwambu that he had already heard the news about his daughter.

"It is good that you are home." Alerted by the noise, Holata Outina came outside just in time to greet his War Leader. He stepped aside in order to permit the man entry. "Bold in Battle and Moon of Winter have always been close," Outina said to the trader, "even though he has lived in his mother's lodge since my sister died. Perhaps he will be able to soothe the girl. I cannot, nor can Walks Tall Woman. And you saw how the Shaman only succeeded in upsetting her further." He shook his head. "It is perplexing, that being favored by the spirits should leave Moon of Winter so distressed. Surely it should be otherwise?"

"I know little about spiritual matters," Kwambu replied cautiously. "But I am sorry that the pearls you gave her failed to delight her. Perhaps, when she is feeling better, she will be able to appreciate them."

Outina brightened a little. "It is true that she scarcely looked at them when I put them into her hand. Do you think she did not even realize what they were?"

"That is possible. Give her time to recover a bit, Holata, then present them again. When she is less . . . confused." He did not think *confused* was the right word to describe Moon of Winter's state of mind, but it seemed politic to use so mild a term.

"I will do that," Outina said. "But I will not make you wait for the bearskin robe and gold ornament I promised you should have in exchange. Indeed, I will give you *two* ornaments, the second one to thank you for your help today. Moon of Winter would have fallen and perhaps injured herself if you had not been so quick this afternoon."

"That is unnecessary," Kwambu protested. But the chief would not be dissuaded, and in truth the trader was not sorry to have the additional gift. Now he could go directly to Apalachee country. Having so much to barter with, he would surely be able to return home eventually with more pearls in his pouch.

But Bold in Battle, his usually imperturbable expression pleated by concern for his daughter, came back into the compound as Kwambu was packing his sledge. "Trader," he called, "I would have a word with you."

Kwambu wondered if Moon of Winter's father meant to press upon him yet another gift, to express his own thanks. If so, he would refuse it courteously. Why should he be rewarded for so small a service?

That was not what the Paracusi had come out for, however. "We met a hunting party from one of our western villages while we were away," he said, "and they gave us news Outina thinks you should hear. A Spanish ship, sailing north, recently passed by one of our coastal towns. Rumor has it that it had already made landfall on the southern peninsula and caused some trouble there." He turned up his hands. "Rumor is not always to be trusted, of course. But there definitely *was* a ship, and you might want to pass on that news to the towns you visit on your way home. When one ship has been sighted, others may follow, and who knows where they may land, or where the pale-skins they carry might decide to travel to? To be warned is to be prepared."

"Did anyone say where in the south this trouble, whatever it was, occurred?" Kwambu's fingers had made short work of lashing down his wares, and he poised himself to leave.

Bold in Battle shook his head. "As I said, most of what I told you is rumor only. There were no details to be had."

The trader tugged at his hauling ropes and the sledge began to slide over the ground. "I must ask you to have Holata Outina send a courier to spread the word," he said to Bold in Battle, "for I will be stopping only when I absolutely must. I mean to go directly south, in case rumor was right when it spoke of trouble there. I am Calusa's man; my place is with his people."

The War Leader did not argue; loyalty to one's leader was a praiseworthy thing, and there were enough runners in Outina's town to carry the alert throughout his province. He moved ahead of the trader to ensure him a clear passage to the palisade.

Kwambu thanked him and passed into the open. Indifferent to the fact that his trip to Apalachee country would have to be postponed, he lengthened his stride and turned his face toward home.

Chapter 11

❦ ❦

"The Spanish on that ship came across a party of fishermen near the place we call Many Small Islands," Headchief Calusa said, pacing the length of a room large enough to hold all of his extended family plus counselors, warriors, priests, and more guests than he was ever likely to play host to at one time. Like the smaller homes set on the broad terraces that fell away from this flat-topped mound, the Headchief's had a raised plank floor with four enormous corner posts supporting a sloping, palm-thatched roof. Here, however, additional vertical posts, spaced evenly, stretched from floor to ceiling, and horizontal timbers ran waist-high between them.

Anger fueled Calusa's muscles, and he swung around and retraced his steps before going on. "There were only four men in the dugout, but a fifth had swum to one of the nearby islands to bag a turtle he'd spotted. Which is how I know"—he flung the words over his shoulder as his feet began to mark off the room's considerable width—"that the Christian soldiers killed two of my fishermen and seized two others. The man who had gone after the turtle saw them flank the canoe with their small boats. Obviously, they expected Calusa's men to try and flee." His contemptuous sniff said how preposterous such an idea was. "Still, for all that they fought back, my men were net-fishing and had only knives with them. They were no match for ten armed soldiers." He turned and looked to where the trader stood. "What will they do with them, Kwambu? With Tireless Swimmer and his grandson Thunder Talker?"

It would be insulting Headchief Calusa to dissemble. "The Christians may have been after slaves," Kwambu said. "My friend Tai-No-Me, who lives in your Arawak village, has de-

113

scribed for you how the people of his homeland were enslaved by the Spanish." Kwambu made a silent vow to go this evening and visit Tai-No-Me. The youth who had come with him to this country had grown up to become one of the Headchief's oceangoing traders and was all too often on a voyage when Kwambu was between journeys. But perhaps things would be different this time, and Kwambu needed to relax; he had wasted little time sleeping and less eating in his haste to return from Outina's town. Indeed, he was so tired now that he had trouble forcing his mind back to the subject at hand. "It is equally likely," he continued, "that the Spanish plan to come again to these shores, to launch an overland expedition as they have done before. Your men would make useful guides, if so."

"No man of mine will guide the Christians!" Calusa said sharply. "Except into the swamps, perhaps." He smiled; men who draped their bodies with metal would have no chance at all in certain swamps that he knew of!

Kwambu hesitated, and the silence spawned by his search for the right words was filled by the rattle of a woman's voice as Calusa's First Wife scolded a servant for some misdemeanor. "They will be given two choices," he said finally. "To guide the soldiers, or to die. And they will not die quickly, if death is what they choose."

"Tireless Swimmer is old, and his grandson scarcely more than a boy," Calusa said morosely, sitting down at last and signaling the trader to do likewise. "I suppose, if one of them is threatened, the other will do whatever is demanded of him." He looked across the room, to where Mask Maker and a pair of youthful apprentices were attaching clan markers, cypress panels the length of a man's arm, to the benches where Calusa and his counselors would be sitting during a meeting later that day. The clan representatives would occupy the second highest tier, three on either side of the Headchief's own seat, an ornately carved stool set on the uppermost level. Calusa's plaque, bearing his clan's Dolphin image, was naturally larger than the others, but all were fine examples of the wood-carver's talent. "Mask Maker," he called, "I have need of your students, if they are willing to act as couriers for me. Can you release them from their duties?

"First," he said to them when the elderly carver had given them leave to go, "I want you to fetch comrades who can also make themselves available to me. Then I will send all of you out, one to the north, one to the south, and two to take a canoe upriver into Lake country, with messages to my Townchiefs. Oh, and I also need someone who is familiar with the river glades; Prowling Panther and his band are hunting near the hammock where the snails wear brown and yellow shells." He did not have to elaborate; everyone knew how the isolated tree-islands dotting the sawgrass ocean were each home to a distinctive breed of snail. "The men must come back, I think," Calusa said, turning to Kwambu. "Until we know if and when the Spanish will come this way again, only small hunting parties should go out. And they will be told not to go far."

The trader nodded. "You are wise, as always, Great Calusa. Will you dispatch a messenger to Mocoso as well?"

Calusa sent Mask Maker's apprentices on their errand with a wave of his hand. "Because of Dancing Egret, you mean?"

"Both your daughter and Ucita's are there. And even though Outina's couriers are certain to have passed the word beyond the boundaries of his province, we have no way of knowing if it has spread all through Timucuan territory as yet."

"Mocoso's town is near to the coast. Surely he keeps sentries posted along the shore?"

"He does. But Mocoso is an arrogant young man who has yet to have an encounter with the Spanish. From different things he has told Kneeling Cypress's husband, I fear he may even welcome them, should they come there."

"Then he is a fool, as well as arrogant," Calusa said, and Kwambu hid a smile. Arrogance was in every syllable of that pronouncement! "Still, I would not have my daughter put at risk. Ucita's daughter removed herself from her father's protection when she fled his town, but it was no more than childish whim that made Egret go with her. So I shall send a message to Mocoso warning him that to offer Spaniards the hand of friendship is an invitation to have that hand cut off!"

A courier bearing that message would most likely have *his* hand cut off, Kwambu thought tiredly. "I will be glad to go to Mocoso for you," he said. "I need to see him, as it happens, for he entrusted me with a commission before I went north to trade. And everyone there knows me. Which will not be the case should you send an ordinary runner."

"Mocoso might not be as eager to welcome one of my runners as he would some sword-bearing Spaniard, I suppose," the Headchief said dryly. "But let the trip wait for a few days. You need sleep, and to fill your belly properly, or I doubt you'll make it to where your canoe is beached."

Kwambu could not deny this, any more than he could have stifled the yawn that had reminded Calusa of the grueling trek his trader had just made. "I will go as soon as I am rested," he agreed. "Like Holata Mocoso, I have listened to Juan Ortiz talk, and have heard him say that it takes the Spanish a long time to arrange any sort of expedition. I expect I could make twoscore trips to Mocoso's town before ships come this way again."

"One trip will suffice," the Headchief said, "but I would be pleased if you would go from Mocoso into the Lake country. It has been so dry here this season that our corn withers on the stalk. If you can get us a supply of zamia root and dates and figs, there will be less cause for grumbling if the rains do not come soon enough to save our first planting."

"Everywhere I have been, people are talking about the abnormal length of the dry season," Kwambu said. "Chiefs will soon be reluctant to part with what food they have."

"If you cannot get a sufficient supply at one or another of my towns, go to Canegacola. Timucuan foodstuffs are as nourishing as ours, and I will see that you take along goods to encourage the exchange."

"If I am going that far," Kwambu said slowly, "I wonder if I might go a little farther. To Outina."

Calusa's eyebrows arched. "That is more than a *little* farther."

"I can go quickly if I do not stop along the way," Kwambu said. "And there is a young woman there who has recently been through a difficult time. I would like to see how she fares."

The Headchief threw back his head and laughed. "So! My trader has discovered heat in his loins at last! I had begun to think such a thing would never happen."

Kwambu shook his head, but Calusa ignored his denial. "What is wrong with our Calusan women, hmm? After all, you are pledged to my service; I would be better pleased if you found a wife here. Indeed, I will find one for you, and make sure she is able to satisfy a man's needs before I give her to you."

"Moon of Winter is Outina's niece, and will wed according to her status," Kwambu said stiffly. "And I doubt that I shall ever take a wife. Like should keep to like, and there are none like me anywhere in this country."

Calusa shrugged his broad shoulders. "The Christian slaves

who have earned a raise in status and found wives or husbands among the Calusa seem content enough. Those not born to the tribe need not concern themselves with the restrictions we have against marrying within one's clan, you know. But you must do as you think best, Kwambu. If you are loath to take a wife, why not get yourself a concubine or two?" He laughed again. "One in the north, and one in the south, perhaps. I would have no objection to that."

When Kwambu made no response, the Headchief decided to have done with the subject. "In any event, go where you will after you arrange for delivery of the food I am sending you to get. So long as you return in good time, I will make no complaints."

Kwambu swallowed a second yawn, made himself show proper appreciation for the Headchief's magnanimity, and was not sorry to be dismissed. He had been careful to conceal it, but it rankled that Calusa was attempting to order his personal life as though he were a slave still. It was as well that he honestly did not intend to wed, or even take a concubine, he told himself bitterly. Then, reminding himself of how much Headchief Calusa had done for him, he squashed his resentment and turned his mind to other matters. He had never been given to feelings of foreboding, yet he knew he would make his visit to Outina's town a brief one. And not just to avoid displeasing Calusa. For no reason he could name, the trader was suddenly certain that Spanish ships would soon be heading this way again, and that their coming would bring havoc to a land he had come to love with all the fervor of those who had the right to call it *home*.

Holata Mocoso set the chunkey stone rolling with a flip of one sinewy wrist. Because of its beveled edges, it described an arc as it moved swiftly over the packed sand of the squareground, and both the chief and Juan Ortiz monitored its progress. The moment the round stone showed signs of slowing down, each cast a long pole toward the spot he believed the chunkey would come to rest.

"Ha!" cried Mocoso. "Mine is the closest, Ortiz."

Juan stalked over to the chunkey, studied the positions of both poles, crouched down to measure with outstretched hand the distance between each one and the stone that lay between them. "You are right," he admitted at last. "There is little more than a finger's width difference, however."

He picked up the stone and his pole and headed back to the far side of the squareground. A grinning Mocoso retrieved his pole and followed him. "We have practiced long enough, I think," he said. "Now we begin the wagering."

The warriors and young boys who had watched the contest thus far cheered the decision and began betting among themselves on the outcome of the next roll of the stone.

Juan Ortiz was not averse to the idea. During the practice, he had proven himself a match for the chief, and wagering was bound to further sharpen a skill he was confident of. "Will you risk your new canoe paddle?" he asked. "The one decorated with symbols to bring you good fortune whenever you go fishing?"

"If you will put up that new vest you are wearing," Mocoso said. He had admired it ever since he'd first set eyes on it. A garment so finely made, its edges trimmed with hundreds of tiny seashells, needed bronze flesh to set it off properly.

His companion shrugged, nodded. Kneeling Cypress could always make him another. He narrowed his eyes as he prepared to set the chunkey rolling. It had arced to the left the last few times, and surely Mocoso would expect it to do so again. If he could make it spin out to the right, Juan thought, surprise might misdirect the chief's toss.

The spectators kept silent as the stone hurtled over the ground, curved to the right, and—at long last—began to lose momentum. Two poles shot after it and thudded into the sand.

"My win!" Ortiz said jubilantly.

Mocoso frowned. "You have my paddle," he said, "but I would still like to own that vest. Shall we wager again?"

"If you will offer something to make it worth my while," Juan said, smiling to hear the praiseful chanting that celebrated his toss. "I shall—" He broke off, frowning in his turn to see the black-skinned trader Dancing Egret was so fond of come past the sentry stations and begin crossing the squareground. "You!" he shouted. "Do not walk there!"

Kwambu lifted his hand and shaded his eyes against the sun. Realizing that absorption in his thoughts had kept him from noticing that a game was in progress, he spread his palms apologetically and retraced his steps, then took the long way around to where the chief stood. A trio of boys hauled a slender, bristly branch to the path he'd inadvertently made, brushed out his footprints, and packed down the sand once more.

"Well, trader," Mocoso said, "I hope you have come to tell me you were successful in getting me what I sent you after?"

Kwambu took a deerhide pouch from around his waist and handed it to the chief.

Mocoso beamed as his long fingers probed the pouch and found it full of hard little globes. Opening it eagerly, he peered inside.

"There are twelve of them," Kwambu said, "and all perfect."

Juan Ortiz moved closer, his annoyance at having the game interrupted supplanted by curiosity, and tried to see inside the bag.

Holata Mocoso was happy to display his treasure. He took out three of the pearls and let them lay in his palm.

Ortiz exclaimed aloud. This was the sort of wealth Panfilo de Narvaez had hoped to find in the new world! "Remarkable!" he breathed. "I had not known pearls were available in this country."

"They are not, except among the Apalachee," the trader told him. "And they get most of theirs from tribes who live to the north of them."

"Is that where these came from?" Juan asked.

"Only indirectly." It was Mocoso who answered him, and he did so without taking his eyes from the fascinating white globes he held in his hand. "My clan-brother, Holata Tocobaga, often takes pearls in exchange for goods he sends to Apalachee territory. These came from him." He raised his eyes for a moment. "Thanks to Kwambu, who was able to persuade him to part with a few for a bundle of egret plumes."

Juan, too, could not seem to take his eyes from the pearls. "Will you wager one," he asked, "on our next round in the game?"

Abruptly, Mocoso fed the pearls back into the deerskin pouch. "You forget yourself, Spaniard," he said sharply. "Only tribal leaders may own such things."

Kwambu did not miss the anger that momentarily distorted Ortiz's features. Fortunately, Mocoso was preoccupied with the pearls. "I bring a message also," the trader said to him. "From Headchief Calusa."

"Let us go into the house, then," the chief said. "I can examine my pearls most closely there." Turning his back on Ortiz, he led the way to the low mound that supported his home.

It was some time before Kwambu was able to deliver his message. First Mocoso spread out the pearls and looked closely at each one; then his wife and mother were summoned to inspect them, and several of his Principal Men. All were suitably impressed, and Holata Mocoso grew more and more expansive as he preened in the glow of their astonishment and admiration.

"You have done well, trader," he said at last, propping himself on one elbow and playing with his pearls as though they were counters in a gambling game. "I shall use these to decorate a gorget, I think," he mused. "No. There are not quite enough for that. An anklet? Or perhaps I can get more of them." He shot a glance at Kwambu. "Tocobaga has many?"

"It is said that he does. And since he was willing to part with twelve, then I think he must." That Tocobaga had also traded seven additional pearls to Kwambu was information Mocoso did not need.

"I shall have him here," Mocoso said thoughtfully. "He can bring his warriors for a week of games and feasting, and while he is my guest I may be able to talk him out of a few more of these beauties. There is nothing he might ask in exchange that I would not give him." He grinned. "Of course, *he* will not know that!"

"Holata Tocobaga may refuse to leave his province any time soon," Kwambu said, "since he has probably already heard the news that I have brought to you from Calusa."

"And that is?"

"A Spanish ship sailed along the lower coast during the last dark of the moon," Kwambu said, "then headed out to sea after the men on board had captured two of Calusa's fishermen. They are almost certainly planning to force the fishermen to act as guides on an inland expedition. Since we cannot know when or where the Christians mean to begin that expedition, Calusa recommends that you prepare to defend your town should the need arise."

Mocoso laughed. "It sounds as though age has turned the Great Calusa into a fretful old woman," he said scornfully. "Has he begun to peer over his shoulder yet, to see if he is being pursued by ghosts?" He laughed again. "You may tell your Headchief for me that we Timucua are not so squeamish. If the Spanish come, I will know how to deal with them."

Mocoso's mother, who had been chatting quietly with his

wife, broke off midsentence and looked with consternation at her son.

"Other Timucuan chiefs are taking precautions," the trader told him. "Even those whose provinces are inland, like Holata Outina."

"Another one who is letting age make a jellyfish out of him," Mocoso retorted. "I still have a spine, however. Besides, Juan Ortiz is precaution enough. I have been an excellent host to him, and am more likely to be rewarded than set upon. So far, though, Christians seem to prefer Calusa country to Timucua."

"The Spaniard who invaded Chief Ucita's town took his soldiers through Timucua country," Kwambu reminded him.

"And did not even know that he did, since he saw so few of us. He and his men finally went on to Apalachee." Mocoso shrugged. "I understand that most of them died there. Blunderers like that pose no threat. Not to the Timucua, at any rate."

Kwambu bit back a stinging retort. While Calusa might feel glad to know he had leaped to his defense, the Headchief would be the first to say that a less than tactful trader was no trader at all. He would be right, too. "Calusa had no intention of dictating strategy to you," Kwambu said quietly. "He only wanted me to pass on this news in case you had not already received it from other sources. And I sincerely hope you are right, that Juan Ortiz is all the protection your town needs against Christian marauders."

"You may depend on it," Mocoso said loftily. "I am a man who plans ahead, trader. And I meant what I told Ortiz when he sought sanctuary with me: he is free to leave with any Spanish that might decide to visit my province." He returned the pearls to their pouch, fondling each one before letting it slip into the bag. "Indeed, I will not be sorry if ships do come, and he decides to take advantage of my offer. The man is beginning to bore me. He has a tendency to get above himself, that one." He studied the last pearl for a long moment before letting it join its fellows. "I would not grieve to see the back of him."

"He has a wife here. And children," Kwambu said.

Mocoso came to his feet, and the trader followed suit. "So he has," the chief said indifferently. "You may tell Headchief Calusa that you delivered his message," he went on, and now his tone was clearly one of dismissal. "You may tell him also that Holata Mocoso pays little attention to alarmists."

Kwambu's jaw tightened, and he relaxed it only with difficulty. "I need to have a few words with Calusa's daughter," he
said. "Then I will be on my way." He would tell Dancing
Egret to go home, and to waste no time doing so. And he
would suggest strongly that she persuade Kneeling Cypress
and her children to go back to Ucita. Kwambu knew that Calusa would approve if he delayed going to the Lake country in
order to act as escort for all of them.

"She is in the women's hut." Mocoso's mother offered the
information. "It is her time of the moon, and she will be there
for some days yet."

"So that is why we had to chase so many children from the
squareground before we could turn it into a chunkey yard this
morning," her son said. "The little ones generally follow Calusa's daughter around like pups stumbling after a bitch," he said
to Kwambu. "She is their storyteller, you see, although the
grownups enjoy some of their tales as much as their children
do. Even I have found them amusing from time to time."

Although his voice was condescending, there was admiration in it, which did not surprise Kwambu. Egret had that effect on people. "Perhaps I will speak with Kneeling Cypress
instead, then."

Mocoso's mother spoke up again. "The Spaniard's wife is
also in the women's hut, and will probably remain there for
some time. The babe she had begun to carry has deserted her
womb. It seems that the woman my son nearly made the mistake of marrying is a puny thing after all." Sour satisfaction
underscored her words.

Kwambu refrained from saying that Cypress had already
given Ortiz three healthy children. He merely thanked her for
saving him a walk to Ortiz's house, then took formal farewell
of Mocoso.

Could he leave a message with Juan Ortiz? he wondered as
he stepped outside. But when he had located the Spaniard and
started toward him, the man swung around and began to stride
in the opposite direction. Kwambu had long since realized that
Ortiz had no use for people whose skins were black, and
doubtless Ortiz was furious because Mocoso had invited the
trader into his house without suggesting that the Spaniard join
them there.

But this left no way to get a message to Dancing Egret. And
if Kneeling Cypress had recently miscarried, Egret would only
refuse to leave here until her friend was well enough to travel.

Kwambu would simply have to make his journey to the Lake villages, and then to Outina, with as much haste as possible. And be prepared to have uneasiness hover around him like a malignant apparition as he went.

Chapter 12

Kwambu, stepping carefully around a clump of gorse, was grateful for the moonlit stream whose meandering course was guiding him to Holata Outina's town. He had probably been unwise to attempt the final leg of his journey while darkness ruled the world, but he had awakened while the moon was still high and known he would not get back to sleep. Without pack to carry or sledge to haul, he'd seen no reason why he should not push on; his successful trading in the Lake country had done nothing to lessen the sense of urgency that had been with him since the start of this mission.

Now his feet found the well-trodden path that bisected Outina's outlying fields, yet it would be foolhardy to approach the palisade before morning's light permitted the town's sentries to identify him. A cluster of boulders marked the midpoint of this path; he could wait there until dawn and then go the rest of the way.

His pace was easy and his moccasins made only the softest of sounds as they met earth worn smooth by the regular passage of those who tended the crops. But his right foot came down with a mighty thud when suddenly a dark shape rose up in front of him.

As he fought to regain his balance, Kwambu wondered briefly if the ghost of his continuing disquiet had managed to put on substance. Then the wisp of cloud that had drifted between earth and moon moved on; light fell upon the fear-pinched features of Outina's niece.

"Do not be afraid," he said quickly, ignoring the hammering of his own heart. "It is only Kwambu." Her tension did not abate; she gave no sign of recognition. "The trader," he said. "I have come to see your uncle." Which was not entirely true; he had come to see the young woman who stood before him now, or at least to learn how she fared.

"The trader from the south," Moon of Winter said faintly.

"Yes. You come often to Outina's town, I think."

"I do. But this is the first time I have arrived at the gates before daylight." He smiled to put her at ease, moved one foot back until he found the base of a boulder, sat down. "Which I will wait for this time, before I hail the sentries."

Moon of Winter was uncertain whether she should suggest that he enter the town now. With her. But what could she do with him once both were inside? None but the guards would be awake. Perhaps she should return to town by herself, and let him make his own way in afterward? No; that would be discourteous.

"You have begun your day early," Kwambu said when she remained silent.

"I . . . I could not sleep. After I had lain awake for what seemed like the whole night, I got up and came out here."

"I am surprised that the sentries allowed you to leave the town unaccompanied," Kwambu said. It was not right for Moon of Winter to be wandering alone through the dark, and might well be dangerous.

She laughed, but the sound was without humor. "These days, I go where I will, when I will." Her laugh disintegrated into a sob. "Everyone believes I am being led by spirits, you see."

"But you do not believe that." The response came before Kwambu could stop himself.

"No." The word was a gusty sigh. "I should have said so at the start," she went on wretchedly. "Now, it is too late."

"Is it ever too late to speak the truth?" Kwambu asked gently.

He felt rather than saw the nodding of her bowed head. "There is a woman," she told him, "who recently delivered a healthy son. It's the first child she has given her husband that has lived beyond a day. She swears that I made it possible."

Kwambu recalled the young matron who had touched Moon of Winter's hair on the day she came home from the forest incoherent and disoriented, remembered, too, his own prayers on the pregnant woman's behalf. But Kwambu need not bear the burden of the new mother's gratitude and praise.

"Now anyone who is ill comes to me," Moon of Winter said, a tremor in her voice. "And some who are not ill come and beg to know if they can expect their good health to continue." She raised her head and peered through the dark at Kwambu. "I don't know these things. I never have, I never shall. And I cannot heal the sick!"

From one of the trees lining the fields, a mockingbird twittered a sleepy *pretty-pretty-pretty*. Kwambu shifted so that he could see the eastern sky. "You are overwrought," he said to Moon of Winter, "and not without cause. Shall we just sit quietly until a new day is born? Then, if you wish, we can talk further."

"I cannot imagine why I am telling you any of this," Moon of Winter said, all at once appalled. "You come here often, yet I've never said a word to you before. You must think me mad!"

"I think you are a troubled young woman," Kwambu said. "That is all. And sometimes it is easier to talk with a stranger than with those you know well. But waiting until sunrise will give you time to calm yourself, and to decide if you truly want to tell me more. For now, just sit. And watch."

He gestured to where a narrow streamer of rose pulsed along the horizon. The mockingbird, in full and handsome voice now, no longer sang alone, and as Moon of Winter obediently watched, the rosy banner expanded, its color strengthened, and it strained against the gray shrouding most of the sky.

"Look," she whispered, pointing to the west. "Moon Spirit does not want to give up her place."

The defiantly glowing round stood well above her appointed destination and did indeed seem loath to move on. "It happens occasionally," Kwambu said. "For a while, sun and moon will share the sky. But she will grow dimmer and dimmer as he comes into his own. Eventually she will disappear, whether she wants to or not."

There was wonder in Moon of Winter's face, and Kwambu exulted that it had grown light enough for him to see it. He could see also that she wore around her neck a pendant fashioned from the pearls her uncle had given her, pearls Kwambu had been so willing to relinquish when he'd learned why Outina wanted them. Moon of Winter had woven thin tendrils of grapevine into a sort of cage to contain the clustered pearls, yet even though their mellow gleam was enhanced as the sky brightened, Kwambu thought they could never be as beautiful as the young woman who wore them.

"I've never watched the day come before," Moon of Winter said. "It's strange how the faraway trees still look black as pitch, while the nearest corn plants and the grass around my feet already wear green. And I can see that the soil around the plants is brown, and that the boulders we are sitting on are gray. But that grassy hill in the distance has yet to take on true color."

Slowly the sky above their heads paled to white, then gradually flooded with yellow. Finally, as though satisfied that man had been given sufficient time to prepare for his appearance, the sun lifted his great golden face and looked upon the world. All the dew-sparkled colors of earth came to life in response, flaunting a purity that would not be theirs again until the next day's dawning.

"It's beautiful," Moon of Winter breathed, "so beautiful I cannot find words to describe it."

"Perhaps it is not meant to be described," Kwambu suggested, "but only to be appreciated."

Moon of Winter looked across at the companion she could clearly see now. Surprisingly, she did not experience the discomfort she had expected. "I thank you," she said quietly, "for showing me such beauty. And for listening to me." She hesitated, made her decision and voiced it before timidity bridled her tongue. "If you are still willing, I'd like to tell you more."

Kwambu felt a warmth that had nothing to do with the sunshine busily dispersing the night's chill. "I am willing," he said.

"You know about the big cat that attacked me? About the . . . the marks it left on my face?" Her hand went up to cover her scars.

Kwambu reached over and lifted it down, patted it. "I know. And I was here on the day you talked with spirits."

"But I didn't talk with spirits," she cried. There was a lengthy pause before she spoke again, while the desire to unburden herself wrestled with reluctance to confess her shame. "I went to the forest that day and tried to kill myself by eating the seeds from a poisonous plant," she said finally, looking down at her clasped hands. "I was a fool to think I knew enough to swallow the right kind of seeds. What I ate only made me shivery and nauseated and caused a peculiar ringing in my head. After a while, the cramping in my stomach eased and the ringing began to sound like a weird kind of music. I think I got up and danced to it. Maybe I was singing, too. I remember wanting to, and people say that I did, but ..." She drew a shuddering breath. "What little I can remember is confused, unreal. The only thing I'm certain of is that I did not talk to spirits, and no spirits talked to me." Her eyes, clouded with anguish, sought Kwambu's. "What I tried to do was a terrible thing. That I have received nothing but praise ever since makes it even worse."

"I have heard," Kwambu said, "that certain plants can bring on delirium if they are eaten. It may be you swallowed the seeds of one of those. But I am glad"—he stared at her sternly—"that it was not the poisonous kind you chose ... as Holata Outina would be, and your father, and the rest of your family, if they knew."

"I would have brought dishonor to all of them," she said in a small voice.

"You would have brought *grief* to them," he said, "and thrown away many years that belong within the measure of your life."

"What good are those years to me?" she challenged. "My marriage will not be taking place, which means there will be no children for me to rejoice in. I've lost what beauty I had, and have been given no powers to compensate for it, despite what Watches for Omens and everyone else may think." She twisted her hands until the knuckles were white as the pearls she wore. "If the rains had not come at last, I am sure the people would have begun to name my supposed powers evil rather than good, Kwambu! They had been seeking me out and pleading with me to do something about the drought that was cursing this season's harvest."

"What did you do, when they asked for help?"

"No more than they were already doing. I sent up prayers to Great Thunder Spirit, even though I knew my voice would sound no louder to him than any of the others."

"You cannot know what a spirit listens to and what he does not. None of us can. But I understand your concern. And you were right in what you said earlier: If you did not deny having spirit powers when first you were credited with them, it is too late to do so now. No one would believe you."

Tears filled Moon of Winter's eyes, spilled over cheeks thinner than they were last time Kwambu had been in Outina.

"You truly do understand! Oh, I am so glad. I have sorely needed someone I can speak with openly about what has happened to me, someone who might be able to tell me how to cope with this dreadful situation."

The town's gates were open now, and women with hoes were coming out to battle the weeds yesterday's rain had spawned. Many recognized the trader and sent smiles in his direction, but their expressions when they looked toward Moon of Winter were more than friendly; they were adoring. Here was proof that Outina's niece was well and truly caught in a snare devised by coincidence.

"The people sincerely believe that you now have the power to heal, and to see into the future, and even to influence the weather," Kwambu said slowly. "I may be able to give you something that will help you live up to some of their expectations."

He took from his pouch the crystal he had carried with him since his second trading expedition. It was about the size of an owl's egg, but instead of being round, the exterior was composed of many smooth-surfaced rectangles which formed sharp corners where they met one another. And it was not opaque like an egg; it was, despite the striations that marked it here and there, a marvel of translucency. Its flat surfaces caught and held the sunlight, and miniature rainbows winked in every angle.

"It's like rainwater made solid by the gods!" Moon of Winter exclaimed. "I have never seen anything like this, Kwambu."

"It is called a crystal," he told her. "Warriors often carry them when they go hunting, for it is said that a properly cared-for crystal will lead a man to more game than he will ever have use for. Perhaps it does; men who own crystals appear to cherish them."

"As you must cherish yours," Moon of Winter said. "Surely this is not what you mean to give to me?"

"In the land of my birth," Kwambu told her, "crystals are held to be magical. That is, they are believed to have amazing powers. It is claimed that they can cure certain illnesses"— Moon of Winter gasped, and he nodded confirmation—"and in our village there was a Wise Woman who vowed she could see the future in a crystal whenever she held it a certain way. I cannot know if these things are true. I was a child when I was taken from my homeland." His mouth tightened as he recalled the night raiders who had brutally killed his warrior-father, then sold into slavery a small boy and his terrified mother, but Moon of Winter was too engrossed in the crystal to notice. "It was because of these childhood memories that I bartered for the first crystal I came across in this country. Yet I am no hunter, and will never be called upon to heal the sick or predict the future." His mouth softened and he grinned. "Such things are not expected of traders, I am happy to say! So I want you to have it, Moon of Winter. I will not promise it can do for you what similar stones are said to have done for others, but I think it may help you if you are willing first to help yourself."

Moon of Winter tore her gaze from the dazzling crystal and looked up into her companion's serious face. "I do not understand," she said. "What must I do to persuade the crystal to serve me?"

"I have noticed," Kwambu said, "that people who do battle against the demons of illness make sure to know all there is to know about herbs and plants. The Shamans most renowned for their healing powers are those who administer potions of their own brewing during the curing ceremonies they conduct."

Comprehension erased the puzzlement in Moon of Winter's eyes. "Watches for Omens does that! And he is so enthused about the plants he collects that he will talk on and on about their properties to anyone who cares about such things." She sighed. "And even to those who don't," she added. "When he talked to me about plants, I did not understand even half of what he was saying. And the little I did understand, I soon forgot."

"Yet your memory is keen," Kwambu pointed out. "The seeds you swallowed when you were in the woods addled your thoughts, yet you were able to describe for me how you felt and acted that day. Most people would probably remember nothing after such an experience. Indeed, the Shaman said something of the sort to your uncle."

"But he thought, both of them thought, that I had been speaking with spirits."

"Which would be a similiar experience, surely. At least in its intensity. The very fact that you can be certain you were not speaking with spirits says to me that you are capable of remembering things clearly and accurately. And what is the lore of herbs and plants but facts that have been committed to memory and passed down to others over the years?"

"But I often forget things that do not interest me in the first place," Moon of Winter said forlornly. "Since I've told you so much, you might as well know that. So how can I hope to learn this lore you are talking about when truly I have no interest in such matters?" She glanced at the crystal Kwambu held cupped in his hands. "Unless . . . would the crystal help me to remember, do you think? Can it do that, too?"

The trader studied the crystal also. It seemed to him that Moon of Winter's future was at stake here. What she had said about the people turning against her, of their naming her supposed powers evil rather than good if she failed to help them when they turned to her, was all too likely. "It is said to increase one's ability to concentrate," he said at last, for instinct told him that to focus on a single object must hone anyone's concentration. He reached for her hand, placed the crystal in it, closed her slender fingers over it. "In a moment," he said, "you will feel it start to warm." This was a quality of the crystal that had always fascinated him, and he knew Moon of Winter would not be immune to it.

She closed her eyes. When she opened them again, he read astonishment in them. "It did!" she said joyfully. "What does that mean, Kwambu?"

"It means that the crystal is willing to work for you," he told her.

"Then it will help me learn about herbs and plants? And to know what is going to happen long before it happens? And . . . and all the rest?"

"So long as you do your part, I think that it will," he said. "If you go to your Shaman and tell him you want to study with him, in time the crystal will help you to become a healer."

"He will think the spirits directed me to do that," she said slowly. "Won't I be deceiving him, Kwambu?"

"Can you honestly say that the spirits are not directing you?" he asked. "From what I have heard, they work in ways we do not always recognize."

She smiled. "That is true," she said, relieved. "And what about foretelling the future? What must I do to have the crystal show me what-will-be?"

"Such a talent will probably be slow in coming," he cautioned. "But I think it can never come unless the person who seeks to know the future learns all she can about what has gone before and keeps herself constantly aware of what is happening now. Only when she is certain she has prepared herself to receive it should she seek a message in the crystal."

"That sounds harder than learning about plants," Moon of Winter said with a sigh. But the crystal she held was not only warmer now, it was throbbing gently within her fist. Surely that was a sign that it was content with her and meant to help her do what she could never do on her own? "I will try," she said solemnly. "I will try everything you suggested."

"And have patience," Kwambu said quickly. "You must not expect all of this to happen within days, or even months."

Moon of Winter sighed again. How often had Walks Tall Woman berated her for being impatient? Scores of times! But perhaps the crystal would help with that as well. "You are certain you want me to have this?" she asked, holding out her hand. "It doesn't seem right that you should give up so marvelous a thing."

"The crystal will be happier with someone who has need of its powers," Kwambu said. "You do realize that you must keep it close to you at all times, and protect it against taint?"

"I will make a special pouch to keep it in," she promised. "I'll cut a small section from the panther skin Swoops Like Falcon gave to me, and make the pouch from that."

"That will be special indeed," Kwambu said, smiling at the confidence in her voice. Perhaps the crystal was already working its magic. He looked up to see the sun halfway to its zenith. "I must be leaving now," he told her. "I gave my word to Headchief Calusa to return to his island as quickly as I could."

"But I thought you wanted to see my uncle."

Kwambu smiled again. "You have been honest with me; I will be honest with you. I came here to see how you fared, Moon of Winter, and for no other reason."

She was plainly perplexed. "But you hardly know me. Or didn't, before today. Why should you care about someone you scarcely know?"

"Perhaps the spirits have somehow led me to care," he jested. "Who can say? But I leave here with a lighter heart than beat in my chest when I came."

"You will come again?" she called after him as he saluted her gravely and turned away.

"I will come again. And soon."

The memory of her pleased smile smoothed his path as he began his long journey back to the southern peninsula, and the specter of uneasiness that had followed him north did not appear again until he was halfway home.

The *Santa Ana*, Spain's red and gold banners topping her three masts, led four sister ships, two caravels, and a pair of pinnaces through a sea bleached of color by the diligent sun. The sun also did its best to erase the red from a cloak worn by the lanky man who stood amidships and peered over the rail toward the east; but the garment was of good quality, and it would be many weeks before streaks of fading marred its elegance.

The cloak whirled as the man spun around impatiently, and sunshine glinted off the gilded metal cuirass that covered his upper torso and flared over his hips. Until they were ready to make landfall, he saw no need to put on his helmet and the rest of his armor. Even though the ocean breeze had the strength he'd begged the Blessed Virgin for, he was hot. His armpits were unpleasantly damp and perspiration sheathed the legs over which his page had stretched thigh-high boots. Hernando de Soto was a fastidious man, as his close-cropped dark hair and beard testified; he did not like to sweat any more than was needful.

"Two days have passed since the steersmen took us through the channel between the Martires and the Tortugas," he said to one of the men standing near him. "Surely we should be able to see land by now?"

Captain Baltasar de Gallegos, a man both taller and broader than De Soto, answered the governor. "According to the map I brought from Spain, the one drawn by a survivor of the Narvaez expedition, we should be seeing it soon, Excellency."

Nuno de Tobar, who had been De Soto's companion in arms during the triumphant conquest of Peru, sought to soothe his friend further. "I heard the screech of a gull earlier," he said. "Keep watching, amigo; you do not want some seaman or slave to be the first person to sight *la Florida*."

Instead of smiling, as Tobar had hoped, De Soto frowned. An agitated snorting and thumping was drifting up from the hold of the ship, and his dapple gray was among the horses hobbled there. He would take stringent measures if some manure-scraping slave had laid even a finger on his favorite mount!

Gallegos tilted his head, chuckled as the sounds dwindled to a disgruntled whickering. "The beasts are as eager as we are to be ashore," he said.

Ashore. Finally, Hernando de Soto smiled. King Carlos had named him Adelantado of the country he would—please God!—soon be setting foot on, as well as Governor of the Island of Cuba. And he had promised De Soto a marquisate, twelve square leagues of the territory he had come here to claim for Spain. In addition to this largesse—which De Soto felt he had certainly earned—as governor, he would be allowed to keep one-half of all treasures taken from heathen temples and burial sites, one-sixth of any ransom received for Florida's native rulers, and as much as he could realize from an unlimited right to take slaves. Hernando de Soto, although by anyone's standards already a nobleman of considerable wealth, intended to make the most of these privileges. He would, for instance, make certain that the tract he selected as his marquisate had a vein of gold running through it. Narvaez, that incompetent, had been unable to find any gold, but this did not mean it was not there. And where it lay, De Soto would stake his claim. The governor smiled again. It was exhilarating to conquer new worlds, but the man who did not profit from his conquering must have the brains of a pig.

His nose wrinkled as he was reminded of the drove of swine brought along on this expedition. Thank the Virgin they were confined on the *San Cristobal*. The stench of pig, unless it was roasted, was more than De Soto could stomach. They would have need of meat on the overland march, though, and unless it was on the hoof, it would spoil before they could eat it all.

Suddenly he stiffened. His hands clutched the rail as he leaned forward, thrust his head out over the side and narrowed his eyes against the salt spray that flew into his face. "Land!" he said. "We are there, comrades."

Now they had only to locate the harbor entrance shown on Gallegos's map, and Florida was his for the taking!

Chapter 13

❦ ❦

Dancing Egret was smeared with mud from head to foot. "After I abandoned the small canoe I used for the river crossings, I came by way of the swamps wherever I could," she told White Gull, who was slowly recovering from the shock of having her younger sister slip into the canebrake that had been sheltering the people of Ucita's town for seven days. "Fortunately, Club Wielder spotted me before I headed toward the bay. Once I'd reminded him that I was your sister, he brought me here." The air in the thicket was heavy and the stench of marshy ground weighted it further. Winged insects moved sluggishly through it and were loath to be brushed away when they lit on arms or legs or face. The tall grass that had been hacked down to make a clearing for the villagers was a decomposing blanket underfoot, and it, too, smelled rank. Hides and bed robes had been spread upon the yellowing grass, and on these the people squatted or sat. Like the air, their mood was torpid; like the insects, their movements were lethargic. "I could have been here sooner, but I was careful to travel mostly at night during the first part of my journey," Egret went on, eyeing the makeshift accommodations White Gull and the other women had made in the midst of the thick-stemmed, tree-high grass. A grid of saplings supported sacks of food, bowls of fresh water, drinking gourds, and neatly folded robes. A doll made of plaited palm fronds and a mischievous-looking otter carved from cypress also lay atop the grid; the few toys the youngsters had been able to bring with them were obviously being treated with respect, and that at least was good.

"You came alone?" White Gull was aghast.

Egret set down her pack of belongings. She was hot and tired and, above all, thirsty. "Can you spare me a drink of water?" she asked, and when White Gull had obliged, "I could hardly ask Mocoso for an escort," she said. "Not after the terrible thing he did."

"Surely he did not attempt to harm a daughter of Headchief Calusa?"

Egret shook her head. "No, no. From the beginning, he and all of his people were good to me." She took another swallow of water and passed the dipper back to her sister. "It was what he did to Kneeling Cypress that sent me running back to Calusa country. My anger was so great that I think I would have killed the man if I had stayed there! As for coming alone, why not? I own two good legs, and have always had an excellent sense of direction. I'm no longer a child, White Gull."

White Gull did not dispute this; Egret was the taller of the two now. And she was anxious to hear what had happened to Ucita's daughter. "What did Mocoso do to Kneeling Cypress, Egret?"

"When Juan Ortiz went to meet the Spanish soldiers, and brought them back to Mocoso's town," Egret said, "I knew at once he would be going away with them. Cypress . . . well, she didn't think he would leave her, or their children. When it became plain that he meant to, she went to Holata Mocoso and begged him to ask Juan to reconsider." Egret's expression said that she would never humble herself in such a fashion, for any man, but this was not the crux of the matter. "A clan-brother of Mocoso, Holata Tocobaga, was with him at the time. He and his warriors had come there to compete in games against Mocoso's warriors, you see. When Cypress appealed to Mocoso, Tocobaga said"—she swallowed hard—"he said that Cypress was a fine-looking woman, one he would not mind having as a concubine, and that if Mocoso was still interested in the trade he'd been trying to persuade him into, he ought to try offering Kneeling Cypress in exchange!"

A baby began to cry, and its mother—who had come with several other women to listen to Dancing Egret's tale—thrust it against one milk-swollen breast. There must be no noise made that might reveal their hiding place to the Christian soldiers.

"Do you mean to say that Mocoso agreed?" White Gull asked her sister.

"Not only agreed, but was delighted to," she said. "Truly, I couldn't believe what I was seeing or hearing. Why, Juan Ortiz himself spoke up and said that Cypress should be proud that she was being given to a man of such stature! Cypress was struck dumb, I think. Even when her children were brought out—for Tocobaga said he would take them, too—she said nothing. And when I spoke in her stead, and insisted that she and the children should be brought home to her father, she seemed as indifferent to what I was saying as the men surely were. She didn't say good-bye to me when she left with Tocobaga and his warriors, nor even look at me when I called to her." Egret shivered. "It was as though the real Cypress had disappeared and a ghost-woman had taken her place. That's when I made up my mind to go home."

"But you must have known by then that the Spanish had come ashore near our town. Why didn't you take the long way to Calusa's island?"

"Someone had to tell Chief Ucita about poor Cypress. Who was there to do it but me?"

"It was foolhardy of you, all the same," White Gull said. She looked behind her to where her husband was conferring with his War Leader. "This will destroy Ucita," she said. "Having the Spanish come here again and make a shambles of his town—" Her voice broke; describing the nightmare made it more real somehow. "—and seize four of our women was bad enough. To hear that Cypress has gone to be concubine to a Timucuan chief will steal what strength he has left."

Dancing Egret followed her sister's glance. She had noticed a stooped and frail-looking man talking with Club Wielder, but since he had been facing away from her, she had failed to recognize him as Ucita. How could only six years have aged him to such an appalling degree? "Is that why you're here in the canebrake, then?" she asked. "Because your town is no more?"

"It is there still," White Gull said, "but so are the soldiers. And they have cast down the Temple, and most of the houses as well, to build quarters for themselves. We had left the town before they invaded it, however. My husband hoped that if they found the town deserted, the Spanish would move on immediately. They did not; instead, they seem determined to try and locate us. Were it not for the swamps that lay between the town and here, they would have succeeded, I'm afraid. But these Christians brought with them Calusans they had somehow captured, to act as guides. Two of them, an old man and a boy, were clever enough to lead a group of Spaniards into the worst of the swamps, and when the soldiers floundered there, the pair followed the path we'd taken and joined us here. They are from our father's island, Egret. The older one, Tireless

Swimmer, I remembered, but I'd never seen his grandson; we came to Ucita before he was born."

"Calusa will be pleased to hear what quick thinkers they proved to be," Egret said. "But what of the women you said the Spanish soldiers seized? Why didn't they leave the town when the rest of you did? And has no attempt been made to get them back?"

"They were women whose bleeding cycles, or recent child-birth, had confined them to the hut near the river," White Gull said, "which meant that they had farther to go. The warriors sent to escort them through the swamps killed one of the soldiers and wounded five. But the Spanish had weapons our people had never before seen, strange-looking sticks that make the sound of a thunderclap and send missiles flying at great speed over long distances. When these missiles strike flesh, they penetrate deeper than dart or arrow ever could."

"They *kill*," said the woman with the infant pressed to her breast. Her face tightened as she fought to hold back tears. "I was there, and saw my man fall. He was dead before I could reach him." Her mouth trembled and she bowed her head over her baby's, held that small, warm body closer to her own.

Egret ached for her. "I'm sorry," she said gently. "But I am glad that you eluded the soldiers, and that you have your child to comfort you." Yet there was nothing gentle about her expression as she turned back to her sister. "Surely Ucita's warriors have tried to rescue the women who were taken by the soldiers?"

"They have tried, but the Spanish are not only well-armed, they are so many that all efforts have failed. Even with the war party Calusa sent to help us, our men are sadly outnumbered, and my husband has said he will send no man to certain death. They are told to harass the soldiers from hiding and to spy on them. That is all."

"It's not enough," Egret said flatly. "And I find it hard to believe that the warriors our father sent are content to do so little."

The other women were moving away now, and signaling to their unnaturally quiet children to come and get food. "We eat no more than we need to," White Gull said, distracted, "since we cannot know how long our provisions will have to last. The smaller children don't understand. They know only that they are always hungry."

Egret watched, too, as the mothers meted out small rounds

of zamia bread and handfuls of dried berries to the youngsters who crowded around them, and saw how not one woman took so much as a single berry for herself. "This is no way to live," she muttered. "How can we let the Spanish do this to us?"

"At least we do live!" White Gull said sharply. "Our bellies may grumble; we may have to sleep in turn at night, to guard the children; but anything is better than being dead, or made prisoners of the Spanish."

"But if a message were taken to Calusa, wouldn't he send more warriors? Enough to make war on the Christian soldiers and drive away those that survive?"

"Many ships, with many men, are in the bay still," White Gull said. "Ucita cannot ask Calusa to leave his own town undefended when no one knows where the ships may go next." Suddenly her face crumpled. "I don't know what will happen to us," she moaned. "Truly, Egret, I'm so frightened all the time that I cannot eat even the paltry bit I'm allowed!"

Club Wielder had melted away into the mangrove swamp west of the canebrake, and Chief Ucita was walking in their direction. Now Egret could see the lines etched deep into his noseless face. White Gull was not the only person who despaired.

Her sister was crying, but before Egret could try to console her, Ucita had reached them. He put out one hand and clumsily patted his wife's shoulder. "Do not weep, White Gull," he said, attempting to smile reassuringly. "Things will be better soon. Club Wielder's scouts report that the Spanish have begun to bring into town those four-legged beasts they ride upon. It may be that they are preparing to head inland. Then we will be able to go home."

He patted her shoulder again, and Egret thought briefly that these two still did not act like husband and wife. Why didn't White Gull turn to him, and the man put his arms around her? Why didn't they admit their fears to one another and face them together?

Instead, "Go home?" White Gull said, raising her tear-streaked face. "How can we, when we have no home to go to!"

"We can rebuild. We have done so before," he said stiffly, letting his hand drop. As he did, he looked closely at Dancing Egret for the first time. "You are not one of my people," he said.

It was half statement, half question. Egret identified herself promptly, but the puzzlement in his pouched eyes was slow to fade. "You are bigger than you were," he said at last.

"And I am covered with mud besides," she pointed out with a smile. "Even someone who saw me yesterday would have difficulty recognizing me, I think."

He did not smile in return, but peered to either side and then behind her. "If you are here, then where is my daughter? Surely Kneeling Cypress came with you?"

Egret looked to her sister for help, but her mute appeal was in vain. "She could not come with me," Egret said slowly. And, reluctantly, told him why.

If she had thought Ucita looked old before, it was nothing compared to the way he looked when she came to the end of her story. Were such a thing possible, she would have believed that his bones had shriveled, for his meager flesh hung from them in dispirited folds. Yet he said not a single word. He simply turned and shuffled away, as though his feet were unsure of the path they were meant to follow.

Dancing Egret led her sister to one of the robes spread out over the decaying cane, urged her to sit, and hunkered down beside her. "White Gull, you are the chief's wife," she said urgently. "If you give in to your misery, how can you expect the rest of your husband's people to endure theirs without whimpering?"

Gradually, White Gull's crying ceased and her slumped shoulders straightened. "I know I should be brave," she whispered. "And I really do try, Egret. But"—bitterness twisted her mouth—"you have no idea how hard it is! I feel as though we've been in this wretched swamp for a whole season, rather than only a few days. And realizing that you will be returning to Calusa while I must stay on and on in this dismal place . . ." Resentment flared in her wide-set eyes. "It's easy for you to counsel me, Egret. It's easy for you to criticize Ucita for not sending our warriors to make war against the soldiers, but what do you honestly know of such things? Ever since the day Kneeling Cypress ran off with that Spaniard, my husband has believed that the gods are chastising him for denying them the sacrifice he had pledged to make. But have you been here to see how her leaving destroyed him? You have not, for you ran away as well. And I suspect that you probably encouraged Cypress to do so. You've always been free with your counsel, sister, even though you lack the experience to advise anyone about anything!"

Egret flinched. Despite the kernels of truth in White Gull's accusations, a stinging retort flew to her lips, and would have been released if two men had not suddenly burst into the clearing. The taller, a muscular young warrior, pushed before him a wild-eyed Spanish youth. The men who had been stationed to guard the women and children made haste to surround the pair. Chief Ucita, who had been standing alone, head bowed, ever since Egret told him about Cypress, put aside his grieving and went to join the group.

"I bring you a prisoner, Ucita," the warrior said to him, and tossed the Spaniard to the ground. "I would have preferred to bring you a full-grown soldier, but this fool fairly fell into my arms when he came out of the town to chase down one of their snorting beasts." He grinned, and all at once Dancing Egret was on her feet and moving toward him. "He makes a sorry prize," the warrior went on, looking down at the cowering lad. "I begin to think I should have let him go and brought back the beast instead."

"Shore Walker?" Egret said, murmuring hasty apologies as she elbowed her way between two of Ucita's warriors. Then, as she finally stood face-to-face with him, "Shore Walker! It is you, isn't it?" Not that they were precisely face-to-face; her childhood companion—if it truly was he—had grown so tall that he stood head and shoulders above the rest of the men. Egret had to crane her neck to look at him.

The warrior stared at the mud-spattered young woman, studied what he could see of her face. "By the gods! It is Dancing Egret, and all grown up, too." His captive made as if to scuttle away, and almost nonchalantly Shore Walker planted his foot in the small of the youth's back. "It's about time you decided to come home, but you chose a peculiar time to do so." He stooped and trussed the Spaniard with leather thongs, stood up again and formally saluted Ucita. "He is yours to do with as you will," he said to him.

"You will take him with you when you go back to your island," the chief said fretfully. "I want no Spaniard in my town, ever again."

"I had thought," Shore Walker said carefully, "that you might try and exchange him for at least one of the women the Spanish are holding."

Ucita showed no enthusiasm for the idea. "How do we conduct an exchange with a people whose language we neither speak nor understand?" he asked wearily.

"Thunder Talker, the boy who helped his grandfather lead the Spanish into the swamps, told me that those the soldiers meant to use as guides were made to learn a little of their language." Shore Walker was keeping his voice even, but Dancing Egret saw the muscles in his jaw tighten, and read determination in his eyes. Once upon a time he had told a fascinated child that only a coward feared to have his thoughts revealed in his face, and it was plain that his attitude had not changed. "I am certain he would be willing to relay a message to the Spanish—from a safe distance, of course—and let them know we're interested in trading hostages."

"I have said I want no one put at risk," Ucita said. "There is no *safe distance* from the thunder-weapons of the Christian soldiers."

"I think there is," Shore Walker said quietly. "And I pledge to shield the boy with my own body while he talks to the Spanish."

"Then I will likely end by having to tell Headchief Calusa that one of his men has died in my service," Chief Ucita grumbled. But he lacked the energy to protest further, and this young islander was reputed to be both clear-headed and quick-thinking. Perhaps his plan would succeed, despite Ucita's misgivings. "Do as you wish," he said. "I will send some of my men to Club Wielder to let him know that the matter is in your hands." He signaled to his own warriors and they trailed him as he moved away.

Shore Walker shook his head. "An excess of caution on one side gives all the advantage to the other," he said. But there was pity as well as exasperation in the glance he sent after Ucita. "The fire has gone out of him," he said quietly, "and that's sad."

"I brought him news that helped to douse that fire," Dancing Egret said, and told Shore Walker what had caused her to flee Mocoso's town.

Unlike White Gull, Shore Walker did not seem horrified that Egret had made the journey on her own. "You always knew where you were going, and how to get there, even as a little girl," he said, and she thought she detected admiration as well as teasing in his smile. The smile blossomed into a grin. "But I do not recall your liking to wallow in the mud when you were small."

"It's impossible to plow through swamps without getting muddy," she retorted. She wished all at once that she had been able to bathe before this surprise reunion with her old friend, but that could not be helped. And she had been waiting to tell him something ever since he and Chief Ucita had begun talking. "Tireless Swimmer's grandson may know a few Spanish words," she said, "but there will soon be someone in the soldier's camp who can easily interpret anything that needs to be said during the exchange you're hoping for. Juan Ortiz'"—she gave the syllables the harshness they deserved—"will be coming there with the soldiers to whom he ran after the ships arrived. He spoke Calusa while he lived in Ucita's village, and will not have forgotten it as easily as he's forgotten his Calusan wife."

Shore Walker nodded slowly. "I'm glad to hear that, Egret. If Thunder Talker can find the words to do so, he will be eager to help rescue one of the women. But he's only a boy, and I had hoped to find a way to communicate with the Spanish without using him. Now, you need only tell me how to recognize this Ortiz and I'll continue my surveillance of the camp until I spot him. Then I will attempt the exchange on my own."

"A description won't help," Egret said. "Before I left Mocoso, Ortiz had put on clothing borrowed from one of the soldiers, and now he looks much like all the other Spaniards. So I'll go with you to keep watch on the camp, and when Ortiz comes, I can point him out to you."

Shore Walker frowned, but before he could respond, White Gull appeared at her sister's side. "That one cannot stay here," she said, gesturing to the Spanish youth. "We have neither space for him nor food and water for him, and would not have him here if we did." She did not wait for an answer before she stalked away.

"White Gull doesn't mean to be discourteous," Egret said hastily. "She's going through a difficult time, as all of Ucita's people are."

"It's only natural that the sight of any Spaniard should distress her, in the circumstances," Shore Walker agreed.

Egret looked down at the boy that lay at his feet. He was too dispirited even to struggle against his bonds, yet his eyes darted here, there, everywhere, as though seeking to understand where he had come to and why. "He is so young, and so frightened," she murmured.

"Too young to have been made a captive, you mean?"

Shore Walker's voice was hard-edged, and Egret, although

she had been thinking something of the sort, decided not to say so.

"He is much the same age as Thunder Talker," Shore Walker went on. "But you haven't yet met him, have you?" He turned and began to walk away. "Wait here for me," he said over his shoulder, then vanished into the tall grass ringing the clearing.

Egret looked again at the terrified boy, looked around and saw that White Gull was at the far side of the clearing talking with the priest. Easing over to the grid of saplings, she picked up a dipper and half filled it with water from one of the bowls. I will drink no more today, she told herself as she carried it over to Shore Walker's prisoner; if I choose to give away my ration, surely no one will complain.

She knelt beside the boy, held out the dipper, put one hand behind his head to help him raise himself enough to drink.

Bound though he was, he managed to twist away from her.

"It's only water," she said soothingly, and tried again.

Once more he flung himself sideways, and this time his knee bumped against the dipper, knocking it out of Egret's hand.

She looked with dismay at the water sinking into the cane. "I wish you hadn't done that," she said, standing up again. "I dare not fetch more."

And he would not drink if she did, she realized. He'd understood nothing of what she had said, and had probably thought she was trying to poison him. She bent and retrieved the dipper, but before she could replace it, Shore Walker came back into the clearing. With him was an old man and a boy.

"Dancing Egret," Shore Walker said, "this is Tireless Swimmer." The elderly man nodded. "And this," he said, putting one hand on the lad's thin shoulder, "is his grandson, Thunder Talker." He looked at the dipper Egret was holding but withheld comment. "They are going to try and find out my prisoner's name."

"I remember you, a little," Dancing Egret said to Tireless Swimmer. "You are one of Calusa's ablest fishermen." As she spoke she tried desperately to focus on the man's face, yet she could not avoid staring at his neck. Around it was an ugly band of raw flesh. A similar pus-oozing welt encircled the neck of his grandson, but that was not the worst of it. When, at Shore Walker's bidding, he and his grandfather went to question the Spanish boy, she saw that Thunder Talker's narrow back was crisscrossed with the puckered scars of other welts, more of them than she was able to count.

"Now you see why I did not hesitate to seize the enemy pup when he offered himself," Shore Walker said grimly. "The Spanish make their prisoners wear collars of metal, each of which is attached to all the rest by metal ropes called chains. This keeps them from escaping, you see."

Egret shuddered. "And Thunder Talker's back? How did that happen?"

"When the soldiers forced his grandfather to kneel and fastened the metal collar around his neck, Thunder Talker broke free from the man who was grasping his arms. He began to flail at those mistreating Tireless Swimmer. For this he was beaten, and then a collar was put on him as well." He saw Egret's eyes darken with horror and revulsion, and nodded. "Now you know why I do not hesitate to hunt down any Spaniard, young or old." He raised his voice as grandfather and grandson, both shaking their heads, abandoned their attempts to speak with Shore Walker's captive.

"What we learned of the white man's language does not let us ask what you would know," Tireless Swimmer said.

"He is too scared to answer us anyway," Thunder Talker said contemptuously. "I was never that scared when we were with the Spanish, was I, Grandfather?"

The old man patted the boy's head. "You were just as frightened, I expect," he told him gravely, "but you were brave enough not to show it."

"You did what you could, and I thank you," Shore Walker said to both of them. "The Spanish will surely know which lad is missing from their camp, so it doesn't really matter that you could not find out what I'd hoped to know.

"It might have confounded the soldiers, though," he said to Egret as the pair went to rejoin their comrades in the swamp, "for me to be able to say the name. And it's always a good tactic to confuse the enemy."

"You should send for Kwambu," Egret said suddenly. "He was only a child when he lived among the Spanish, but he has told me that he found it easy to learn their language."

"Then I wish I could send for him. But he was gone from the island when I left it, and there seemed to be some question of how soon he would return." He shrugged. "I'll have to make do with this Juan Ortiz you've told me about."

"When I left Mocoso, Ortiz and the soldiers were already

preparing to come back here, so it shouldn't be long before he arrives in the Spanish camp," Egret said. "Perhaps we ought to go now and—"

"We?" His interjection was forceful. "You will not be going, Egret. It's far too dangerous."

"Why is it more dangerous for me than for Tireless Swimmer?"

"It is different. You are Headchief Calusa's daughter."

"And like him, I am no coward," she snapped.

"It's not necessarily a sign of courage to expose yourself to danger," he said firmly.

"You will be doing so."

"I am a warrior. It's my place to do so."

Egret felt all at once that the years had been blown away, that she and Shore Walker were the same children who had never hesitated to argue heatedly when they disagreed about something. "We are wasting words, and wasting time," she said, making herself adopt a reasonable tone. "You need my help to identify Juan Ortiz. If the Christian soldiers haven't yet spotted the warriors who spy on them regularly, they will not see me, either. And as soon as I have pointed out the man, I'll return to the canebrake. That way, I will be in no danger whatsoever."

Shore Walker, as she had hoped, took the time to do some reasoning of his own. Egret had never been one to make promises lightly, and he wanted very much to pinpoint the man he would have to negotiate with, to be able to watch Ortiz's face in order to search for signs of deception in it. "You'll give me your word to come back here when I tell you to?"

Dancing Egret met his penetrating gaze directly. "I give it."

"Then I will take you along. We leave at first light tomorrow." He saw the question in her eyes, gestured to the sky. "It will be dark soon, and time for everyone to settle in for the night. I must go to my post in the swamp." He considered her for a long moment, then shook his head slowly. "I haven't seen you in nine years," he said, "but in many ways you have not changed at all, Dancing Egret."

As she helped the other women lull the children to sleep, Egret puzzled over his final words. Had they been intended as compliment or complaint?

Even though she lay awake long after most of the others slept, she still could not be sure, and her uncertainty was more

of an irritant than the mosquitoes that plagued her all through
that humid summer's night.

Chapter 14

⇒ ⇒

"We'll take a canoe part of the way," Shore Walker told
Dancing Egret as they stepped into the ankle-deep water covering the marsh that spread itself around the canebrake. In the
hushed gray of predawn the splashes their moccasined feet
made seemed loud indeed, and Egret kept a wary eye out as
she scrambled over a network of mangrove roots lest she create an even bigger splash by falling on her face. "For now," he
went on, looking back at her briefly, "just follow me. The
stream we're making for is some distance away."

The mud with which Egret had smeared herself was starting
to solidify. She fought the urge to scratch her cheek, then forgot about the annoying itch as a misguided step wedged her
left foot between two partially submerged roots. Fortunately,
she managed to free it without Shore Walker noticing her
clumsiness. Trying to keep up with him was the problem;
when she had maneuvered through swamps on her own, on her
journey south from Mocoso, she had done well enough. But
Shore Walker's strides, even among the mangroves, were
longer than hers, and she dared not ask him to slow down. He
might begin regretting that he'd said she could go with him,
and that would never do.

Somewhere in front of them a heron squawked. What she
could see of the sky between the huge green heads of the trees
was lightening rapidly, and the world was waking up. She
sloshed through a pool of brown water, clambered again onto
the arching roots of the mangroves that made this swamp impenetrable to anyone not bred to such terrain. She risked a
glance ahead, and almost wished she hadn't. They were ap-

proaching a veritable jungle; beneath rank upon rank of ancient, moss-hung trees the spirals of humping roots were nearly as tall as she was!

"There is only one way to go on from this point," Shore Walker called softly. "I hope your arms are strong, Dancing Egret."

With that, he jumped up and grasped one of the interlocking branches of the nearest mangrove, a limb growing well above the basketwork of prop roots. From there he swung himself forward until he could reach out one hand and seize a branch of the next tree along. When he was dangling from it by both hands, he looked back at Egret. "Just do what I did," he told her, "and you have nothing to fear."

She smiled. She had begun climbing trees nearly as soon as she could walk, and swinging from their branches had been one of her great pleasures. She balanced on a root broad enough to support her feet, crouched, leaped, and grabbed the limb Shore Walker had released. "Move on," she called airily. "I'll be right behind you."

It was, she admitted to herself when their airborne journey had gone on for some time, somewhat different to be moving through a forest this way, and not quite so pleasurable. A dull ache had invaded her underarms, the muscles in her shoulders were protesting, and her hands were sweaty enough to threaten the security of her grip before she saw Shore Walker swing forward a final time, then drop to the boggy ground bordering a narrow stream.

She was not sorry to be able to jump down beside him, and when he knelt and began to drink from the stream, she was glad of the opportunity to catch her breath and do likewise. "Is your canoe near here?" she asked when she had twice gulped from her cupped hands.

He nodded, water dripping from his chin as he stood up and pointed to a large vegetation-covered mound surrounded by uprooted cattails. "It's in the bushes beyond the gator's nest." At Egret's disbelieving look, he grinned. "Far enough past it that I don't disturb Mother Alligator when I take it out or bring it back. I want no toothy monster hissing at me, especially since it violates the laws of hunting to kill a female gator before her babies are hatched."

They gave the nest a wide berth, then waded the narrow stream to where a small canoe had been thrust into a confusion of brambles and marsh grass. The water was thigh deep here, and tiny fish darted between Egret's legs as she looked up at the branches over her head. So intermingled were they that light from the new-risen sun pierced them only intermittently to cast golden flecks upon water stained red by the mangrove roots it flowed over.

"If you're thirsty still, then drink again while we're here," Shore Walker said, guiding the dugout into a channel no wider than the canoe itself. "Very soon the water will become brackish and undrinkable."

"Are we that close to the coast already?"

"We have some way to go yet, but in certain places the salt water reaches in farther than most people realize. And we won't be going all the way to the coast; Ucita's second town does not sit as near to the bay as his first one did, if you remember."

They sculled through a twisting tunnel of dusky green, for the meandering stream was slow to widen. A foraging raccoon lifted its masked face curiously before returning to its breakfast, and a brown-black moccasin slithering along the bank swirled into a coil and opened its white-lined jaws to warn them off. An unseen hawk shrieked from the sky high above them, and a limpkin hunting snails lurched unconcernedly through the multiple stiltlike roots of a black mangrove. And still they glided on, except where the stream narrowed so much that both Shore Walker and Egret put out their hands and forced the dugout forward by grasping whatever roots or overhanging branches offered themselves.

They spoke little, for the morning was maturing. Although Shore Walker had said that the Spanish soldiers seemed reluctant to wander far from camp, it would be rash to assume that their leaders were never moved to send out scouts. Occasionally they approached a break in the monotonous parade of trees and glimpsed a bit of coastal prairie thickly carpeted with glasswort and sea purslane, but it was never long before their serpentine tunnel closed around them again.

"We are going to come upon Ucita's town from the northeast," Shore Walker told Egret. "On that side, the swamp ends just before the town begins, and will conceal us until we're almost to the Temple mound. There is always a sentry atop the mound, but I have watched him closely, and he makes a habit of pacing back and forth while he stands guard. We'll move forward only while his back is to us. Do you recall the clumps of sea grape that grow behind the mound?"

Egret wrinkled her brow. "I think I remember the men removing and replanting the bushes so they could level the ground for the mound-raising," she said finally. "I suppose they left some on its far side?"

Shore Walker nodded. "They would have dug up no more than was needful," he said. "Since then, those they left undisturbed have spread halfway around the mound. We'll have to crawl on hands and knees, and sometimes creep along on our bellies, but there are enough bushes now to give us cover while we look into the Spanish camp." He guided the canoe past yet another bend, and she saw that there were gaps in the trees ahead, and that the trees themselves were younger and smaller than those they were leaving behind. "From here," he warned softly, "we must not talk at all, nor make any sound."

As the stream widened and exited the swamp, Egret's heart began to thump in her chest, and all at once she wished she had not insisted on coming along. What did she know of sneaking up on an enemy? If she inadvertently called attention to the pair of them, she had no doubt whatsoever that Shore Walker's life would immediately be forfeit. To put herself at risk was one thing; to endanger someone else was another thing altogether. And why hadn't she considered all of this sooner? White Gull was right, she thought dismally, when she said this woman was too much given to speaking her mind on subjects better left to those who knew what they were talking about.

Well, it was too late now for self-reproach. Shore Walker was easing the dugout toward the bank, and she could only pray that her ignorance would not lead them into disaster.

She stepped out of the canoe as silently as he had, stood unmoving as he secured it to the slender mangrove she waited beneath, then followed close behind as he scrambled up a muddy incline that took them onto higher ground. Here, rough-textured grass grew waist high, and when he got down on his knees to crawl through it, she followed suit, stifling a sneeze when puffs of dirt rose into her face. A shiny beetle scurried out of her way, but a small brown spider hopped insouciantly upon her shoulder when she paused to rest for a moment. She shook him off and continued doggedly on.

Shore Walker came to a halt, signaled for her to come up beside him. "The sea grapes begin just ahead," he murmured. "They are so dense that we shall have to imitate snakes from here on."

"Then we're coming to Ucita's town?"

"To what *was* Ucita's town, yes." He parted the grasses in front of them, gestured. "There is the mound."

She lifted her head cautiously, saw the massed, round-leafed shrubs they would soon be slithering beneath, looked up and saw the sky-reaching mound that had once supported a Temple. A soldier clad in metal armor marched slowly across the mound's flat crest. When he reached the side facing the town, he paused, wiped one hand across his face, then turned and began to retrace his steps.

Egret ducked her head swiftly, and Shore Walker nodded approval. "The sun is in his eyes when he looks this way," he whispered, "but caution is called for nonetheless."

When the sentry had recrossed the mound, surveyed the landscape, and swung around to pace in the direction of the town again, they moved. Crooking his arms and using elbows and angled knees to pull himself along, Shore Walker slid ahead of her into the expanse of sea grape. Dancing Egret, after one false start, wiggled her way beneath the sprawling leafy branches. Now it was a miniature jungle they were in as they hugged the ground and inched along, a place of eerie half-light pungent with the odors of tropical growth and moist, sandy soil. Pebbles loomed big as boulders and felt as big when bare flesh pressed down on them. Lizards skittered away from the giants invading their province, and Shore Walker's leveling of an anthill left Dancing Egret to crawl over the agitated insects who spilled out to protest the razing of their town. She could not blame the ones alert enough to bite her; how could they know that it was not Egret, but her companion, who had left them homeless?

It did not take Egret long to realize that Shore Walker was following a trail of sorts, one that he had made for himself through this maze. With no hesitation, he veered this way or that to evade branches sturdy enough to impede them, and he took them unerringly between shrubs that seemed to have no beginning and no end so far as Egret could tell. The summer sun poured heat upon the huge leaves that made a low ceiling over their heads, and perspiration trickled down Egret's face. She blinked it out of her eyes and forced her abused elbows to drag her weary body in Shore Walker's wake.

Just as she had begun to wonder if they would ever reach their destination, Shore Walker pushed his way beneath yet another sea grape bush and came to a halt. Egret crept up beside him and let herself collapse, closed her eyes and waited for the muscles in her arms and legs to unclench. Only then did she become aware of the din. Her eyes flew open as the rattle of scores of voices, the thud of hundreds of footsteps, and the clinking and clanking of metal assaulted ears that had been deaf to them before. Could she have been so preoccupied with their tortuous progress that she'd been incapable of noticing anything else?

Obviously she had been, which was a phenomenon she would have given much thought to had time permitted. But Shore Walker was signing for her to watch, so she fixed her eyes on him as he reached out and slowly lifted two branches of the shrub they lay beneath.

Without raising her head, Egret was able to see that they had come to the sunrise side of the mound. During some earlier surveillance, Shore Walker had apparently cut away any underlying greenery that interfered with his view of the Spanish camp, for with the slight elevation of that single pair of sturdy branches, the better part of Ucita's squareground could be seen.

It literally teemed with men, but women were there as well, and the huge beasts the Spanish called horses. Dogs, big and lean and long-headed, lay panting in the sun or growled at one another as they fought over scraps tossed to them by the grinning soldiers, who were surely wagering on the outcome of each fight. The smell of a meat Egret did not recognize drifted from a huge black pot hung over a cooking fire in the center of the plaza, and on the far side of the square stood the rectangular timber structures the Spanish had erected for themselves to sleep in. Except for narrow door openings, they were entirely enclosed, and Egret was amazed that even the Spanish could be so foolish as to deliberately shut out the soothing coolness of night's breezes.

A sound that was half grunt, half squeal drew her attention to a rude pen sitting not far from where she lay. Within it were a huddle of strange-looking animals whose egg-shaped bodies were mounted on short, stubby legs. They had no necks at all, and on their round heads tiny eyes flanked peculiarly flat noses. Or did the Spaniards make a habit of lopping off noses, even those of animals that, for some reason, they saw fit to confine?

Shore Walker, apparently realizing what she was puzzling over, gently touched her shoulder. His eyes said that she should not waste time over such things, and shame made her cheeks burn. She was not here to learn what the camp of Christian soldiers looked like, but to identify Juan Ortiz. If Ortiz had arrived yet, that is.

She began at one end of the squareground and examined each dark-haired man whose height and weight said this might be the person she sought. Some she could eliminate with a glance; others, she had to study more closely. She lingered over a gesticulating man whose scarlet cloak and golden body armor suggested he was the leader of the soldiers; his facial expression bordered on the melancholy, but his movements were vigorous and hinted of impatience. Then she looked beyond him, and was hard put to restrain a gasp. Not only had she spotted Juan Ortiz, but coming into the plaza behind him was Holata Mocoso and a full escort of warriors!

Shore Walker had seen them, too, had felt Egret start and guessed at once who the newcomers were. His hawk-nosed face hardened as Ortiz approached the man in the red cloak, bowed, and said something to him in their native tongue. The soldiers' leader made brief reply and Ortiz beckoned to Mocoso, who came forward without haste to be presented.

The corners of Egret's mouth turned down in disgust as she saw Holata Mocoso drop gracefully to his knees and turn up his palms in a gesture of submission. To put on the traditional attitude of respect in such circumstances robbed it of dignity. But the Spanish leader seemed pleased and indicated that Mocoso might feel free to speak.

Egret looked toward Shore Walker and managed with signs to tell him she would be able to understand most of what would pass between the Timucuan leader and the Spaniard. She could not think how to indicate that she would repeat it to him later, but surely it was unnecessary to communicate the obvious.

Mocoso had come to his feet. Now he clasped his hands in front of him and began to speak. "Most high and powerful Chief Hernando de Soto," he intoned, "I have come before you in the full confidence of receiving your favor." He paused, nodded to Juan Ortiz, waited while Kneeling Cypress's erstwhile husband repeated his words to the man in the red cloak. "I expect this not in requital of the trifling service I rendered by setting free the Christian while he was in my power. This I did not do for the sake of my honor, or of my promise, but because I hold that great men should be liberal."

If Mocoso had not been Holata, he would have made a fine Chief Speaker, Egret thought wryly. His words were strung as elegantly as perfectly matched beads on a string, and were as colorful. But that the man who had so callously disposed of poor Cypress could refer to himself as liberal galled her beyond the describing.

"As much as in your bodily perfections you exceed all others," Mocoso went on after Ortiz had once again dutifully translated, "and in your command over fine men you are superior, so in your nature are you equal to the full enjoyment of earthly things. The favor I hope for, great Lord, is that you will hold me to be your own, calling on me without hesitation to do whatever may be your wish."

With a self-satisfied smile he nodded once more to Juan Ortiz, then folded his arms and awaited Hernando de Soto's reply.

Egret had to wait, too, until Ortiz had heard it and reshaped the Spanish words to fit the Timucuan language. Then she felt a trifle gleeful, for it seemed that Mocoso's fulsomeness had been wasted.

"In freeing Ortiz and delivering him to me," the Spanish leader said, "you do no more than keep your word and preserve your honor. But I am a generous man, so I thank you nonetheless, and will have gifts brought to you to express that thanks."

He clapped his hands as soon as Juan Ortiz had delivered this terse little message, and the youth who came running in response dashed away and returned with a shirt and other articles of white man's clothing. These De Soto took from him and presented to Holata Mocoso.

Mocoso's smile did not falter, for which Egret gave him grudging credit, and he inclined his head courteously before he passed the bundle to one of his warriors. "Tell him," he said to Ortiz, "that he and his men are welcome to visit my town before they travel on, that all will be treated as honored guests there."

Egret frowned. What did Mocoso have in mind? But the man called De Soto was speaking again, and she strained to hear his words relayed by the obliging Juan Ortiz.

"The governor wishes to know," Ortiz said to Mocoso, "if there is gold in your town. I have told him there is not"—he smiled apologetically for having departed from his role as interpreter—"and he wishes me to ask you where in this country gold can be found. It seems that one of the guides he brought with him has spoken often of *oro*, which in our language means gold. So he is confident that he will find it somewhere in this land."

"It may be," Mocoso said with a shrug, "that this guide you mention was trying to tell him that *Ortiz* was here in this country, not that *oro* was. Certainly there is no gold anywhere in my province. But I will be glad to direct him to my brother-in-law, Canegacola, who lives some distance inland. It is possible that the gold Hernando de Soto seeks"—he bowed in the Spanish leader's direction—"can be found in the north; I do not know if this is so, but Canegacola will. We Timucua," he added loftily, "are not much interested in gold."

This from a man who had nearly as extensive a collection of gold ornaments as Headchief Calusa, Egret thought scornfully. Not to mention the pearls he set such store by! But she could not deny that his tactics might well speed the Spanish on their way.

De Soto's response to this was to tell Ortiz to bring Mocoso to his quarters for further talk. When the Timucuan chief had agreed to this, his warriors spread themselves almost casually along the perimeters of the squareground, two of them stationing themselves perilously close to where Shore Walker and Dancing Egret lay in hiding.

Shore Walker did not need to signal for Egret to crawl backward until she reached a place wide enough to turn around; she did so promptly, but with infinite caution. The Christian soldiers, inclined as they were to incessant conversation, would be unlikely to hear rustlings in the underbrush. This could not be said of the Timucuan warriors.

As swiftly as they could, Egret and Shore Walker put space between them and the Spanish camp, did not even rise to a crouch as they made their way through the tall grass that led to the river and their canoe. In silence, Shore Walker relaunched it, and in silence they stepped into it and let the current carry them to where the water funneled into the narrow stream once more. Only then did they risk talking, and in voices soft as the bay breezes that briefly followed them into the mangroves.

"It does sound as though Chief Mocoso is trying to persuade the Spanish away from the coast," Shore Walker said when Egret had reported all that she'd overheard. "Perhaps he feels

that by inviting this De Soto to his town, he will convince him
that there is really no good reason to go there."

"It's true that the Spanish delight in going where they are
not wanted," Dancing Egret said bitterly. "But I think Mocoso
is a fool to risk their accepting his invitation. My father would
not take the chance of putting his people in danger that way."
She brooded for a moment. Then, "I didn't see the women
from Ucita's village in the camp," she said suddenly.

"They are usually kept in the hut by the river," Shore
Walker told her, "and well guarded. I've seen them from time
to time, though, and they don't appear to have been ill-
treated."

"So far," Egret retorted, and he nodded gravely.

"So far," he echoed. "But now that I've seen for myself
how efficient an interpreter Ortiz is, I have every hope of being
able to win back at least one of them."

"I don't see how you can possibly go alone to the camp,"
Egret said. "The Spanish will seize you as soon as you try to
hail Ortiz. I know they will." She spoke evenly, but Shore
Walker did not miss the tightness in her voice.

He smiled. "The warriors I brought from Calusa's island
will be with me, and many of Ucita's as well," he said reassuringly. "They'll hide themselves around the village, and keep
their dart throwers at the ready. And we warriors know how to
convince the enemy that we number more than we do in fact.
So long as Mocoso is gone from the Spanish camp and cannot
betray our tactics—for the Timucua are adept at the same sort
of thing—I think the man called De Soto will listen to me."

"But the Spanish have powerful weapons, weapons that
make noises like thunder!"

"We will be gone before they have time to fire their
thunder-sticks, or even their arrows. The Spaniards' weapons
have power, yes, but even their bows are unwieldy. The soldiers have to prepare for every shot they make, and I've noticed that they cannot do so quickly."

"But I saw today that many of them carry spears."

"What good are spears against our death dealers? Do not be
concerned, Egret; let Chief Ucita do the worrying. He'll do
enough for the both of you, and most of it wasteful." With this
jest, Shore Walker rounded a bend in the stream and pointed
the dugout smoothly toward the bank he used as a mooring
place.

Egret went first as they waded through water warmer than it

had been on their outward journey. Its caress leached some of the soreness from her muscles and soothed the scratches and ant bites on her legs. Smiling, she turned her head to tell Shore Walker how pleasant it felt. And immediately slipped, then tumbled sideways into the stream.

It took only a moment to push herself erect again, but in that moment a lumbering body shot out of the underbrush just ahead and crashed into the water.

"Gator!" Shore Walker shouted. He put out both hands, grasped Egret's buttocks, and heaved her out of the stream.

The breath whooshed out of her as she landed facedown on the bank, and she was dizzy and gasping as she scrambled to hands and knees while an ominous splashing went on behind her. Frantically she swung around, looked for a rock, a stick, anything that might serve as weapon.

There was nothing, *nothing* to help the man in the stream fend off the angry alligator. Egret's hands balled into fists as Shore Walker tried desperately to shove the beast away, and she screamed shrilly as the gator's huge jaws opened, clamped over Shore Walker's left forearm and dragged him beneath the roiling water.

Dancing Egret leaped back into the stream, threw herself forward just as the two surfaced, and began to pound on the twisting reptile's snout. Shore Walker's blood added crimson streaks to water already painted brown by churning mud, and she pounded harder, harder still, while shrieks of gut-deep fury erupted from her mouth. The gator's bulbous eyes mirrored its contempt for so puny, so ineffectual an attack, and its terrible teeth crunched deeper into the flesh of its hapless prey.

Shore Walker grunted. It was the only sound Egret had heard him make since this fearsome battle began. Now he raised his right arm, and she saw his shoulder bulge as he brought it forward with all his strength and thrust his broad thumb into the reptile's left eye.

On the instant, Egret stopped her useless battering of the beast's snout and drove one fist into the gator's other eye, threw all the power she could command behind it and rotated her knuckles back and forth, back and forth. She was no longer shrieking; her mouth was set in a snarl that was animallike in its intensity.

Abruptly, the alligator gave up. Releasing Shore Walker's arm, the reptile retreated from the awful pressure on its eyes, revolved its cumbersome body once and submerged to swim downstream.

Egret let out a shout of triumph, a sound cut short as Shore Walker toppled into the murky, bloody water. She grabbed for him, jerked him upright, a sob catching in her throat as she spied the pulpy mess between wrist and elbow that made a jagged frame for the skeletal white of exposed bone. She had thought herself drained of energy, but terror refueled her, let her drag him to the bank and somehow maneuver him up and out of the water.

Blood began to gush from his mangled arm and Egret whipped off her moss skirt and wadded a strip of it around his wound, pressed down upon it.

Shore Walker moaned, opened his eyes.

"I must stop the bleeding," she said through chattering teeth.

He nodded, closed his eyes again. "Tie it," he mumbled. "With my breechclout."

She continued to apply pressure with one hand while the other fumbled with the fastenings of his loincloth. When she had loosened them, he opened his eyes a second time and used his own right hand to hold the moss firmly in place while she tried to remove the fabric he wore around his genitals. Her movements were clumsy, uncertain, and he smiled briefly. "Don't be afraid of hurting me," he told her.

His voice was stronger, which heartened her. She put one hand beneath him, lifted, and unwound the fabric, shook it out, and wrapped it around his arm, knotting it firmly.

He tested the knot. "It will serve," he said. "Can you make it back to the canebrake on your own?"

She would not let herself doubt. "I can. I'll leave as soon as I've made you more comfortable."

"I'm fine as I am," he said. "Go Egret."

She ignored him, ignored his shouted "No!" as she stepped again into the stream, ignored the fear that boiled in her belly as she waded to the place he had stashed the canoe, yanked it out of the reeds, and pushed it ahead of her back to where Shore Walker lay. When she had tugged it out of the water, she dragged it to the sunniest spot she could find, then returned to her companion. But when she bent to try and drag him also, he raised himself on his good elbow. "If you'll help me, I can walk that far."

To walk would probably hurt him less than to be dragged, she told herself, and managed to get him to his feet. Together they stumbled to the canoe, and as gently as she could, she lowered him into it.

"I wish I had something to cover you with," she said anxiously, eyeing the sweat that beaded his wide forehead and glistened on his sallow cheeks.

"The sun will soon warm me," he said, and tried a grin. "I shall probably sleep while you are struggling through the mangrove swamps. Which hardly seems fair."

Yet anxiety underscored his voice. Egret did not know the way; to travel it once was not enough to memorize that confusing labyrinth! "Be careful," he said. But already the weakness was threatening again, and he could not put force behind his warning.

Egret understood the reason for his concern, but blood was seeping through the moss and staining the bindings she had fashioned from his breechclout. If she did not hurry, Shore Walker might die before help reached him. She laid one hand lightly on his clammy forehead and smiled reassuringly.

Then she was gone, running like a deer to where the mangroves began.

Chapter 15

Although the need for haste was uppermost in her thoughts, Dancing Egret had never forgotten the hunting Legends that were part of the lore of her people. The tales plucked at the corners of her mind now, and persuaded her to stop running. While her breathing quieted, she stilled her racing thoughts as well, and prepared to emulate the hunters of myth by offering herself up to the spirits of the swamp she would be entering. To do this properly, she knew she must somehow abjure her humanness and allow her senses, her movements, even her thoughts, to merge with that twilit place. The animals who made their homes there, and those who foraged and preyed there, did this instinctively; Dancing Egret knew she could do so only by surrendering her will, her control of self, until her blood pulsed to a new and slower rhythm, one dictated by the earth that sustained them all. Only by deliberately slowing down could she hope to travel swiftly and surely through the swamps that stood between her and the canebrake.

She closed her eyes, made herself listen until she could identify sounds beyond those she ordinarily heard: the faint flutter of leaves that formed the crown of the tree she stood beside, a hesitation in the river's song as a school of minnows flashed by, the moist plodding of a turtle's feet as it crept across a fallen branch. She flared her nostrils and inhaled, did it again and again until she could distinguish the aroma of sunwarmed grass from that which grew in the shade, tell wet bark from dry, recognize that fresh bird droppings decorated one of the mangrove roots on her right. An errant breeze gifted her with the merest scent of the white orchids it had blown across on its way, and she knew at once when a water-logged bit of carrion floated by.

She quivered as the expansion of all her senses continued, was filled with wonder as the heartbeat of the swamp began to regulate the blood that beat in her own wrists and throat. Even her skin began to respond to stimuli that would ordinarily go unnoticed. She felt patches of it warm as sunshine dappled her back, cool instantly as a cloud drifted across the face of the sun; was aware of a mole cricket burrowing through the ground beneath her moccasined foot; knew when a nectar-seeking butterfly hovered just above her head. She was unsurprised when she heard a mangrove seedpod plop into the mud directly in front of her; presentiment had made her shrink back so as not to impede its descent.

She was ready. Opening her eyes, she looked confidently toward the tunnel of green and brown whose mazelike twistings would take her back to the canebrake. She flexed her arms, bent her knees, thanked the spirits who inhabited the marshy places of her world for the smoothness with which her muscles responded, for the water that scarcely rippled as she stepped into it, for the air that flowed with rather than against her as she climbed upon an arching root, leaped lightly upward, and curled her fingers around a springy branch. Effortlessly, she swung herself to another, and another, and another, until the gallery of centuries-old trees had taken her in, welcomed her, and sanctioned her passage through its darkling corridors.

When the narrow creek in which the mangroves stood diverged, Egret knew no hesitation. She swung herself to the left and continued on, knew that the bullfrog that croaked a greeting was cheering her progress, never doubted that the snake coiled around one of the limbs she reached for would let her pass in peace, or that the ubiquitous mosquitoes would, for now, disdain this woman's flesh. Even the perspiration that puddled on her brow refrained from dripping into her eyes.

She felt no strain as she skimmed from branch to branch to branch; she had become oddly weightless, almost insubstantial. A young bobcat lapping from the stream paid no heed to the feet that briefly dangled above his spotted rump, and despite the urgency of her mission, Dancing Egret knew that much of her buoyancy derived from elation. She had truly become part of the brooding splendor of this mangrove swamp. Its tangled depths were no longer a mystery to her; they spawned joy instead of apprehension.

She was almost sorry when the trees thinned and sunlight began to gild the dark little stream that had murmured encouragement to her all along the way. She dropped lithely into its shallow water, then hoisted herself onto the complexity of roots she would be crossing now. With the same incredible delicacy that a broad-chested stag was capable of, she fairly ran across them. No chance of missteps this time; the unique, the bizarre, had metamorphosed into the familiar, the beloved, and she flowed as easily over the humped roots as the stream did beneath them.

Now the thicket of tall, close-growing cane was ahead of her. She had made it! She closed her eyes, sent up a prayer of thanks, promised to cherish forever the miracle that had been granted to her this day.

"Where is Shore Walker?"

Club Wielder, who had been keeping watch, emerged from the brake as he spoke. At once Dancing Egret's euphoria fled. Pain leaped into every muscle and tendon; her shoulders slumped and soul-deep exhaustion weighted her feet. She could not move, could not make herself take the few steps necessary to reach the War Leader. The enchantment that had sustained her had been stripped away; she was merely a woman whose reservoir of energy had been drained. "He is hurt," she managed, and began to crumple to the ground.

Club Wielder strode forward and caught her. "You must tell me where he is," he said urgently, lifting her and starting back into the canebrake.

His voice seemed to come from far away, but Egret feared that hers might not be audible at all, to either of them. "Beyond the swamp," she tried. "Near the place where his canoe—"

It was a mumble only, but the War Leader made out her words and, more importantly, understood what she meant. He shouted, and two warriors came running. "Take her to Chief Ucita's wife," he told them, "then return to me. Bring with you one of the slings we use to carry the wounded home from war. The warrior from Calusa's island is injured. We must go for him."

"It . . . it was a gator," Egret faltered as the young men cradled her in their linked arms. She shuddered, then let her head droop. She could say no more, however desperately she wanted to.

"Tell the priest to prepare himself," Club Wielder called as she was borne away. But Dancing Egret did not hear him.

Someone was trying to coax her to drink. "It's water, with honey in it," a voice said. "Open your mouth, Egret."

She parted her lips and swallowed when cool, sweet drops of liquid met her tongue.

"That's good." It was White Gull's voice. "Drink a little more, Egret."

She opened her mouth again, swallowed again. Then she opened her eyes. For a moment the world spun dizzily; White Gull's face was a blurred oval that would not stay in one place. Then the mists cleared, the world settled down, and she could recognize the worry in her sister's face. "Shore Walker?" she croaked.

"The men have brought him back, and Tradition Keeper is tending to him."

Egret struggled to sit up, and her sister put a supporting arm around her. "Perhaps you ought to lay still for a little longer," she said anxiously.

"No. I'm all right now. Just a bit weak." She reached for the dipper White Gull was holding and took it in hands that were able to grasp it despite their shaking. She raised it to her mouth, gulped down the rest of the honey water. "This helps," she said.

"It's a strengthener. Tradition Keeper says it is probably all you need. Except for salve for your scratches and insect bites, perhaps." There was no sign now of the anger and resentment that had marked her face the last time Dancing Egret looked upon it, which did as much to strengthen the younger woman as the priest's potion.

"And what does he say about Shore Walker?"

"That he'll survive, and that his arm, although it will take a long time to heal, should be nearly as good as it was, eventually. He needs stronger medicine than you do, Egret, and Tradition Keeper will do a healing ceremony for him besides. But he will survive."

"It was my fault," Egret burst out. "If I hadn't fallen into the water and made such a loud splash, that gator would never have known we were there."

White Gull said nothing for a moment; when she'd learned where her sister had gone, she had been aghast. A woman had no right to trespass in a warrior's province. But concern had eroded her disapproval, and Egret was looking so miserable! "I don't think he will blame you," she said gently.

"Perhaps not," Dancing Egret said. "But that won't stop me from blaming myself. You were right, White Gull; I say what I shouldn't say, and go where I shouldn't go." But as she spoke, it was coming back to her, the exhilaration she'd known when the spirits of the swamp adopted her and saw her safely back to the canebrake. Sincere though her penitence was, she knew she didn't regret the wonderful thing that had happened to her because she had gone to the Spanish camp with Shore Walker. And she had been able to do as she'd promised; she had located Juan Ortiz and pointed him out, had even been able to interpret what passed between Holata Mocoso and the Spanish leader.

Yet that small success would have no meaning until Shore Walker was able to return to the camp and attempt an exchange of prisoners. Which he could be doing right now if she had not alerted the alligator to the presence of strangers near its nest. It was solely due to her that the furious reptile had rushed into the stream, seized Shore Walker's arm, and torn at it with those terrible, terrible teeth . . .

Tears pricked at her eyes and she lay back down, averting her face so that White Gull wouldn't see them. Egret had no respect for women who wept, had long since vowed that she would never, ever display such weakness. "I need to sleep again," she muttered.

White Gull nodded. The priest had said that her sister would crave sleep, and that this was as it should be. "When you waken, I'll bring you broth," she said. Confident now that her sister would be herself again soon, she tiptoed away.

Dancing Egret made herself swallow her tears, and was glad to take refuge in sleep when finally it offered itself.

By the time she felt strong enough to approach Shore Walker, she knew that the Spanish had sailed away in the ships that had brought them to these shores. There had been no exchange of prisoners, and now there never could be. Egret ached for the four women from Ucita's village. What would happen to them now? But when Club Wielder's scouts reported the Spaniards' departure to Chief Ucita, he had seemed more relieved than anything else.

"Yet he is in no hurry to go back," White Gull told Egret fretfully. "Not that there is much left to go back to! But anything would be better than remaining in this awful place." She slapped at a mosquito and sighed. "Some of our people are making plans to visit kin in other towns," she confided. "I think that many, if not all, will stay there if they can. Like my husband, they have begun to think that any town of Ucita's must be cursed."

White Gull believed that, too, Egret thought, and thought as well that all of them were being foolish. She did not say so, however; she had learned her lesson, and learned it well: no more impulsive speaking out, particularly on matters she was no expert in. It was for the priest to say if a town could be cursed or not. "I'm hoping Tradition Keeper will let me see Shore Walker today," she said instead.

"He allowed Ucita to see him this morning," White Gull told her. "And when Shore Walker insisted upon it, Club Wielder, too."

"He is better, then?"

"So it seems. Certainly he is eating a good amount of the herb broth Tradition Keeper showed me how to make."

"I'll make the broth, and help with all the other chores, too, now that I'm feeling so well," Dancing Egret said firmly. Until today, everyone had insisted she continue to rest, but idleness was no friend of hers. If the children hadn't come begging to hear the stories she had once told to their older brothers and sisters, she would have been up and about much sooner, no matter what anyone said. "Right now, however, I want to see Shore Walker."

The priest had had a shelter of sorts constructed on the far side of the clearing, and Shore Walker lay on a pallet beneath a canopy of palm fronds. His face looked thin to Egret, and shorn of the strength that had governed his features before, but he smiled when she crawled under the fronds and sat down beside him. "I had hoped you would come," he said simply, and a tightness in her chest suddenly unknotted itself and permitted her heart to beat naturally again.

She looked at the arm Tradition Keeper had wrapped neatly in clean deerhide. "Your wound is healing?"

"Healing nicely, according to Ucita's priest," he told her. "The bone wasn't broken, you see, and he knew how to stitch the flesh together over the wound. He used an awl much like the kind you women use for sewing garments."

"That must have hurt," Egret said.

Shore Walker smiled again. "I was unconscious at the time, so I don't know if it did or not. I didn't waken until after the healing ceremony had been performed."

"I slept a good deal, too," Dancing Egret confessed. "And I wasn't even injured."

"To come back here through that swamp, alone, must have demanded more of you than you could spare," Shore Walker said. "I'm still amazed that you were able to do it, Egret."

Should she tell him of her wondrous experience? Someday, perhaps, but she was awed by it still and would not risk demeaning the extraordinary by trying to put into words something that was in truth indescribable. Besides, Shore Walker might think her fanciful when he heard, and this she could not abide. "What matters is that I did do it, and that you were rescued before too much blood spilled out of your body," she said.

"And that I'll be able to use my arm again, as easily as I did before," he said. "For a while I feared my warrior days might be over, that I might have to put on a moss skirt and live among the berdaches."

"You? Never," Dancing Egret told him. "You would have become a trader, like Kwambu. Or a woodcarver, like your grandfather." She shifted herself, plucked from the waistband of her skirt the flute he had made for her years before. "You were a boy still when you carved this," she said, caressing the smooth wood with her fingers, "and it's truly beautiful. What a boy can do, a man can do, only better. Your fingers are as talented as Mask Maker's, Shore Walker."

"But if I had been left with the use of only one arm, I could not be a woodcarver," he said gently.

Egret bowed her head; she had spoken thoughtlessly again! "Shore Walker," she said, "you can't know how sorry I am that I put you in such danger. Just because you will heal and be able to use your arm again, doesn't alter the fact that I was the cause of your being hurt so badly that you might well have been crippled."

Her face was a study in wretchedness, an expression that did not suit those strong features. And there was no reason for it. "Egret, you *saved* my life," Shore Walker said. "I'm the one to apologize, for you were in as much danger as I was. And none of it would have happened had I not chosen to keep my canoe so near to an alligator's nest. It was my fault, and mine alone, that the mother gator finally decided she'd had enough of humans coming too close to the eggs she is hatching."

She raised her head. "I was the one who carelessly fell into the stream and told her we were there."

He laughed. "If you think the gator didn't already know that, then you don't know gators! No, Egret; do not blame yourself for something you didn't do. Instead, remember how courageous you were. I know few women daring enough to throw themselves into the water to fight off an alligator! I would have made a dinner for that beast without your help. And then you hauled me out of the water, and bound up my wound, and went for help . . . Egret, you have nothing whatsoever to blame yourself for, only a great deal to take pride in."

"I don't feel proud," she said. Then her mouth curved into a smile. "But I don't feel shame anymore, either. Thank you, Shore Walker."

He did not respond, but only looked steadily at her.

"Why do you stare at me?" she asked when she began to feel uncomfortable under his scrutiny.

"It's the first time I've seen your face without mud all over it," he said. "You have grown into a handsome woman, Dancing Egret."

"Now I know you're twisting the truth," she said. "It may be that I wasn't responsible for the gator attacking you, but I have seen my own face. I know there is nothing handsome about it."

"You have not looked at it through my eyes," he said quietly, then turned his head as a shadow fell across them. "I think it's time for me to swallow more of Tradition Keeper's bitter potion," he added.

Egret looked up to see the priest standing just outside the shelter. "I must leave you, in any event," she said, moving out of his way. "It's time for me to help my sister give out the shellfish some of Club Wielder's men harvested this morning. Everyone will be having a fine treat today."

Although she distributed her share of the oysters among children who had gone too long without seafood of any sort, Egret felt obscurely that she, too, had been given a treat this day, one infinitely more nourishing than oysters and clams could ever be.

White Gull had been right. Slowly but surely, the people began to drift away, to explain haltingly that they were going to visit a cousin on Muspa, an uncle living in the Lake country, an old grandmother whose village was on the southernmost coast. By the time Shore Walker was up and about, none of the leave-takers had returned; it seemed certain that they had found homes elsewhere.

"Club Wielder and the warriors he has left want to offer their services to Calusa," Shore Walker told Dancing Egret. "They'll be returning to the island with us."

"So will Ucita and my sister," she said. "White Gull told me this morning. It's sad, Shore Walker."

He nodded. "It is. But Chief Ucita has had more than he can stand. He's not a young man, and everything that has happened has aged him beyond his years."

"My father will understand," Egret said. But she wondered if he truly would. The Calusa she remembered had always seemed to despise weakness of any sort.

Shore Walker looked doubtful, too, but said nothing, only went to help the other men tear down the few shelters the people had erected and restore the clearing to its natural state. The cooking fire had been buried beneath a heap of damp soil, and its encircling stones returned to the river they had come from.

It was a pitifully small band that made the trip to the inlet where Calusa's island lay. The three long canoes they had retrieved from Ucita's village carried all of them easily, and the ocean was tame enough for them to be able to move parallel to the coastline all the way.

"Does anyone know where the Spaniards went, when they left?" Egret asked, moving her feet cautiously so as not to kick the Spanish boy who lay in the bottom of the dugout. Only his hands were tied now, but even that hardly seemed necessary. Fear fettered him more effectively than the thongs linking his thin wrists.

Club Wielder, the muscles in his broad back rippling as he dipped the paddle he held, answered her. "They sailed up the coast to Mocoso's village, then marched inland."

So Mocoso had done as he'd promised, and sent them on to his brother-in-law, Egret thought. Who would doubtless send them north, out of Mocoso territory altogether.

"They will go north from the Lake country," Shore Walker said, feathering his own paddle as they approached the narrow channel leading into the island. Dancing Egret smiled, and was glad she had held her own tongue. It had not been her place to make the prediction.

The three canoes went single file until the channel widened to form the water court that flowed behind the Temple mound, then glided together toward its shell-built rim. They tied up side by side and the passengers scrambled one at a time onto the raised ground on the north side of the water court. Already people from Calusa's town were congregating there, for sentries had reported the canoes' coming long before they'd entered the channel.

Egret looked upon a sea of faces, tried desperately to find one she recognized. It did not seem right, to feel so like a stranger on her own father's island. Finally she spied a gray-haired man whose nose was as hawklike as Shore Walker's, whose pouched eyes, although age-dimmed, were as expressive as the warrior's were. "Mask Maker," she called, and ran to embrace him.

He looked down at her, puzzled at first, then smiled. "Dancing Egret. Your father will be pleased to welcome his daughter home."

"And not beforetime." A woman's voice, with a touch of asperity in it.

"Trailing Vine," Egret said, turning to her father's First Wife. "And Herb Gatherer, too," she added, noticing the plump woman who stood beside her. She hugged both of them as well. Never mind that the child she used to be had diligently avoided the sharp-tongued Trailing Vine, or that Herb Gatherer had always been too busy with her own flock of daughters, or mixing her various balms and potions, to bother much with a motherless little girl. "Oh, it's so good to be back."

There were others she could not place until they told her who they were, among them Herb Gatherer's oldest daughter, Brown Pelican. "We were both children when I went to Ucita," Egret exclaimed, looking with astonishment at the pretty young woman, the baby in her arms, and the toddler clinging to her leg. "Now you have children of your own."

"I married Prowling Panther," the wife of Calusa's War Leader said proudly. "You are a maiden still, Dancing Egret?"

Egret thought of the young warriors in Mocoso's town who would have been more than willing to alter that status, and sighed. "I am." It was as well she'd rejected them, she told herself, else she would not be here now. And suddenly this was the place above all others that she wanted to be. "Is my father in the house?" she asked Trailing Vine.

The older woman nodded. "He is meeting with his counselors to make final arrangements for the Harvest Ceremony." But she spoke absently; she had finally noticed White Gull and Ucita, who were waiting a little apart from the others. "Why is your sister here?" she demanded. "And who is that old man with her?"

"That is her husband," Egret said. "They have come to visit Calusa." Let White Gull explain to their father what had brought the two of them here; it was not for Egret to do so, and certainly not to Trailing Vine. She was relieved to have Brown Pelican touch her arm.

"You must meet your father's Fourth Wife," the young woman said, leading forward a truly beautiful woman who had a mischievous-looking little boy in tow. "Watchful Doe is my husband's sister, as well as Calusa's wife," Pelican finished.

Egret took Watchful Doe's proffered hands, squeezed them lightly. "If you are my father's latest wife, then this must be the son I've heard so much about," she said, releasing them and squatting down in front of the boy. "Hello, Crested Heron. I am your sister, Dancing Egret."

"Will you play with me?" the child asked eagerly, and Egret laughed.

"I will, indeed, as soon as I've paid my respects to our father," she told him.

"Grown women do not play," Trailing Vine said repressively.

"This grown woman does," Egret retorted. "Can you think of a better way for me to get to know my new brother?"

Trailing Vine contented herself with a sniff, and turned away. "The counselors will be ready to take refreshment," she said. "Since Calusa's other wives seem more interested in welcoming someone who should have been sensible enough to come home long ago, I suppose I will have to prepare food and drink for them."

"I will help you," Herb Gatherer said hastily, and with a distracted smile toward Dancing Egret, followed Trailing Vine back to the domiciliary mound. Watchful Doe shook her head, tugged at Crested Heron's hand and hurried after them.

"You mustn't mind Trailing Vine," Brown Pelican said. "As First Wife, she feels responsible for everything. But my mother and Watchful Doe make sure to do their share of the work, I promise you."

"I don't doubt it," Dancing Egret assured her. "I remember enough of my childhood to know that Trailing Vine has always been that way. She's older now, of course, but I can see that she hasn't changed."

"If anything, she has gotten worse," Brown Pelican said in a whisper, and grinned. "Why don't you come to my house, Egret, until Headchief Calusa is able to see you? You're probably more in need of refreshment than the counselors are, and I have new-baked corn bread there, and plums I picked only this morning."

"I'm both hungry and thirsty," Egret said, pleased to have found a friend so quickly. "You are kind, Brown Pelican, and I accept your invitation."

She picked up her sister's older girl after they had crossed the plaza, made her giggle by nuzzling the top of her head, then carried the child on her shoulders to the second highest level of the mound. It truly was good to be home, and so she would tell Calusa when finally she saw him.

Chapter 16

◆ ━ ◆

He was not as awesomely tall as she remembered. That was Dancing Egret's first thought when she had been summoned to the huge house that looked down on the homes of Calusa's priests, counselors, warriors, and—far below—on the simpler dwellings snuggled around the vast elevated base of the mound. Among the naturally tall Calusan men, the Headchief's height was still impressive, but Egret stood on a level with his broad chest now; his head, with its flowing mane of silver-black hair, no longer seemed to loom against the sky, as it had when she was a little girl.

"So. You have come home at last." Calusa's piercing eyes measured her growth, lingered on the square face that bore features remarkably like his own. The chin had a stubborn cast to it, and her gaze—like his—was direct and appraising. No one would ever question who had sired this girl! Of course, appearances only told part of the story. "What have you to say for yourself, Dancing Egret, to persuade me that you had good reason to stay away so long?"

"You did not object when my sister asked to take me with her to Ucita's town, after you arranged for her to wed its chief," Egret said swiftly. Indeed, he had seemed indifferent to the whole situation, if she remembered correctly, and if the memory of a five-year-old was to be trusted.

"That," her father said, "was many years ago. "My house was glutted with daughters then. And you had no mother to tend to you; White Gull was both willing and eager to do so." He suppressed a grin. The trader had been right; there was nothing timid about Dancing Egret. "What I asked is why you did not come back sooner to the place that is, after all, your home."

170

"I made friends in Ucita's town," she said. "Kneeling Cypress, Ucita's daughter, was my dearest friend. When she had to leave suddenly, naturally I went with her. She had no one else."

"She had a husband," Calusa said dryly. "A Spanish husband, who ought by rights to have been a sacrifice. Or at least a slave. He was the reason she ran away and asked sanctuary of a Timucuan chief. You had no such reason."

"A husband who has since deserted her," Egret shot back. "Deserted Cypress and their three children." She knew full well that Trailing Vine and Herb Gatherer, supposedly engrossed in sewing white plumes onto Calusa's ceremonial headband, were listening avidly. And disapprovingly. But she did not care. "I have never understood why you didn't intercede between Cypress and Ucita when all of this happened. Surely you knew of it. You know everything that goes on in your provinces. It's shameful, that a daughter of the Calusa should have to flee to a Timucuan to find justice."

His eyebrows soared. "Is justice what Holata Mocoso dispensed? I have heard that he merely suffered the presence of you and Ucita's disobedient daughter so that he might, at last, have a Spaniard in his town. His warriors never had brought him one, for all that he pressured them to."

"I was content enough in his town."

"Can you say the same of Kneeling Cypress?"

Dancing Egret hesitated. "She had her children. And her husband, for a while. But now . . . Father, Holata Mocoso *traded* her to a brother chief, Tocobaga, after Juan Ortiz decided to leave with the Spanish leader called De Soto. She had no wish to go and be concubine to that man! You must know all this, too. Why haven't you sent warriors to bring her and her children back? How can you be so unfeeling?"

She hadn't meant to let all of this pour out, not yet. But speaking of poor Cypress had resurrected her anger and frustration, and she could not help herself.

"Your friend chose to turn her back on her father. By doing so, she turned her back on her tribe. I could not afford to jeopardize my hard-won safe-passage agreements with Holata Mocoso by interfering when she fled to him. All that has happened since has sprung from that, from Kneeling Cypress's own foolishness. Had you been mistreated in any way, it would have been different; you were still too young to know better when you left Ucita's town. But you yourself have just confirmed what I have been told all along: that you were treated well enough by the Timucua." He smiled. "And I have been told that you might have learned a thing or two from them, as well." He had had a long and interesting chat with Ucita's War Leader, and another—even more interesting—with the convalescing Shore Walker. But he would choose his own time to discuss what he had learned from them with Dancing Egret.

"I can speak their language," she admitted. "And I know many of their Legends, also."

"So you are as fond of stories now as you were when you were small?"

Dancing Egret started; she'd never realized that Calusa paid her enough heed to know how she had loved to listen to the Legends of their people. "I am. I like to tell them, too, especially to children."

"Well, there are children enough in my town to be glad of that. We have had no proper Story Singer here since Tale Spinner died."

Briefly, Dancing Egret bowed her head. She hadn't known that the old matron whose stirring tales made you forget her twisted back had gone to join her ancestors. How many others that she remembered were no longer around? she wondered. "I can never be as good as Tale Spinner," she said slowly, "but I'll be happy to entertain the little ones as best I can."

Calusa smiled again, and not just because he had succeeded in distracting this outspoken daughter of his. "That is good. Legend Singing is a suitable occupation for a Headchief's daughter. Now that you are home again, you must take care to remember your status, you know. You will only confuse the people if you do not."

Status was not something Egret had ever given much thought to, growing up as she had. She knew the rules, of course, and was familiar with the system that kept the Calusa strong. Her own Dolphin clan was the ruling clan; then came the priests, the Counselors, and the warriors. Each group had its privileges and responsibilities, and were required always to look after those born to be servants or slaves. Artisans and traders might arise from any group, of course, and berdaches might come from any group except the ruling clan. But Egret had never sought privileges, and her sole responsibility, for most of her life, had been to look after herself. And to take care of her friends, whenever she was able to. Which reminded her . . . "What of Kneeling

Cypress?" she demanded. "Surely you will help her, Calusa? Even if you name her foolish, the daughter of a Calusan chief should not be concubine to a Timucuan!"

His eyes were suddenly cold. "Dancing Egret, this is something only the Headchief can decide. I do not expect you to understand, but I can do nothing to help Kneeling Cypress. Since I cannot, we will talk no more of this, now or ever."

She did not doubt that he meant it, and she knew that nothing she said would sway him from his decision. Bitterness flooded through her, but she merely inclined her head and began to back away.

"Wait," he said. "Trailing Vine tells me that you came to my island unattended. Where is your serving woman, daughter?"

She struggled to keep exasperation from her voice. "I've no need for a serving woman, Father."

"You will have one anyway," he said imperiously. "Your status demands it." He turned his head, called to Trailing Vine. "Send for the Spanish woman who helped the berdaches during the time of sickness three seasons ago."

Despite herself, Egret was intrigued. "How did a Christian slave come to help the berdaches? And how serious was the sickness you're speaking of?"

Calusa's expression was grave. "It was bad," he said bluntly. "Many of our people suffered from a heating of the blood which caused their flesh to erupt. The priests could do little for them, and far too many were dying. Then this slave I just sent for went to Vision Seeker and told him that she recognized the disease and knew what to do with those who were ill."

Egret was puzzled. "How could she tell him all of this? Surely Vision Seeker doesn't understand the Spanish tongue. And why did I hear nothing about this sickness? Kwambu came often to wherever I happened to be, yet he never spoke of it."

"The Christian woman spoke in our language," her father said. "One of our fishermen took her for a wife three years after we rescued her from the sea following the wreck of a Spanish ship. In time, she learned to talk as we do, although not so smoothly. As for your not knowing about what was happening here, the worst occurred while the trader was in the north, and I forbade him to mention it to you afterward. Or to anyone. It would not do for my enemies to learn of many deaths on Calusa's island; some might be rash enough to try and take advantage of such a thing."

Egret could not argue with her father's reasoning, so she focused on the answers to her other questions. "The Spanish woman," she said. "Her advice proved good?"

"She persuaded Vision Seeker to have a large shelter built apart from the town, and keep all who were sick there together. Not only was it easier for the berdaches to tend them that way, but most of those who had not fallen ill remained healthy. Why, I cannot say; Vision Seeker suggests that isolating the sick lured away the demons who brought the illness to our town, and that his prayers were able to confine them in one place. He may be right. But the Christian slave stayed in the house of the sick to help the berdaches, and she did not become ill with the fever. Perhaps our demons are not tempted by people whose flesh is unappetizingly pale." He shrugged; no one knew the truth of it.

"She sounds wonderfully wise," Egret said. But the plump, motherly-looking woman who came into Calusa's house did not look particularly wise; her round face registered bewilderment and anxiety more than anything else.

Puffing audibly from her climb to the top of the steep mound, she crossed the floor and prostrated herself before Trailing Vine. "It is the Headchief who wants you," Calusa's First Wife said impatiently. "Go to him."

Calusa acknowledged her salutation, then told her to stand. "From now on," he said abruptly, "you are not a slave. Instead, you will act as serving woman to my daughter, Dancing Egret."

He waved a hand in Egret's direction, and the Spanish woman turned soft brown eyes toward her. The puzzlement in them slowly gave way to comprehension. "*Gracias,*" she said quietly. Then, hurriedly, "I mean, I thank you for your kindness, Great Calusa. It will be as you say."

The Headchief waved his hand again, this time in dismissal of both women. Neither moved until Egret realized the Spaniard was waiting for her new mistress to precede her.

Dancing Egret was certain her father was tempted to smirk when he sensed her discomfort, and this did not please her at all. She threw back her shoulders, held her head high, and led the way with as much dignity as she could muster.

Crested Heron was sitting outside waiting for her. "You promised to play with me," he said, jumping up and snatching her hand.

"But I didn't say precisely *when*," she told him, smiling down into his eager face.

"It must be now," he said, his lower lip protruding. "Everyone else is busy making ready for the Ceremony of First Harvest, and I have nothing to do."

"Are all of your friends busy also?"

"No. But I don't feel like playing with them today. I want to play with you. As you promised."

Dancing Egret sighed. She had wanted time to talk with the Spanish woman Calusa had foisted upon her, to ask her more about the sickness Calusa had described and to let her know—gently—that her services would be needed rarely. What on earth did one do with a serving woman, anyway? Egret knew that until she found out, she would feel as though she walked always with a substantial shadow lumbering after her. "I have an idea," she said to her brother. "Instead of a game, how would you like me to tell you a story? If you go and get your friends, I'll tell it to all of you. It's more fun that way, you see. And I might even teach you children to sing the story. If you do it well enough, and if our father agrees, perhaps you can sing it on one of the days of the Ceremony."

Crested Heron's eyes lit up. "Then we can be busy making ready for the Ceremony, too!" He released her hand. "I'll bring my friends," he said, preparing to dash away.

"Bring girls as well as boys," she told him before he ran out of hearing. "We'll need all the voices we can get."

He made a face, then grinned, and headed for the plaza.

Dancing Egret turned to the woman standing behind her, was suddenly appalled to realize she did not even know her name. "I am Ysabel," the woman said when Egret apologized for her father's oversight. Her voice was as full as her breasts, and the way she shaped her words reminded Egret of Juan Ortiz.

Dancing Egret told herself firmly that she must not take against this woman because of that. "I know that you have a husband," she said to her. "Do you have children also?"

Ysabel nodded. "Two," she said.

"Then why don't you go and get them, and bring them to listen to my story with the other children?"

Ysabel's confusion was plain. The Headchief might object to her son and daughter mingling with Crested Heron and his friends, yet if she were to serve the Headchief's daughter, then surely she must do as the young woman said?

Egret had no trouble interpreting the expression on that round face. "Their father is Calusan," she said decisively. "So are they. They should learn our Legends."

For the first time, Ysabel smiled, and Egret glimpsed the pretty girl she had once been. "It will be as you say," the Spanish woman said. She turned away, turned back. "I think," she said slowly, "that I will be pleased to serve you, Dona Dancing Egret."

Whether Crested Heron was the sort of child to have a great many friends, or whether no one dared refuse the invitation of the Headchief's son, Egret didn't know. But when finally she had persuaded the children to seat themselves in a semicircle, she found herself looking upon scores of expectant faces. "I'm going to tell you the tale of our creation," she said. "When I've finished it, I'll sing you a simpler version, and those who wish to learn it are welcome to."

As she had expected, some of the little ones appeared excited at the idea of learning a story-song; others seemed decidedly doubtful. But all retained their air of expectancy, so it was obvious that they wanted to at least listen to the creation Legend.

"In the Beginning there was only the sky, with the islands we call clouds floating in it," she said, and smiled when most of her audience looked up. "During the day, Sun glided through the sky in his canoe, visiting the islands on which Thunder Master and Rain Chief and Wind Maker lived. Spirit ancestors of the animals lived on other islands, and Sun visited them also. At night, Moon paddled a canoe through the same waterway and watched over the animals as they slept."

Ysabel's children, huddled together at the back of the semicircle, kept their big eyes fixed on Egret's face as she talked, and she knew instinctively that they had never heard this story before. "One day," she went on, "Sun, Moon, Thunder, Rain, and Wind met in Council. 'We are all powerful gods,' they said. 'There should be lesser beings who recognize this, and pay homage to us.' So it was agreed that the Calusa should be made."

She went on to tell them how the Council had realized that a home must be made for the Calusa, and how Thunder, Wind, and Rain worked together to make an ocean beneath the sky. "The animal spirits had been watching," she said, "and now they spoke. 'That is a fine home if your Calusa are to have gills and fins,' they told the gods. 'But if they must breathe air, as we must, then they cannot survive unless there are islands below just as there are above.'

"This made sense, but no one could agree on how an island should be made. 'Leave it to us,' said the spirit ancestors of the animals, and sent Turtle down to build one. Well, he swam all the way to the bottom of that ocean, scooped up mud, and carried it on his shell to the surface. Then he dove again, for although Turtle is slow, he is a patient creature and meant to dive as many times as might be necessary to make an island. Unfortunately, each time he swam back up again, the mud he'd already brought up had dissolved." She grinned. "As I have said, Turtle is rather *slow*."

The children snickered. How foolish of Turtle to think he could build an island!

"Then Sea Gull and Fishhawk went to a deserted cloud-island and took opposite corners in their beaks. Holding it securely, they flew down and laid it gently on the ocean. It looked very pretty, but when Deer went down to test it, his delicate hoofs sank into the cloud's surface and soon he was belly-deep in water. 'If the Calusa are to walk, they will need a firmer surface,' he said. 'And we animals will need grass and trees besides, if we are to survive on this earth you wish to make.' For the animals had asked permission to live in the Calusa's world, and this had been granted.

"Sun and Moon, who had been debating what form the Calusa should take, agreed. 'The people we make will need a solid island,' they said, 'for we have decided to give them two legs apiece so that they may walk upright, which will set them apart from the other creatures. They will breathe air, though, as the four-footed animals do, and will be able to swim, as fish do, and to sing sweetly, as birds do.' "

Crested Heron, sitting directly in front of Dancing Egret, reached forward and poked her with his forefinger. "*You* sing sweet as the birds," he said, and several of his friends nodded vigorously.

Egret beamed. Praise from children was always sincere; even if undeserved, she cherished it. "Dolphin," she said, going on with her story, "was a serious-minded animal whose natural home was the water. He thought it a fine thing that the Calusa would breathe air, as he did, yet be able to move through water, as he did. 'I think I can make the kind of island you want,' he said to Sun and Moon. Since he was such a sober fellow, they had faith in him and allowed him to try.

"He dove out of the sky and into the ocean, kept on going until he touched bottom. But when he swam to the surface, he carried with him more than mud: he brought along several shells as well, and used the mud to glue them together on top of the water. They floated calmly there while he dove again and brought back more mud and shells. So long as Sun's bright eye watched him, Dolphin continued in this fashion. When it came time for Sun to seek his bed in the west, a large island had already been formed."

"It was *this* island," a little girl shouted.

"Many think so," Egret said solemnly. "The Legend does not tell us for certain. It only says that Dolphin continued to work beneath the paler eye of Moon. Now he was bringing up a thick layer of mud to lay upon the shell foundation. 'Be certain to leave room for rivers to flow through it,' Moon called softly, so just before Sun lit the morning fire in the east, Dolphin used his flippers to score the island's muddy surface.

"After Sun came into the sky and gazed upon the island for a little while, plants and trees began to push their way through the mud to reach for warmth and light. And when Rain saw the troughs Dolphin's flippers had made, he poured fresh water into them so that the roots of the plants might be kept moist. As the trees grew taller and taller, Wind brushed their branches with his fingers, and when Sun's gaze grew so strong that the plants began to wilt, Thunder sent a storm to cool the island."

Egret glanced around the half-moon of intent faces. " 'We have done well,' the gods said to one another. Then they turned to Dolphin. 'But you have done best of all. You have made a home for all the animals and for the Calusa as well.'

"Their praise made serious Dolphin smile and smile," she finished. "And he smiles still to see how much the Calusa enjoy the islands, big and small, that he made for them to live on."

Crested Heron grinned as his friends thanked Dancing Egret, and preened himself as though it had been his idea that she should tell the story. "Now teach us the song," he said loudly.

And Egret grinned, too, to have so many of the children decide to stay and learn the simpler creation story she had devised while living in Ucita's village.

Headchief Calusa looked upon the face of his old friend and almost failed to recognize it. Age had seized Ucita and wrung all the juice out of him, and Calusa was saddened to see a man who had once been a proud warrior reduced to the haggard elder who stood before him now. "You are welcome here," he said, "but I am sorry for the tragedy that has brought you to my town."

"Many tragedies have arisen to plague me since last we met," Ucita said, and shrugged. There was no need to elaborate; Calusa would have heard of all of them. "So many, that I have come to accept that I have fallen out of favor with our gods."

And having accepted that, you are no longer inspired to fight adversity, Calusa thought. "You have made up your mind to abandon your town?" he asked.

The noseless man nodded. "Why rebuild when the gods will only see that it is cast down yet again?" There was weariness in his voice and resignation in his eyes. "And I no longer have enough people left to accomplish such a thing. They know as well as I do that it would be no use."

The Headchief hoped that the man had not infected all of his people with his own dispiritedness. They would no longer be fit to be called Calusa, if so! "Have you considered turning over the leadership of the town to Club Wielder? He is of your clan, and seems to me to be a man of intelligence as well as courage. Your people might be willing to return, if you do this. And you could act as Senior Counselor to him." Whether Club Wielder would ever feel inclined to take advice from Ucita was of no importance; this would still be a way of saving face for the old chief, and Calusa would see that Club Wielder understood that. "You know better than anyone how much I need a border town in that area," he added encouragingly.

Ucita shook his head. "I will not go back there." For the first time, there was strength in his voice. "You might be able to persuade Club Wielder to, and I agree that he would make a good chief. But I will not go back."

"You wish to stay on here, then?"

Again Ucita shook his head. "Not permanently, no. What I wish . . ." He sighed, made an effort to straighten his slumped shoulders. "What I wish most earnestly is to have done with this life. A man the gods frown on is doomed to misery, Calusa, and I have had enough of it. Of misery, and of shame. For I carry a huge burden of shame to know that I must have offended the gods so dreadfully. And I can think of no way to be rid of it except by dying."

"To take your own life would offend the gods more seriously than anything you could possibly have done so far," the

Headchief said sternly. "You must not think of such a thing, Ucita."

"You misunderstand," Ucita said. "I wish to make amends to the gods, not to offend them further."

Calusa frowned. "And how do you propose to do so?"

A trace of eagerness lit his companion's face. "With your help, I can atone," he said. "Only let me be the sacrifice during the Ceremony of First Harvest, and I will offer up my life with a joyful heart. Then the gods will know that I am truly repentent and will not condemn my three souls to walk this earth forever. My life may have been riddled with shame and misery, but my death at least shall be glorious!"

Dancing Egret had not known Shore Walker was standing behind her until the children, finishing for the third time the song she was teaching them, began to nudge one another and giggle.

"Did you hear it all?" she asked after she had turned and greeted him. "Did they sing clearly enough for you to understand the words?"

"They did, and I enjoyed listening very much," he said gravely. "They sing as well as most grownups do."

The children giggled again, this time to cover their own confusion at being praised by a warrior. "That's enough for now," Egret told them. "I'll speak to Calusa as soon as I can and tell you tomorrow if you will be permitted to sing at the Ceremony."

She watched them scamper away, then turned a questioning look on Shore Walker when Crested Heron ran back long enough to ask if his toy was finished yet. "I'm carving a double canoe for him," Shore Walker explained, "a small replica of our seagoing dugouts. Carving is a good way to strengthen my arm, yet I dare not try and help my grandfather finish the Ceremonial masks he is making. I'm too clumsy yet for that. The boy won't notice if his plaything is not perfect, however."

Egret laughed. "He probably will, you know. Children notice more than we think they do. But he'll be happy anyway to have a new toy. It's nice of you to do this for my brother."

"He asked if I would," Shore Walker confessed, and Egret laughed again. She was beginning to recognize Crested Heron's determination to have what he wanted, when he wanted it. It was only natural, she supposed, for the boy must have been made aware of his status almost from the day of his birth. And surely he would learn tact as he grew older.

"Well, make certain that he thanks you properly for it," she advised. "I'm already fond of my little brother, but it would be wrong to allow him to believe that toys upon demand are his due. Children are often self-absorbed, but the son of a Headchief should learn early to be considerate of others."

"You understand children rather well, it seems."

"I've known a great many," she said. "Perhaps that's why. Or perhaps I'm still a child myself in some ways."

He stood back, surveyed her from head to toe, then grinned. "But not in others," he said.

Egret felt her face grow warm, and was relieved to hear someone calling her name. Relief and embarrassment gave way to delight when she saw who it was. "Kwambu!" she said, running to him and hugging him. "Now my homecoming is complete."

"I am happy to see you, too," he said when she released him, "and happier still to see you here. I learned you had left Mocoso, so I stopped at Ucita's town on my way back to the island. Worry tied wings to my feet after that! What happened there?"

Between them, Egret and Shore Walker told the trader about the Spanish invasion. Kwambu's expression registered shock, anger, dismay. "And you believe they went north from Canegacola?" he asked Shore Walker.

"I do. Canegacola is no fool; he would have thought of some way to send them on. And the Spanish, having been unable to find any gold to speak of in the south, would naturally head north, I think, if only because the going is easier. To turn back south, even southeast, would have brought them to the river glades. One look at that seemingly endless maze would surely convince them that none of the yellow metal they prize so highly can be found there."

"They were not told about the traders' road," Kwambu said almost to himself, "or I would have come across them somewhere as I was returning home. But if they marched directly north after leaving the Lake country . . ." He closed his eyes, visualized this and that route they might have taken. Every path he could think of led, eventually, to Outina! "I must speak with your father," he said to Egret. "Is he in the house?"

"He must be," she told him. "I haven't seen him come out."

Kwambu, without bothering to excuse himself, spun around and hurried up the ramp. Such discourtesy was not like him. "He seems upset about something," Dancing Egret said.

"He does," Shore Walker agreed. "Doubtless Calusa will be able to help him with whatever it is. Meanwhile, why don't you come with me to Mask Maker's? I want to show you the canoe I'm carving for Crested Heron. You'll have plenty of opportunity later to talk with Kwambu. There will be no trading expeditions now until the Ceremony of First Harvest has been celebrated."

But pleased as she was to accept Shore Walker's invitation, Dancing Egret could not stop wondering what had agitated the usually phlegmatic Kwambu. She would have been mystified had she heard the trader begging to be allowed to set out again immediately for the northern Timucuan provinces, and would have been puzzled indeed to see his distress when this plea was met with an emphatic *"No!"*

Chapter 17

Rain clouds shrouded the eastern half of the sky, muting the sunset's glory in the west; only a lambent coral marked the ending of the third, and last, day of the Ceremony of First Harvest. But the sun departing so unobtrusively had risen in splendor that morning. The god's golden face had looked upon an altar then, and smiled upon the man who spread himself upon it unassisted. Chief Ucita had smiled, too, when the priest bearing the ceremonial dagger lifted his arm and began the incantation that offered up Ucita's spirit as an act of atonement, and his blood to ensure the bounty of good harvest. With his dying, Chief Ucita had won the admiration of all those who witnessed it; his spirit had been borne out of this world on the tide of their respect.

Now the time had almost come to hold back the night with the new-kindled fire of a New Year, and Egret summoned the children to lead them in the story-song she had taught them.

They stood around her, their little faces solemn as she put her flute to her mouth, piped a spill of sound, and signaled them to begin.

> "Once there was only the sky
> with cloud-islands where spirits lived."

The children chanted in unison. Egret smiled encouragingly.

> "Sun and Moon and Rain,
> Wind and Thunder, too.
> And then the Calusa were made."

As she had told them to do, they raised their voices at the end of the verse, then lowered them for the next one:

> "Rain and Thunder and Wind,
> created a sea far below.
> Sun and Moon agreed
> islands must be built
> to give the Calusa a home."

Now they waited while she imitated the cadence of their voices with her flute. When she had finished, they started to sing again:

> "Turtle shaped one out of mud
> but it quickly dwindled away.
> Sea Gull and Fishhawk
> flew down with a cloud
> but Deer proved that this was too soft."

One of the boys faltered, then rushed to catch up with his companions. Laughter rippled through the crowd, sympathetic laughter that was over before the children began the final verse:

> "Only the Dolphin was wise.
> He brought up both seashells and mud;
> he made an island
> fit for Calusa.
> We honor him still, and he smiles."

Watchful Doe was the first parent to rush forward and embrace Egret after the children had been praised for their performance. "It was a fine idea, to have the children sing," she told her, her eyes resting fondly on her son. "I hope you will teach them other songs, so they can sing whenever there is any kind of ceremony."

"That will be up to Calusa," Dancing Egret said, and both turned to look toward the Headchief, who had come forward to congratulate the boys and girls. His delighted expression suggested that he would not be averse to the idea.

"Crested Heron will be too excited to sleep tonight," Watchful Doe said. "He looked so proud when he came and told me he and his friends would be singing at our ceremony, but that was nothing compared to what he is feeling now."

The boy was running toward his mother, and even in the gloom his face glowed. "My father said I sang well," he said. "Did you hear him say it, Mother? Did you, Dancing Egret?"

"We both heard," Egret said, "and he spoke truly. You did sing well, all of you. My song has never sounded better."

Crested Heron's face fell a little. "I thought *we* were the very first to sing it," he said.

"You were the first children to sing it so beautifully," Egret said quickly. Over the top of his head she saw Vision Seeker and his helpers walking toward the pyre the warriors had built at the foot of the Temple mound. "It's time for the fire-lighting now," she added, and took one of his hands while Watchful Doe took the other. The three moved into the circle the rest of the people were forming and gave all their attention to the priest.

Vision Seeker, holding sacred tobacco in his cupped hands, murmured an invocation as an acolyte inserted a ceremonial fire-stick into the hole bored in a decorated plank, a prayer that cleverly shaped itself to the rapid twirling of the fire starter's fingers. He ended it with a *"Hah!"* as sparks began to flicker and a second acolyte thrust a bit of dried moss among them. When the moss was smoldering nicely, the youth presented it to the priest, who laid it beneath the kindling at the foot of the pyre.

The people stood in silence while Vision Seeker tossed tobacco on the New Fire and begged the gods to favor the Calusa until the next First Harvest. By then, heartening flames were ascending into the night sky, while scented smoke purified the island and its inhabitants, and it was time for the communal dancing that was the joyful conclusion to all such occasions.

Much as she enjoyed dancing, Egret slipped away from the Temple plaza then. White Gull, widowed only that morning, had been sitting alone in their father's house ever since; it did not seem fair that she should be by herself any longer. So Egret used a canoe to cross the canal that separated the Temple mound from the domiciliary one, and went to comfort her sister.

Egret's efforts were not so much in vain as they were made mock of. "How can a woman who has never been wife be a widow?" White Gull demanded. "I will not mourn a man who was incapable of being a husband to me."

"But you lived with Ucita for nearly ten years!" Egret was unable to conceal her shock. "Do you mean that he never once—"

"Not even once!" White Gull snapped. "He treated me like daughter, not wife, yet—despite what she did to him—all his fatherly love was for Kneeling Cypress. So I had nothing from Ucita save misery and aggravation. I do not need comforting, Egret, so go back and take part in the dancing. I would come with you if I dared, but our father would only rage at me and send me away. My youthful years were stolen from me, but you might as well make the most of yours. While they last."

Egret put up only token resistance to leaving her sister. White Gull's final words had been a warning, she knew; it would not be long before Headchief Calusa found a husband for Dancing Egret, and there was no way of telling who this would be. Out of the night, which wore no moon or stars to alleviate the dark, came words Kneeling Cypress had spoken years before: *I can wish nothing better for you than to wed the man of your choosing.* She had said that during the early days of her own marriage, and her face had been radiant with happiness. For a while, at least, Cypress had loved and been loved. Would Egret, like White Gull, be denied the opportunity to experience such bliss?

Although the night air was oppressively hot, Egret shivered as she launched the dugout again and made her way back to the Temple squareground. Drums were throbbing and shuffling circles contracted and expanded as boys and girls made room for grinning grandparents, or young warriors enticed giggling maidens to leave the women's circle and join theirs. Where feet had caressed the hard-packed earth at the start of the evening, now they stomped upon it. Soon smaller circles, composed of paired warriors and maidens, would form within the larger ones and the drumbeats would accelerate until those separate groups, revolving independently, were spinning with such frenzy that dizziness overcame the dancers. Members of collapsing circles were expected to rejoin the larger circles that had kept to a more stately pace. And so it would go on until only one group of warriors and maidens remained to proudly receive the praise of those they had outlasted.

Brown Pelican spotted Egret as the unwieldy circle she was a part of began to move sunwise around the pyre. She pulled her sister into the circle and danced in place until Egret's feet were moving in time with the others. A shatter of thunder tried to drown out the drummers, but no one even looked up. Egret told herself that she would ignore her gloomy thoughts the same way everyone else was ignoring the coming storm. She closed her eyes, smiled as she lost herself in the passion of the dance.

Someone else grabbed for her, and her eyes flew open, fastened on Shore Walker's face. He tugged again and, laughing freely now, she let herself be pulled into the warrior's circle. When two other warriors and the maidens they had chosen broke out of it to make their own inner circle, Shore Walker's glance was enough to persuade Egret that they should join them. Spinning with abandon, she threw back her head and watched the black sky reeling, told herself she would not get dizzy, that she and Shore Walker and his friends would dance, dance, dance, until even the drummers conceded defeat.

Lightning split the sky, and before its eerie afterimage could fade, Thunder Master hurled more spears after it. Faster and faster he threw them, roaring a challenge as he did so. Wind Maker was quick to respond. He stirred the sultry air with his mighty club, and Egret's skirt whipped around her legs. Sand and bits of dried leaves flew up and began their own peculiar dance.

Mothers and grandmothers were snatching up children and hurrying them toward the boats lining the canal bank; elders retreated more slowly, shaking their heads in dismay that the dancing must end so precipitately; a few of the maidens squealed dramatically at the next flash of lightning, and their warrior companions escorted them gallantly to waiting canoes.

Egret noticed all of this peripherally. The drummers were still pounding away, and the couples left in the squareground were determined to go on circling the fire as long as it blazed. Thunder and lightning? They only added excitement to the dance!

But Rain Chief would not be denied his moment of glory, the opportunity to remind these mortals that, just as death conquers life, water can always vanquish fire. Suddenly the rain cascaded down, silvering the night and pelting the young people who had dared to defy their aquarian god. Within seconds the pyre had been reduced to smoldering faggots and sopping ash.

Egret shook out her dripping hair as Shore Walker upended the canoe that had brought them back to the residential part of Calusa's town. "It was fun, dancing in the rain," she said. "And I feel cool now, truly cool. I'll sleep well, I think."

Shore Walker smiled down at her. Water trickled from his hair, too, and from the bandage Vision Seeker had only yesterday fastened around his healing wound. "I enjoyed it as much as you did," he said. "I just wish we could have danced longer; I had hoped to be with you until dawn this night."

Egret dropped her eyes. It would be better for her composure if Shore Walker occasionally refrained from letting his thoughts show in his face. "Should the rain continue," she said quickly, "there might not be a dawn tomorrow. Not a proper one, anyway."

He laughed softly. "All the better," he said. "We should never have known when to come home without a sunrise to warn us." He reached out and put one hand beneath her chin, tilted it so that she had to look at him again. "Would you have minded that very much, Dancing Egret?"

She shook her head, moving it against the warmth of his fingers. "I think I would have been glad," she whispered.

Then she, who had never before been troubled by shyness, discovered that it had been lying in wait for her all along. "I must go in now," she muttered, and backing away from him, fled to the house at the top of the mound.

The flesh beneath her chin, where Shore Walker's hand had rested, did not cool until long after she had fallen asleep.

Calusa surveyed the pelts spread across a lower bench, the baskets of beans and berries, zamia flour and smoked bear meat, the strings of dried plums and grapes that slaves were looping from the rafters in the storage area of his house. "Considering the severity of the dry season this past year, the tribute is commendable," he told his clan leaders. He leaned forward and poked at the collection of gold and silver ornaments certain coastal townchiefs had sent in lieu of foodstuffs or skins. "What came from Tequesta was not enough to make up for the whale meat he generally gives, however," he said, frowning slightly. "Surely a long dry season does not lead to a scarcity of whales in the ocean?"

The leader of the Kingfisher clan wrinkled his own forehead. "I cannot see that it would," he said. His voice was so resonant that it interfered with the lively conversation of the women clustered at the far end of the room, but Calusa's Chief Speaker had trained himself to put force behind his words, and never even noticed when he did so inappropriately.

"His is a gift of courtesy, though, and should not be subject to the laws of tribute." This from Twisting River of the Conch clan. He, too, was frowning, but his frown indicated concern rather than censure. It might lead to unpleasantness if Calusa were encouraged to think that Tequesta meant insult by the paucity of his gift.

"Any gift to Great Calusa should be in keeping with his status," Shark Fin snapped. The leg wound that had prematurely ended his days as warrior had left the leader of the Seagull clan with a reservoir of unvented spleen. "Tequesta knows that! And he needs to remember that his men are allowed to hunt freely throughout the river glades, even though most of the land is Calusa territory. I say we should teach him how to be properly grateful."

Mask Maker, representing the Cormorant clan, said nothing, nor did the delegate from the Alligator clan. Both were older men, and rarely spoke without first taking the time for prolonged thought.

The Headchief held up a brooch of Spanish gold encrusted with colored stones. "He has sent me ornaments that enchant the eye, however," he mused. He tossed the bauble back into the basket; he would have Trailing Vine sew it onto his second-best cloak later. "I will consider what all of you have said," he went on, turning back to his counselors. "Before making any decision, I mean to have my trader Kwambu investigate conditions on the eastern shore. He will spend time with Tequesta before he goes on to the towns that lie between there and Oathkaqua's province. He will also visit Oathkaqua. The man may be Timucuan, but he has always been a friend to us and feels greater kinship with other coastal chiefs than he does with many of the leaders within his own tribe. When

Kwambu returns, we will learn the extent of drought damage in the east. For now, we have other matters to discuss. Although most of the Christian soldiers left my province, some remained behind. Prowling Panther reports that they seem to be settling in to the town Ucita abandoned. They have even built around it a log fence similar to those the Timucua put up to protect their villages."

"This is indeed a matter requiring discussion," the Chief Speaker echoed sonorously. "The Council must consider the matter of the Spanish settlement before we talk of anything else."

Calusa's advisors settled into their accustomed seats and waited courteously for their Headchief to speak further.

Kwambu, who had been lingering a little distance away in hopes of having a word with Calusa, sighed and walked silently out of the house. Although the Headchief had given no sign that he was aware of Kwambu's presence, it was certain that he'd intended his words to be overheard by him. It had been a mistake to let Calusa see how anxious he was to return to Outina, Kwambu reflected. Now it would be a long time before he was sent north again, a long time before he could discover whether or not Outina's town had lain in the path the Spanish soldiers had taken.

Hernando de Soto rolled up the parchment his secretary had been writing on, tapped it against the palm of his other hand.

"It is a marvel that we were able to complete your report," the secretary said as he bundled ink and goose quills and fastened them securely to his belt. "The din is incredible."

"It is a matter of discipline, to be able to concentrate on business without regard to what goes on around you," the governor said. But he was scowling. "There is no need for so much noise, however," He turned to the captain of the sixty halberdiers that formed his personal guard. "I would have it quieter. Now!"

The Captain of the Guard saluted, and promptly took steps to make the governor's wishes known throughout the camp.

"It will not be easy to still the cursing and grumbling," Baltasar de Gallegos told De Soto. "Even the seasoned soldiers are disgruntled; they see no purpose in setting up a new camp every other day. As for the women and the servants"—he shrugged—"ever since your steward died, when we traveled across that plain where the sun burned as fiercely at dawn as it did at midday, they have been looking for signs of illness in themselves."

"My steward died of thirst," De Soto said, refusing to permit the doubt in his own mind to reach maturity. He had told no one of the red spots that had marked the flesh of the youth, and had made sure Indian slaves wrapped the body securely before its burial. "He was fool enough to guzzle his ration early in the morning, then stumble on through the heat with no water to drink. As for the men being unhappy about moving so slowly toward Outina, it is not their place to see purpose in anything, but only to obey orders."

He looked behind him to where half-a-hundred cavalrymen were saddling their horses while dog handlers chained snarling war hounds together. The mutts the provisioner had seized in Chief Ocale's territory circled the pack, yipping and yapping, or rashly nipped at the heels of restless mounts. Servants rushed about obeying their masters' shouted injunctions and mules brayed in protest as their backs bent beneath too-heavy loads. The inevitable camp followers talked shrilly among themselves as they swung sacks of belongings over their shoulders and fell in behind the foot soldiers; they were sorry now that they had not elected to remain in the fledgling colony on the coast. De Soto had seen to it that enough Indian women were taken from each town along the way to pleasure all of his men, and a fascination with the unusual had left the Spanish women virtually abandoned by their former patrons.

Only the slaves had grown quiet since the halberdiers passed the word that the governor was displeased with so much noise. They knew better than to ignore De Soto's commands; the dogs were always hungry, and rejoiced to feed on human flesh. The Indian prisoners made no sound, either, but then they never did. It discomforted the governor from time to time, this unnatural stillness of theirs. Even the chief of Caliquen and his young daughter rarely spoke, and *they* were not in chains. Their sullen silence was the sort De Soto had sometimes observed in wild animals that had been caged. In truth, the savages were much like animals; they even smelled like them, something that was only partially explained by their revolting habit of smearing themselves with bear grease. Juan Ortiz maintained that they used the stinking stuff as protection against insect bites, pointing out that mosquitoes invariably found Spanish flesh preferable to Indian flesh. De Soto snorted; that was only because, even to a bug, noble blood must surely be richer and more satisfying than that which flowed through the veins of inferior beings.

"Attitudes will probably improve once there is treasure to fatten empty pockets," De Soto's secretary offered. "Which should happen when we reach this Apalachee province we keep hearing about. Both Chief Mocoso and his brother-in-law said that there is much gold there."

"Let us not forget what Juan Ortiz vows he heard two native chiefs say to one another, however," Gallegos cautioned in a rumble. "It may be that Narvaez found no gold in Apalachee because—despite what we have been told—there is none to be had there."

De Soto raised his eyebrows. "The heathen of this land lie as easily as they breathe. Which leaves me suspicious of everyone, including those who insist there is no treasure in the country we are marching through; the Indians are hiding it from us, I am certain, which is why we are pushing on to Outina. I am especially suspicious of a man who daily sends emissaries to warn me away from his borders. Even the fact that I hold hostage his brother and his niece does not prevent Outina from vowing to bake half of us and boil the rest!" There was derision in De Soto's ordinarily lugubrious face; such infantile rantings could hardly be regarded as proper threats. Of course, these Indians *were* children in many ways. The priests were right: they sorely needed Mother Church to guide their lives. They would have Her, too, in exchange for the precious metals whose value such a backward people could not possibly appreciate.

He swirled his red cloak over his shoulders and mounted the prancing gray steed a hostler brought to him. Eyes passing indifferently over the litter of cornhusks and gnawed bones that lay around the drowned campfire, the odds and ends of grubby clothing and bent metal utensils many had decided to leave behind, and heaps of animal dung studded with buzzing flies, De Soto pointed the stallion's aristocratic nose toward the north. Raising one gauntleted hand, he signaled to the musicians at the front of the procession. "We go forward," he said as the trumpets blared. "One more encampment, and we will have convinced the Indians that this is the unvarying tempo of our march. Then we will move with all speed to Outina."

Chapter 18

⊷ ⊷

Holata Outina looked toward the young Spaniard who sat between him and Hernando de Soto. "Tell your chief that my brother and his daughter were grateful for the gifts he gave them before they began their journey home." Outina had no idea what use Caliquen could possibly find for white man's clothes, and strands of colored beads and a shiny rectangle in which she could see her face could never erase from the girl's mind the memory of being dragged from her home by rough-handed soldiers. And where was compensation for fields stripped of corn and pumpkins, for storehouses virtually emptied of foodstuffs being saved for the winter? Still, it was the courteous thing to say, and Outina was determined to be courteous. For now.

Juan Ortiz relayed the message.

"The words must be bile in his mouth," De Soto said to Ortiz. "I am certain the taste was far more pleasing when he was threatening to have the earth open up and swallow me, or to send birds to drop venom from their beaks upon my expedition." Outina's final message, arriving just as the governor was preparing for a full-scale assault on the town, had been quite the opposite of a threat, however; it had been an invitation for the Christians to visit him. Satisfaction at having made the Indian leader capitulate had outweighed De Soto's disappointment by only a little.

Ortiz kept his expression bland. "Governor De Soto thanks you for having been so exemplary a host this week," he said smoothly.

Outina inclined his head. The young Spaniard lied; both of them lied. And so did Outina. He suppressed a sigh. He wished Walks Tall Woman could be here. She had a talent for

putting words together and would have been able to help him
think of something that, while true in itself, would still have
misled the Spanish leader. Then there would have been no
need for him to soil his tongue with falsehood.

He studied De Soto. An honest enemy would be easier to
deal with; Potano for instance, or Holata Saturiba. Outina need
not have sent elders and women and children to stay with his
cousin had either of them been his guest. Even Timucuan
chiefs who were sworn enemies of one another could be
trusted not to breach the laws of hospitality.

He looked toward Juan Ortiz. "On the day Holata De Soto
accepted my invitation to come here, I arranged for a splendid
meal to be served in his honor. Please say that the feast will
take place tomorrow, and that all of my forty Townchiefs are
sending emissaries with gifts for him."

Ortiz turned to the governor and translated.

"I was confident that forcing Outina to receive me would
make lesser chiefs rush to placate me," De Soto said, "but let
us hope their emissaries are bringing food with them. God
knows, there is not enough left here to prepare an ascetic's
meal, let alone a feast." The hearty appetites of his men, and
his provisioner's seizure of any foodstuffs deemed portable,
had seen to that.

"The governor hopes your generosity will not rob you and
your people of food you may need for yourselves," Ortiz said
to Outina.

"My men will be hunting today," Outina replied, "and my
nearest subchief is sending bearers with flour for bread-
making. I have suggested that grass be brought also, for your
horses to eat, since the open fields around here have been
stripped bare." He did not reveal, by word or gesture, his anger
when he had seen soldiers leading the beasts into the planting
fields to feed upon the new growth there. He would have his
revenge, for that and for everything else. When the time came.

De Soto scowled. "His men may go hunting only if an equal
number of my soldiers go with them. These Indians are perfidious devils; left to themselves, they might sneak back and attack us."

"The governor would like his men to observe your hunting
methods," Ortiz said to Outina.

Outina nodded. Let the Spanish go along. They lumbered
through the forest like bears grown old and crippled; certain
warriors he knew would have no difficulty eluding them in or-

der to carry messages to the Holatas Outina wanted them to reach.

De Soto stood up. "I will have my men make ready," he said, and waited while Ortiz translated before going to find Tobar. He would put Nuno in charge of the hunting detail. Then, when they began making their plans to head northwest, Tobar would be able to tell him which of Outina's warriors were the strongest and most agile. Some of the mules were showing signs of exhaustion; the savages Nuno recommended could be chained and made to act as substitute beasts of burden on the journey to Apalachee.

Juan Ortiz tried to conceal his contempt as he listened to the Indian interpreters who had sought him out. A cavalier would endure the most excruciating torture and never betray his fellows, but these heathen ... merely the prospect of punishment was enough to transform them into traitors.

"It is true," the young warrior from Ocale's province was saying. "Holata Outina means to group his warriors in the open space in the forest north of town. He will ask your chief to go there with him to choose those he wants to take along as guides when he leaves here. The warriors' weapons will be concealed in the tall grass and behind bushes, and when your chief goes among them, he will be seized. Any soldiers he has with him will be slain."

"At the same time," put in the man whose brother had had his head cut off when his clumsiness slowed the rest of the bearers during the march from Potano's province, "other warriors, pretending to be servants carrying firewood and water, will kill any soldiers left in the town."

"I cannot think where you heard such foolish talk," Ortiz said, making a convincing display of skepticism.

"We heard it from Holata Outina himself," said Ocale's warrior. "He wants us to help his men. In return, he has promised to send us home to our families."

Juan Ortiz studied the man. This one had fought against being taken along by De Soto until a knife had been put to his old grandfather's throat. He'd been docile enough after that. "You have no faith in his promise?"

The savage hesitated. "Perhaps," he said reluctantly. "But you have more fighting men, and your weapons are more deadly. Holata Outina's plan cannot possibly succeed."

So you are protecting yourself against its certain failure,

Ortiz thought scornfully. "You are certain about what you say?" he asked. But he no longer doubted them; this explained why there were only men in the town, something that had been bothering both the governor and Ortiz.

The two nodded vigorously.

"Then I will speak with the governor, and at once. Meanwhile, you will say nothing about what you have told me. You understand?"

The informers looked at each other. Who would they tell? Their comrades, who meant to go along with Holata Outina's wild scheme, must never learn who had betrayed it to the Spanish, and Ortiz was the only one among the Christian soldiers who could understand the Timucuan language.

They were relieved to be dismissed, and went in different ways as soon as they were in the open. Not even between themselves would they talk of what tomorrow might bring!

Outina, his Principal Men standing around him, made himself smile at Hernando de Soto. "As you see," he said, indicating the topknotted men massed on one side of the spacious glade, "I have many, many warriors. I can easily spare some to guide you to Apalachee." It had worried Outina at first, to see how Spanish soldiers had arrayed themselves on the other side of the clearing and how soldiers on horseback made a living fence between the foot soldiers and his warriors, but he had told himself that his men were surely capable of dealing with even this metal-clad army.

De Soto, too, was escorted, by half of his personal guard. The rest stood among the soldiers ranked on the left side of the field they were surveying. Close-growing trees rose behind them, but the men in the rear had been told to face backward; that way, no savages would be able to burst out of the forest and fall upon the Spanish. "Tell Outina," he said to Ortiz, "that both of us may be proud of our fighting men."

While Juan Ortiz translated, his eyes moved appraisingly over the congregation of savages, noting particularly those who stood nearest to the man supposedly brought here to review them. If the attack Outina planned should somehow take place, the warriors best able to reach De Soto would be the ones who attempted to seize him. Ortiz's gaze rested thoughtfully on two lakes, one large, one small, that lay a little distance behind the heathen warriors.

"Those lagoons look deep," Baltasar de Gallegos said quietly, "and our cavalry is in good position. As soon as the trumpet sounds, they can drive into the water any Indians they do not kill. Later, we can seize at leisure those who do not drown outright."

He and Nuno de Tobar, mounted on horses trained to be patient until hands tightened on the reins, were directly behind Ortiz, who nodded appreciation of the strategy Gallegos had decided upon.

Outina turned to De Soto, gestured toward the Spanish cavalry. "Your horses enjoyed the abundance of fine meadow grass my subchiefs brought for them?" In truth, the bundles contained more than hay; they had bristled with spears and with bows and arrows. Of course, these had been safely stashed before the fodder was turned over to the hostlers.

Ortiz, translating De Soto's reply, saw the governor lift his right hand and tug at his beard. As he did so, a musician standing in the second rank of soldiers put his trumpet to his lips and blew a single piercing note.

Three of De Soto's men flung themselves upon Holata Outina and wrestled him to the ground. Simultaneously, his personal guard surrounded Outina's Principal Men. Tobar and Gallegos spurred their horses forward, separated on the gallop, and led two columns of cavalry thundering toward the savages, who somehow managed to retrieve their weapons before scattering in all directions. Neatly dodging swinging swords and pounding hoofs, they were nocking arrows and firing repeatedly at the Spanish troops. The mingled shrieks of wounded animals and stricken men proved that Timucuans need not stand still to aim accurately. Other warriors burst out of the forest, zigzagging as they came to avoid making themselves easy targets for the soldiers' rear guard. Some succeeded; others fell before they could manage even single swipes of the clubs and axes they brandished.

Ortiz and De Soto were mounted now, but as the interpreter made ready to follow his governor into the thick of the fighting, Bold in Battle flung aside the body of the guardsman he had knifed and grabbed his bow. The four arrows he released in rapid succession struck the knees of De Soto's gray stallion; the next four, released as the beast collapsed, buried themselves in its chest.

As the governor shouted for a fresh mount, Ortiz swung his horse around and rode straight for Outina's Paracusi, sword thrust out in front of him. The blade was deflected by a mighty blow from the War Leader's club, and Ortiz swayed in the saddle as he angled away. Bold in Battle did not wait to see if the Spaniard meant to return and resume their fight; instead he dashed to his right to try and reach his fallen chief. His club rose and fell, rose and fell, and his knife blade flashed in the sun, but the halberdiers fighting to subdue Outina's Principal Men blocked his way. Bold in Battle veered, ran out onto a meadow already littered with wounded and slippery with blood. "First destroy their horses!" he shouted when he was close enough for his warriors to hear him. Immediately, arrows surged from bows like wasps from a nest, and more than a few found their mark.

Outina, blood pouring from a gash in his forearm and a lump rising behind his right ear, had been trussed hand and foot by his assailants. Guards stood around him, but between their booted legs he could see into the glade that was to have been the scene of a far different battle, one in which the Timucuan warriors overcame the Spanish Christians, one in which the man called De Soto, and not Outina, lay sprawled in an ignoble heap on the ground.

He moved his head a little, dislodging a column of ants that was exploring the corner of his eye, but was able to see only a confusion of feet and legs, some human, others belonging to the huge beasts who trampled the wounded and dead while their riders urged them in pursuit of those warriors still able to fight. And they were fighting still, his men, fighting fearlessly and well. Many of the fallen wore garments made of metal. The heads of some had been crushed by Timucuan clubs; others had arrows protruding from neck or thigh. All, like Outina, lay in puddles of their own blood.

The curses, the moans, the ululating cries that decorated the afternoon like the calls of improbable birds, confirmed that the battle was not yet over, but Outina would not let himself be deluded. Too many of the casualties were warriors. The only thing that cheered him was the sound of repeated splashing from the direction of the lakes on the sunrise side of the clearing. If the soldiers were not flinging the dead into the water—and this seemed unlikely—then Outina's beleaguered warriors were jumping in to escape the persistent Spanish. And these were men who could swim as though they had been born with tails and fins.

Perhaps all was not lost after all, Outina thought. Perhaps

this battle only marked the beginning of a war, a war his people still had a chance of winning.

"Have the rest of the savages come out of the lagoon?" Hernando de Soto barked the question. Yesterday had been a long day; it had been midnight before his interpreters, endlessly repeating the governor's promises of clemency, had been able to persuade a handful of Outina's warriors to emerge from the lakes in which they had found sanctuary of a sort. Defying the hundreds of missiles directed into the lakes by guns and crossbows, they had made sporadic use of the bows and arrows they had taken into the water with them. Those who had swum into the center of the large lagoon, where the water was deep indeed, had actually stood on the shoulders of willing comrades in order to shoot at the Spanish!

"The smaller lake, the more shallow one, is empty," Baltasar de Gallegos reported, "and they are leaving the bigger one in droves now. Nearly two hundred have swum to shore since dawn, and they are in sorry shape, I assure you."

"Are any still in the water?" De Soto asked impatiently.

"A half dozen or so only," Nuno de Tobar said.

"According to Ortiz," Gallegos put in, "most of them are the chief's advisors. One is leader of his warriors as well. Such men would naturally be suspicious of your promises, Excellency."

De Soto looked toward the far end of a vast hall that had doors set at each of the four compass points. There, in the largest of the numerous apartments built against the walls, Holata Outina was being held. Should he send the guards for him, and make the chief himself speak with the recalcitrants? No; enough time had already been wasted. He turned to Gallegos. "Send into the lagoon twelve soldiers who are strong swimmers," he told him, "and tell them to take swords or knives along. If possible, they are to force the bastards onto land. If not, they are to kill them. Let the water these pagans love so dearly serve as their common grave."

"But in truth you mean to slay them anyway, do you not?" Tobar asked when the burly man had gone out. "We lost a fair number of men to those savages yesterday, and you lost your prized gray as well. Since we cannot determine who among them was responsible for these deaths, surely you will punish all of them?"

The governor smiled. "I am a man of my word, Nuno," he

said softly. "I will spare their lives. But it is equally true that punishment must be meted out. And it will be. It will be." He snapped his fingers to summon his secretary to him. "Prepare a parchment and sharpen your quills," he told him. "Soon the Indians that remain alive will be brought to this house. I want you to record my disposition of them."

It did not happen as quickly as he'd hoped, but by the time he had sent for interpreters and arranged for Holata Outina to be brought out of confinement, his soldiers were herding scores of naked savages through the quartet of doors and forcing them to stand in more or less orderly rows. At a signal from the governor, Gallegos led to the forefront Outina's Principal Men, those who had finally been hauled from the lake they had sought refuge in. There proved to be seven of them, and three were old enough to earn De Soto's grudging respect for their stubborn courage. Their skin was waterlogged and wrinkled, and the occasional involuntary shiver said that they were suffering the effects of their ordeal.

"Give the old ones blankets or cloaks to wrap themselves in," he said to Juan Ortiz. But when these were offered, they were refused.

"They say they continue to prefer death to dishonor, that they did not leave the lagoon by choice and would have died there rather than surrender," Ortiz said to De Soto.

"Then they are fools," the governor said.

Beside him, Outina smiled slightly. His eyes lingered on each of his Principal Men, and the seven recognized the commendation in his gaze and stood proud in the warmth of it. When Outina glanced toward Bold in Battle, the Paracusi nodded almost imperceptibly; their defiance had not ended, and would not.

"Tell the savages," De Soto ordered the interpreter, "that I will keep my vow. None will be put to death for what they did. Or tried to do. The chief's advisors will, like him, be kept under house arrest until we leave here. The rest"—he shrugged his shoulders—"well, they can hardly expect to escape just punishment, and Outina can scarcely hope to have his army around him again, inept though it be. Each warrior will be given to one of His Majesty's soldiers as a slave. The cavaliers may choose first, of course, but there are enough to go around, I believe."

There was no sound, not even an indrawing of breath, when Juan Ortiz made the pronouncement. Not even the fitting of iron collars around Timucuan necks or the fastening of chains on wrists and ankles brought any sort of protest. And if the Indian interpreters, or the guides De Soto had impressed as the expedition passed through the various provinces, were moved to sympathy by the plight of the men of Outina, they did not show it. Indeed, the youngsters from Caliquen, who were being trained as fetchers and carriers by the soldiers, or had been kept to service those who preferred to share their beds with boys rather than women, were chattering together and laughing now and then as the new-made slaves were led away.

"They are like animals," the governor said to his secretary, who knew better than to record this statement. "Now that they are fettered, they will give us no trouble."

Holata Outina did not know what De Soto had said to the man who was making strange marks on the barklike stuff these Spanish were forever busy with. Nor did he care. The clanking of chains cut into his soul with the agony of dull knives sawing at tender flesh. Someday the Spanish Christians would pay for what they were doing here this morning. If the gods could be persuaded to take a hand, perhaps someday might come sooner rather than later.

Chapter 19

⊷ ⊷

It was Bold in Battle who suggested asking the youngsters from Caliquen to deliver Outina's message to his enslaved warriors. "The Spanish let them move around freely. After all, what harm can mere children do? And the boys made it a point to jeer at the chains our warriors wear, which makes De Soto believe—wrongly!—that they care nothing for what has happened in this town. Lately he has been assigning them to carry food to the warriors. When the men are allowed to eat, that is. Which is seldom." The Paracusi's face, as markedly handsome as his daughter's had once been beautiful, reflected his anguish. Those who went in chains and were kept half starved were men who had trusted in their leader; he felt responsible for the sorry state they had come to.

Holata Outina nodded and resumed making fists with his left hand to reassure himself that his wounded arm had lost none of its mobility. "But our warriors have been bound in such a way that only limited movement is available to them. Will it be enough, I wonder?"

Bold in Battle nodded. "Their hunger for revenge will give them all the agility they need," he predicted.

"This is so." The confirmation came from the oldest of Outina's Principal Men, a man who had been a warrior to contend with before the weight of years slowed his reflexes. "But the instructions you give to the boys must be contained in a dozen words or less, Holata. Always the interpreters"—he took a moment to spit out the aftertaste of the vile word; they all knew now who had betrayed them to the Spanish—"hover around us when our meals are served. What you say must sound like an expression of thanks only, or their suspicions will be aroused."

The warning made sense. Indeed, this was the first time that the town's leaders, those who had been placed under what De Soto termed "house arrest," had been able to talk freely together. But today De Soto had ordered even the interpreters to begin building long trestle tables for a victory feast, and to oversee the slaves who were harvesting crops that ought to have remained unpicked for several weeks yet. Clearly, he meant his celebration to be impressive. Equally, clearly, he meant to leave Outina's town raped of sustenance when he departed.

Learning about the celebration had spawned the idea of an uprising, for Outina and his Principal Men had been invited to sit with the Spanish during the feasting. *I am a generous man*, the governor had said. *You will have the opportunity to sample good Spanish cooking before we go on to Apalachee.* The smile he wore during this announcement confirmed Outina's suspicions that the meal would consume all that remained of the town's food supply.

"We have four days," Holata Outina said slowly. "If I alert the boys when they bring our food today, then give them the actual message tomorrow—and I will make it brief—perhaps the interpreters will be fooled into thinking I am only offering thanks to our servers."

Bold in Battle managed a laugh. "It is good that you have never failed to say thank you for any service. The spies will be unsuspicious."

Outina nodded gravely. "Let us hope so," he said. "Everything depends on our warriors being notified in time. Everything."

The chief and his Principal Men had seated themselves cautiously on the tall wooden stools ranged alongside tables heaped with food. Between each of them sat one of the governor's own principal men. De Soto, as he had pledged to do, sat beside Holata Outina at the head of the table, which greatly relieved the Timucua. If he had not, the plans Outina and his Paracusi had crafted so carefully would have been doomed from the start.

Bold in Battle, flanked by Nuno de Tobar and Baltasar de Gallegos, avoided looking at Outina. He did permit himself to peer at the sky, however; the sun was approaching its zenith. He smiled slightly, and chewed absently at a piece of deer meat.

The feast was being held in the open space in front of Outina's house, as had been arranged, for the governor had thought it might be amusing to have Outina witness the chained warriors waiting upon their new masters. He had expected the chief to be discomforted by the sight of them fetching beakers of wine from the kegs the provisioner had set out, and getting cuffed by the Spanish if they were not quick about it; but the man's face remained impassive even when one warrior was knocked off his feet by a blow delivered by that hothead, Tobar.

De Soto took out his handkerchief and wiped perspiration from his face. Perhaps they should have moved the tables into the hall; it was too hot out here for a man to enjoy his food properly. And it looked as though food would be all the enjoyment he could count on today.

The sun burned even hotter as it moved to stand directly overhead. In that moment, Holata Outina put down the bread he had just picked up. Slowly, deliberately, he allowed himself a final sip of sassafras tea. Then, rising so abruptly that De Soto dropped the beaker he had been raising to his lips, Outina gave a mighty shout. With one hand he seized the governor by the back of his coat and jerked him from his seat. His other hand clenched into a fist, and he drove it straight into De Soto's mouth.

Before the unconscious governor could hit the ground, halberdiers swooped upon his assailant. As a dozen spikes pierced Outina's chest and abdomen, one guard reversed his weapon; with its axelike blade, he split the skull of a man already dead.

Bold in Battle and the rest of the Principal Men had leaped up when Outina did, each attacking the Spaniard sitting on his right. At the same time, the warriors-made-slaves responded to the message they'd received from their chief. Despite their chains, they managed to grab heavy crocks from the table, blazing faggots from the cooking fires, the stools they had been forced to help construct. Whooping and shrieking, they fell upon the soldiers they had been given to by De Soto.

Outina's Paracusi, struggling with Gallegos, fumbled for the pot of bubbling beans a servant had recently placed on the table. He hefted it, poured the boiling mess over the man's head, then butted him in the belly. When Gallegos fell, Bold in Battle swung around and used the metal pot to bash the nose of a soldier whose knife was poised to plunge into the War Leader's back. The Spaniard tumbled backward onto the trestle table; the table teetered, tipped, and went over, splintering as it fell. Bold in Battle snatched a jagged-edged plank in one hand, took the fallen soldier's blade in the other, paused to take stock of the situation. Excited mongrels were darting through a network of flying feet, their shrill yelps a counterpoint to the baying of warhounds surging against their restraints; from human mouths, screeches of triumph alternated with death cries; and the clatter of iron pots being knocked from tripods was punctuated by intermittent bursts from Spanish matchlocks. Bleeding men lay in puddles of spilled food; others, their hair and clothing aflame, were crawling out of the fire pits they had been shoved into. Although many of them were warriors, many were not. Pride filled Bold in Battle's soul to know that the men he had trained had fought so magnificently.

And the fight was not over. Outina may have been slain, but his people would not let themselves lose heart. Even the youngsters from Caliquen, whose cooperation had made this revolt possible, were throwing themselves into the fray. They had collected rocks and boulders, and were heaving them with commendable accuracy at Spanish heads. One of Bold in Battle's warriors, chains clanking almost insolently, was scrambling to the top of a corncrib as he flourished a lance belonging to the Spaniard he had just killed. Soldiers with arquebuses rushed in his wake and made ready to shoot him down. But the warrior lay about him with the lance, slicing into three before the rest backed off. The remaining soldiers knelt at a safe distance and took aim, and the warrior flung the lance just as they fired in unison. He took one of his slayers with him into death.

Bold in Battle sent a silent salute to the warrior's brave spirit, then charged a trio of halberdiers who were rounding up wounded warriors and chaining them together. He meant to avenge his chief's death tenfold, and if he could rescue some of his own men while doing so, all the better! Swinging the heavy plank as though it were a club, he felled two of the governor's guardsmen, stooped to run under the third man's menacing halberd. But as the War Leader lunged with the knife he'd appropriated, the soldier brought his weapon down with all the power he could command. Bold in Battle, blood spewing as the muscles in his right shoulder were severed, descended into darkness.

When he came to, he knew before he opened his eyes that the fighting was over, knew also that the Spaniards had won again. Although the air was still thick with the smell of blood, none of it was new-shed; although the rattle of weapons still rang in his ears, it was the sound of metal swords being honed and resheathed.

He did not want to look upon defeat, but it served no purpose to pretend it had not happened. Slowly, he opened his eyes.

Nuno de Tobar grinned down at him, then beckoned to a pair of soldiers standing nearby. "You savages do not learn lessons easily," he said as the soldiers yanked Bold in Battle to his feet and wrapped chains around his ankles. "No, no," Tobar said as one of them went to fasten the Paracusi's wrists together. "Why waste a chain? It is certain that this one will never again use his right arm, and I will see that he dies if he dares to raise the other one against us."

Bold in Battle, head reeling from the blood he'd lost, blinked to clear his vision. Three Principal Men, one of them the elderly former warrior, were being chained also. Doubtless the others were already dead. His warriors, who had fought so courageously in circumstances that would have daunted lesser men, had been lined up and were being brought one by one before Hernando de Soto. The Spanish leader's mouth was puffy and bloody, and from the look in his eyes, he, too, had only lately emerged from unconsciousness. The blow Outina dealt him had been a forceful one!

The thought heartened the Paracusi, and kept him company when it was his turn to stand before the governor. He did not listen to Juan Ortiz's translation of De Soto's mumbled words, but spent those moments praying that Moon of Winter would not be overcome with grief when she and the others came home. Instead, let the memory of her father's love console her and strengthen her spirit. She would need all the strength she could summon, as would all of those who had been sent away; they would be returning to a town where there was not a man left alive to protect them.

Holding himself as tall as pain and weakness would permit, Bold in Battle joined his comrades in front of a firing squad made up of Indian guides and interpreters. This was the Spanish leader's final effort to provide himself with the entertainment he had so far been cheated of. Despite his injuries, De Soto smiled as, one by one, the savages were executed by others of their kind.

The bodies lay tumbled upon ground unable to absorb so much blood and urine and feces. From a cloudless sky the sun reached down and drew up the stench of death, inhaled it, breathed it out and let it settle once more upon Outina's town.

Hernando de Soto held a square of scented linen to his nose as he looked around him. "Have the handlers bring the mules and command our slaves to begin loading them," he said to Nuno de Tobar, "and order the foot soldiers and cavalry to prepare to march." His words came thickly; mouth and jaw were swollen, and the holes where his front teeth should have been were once more leaking blood into his mouth. "Anyone who is not ready to leave by midafternoon will be left behind."

Tobar grinned. "All will be ready, Governor, even those malingerers who have been moaning about feeling unwell. No one will risk having to remain in this hellhole."

De Soto lowered his handkerchief long enough to spit. "Your description is apt, Nuno. This place is fit only for carrion-eating birds, and they are welcome to it. But that will be a feast I do not care to attend, so let us make haste and be on our way to Apalachee before our taloned guests have assembled."

* * *

The vultures and their kin had long since consumed their monstrous dinner and taken their bloated bellies elsewhere by the time Watches for Omens led home the elders and women and children of Outina. Because they had come upon a small boy wandering alone on the path they were following, a boy whose dreadful tale spilled out along with the tears he could no longer contain, they thought they were prepared for what they would find when they reached the town.

They were not. A hundred boys, telling a hundred versions of the same heart-chilling story, could never have prepared them for such horror. Their fathers, husbands, brothers, sons, were virtually unidentifiable, mere skeletons with shreds of flesh clinging here and there. Most had only gaping sockets where there used to be eyes that looked with tenderness upon loved ones and brightened with laughter when a good joke was told. The boy from Caliquen had told the truth; there was no one left alive in Outina.

Except for those who stood in frozen silence, or clung together keening, in front of the Principal House. Finally:

"Who will bury our dead?" wailed a young matron. She held a baby in her arms and looked despairingly upon the bleaching bones of the man who had been her husband. Only the pair of hawk feathers fastened in his blood-encrusted hair told her this; she herself had bound the feathers together with that strip of crimson-dyed doeskin. He had smiled to see what she had done, and boasted that his comrades would envy him such a fine decoration.

Walks Tall Woman averted her eyes from the mutilated body of her brother. "We will," she said shortly. She turned to her son. "You and your friends will go into every house and collect bed robes and cloaks and softened hides. If there are not enough, then search the homes beyond the planting fields for more."

Swoops Like Falcon could only nod. His face was tight from damming the tears a fledgling warrior must not shed.

Moon of Winter's face felt as stiff as her cousin's looked. She put one arm across his thin shoulders. "I'll help you," she said when she was able. "So will the other maidens, I am sure."

"You maidens will be too busy helping the matrons," Walks Tall Woman said. "The younger boys can go with the warriors to fetch the skins with which we will wrap our dead."

Warriors. The word hung on the putrid air like an eagle poised in midflight. Black Wolf Running and Sends a Signal had been the first of his friends to volunteer to go with Swoops Like Falcon. Now the three stared at Falcon's mother. As did all of those who had heard what she said.

Yet it was true. In this town, the warriors-in-training had been thrust into full manhood by awful circumstance. Youths of fourteen and fifteen were all the men they had.

Moon of Winter saw her cousin's chin lift and his spine straighten as pride relieved some of his grief. Falcon's friends, who had been contending with their own sorrowing, also stood a little taller. She looked with new respect toward her aunt.

"When you return," Walks Tall Woman was saying, "there are scaffolds to be built and a trench to be dug in the Temple floor for Holata Outina's burial."

The Shaman had been trying to comfort his niece's young daughter. Her mother had died the preceding year; now her father was dead, too. And Palm Tree Bending's grandfather—the elderly Principal Man who had been a cherished friend of Watches for Omens since childhood—must also lie among these fleshless corpses. . . . Giving the sobbing girl's shoulder a final pat, he went to stand between Outina's sister and the trio of youths. "It must be dug on the right-hand side," he told them, his own grief thickening his voice, "and there is a ceremony attached to the digging. Do not begin until I can be with you."

Falcon promised that they would not, then went with his friends to join their peers and boys several years younger who were already grouping. As they skirted the dead littering the plaza, he focused intently on the job to be done. Timber for the scaffold-building could be gathered while they were outside the town, so it might be wise to take a sledge along. The littlest boys could easily pull an empty one, which would make them feel important and keep them from pestering the older boys—no; Falcon corrected himself; from pestering the *warriors* on whom the bulk of the work would fall.

"What of the little girls?" Moon of Winter said to Walks Tall Woman. "Surely they should be sent away as well."

Walks Tall Woman frowned. In her opinion, girls were stronger in certain ways than boys, and grew up to have greater spirit strength than men. Still, there were some here that were very small, and perhaps they were too young yet to be taught this. "You women who are experiencing your monthly bleeding," she called to a huddle of matrons who had carefully kept themselves apart from everyone else during the long walk home, "take any child under five with you to the hut you will be staying in until your menses have ended. They will be in your charge until someone is sent to bring them back into town."

Watches for Omens murmured a few words. "You understand that those of you who are still bleeding will be unable to take part in the burial ceremony?" she added. They did know this, of course; every woman here had been properly instructed at puberty. But the Shaman was as distraught as anyone else, and he was an elderly man; she would refrain from pointing this out to him.

The women she had been speaking to nodded as they moved away, carrying or herding in front of them the little ones who would be going to the menstrual hut with them. This was against tradition, of course, but not even Watches for Omens protested. For now, tradition must give way to expediency, in minor matters at least. Besides, the idea had been Walks Tall Woman's; no one cared to question her judgment.

But it was Walks Tall Woman's niece that many eyes rested upon before the maidens and matrons went to walk among the skeletal dead and identify them as best they could. Not even soul-deep grief can prevent the sprouting of fear, and all of them were aware that no small band of youths, however skilled, however dedicated they might be, could possibly take the place of full-grown warriors. And how safe was a town that had no warriors to defend it? With no human help available to them, the people of Outina must look to the spirits for protection. Moon of Winter had been marked by the gods; surely she would be willing to appeal to those gods on behalf of all of them?

Moon of Winter was unaware of their scrutiny. All her attention was focused on trying not to succumb to hysteria as she knelt beside corpse after corpse and attempted to determine—by the paint on a bow that had dropped from fleshless fingers, or the symbols etched on the gorget that lay within a rib cage—what names belonged to the dead. More and more, her right hand sought the panther-skin pouch that hung around her neck, and clutched the crystal nestled within it. *Help me to be strong enough to do this,* she begged it. *Please, do not let me disgrace myself and my clan by giving in to nausea or surrendering to the darkness that threatens to wash over me.*

And the crystal heard her and responded. Even when she and Walks Tall Woman bent to examine a body whose right arm lay almost perpendicular to it, and Moon of Winter recognized at once the wide copper bracelet that still encircled that half-severed arm, she did not faint or release the bile that bubbled into her throat. Only a small moan escaped her mouth before she could form the words she knew it was her place to say: "We have found my father."

The day's sun was heeling into the west before the job was done and the dead had been gently wrapped in the hides and cloaks and robes brought into the compound by Swoops Like Falcon's band. The youths had helped widows and bereaved mothers to raise their loved ones onto scaffolds that had been erected in front of each house, and four of them had gone into the Temple with the Shaman and dug a neat trench in its floor. Now the townspeople were gathering for a ceremony that would culminate in Holata Outina being laid to rest in the grave that waited for him. Here he would lie until the Shaman could disconnect his bones and place them in a special basket that would remain forever in a prominent place in the Temple. The rest of the dead, when time had dissolved the tendons that gave their skeletons shape, would be buried beneath the floors of the houses they had lived in; their spirits would watch over the families they had left behind.

Watches for Omens had put on a headdress with red feathers hanging from it, and feathers of both red and black were sewn to the sash girdling his waist. His face and arms had been daubed with red paint. Earlier he had spoken with the Holata's family and it had been agreed that—even though Outina had been a Headchief worthy of the utmost honor and respect—there was no need for the ritual strangulation of clan kin and servants that sometimes accompanied the interment of exceptional leaders. "His Principal Men are already dead, and all of his warriors," the Shaman said. "They are sacrifice enough. His spirit will not lack for worthy attendants."

Now Watches for Omens left Outina's home followed by Swoops Like Falcon, who, since there was no longer a Paracusi in the town, carried in one hand a pole from which hung Outina's battle trophies and in the other the Headchief's ceremonial pipe. Behind him came four of Falcon's comrades bearing the litter on which the Holata, his bones already anointed with red pigment, lay. Walks Tall Woman and Moon of Winter moved into the compound after them and walked with measured pace between the rows of women and children who stood in solemn silence to honor Holata Outina.

The procession circled the Principal House three times, then turned and marched slowly to the Temple. The rest of the mourners fell in behind them and made a circle at the foot of the mound.

Moon of Winter heard little of the Shaman's eulogy. Although she made no sound, the tears of grief she had been repressing began to leak from her eyes and trickle over her cheeks. She did not wipe them away; now, finally, it was permissible for them to be shed, and she was not the only one who was crying. Even Watches for Omens, although his eloquence was undiluted by them, had tears standing in his eyes.

This time, she did not reach for her crystal. She had spent the day surrounded by death, immersed in death. It was not strength she needed now, but consolation. And no crystal, however magical, could possibly offer that.

Chapter 20

🦴 🦴

"Would you have me encourage your sister to go against tradition?" Headchief Calusa glared at Dancing Egret.

Her Spanish serving woman, still in diligent attendance, took two unobtrusive steps backward to remove herself from the sphere of Calusa's anger, and Egret sighed. Last night she had tried hard to make White Gull see reason, and been rewarded with alternating rage and tears; now, it seemed, she was going to have her father furious with her, too. Sometimes families were impossible to deal with. "White Gull is willing to let her hair be cut to satisfy tradition," she repeated patiently. "She asks only that it be a token cut, leaving enough to let her plait what is left. She has promised to keep the braids wrapped around her head during her time of mourning, Calusa."

"She must have all of it cut off."

Egret was not about to give up. "My sister has been through so much," she said. "Her husband's nose was chopped off by the first Spaniard who came to their town; she has twice lost her home; although she was as frightened as anyone else during the time the people hid themselves in that canebrake, she had to pretend to be brave in order to set an example for the others." Dancing Egret hoped her father would not see in her eyes that her last statement was not entirely true; he must never know how White Gull had strongly resisted setting a good example for Ucita's people. "And she has spent years trying to console a husband who grew more and more despondent because he feared that the gods had turned their backs on him. Furthermore, Ucita died by his own choosing; he would not want White Gull to grieve excessively when he was so happy to go to his death."

Her father scowled. "There is nothing excessive about adhering to tradition. Particularly when White Gull is my daughter, and widow of a Townchief. All along, she has done only what her status demanded of her."

"As she means to do now," Egret said swiftly. "So long as her hair is not left unbound, tradition will be satisfied. And my sister is already living in seclusion." She gestured to where a corner of the huge hall had been screened off. In the two weeks since the Ceremony of First Harvest, White Gull had confined herself to that small area. From behind her woven-frond screen, she was no doubt listening avidly to this exchange between Egret and Calusa. "She'll continue to live apart from everyone while the moon waxes and wanes three times, just as the widow of a Townchief should. And when she emerges, she will smear her face with ash, just as though Ucita had died in the fullness of time, or she had lost him in battle or to disease demons, until our priest says that men may be permitted to look upon her once more."

Calusa's right hand went to the gold ornament he wore around his neck. "No man will waste time looking upon a woman whose barrenness has been amply proven," he said, fingering its smooth surface. "It is possible that Vision Seeker may decide it will be unnecessary for your sister to conceal her face once she is brought out of seclusion. As for the rest . . ."

He frowned again, but his furrowed brow signaled thoughtfulness this time.

Egret bit her lip to keep from telling what she knew about White Gull's unconsummated marriage. She had given her word and must keep it. And, for the moment, silence might be her best ally. She made herself relax, stood quietly and respectfully while her father pondered.

"Very well," he said at last. "I do not see the reason for White Gull's aversion to having her hair cut off, but wearing it tightly bound will serve the same purpose, I suppose." For the first time, he smiled. "You are a born negotiator, Dancing Egret," he said, only half jesting. "You not only speak persuasively, but you argue as logically as anyone I have ever had dealings with. Were you a man, and not my daughter, you would surely be serving admirably on the Headchief's Council."

He got up and began to pace. "Take this matter of the Spanish soldiers occupying Ucita's abandoned town, for instance. I considered telling our warriors to attack in force and slay them all, but in the end it seemed more sensible to have Prowling Panther lead small raiding parties against them. To harass them, you see, and make them understand that I will not have them in Calusa country." He grinned more broadly. "It is good training for the newer warriors, too: one day, they approach the town by land; on another, Prowling Panther sends war canoes to creep up on the place. Our young men are learning every manner of warfare, and the Christian soldiers are helpless against them. Spanish weapons may make a great deal of noise, but who can take aim at what he cannot see? Prowling Panther's warriors release their arrows in silence and are gone before the enemy can discover their hiding places. We are eating away at the Spaniards the way the waters of the bay nibble at the shore, bit by bit. Soon those that survive our raids will have had enough, and when they flee, they will let others of their kind know that the province of Headchief Calusa is a place to be avoided."

Dancing Egret nodded. "And all of our warriors come home safe each time, which might not be the case if a great war party was sent against those who have taken over Ucita's town."

Her father looked at her approvingly. "I will say it again: you would make a fine addition to my Council. Instead, I have the likes of Shark Fin and Twisting River. Shark Fin did not approve my plan; he insisted that to kill every last Spaniard would send a stronger message. He cannot understand that this would leave no one alive to deliver the message! He is always ready to urge war, that man, whether there is true need for it or not. On the other hand, Twisting River never recommends sending our warriors out, not even on raids to remind disgruntled Townchiefs of their allegiance to me. He will suggest making any concession—even foolish ones—to avoid ruffling the still waters of peace." He plucked a grape from a heaped basket his First Woman had brought to him earlier. "Then there is my Chief Speaker," he went on, his words muffled until he swallowed. "That one will only repeat what I say first. I begin to think he has not had a thought of his own in years."

Egret could not resist. "He dresses yours in elegant garments, however," she said dryly.

Calusa stopped his restless pacing and laughed delightedly. "And that is the primary duty of a Chief Speaker!" he said, nodding agreement. Then he sobered. "But he does not advise me, Egret. Which is what he is supposed to do when we meet in Council."

He sat down again and, after a moment's hesitation, Egret sat down too. Her father did not object, and she relaxed further. "If the Spanish lacked food," she said slowly, "they would be gone before the dark of the moon comes again."

"The bay and all of our rivers teem with fish," her father pointed out, "and there is game to be had all around them." His eyes crinkled suddenly. "They are having a few problems hunting, however, with warriors waiting to pounce on any soldiers that leave the town! But as I said, they have an abundance of fish and shellfish near to hand. And Prowling Panther's scouts say that they are making planting fields north of the town, where they felled all the trees in order to have wood to build their homes and fences." His eyes hardened. "They are stupid people, Egret. Some of those trees had stood there for centuries. Their roots held down what little soil there is so close to the coast. If they could stay here long enough, the Christians might be able to grow a single crop, perhaps even two. But soon there will be nothing but thin sand in the fields, and any seeds planted after that will refuse to grow."

Egret was still concentrating on some way to keep the Spanish from filling their bellies with fish and shellfish. "If some of your warriors could patrol in canoes from dawn till dusk," she ventured, "wouldn't the Spanish fishermen become as frustrated as their hunters are?"

Calusa did not make mock of the suggestion. "There would be no cover available to men in canoes, as there is for those on land," he said. "Yet the Spanish have only three small boats, boats that hold six soldiers apiece at best." He helped himself to a handful of grapes this time, wiped his blunt chin as juice trickled out of his mouth. "And Shore Walker tells me that their clumsy weapons need firm support, something that is hardly to be found on any sort of boat."

"Yet our warriors can use their dart throwers as easily on water as they do on land," Egret put in softly, "and as accurately." In the past, Calusa's warriors had often carried out highly successful raids against the coastal Timucua.

"That is so," the Headchief said, then abruptly signed for her to leave him. His War Leader was coming into the house, and Prowling Panther would be discomforted if Calusa outlined this interesting new strategy with Dancing Egret present. Should he learn that the idea had been hers to start with, he would dismiss it out of hand, as most men would. Headchief Calusa, however, was not like most men; when a plan had merit, why should it matter where it came from?

Egret was glad to be dismissed. She invented a task to keep Ysabel occupied elsewhere, and did not even pause to whisper to White Gull that her wish had been granted; her sister would have overheard enough to know that, in any event. And Shore Walker had come to Calusa's house just after dawn to ask Dancing Egret if she would like to go with him when he took a canoe into the river glades. "I'm not assigned to today's raiding party," he had explained, "and it's been a long time since you have traveled through the glades."

It had indeed. During her years in Mocoso's town, she had not been permitted to go so far. In truth, she had rarely been allowed on even the smaller streams that curved around his town, and to be denied that simple pleasure had chafed at her.

Shore Walker's strong strokes carried them swiftly from the island and into the mainland river that pointed toward the glades. His companion, eager for her first glimpse of a sea of sharp-bladed grass stretching from horizon to horizon, did not notice when occasionally one of his strokes faltered, did not see Shore Walker wince as pain stabbed at the arm he had told everyone was nearly healed now. For this, he was grateful; it was not pity that he wanted from this woman.

As the peculiar silence of the glades closed around them, Egret murmured contentedly and trailed her fingers through the yellow-gold blossoms of the bladderwort that, in the shallows, lived companionably with spike rush and sawgrass. Gossamer-winged dragonflies perched on gently waving stems, and the glossy pink eggs of apple snails decorated stalks of pickerel-weed. Ahead of them she could see a stately blue heron watching for the tiny killifish that abounded in these warm brown waters. Beyond the motionless heron, one of her namesake birds was stalking its own meal, its elegant white head turning this way and that, then vanishing briefly as it fed. And far in the distance lay an island of lush green, the teardrop-shaped hammock Shore Walker had said they were making for. Over all of this the summer sun decanted heat and light, and Dancing Egret lifted her face to receive its singular blessing. "I had almost forgotten how special the glades are," she said after a moment. "I am happy you asked me to come with you today."

"You may not be so happy if a storm decides to visit us while we're out here," he teased.

"I've never worried about summer storms," she said. "They are fascinating to watch, and over quickly."

"When you were little, you used to think thunder and lightning were signs that the gods living on the cloud islands were doing battle."

"And you, who felt that you knew more about war and warriors than any girl ever could, would laugh and say that gods don't go to war, only men do."

"Which is true," he said, and angled the dugout toward the right, where the going was easier. The grass grew higher here, proving that this was a river that would carry them into the true channel of the river glades. When they had progressed a bit farther, the sedge would be tall enough to obscure their view altogether. "I never said that the gods do not want to keep us mindful of their enormous power, however." He looked up into an expanse of blue so brilliant that his eyes stung briefly. "They don't seem inclined to do so any time soon, though, so we should be able to make the most of exploring the hammock I told you about."

"The one where the snails' shells have green stripes on their spirals," she said.

He nodded. "I have been there often while hunting. It's one of the larger hammocks, and I think you'll enjoy visiting it."

The channel veered, became no more than a narrow stream,

and he peered around him. The close-growing grass guarded its secrets, and not even by standing would he be able to look over it and discover where the deeper waterway could be picked up again. Laying the paddle across his knees, he cupped his hands around his mouth and chanted "Yi-Yi-Yi-Yi," swiveling his head slowly as he did so.

"What are you doing?" Egret asked.

He chanted twice more, then nodded in satisfaction and forced the dugout around until it faced the wall of sawgrass on his left. "I was sounding the way," he said when he had inverted the paddle and poled them into a wider and deeper stream. "Where the sedge is truly dense, my words come back to me at once. They take a bit longer to return when the grass is merely a screen between channels."

Dancing Egret was intrigued. "May I try sounding next time?"

He nodded. "There will be opportunity enough for both of us to grow hoarse," he said with a grin. "You know that there is never straight passage through the glades, and this season the rains have been coming regularly. The sawgrass is responding by forming clumps and reaching for the sky. Since we can't see over it or through it, we have to sound our way to the hammock."

This was certainly true. Surrounding them now was a living palisade of sawgrass, elongated pale green blades folded lengthwise to protect their blossoming spikes, the outer surfaces edged with vicious miniature teeth. The breeze she had relished earlier must still be blowing, for the tips of the sawgrass swayed in response to it, but she felt no stirring of the humid air. It was as though they moved through a separate world, a world that held its breath as their canoe slid through its glinting waters.

"If the rain continues to visit us," Shore Walker was saying, "passage will be easier later in the season. The channels will be swollen with water then, and most of the sawgrass will lie beneath it."

"It was like that when last I came here," Dancing Egret told him, "and there were fish—big fish—everywhere I looked."

Shore Walker nodded. "They find their way here when the streams deepen." He dipped his paddle twice, and once more they were facing a wall of grass. "Now is your chance to decide which way we should go," he said.

Egret lifted her head, inhaled, and opened her mouth. "Um-

A-La, Um-A-La," she chanted, then listened intently before shifting position. "Um-A-La, Um-A-La," she sang again, trying to gauge the return of sound to her ears each time. Finally, she faced backward, the way they had come, and chanted yet again. There *was* a difference, and now she recognized it! She grinned at Shore Walker, and began the whole procedure over again, this time stopping when her voice lingered a little before coming home to her. "We go this way," she said to him, pointing.

He turned the canoe obligingly, forced it through a seemingly impenetrable barrier, and in moments they were gliding on the surface of a sedge-rimmed pool where gatorfleas played tag on the hanging roots of duckweed. "You did well," he said, "and certainly your voice is prettier than mine. I've often frightened away feeding herons with my sounding; for you, they would doubtless come closer, to hear more."

Egret's cheeks, already glowing from the unremitting touch of the sun, grew warmer still. She fumbled for something to say. "Will the warriors be raiding the Spanish village again tomorrow?" she asked, the voice Shore Walker had just praised raspy all of a sudden. She knew he was grinning at her discomforture, and refused to look at him. "Will you go with them, if they do?" she persisted.

He released her from a confusion he found both endearing and encouraging. "They will, and I shall be going with them," he said. "And this time we'll concentrate on killing a soldier or two, instead of on kidnapping those odd-looking beasts that the Spanish use for food. You remember; we saw them when we spied on the village when Mocoso came there with Juan Ortiz."

"The round animals with the strange noses and tails," Egret exclaimed. "You mean people actually eat the flesh of such creatures?"

Shore Walker nodded. "So we discovered. Which is why we destroyed the pen the Spanish kept them confined in when last we raided. We caught several of the creatures and brought them back and roasted them. A few liked the flavor, but the meat was too sweet for my taste." He took them into a channel leading out of the pool. "The rest of the squealers made for the swamps once we'd freed them; if panthers and gators haven't already pounced on them, I expect our hunting parties will bring home others from time to time."

"I can't understand why the Christian soldiers brought such

animals with them," Egret said. "Surely it would be easier simply to hunt wild game?" But she spoke distractedly. Shore Walker's mention of Juan Ortiz had reminded her of someone who was never far from her thoughts. Where was Kneeling Cypress at this moment? Was she heartsick still at her husband's rejection of her and their children? Did she burn with hatred for Ortiz and Mocoso, and for the man whose concubine she had become? Would she ever understand why no one had come to rescue her and bring her back to where she belonged?

Shore Walker had been studying Egret's face. "What's wrong?" he asked gently.

"I was thinking about Cypress," she said, and when he nodded sympathetically, suddenly found herself telling him everything that Headchief Calusa had refused to listen to. "She must be so unhappy," she finished. "She will never even know how hard I tried to persuade my father to send warriors to fetch her home. She'll think no one at all cares about her."

"You were friends for a long time," Shore Walker said. "She'll know that you care, that you will always care. And she was daughter to a chief; she'll know, too, that Calusa may have his reasons for not rescuing her."

"But she will not understand," Egret said stubbornly. "I heard his reasons, and I don't. Were I a man, I would disobey my father and go after her, I swear I would."

Shore Walker smiled. "I believe you would," he said. "But would you find any warriors willing to risk Calusa's wrath by going with you?"

"If I couldn't, I would go alone!" she flashed back. Then, recognizing the futility of that, "Which wouldn't help Cypress at all, would it?" she whispered.

"No. And you must be fair to your father, Egret; just because you neither understand nor agree with his decision doesn't mean it wasn't a wise one." He watched her begin to deny this, saw her soul-deep honesty intervene and seal her lips. "We must seek out the channel again," he said quietly. "Will you sing us to it, Egret?" In truth, he'd already spotted a telltale glimmer of water diagonally ahead of them, but his heart ached to see her so miserable. To concentrate on sounding the way would give Dancing Egret an opportunity to compose herself.

"If I've reckoned properly," he said with her *Um-A-La* still echoing sweetly in his ears, "we should be at the hammock of the green-striped snails very soon."

Egret made herself put aside a dilemma that seemed incapable of resolution, focused on being the first to see the upthrusting green of a jungle island. Her gaze swept the sky, a sky the mounting sun had leeched of blue, swept it again and again as Shore Walker paddled with renewed vigor. Suddenly, above the monotonous line of the sawgrass, a thin arch of darker green appeared. "I see it!" she cried triumphantly.

Shore Walker, who had kept his own eyes deliberately lowered, looked up to see the arch expanding and thickening. "Get ready to go exploring," he said to his companion. "This stream will take us directly there."

A delicious coolness met them as they stepped onto the rock-based plateau and eased their way through a shoulder-high thorny thicket. Closely spaced saplings, offspring of the live oaks that filled the heart of the hammock, were draped here and there with delicate spiderwebs that occasionally dipped low enough to attach themselves to the tips of the ferns that proliferated beneath them. Laughing, Dancing Egret and Shore Walker dodged the sticky webs, skirted solution holes half concealed by leaf litter, went without haste into the dimness beyond.

"Look! There are some of the snails that give this hammock its name," Egret said, gesturing toward the furrowed bark of the first mature oak they came to.

"You'll see a great many of those before we leave," Shore Walker told her. "And a great many of these as well."

She turned her head, gasped to see a cluster of purple orchids clinging to one of the tree's lower limbs. On other limbs bromeliads grew one atop the other, and a motley collection of hovering butterflies drew her gaze to a larger grouping of orchids, yellow ones this time. "How beautiful," she murmured. It was not awe alone that softened her voice; the hush that hung over all the river glades was more pronounced here, more intimate. The buzzing of gnats and mosquitoes, the drone of lazier insects, even the cry of a barred owl from the far side of the hammock, only emphasized the peculiar hush. Now and then birds offered up abbreviated trills of song, but these, too, were rapidly absorbed by the canopy of silence that hung over this fascinating place.

"Come this way," Shore Walker urged, taking her hand. She did not resist, but grasped his firmly and allowed him to lead her between bay tree and cocoplum shrub, around tangled passion vines and sprawling patches of resurrection fern, to a place where the jungle petered out, revealing a small glade centered with a limestone-edged pond. Its clear, pale brown water was as serene as the vegetation-scented air, and yellow duckweed floated placidly on its surface.

"What a lovely spot," Egret said, grinning to see a turtle emerge from a mass of palmetto then—at the sound of her voice—swiftly draw his head into his black-and-yellow shell.

"It's only another sinkhole, a much larger one," Shore Walker told her, "but it is a pleasant place, isn't it? Deer often stop here to drink, and there are almost always smaller animals around, otters and possums and the like. I even saw a panther here once."

His companion found an outcrop of rock that was not playing host to a community of air plants and sat down. Shore Walker joined her and together they watched a diminutive tree frog navigate a frond of palmetto, then tried to discover designs in the lichen embellishing the trunk of a tree on the other side of the pond.

"There, near the branch that's dangling over the water," Dancing Egret said. "Doesn't that look remarkably like my father's ceremonial headband?"

"Except for the fact that there are no egret plumes dangling from it," he agreed, laughing. The slab of rock they were perched on was not very wide, and her hip rested temptingly near his. It was becoming increasingly harder for him to concentrate on such things as tree frogs and lichen, with that gentle round of flesh so close.

The *whoo-whoo-whoo-all* of the barred owl came again, and Egret turned to him. "It sounds like he is asking who has come to his hammock," she said, then lifted her head and imitated the bird's call. The owl responded, and she tried again.

This time, however, she was met with silence. "He can be fooled only once," she said, laughing in her turn.

Delight animated her face and drenched it with softness. Shore Walker lifted one hand, traced the outline of the brows crowning her expressive eyes, the strong bone of her nose, her curving lower lip.

Egret ceased to laugh. He was so close to her that the warmth of his lean body was like a different kind of sunshine, concentrated rays that pulsed disturbingly against her own flesh. And he was looking at her oddly. Very oddly indeed.

Now his fingers were caressing her broad cheeks. "You are a beautiful woman, Dancing Egret," he said, "and a desirable one. I still find it hard to believe that you were once a chubby little girl with tangled hair and a face that was always streaked with dirt."

There was something wrong with her breathing. It had speeded up, become uneven. "I had dirt enough on my face when we met in the canebrake not long ago," she said quickly. But there was something wrong with her voice as well; she did not sound at all like herself.

He smiled. "Which is probably why I was able to recognize you so quickly, even after so long a time. For the rest of you had certainly changed!"

She wanted to stay where she was; she wanted to move. She wanted Shore Walker to go on talking like this; she wanted him to stop. For the first time in her life, the daughter of Headchief Calusa did not know in the least what she *did* want, and this frightened her.

She edged away from him; he smiled again and closed the gap she'd made between them. She moved a little farther; he did the same. She pushed herself away yet again . . . and tumbled off the outcrop of rock and into the pool.

He stood, reached down his hand and hauled her out. "You should take that as an omen," he said, picking strands of duck-weed out of her hair. "You are not meant to put distance between us, Dancing Egret."

With that, he pulled her dripping body into his arms and wrapped them tightly around her. "One day soon, I hope we shall be even closer together," he murmured against the top of her head. "And I think you feel the same."

The thudding of his heart made hers pound the faster, and suddenly she no longer wondered what she wanted. She knew; clearly and certainly, she knew.

She drew back a little. "I do," she said simply, then fitted herself against him once more and closed her eyes.

The green tree frog went on with its explorations, and the turtle with the yellow and black shell came all the way out of the palmettos. The water in the pond settled, and the torn duck-weed mended itself and stretched comfortably across it. There was no sound of footfalls, and no twig snapped anywhere. But the air quivered suddenly, in the way that it does when it in-sinuates itself around an obstacle. And then someone coughed.

The man and woman in the glade sprang apart, turned as

one to see a tall dark man regarding them with undisguised interest.

"I honestly did not mean to intrude," Kwambu said. "I frequently stop on this hammock when I'm returning from the eastern coast, and I had no idea anyone else was around." He smiled. "You were not exactly making a great deal of noise," he added dryly.

"Shore Walker comes here often. With hunting parties," Egret said breathlessly. "Which is why he wanted to bring me here. To show me what a beautiful place it is, I mean."

The tension that had poured into Shore Walker when he'd realized they were no longer alone drained out of him. "You ought to be warrior instead of trader," he said feelingly. "You walk so quietly that even the creatures that live in this hammock must have been unaware of your coming."

Kwambu shrugged. "A man who nearly always travels alone needs to be able to move soundlessly, just as much as any warrior does." He looked from one to the other of the people he had startled. "He also needs to know how to forget much of what he sees along his way," he added blandly. "I am good at that, too."

Egret, her flesh still tingling from the excitement of Shore Walker's embrace, only laughed. "I don't care if you speak of what you saw," she began, but a look from Shore Walker silenced her.

Kwambu and the warrior exchanged glances. "I think I will forget about it nonetheless," the trader said, and Shore Walker nodded his thanks.

"You are both being foolish," Dancing Egret declared, but she had too many pleasant things to think about to waste time dwelling on the eccentricities of men. She shook out her hair so that the sun could finish drying it, and went to sit down on the rock again.

"We should be heading for our canoe," Shore Walker said, shading his eyes and studying what he could see of the sky. "The clouds tell me that this day will be ending with a storm, and I'd like to get you safe home before it begins."

"You are right," Kwambu said. "Those clouds are the kind that swell and darken rather abruptly."

Reluctantly, Egret started out of the glade, followed by the two men. "Do you think the spirits of the hammock will object if I pick a single blossom to take home with me?" she asked over her shoulder. If they had to leave it so soon, she would love to have at least a reminder of this enchanted place.

Shore Walker smiled into her radiant face. "I think they will feel honored if you do," he said, and his smile stretched into a grin as she dashed away to find the tree where the orchids grew in such profusion. He picked up his own pace, but Kwambu laid a restraining hand on his arm.

"Before you leave," he said urgently, "I am going to tell the both of you about a plan Headchief Calusa has in mind. Please understand that I will be revealing it only because I have always had a special affection for Dancing Egret." He saw Shore Walker's eyes darken and laughed a little. "No, no. Not in that way. I speak of friendship only; but mine is a feeling that matches yours in strength, even if its quality is somewhat different."

They caught up with Egret just as she was tucking a purple blossom behind her ear. "That is fitting adornment for you," Kwambu said gravely.

Shore Walker only looked at her, but it was a look that repeated what he had said earlier: that he thought her beautiful. Dancing Egret felt as though her heart might sprout wings and flutter out of her chest.

Kwambu cleared his throat to recapture their attention. "You should know," he said slowly, "that Chief Tequesta has accepted Calusa's invitation. He and his warriors will be coming to the island during the first full moon after the end of the rainy season."

Egret stared at him, bewildered. Why was he telling them this now? Tequesta had often come for a week of games and feasting, so it was scarcely news that he had agreed to do so again.

"Headchief Calusa," Kwambu went on, suddenly looking at neither of them, "will be glad to know this. He is looking for an opportunity to have a private talk with him. You see, Calusa is thinking seriously about trying to arrange a marriage between Chief Tequesta and Dancing Egret."

Chapter 21

❦ ❦

"You can do nothing about it," Brown Pelican said. She took the sleepy baby from her breast and laid her in the carry sling stretched above the sleeping bench. "Our father is the same as he was when the two of us were little: once he makes up his mind, nothing short of a raging hurricane can change it."

Dancing Egret's sister had smiled when she heard how Egret went into the glades with Shore Walker, then pressed her hand sympathetically when Egret described the dreadful news Kwambu had delivered to them there.

"Calusa arranges marriages for all of his daughters," Pelican went on. "I count myself fortunate that he wasn't trying to improve relations with some Townchief or tribal leader when my turn came. I did not have to leave this island, and I've grown to love Prowling Panther in the years since we were wed." She looked to be sure her older daughter was still playing happily with the shells Egret had brought along, then turned back to her visitor. "So far as I know, all of our sisters are content in the marriages Calusa arranged for them. And Chief Tequesta is a fine-looking man, Dancing Egret. He is fairly young still, only a few years older than my husband, and has already fathered half a dozen children. You, who love children so much, should be able to take heart from that, at least."

"I won't deny that I long to have children, a great many of them," Egret said. "But I want Shore Walker to be their father." Her voice was tight. She ached to shout out that not all of Calusa's daughters had found contentment in their marriages; White Gull certainly hadn't. But her tongue remained fettered by the promise she had given Ucita's widow. "I never expected to fall in love," she went on. "While I was living in

Mocoso's town, more than one warrior wanted me for a wife. I liked them well enough, but I certainly didn't love them. So I told them I could not wed until Headchief Calusa said I might, and then it must be to a man of his choosing." Bitterness laced her voice now; was it possible that tempering her refusals with that excuse had influenced her life thereafter? Had she, without knowing it, been predicting her own distressful future? "I should have accepted one of them," she said morosely. "Then my father would have been powerless to give me away to someone like Tequesta. A man may have many wives, but no woman is permitted more than one husband at a time."

Pelican waved away her words as though they fouled the air like smoke from an ill-made fire. "You would not have wanted to live out your life among Timucua."

"I suppose not." Egret thought again of Kneeling Cypress, who was doing just that. And all because she *had* been allowed to marry the man she loved. Should her sad story be regarded as an omen? No, Dancing Egret told herself; their situations were far from similar. She would think instead of something Kwambu told her a long time ago, that she must learn to consider what was best for Dancing Egret. In this instance, she was confident that she knew what that was, and she meant to have it, too. Somehow. "Do you know if Chief Tequesta has a daughter old enough for marriage?" she asked suddenly.

Pelican laughed. "What an odd question. I doubt that he does. As I told you, he's close to Prowling Panther's age; he would have had to marry very young to have a grown daughter."

"Has he a sister?"

Brown Pelican shrugged. "I haven't heard, one way or the other. Probably he has. Like the Calusa, the Tequesta tend to have big families."

"If he has a sister," Egret said, "then why can't Calusa's brother's son—Burrowing Kingfisher, is it?—take her for a wife? That would establish kinship bonds between Calusa and Tequesta, wouldn't it?"

"Of a sort," Pelican said. "But Burrowing Kingfisher is already married, Egret. In fact, his wife gave birth at the same time I did, only she had a boy. They call him Swift Eagle. Kingfisher is all puffed up with pride about his son. And even if he agreed to take a second wife so soon, and Chief Tequesta should have a sister and be willing to send her to him, it won't be the same as your marrying Tequesta and going to live in his town."

Dancing Egret rolled between her palms the snail shell she had brought back from the hammock. She'd found it among the ferns at the foot of the tree she plucked the orchid from. Some hungry bird had stolen its occupant and, since her beautiful blossom was doomed to fade and die eventually, Egret snatched it up so that she could have a lasting memento of the place where she had finally learned what it meant to love and be loved.

She slid the shell into the pouch she wore at her waist and stood up. "Someone once told me that I was very like my father in certain ways," she said to Brown Pelican. "I think perhaps this is so. It will take more than a hurricane to change *my* mind."

She was plotting so busily as she left that she failed to stop and admire the shell design Pelican's two-year-old had laid out for her inspection, and Brown Pelican forgot her own bewilderment as she hurried to console the child.

"My husband helps to repair the causeway," Ysabel said proudly, gesturing toward the line of men sloshing through muddy water to pound conch shells into the gaps left by the battering of a violent storm. "He is very good at guessing which size shell will best fit any place that needs mending."

The man she indicated was as big as any of his fellows, and burlier than most. The Spanish woman must feed him twice a day, Egret thought, and came close to smiling. It was plain that Ysabel heaped her husband's plate as generously, and as often, as she did her own.

Her serving woman was watching her. Ysabel had been elated to see that half smile and was crestfallen to have it disappear before it could transform Dona Egret's face, gentling it and making it more feminine. The way a woman's face should look, so far as Ysabel was concerned. "What troubles you?" she asked softly.

Dancing Egret frowned. Was she that transparent? If so, she must take care. It would not do for everyone on the island to begin to wonder what was wrong with her. Calusa would surely hear of it, and if he questioned her, she might be tempted to tell him how the plans he was making for her had ruined her life. "I didn't sleep as well as I usually do," she said to Ysabel. "The storm kept me awake most of the night."

Ysabel nodded. "So much noise," she agreed. "And that wind! My husband could not sleep, my children could not sleep. So I did not sleep much, either." But she did not think that the storm alone had caused Dona Egret to lie awake. Hadn't she seen with her own eyes the way the handsome young warrior, the one called Shore Walker, turned aside when she and her mistress came upon him yesterday? Hadn't she seen the greeting Dona Egret was about to give swallowed like a dose of vile-tasting medicine, and the hurt in her eyes as she'd watched him walk away? "My husband complained more than my children did," she went on, "which should not surprise me. Men are much like little boys in some ways; it is a miracle we women are willing to put up with them."

Dancing Egret scarcely heard her. She, too, was remembering yesterday. It hadn't been the first time Shore Walker avoided her since their trip into the river glades. That had been on the day she'd visited Brown Pelican and been suddenly gifted with the glimmerings of a scheme that might let her marry the man she loved. But Shore Walker had merely offered her courteous greeting when she found him, and made no motion to take leave of his friends, as she'd hoped he would. He had smiled impersonally, and gone back to talking about the new fish basin the men were making on an offshore reef.

It had stung, that rebuff, but she'd told herself that a man might be hesitant to have his comrades discover how much some woman meant to him. Warriors seized upon any excuse to tease one another, after all. But there had been additional rebuffs, and yesterday she'd made herself face the fact that the afternoon they'd spent at the hammock had not meant to Shore Walker what it had to her.

"I'm going into the house now," she said to Ysabel, and spun on her heel.

The Spanish woman began to breathe heavily as she hurried after her across the squareground and up the ramp. Why was Dona Egret in so great a hurry to return to the place they had left such a short time before?

In truth, there was no reason for haste, save for Egret's need to run away from her own disturbing thoughts. Once inside, she made straight for White Gull's corner; her sister was always glad to have company, and a flood of distracting conversation was what Dancing Egret craved right now.

But White Gull was in a complaining mood this morning. "The hours pass so slowly," she began as soon as Egret slipped behind the screens to join her. "I feel as though a whole season has gone by since Ucita died, yet I have weeks of confinement ahead of me. And I am already tired of sewing and weaving baskets. Soon I will be going outside to relieve myself more than I need to, just to feel the sun and catch a glimpse of other people." She compressed her lips. "I'll have to keep my head lowered, of course, and pretend that I see no one. Trailing Vine will certainly notice if I do otherwise, and then there will be trouble."

"But you've had visitors every day, haven't you? Whenever I've been in the house, it seems as though someone is in here chatting with you."

"Other widows come," White Gull said, "to grieve with me. They cannot know that my grieving is very different from the kind they knew, and I dare not tell them the truth. So I have to pretend all the time they are here. That's hardly cheering, Egret. And Trailing Vine, when she brings my food, lingers to remind me of my duty and to tell me how fortunate I am to have such spacious quarters. Were I not Calusa's daughter, she tells me, I might be spending my mourning time tucked away in the corner of a much smaller house, with scarcely room enough to turn around, let alone sufficient room to spread out the bed robes she invariably brings me to mend." She pointed to a heap of frayed coverlets to prove what she said. "Sometimes it's Herb Gatherer who fetches my meal; she tries to be nice, but she's such a ditherer that half the time I can't figure out what she's saying. She's always hurt when I refuse to accept the tonics she makes for me, yet I cannot drink any more of them; they taste abominable, and they neither strengthen nor soothe me. If Watchful Doe visits, she doses me, too—with endless anecdotes about Crested Heron! You'd think he was the most amazing boy-child ever born, to listen to her; yet everyone knows he is nothing but an overindulged child who is much in need of discipline." She tugged at the plaits wrapped tightly around her head. "And I begin to think I should have agreed to have all my hair cut off; I'm uncomfortable, wearing it this way."

"Then it seems I wasted my time appealing to Calusa for you," Egret said. Her own mood was not the best, and her annoyance showed.

"I didn't mean that, exactly," White Gull said hastily. If Egret left, she would be alone again. She did not want that. "It's just . . . don't ever be a widow, Egret, if you can help it."

Ordinarily, Dancing Egret would have laughed at such a silly remark. Today, she did not. "What you're saying is, never be a wife. To be a wife generally means that someday you will be a widow, doesn't it?"

"Being a wife is not such a fine thing, either," White Gull said, "so perhaps that's what I do mean." She sighed. "Oh, don't listen to me! I'm only feeling sorry for myself. Many women have good marriages, and feel genuine grief when their husbands die. You will doubtless be one of them. I wish I could have been, that's all."

"You are scarcely ancient," Egret said. "When you marry again—"

"Marry a second time? I think not. You forget that I am supposedly barren, Dancing Egret. What man would have me, knowing that I was married for twelve years and never once bore a child?"

"Then why not be sensible and tell the truth? At least to Calusa. You can't be the first woman to have an impotent husband, White Gull."

"Ucita sired many children," White Gull pointed out. "Who will believe that my childlessness was his fault?"

"I think our father would, if he heard the whole story." Despite Egret's current disaffection for Calusa, she could not let herself be less than fair to him; stubborn and opinionated he might be, but he was too honest himself not to recognize truth when he met it.

"I can't speak of such things to him. Or to any man."

Dancing Egret shook her head. "Then you are condemning yourself to many, many years alone," she said. "And you don't like being alone, White Gull."

White Gull looked around her at the boxlike area she was confined to. Screens had been set against its outer walls also, since no man must look upon her during this time, and only faint light filtered through them. "I certainly hate being alone here," she said. "When my mourning ends, however, I will be free to go wherever I wish. I'll hardly be alone then. Husbandless, yes; but not alone. Unless I choose to be."

She tried to sound as though she might make just that choice upon occasion, but Dancing Egret was not deceived. Her sister deserved better than a lonely old age, and even if it meant breaking a promise, Egret told herself, she was going to do what she could to see that White Gull had a chance at the sort of rich, full life every woman is entitled to.

If only she were able to do the same for herself, she thought bleakly, then attempted a smile as her sister leaned forward and touched her hand.

White Gull's expression was contrite. "I shouldn't have snapped at you," she said. "Your visits are the ones I look forward to, yet here I am making you listen to my tale of woe. Let's talk of something more pleasant, shall we?" She settled back on her heels. "I'll tell you what Herb Gatherer told me about our father and Trailing Vine, something I'll wager you've never before heard. Herb Gatherer swears that Calusa was so enamored of Trailing Vine—who was, according to Herb Gatherer, a real beauty when she was young, and had many warriors sighing after her . . ." White Gull rolled her eyes and won a giggle from Egret; neither could picture the pigeon-busted, caustic-tongued Trailing Vine as young and desirable. "Anyway, she says that Calusa threatened to steal Trailing Vine from her village if her father would not give her to him. Can you imagine that? And he was so set on having her that he agreed that Herb Gatherer, when she was old enough, might come to him also. Their father, like ours, had a great many daughters to find husbands for, I guess. In any event, Herb Gatherer insists that Calusa and Trailing Vine were much in love. Of course, she says that in the beginning they disagreed a great deal also, because both were strong-willed."

Egret nodded, fascinated now with this tale of long ago. The two were still strong-willed, so this part of it she did not doubt.

"They even enjoyed quarreling with each other, so Herb Gatherer says, and she says, too, that they have never stopped caring deeply for one another. Which is why Calusa's other wives have always avoided crossing Trailing Vine. To this day, Calusa will take her word over anyone else's should there be any sort of dispute."

White Gull's discontent had been vanquished, at last temporarily, by her eagerness to share this gossip, and Dancing Egret was glad. But when she left her, after they had idled away a few moments comparing the Trailing Vine they knew with the one Herb Gatherer had described, she could not help but think how ironic it was that it had been a love story of sorts she'd been treated to. And the last thing Egret wanted to think about was love.

The huge room was bustling with people now. Calusa's three wives were finally reaching agreement on distribution of the household goods Kwambu had brought back from the eastern coast, and a bevy of slaves waited to be told where to deliver them. Not far from where they stood, two of her father's counselors were arguing heatedly about something; Egret was amused to see that they were the pair Calusa had so graphically described to her. And Crested Heron, to the obvious dismay of Herb Gatherer's young daughters, had brought in a group of noisy friends who sprawled in the middle of the floor as they compared the seagoing canoe Shore Walker had carved for Calusa's son with toys made by their various fathers and uncles.

Shore Walker. No matter what trail Egret's thinking took, always it ended at Shore Walker. This would never do.

She looked to the far end of the room, where her father sat. He was speaking with the trader, but Vision Seeker waited nearby and servants were tending to various chores in the area. Since there seemed to be nothing particularly private about their conversation, Dancing Egret wandered in that direction. When they were finished, she'd walk outside with Kwambu and talk with him for a while. Perhaps she could get him to describe more of his trading adventures; that should go a long way toward taking her mind off . . . certain people.

"So Oathkaqua continues eager to receive goods from Calusa," the Headchief was saying. "That pleases me."

"Holata Oathkaqua has always valued your friendship," Kwambu said, "and has never failed to appreciate the favorable trading agreements that arose from it. And I think he trusts you more than he does certain chiefs among his Timucuan kin."

"That is because he has so often had to repel raiders sent south by the wily Chief Saturbia," said a grinning Calusa, who had heard about these raids from Kwambu. "He has never had to fear something similar from me, since so much land separates our two provinces."

"After I left Oathkaqua," Kwambu said, "I met a pair of Timucuan traders who were traveling from Saturiba to Mocoso's lake villages. They told me that the Spanish who landed here have been causing considerable trouble inland, in the regions of Ocale, at least. Apparently they have been seizing Timucuan men—and even women and children in some instances—and taking them along as slaves." He took care that his voice did not betray the anxiety he'd felt as he questioned the traders, how upset he had been when they could tell him no more than that.

"The Christian soldiers took no slaves among the Calusa," the Headchief said with satisfaction. "The Timucuan chiefs who permitted such a thing must be either fools or cowards."

"The Spanish policy is to force each Townchief to go with them until the next town is reached. Seeing their chief made prisoner convinces the people not to resist when some of them are herded up and made to go along also. But although the chief is usually released eventually, most of the others are not."

Calusa had caught sight of Dancing Egret and knew that she was listening to them. Signaling her to come closer, he raised his eyebrows. "Can you see any pale-fleshed soldier forcing *me* to leave my home?"

"I cannot. And even if an entire army pounced on you and bound you hand and foot, I can't see your people being so foolish as to trail along when they took you away. The Calusa are not a herd of timid does unable to exist without the stag that leads them."

Her father laughed. "They would scarcely be leaderless if Dancing Egret were with them, I think." He turned to Kwambu. "Do you agree, trader, that this daughter of mine ought to have been born a boy?"

Kwambu tamped down his personal concerns. "That would hardly be fair to the young men of your island," he said courteously. "Where would they turn their admiring glances then?"

It pleased Calusa to hear that his daughter had attracted the attention of the warriors; she was not as pretty as her sisters, and he had worried that this might detract from her appeal. It gave advantage to any chief who wanted to arrange a marriage when the prospective bride was known to be admired by the men of her town. He wondered briefly why Kwambu's compliment had made Egret frown instead of smile, then turned again to the trader. "After our next harvest of conch, I will send you out again," he told him. "For now, rest from your journeying."

"I have no need to rest," Kwambu protested. "My trip to the eastern coast was lengthy, but it was far from tiring. If the conch harvesting is not to be soon, I thought I might go north again and see if I can bring back a supply of dates and figs, and bundles of the medicinal herbs that do not grow around here. Your Second Wife tells me she would like some to make her potions and salves." He had persuaded Herb Gatherer to the idea, but it was a good one nonetheless, and the priest had enthusiastically endorsed it. As Kwambu had known he would.

But Calusa was a shrewd man, one who rarely forget anything told to him. "I suppose you would like to go to Outina?"

Kwambu nodded. "Among other places, yes."

"I will consider it," the Headchief said, and his tone was one of dismissal.

Kwambu hoped Calusa was not dismissing the proposal as well as the proposer, but it did not seem politic to ask. He turned and made his way to the door, with Dancing Egret close behind him.

"Why did you say what you did?" she whispered as soon as they'd emerged into the sunlight. "About the warriors admiring me."

"Should I have said that none of them pays you the slightest attention? You are a strange woman indeed if you would want that said about you."

"You know what I mean," she said. "I don't want my father to suspect anything. About Shore Walker. And me."

Once again Kwambu put aside his own concerns. "I said nothing to make him suspicious of such a thing. Nor would I. But, Egret, now that you know your father's plans for you, surely there is nothing for Calusa to be suspicious about?"

She sighed. "I wish I could say that there were," she told him. Here at last was someone she could speak freely to, and she realized it was not distraction she'd hoped for from Kwambu, but advice. "Shore Walker has scarcely looked my way since the day we went to the hammock," she confessed. "Apparently I made too much of what happened between us there." She stumbled as they descended the ramp, and the trader put out a hand to steady her. "I know that some warriors make almost a game out of dallying with this maiden and that, at least until they're ready to wed. But I didn't think Shore Walker was that way."

"He is not," Kwambu said soberly. "What Shore Walker is, is a prudent man. Now that he understands you are meant to be wife to Chief Tequesta, he will stay away from you as much as he can. This is not a sign that he no longer cares for you; it is only that he knows it will cause trouble for the both of you if he permits the growth of something that can never see fruition."

Dancing Egret's step was suddenly more confident, and the heaviness in her chest had disappeared altogether. "You're certain of this?"

Kwambu nodded. "I have known Shore Walker even longer

than you have, for there were many years when the two of you did not so much as see one another. He is not light-minded, Egret. But"—he stopped walking and studied her face—"he has the good sense not to oppose your father. Which I hope, sincerely, you do also."

"I don't mean to oppose him," Egret said. "Not outright. But I do mean to try and persuade him to alter his plans for me."

"So that you may marry Shore Walker?"

His companion nodded.

"It will not work, Egret. Calusa is not Ucita. He will resist with ease any tearful pleading on your part."

"I'm aware of that, and I'm not the sort to weep and beg in any event. All you're telling me is that I must be both subtle and clever. Which I will be." She was grinning now, and full of renewed hope.

Kwambu shook his head. "Shore Walker, although a fine warrior, is no Townchief. And your father wants you to make an advantageous marriage."

"Advantageous for Calusa, you mean. He wants to ensure a permanent alliance with Tequesta and his people."

"He is wise to want that. The Spanish have come here three times, and who can say when others of their kind will decide to do likewise? They are able to raise huge armies, Egret. But if Calusa and Tequesta become firm allies, and agree to unite against any invasion of the southern provinces, they will have far better chance of repelling even a vast army of Christian soldiers." And the last ones to land in Calusa's territory, those who marched north, where were they now, and what were they doing? Kwambu did not know, would never know, unless Calusa granted permission for him to go back to Outina. But he said none of this to Dancing Egret; she had her own worries, and could do nothing to alleviate his.

"I've never doubted my father's wisdom," Egret said earnestly, "and I'd already guessed at his reasons for wanting to form kinship bonds with Tequesta. But I am going to do everything in my power to see if he can't achieve his aim without sacrificing my happiness." She thought of White Gull, of the years she had spent trapped in a passionless marriage, and shuddered.

"I wish you good fortune, then," Kwambu said. "I only hope you will use caution, Egret. Your father seems to feel easier with you than with any of his other daughters, and I can see that he is proud of you as well. I do not deny that he likes to organize people's lives for them"—his mouth twisted as he said that, and Egret knew suddenly that he was speaking of himself as well as of her—"but Calusa is a good man, and worthy of all your honor and respect."

"Those I give him, without stinting," she said. Then her brow furrowed as she thought again about White Gull. If she used the caution Kwambu suggested, and a good deal of common sense besides, it was just possible that she might be able to solve her sister's problems as well as her own, and all without any thwarting of Calusa's plans. Rearrangement, yes; but where was the harm in that? Indeed, her father might have even more cause to take pride in her if she could accomplish this. "Sometimes," she said to Kwambu, "a direct approach works better than any other. Doesn't it?"

He gave the question serious consideration. "It does," he agreed.

And wondered if the direct approach might not be what was called for in his own dealings with Headchief Calusa.

Chapter 22

The first thing Kwambu noticed when he reached Outina was that the warriors standing sentry were unfamiliar to him. Well, not unfamiliar exactly; some he recognized, but it was not in Outina's town that he had seen them before. He paused only long enough to return their salutations, then went swiftly into the town and made for the Principal House.

Along the way he saw other warriors who simply did not belong where they were. And, most disturbing of all, he saw not one of the men he was accustomed to meeting when he came here. The women he had passed in the planting fields were residents, he was certain, and the children sitting in front of the round-roofed houses or playing tag in the compound were youngsters he had seen before. But even though it was not yet the season for large hunting parties to depart for the thickly forested areas of Outina's provinces, there seemed to be too few people of any description in this town.

He quickened his pace further; something was askew, and only Holata Outina could tell him what, and why. Worry, like an ill-tempered mutt, nipped at his heels; he hurried past a quartet of warriors knapping flint for arrowheads, skirted the circle of young women shaping wet clay into pots, and was nearly running as he approached the center of the town.

"Ho! Trader!" Swoops Like Falcon stepped into Kwambu's path and brought him to a halt. "If you always cover ground at such a rate, I'm surprised it's been so long since we've seen you."

"I have been busy in the south," Kwambu said, relieved to see the young man grinning at his own jest. Whatever was amiss here could not be too serious, surely.

"Well, you've come at last," Falcon said, "and I hope you have brought along a good supply of those purple shells my mother got from you once before. I would like them used for decoration on the cloak Walks Tall Woman is making for my marriage ceremony."

Even though the youth was strolling away from the Principal House, Kwambu fell into step beside him. Swoops Like Falcon was Outina's nephew, and it would be discourteous to take premature leave of him. Also, he seemed in a mood to chat; he might inadvertently answer questions before they needed to be asked. "I had not known you planned to wed," he told him. "As I recall, you were not even old enough to be a full-fledged warrior when I was here last."

Falcon sobered abruptly. "I am warrior now, and have been for some months. So"—he spread his hands, smiled once more—"I'm old enough to take a wife as well. I will be marrying Palm Tree Bending, the daughter of Watches for Omens's niece."

"Your Shaman must be pleased to have his family so honored," Kwambu said. "And Holata Outina and Walks Tall Woman—they are happy that you choose to marry so young?"

"My mother urged me to do so," Falcon said. "As for Holata Outina . . ." He hesitated, then drew himself up tall. "Although my tattooing has had to be postponed, I am Holata Outina now." But his voice, so confident only moments before, was suddenly stripped of substance; clearly, the confidence had been a mask put on for Kwambu's benefit. "My uncle," he said with conspicuous difficulty, "was killed by the Spanish. Everyone who was in the town was killed when they came here. Except for one small boy the Spanish brought with them from Caliquen. And he has died since."

Kwambu's feet, always so certain of their way, forgot their appointed path. "Your mother? And . . . and your cousin?"

"Had been sent away, to stay with a nearby Townchief. As I was." Now Falcon's voice betrayed bitterness as well as pain. "My uncle would allow only warriors to remain with him when he finally realized he could not avoid a meeting with the Spaniard called De Soto. But if I'd been allowed to stay, perhaps . . ."

The trader wanted to put a sympathetic arm across the boy's shoulders. How well he understood what Falcon was feeling now! But Falcon was boy no longer; what had happened here had transformed him to man, to chief. "You would only have been among those slain," he said gently. "If you had died, who would have led your people?"

"My mother says the same," Swoops Like Falcon told him. "She says that's why my uncle made me go. But it seems strange to have everyone call me 'Holata' when I've never even had the chance to be warrior. My friends are all warriors now," he said enviously, "but I was one for only a few short weeks. And there was no time for wars or raiding then."

"When there is time for such things, and need, you will be the one to say so," Kwambu said. "And your Paracusi will come to you with his war plans, for your advice and approval."

Falcon considered this, smiled. "You are right. And there's no reason I cannot go along with them from time to time, is there?"

"That will be for you and your Principal Men to decide," Kwambu pointed out.

"I haven't yet chosen my Principal Men," Falcon confided. "At first, I planned to make Black Wolf Running my War Leader, so he could be one of them. He's my good friend, you see, and brother to Palm Tree Bending. But once there were more experienced warriors in the town, those that came from Caliquen, my mother said that to set someone so young over them would be a mistake, and might even make them decide to go back where they came from. So even though Black Wolf

Running was unhappy about it, I took my mother's advice and told the warriors to elect their own leader."

"How is it so many young men left Caliquen to settle in your town?" Kwambu asked, realizing at last why the faces he had seen had been both familiar and unfamiliar.

"As soon as Watches for Omens pronounced me inheritor of the leadership of this town, and of all of my uncle's provinces, I sent emissaries to invite them to come here and find wives. We had heard, you see, that the prisoners the Spanish took from Caliquen were mostly women." All traces of boyishness vanished as his jaw tightened. "They use them as slaves and concubines," he said harshly. "I'm grateful that my uncle was wise enough to send our women elsewhere, or they would surely be in that same sorry situation now."

Kwambu contented himself with a nod of understanding; it would serve no purpose to tell Swoops Like Falcon that he, too, was devoutly thankful for that.

"In any event," Falcon went on, "since Caliquen lacked marriageable women, and our women were without husbands, it seemed sensible to approach the Townchief with our invitation. Now, there are men for our women to wed, and Outina is no longer virtually defenseless." It had been hard for Swoops Like Falcon to accept that he and his comrades were not enough to protect the town, but in the end reason had prevailed over pride.

He turned to the trader. "You are a good listener," he said. "I haven't told even my mother all the things I'm telling you."

"There are some subjects," Kwambu said, "that men discuss with women; others, they discuss only with men—and often they feel the need to talk with men older than themselves. You probably are not yet wholly at ease with the warriors from Caliquen, which leaves you only elders like your Shaman to speak with. All the rest . . ."

"Are dead," Falcon finished bleakly. "Which is another reason I haven't named my Principal Men. Caliquen's warriors are still strangers to me, Kwambu, as you said, and what good is a Council made up solely of elders? Why, some of them might even treat me like a child, even though I'm Holata now."

Falcon's voice cracked as he hinted at a situation he misliked even imagining, and Kwambu hid a smile. The smile came out of concealment as the youth lifted one hand and inclined his head to acknowledge a greeting sent his way by the snaggle-toothed old man who was the town's toolmaker. The benevolent gesture was one the trader had often seen Falcon's uncle make.

"Well, at least I can have my cousin consult her crystal whenever I am uncertain about something," the new Holata went on more cheerfully. He grinned again, and was—briefly—given back the youth events had cheated him of. "You don't know about that, do you? Moon of Winter didn't have her crystal when last you came. It's a wondrous thing; it told my cousin I should bring the men of Caliquen here. And Watches for Omens says it will reveal more and more to her as time goes on. So, between my mother—who always knows how things should be done—and Moon of Winter, I'll never lack for advice. Which means I can afford to wait awhile before selecting my Principal Men."

Kwambu contrived to look surprised at mention of the crystal. If the girl wanted to keep secret where it had come from, he would not spoil things for her. After all, he ought not feel hurt that she had failed to name him as the giver; he should feel glad, instead, that she had learned to make good use of it so quickly. And what was important right now was that Swoops Like Falcon seemed too much inclined to look to Walks Tall Woman for guidance. However powerful the bonds that linked him to his mother, it was vital that this particular young man see the importance of severing them. "I would not wait overlong," he said carefully. "Other Holatas might make mock of a chief who seems to prefer the counsel of women over that of men."

"I'd feel the same," Swoops Like Falcon said easily. "But I don't want to be hasty about something so important, so I'm going to give myself time enough to learn all I can about the warriors from Caliquen. Besides, most Holatas will envy me for having a cousin who is a crystal diviner. Even if she is a woman."

He was right, and his shrewdness impressed the trader. Falcon still had some growing up to do, but he was not so far, after all, from true manhood. "You are going to be a fine leader," Kwambu said. "Your uncle's spirit must be rejoicing."

Falcon turned his head away, but not before the trader saw tears mist his eyes. This, too, was good; the greatest chiefs he had met in this country were those whose strength was tempered by sensitivity. "Shall we go to your house?" he asked after a moment. "I will retrieve my sledge from the sentries, and you and your mother and cousin can look over the goods I've brought with me. I do have those purple shells you mentioned earlier, as well as other things Holata Outina might be interested in trading for."

He emphasized the formal address, and the youth flashed him a smile as they turned to go back the way they had come. "I hope you have some fine big conch shells with you, too," he said as they neared the Principal House. "It's tradition for a Holata to have his own for the ceremonial drinking of cassina tea. But I warn you, I mean to be as sharp a bargainer as my uncle always was."

Kwambu smiled, too. "I would be disappointed if you were not," he told him, then followed him into the dimness of the rectangular hall.

It was gratifying to have the women within welcome him warmly. Walks Tall Woman ordered the servants to bring refreshment, and Moon of Winter smiled with her eyes as well as her mouth when she greeted him.

"I was sorrowed to learn of your troubles," Kwambu said as he set out stacks of pelts and automatically displayed shells and feathers to best advantage on the packed earth floor. "The former Holata Outina was a good man, a wise man, and will be missed."

"My son will win such praise for himself eventually," Walks Tall Woman said.

"I believe he will," Kwambu told her, and was glad that he was able to say so sincerely.

She awarded him a smile. "He is to be married, you know."

"So he tells me. And that he would like his ceremonial robe trimmed with some of the shells I have brought from the southwestern coast." He indicated the glistening purple shells, and Walks Tall Woman picked up a handful and examined them.

"I haven't much to trade with," Moon of Winter said hesitantly when she saw Swoops Like Falcon studying an assortment of busycon shells, "but I'd like to give my cousin and Palm Tree Bending fine skins to be made into cloaks they can wear on cool mornings."

"These doeskins might be just what you are looking for," Kwambu said, passing them to her. "And if you can give me a few medicinal herbs, or the kind used to make dyes, they are yours. One of Calusa's wives commissioned me to bring back such herbs."

"I can, and I will," she said, and Kwambu realized that Moon of Winter had not only learned to use her crystal, she was also becoming familiar with the properties of healing herbs. Calamity had accelerated her maturing, just as it had the new Holata's.

He turned his attention back to Walks Tall Woman, who had selected both janthina shells and an array of the colorful glass beads Kwambu had traded for while he was in Tequesta territory.

Swoops Like Falcon was delighted to have them chosen as additional decoration for his wedding finery. "Some should be put aside for Palm Tree Bending's garments, though," he told her. "Since she has no mother to help with the sewing," he said to Kwambu, "Walks Tall Woman has offered to do so."

"The bride might prefer to choose her own decoration, however," Moon of Winter murmured. But neither her cousin nor her aunt paid her any heed.

When the bartering was concluded, Moon of Winter walked outside with Kwambu. "They listen to me only when I have been sitting and staring into the crystal you gave me," she told him. "If they but knew . . ." She bit down hard on her lower lip. "Kwambu, I look and look into that crystal, and still I see nothing but reflected sunlight!"

"But your cousin said a vision in the crystal led to the warriors from Caliquen coming here."

She lowered her head, embarrassed. "So everyone believes. Things were so bad, you see. All of our warriors were . . . gone; we had no food, no skins to make into winter garments. And rumor said that Holata Potano was planning to claim Outina and annex all the provinces that lay between our town and his. The women hoped I would be able to invoke spirit protection, since we had no other kind. They begged me to use the crystal."

"And?" Kwambu prompted.

Moon of Winter sighed. "This time, I expected to find something in it," she said. "During the first awful days after we arrived home, it had seemed to comfort and strengthen me. Having done so much, I thought it might be willing to do more, that it knew how great was our need and would respond to it. I was wrong, but I couldn't let myself disappoint those who were counting on me. So I gave the only advice I could think of: to bring men here from another of Holata Outina's towns, men willing to defend us in return for finding wives among our women. Walks Tall Woman was the person who named Caliquen as the most likely town, and said that any warriors who accepted our invitation should bring food with them, as gifts for those they hoped to wed."

"Your advice was excellent, and your aunt's suggestions arose from it," Kwambu said. "Does it matter that the spirits, rather than painting images in your crystal, whispered in your ear?"

"I heard no voices, save those of the women pleading for an answer to our problem."

"Perhaps the spirits whisper soundlessly, Moon of Winter."

"Then I wish they would do so again," she said wearily. "We have illness here, Kwambu. It began with the boy from Caliquen we met on our way home. His skin grew hot some days later, and a rash—the sort you sometimes get when you touch certain bushes—appeared on his flesh. None of Watches for Omens's salves could send away the rash, and none of his potions could cool the boy's blood. When the poor child died, the Shaman said that perhaps his spirit had been taken by alien demons brought here by the Spanish. But when others—mostly children and old people—became ill, and some of them died also, I turned again to the crystal. Again it told me nothing. The people expect me to be healer as well as prophetess, and I am neither. And what if the sickness visits more of us, and the warriors from Caliquen hear about it? They came here willingly enough, but are they likely to stay once they know they might be putting themselves at risk by doing so?"

"The children and old people who were ill," Kwambu said slowly. "Did any of them live in the same household, Moon of Winter?"

"Many of the elders who died were grandparents of boys and girls who somehow recovered from the sickness," she said. "Sometimes death came to both young and old in the same family."

"In the south," the trader said, "the people have learned to move their sick into a house set apart from the town. Isolating them seems to thwart the demons that bring the illness."

"But who cares for them in this separate house?"

"The priest—who is like your Shaman—conducts healing ceremonies and provides what medicines he can. But they are mostly tended by those your people sometimes refer to as 'half-men,' the berdaches. And I will not tell you that no sick people die; that would be untrue. Yet whenever disease invades a town, fewer become ill when this procedure is followed, and fewer die in the end."

"Do you think something similar would work here?"

"It cannot do harm. Why not approach Watches for Omens with the idea, and tell him it is a practice of the Calusa?"

She looked uncomfortable. "I think I will avoid mentioning the Calusa. We Timucua consider the southern tribes somewhat primitive, I'm afraid, and Watches for Omens might reject the idea on that account."

Kwambu laughed for the first time since entering Outina. "And the tribes in the south think that those in the north cannot be nearly as advanced as they are," he said. "It seems that people everywhere have difficulty admiring those who are in any way different. Except for my friend, Dancing Egret; she finds all people fascinating, even those she has never seen. I have told her about the people here, for instance; now she asks about you each time I return from the north."

"And what have you told her about us?"

"I told her what a praiseworthy chief your uncle was, and what an outstanding warrior he had been. I even told her how his voice was inclined to squeak when he became excited."

Moon of Winter laughed. "He worked hard to overcome that," she said. "And what did you tell your friend about Walks Tall Woman?"

"That she is a commanding woman," Kwambu said solemnly, and the young woman laughed again. "I also told her about the lively boy who is now Holata. Egret will be interested to hear that, and saddened to know how it came about."

"What is she like, this Dancing Egret who is so curious about us?"

"Egret is curious about everyone. And everything," Kwambu said, and continued to speak of her, and of Shore Walker, as he and Moon of Winter crossed the square in front of the Temple.

"In her own way, your Dancing Egret is as brave as any warrior," she said when he had finished. "I hope she is able to marry the man she loves." She gave him a shy, sidelong glance. "Have you said anything to her about me?"

"I have. She was most intrigued, and much impressed with your courage." When Moon of Winter opened her mouth to protest, he added quickly: "As you implied, there are many kinds of courage, and those who see it in others often fail to recognize it in themselves."

He led her around a steaming pot in which slabs of bear meat were being rendered, and was pleased when the women tending it called out to say that Moon of Winter would be given the first batch of scented balm made from the oil.

"Their daughters have found husbands since the warriors from Caliquen came," Moon of Winter murmured as they moved toward the palisade's gateway. "That's why they want me to have it." She sighed. "I've no need of scented oil, but I can give it to Palm Tree Bending, to use on her marriage day."

Kwambu pulled his sledge through the gateway, paused in the shade of a solitary oak that grew near the edge of the first cornfield. "Why not save it for your own?" he asked. "Surely the woman who conceived the idea of bringing marriageable men to the town should have had first choice among them?" He tried hard to inject a teasing note into his voice, and failed miserably.

Moon of Winter noticed, and misinterpreted. "You are trying to be nice," she said, "but you know full well that no man, however desperate he may be for a wife, will want to marry a women as ugly as I am." She turned so that her scarred cheek was exposed to the light; but the sun, no respecter of intentions, revealed as clearly the anguish in her dark eyes. "I'm not nearly as brave as the daughter of Headchief Calusa, you see. I prefer not to risk rebuff. And to have a warrior accept my offer only because I am cousin to Holata Outina would be worse than rebuff."

"They are fools, the men of Caliquen," Kwambu said hoarsely. "If they cannot see the lovely woman that wears your face; if they cannot see the beauty in your eyes, in the softness of your hair . . ." He cleared his throat. "Were my skin red instead of black, I would be proud to be your husband, Moon of Winter."

She flinched and drew back into the dappled shade, turned her head away from him. "I didn't expect cruelty, not from you. Please. Don't taunt me by saying such things."

He should have bade her farewell within the town, Kwambu told himself. By now he should be trading with the smaller householders who lived beyond the planting fields. Instead, by letting impulse rule his tongue, he had destroyed the self-assurance he'd been so delighted to see in Moon of Winter, a self-assurance it must have cost her enormous effort to achieve.

Yet he had spoken honestly. Surely she did not think otherwise, did not truly believe he had meant to mock her! That she might have misunderstood to such a degree appalled him. He stepped close to her, laid one hand gently on her shoulder. "Moon of Winter, I ask your pardon. I had no right to speak as I did. However much I admire you, I had no right to make such a declaration to a daughter of the ruling clan of the Timucua."

For a long moment she stood motionless and said nothing. Then, still without moving, not even to shrug off the dark-skinned hand that rested on her bare shoulder, she said something in so soft a voice that he could not make out her words.

"Are you saying you do forgive me?" Kwambu moved closer, strained to hear her answer.

She swung to face him. "I am saying," she said, her tear-stained face a study in confusion, "that I still don't know what you're trying to tell me." She swabbed at her cheeks with both fists, as a child might do. "It sounds as though you . . ." She shook her head. "No. You cannot mean that."

Her expression said far more than her words, and Kwambu at least was suddenly no longer confused. "If you started to say that it sounds as though I wish I could take you for my wife," he said, "then you are right. But if somehow I could be transformed into a native of your land, that still would not make me my own man. Calusa's traders go nowhere without his permission, and go only where he tells them to go. Even if I were not so far beneath you in status, Moon of Winter, you surely would not want for a husband any man who is at the beck and call of another."

"You mean what you're saying, don't you?" she asked faintly. "You really mean it."

Kwambu nodded; he did not trust himself to speak further. And although he knew he should leave at once, should leave and give Moon of Winter ample opportunity to forget this fool of a trader, he could not make himself do it.

She continued to stare at him. "But how can you mean it? We scarcely know one another, you and I."

"I have known you since you were a child," Kwambu said. "You seldom noticed me when I came here; why should you? But I have watched you grow up, stood in awe of the beautiful maiden you became, and wanted to weep for you when your encounter with the panther seemed to put an end to all your dreams." His lips curved in a smile. "And my heart swells

with joy to see how you have stepped over the pieces of your
shattered dreams and transformed yourself into a woman I can
respect as well as admire."

Moon of Winter's eyes continued to shine, but there were no
tears in them now. "Don't you realize that any change in me
is due in part to you? No, no; I don't mean just because you
gave me a crystal, a crystal that still withholds most of its secrets from me, after all. But on the morning you gave it to me,
you talked to me as no one has ever done. I spent a long time
thinking about what you said, and from that day I made an effort to put aside my self-pity. I went to the Shaman, as you'd
suggested, and asked if I could study with him." She laughed
a little. "Watches for Omens is not an easy taskmaster; he soon
had me so busy that I had no time to think about my scarred
face. And other people seemed to stop thinking about it when
I did, or perhaps they just grew accustomed to the way I look."
She reached up and fingered the puckered scars, and her voice
hardened. "But I will not lie to myself, Kwambu; I am an ugly
woman. And even if I have somehow earned your respect and
admiration, you deserve better than an ugly wife."

Kwambu released his grip on her shoulder, let his hand fall
to his side. "Before the cat attacked you," he said, "you were
an exceptionally beautiful woman. Because you knew that, you
were also somewhat vain. Until this moment, I believed all
vanity had been leeched from you, and was glad. Now I see I
was wrong; you may be vain in a different way, Moon of Winter, but you are vain still if you feel you have the right to say
who a man should or should not love."

"You said that you admire and respect me. Are you saying
now that . . . that you love me?" Moon of Winter's voice was
no more than a flutter.

"I have been saying that all along," he said simply. "I know
I have no right to, none at all; but love you I do."

She looked down at the ground. "What isn't right," she said
finally, "is that you should feel you must apologize for . . . for
loving me. You're a good man, Kwambu the trader, and a
kindhearted one. And you are easier to talk to than any man I
know." She looked up again, managed a small smile. "You're
a fine-looking man, besides, which many women feel is important in a husband. But it had never occurred to me that you
might love me, and I don't know whether to laugh or cry now
that I know you do." With hands that shook noticeably, she
pushed back the hair a wayward breeze had draped over her

nose. "I guess I'll just be honest with you," she said in a voice no steadier than her hands. "I think you are the sort of man I would dearly like to have for a husband, yet I cannot say that I love you. I'm not even certain that I know how it feels to love. When I was pledged to Potano, there was no question of love between us; ours was to be a political marriage, and it didn't bother me that I did not love him, or him me. With you it's different, very different, and I must ask you to give me time to consider before I made a decision."

"That you are willing to consider me at all astounds me," Kwambu said when he could trust himself to speak. "Like you, I wonder whether I should be laughing or weeping. It is a strange feeling, is it not?"

She solved their mutual dilemma by laughing softly. "It is, but I don't find it unpleasant," she said, and hope kindled a fire in Kwambu's brown eyes. "I won't keep you waiting long," she added. "If you can remain here until the next full moon, when Falcon's marriage ceremony takes place, I will have an answer for you then."

Would he risk annoying Headchief Calusa by prolonging his visit? Probably. But suddenly Kwambu cared nothing about that. "I will stay," he said. In truth, tenscore of lance-bearing warriors would lack the power to drive him away!

The day of the new Holata Outina's wedding dawned cool but sunny, a good omen. Townspeople and visitors lined three sides of the Temple square, and on the fourth stood Watches for Omens and the newly tattooed Headchief. He looked, Kwambu thought, too young to be waiting for the fur-lined litter that was being borne by a quartet of hefty warriors, a litter carrying to him his even younger bride. Her arrival was heralded by a pair of men coaxing exultant notes from flutes made of rolled bark, and behind the litter danced the maidens of the town, each carrying an intricately woven basket heaped with fruits and berries. Bringing up the rear were the rest of the warriors, both the men who had come from Caliquen and the much younger warriors who had been Swoops Like Falcon's comrades since childhood.

It was Palm Tree Bending who caught and held everyone's attention, however. She was so delicately made that she looked younger than her fifteen years, and so shy that she continued to keep her eyes cast down when the Shaman helped her from the litter, then placed her left hand in the youthful Holata's right one. Nor did she look up as the pair mounted to the shoulder-high platform that had been built for them to sit upon while the people celebrated their marriage with dancing and singing, feasting and games. She seemed grateful for the feather fan that was part of her wedding finery; although her new husband enthusiastically applauded the skills of those who performed in his honor, Palm Tree Bending only peeped around her fan to watch them. Even when her husband stood and spoke eloquently to praise the bride he had chosen, she hid behind her fan; yet she responded gracefully, if briefly, to his speech, and the people shouted their appreciation of her when she was done.

Walks Tall Woman ordered the setting out of the feast when it was time, and although she had managed a lavish one, Kwambu had no interest in roast venison and palm berries, heaps of nut bread and corn fritters, or jelly made from the seagrapes he had brought from the south. For weeks Moon of Winter had been busy helping the Shaman direct the isolation of the sick and overseeing their care. Until the Calusan method proved effective, Kwambu had seen her only intermittently, and after that she had been involved with her cousin's wedding preparations.

Kwambu had understood, or tried to, even when he'd had to dodge a Principal Woman who kept demanding to know why "that malingering trader" was "skulking" around the town. But today, the day he had been alternately anticipating and dreading, he still had caught only frustrating glimpses of Moon of Winter. He realized she must have assisted with the dressing of Palm Tree Bending and had probably helped her aunt with the food, but surely she could have found a moment or two to seek him out? If she had wanted to. What frightened him, what made his stomach quiver like the sun-warmed seagrape jelly was doing, was the possibility that Moon of Winter was deliberately avoiding him.

The dancing, the singing, the contests between grinning warriors, and the games of chance that everyone took part in could not hold the trader's attention. He wandered away from the chattering throng, sought a quiet spot near a recently filled corncrib, and sat down on the bit of grass that grew in front of a healthy looking tobacco patch. He would wait until first dark; if Moon of Winter had not come to him by then, he would slip out of the town and go on his way. Her failure to seek him out would be answer enough; there was no need to put her through the discomfort of telling him she did not care to marry him.

The sky was painted with coral and gold, and the mauve that streaked it was deepening to purple before she came. "I had begun to think you were hiding from me," she said, looking down at him.

He sprang to his feet. "Would I have remained here so long, only to hide from you on this day of all days?" he asked, and attempted a smile. But his hunger for the answer he was waiting for was plain in his eyes.

Moon of Winter looked into them and held out her hands. "If you want me still," she said in a small voice, "then I would be happy to have you for my husband, Kwambu."

The purpling sky darkened further; night came to Outina. But for Kwambu the trader the sun was shining as it had never shone before.

Chapter 23

The contests between Calusa's warriors and those from Tequesta had gone on longer than planned, and the extension had been at the behest of the chief from the eastern coast. Tequesta, Egret thought, watching as he shouted insults at the men competing with his club hurlers, was a man of lusty appetites. He gestured broadly when he spoke, feeding words to his listeners with both hands, then dined heartily on their responses. He had proven himself a glutton for physical activity, too, especially wrestling; in everything, he was a man who always wanted more.

Egret was certain she could never be happy with Tequesta. She admired his exuberance, and the good humor he had shown despite the fervor of his rivalry, but her need was for a man who refreshed himself from time to time by bathing in the pond of serenity. And she suspected that, if calmness ever visited Chief Tequesta, it would be much like that found in the eye of a hurricane: deceptive and soon over.

Dancing Egret needed a man like Shore Walker. No, not a man like him—she needed Shore Walker himself, and no other. White Gull, on the other hand . . . Egret looked toward her sister, who sat between Watchful Doe and Herb Gatherer in the circle of chattering onlookers. Unless Egret was much mistaken, White Gull was impressed with Tequesta. Certainly she was giving him all her attention as he hefted his spear and narrowed his eyes at the target set up for the next match. And wouldn't such a man be good for her, wouldn't he set her afire with his own enormous enthusiasms, and more than compensate her for the passionless union she'd had with Chief Ucita? Ignoring the cheers that saluted Tequesta's successful cast, Dancing Egret studied her sister more closely. White Gull had been looking remarkably pretty these past few days. Unbraiding her hair, and brushing it until it gleamed, had been the first thing she'd done on emerging from widow's confinement. Now it made a gleaming fall down her back and a fitting frame for a face that glowed with a light absent from it for many years. Egret had not been the only one to appreciate White Gull's appeal, either; she'd seen Chief Tequesta's eyes seek out her sister, and admiration had been plain in them.

He had not looked upon Dancing Egret that way, but she'd taken pains to ensure that he wouldn't. She had deliberately refrained from her usual practice of washing her hair each time she bathed, she wore her shabbiest skirts each day, and pretended she had misplaced her collection of earbobs and necklaces. She'd kept a smile from her face, too, as often as she could. Which hadn't been easy when Shore Walker was participating in the games! She'd worried at first that someone might notice what she was doing; Trailing Vine was generally quick to spot any deviation from the ordinary, and Egret was all set to vow that she felt a little unwell from so much feasting and tired from the prolonging of the games. But there had been so much confusion, what with finding lodging for Tequesta and his men and for the many guests that had come here from other towns, and overseeing the daily preparation of food for everyone, that Calusa's First Wife had found no time to pay much heed to a girl she had always considered nondescript anyway. Watchful Doe had expressed concern, until Egret offered the excuse she'd prepared for Trailing Vine, and Brown

Pelican had sent a few considering looks her way, but that was all. And there had been no risk that Shore Walker might see her at her worst, she thought unhappily; he continued to avoid her assiduously.

Well, that would change. She hoped. But first she must attend to the furthering of her plan by somehow convincing her father of its feasibility. Which would not be easy.

She lent her voice halfheartedly to the rousing shout going up to applaud the start of yet another game, and pondered the best way to go about it.

In the end, she did not have to devise an excuse to speak to Calusa. He sent for her early on the final day of Tequesta's visit. "While our guests are bathing," he said when she responded to his summons, "I wish to talk with you."

Egret's heart transformed itself into a stone plummet and sank into her stomach. "I am listening, Father," she murmured.

He laughed; clearly he was feeling expansive. "From you, Dancing Egret, I expect more than just listening. Since you returned home, we have talked together enough for me to know that I will do a certain amount of listening also. Which I have more than once done, and been glad to." He spoke jestingly, but there was respect in his voice. The riverine raiding of the Spanish in Ucita's old town was having the desired results, and Calusa would never forget that the idea had originated with Dancing Egret.

She smiled; perhaps this meeting would go more smoothly than she'd hoped.

"Indeed, I have decided that your acumen should be rewarded," he went on, and took up a pair of splendid white plumes. "These feathers are traditionally worn by me alone, as you know. But I hereby decree that you shall be permitted to wear two of them whenever you are dressed for ceremony." His face was solemn now. "They are tribute as well as gift, Dancing Egret," he said, "and I shall let it be known that they are."

The hand she put out to receive the egret plumes shook a little. "I have done nothing to deserve such tribute," she said faintly. How oh how could she defy Calusa after this?

He smiled again. "That is for me to decide," he told her, "and I say that you have. I had never expected to have a daughter with whom I could discuss matters political and know that she understood what I was talking about, but the gods have seen fit to give me one, and that pleases me."

Her father's three wives were sitting only a little distance away, but Egret dared not look at them to gauge their reaction to the praise Calusa was heaping upon her. Still, her father did nothing without purpose, and perhaps they already knew what this tribute, however sincere, was going to cost her.

"It would be a pity to waste the talent you obviously have for understanding the problems a tribal leader faces," Calusa said next, and Egret's heart was once again a pressing weight in her chest. "Therefore, I am going to see that you have a husband who will appreciate that talent and make use of it. When Chief Tequesta returns to his town, you will go with him. As his wife."

It was now or never. "I wonder," she said slowly, "if Chief Tequesta would be happy with a woman whose only asset is a talent for understanding his problems. He seems to me a lusty man, and lusty men surely look for other things in a wife. Things I could not bring to a marriage with him."

Calusa spread his large hands. "Nonsense," he said. "I have told Tequesta he shall have my daughter for a wife, and he was delighted to hear it."

Egret swallowed hard; in the next few moments she would win or lose her heart's desire. "But did you tell him which daughter, Father?"

"What do you mean, 'which daughter'? My other daughters are already wed and—except for Brown Pelican—gone from this island."

Egret shook her head. "You have one other who is available for marriage," she said. "White Gull."

"Do you think I would foist off a barren woman on Tequesta?" he roared. "Any treaty made between us would be nullified as soon as he realized what I had done. I would make an enemy of a man I want as ally if I gave him your sister as wife."

Silently, Dancing Egret begged White Gull's forgiveness. "White Gull is not responsible for her childlessness," she said strongly. "For some reason, Chief Ucita suffered impotence whenever he approached her. She has been widowed, but my sister has never yet been wife." Calusa's astonishment rendered him speechless, and she rushed on. "And White Gull is the one Chief Tequesta has been admiring since the day he came here. I've seen that with my own eyes." She swung around, confronted the three women who were listening avidly. "Surely you have noticed it, too?"

The trio exchanged glances, then Trailing Vine turned away and began to sort through the strings of dates and figs laid across the bench beside her; if Calusa was set on this alliance, it was Egret's duty to see that it took place. Herb Gatherer hesitated, gave a frightened little nod, then turned away also. Watchful Doe, however, did more than just nod. "I have seen the way he looks at her," she said softly to her husband. "Dancing Egret is right, Calusa."

The Headchief got up and began to pace. "I have seen nothing," he said.

"You have been focusing on the games and contests, I expect," Egret said quietly. "But if you could see it for yourself, would you at least consider letting White Gull marry Tequesta, instead of me? You would still have your alliance, Father. And"—she planted herself in his path and grinned at him—"you'd still have me around to talk to and argue with. Which you have said pleases you."

He looked down at her, this daughter of his spirit as well as his loins. "You are certain of what you told me, about Ucita's impotence? He fathered a fair number of children before he took White Gull as wife."

"I know that. But he was younger then, and it may be that age affects some men that way."

Calusa thought this over. The years had not played havoc with his virility; far from it. But other men were not of the caliber of Headchief Calusa, and he had heard rumors of that sort about more than one man of his acquaintance. "Why did White Gull conceal this from me?" he asked.

"She was shy of speaking about such a thing," Egret said truthfully. "And ashamed as well, that nothing she could do enabled Ucita to consummate their marriage."

Her father resumed his seat. "Always you are trying to persuade me to something I do not want to do, at least where White Gull is concerned," he said. "That is not the sort of conversation that pleases me, Dancing Egret."

"And I do want to please you," she said swiftly. "But would it have been right to let you remain in ignorance of what I'm telling you? Especially when altering your plans just a little might make Chief Tequesta even more grateful to you?"

He stroked his jaw with one hand, looked at her through half-lidded eyes. "Sometimes I think you are too much like me," he said. "Still, if you can prove to me that Tequesta and White Gull are interested in one another, perhaps I will make a minor adjustment to my original plan."

Egret smiled. This, she had anticipated. "There will be dancing tonight, to mark the end of the festivities," she said. "If you will be watchful, I think you'll find all the proof you need. Only notice who it is Chief Tequesta chooses to dance with." She smiled more broadly. "It will not be me, I promise you."

His sleepy look vanished. "It surely will not be, if you continue to look disreputable," he said. "I promise to be watchful, Egret, but in return you must promise to take off this mask of dowdiness you have been wearing. Dress in your finest, and wear the plumes I have given you in your hair. Which I trust will be neatly combed for the occasion." He smiled with satisfaction to see her taken aback. "Would it be right to let you go in ignorance of the fact that I have been aware of what you have been doing?" he said, deliberately using the same words she had challenged him with. "Tonight's must be as fair a contest as those that have been taking place in the squareground these last ten days," he said. "Do I have your word on it?"

Her face warm, Egret nodded. "You do," she said. And fled the room with his laughter ringing in her ears.

Three days later, after a stunned but happy White Gull had departed with her brand new husband, Kwambu the trader returned to Calusa's island. Dancing Egret spied him first, and she flew to meet him. "Kwambu, I've done what I said I would do," she called, her excited words rushing before her like a swarm of butterflies. "Tequesta has gone home, and I am still here. As you see." She fell into step beside him and told him the whole story as he made for the domiciliary mound. "Now I have only to persuade my father that I should marry Shore Walker," she finished.

Kwambu halted midstride, turned and looked at her. "You would have been wise to have done so before I came home," he said. "I am bringing him news that will not exactly put him in a pleasant frame of mind."

"The Spanish?" she asked anxiously.

He managed a smile. "I do have news about the Spanish," he said, "but it is nothing you need be concerned about. No. What I have to tell Headchief Calusa, after apologizing for my delay in returning, is that I have taken a wife among the Timucua."

"Moon of Winter," Egret said at once, and he started. "Oh, it's been obvious that you have a great fondness for her, Kwambu. Your eyes go all soft whenever you speak of her, you know. I'm glad for you, my friend. Very glad."

"Your father will not be," Kwambu said. "I am not looking forward to telling him about it, Egret."

"I'll go into the house with you," she said promptly.

He raised his eyebrows. "Do you think I lack the courage to face him alone?"

"Not at all," she said. "But why stand alone when there is someone sympathetic willing to cheer you on while you talk to him? Silently, of course," she added, grinning. "I'll have my own share of his wrath to deal with soon, so I might as well learn what to expect. Perhaps being there with you will help me to better prepare myself for it."

For the first time, he smiled. "Egret, I love my wife, love her to the depths of my soul. But you are truly the best friend I have ever had, or ever hope to have. And while I should be too proud to take advantage of your generous offer, I am not." He set aside the pack he had carried across the squareground. "I doubt that watching your father respond to what I have to say will teach you anything useful, but I will be glad to have you there just the same."

It disconcerted Dancing Egret somewhat to discover that Prowling Panther and certain of his warriors were in the house at the top of the mound, particularly since Shore Walker was one of the group, but she had given her word to Kwambu and would not desert him now. This time, however, it was she who carefully avoided looking at Shore Walker, rather than the other way round.

"Look who has come home, Father," she said, going directly to where Calusa sat talking quietly with Trailing Vine.

The Headchief looked up, and his heavy brows met above his impressive nose. "And ready to give me good reason for having been gone so long, I trust."

"I have reasons to offer," Kwambu said. "It is for you to say if they are good, or not."

Calusa sat up straighter. "That is true. So spread out your excuses, trader, and let me examine them as though they were goods you were offering for barter. Persuade me that I should forgive your tardiness in exchange for them."

Kwambu inhaled deeply. "I have several things to tell you," he began. "First, one of the reasons for my lateness in coming back was that I followed the Spanish into Apalachee country after I left Outina." Soberly, he outlined what had happened in Outina's town, and although he did not raise his voice, the passion in it caused everyone in the vast room to fall silent and listen to what he had to say. "It was not hard to track their progress," he went on. "De Soto's expedition left a trail a blind man could pick up. I called upon the chiefs of several towns he had stopped at, and everywhere the story was much the same as those I had heard in Timucuan country. The Spanish had put certain towns to the torch; elsewhere they helped themselves to foodstuffs and slaves. Most of the captives they had taken from among the Timucua died early on, it seems. Or were slain for their rebelliousness, perhaps." His wide mouth twisted as he thought of men, women, and even children mercilessly slaughtered simply because their chains prevented them from walking fast enough to suit their captors, or because they happened to look askance at a guard shouting something in a tongue they did not know.

"I am more than ever grateful that Tequesta and I reached agreement about defending the southern peninsula," Calusa said. "Did you learn anything else that might be of use to me, Kwambu?"

"I went as far as the inlet where the Spanish camp was," the trader told him, "and lingered long enough to spy upon it for a day and a night. After dark I was able to creep close enough to overhear De Soto speaking with his men. The Spaniard means to send ships back to Calusa country"—he lifted a hand as agitated murmurs arose among his listeners—"to take north the Spanish that settled in Ucita's old town," he finished. "They might already have done so; for all that I hurried back from Apalachee territory, the ships could have arrived before me."

Prowling Panther spoke up. "There has been no sign of them so far."

Calusa smiled. "And when they come, we will give them something to remember us by, will we not, Prowling Panther? We will not stand in the way of their sailing again, and certainly they must take their countrymen with them. But I am confident that my warriors will speed them on their way with a hail of arrows, and make their departure a decidedly undignified one." His War Leader nodded, then began a low-voiced conversation with his comrades, and the Headchief returned his attention to Kwambu. "You did well, taking it upon yourself to trail the Spanish into Apalachee country," he said. "I will not forget that you exposed yourself to danger to obtain this information for me."

"I hope you will bear that in mind when I tell you the rest of my news," Kwambu said, too tense to return Calusa's smile. "You will recall that, when I asked your leave to go north this time, I confessed my concern for Holata Outina and his people? And how I mentioned on a prior occasion that Outina has a niece called Moon of Winter?"

Calusa sat still as stone. "I recall all of this."

The trader would not let himself flinch from Calusa's stare. "I have taken Moon of Winter for my wife," he said.

"You did not," Calusa said harshly, "receive my permission for that."

"You are right, for I had never anticipated such a thing happening. Indeed, I continue to be surprised that I dared tell Moon of Winter of my affection for her, and I shall forever be amazed that she was willing to marry me." He would not say that she returned his affection, for he was not a man given to self-delusion; she cared for him in a way that was spawned by gratitude and nurtured by the ease she felt when she was with him. Which, after all, was beyond anything he had ever dared hope for.

"I offered to find you a wife among the Calusa," the Headchief said. "You would have done well to accept that offer. Of what good to me is a trader whose loyalties are divided?"

"Moon of Winter understands that my primary allegiance is to Headchief Calusa," Kwambu said. "Both of us know that we can be together rarely, that I will be able to be with her only when you allow it." He hesitated. "Please believe that I have never lost sight of all you have done for me, of how much I owe you. But however great that debt, and however sincere my determination to repay it, it is not possible for any man to dictate the desires that arise in another man's heart, Great Calusa. I love Moon of Winter, and whatever punishment you might see fit to mete out because I wed her without consulting you first will not alter that. Nothing can alter that."

"Love!" Calusa came to his feet. "What nonsense! You deceive yourself, trader. I have no doubt that it is mostly lust that you feel for this Timucuan woman. And lust can be satisfied without recourse to marriage. Any sensible man knows that."

Kwambu stiffened. "Moon of Winter," he said, "is a daughter of the ruling clan among the Timucua. And she is my *wife*. I will not have her spoken of as though she were the sort of woman a man may pleasure himself with, and then abandon!"

His eyes were ablaze with an anger Dancing Egret had never before seen in them, and suddenly she was furious with her father, furious enough to speak up before he could unleash the angry words hovering on his own lips. "Why do you mock love between man and woman, Father?" she demanded. "I would not have thought memories leaked from your mind like water from a cracked jug."

Calusa's wrath was fueled further by the interruption. "I have not given you permission to speak."

"No, but someone must speak if you are to be reminded that you have not always held love up to scorn. I've heard that there was a time when love moved you to threaten to steal a woman if her father would not give her to you for a wife." She swung around, faced Calusa's First Wife. "Isn't that so, Trailing Vine?"

The huge room had fallen silent once again, and her words dressed themselves in echoes. Egret saw Herb Gatherer look guiltily toward her sister, but Trailing Vine did not notice; her gaze was traveling slowly between her husband and Dancing Egret. Calusa pretended unawareness of it, but when Trailing Vine did not immediately deny what Egret had said, he let his eyes rest briefly upon the woman who had, long ago, inspired a love that had suffered no erosion in the years since he had married her. Suddenly, unexpectedly, he smiled.

"I have always prided myself on being an honest man," he said, "and a fair one. How you came by this information, Egret, is something I do not wish to know. But I will admit the truth of it." He turned to Kwambu. "Which means, I suppose, that I should ask your pardon for insulting the woman you married, even though I did not intend that when I said what I did. I meant only that a man's lust need not be spent on any particular woman, that purely physical hunger can be easily sated. You were right to rush to Moon of Winter's defense, even though you had misunderstood me, and even though there was injudicious lack of respect in your response."

"You have my pardon," Kwambu said after a moment, "and I hope I have yours for a disrespect I did not consciously intend, and—more importantly—for marrying so precipitately and without your express permission." The courteous words squeezed themselves out; anger still simmered deep in his belly, anger fired by his resentment that he needed any man's permission to take a wife.

Calusa nodded. "It is yours. Also yours is the problem of keeping your woman happy when you will be seeing her so seldom. For you were also right when you said that your first allegiance is to me. I expect you to conduct yourself accordingly."

There was a general release of withheld breath; it would not have surprised anyone if Headchief Calusa had withdrawn his sponsorship of the trader and reduced his status to servant or even to slave.

Dancing Egret smiled. Matters had gone well after all for her friend. She raised both hands to push back her hair and, in the process, glanced to her right. Shore Walker was watching her.

Before he could look away, she saw in his eyes what she had hoped to find there ever since their day in the river glades, and she knew at once that she dare not let this moment pass. Now, while Calusa was preening a little as he basked in the people's praise for his largesse, was the time to present her own case. "Kwambu is not the only one who has lately learned what it is to love and be loved, Father," she said clearly. "I would like to ask your approval of the man I want for my husband." She clenched the hands that were twisted in the folds of her skirt; she was trembling, but she had no intention of letting her father see that she was.

Calusa's smile faded. He fixed suspicious eyes on her face. "What man is this?" he demanded.

She swallowed. Twice. "Shore Walker," she said. And prayed that the warrior would understand why she had chosen to make public declaration of the way she felt about him.

"You want to wed a man whose status is so far beneath yours? You are daughter to a Headchief, Dancing Egret; you are destined to be wife of a Townchief, at the very least."

"I do not want a Townchief. I wouldn't even want a Headchief, were one available. I love Shore Walker, and I want only him for my husband."

"For my trader to wed the woman of his choosing, and without my consent, is one thing. But for you to speak of marrying for love, Dancing Egret, is nothing short of ridiculous. Women who belong to a tribe's ruling clan do not do such things." The cords in his neck swelled to mark his rage, and his expression was fierce.

Egret wrestled with trepidation, and bested it. "Kwambu's Moon of Winter did. And you allowed Brown Pelican to wed your War Leader."

"We are not Timucua! As for Pelican, there was not, at the time, any tribal or town leader I needed to bind to me."

"Nor is there now," she retorted. And was grateful indeed that her father had formed the habit of taking her into his confidence about so many things.

"There is no telling when a situation might arise where I find myself wanting to improve relations with a man whose support I crave."

"So you hope to keep me unwed for how long: A year? Two? Five? Until people whisper that Headchief Calusa has a daughter who will forever be a spinster, and begin to wonder why?"

"You exaggerate, Dancing Egret." Calusa's voice was spear-sharp. "And it is inappropriate for you to have raised this issue at such a time. If we discuss it further—which I doubt—it will be privately." He turned away from her, beckoned to Prowling Panther. "I am interested in hearing your plans to harass the Spanish ships," he said to him.

His War Leader stepped forward, halted when Dancing Egret thrust herself ahead of him. "Father," she said desperately, "you are being unfair. You were willing to let Kwambu speak, and were generous enough to admit to him that love can be a compelling influence on a man. Won't you hear me out as well, and let me try to persuade you that a woman can love as strongly, and as enduringly, as any man?"

Calusa scowled, but he prided himself on his even-handedness, and everyone knew this. "I warn you that you risk bringing shame on yourself by talking about such things where there are so many to hear you," he said. "But I have never been accused of unfairness, nor will I be now. Speak on if you must, but keep it brief."

Egret turned toward the group of warriors, looked pleadingly at Shore Walker. Without hesitation, he left his friends and came to stand beside her, and when Egret reached for his hand, he gave it gladly. His firm clasp heartened her. "Great Calusa," she said, "I love this man, and he loves me. We wish to spend the rest of our lives together, and our shared life would be the happier if you would agree to our marrying." She inclined her head. "That is all I have to say."

In truth, there was nothing more she could say, and she

knew it. In the ensuing silence, she raised her head again, smiled at Shore Walker, then looked steadily at her father. And waited.

The wait was long, long enough to seem endless. But Egret stood tall, as did the man beside her, and despite the thudding of their separate hearts, neither betrayed impatience.

Calusa looked from one to the other, did so a second time. He struck a brooding posture and watched covertly to see if either could be discomfited by his continuing silence. He had been reasonably certain his daughter would not be, but the warrior, despite his reputed bravery, might well deem it politic to forswear the girl rather than incur the wrath of his Headchief.

When the waiting had gone on so long that some of the onlookers began to shuffle their feet, he accepted that Shore Walker would not back down. What kind of marriage would they have, Calusa wondered, if these two carried such prideful adamance into the disputes that arose naturally between any man and wife? Much like the sort he and Trailing Vine had, he supposed.

He stifled a grin at the thought of it, then made his pronouncement. "If you still feel the same after five round moons have come and gone," he said, "then I will arrange a ceremony of marriage for you." The angles of his face softened as he released his smile. "And I will be the first to wish you joy of one another."

Chapter 24

Dancing Egret stood in the center of the neat little house Shore Walker had built for them. Her bare feet rested on the mats she had made to cover the floor, mats she had woven loosely so that air would filter up through them. Those Shore

Walker was raising against the open sides of the house, mats generally set in place only to shut out sharply angled rain, were more tightly woven, but even these encouraged air to come in. Which was good; it was some time yet until the Ceremony of First Harvest, but this day would have been uncomfortably hot had it not been for the breezes that came to the island across the water surrounding it.

Shore Walker looked over his shoulder and smiled at her. The light from the huge fire in the plaza had been reduced to a dim glow by the placement of the shutters, but although she could not make out the expression in his eyes, she sensed the desire in them. She turned away in some confusion and pretended absorption in the stools and benches he had carved. His special talent revealed itself in the perfect symmetry of the supporting legs, in the satiny smoothness of the wood slabs that were designed to hold everything from their combined belongings to the visitors they would eventually be entertaining, and the two of them when it was time for sleep.

Hastily, she averted her glance from the sleeping bench with its heaped bed robes, robes she had sewn from the softest skins she could find. She had been unhappy at first when Calusa decreed they must wait so long to marry, but both Egret and her new husband had put the waiting time to good use. The narrower stacked benches on the opposite side of the room were lined with new-made pots and bowls, with baskets painstakingly plaited, with a goodly supply of gleaming conch shells and hollowed-out gourds. Egret and Shore Walker were beginning their life together with everything new, which was surely appropriate.

Shore Walker had fastened the last of the shutters firmly in place, and the din from outside, where dancing would go on well into the night, lessened abruptly. There had been no more room on the domiciliary mound, and the two had courteously refused Mask Maker's offer to share his home with them. Instead, Shore Walker had built a new house on the far side of the squareground, setting it on sturdy posts that were sunk deep into the ground, and constructing an equally sturdy ladder for them to use whenever they entered or left it. He'd done a fine job; it was a house anyone would be proud to live in.

She started. Shore Walker had come up behind her and put his arms around her. "What are you thinking about?" he murmured.

"About how much work you did, building our house," she said truthfully. "And about how much I love it."

"I'm pleased that you do," he said gravely. Then a smile crept into his eyes. "But I am far more pleased that you love the man who built it."

She turned into his embrace. "You must be very pleased, then," she whispered, "for I love you very, very much." She pressed her head against his shoulder. What she said was true; she loved this man so much that she was overwhelmed by the immensity of the feeling. So why, on the day she had waited so long for, was she deliberately searching for something else, anything else, to think about?

"My father arranged a lovely ceremony for us, didn't he?" she said, her words muffled.

The festivities had begun at dawn, with the young women of the town chanting softly outside the house at the top of the mound. Her father had wished her well then, and taking with him a sleepily protesting Crested Heron and the male slaves who had attended the two upon their awakening, left the house to Egret and her female relations. Ysabel had come in shortly afterward, an Ysabel whose smile was as brilliant as the sun chinning itself on the mangroves bordering the island's eastern perimeter. To dress Dona Egret for her wedding was a privilege she would not relinquish to anyone, not even to Headchief Calusa's officious First Wife.

After she had draped her mistress in a skirt sewn from bleached doeskin, Ysabel slipped shell bracelets around wrists and ankles and fastened a shell necklace in place. She made slender plaits of hair to frame the lower half of Dona Egret's face, and wove into them the egret plumes Calusa had given to his daughter. The rest of Egret's hair she swept back with the wooden combs Shore Walker had carved for his soon-to-be wife, delicately curved combs to which—using dabs of mortar begged from the causeway builders—Ysabel had fixed in pretty patterns the eight pearls Kwambu had brought to Dona Egret for a marriage gift.

Calusa's wives had led Dancing Egret outside then, and preceded her down the ramp and across the square, where a throng of townsfolk and visitors parted to make a path for them. As Egret passed, many tossed flowers and bits of greenery for her to walk upon, and the new-risen sun lit the way to where Shore Walker, flanked by her father and his priest, waited for her within a circle of polished busycon shells. Be-

hind them was a tall trellis, its outer borders adorned with elegantly carved images of land and sea creatures. The male and
female of each species was represented, and the slats of the
trellis had been wound with vines so fresh-cut that dew still
sparkled on them. Mask Maker's grin when Egret passed him
told her that Calusa had commissioned the woodcarver to
make the trellis, and that Shore Walker's grandfather had spent
weeks and weeks working his particular magic to produce
something unique.

When Egret had stepped inside the shell circle, she and
Shore Walker faced one another, and the shadows of gently
rustling leaves played upon their faces. A hush fell over the assembled onlookers as Headchief Calusa proclaimed that, from
this moment, these two were husband and wife. Vision Seeker
had called upon the gods to witness and smile upon their
union, and—as a surprise for Dancing Egret—the children had
joined hands, danced in a ring around the couple, and sung one
of the Legends she had taught them. Then the games and
feasting had begun, and—thanks to the fish and game brought
in by Shore Walker's comrades, and to Trailing Vine's raids
upon the community's storehouses—the usually abstemious
Calusa would be able to eat and drink their fill until dawn.

Except for the pair the celebration honored, of course. At
moonrise they had been escorted to their new house by a rau-
cous band of Shore Walker's friends, warriors whose bawdy
jests had propelled Egret up the ladder with unseemly haste.
Now they were alone, and the mats Shore Walker had been
quick to set in place ensured that they were safe from prying
eyes as well.

"It was an impressive ceremony," Shore Walker said against
her hair, "even if it did go on rather long." He pulled back a
little and looked down at her. Her eyes were luminous in the
dimness, and he ached with his need for her. "Since midday
I've been dreaming of the moment when I would have you to
myself."

Once again shyness visited Dancing Egret. "Watchful Doe
told me it was Crested Heron's idea that the children sing.
Wasn't he nice to want to do that for us?"

Shore Walker laughed. "I've no doubt the boy meant their
song as a sort of marriage gift, but I expect he wanted a part
in the proceedings on his own account as well. Your brother
doesn't like being left out of things."

"He does enjoy feeling important," she said, "but he is truly fond of me, I think. And of you. I believe he was more interested in pleasing us than in calling attention to himself."

"Perhaps you're right," Shore Walker conceded, letting his hands slip from her shoulders to her waist. "It's remarkably easy to be fond of you, Dancing Egret. And I am of a mind to please you also."

His strong fingers explored the enticing roundness of her hips, slid upward until they found the firm, pink-tipped globes of her breasts. His touch was light, almost teasing, and Egret caught her breath sharply as her nipples hardened in response. "Am I pleasing you?" he asked softly.

She nodded, and swayed a little. Shore Walker steadied her, then picked her up and carried her to their bed. "Let me see if I can find more ways to please you, then," he murmured, untying her skirt and letting it slip to the floor. He laid her atop the thick bed robe that padded the bench, then went down on his knees beside her.

Gently, he removed the clustered shells that girdled her ankles and wrists. He took the pearl-studded combs from her hair and watched the dark mass tumble down, but when he started to reach for the egret plumes, he stayed the motion. "Those, I will leave," he told her, "so that even when the fire outside burns so low that our home is filled with shadow, I'll still be reminded that it is Egret I have wed this day, that it is Egret who shares my bed, that—amazingly—it is Egret who loves me." His voice thickened and he buried his face in the hair cascading over his arm, breathed deeply of the fragrant herbs she'd washed it with. "For I can't quite believe it, you know. Even now."

The remnants of her inexplicable constraint disappeared, and Dancing Egret raised one hand, began to stroke the nape of Shore Walker's neck and the bunched muscles in the shoulder nearest her. "I can't believe it, either," she said. "But"—she shifted as he raised his head, and put both arms around his neck—"we are not exactly sharing a bed yet, are we?"

"You think not? Then I must persuade you otherwise." He leaned forward, found the pulse at the base of her throat, took its measure with his tongue while his hands moved caressingly over her body. When her heartbeat quickened, he let his tongue follow the trail his hands had blazed, pausing along the way to take each distended nipple into his mouth, to probe the maze of her navel.

The paths he traced upon her flesh heated her blood; it bubbled through her veins, spilled into some inner cauldron and splashed upon sinew and bone. She was melting inside, she knew she was, yet the thought failed to frighten her. And when she moaned, the sound was spawned by pleasure, not pain.

Shore Walker turned his head slightly, smiled. "Am I sharing your bed yet?"

In reply, she caught his head between her two hands and pressed it back against the down-covered mound his journeying had taken him to. Without haste, he parted her legs, initiated an investigation of the cleft that concealed her womanhood.

Egret moaned again and her fingers clutched his hair as he thrust his tongue inside of her, licking, savoring, feeding the fire that was raging now throughout her arched body. Like his, her flesh was sheathed with perspiration; like his, the pulses that signaled each heartbeat resounded like manic drums.

The moment had come. He knew it, and she knew it. Trembling, Shore Walker came to his feet, dropping his breechclout as he stood up.

Egret looked without shyness upon the rigid phallus that jutted from his loins. Her right hand stole out, closed around it, understood its throbbing signal. "Come to me," she said. "Let this become a marriage bed in truth."

He lowered himself upon her, gloried in the searing contact of flesh with flesh, desire with desire, hunger with hunger. Instinct told her to open herself to him; instinct led him to find his way without groping into her passion-slick vagina; instinct synchronized their movements, the alternating thrust and retreat that carried the both of them to the towering pinnacle that must be surmounted before release can be granted. But it was love that took them over it, love that cushioned their slide down, down, down that glossy mountain, love that landed in the peaceful aftermath of true togetherness.

Dancing Egret was hesitant about leaving their home next morning. She was certain she and Shore Walker would be met with knowing smiles, or even with a recurrence of the previous night's ribaldry, should they come across any of Shore Walker's fellows. But the people they encountered in the plaza merely gave them cheerful greeting. Egret, euphoric from a surfeit of physical and emotional sensation, found it hard to adjust to the fact that, for everyone else, this was just an ordinary day.

When they had made their way into the house crowning the mound, even her family did little more than offer abstracted smiles. Only Crested Heron made much of their entrance. "What is it like to be married?" he demanded. "Will you still teach us songs, Dancing Egret? And did you like the one we sang for you yesterday? When can I come and visit you and Shore Walker in your new house?"

Egret held up her hand. "Being married is most enjoyable," she said primly, her face warming as Shore Walker surreptitiously patted her rear. "As for the rest of your questions: I will; I did; and you are welcome any time. During the daylight hours," she added hastily, as her new husband prompted her with a gentle pinch.

Calusa, whose ears were sharp as any stag's and whose eyes missed nothing, laughed. But all he said was, "You must learn to ask your questions one at a time, Crested Heron. They are not grapes, to be served in bunches."

He had been speaking with four men sent by Chief Tequesta with marriage gifts for Shore Walker and Dancing Egret. Now he gestured toward an intricately worked headband, one embroidered with symbols representative of the Cormorant clan, and to a chain forged of Spanish silver onto which had been tied glistening shells of graduated sizes. "Your sister and her husband wanted to bring these to you, but it seems that White Gull is carrying a babe, and Tequesta felt it would be unwise for her to attempt so long a journey. Instead, they will visit us after the babe has safely arrived, and personally deliver their good wishes then."

Egret's heart sang. How happy White Gull must be, with a child on the way and a husband so devoted he would not leave her even upon receipt of a summons from Great Calusa! And perhaps, by the time her sister came to the island, she herself would be heavy with child. Shore Walker's child.

She slipped the silver necklace over her head, was delighted to see how well the warrior's headband suited Shore Walker. "Please tell your chief and his wife that their gifts made us glad," she said to Tequesta's emissaries. And for the first time noticed the Spanish boy standing a little behind them.

He was young, no more than twelve or thirteen, she guessed, and something in the way he held himself, and in the quality of the disheveled clothing he wore, told her he must be the sort of Spaniard the perfidious Juan Ortiz had once been.

Calusa saw her looking at the boy. "Tequesta sent me a gift

also," he said. "A ship sank recently off of his coast, and he has given me one of its survivors for a slave. The lad looks bright enough, and will doubtless grow in stature if he escapes being our ceremonial sacrifice at the time of First Harvest. He speaks and understands only Spanish gibberish, of course, so I have had one of my servants go in search of"—he broke off as someone came through the wide doorway that faced the mound's ramp—"Kwambu," he finished, and beckoning the trader forward, repeated what he had just said to Egret. "Find out his name," he told him. "And let him know what his status will be in my town." He turned back to his daughter. "Perhaps your serving woman will take him in, and teach him to speak like a civilized Calusan."

Ysabel had done this for other newly arrived Spaniards, and Egret knew she would agree; that woman would mother the world if she could! And Egret had no doubt whatsoever where Ysabel was at this moment. As soon as she and Shore Walker left their house, Ysabel would have scurried up the ladder and begun to neaten the place in anticipation of their return.

Kwambu was talking quietly with the Spanish boy, who responded as much with gesticulation as with speech. "He says his name is D'Escalante Fontaneda," the trader said to Calusa. "The ship he was sailing on was supposed to be taking him and his brother to Spain for their"—he frowned; the Calusa had no word for *schooling*—"to be taught the history and Legends of their people," he said instead.

"Fon-tan-e-da," Calusa said. "These Spaniards have names that make no sense, and are difficult to wrap one's tongue around. But you may tell him that, for now, he will be living with someone who is a native of his homeland." He raised his eyebrows and Egret nodded; she would send Ysabel to fetch him.

As she prepared to leave, one of the couriers from Tequesta addressed Kwambu. "You are the only black-skinned trader I have ever seen," he said to him, "so I wonder if it was you that a bluejay feather-wearer from Timucua country was referring to. I met him just before I came west, while I was in the territory of one of the northern coastal chiefs."

Kwambu smiled courteously. "I am the only black trader in this country, so it must have been."

"You wed a cousin of one of the Timucuan chiefs?"

Kwambu stiffened. "I did."

"That's what he told me, but I didn't entirely believe him,"

Tequesta's courier said. "Well, I'm glad to meet a man who realizes that birthing babies is woman's work." He began to laugh. "Our chief's wife is not nearly so close to delivering as the trader said yours is, yet obviously you weren't afraid to leave her and go about a man's business. Tequesta hovers over his pregnant wife like . . ."

Kwambu did not hear the affectionate but somewhat vulgar comparison. Astonishment washed across his face like an ocean wave over exposed rock.

Egret delayed her leaving long enough to run to her friend and congratulate him, but by then astonishment had been replaced by worry and—as Kwambu looked up at Calusa—a tense wariness.

The Headchief sighed. "Will someone tell me why my life is suddenly complicated by such things as marriages and childbirth, matters which by rights should cause no upheaval whatsoever? They are hardly uncommon events, either of them." He watched Kwambu struggle to find words in which to clothe the request Calusa knew was coming, and decided to make it easy for him. "I was much taken by the pearls you gave my daughter," he said, "the ones she wore for her marriage celebration. And I find myself with an excess of those colored stones the Spanish decorate gold ornaments with. If you promise to find a town where you can exchange the stones for pearls, then you may head north as soon as you can be ready to go."

He waved away Kwambu's thanks and sighed again as he watched him follow Shore Walker and Egret out of the house. Silently, his First Wife handed him a dipper of cool water.

"I must be growing old," he said dolefully, wiping his mouth. "All this youthful ardor"—he shook his head—"tires me out."

"It was staying up all night that fatigued you," Trailing Vine said. "You sat by the fire until nearly dawn, Calusa. When you were not gaming or dancing, that is. Many of the young warriors had already sought their beds before you came to yours."

"That is true," her husband said, brightening, and handed back the empty dipper. "And it was your bed I went to, not my own."

"Nor did you go to one of your other wives'," she pointed out, "although both of them are younger than I am. The passing years can be blessing rather than curse, Calusa, when there is someone you care for growing older with you."

"And whose memories are your memories, too," the Headchief said softly as she hurried away to assign chores to a huddle of idle servants. It did not matter that Trailing Vine could not hear him; had she been able to, she would agree. And he would say it again, only without words, when he made her a gift of the pearls Kwambu had been commissioned to find for him.

Kwambu walked back and forth, back and forth, in front of the woman's hut that stood by itself in the shadow of the palisade. His face was haggard with weariness, but concern and frustration kept him on his feet. Within the small building was Moon of Winter, attended by Walks Tall Woman and two other matrons, but the trader had not seen her; would not see her, as her aunt had informed him sternly, until the babe had been born, the cycle of birth-bleeding ended, and a purification ceremony performed.

The aroma of burning herbs crept out of the hut and insinuated itself into air weighted with the pressure of a slow-building summer storm. To think he had come so far so fast, only to arrive too late to see his wife before her labor began! All the way to Outina, Moon of Winter's image had gone before him, an image that beckoned constantly, that urged him to plunge through swamps rather than take the time to skirt them, that allowed him to sleep only in snatches, that often made him forget to eat until dizziness warned him that he must. He had paddled along rivers with such strenuous strokes that the muscles in his arms protested, and raced across meadows until his lungs were on fire. And all for naught. All for naught.

A groan, pain-swelled, followed the path taken by the scent of smoldering herbs. Kwambu clenched his fists; it was not the first such sound to seep from the women's hut, and each time he felt as though a lance had pierced his heart. A day and a night and half a day had gone by, and Moon of Winter continued to suffer in an effort to bear the child that had grown from his seed. It was wrong that women alone must endure this agony when it took man and woman both to make a child. If any god had the power to grant such a boon, Kwambu would pray to be allowed to take his wife's place during the birthing of their baby.

Since this was impossible, why must he be prevented from offering the pittance he was so anxious to offer: his encouragement, his support, his love? Why did tradition keep man and woman apart at a time when they needed so desperately to be together? Why was there nothing, nothing at all, that he could do to help Moon of Winter?

Walks Tall Woman slipped out of the hut, frowned when she saw him. "Why are you still here?" she asked. "I told you to go to the Principal House and wait. Falc . . . I mean, Outina, is there, and the Shaman. Go. Go." She flapped her hands at him as though he were a rodent that had invaded her cornfield.

"Why is it taking so long?" he asked her. "How can Moon of Winter endure so much pain? Had I known it would be like this—"

"What would you have done? Kept from your wife's bed?" Scorn was in Walks Tall Woman's face, in every inch of her angular body. "Tell me something I will believe, trader."

A prolonged grumble of thunder gave Kwambu excuse not to attempt reply. Even if he could say honestly that he would have made such a sacrifice, Walks Tall Woman's scorn would not have abated. She had little respect for any man, and none at all for the trader from the south her niece had been fool enough to wed. He watched her go to the stream bisecting this corner of the compound and fill the clay pot she had brought out of the woman's hut. Then they both spun around as a shrill scream sliced another growl of thunder in half. When Walks Tall Woman came rushing past, water sloshing from her pot, Kwambu thrust out his hand, caught her by the elbow.

"It is not natural, is it, for a babe to take so long being born?" he said hoarsely.

She tried to shake herself free and could not. "It has happened before," she said. "Now let me go to her."

"Is there nothing anyone can do to make things easier for her?" His fingers tightened, his eyes burned into hers.

For the first time, she recognized the anguish in those eyes and understood that this man might be different from most. "We are helping her all we can," she said. "And Watches for Omens has begged the gods to help her, too. It is only that"— she hesitated; ordinarily, she would not go into such detail except with another woman—"Moon of Winter is small-boned, and the child appears to be big. Birthing takes longer when that is the way of it."

He loosened his grasp. "And hurts more," he said.

She nodded and moved toward the hut. "You will do better to go and wait with my son and our Shaman," she said over her shoulder, but another shattering scream drowned her out.

Kwambu leaped forward, grabbed Walks Tall Woman's arm again. "Tell me," he said urgently, "does Moon of Winter still wear her pouch around her neck, the one made from pantherskin?"

Walks Tall Woman wondered if demons were beginning to addle the trader's mind. "It would complicate the birth, to have a knotted thong, or any kind of knot, within the hut," she said. Was it possible that, where he came from, people were ignorant of such things? "Now let me go. Moon of Winter needs me."

And does not need me, Kwambu thought miserably. But perhaps she did, perhaps there was a way he could be of help to her after all. "Her pouch," he said, "where is it now?" Walks Tall Woman scowled; her patience was at an end. But as she pulled away from him, he held out his hands beseechingly. "Please. That was no idle question. Her crystal is in that pouch, and holding it might enable Moon of Winter to deliver our child more quickly. If nothing else, the crystal will comfort her, and help her to withstand the pain."

"I will see that it is given to her," Walks Tall Woman began, for what he said made sense.

But Kwambu was shaking his head. "No," he said. "If a strange hand touches the crystal, its magic will be diminished. Only its owner may handle it."

"Then how is she to take hold of it?" Walks Tall Woman demanded. "If you think that my niece is in any condition to unfold that pouch and take the crystal from it, then you know nothing about the rigors of childbirth, trader."

Her words confirmed what Kwambu feared most, that Moon of Winter had weakened to an alarming degree. "Listen," he said, praying that Walks Tall Woman would believe him, "I was the one who gave the crystal to Moon of Winter. I think that the crystal will remember the feel of my flesh and be unaffected by it. I can remove it from the pouch and place it in Moon of Winter's hand."

"But you may not go into the woman's hut," Walks Tall Woman said stridently. "That is forbidden, as well you know." Her expression softened a trifle. "I am sorry, trader. But unless there is some other way of giving it to her, then my niece will have to manage without her crystal."

Kwambu looked at the low door of the hut, looked back at the woman who barred his way into it.

"I know better than to go against your traditions," he said.

"But if you could bring me the pouch, and see that my wife is moved close enough to the door so that one arm will reach through it . . ."

Walks Tall Woman's response proved that her reputation for quick thinking was fairly earned. "Wait here," she said, and went swiftly into the hut.

It seemed an eternity that he paced the ground beneath a rapidly darkening sky, but in only a few moments she rejoined him and gave him the pantherskin pouch. "Moon of Winter's strength is unreliable," she cautioned. "We will have to move her arm for her, but I have warned the others that we must not touch the crystal once you have put it in her hand."

Before he could thank her, she was gone again. He moved close to the hut's doorway, crouched and waited.

The arm that was eased out into the eerie, prestorm light was oiled with perspiration, and the hand Kwambu reached for nearly slipped from his gentle grip. He felt for the pulse in Moon of Winter's slender wrist; its rhythm was feeble and erratic, and the trader's fear increased tenfold.

He had not, when this plan first occurred to him, thought to take advantage of his wife's nearness by talking to her, and he did so now without conscious decision. "Moon of Winter, I have taken the crystal from your pouch and am placing it in your hand," he said quietly but distinctly.

She made no response. Well, he had not expected any, for all that he'd hoped for one. With infinite care, he closed her flaccid fingers over the translucent stone. "Now you are holding your crystal," he told her. "Feel its power flow into you, Moon of Winter. Feel it replenish your strength."

He cocked his head. That faint murmur; had it been Moon of Winter's voice? He tightened his grip on her closed fist. "It is soothing you also," he went on. "Your pain will dissipate as the crystal fills you with serenity, for even womb-pain can be eased by true serenity. And the babe that has been fighting to leave your womb will find his passage made smoother. Soon he will slide into life as easily as an otter slides down a mudbank into the river that is his proper home."

His voice rose and fell, rose and fell, as though it were a lullaby he chanted. Where the words came from, he did not know, would never know. "And more than the crystal seeks to comfort you," he said. "The hand that is wrapped around your hand is lending you whatever strength I possess. Let it pass from my flesh to yours; accept it as you have accepted my love, and let me be a part of what you are going through. Your pain, I take upon myself; I yearn to suffer in your stead." His voice trembled, and suddenly his flesh wore the same sheen of perspiration that Moon of Winter's did. "You are my wife, and I love you," he said brokenly, then said it again, more strongly, as Thunder's voice vied with his.

The hand that he held, the one clutching the crystal, stirred. He felt Moon of Winter's fingers tighten around the stone even as she gave a great cry. And although there was pain behind the cry, it seemed to him that there was triumph in it, too.

"Release her hand, trader." The command came hard upon the heels of an agitated whispering within. Reluctantly, Kwambu obeyed, then came shakily to his feet. Head bowed, he stood with his eyes closed, heedless of the huge raindrops that signaled the onset of a downpour. He had so hoped to be able to help, had thought, briefly, that he'd done so. But obviously he had not. And there was nothing more he could think of to do.

Then another cry came to his ears, a cry so thin it might have been the wailing of some lost and lonely spirit. Kwambu's flesh puckered and he scarcely breathed as he tried to interpret the sound.

The cry, more lusty now, was repeated, and a moment later Walks Tall Woman emerged from the hut.

She looked at the man who seemed unaware that water was gushing now from the clouds he stood beneath, and her mouth curved in what, for her, was a smile. "My niece," she said, "insisted that you be told at once. She has given you a son and"—she shook her head, amazed to be delivering such a message from someone so exhausted she could not speak above a whisper—"she promises that he is only the first of the many sons she hopes to bear for you."

Kwambu exhaled his pent breath, turned his face into the cooling rain and drank deep of the joy that flooded into him.

PART II

1550–1567

Chapter 25

Dancing Egret refused admittance to the tears that crowded behind her eyes. For thirty years she had been schooling herself against crying; she would not do so now, however great the provocation. "Vision Seeker is waiting outside," she said quietly. "He has a new healing ceremony. . . ."

Headchief Calusa shifted, grimaced, resettled himself. "No. No more rattle-shaking and chanting, no more vile-tasting medicines. Let us have done with pretending that my life can be prolonged." He grinned, and his awful gauntness was temporarily relieved. "It is enough for me that I can sit here and look back on my life with no regrets. I have made enemies—what man does not?—but I have made good friends, also. And I have always taken care of my people. I have done well, have I not, Egret?"

"You have," Egret said unsteadily, "and will be remembered for it." She hesitated, rushed on: "And I will remember, always, how you have been kind enough to ask my opinion on so many matters that women are not usually consulted about."

"I was being shrewd, not kind. Most women are not like you. Just as most men are not like me."

His pronouncement echoed in the vast room, for it was empty of everyone but the two who sat talking. The rest had departed at Calusa's command; their Headchief might be dying, but his word would be law until the end.

Calusa had closed his eyes. Now he opened them again. "Your brother . . . I wish he were more like you."

"Heron is barely sixteen," Egret said cautiously. "It's only natural that he wants to spend most of this time sporting with his comrades or trying to impress pretty girls."

But her father was shaking his head. "He has neither the

skills nor the temperament to be a good Headchief. He will need help, Egret. Fortunately, he has grown accustomed to your waiting upon my counselors whenever I meet with them." He cleared his throat; how he detested the unreliable rasp his voice had become! "He will think it natural for you to do the same when he is sitting in my place," he finished.

Egret held back the protest impulse prodded her to make. Her father was asking her to act as advisor to her young brother, even correct him when necessary. Which would not be easy; since he'd been a small boy, Heron had blithely ignored correction. "I will do what I can," she said reluctantly.

"I know you will. And my son can have no better guide than the daughter I myself have trained." A small smile played about his mouth, and his eyes closed once more.

Sleep had reclaimed him, and Egret was unable to ask the question that leaped into her mind. Was it to create a mentor for Heron that Calusa had insisted she spend so much time talking about matters political, why he'd made her privy even to information he occasionally saw fit to keep from his own counselors?

And did he understand what a burden he was laying across her shoulders? Most likely, she thought wryly. But at least she would have Shore Walker to lean on when the load threatened to crush her. Which was doubtless the reason Calusa had decided to favor their marrying. Nothing was beyond her father. He was a man without equal, and when he awoke next she would tell him so.

She smiled briefly as she realized that he would be quick to agree with her; Calusa had never pretended to modesty!

There came a gentle stirring of the air; a single strand of Egret's hair lifted, drifted across her forehead. Then the breeze, if breeze it was, was gone, and the ponderous heat resumed its reign in the house at the top of the mound. It impregnated the silence, altering the substance of it, adding an unnatural stillness to what had, before, been merely lack of sound.

And she knew, before she turned to look at the figure sprawled against the rolled bed robes, what had brought about the change. Slowly, carefully, she came to her feet; squaring her shoulders, she walked to the wide doorway that gave upon the ramp.

The rest of Headchief Calusa's family waited outside, and one glance at Egret's face told them all they needed to know.

Dancing Egret went and stood before Crested Heron. "You are Calusa now," she said.

They came from everywhere to show their respect for a man who would be sorely missed: each town in Calusa's province was represented by its chief and an escort of warriors; the Timucuan Holata, Oathkaqua, came, with his youngest wife and three of their daughters; and Tequesta and White Gull brought along a full complement of warriors to stand sentry so that Calusa's own warriors might devote themselves to mourning their Headchief.

Egret stood in her house and looked out at the scaffold on which her father lay. Instead of resting upon the usual plain wooden grid, Calusa's body had been placed on the elegant slatted trellis old Mask Maker had carved for his grandson's marriage. Next to the scaffold stood the priest, overseeing preparation of an altar that would receive the slaves selected for ritual sacrifice, and underneath it warriors were laying faggots to make the funeral pyre. Crested Heron was not with them, of course; tomorrow he would put on the feathered ceremonial cloak, fasten egret plumes to a headband decorated with their father's sun-shaped, sun-colored emblem of authority, and receive homage from those who had come to bury one Headchief and vow fealty to another.

Egret turned as White Gull came into the house. Her sister's eyes were swollen and her cheeks damp, but she had finished with her crying. "I wish I had brought my children along," she said. "If only our oldest had not fallen and injured his leg. . . ."

"It would have been unfair to bring the rest if he had to stay behind," Egret assured her. "You made the right decision, White Gull." Her sister had grown plump as a well-fed dove, and as contented. A good marriage, one that had gifted her with four sons and two daughters, was the reason for it, of course.

"Will the children be singing tomorrow?" White Gull asked. "I think our father's souls will be glad if they do."

"They will. Naturally, they are not the same children who sang when you last visited the island. Those have all grown up now."

White Gull laughed. "I am aware of how fast children grow," she said. "One moment they are babies, the next they are training to be warriors."

Dancing Egret stifled a pang of envy. The only children she

had were those who came to her regularly to learn the Calusan Legends, and much as she loved every one of them, she was never able to forget that they belonged to other women. More fortunate women. "Let me show you the burial box Shore Walker has made for Great Calusa," she said, and was prompted to smile when White Gull exclaimed over the twin dolphins incised on its inner lid. "Shore Walker is a fine craftsman," Egret said proudly. "One day, when he has put aside his warrior's weapons, he will stay at home with me and make masks and plaques and all manner of things from wood."

White Gull smiled, too. "And you will be happy to have him with you all the time, won't you?"

"I will," Egret said. "He is so often away—hunting, patrolling our territory's borders, escorting message-bearers to this town and that. I miss him when he is not here."

"It's a good thing, when there is love between husband and wife," her sister said. "Thanks to you, I know how wonderful that kind of love is. Even though I once accused you of meddling in matters that were not your concern, I must confess that I will be forever grateful for the meddling that made it possible for me to wed Tequesta."

This time, Dancing Egret found it impossible to return her sister's teasing smile. It suddenly occurred to her that what Calusa had termed "guidance" when he spoke of Egret's advising Crested Heron would be, in actuality, only another form of what White Gull rightly called "meddling." And her long-ago friend, Kneeling Cypress, whose world had ultimately been shattered because she had heeded Egret's advice ... wouldn't she use an even harsher word to describe this woman's appalling habit of interfering in other people's lives?

After her sister had departed, Egret continued to puzzle over this, and was left so downcast that Shore Walker asked gently if she were dreading the ceremony that would begin with the next day's dawning. Egret shook her head. "No," she said. "It will be an impressive ritual, and no one loved ceremony better than my father. I will think about that, instead of my grief. What bothers me is something White Gull said today." She repeated her sister's words and admitted to the unsettling thoughts they had spawned.

He put his arms around her and nuzzled her neck. "You may meddle in my life whenever you choose," he declared. "If you hadn't done so twelve years ago, we would not be here now." He stroked her back, long, lazy strokes that relaxed her but at the same time quickened her breathing. "And I can think of no place I would rather be, or of anyone I would rather be with."

Thunder, the fretful kind of thunder that rarely brought them the rain they craved, rumbled in the distance as he led her to their bed. "When you care about people as wholeheartedly as you do, Egret, it's natural to try and bring about what's best for them. Don't waste time blaming yourself if occasionally something goes amiss. The gods make the final decisions, you know, where all of us are concerned." He bent his head and teased at one breast with his tongue, drawing circles around and around the nipple. In a moment Egret's worries had been obliterated; even the ache of emptiness her father's dying had left her with disappeared as she gave herself up to the joy of lovemaking.

The smoke sent up by the roaring pyre lingered long in the plaza, its last trailing wisps filling the leaden air with the aroma of Vision Seeker's sacred tobacco and the sweet herbs Calusa's surviving widows had cast into the flames. A tendril of it curled around the head of the new Calusa, the young Calusa, who stood on the second tier of the Temple mound to acknowledge the salutations of the dignitaries who had come to the island. One by one they approached him, knelt, and turned up their hands in a gesture that had originated with the ancients.

Crested Heron was conducting himself magnificently, his sister thought. He had been suitably solemn during the burial rites for their father; now, he turned a beaming smile upon the men who were accepting him as leader or ally. He even offered a few personal words to each of them, which was clever of him. Many must have had reservations about swearing allegiance to so young a leader, but whatever he was finding to say seemed to be restoring their confidence in the choice they were making.

"My son even looks like a leader." Watchful Doe's eyes, so sad this morning, sparkled now. "He will do well, Dancing Egret."

"He looks like his father did at his age," Herb Gatherer put in softly, "so tall and broad of shoulder. And he bears himself proudly, as Calusa always did."

Egret looked at the woman who had become her father's wife only because she was Trailing Vine's sister. She had not been chosen by Calusa, as his other wives had been. Even after

Trailing Vine died, more than a year ago now, Herb Gatherer
had not been accorded the status of First Wife. Was her grief
today greater or lesser because Calusa had never even pretended to love her? Perhaps, in her quiet way, she had been
grieving about that most of her life.

But what she had said about Heron was true. If the Sun God
ever put on human guise, he would probably resemble the new
Headchief; Crested Heron's handsome face glowed, and the
oiled flesh that covered his sinewy body reflected the sunset.
And Watchful Doe was probably right about him also; in time
he would become as great a leader as his father had been. She
told herself it was wrong to be uneasy about him merely because he had been less than pleased that morning when she
fixed in her hair the white plumes Calusa had given her. *Despite your name, the Headchief alone wears the plumes of an
egret,* he had told her, frowning, and only gave in when his
mother and Herb Gatherer confirmed that Calusa himself had
years ago decreed that his daughter might also display such
plumes. He had been nervous, she told herself now, as what
youth wouldn't be who must put on the mantle of leadership
so abruptly? And he had offered her a genuine smile, a grateful
smile, when she'd told him that she had arranged for the children to sing a song of praise for him in addition to the one
they would be singing to honor their dead Headchief's spirit.

The time had come for the island's warriors, led by Prowling Panther, to salute the new Calusa, and behind them came
the town's artisans and traders. Egret smiled. Kwambu towered
above the pair of Spaniards who had recently earned their
bluejay feathers, Fontaneda and a lad who had come here
shortly after he had. Gomez, that was his name. They were
names that Egret could pronounce correctly, thanks to the tu-
toring she had received over the years from her obliging serving woman.

It was all over but the feasting, a meal that, sadly, would
be sparse indeed by ordinary standards, but—thanks to Kwambu—there would at least be an abundance of sassafras tea to
wash it down with. From his latest trip to the place Egret knew
he now thought of as home, he had brought back a bundle of
the fragrant root, hoping that an infusion of it might lend
strength to the ailing Headchief. Nothing could have done so,
but the tea had comforted Calusa while he was still able to
swallow sufficient quantities of it. She must remember to tell
Kwambu that.

The opportunity presented itself after most of the guests had gone to their temporary quarters to get a good night's sleep before beginning their homeward journeys. Shore Walker brought the trader to their house, and the three settled down to talk of the man whose flame-purified bones the priest had sealed into the box Shore Walker made to hold them.

"I had forgotten, until Vision Speaker begged our gods to welcome my father's soul, that his birth name was Sunquene," Egret said. "His father—my grandfather—died before I was born, so I never heard him called anything but Calusa. It's sad, that I should have to be reminded of the name his mother gave him, a name Trailing Vine must surely have used when she and my father were young."

Shore Walker pressed the hand that rested in his. "The people our parents were in the days of their youth must always be strangers to us," he said. "This is only natural, Egret, and nothing to be sad about."

"I suppose it would not be, ordinarily," she said. "But today . . ."

"Today is a day for sadness," Shore Walker said, and she gave him a grateful smile. How comforting it was to be understood.

She was even more grateful when her husband went on to tell of the time Calusa had challenged his new-made warriors—one of whom had been a decidedly nervous Shore Walker—to pit their skills with the dart thrower against their Headchief's. And when Kwambu countered with a hilarious tale about Calusa taking subtle revenge upon a glib trader who had tried to foist ill-cured buckskins upon his youngest wife, she found her sadness receding.

"I wish I could have spoken one last time with your father," Kwambu said to Dancing Egret when they had finished the reminiscing that dulls sorrow's sharper edges. "I do not wish to worry the new Headchief so soon, but I am not certain that it will be wise to allow Fontaneda and Gomez the freedom of movement traders are usually entitled to." He shrugged apologetically. "I should have mentioned this months ago, I suppose," he said, "but I continued to hope that I might not have to."

"You have reason to mistrust the two?" The question came from Shore Walker.

"Specific reason? No. Which also made me hesitant to speak of it before. But I can see no sign of true loyalty in either of them, no appreciation for their having been given the chance to serve Calusa as traders rather than live out their lives as slaves. Instead I see resentment, particularly when treasure is brought to the island from a ship wrecked off the southern coast. It is Spanish gold, they tell one another, and the Calusa have no right to it. They would lay claim to it if they dared, but"—his expression was carefully neutral—"I notice that they never speak of wanting to see such treasure distributed among all the Spaniards who live in Calusa country."

"I wish my father had known this," Egret told him, worry puckering her forehead. "My brother has no experience to call upon as yet, and will not know what to do about it."

"Nor am I anxious to go to him and tell him that, although he can safely place his trust in his African trader, he ought to be suspicious of the Spaniards," Kwambu said. "I will probably only succeed in making him suspicious of me as well. Your brother is bound to tell himself that all three of us came from beyond the eastern ocean, even if our homelands were not the same; all of us were originally slaves; and all of us are aliens in this land."

Egret laughed. "Kwambu, not only do you know this land better than I ever can, or even Shore Walker, you have a wife and three children who are native to Timucua country! How can you call yourself alien?"

"I was not born here; although I speak your language, and Timucuan, neither is my native tongue; and"—he held out his arm—"no one in this country has flesh the color of mine."

It was Shore Walker's turn to laugh. "You make much out of nothing," he said easily. "My flesh is browner than my wife's; her brother's flesh is lighter than both of ours. As for where you were born, what can that matter? You described for us once how you leaped over the side of a huge ship because you were so eager to come to Calusa's island. Which means that, unlike the two Spaniards, you came here voluntarily. Why, you've lived most of your life in this country! If that does not make you one of us, I cannot imagine what does."

"And," Egret added, her eyes twinkling, "you are wrong about being the only black-skinned person in this country. Aren't you forgetting about your children, Kwambu?"

He considered, smiled. "You are both right and wrong when you assume that, because my skin is black, theirs is also. Hawk Flying High, although he has my features, has flesh only a little darker than his mother's; Red Fox Barking has skin the color of a hickory nut; but my daughter, Kaia"—he smiled more broadly—"who has inherited Moon of Winter's beauty, did indeed inherit my flesh."

"*Kai-yah,*" Egret and Shore Walker said in unison. "Your daughter's name has music in it," Egret added, and Shore Walker smiled agreement.

"Among my people," the trader said, "Kaia means 'lovable.' Which my little Kaia has been since the day she was born."

Shore Walker slid his left arm across Egret's shoulders. Although she was careful not to show it, he knew full well that she was wishing desperately she had been able to give her husband children he could boast about. As Kwambu went on to talk further about his sons and daughter, his voice swelled with pride, and nothing would ever convince Dancing Egret that Shore Walker did not envy him. Which, in truth, he did; but only a little. To have Egret for his wife was far more important to Shore Walker than to have fathered a score of children.

They were still talking when full dark descended, a humid dark that hung around them in stifling folds. Shore Walker flexed his fingers surreptitiously; any extreme of weather brought a debilitating ache to the tendons beneath the scar that ran from wrist to elbow. During his last trip into the glades, when he'd had to swing his club to finish off the single bear the hunters had found, he had come close to losing his grip on the weapon. Nobody had seemed to notice, and he meant that no one ever should. Much as he enjoyed making things out of wood, like his grandfather before him, he had no wish to settle to sedentary work until he was considerably older than he was right now.

Egret turned and smiled at him when she felt his arm move, and he tightened his grip on her shoulder. It was essential to Shore Walker that Egret never realize how his encounter with the alligator had left him with a weakness that might label him unfit to be a warrior. She would only worry over him if she knew, and she had enough to worry about now that her young brother was Headchief. Egret had promised her father to see that Heron became a good chief. Shore Walker hoped it would be an easy promise to honor, but somehow he doubted it.

His doubts burgeoned as White Gull burst into the house and began to speak agitatedly even before she had been given welcome. "Egret, you must speak to Crested Heron. Tequesta asked him if he will send food to our town if the drought continues, as our father has always done. And he has refused to do so!"

Chapter 26

"Your accusation is unjust, Egret. I did not refuse to send food to our sister's husband."

Her brother's dark eyes were wide with hurt, and Dancing Egret found herself wishing she had taken the time to question White Gull further. Last night she had been too intent upon reassuring her to do so, and this morning she had waited only until it was light enough before racing across the squareground and up the mound. "I did not mean to sound accusing," she said more moderately. "Truly, Heron. But it does seem as though our sister misunderstood. Or perhaps Chief Tequesta did, when you were speaking with him."

A smile transformed the young Headchief's face. "I should imagine it was White Gull. That sort of thing happens when women concern themselves with men's affairs." His smile expanded. "As you are doing now, Dancing Egret," he said affectionately. "You look upon me still as your little brother, I think, but—since you were always my favorite sister—you can be forgiven for that."

She returned his smile. "It's hard to change the shape of my thinking," she admitted. "But I'm so glad I may tell White Gull she was wrong, that you will send foodstuffs to Tequesta should they have need of them."

He nodded. "Of course I will. Naturally, I must tend first to the needs of my own people, not only those on the island, but the people in all of my towns. What is left—if any—will go to our friends in other tribes."

"But our father, whenever food was scarce, always divided what food we had equally among our own Townchiefs and our allies," she reminded him. "He used to say"—she seemed to hear his voice as she repeated his words—"that it was better for all of us to be a little hungry than for anyone to starve. His allies knew and appreciated this, Heron. That's why they remained his allies."

"As White Gull's husband," her brother said, "Tequesta is bound to us by ties of blood. Food or no food, that will not change."

Dancing Egret, telling herself that Crested Heron was too young to have a memory as long as her own, kept both voice and expression uncritical. "In the past, such ties have been known to loosen when slights were imagined or offense taken for some reason. Our father was always alert to such threats to the alliances he worked so hard to make and to keep."

The new Headchief laughed at her earnestness. "There may have been a time when alliance with Chief Tequesta was vital, during the years when the Spanish came often to these shores. But, except for shipwreck survivors, the only ones to come here since I was a child were those three black-robed fools that lacked the sense even to carry weapons. And in spite of the warning taken to them by that Spaniard your husband seized when De Soto invaded Ucita's town, they were dealt with quickly and efficiently, were they not? So I did not put anything important at risk by speaking honestly to Tequesta. Which is all that I did, Egret. Certainly I said nothing to offend him. Indeed, I spent much of our meeting heaping praise upon the man for insisting that his warriors train as rigorously at sea as on land. 'Your people will never lack for food,' I told him, 'so long as your ocean continues to teem with fish and manatee and whales.' "

"People cannot eat fish alone and remain healthy," Egret said mildly. "And White Gull tells me that this season's crops have withered in the fields, and that the berries and roots the women usually gather are poor, shriveled things. They are merely asking for food to supplement the fish, Crested Heron. And so long as we are fortunate enough to have it to give . . ."

"But we have no excess," her brother said. He stood up and went to look out over the plaza, waved to acknowledge the greetings sent up to him by a trio of warriors. "In truth, if it were not for the new treaty I mean to force the Timucuan Mocoso to agree to, I would not dare plan to marry so soon." He swung around, turned his engaging grin in her direction.

"You are surprised," he said with satisfaction. "You did not know I planned to wed."

"I did not. I thought you enjoyed the attentions of all the maidens far too much to settle for just one." And what did this, surprise though it certainly was, have to do with sending food to Tequesta should the need arise?

"My father's old friend, Oathkaqua, has a particularly lovely daughter," Crested Heron said. "As soon as I saw her, I knew I must have her. And by making her my wife, I am reinforcing our ties with Oathkaqua. Which would have pleased my father, I am sure. In any event, she will be coming to me after the moon has three times shown all of her faces to us. And I mean to celebrate our marriage in suitable fashion, not with the sort of miserly feasting we had yesterday. That means we shall be needing all of the foodstuffs we have stored away, and more besides. Which is why the emissaries I shall be sending to Mocoso will tell him that his brother-in-law may no longer expect to receive so great a portion of the goods our traders carry when they pass through Canegacola's territory. Half that much is sufficient payment for their safe passage."

"Suppose he thinks otherwise?"

The Headchief shrugged. "Then Kwambu and the Spaniards will have to find another route north."

Dancing Egret tried not to let her exasperation show. "That will mean making a treaty with yet another Timucuan chief. And the terms he demands may not be to your liking, either."

Crested Heron raised his eyebrows. "But only Canegacola has a host of superbly trained warriors that no sane man will tangle with. The lesser chiefs can always be persuaded to my terms by force if necessary." He smiled again, broadly. "You see, Egret, I have thought everything through carefully. I am more like my father than you thought I would be, am I not?"

Her head was reeling. What he said was sensible enough that any argument she put forth would sound ridiculous. And if she gave Heron cause to laugh at her now, she could never hope to influence him in the future. Yet there was so much he did not understand, could not understand, because he had never been privy to their father's methods of dealing with both friend and potential enemy. "The counselors are in favor of all of this?" she asked quietly.

"I have not discussed it with them, but I see no difficulty convincing them that my ideas are sound. Those who disagree can easily be replaced, after all. And will be; I have no desire to be badgered by a group of quarrelsome old men."

He swung around as Watchful Doe, Herb Gatherer, and Brown Pelican, followed by basket-toting servants and slaves, came in. "I expect the women will be needing your help with something," he said to his sister. "I will not keep you longer, Egret."

Despite his smile, it was a dismissal. Dancing Egret, her brow puckered, ignored his pointed suggestion that she occupy herself with women's work and went to find a place where she could do some uninterrupted thinking.

Egret scrambled down the sloping sides of the raised squareground and took the path leading to the lagoon their ancestors had dug to make a water court behind the Temple mound. Last night's humidity had not abated, and swarms of gnats hung motionless in the thick air. Beneath her feet, the ordinarily soggy ground was almost gritty for want of moisture, and the palmetto shrubs she skirted bristled with dusty fronds. She was prepared to find that the water in the lagoon lay well below the level of the seawall that girded it, but its color was strange, too; it had taken on the same yellowish tinge the sky had been wearing ever since she arose that morning. It looked as though the sun had decided to leak its color across the Upper World rather than pouring it upon the earth. Yet if earth had been deprived of the sun's gold, it had been spared none of its heat; waves of it shimmered everywhere she turned, blurring the outlines of the familiar.

She hunkered down on a curved section of seawall and concentrated on the problem of her brother. It was not uncommon for a sixteen-year-old to believe that he knew, essentially, all that he needed to know; those who had grown beyond this youthful arrogance usually withheld comment and let experience serve as instructor. But Crested Heron was Headchief; whatever he said or did affected all their people, and Egret had pledged to see that he did not act unwisely. Her father had offered no suggestions on how to live up to that pledge, which had shown lack of wisdom on his part, she thought wryly. And the least wise of all of them was Dancing Egret for letting herself make such a promise in the first place.

Not that she'd had much choice in the matter, or even time to give it proper consideration before she'd agreed to do what her father asked of her. Everything had happened so fast, was still happening so fast. . . .

"Do you want to be alone, or may I join you?"

Egret came out of her reverie and motioned Kwambu down beside her. "You have given me advice in the past," she told him, "good advice. Perhaps you can do so again." And she told him about the conversation she had just had with her brother.

"It may be that you are upsetting yourself prematurely," Kwambu said when she came to the end of her story.

"I hope I am," she said. "I love my brother, and will be overjoyed if he proves himself an able Headchief."

"You must allow for his youth," Kwambu said. "Some things Heron can only learn for himself, despite your desire to forestall his mistakes. At least he has shown that he is capable of making decisions, which Moon of Winter's cousin, at the start, had trouble doing. You remember my speaking of him? He was another who had leadership thrust upon him before he was fully ready for it."

Egret nodded. "You have mentioned him before."

"Well, his failing was the opposite of your brother's. In the beginning, he allowed his mother to guide him to every decision. It was hard not to, I suppose; he has no sister, so his mother continued as Principal Woman of the town. Which meant she went on speaking her mind on virtually all matters, something Principal Women are permitted to do. Outina listened, of course, and since his mother had experience to call upon and he did not, he was too often persuaded to echo her opinions. That could have cost him the respect of his people, but as he gained confidence, my wife's cousin gradually learned to trust his own instincts. Now he shows signs of becoming a truly praiseworthy leader." He laughed. "Walks Tall Woman has blinded herself to his maturing; she continues to feed him advice along with the meals she prepares for the family, and will not see that he only pretends to swallow most of it."

Egret laughed. "This Walks Tall Woman does not sound particularly likable."

Kwambu shrugged. "She is a person worthy of respect, however. She is"—he grinned—"a woman of commendable strength. As you are."

Egret grimaced. "And, like her, I am trying to direct the actions of a tribal leader. Are you hinting that I might jeopardize Heron's authority by doing so?"

He shook his head. "Indeed not. You have more subtlety than Walks Tall Woman, for one thing. Also, you will recognize when advice is needed and when it is not. And your father was right: Crested Heron has need of guidance, for a while at least."

"If the Calusa recognized Principal Women," Dancing Egret said, "my task would be made easier, wouldn't it? Indeed, all towns would probably benefit from having Principal Women." She was not speaking idly; there were often times when a woman's instincts might be more reliable than a man's reasoning, or when a woman's preoccupation with the immediate should temper the long view taken by most men. She sighed; why should she think the practice of a faraway people would be a fine thing to adopt, but have so little patience with her own brother for not strictly adhering to the ways of their father?

She realized suddenly that Kwambu had stood up, was trying to urge her to her feet. "What is it?" she asked.

He pointed toward the canal, and she looked up to see a spiral of smudge-colored clouds racing in their direction. Beneath the clouds, the waters of the bay were mounding into spume-crested billows. "A rain squall," Kwambu said unnecessarily, as the advance surge of a gusting wind reached them, "with more behind it."

"Thank the gods," she said fervently as they headed back to the town. "I had begun to fear it might never rain again."

And realized that one of the problems she had come out here to mull over might have solved itself: If the rain that was beginning to pelt them signaled the tardy beginning of the wet season, game animals would return to the glades, crops would flourish, and there would be no need to find a way to persuade Crested Heron that food must be sent to their allies as well as to subject towns.

The rest she could worry about later.

Intermittent squalls dumped torrents of water upon the island throughout the rest of that day and into the night, but the eerie stillnesses that marked the intervals between storms were packed with heat. Sleeping was difficult, even after the final storm had deserted the island to swing out over the river glades. No one was sorry when morning finally came, although it was a morning sullen in both appearance and temperament. The clouds in the sky were mounding like slow-moving, spume-tipped waves; their crests were pale as bleached doe-skin, yet they were dark on the bottom and yellow-gray oozed from their midsections. And the air hung heavy over the town, just as it had the day before.

The hair on Dancing Egret's arms prickled, and she found herself feeling grateful that White Gull and Tequesta, who had left the island early the preceding day, were surely safe home by now. "It's odd," she said to Shore Walker, "but I feel as though we are being made to wait for something. Something none too pleasant."

Shore Walker did not laugh, as she had expected him to. "It has been a long, long time," he said, "and I was only a small child. But I can remember another day like this one." He hugged her to him, rested his chin against the top of her head. "Before it was over, a monster storm had raged in from the ocean, bringing thunder and lightning such as I'd never before seen. Waves began crashing against the seawall, then leaped over it to swoop upon the causeways and flood the town. And the wind . . . its shrieking I will never, ever forget."

"You are talking about a hurricane," Egret said. She had heard about such storms but had never experienced one.

"I am. And I overheard some of the elders talking among themselves. Their memories of the last storm are clearer than mine, and they were saying that we would be wise to make ready for one."

"How do we do that?"

"Every boat on the island will be taken to the mangroves that line its eastern side. They will be secured among the trees, and that is where the people will go for sanctuary from the storm."

Dancing Egret stared at him. "A canoe is safer than a house?"

"If the storm is powerful enough," he said grimly, "there will be no houses left standing afterward. And it's not that the boats themselves offer safety; the mangroves do that. Even the strongest of winds rarely topples a full-grown mangrove."

Egret looked around her. "If our house is blown away," she said slowly, "everything we have will go with it."

"Some, we can take with us," he told her, "in a small pack, one that can be carried on my back and will not impede move-ment. I will leave it to you to decide what to put in it."

Ignoring the flutter of panic beneath her breastbone, Egret moved away from him, began to select this and that from the shelves. The animal carvings Shore Walker had been working on prior to her father's dying must go with them, even if everything else had to be left behind. She fingered the doe's head that was one of her favorites; the animal's huge eyes, the perfectly shaped ears that fit into the neat sockets Shore Walker had reamed to hold them ... even Mask Maker had never made anything so beautiful. It calmed her merely to look at it. And the alligator with its hinged jaw, the pelican's head with its elegantly curved beak, those must go also. Shore Walker had found a darker wood to make the kneeling panther he had still to finish; or was it supposed to be a priest wearing a panther-face mask? It was too soon to tell, but the carving must go with them, certainly.

When he realized what she was doing, Shore Walker protested. "Egret, I can always make more. And better. By the time I have grown old enough, and good enough, to become the town's woodcarver, I will probably want to hide those trinkets away."

She smiled and went on wrapping them and fitting them into a tidy pack. "I like them. And while cups and platters and even clothes can be easily replaced, these cannot. I think I appreciate your talent more than you do, Shore Walker." She touched the small sack she wore at her waist. "The flute you carved for me long ago ... it has been with me ever since, and always will be. Even then I could see how skilled you were."

He laughed and hefted the pack. "You did put in your egret plumes?"

She nodded. "Also the combs you made for me for our marriage day, the ones decorated with Kwambu's pearls. And your ceremonial headband, and the shell necklace that was a gift from White Gull. All of them are treasure to me." She took the pack from him. "I will carry it," she said. "My back is certainly broad enough, and you might need to be moving around more than I will."

"That's possible," he said, "but a pack this small will not get in my way."

"It goes on mine," she repeated firmly. "You will have enough to do without guarding our treasures."

He pulled her to him. "At least they will rest against a more beautiful back than I can offer," he teased. Then he sobered and looked down into her face. "A hurricane is a fearful thing,

Egret, and while I hope I can be with you during the worst of it, that may not be possible. Please, promise me that you will take care, that you will not let yourself get so concerned about everyone else that you put yourself in jeopardy. If anything should happen to you . . ." His embrace tightened almost hurtfully.

"If you will promise the same," she whispered. "Shore Walker, I would not want to go on living if you were taken from me."

By late afternoon the sky was furred with gray and Egret was not the only one whose flesh tingled mysteriously. People abandoned the chores they had been doggedly attending to and stood around in restless groups, chatting uneasily. Children, even those old enough to roam at will, were confined to the plaza, and anticipation of something momentous infused them with an excitement that added shrillness to their voices.

The new Headchief came into his own then. He descended from the house at the top of the mound and walked among his people, speaking an encouraging word here, unleashing an unexpected jest there, smiling confidently as he reminded everyone of the signal that would send them to the canoes securely moored among the close-growing mangroves on the landward side of the island. Some of those mangroves were centuries old, he informed them, and had never fallen victim to a single hurricane. The people who sheltered among them might trust in their protection.

Who had told him this? Egret wondered. Herb Gatherer, perhaps. Or it might be that Heron had seen fit to consult with his counselors; those he had dismissed as "quarrelsome old men" would have been able to explain how the islanders had protected themselves in the past when monster storms came.

A dull drizzle began, blew fitfully around the town, stopped abruptly. Overhead, the sky darkened, adding a tinge of green to the weird yellow that persisted along the southern horizon. A squall, similar to those that had begun the day before, blew in on a sudden gale of wind. Rain angled into the houses, leaving the people who had not congregated in the squareground as drenched as those who had elected to remain outside.

The Headchief, water cascading from his long hair, but smiling determinedly still, made his way to where Egret and Shore Walker stood. "Everyone must go to the mangroves before night comes," he told his sister's husband. "Prowling Panther is assigning families to the warriors. Each man will be responsible for taking at least one family to the boats and seeing that they stay there." His smile gave way to the soberness that underlaid it. "No matter what happens when the storm finally arrives."

Shore Walker nodded, pressed Egret's hand, and headed across the plaza to report to the War Leader.

Heron turned to his sister. "I am leaving it to you to take my mother and Herb Gatherer to the mangroves," he told her. "Prowling Panther should not have to spare a warrior to protect three sensible, healthy women; the men will be needed more where there are groups of old people and small children to be guarded."

Her brother did not look as young today as he had yesterday, but Egret rejoiced to see how precisely he was arranging for the safety of their people. "And what of you?" she asked. "You will be joining us there eventually?"

"Prowling Panther and I will come when everyone else has left the town," he said, "but there may not be space in your canoe by then. Although families will object to being separated, I plan to have several children placed in each boat. That way, there will be at least one adult to care for each child until the storm has passed."

"I will welcome the ones sent to us, and try to comfort as well as protect them." She reached out and touched his arm as he started to walk away. "Our father would be proud of the way you've taken command," she said.

"That," he said, grinning, "is what a Headchief is supposed to do."

Egret shivered uncontrollably as she fought to keep in place the small bed robe she had wrapped, skin side down, around one of Brown Pelican's four-year-old twins; beside her, Watchful Doe wept with frustration as she struggled to do the same for the little girl's brother. The wind, a malevolent, howling creature of the night, seemed bent on thwarting their efforts. It wrestled them for possession of the robes, seized the end of the one Egret was grappling with and whipped it across the frightened child's face, making her cry the harder. Wind was not satisfied to be terrifying the children with its ear-shattering screams, Egret thought furiously; it wanted to make certain that the little ones were thoroughly soaked by the rain borne on its huge, relentlessly flapping wings.

Herb Gatherer, huddled in the bow of the dugout, clutched to her ample bosom the baby her youngest daughter had left in her care. The child's parents had gone to visit clan kin on Muspa after attending Great Calusa's burial rites, and Herb Gatherer had been delighted to be entrusted with her youngest grandchild. Having him around diluted her loneliness, and she had looked forward to five days of coddling and cuddling the tiny boy, of showing him off to friends and reveling in their compliments on his huge black eyes, the soft dark hair that grew in such abundance on his small head, the way his dimpled fingers grasped whatever was held out to him. Now she could only beg all the gods of the Calusa to help her keep him safe from the splintered tree limbs that were falling all around them, from the foaming water that surged into the boat, from the spears of lightning sent their way each time Thunder roared a warning. The baleful rain beat upon her hunched shoulders, the canoe canted sharply, and the sloshing water in the bottom of the boat vaulted into her lap. Herb Gatherer clung to her swaddled grandson, looked anxiously at the grandchildren Egret and Watchful Doe had taken responsibility for, and wished that her husband might be alive again and here with them. Not even a hurricane could have triumphed over Great Calusa.

Reason told Dancing Egret they had been here only half a night; her bruised and battered senses insisted it had been much, much longer since the western edge of the deceptively serene sky had been the aquamarine color of a new-caught snapper's scales. When the last of the color faded, the sky had not taken on the black of ordinary moonless, starless nights; the approaching storm had stolen the dark from it, and the people in the mangroves marveled at this while the rain visited them once more, a rain so cold it chilled them through and through. Then the wind had begun to gust so strongly the trees bowed before it, their many-fingered branches scrabbling against the sky as they threw up their limbs in despair. Lightning tossed phosphorescent sheets somewhere beyond the boiling clouds, and the icy rain had started to come at them horizontally while the wind that drove it bellowed in exultation. The hurricane had found them, and it did not want to let them go.

Dancing Egret bent her sopping head over the child she held. Time had lost definition in the moment the hurricane changed their world into a nightmare place where the dark was filled with caterwauling demons, a place that abjured stillness in favor of constant, dizzying motion and assaulted those imprisoned in it with every imaginable horror. The rain they had prayed for had grown fangs that mauled the flesh; the bay Egret had always loved was a voracious, swag-bellied monster seeking to swallow everything that lay in its path; and the wind . . . that was the most frightening beast of all. It hammered at the boats lashed to the flailing mangroves and to each other, lifted them, dropped them, swung them from side to side, strove ceaselessly to career them and dump their occupants into the bay for the roiling waters to devour. And all the time, it screeched at them, yowled at them, taunted them with the ululating cries of a thousand evil spirits.

She shifted the child so that she was wedged beneath her left arm, used her right hand to try and bail some of the debris-laden salt water out of the canoe. The rain clawed at her, bit at her, and replaced with a deluge of fresh every dipper of briny water Egret scooped over the side. She shook the rain out of her eyes, squinted, peered through the churning night; she knew there were boats on either side, boats near enough to reach out and touch, but she could not see them, could not see if the people in them were all right, if they had remembered to tie themselves each to another the way Shore Walker had told them to do.

Shore Walker. Where, in this spinning, cacophonous world, was Shore Walker? She'd seen him last when he had brought the twins to her. "Pelican has her older girls and the baby to care for, and has asked that these two be taken to the boat their grandmother is in," he had said. "She will trust you and Watchful Doe to care for them. Prowling Panther cannot be in the boat with her, you see, any more than I can be with you. We will be in a separate canoe, one of the bigger ones, so we can patrol the inlet. A second canoe, with your brother and another warrior in it, will also be patrolling. That way, we will not miss seeing any boats that might somehow go adrift. Not that this is apt to happen, as tightly as we have lashed them, but we want to take every precaution."

"You cannot patrol during a hurricane," she had protested.

"No. Before the storm strikes, we will head in and anchor ourselves among the mangroves, one canoe on each side of the inlet. We'll be at the outer limits of the crescent, but we will be perfectly safe, I promise you."

She had known better than to argue further; it was Shore

Walker's place to be where he was, and hers to be here, while the great bird of prey the wind had become screeched in her ears and tore at her flesh and tried to wrest Pelican's daughter from her arms. Egret tightened her grip on the child and curled in upon herself to thwart Wind's fiendish designs. She told herself she would survive, that they all would survive, that morning would come in the end, and with it, peace.

Chapter 27

Just after dawn, a dawn invisible to those who had found shelter of sorts within the complex basketweave of mangrove roots, the hurricane vanished. Contrary to their expectations, the storm did not diminish gradually until its contours became familiar to the exhausted islanders; between one heartbeat and the next, it simply disappeared. The beaked wind roosted; it folded its monstrous wings, and the sheeting rain became droplets the astonished people could count as they plopped into the water-filled dugouts. The obscenely swollen bay, deprived of its allies, tried futilely to slink away. Overhead, a disk of blue appeared and blossomed into a sky so untroubled it stunned those who craned their necks to see it.

But most blessed of all was the silence, a silence so profound and so heart-soothing that for some time no one intruded upon it. Then the smaller children began to whimper; during the endless night they had become conditioned to terror, and even the death of the hurricane frightened them. Mothers and grandmothers murmured comfortingly, and soon the cove was home to a babble of voices as everyone began to talk at once.

"My children are safe?" It was Brown Pelican, calling hoarsely from a dugout some distance away. "And my mother, and my nephew?"

By way of answer, Dancing Egret gently turned the small

girl she held toward her mother. Watchful Doe did the same with her brother, and Herb Gatherer interrupted the lullaby she was chanting to further reassure her daughter. Pelican's anxiety fled on the instant. "Your baby sister is also fine," she told her twins, indicating the one-year-old cradled in a sling beneath her breasts. Nodding toward the pair of huge-eyed girls huddled in the stern, she added, "So are your big sisters." She shaded her eyes with one hand, looked toward the outer limits of the small cove. After a long moment, she looked back toward her children. "I can see your father, too," she said exultantly. "We are safe. All of us are safe." She sent a smile in Egret's direction. "Shore Walker is with Prowling Panther," she said. "I could not see him at first, because he was bent over. But when he straightened, I recognized him."

Egret had to see for herself. Stretching as high as she could without putting undue strain on the cord that still bound Pelican's little girl to her aunt's waist and the both of them to the dugout, she peered over the incredible tangle of tree limbs heaped in the inlet. And there he was, a wide swing of his muscular arms punctuating something he was saying to the War Leader. Dancing Egret felt tension drain out of her.

Watchful Doe was trying vainly to see as far as the other end of the cove. "There are so many branches in the way that I cannot find my son," she said. She fished in the water slopping around her thighs. "Egret, where is the skinning knife we used to cut the fiber cords when we fastened the children to us? Is it near you, perhaps? I want to slash the cord that's tying me down so I can stand up. Then I might be able to see Crested Heron."

"I have it," Herb Gatherer told her. "It was here in the bow, and I am using it to cut the cord that is keeping me confined. I will pass it across to you in a moment." She applied the blade expertly, then eased herself into a crouch, still clutching to her bosom the infant who was crying shrilly despite all her efforts to quiet it. "Poor babe," she crooned, absently thrusting the knife into her belt. "You are hungry. And so wet!" She tried to fold back the sodden skin he was wrapped in. "He is shivering from being so wet," she said worriedly, her blunt-tipped fingers tugging at the bindings that held the robe around him.

"Herb Gatherer," Watchful Doe said with uncharacteristic sharpness. "I must see if my son is all right. Please, the knife."

From the canoe on their left, Vision Speaker spoke. "Word

is being passed from our Headchief that no one is to loose the cords that kept us safe during the night."

Watchful Doe looked into a face more deeply creased than it had been before the storm. "You are certain it was my son who said this?"

The priest nodded. "The message is from him. Please pass it on."

She relaxed visibly and did as he asked.

Herb Gatherer rested her buttocks against the bow, looked up at the sky. It was rimmed with dark clouds, true, but surely that shimmering blue was steadily pushing them back? "That is nonsense," she declared. "Anyone can see the storm is over. Why should we continue to sit in water? Why should the children go on being miserable? Why must my daughter's son go on crying when there is no need for it?"

Dancing Egret understood her concern for her grandchildren. "It is confusing," she agreed, "but my brother must have reason for saying what he did."

"He is young," Herb Gatherer said firmly. "He has never been through a hurricane. Those that I have seen have always been over when they are over. The winds have never stopped so quickly before, as I recall, but how can that make a difference?" She took the knife from her belt, sliced through the complicated arrangement of cords she had rigged to keep the infant securely swaddled. "At least I can dry my nestling off," she said, "and warm him."

She slid him out of his drenched cocoon, held him so a sliver of pale sunlight fell on his naked body. "Now," she said, smiling into his little round face, "isn't that better?" Her smile broadened, brought a touch of youth to her age-crinkled face, when the baby's chubby arms lifted as though to embrace the warmth she had found for him.

Egret tipped up the tear-washed chin of Pelican's daughter. "Look," she said. "Morning is here, and the gods are giving us a beautiful day to make up for the awfulness of last night." Calling her attention to that patch of silver-blue sky was far better than encouraging the girl to look around her and see how the huge mangroves that had outwitted the storm had nonetheless bent low before it, how the limbs that had not been wrenched from their trunks had been stripped of leaves and, in places, of bark. Younger and smaller trees had been violently uprooted; some had come to rest against the parent trees; others added to the confusion of debris in the water around and beyond them. And the shoreline of the mainland, even from this distance, was altered past recognition. They had survived the hurricane, only to find themselves in an alien world.

All around her, others were discovering the same thing. Shock and disbelief warred in the faces she could see, and hushed exclamations fluttered into the air like a bewilderment of sparrows.

"What will it be like in the town?" Watchful Doe whispered. "Our homes . . ."

"We can only wait and see," Dancing Egret said with a steadiness she did not feel. She watched a pair of rattlesnakes slither past a mouse that had also found sanctuary among the mangrove roots; mice were the natural prey of such reptiles, yet neither paid heed to the other this time. Nor were these the only creatures who had fled to the cove for safety. Raccoons and squirrels, rabbits and opossums, skunks and otters, the dogs who usually lived in and around the town . . . a host of furry creatures had come here and, like the Calusa, were continuing to bide on the landward side of the island. Did they, too, fear that their nests and burrows and dens had been destroyed? Were the animals, like the people, reluctant to find out if those fears had merit?

She invited Pelican's twins to guess the names of those animals daring enough to expose more than their snouts, and the strain in their faces eased a little as they vied with one another to identify the bedraggled things. "If anything has happened to our homes," Egret said to Watchful Doe, "we will rebuild. When Ucita's town was burned by Mocoso's raiders, his people built a whole new one. What they could do, we can do. If it is necessary."

Herb Gatherer, rocking her grandson to soothe him, shook her head. "Ucita's town was smaller than ours. Much smaller."

"We have more people to do the work," Egret pointed out, raising her voice to be heard over the baby's squawling.

But Herb Gatherer had lost interest. She was moving the arm that cradled the baby, seeking the stream of warmth that for some reason eluded her now. Even though Dancing Egret and White Gull took to persuading themselves that the damage to the town might be less than they imagined, even when those in the canoes on either side joined in and the conversation became positively animated, Herb Gatherer was oblivious to it; all her attention was on her grandchild.

"Is it any wonder that Sun is one of our gods?" she murmured to him. "If he had not returned when he did, you might have sickened from being so damp and cold." But the boy was shivering again; she must get him closer to the source of that elusive warmth.

For that, Herb Gatherer had to stand upright. Well, she had the knife still, and even if Calusa's son ranted at her later for being a stubborn old woman, she would use it again. Severing the thicker cord that tethered her grandson and her to the dugout, she came shakily to her feet, then lifted her arm so that he rested on the shelf of her ample bosom. Ah, yes. This should do it!

She swayed as the canoe rocked suddenly, spread her legs a trifle to achieve better balance. The babe continued to cry. Poor thing. He was more than just cold and wet; he was exhausted and hungry besides. As she was. As all of them were. A steaming pot of cornmeal gruel would mend that, however. And if a few chunks of venison could be thrown in to flavor it—

The gust of wind came out of nowhere. It slammed into Herb Gatherer's chest with the force of a hundred hammer stones and flung her backward. Backward to where the water crested and surged once more as a transfusion of driving rain revived the demon that had been lurking beneath the surface.

Watchful Gull's scream sent Egret's head swinging around as the wind struck. She thrust Pelican's daughter between her knees and, arms outstretched, lunged forward. But the cord that was fixed to her waist would not let her reach Herb Gatherer. For one agonizing moment the two women looked at each other, and in that moment both acknowledged that there was no hope of rescue.

As if in compensation, the gods suddenly granted to Herb Gatherer a strength and agility she had never before owned. Even as she was swept over the bow of the canoe, she used her knife one last time, to slash the cord that linked her with her grandson. Then she tossed the baby at Dancing Egret.

If the wind had not been gathering itself to blow the harder, the maneuver would have failed. But before it could unleash its fury again, Egret's grasping fingers closed over the howling baby's ankle. She jerked him to her, wedged him between Pelican's daughter and herself, and wound her arms tight around the pair of them.

But she understood, even before she tried to peer through

the undulating gray curtain thrown up by the wind and rain and churning sea, that already the roiling waters had swallowed Herb Gatherer.

Triumph added shrillness to the hideous screech of the wind. The hurricane, cleverly mounting its second siege from the opposite direction, had succeeded in claiming a sacrifice.

The battering was as vicious as before, the bellow and whine of the wind as tormenting to the ear as the ruthless flail of the rain was to the flesh. Man, woman, child, and beast attempted to shrink into themselves to avoid what could not be avoided, and their minds as well as their bodies steeled themselves against the reprise of a torture they were, this time, only too capable of anticipating.

When it was over, when it was well and truly over, they were numb within and without. When the word was sent around that those who could should extricate themselves and go to the aid of the ones who could not, their movements were sluggish, uncoordinated. No one, this time, bothered to gaze entranced at a sky that was smiling sincerely now. Indeed, they scarcely spoke as they freed limbs that were cramping from being so long in one position, helped one another out of the dugouts, pressed strips torn from sopping moss skirts against the more serious scrapes and gashes.

Hefting toddlers and supporting the elderly, they slowly made their way across a seemingly endless grid of mangrove roots. Even when the going became easier, people continued to stumble. No one smiled to see a twitchy-nosed hare hopping along in their midst, his long feet splashing through the ankle-deep water. And although Brown Pelican's anguished cry, when she discovered her mother was no longer with them, told the islanders that a kindly, much-respected woman had been seized and devoured by the storm, no one had the energy to mourn; the only tears shed were shaped from sap and clung to raw wounds of the trees they passed.

They came, eventually, to their town. Many wished they had not, that the journey from the eastern side of the island might have taken twice as long. Across the canal, the wattle and daub Temple with its to-the-ground thatch roof was still standing; Calusa's bones were safe, as were those of his father and his father's father. But the palm fronds that roofed the house on the top of the domiciliary mound had been ripped off and shredded, its pinewood frame had been blown away, and two of the building's walls were demolished. Of the houses on the levels descending from the upper one, some had been reduced to rubble while others, although still upright, threatened to collapse with the next lively breeze. And the homes circling the flooded plaza either listed crazily or had been razed by the malicious winds.

Dancing Egret was afraid to turn and look toward the place their house should be. If it had been one of those the hurricane had chosen to destroy, she would be tempted to weep. And exhausted as she was, and shaken by Herb Gatherer's death, she did not trust herself to resist that temptation. Not yet.

She studied the squareground instead. It was littered with possessions: stools of all sizes, most splintered but some surprisingly undamaged; pots, baskets, dippers, children's playthings; the tools and weapons men had tied to the rafters of their houses, the remnants of the bundled skins and mosses their women had wedged against the roofs; many of the rafters themselves, or jagged pieces of them. Draped upon those bushes that had not been savagely jerked from the ground was everything from a child's breechclout to Word Weaver's oncemagnificent ceremonial cloak. The elevated pavilion where the matrons gathered to cook was gone; only skewed and gapped rings of conch shells marked the areas where their fires had been kindled each day, with a single splintered post leaning crookedly over one of them.

Egret studied the faces of the people closest to her. Every one, from the youngest to the eldest, wore the same bemused expression. The eyes said that they recognized what they looked upon, but something deep within each person denied the reality of it, begged to be told that this was only the sort of dream sent upon occasion to plague those who had hoped to sleep peacefully and awaken refreshed. But this was no demon-sent dream; there would be no awakening from it.

A child began to sob, and Egret turned to see a little girl holding up a doll she had snatched from the wreckage of a nearby house. The toy had been shaped from a cypress knee and dressed in a beaded cloak. Now only a few colorful beads hung dispiritedly from a remnant of snarled deerskin, and there was naught but a shaving of wood to indicate the neck that had supported the head with its brightly painted face.

Egret looked down at the babe in her arms. At least Herb Gatherer's grandson was too young to know what was going on or to remember it. That was good. But it was sad that he was too young also to remember the grandmother who had kept him safe during a monstrous storm, the grandmother who had lost her life through her ongoing concern for his well-being. When Herb Gatherer's daughter returned from Muspa and learned what had happened, she must hear how quick-thinking and selfless her mother had been. It would help her through her grieving, and she could tell the tale to this tiny boy when he grew old enough. Egret would make a point of telling it to Pelican's children as well. Usually, fathers and uncles and grandfathers were the heroes of family legends, but Herb Gatherer had earned the right to the praise-singing ordinarily reserved for men. Dancing Egret meant to see that her spirit received what was owing to it.

She blinked away the tears filming her vision when a familiar hand closed itself gently over her shoulder. "I will build us a new home," Shore Walker said, hugging her to him with his right arm. His left elbow had been grazed by a wind-flung branch during the storm, reviving the debilitating ache in his forearm, but that could be ignored. In the circumstances, it would have to be. "When I am done," he told her, "we will have a bigger house. A better one."

With her husband at her side, Egret found at last the courage to look in the direction he was looking in, was even able to summon up a tremulous smile despite the fact that, where their home had been, there was nothing. Nothing at all.

"And I will help you do it," she told him. "But first, I would like you to carve a new doll for a little girl who is weeping over a broken one."

There was no surprise in his eyes as he nodded gravely. Which was one of the wonderful things about this man of hers.

Dancing Egret stood in the midst of her ruined town and sent up a prayer of thanksgiving to all the gods of the Calusa.

Chapter 28

⋙ ⋙

"The Calusa had already begun to rebuild before I left the island," Kwambu said, "and the land had started to rebuild itself: the vines whose leaves were torn away by the wind are tipped with red now, and the naked branches of the trees and bushes have started to put forth buds. And in the river glades the trampled sawgrass is springing upright once more." He took the dipper of water Moon of Winter was holding out and drained it. His throat had grown dry from so much talking.

Kaia looked up at her father with troubled eyes. "What happens to the birds when those awful storms come?" she asked.

He leaned forward and took her onto his lap. "Birds know how to protect themselves," he said, smoothing her distinctive black curls. "I expect they hide in low thickets or underneath dense bushes and wait until the hurricane ends. When it does, they dry their feathers and soar into the sky once more. The first thing I saw when we came out of the mangroves was a woodpecker, the kind that wears a red cap on its head. Other small creatures also seem quite capable of looking after themselves. The Calusa had scarcely finished roofing their Headchief's new house before a pair of lizards and several spiders were making their own new homes in the thatch."

"We have a tiny mouse underneath our roof," Kaia said. "When it is quiet, he sometimes peeks out at me." She peered upward as though willing the creature to appear and prove her right.

Her brothers hooted derisively. "Kaia calls it *her* mouse," Hawk Flying High said to his father. "She has even given it a name." He rolled his eyes to show his scorn for such silliness.

"She calls the mouse Corn Nibbler," Red Fox Barking confirmed. "And until Walks Tall Woman found out and stopped her, she was leaving out bits of food for it to eat."

The little girl sat up straight. "My mouse probably has a family to feed," she said, "and if the boy mice eat as much as you and Hawk do, there is probably never enough to go around!"

Moon of Winter signaled for quiet. "I am sorry to hear that Great Calusa died," she said to Kwambu. "His people will miss him, and I know you will, too. But I am glad your friends survived the hurricane and will be able to rebuild their town."

Walks Tall Woman sniffed. "To live on an island where such storms are certain to come sooner or later seems foolish to me," she said. "The Timucua who prefer to live near the coast have the good sense not to make their homes on islands."

Outina's wife stiffened; why must her husband's mother always have so much contempt for anyone who did not think precisely the way she did? Palm Tree Bending had more than once suspected that Walks Tall Woman felt contemptuous of her son's wife merely because—unlike the Principal Woman—Palm Tree Bending was not given to speaking her mind on any and every subject. The young woman looked down at the two boys sitting on either side of her; if Walks Tall Woman should persist in a certain scheme she had lately begun to promote, however, she would quickly learn that Palm Tree Bending was no longer averse to making her opinion known. Or of defending it!

Outina was unperturbed by his mother's tactlessness; it was the way she was, and he was accustomed to it. "I suppose you helped the Calusa with the first part of their rebuilding," he said to Kwambu.

"I helped mostly in the Arawak village," the trader said. "I spent the night of the hurricane in a dugout with my old friend's widow and her family, so I naturally went back with them when it was over. But I had done little more than clear away some of the debris before the Headchief summoned me and asked me to come north."

"The Arawak family lost a home also?" Moon of Winter asked.

Kwambu nodded. "They did, but—like all those left homeless—they are building another."

Kwambu helped himself to a piece of the mulberry bread the Principal Woman had brought from her hearth. "I wish to speak with you about letting me have certain goods, skins and the like, to take back to Calusa country," he said to Outina. "They are in need of virtually everything, so I have nothing with me to barter with this time. But I will bring whatever you ask for in exchange just as soon as I can."

"Our hunters were successful last season," Outina said. "We have hides to spare, and you might take them some smoked meat, also. We can give you beans and squash, too, and perhaps some mulberries; they will not take up much room, and you can introduce the Calusa to the kind of bread we are eating now."

Kwambu thanked him. "Once they have tasted it," he said, "I will probably be told to trade for the berries on future expeditions."

"They are not always plentiful," Walks Tall Woman said swiftly. "It will take more than a handful of shells to exchange for mulberries. We may well demand as much as a sack of salt for each sack of the berries. Be certain they understand that."

Outina laughed. "I have never known a season when our bushes were not laden with the things," he said. "As Kwambu knows. Save that kind of bargaining for the strangers who pass through our town, Mother. Do not waste it on my cousin's husband."

"As a trader, I appreciate shrewd bargaining," Kwambu said placidly. "It makes my life more interesting." He set his daughter on her feet and looked toward his wife. "I feel the need to be up and moving," he told her. "Will you walk with me?"

His sons spoke in unison: "I will walk with you, Father."

Kwambu shook his head. "You walk too fast," he said. "I have just finished traveling a great distance, so I want to amble, not run a race. Especially when it is a race you would easily win! Go and practice with your bows and arrows instead, and when your mother and I return, I will come and see how greatly your skills have improved since I was home last."

A small hand tugged at his. "I would not run," Kaia said.

"But you have promised to help Palm Tree Bending decorate the moccasins she is making for you," Moon of Winter said gently, and looked an appeal at her cousin's wife.

When the child, her lower lip protruding slightly, had been led away, Kwambu and Moon of Winter slipped out of the Principal House. With one accord they hurried through the town and out the palisade gateway. Nor did either have to ask the other which direction to take next; side by side they made their way to the forest and continued into it until they came to a small glade overhung with the branches of a huge magnolia tree. Only then did Kwambu spread wide his arms; only then did Moon of Winter step within the wonderful, warm circle of his embrace.

"I thought we would never find a reason for coming away this time," she murmured, breathing deep of the wood-smoky scent of his dark flesh. "And I have missed you so much. So very, very much."

"No more than I have missed you," he said, his voice a rumble in the ear that was pressed against his heart. "But you should have known I would find a way for us to escape to our place of magnolias."

They had discovered the glade on the day of their marriage, more than a dozen years earlier. Indeed, they had literally stumbled upon it after fleeing the Principal House in the face of Walks Tall Woman's vociferous disapproval of the man her niece had chosen for a husband. There had been no elaborate ceremony for Moon of Winter and Kwambu the trader; she had known that to attempt to take a husband in the traditional way would only bring her up against the full strength of her aunt's objections. So, making valiant effort to conceal her nervousness, she had simply taken Kwambu to the new Holata and announced that they were pledged to one another, that whenever Kwambu could be in the north, he would be sharing Moon of Winter's home, and her bed.

But neither wanted to stay in the Principal House that night, to have to come together for the first time with other people around. And it had been a day of sunshine and birdsong, promise of a beautiful night to come. What could be more natural than to steal away to the forest? When they had happened upon the magnolia glade just as the western sky faded from crimson to rose-dappled mauve, they knew they had somehow been led to a place of enchantment, a place surely meant to be theirs alone.

Afterward, they made a habit of coming here each time Kwambu returned from his journeying. As they had done this day. Now, Kwambu guided his wife down to the soft earth that was perpetually shaded by a canopy of waxy foliage. "Shall I show you how much I have missed you?" he asked, stretching out beside her.

She nodded, and her lovely eyes explored his face, rejoiced in every nuance of expression as he unfastened the garment draped over her left shoulder, then eased the skirt over her slender hips, her knees, her ankles. The afternoon sunlight, filtering between whispering leaves, vied with shadow to kiss her face, her breasts, the gentle curve of her stomach, her firm-muscled thighs, but Kwambu would not surrender to them his right to caress her, possess her. His broad-palmed, dark-skinned hands made more substantial claim to her bronze flesh. His lips, gentle yet urgent, brought her to tingling arousal, awakened in her yet again the realization that this man truly loved her, that even if it had been only pity that drew him to her in the beginning, it was love, soul-deep and enduring, that brought him home to her again, and again, and again.

Kwambu looked up as her fingers began to trace designs on his sinewy back, to feather the hair on the nape of his neck, and her luminous eyes told him the direction her thoughts had taken, told him, too, that his great love for her was returned in kind. He remembered how he had warned himself long ago never, ever to hope for this, but to be content that Moon of Winter respected and trusted him. It amazed him still that trust and respect had somehow blossomed into a love so infused with both tenderness and passion that he never ceased to be awed by it, inspired by it.

He shifted position, poised himself over a body already arching to meet his, slid slowly into the moist valley waiting to receive him, felt it close around him and shut out the world.

Kwambu the trader was truly home again.

Their return to the town was unhurried. They dawdled beside meandering streams, gathered acorns as they passed through a grove of oaks. When they came across a patch of rattleweed, Kwambu obligingly dug up some of the roots to add to his wife's store of medicines while Moon of Winter plucked leaves and stems so that her daughter's winter cloak might be dyed blue. Finally, they paused to watch a brightness of butterflies hovering over the tall grasses dancing in a meadow. And all the while, they talked—of everything that had happened during the weeks they were apart, of their children, about their plans for the future.

"Maidens still come to me begging for love potions," Moon of Winter said suddenly. "I used to send them away empty-handed, but lately I have begun to feel such pity for them, Kwambu. They are so young, and so yearning. So I have taken to giving them small pots of oil scented with the magnolia blossoms you picked for me the last time you returned from the south."

He smiled. The trees had been blooming profusely then, and the aroma had added something special to their reunion. "I remember," he said, tightening his grip on her hand.

"Each time, I warn them that there is no magic in the oil, but I know they do not listen. Their faces are so shining with hope when they leave me that I feel ashamed. It's wrong to mislead them, even unintentionally, yet that is what I'm doing, isn't it?"

"Were any of them successful in their quest for a husband?"

Moon of Winter nodded abstractedly. "Most were. But not because of anything I did, Kwambu. I feel like hiding away when later they bring me gifts and go about singing my praises."

"The trees were not blooming today," her husband said quietly, "yet all the time we were in the glade my head was filled with their perfume. I can smell it even now."

She laughed. "I use the oil myself," she said. "That was why I made it in the first place."

He drew her closer to him, rested his cheek against her hair. "It may be that the fragrance of magnolias does act upon a man's senses," he said, "and moves him to thoughts of love. Some part of you probably recognized this long ago. Which makes your scented oil a love potion of a sort, I think." He hugged her tighter. "You have no real need of it, however," he said. "Your flesh has always owned a sweetness no flower could ever hope to imitate."

She clung to him briefly and let her concern dissipate. Giving sweet-smelling oil to girls was certainly doing them no harm. And she would rather be asked for a love potion than to have someone beg her to consult her crystal for the answer to some unanswerable question! "As always, you have made me feel better," she said. Her eyes lit with a mischievous gleam. "In every way," she added.

Looking down into her face, Kwambu felt desire rising in him again, but when Moon of Winter realized that, she eased away from him. "We had better wait," she said. "We have been gone overlong as it is, and everyone will be wondering where we are. Our children are growing older, you know; Hawk has surely reached the age where he can guess why we go off alone together each time you come home."

Kwambu sighed and matched his step to hers as she started

through the knee-high grass. "Red Fox Barking probably suspects also. He has a lively mind and a curiosity to match. One of these days, he will no doubt follow us to prove his suspicions."

Moon of Winter glanced uneasily over her shoulder.

Kwambu grinned. "Not yet. I would have known. And will, if ever he tries it. A trader learns early to sense whether or not he is alone in a forest."

"I'm certain Kaia is too young to think about such things," Moon of Winter said, "but you may be sure she will be watching for us also. She adores you so much that I think she's jealous whenever I take you away from her. And of course Walks Tall Woman knows why we slip away." She pursed her lips in an attempt to replicate the expression her aunt would be wearing when they got home. "When her husband was alive, I suppose they shared a bed only once: before the Holata was born."

He chuckled, but there was a hint of resignation in the sound. "It does not worry me if Walks Tall Woman disapproves of our hunger to be together. I shall never win her approval anyway. It's plain that she considers traders inferior to *real men*, and I am no exception. Quite the opposite, in fact."

Moon of Winter smiled. "That is only because she does not, *can* not, know you as well as I do," she murmured. Then she looked at him from beneath her lashes. "She suspects that you have a woman in the south, as well as me."

Kwambu stopped short. "Surely you were not so foolish as to believe her?"

"I don't, now. But there was a time, I confess, when I wondered a little about this Dancing Egret you speak of so often. Then, after your Arawak friend died . . . well, a man often takes his brother's widow as a second wife. And you and the Arawak were much like brothers. I thought you might. . . ." She looked at him fully, saw the pain in his eyes. "But I no longer think that, Kwambu. I never would have, I suppose, except for the fact that you are in the south so much and here so seldom."

And because your self-esteem continues to be a fragile thing, Kwambu thought. He reached out his hands and smoothed the hair back from her brow. "Many of the men in this country live contentedly with several wives, but I will never be one of them," he said. "There is but one woman for me, and that woman is you. Now and forever, it is you."

Moon of Winter smiled and let the last of her doubts drift away with the butterflies that swarmed from the meadow.

Outina went with Kwambu to watch the trader's sons demonstrate their skill with the small-scale weapons they longed to exchange for man-sized ones. Hawk Flying High approached the exercise with an attention to detail that was typical of him, and every one of his feathered shafts hit the target. Red Fox Barking lacked his brother's patience, and occasionally sacrificed accuracy for speed. Nonetheless, most of the arrows he released somehow found their way to the target, also.

"They are good," the Holata said. "Your sons will make fine warriors, Kwambu."

"Fox needs to learn that faster is not always better," Kwambu replied, "but I will not pretend; I am proud of both of them. And grateful to you for overseeing their training."

"I am as near to an uncle as they have," Outina said, "and it is an uncle's responsibility to teach his nephews warrior skills. But Palm Tree Bending's brother has also worked with your sons. As he will be working with mine, once they are old enough."

"Then I must be sure to thank Black Wolf Running, also," Kwambu said. "And to congratulate him on being chosen Great Warrior, too, I understand."

"My old friend waited a long, long time to become Paracusi," Outina said, "but I think he has finally forgiven me for not naming him Great Warrior at the time I became Holata." He grinned. "That doesn't mean we have put aside our rivalry, however. As you shall see during the Ball Game tomorrow."

"Moon of Winter mentioned that a game was scheduled. She told me that you have been encouraging the warriors to hold such contests regularly so that they will be fit for your annual game with the warriors from Potano."

"I have. It seems to me that if we can continue to best Holata Potano's men in the Ball Game, then it is unlikely that he will consider going to war against us. As he has been too much inclined to do in the past."

"Your games are close kin to battles, in any event," Kwambu said feelingly. He had participated in practice games from time to time, when he had happened to be in the north long enough to prepare for them. He had the scars to prove it.

"Indeed they are. They are meant to be. Now, if I could just persuade my uncle's old enemy Saturiba to bring his warriors here so we can humble them also ..." He turned to examine the bow Hawk brought to him, nodded approval when he saw how the boy had tightened the string. "That is enough practice for today, though," he said to him. "You and Red Fox will want to help prepare the field for tomorrow's game, and that must be done before dark." He watched the pair race away, then turned back to Kwambu. "By next season, Hawk will be ready to compete in certain of our contests. And his brother will not be far behind him."

"They will be pleased to hear that," Kwambu said. But he frowned a little. His sons, all of his children, were growing up so fast. Too fast. If only he could be with them more often, and stay longer each time he came. But at least Hawk and Fox would have the opportunity to become warriors and win praise for themselves, an opportunity that had been denied their father. They might never be able to boast about him, but Kwambu was confident that someday he would be boasting about them.

Moon of Winter knew the instant she entered the Principal House that Walks Tall Woman had once again been trying to convince Palm Tree Bending that the older of Outina's two sons should be adopted by his grandmother. Doubtless the argument she had offered had been the same this time as it was before: that neither of his sons were eligible to be Holata after him, yet if Walks Tall Woman took one of them into her clan, that boy could grow up to take his father's place as leader of their people. She sighed; it had been a lovely day so far, and she hated to have it spoiled. But the tension in the house stretched between the walls like a giant spider's web, and there was no way Moon of Winter could avoid walking into it.

She gave courteous greeting to both women, then hurried over to her daughter. Perhaps, if she occupied herself with Kaia, she could avoid entangling herself in a matter she wanted no part of.

"I have brought home some acorns," she told Kaia, "and your father has said that he will take you to the oak grove soon and let you gather more. When there are enough, you may wash them and help him bundle them to take to his friends in the south."

"To the people who have no food because of the hurricane?"

Moon of Winter nodded. "You would like to help them, wouldn't you?"

"Will Kwambu tell them that I gathered and washed the acorns for them?" the little girl asked eagerly.

"He will, indeed. And they will praise you for it."

She tumbled the acorns onto the floor, and Kaia promptly took up a basket and began filling it with the biggest ones. "I want the Calusa to see that Timucuan acorns are the finest there are," she explained, "so I will not let my father take them the small ones." She looked to see if Walks Tall Woman were nearby. "Perhaps I can give the smaller ones to Corn Nibbler," she whispered.

Moon of Winter, seeing her aunt coming toward them, merely grinned and nodded. "You will be making the black drink for the warriors to cleanse themselves with tonight?" she asked Walks Tall Woman.

The older woman gestured toward her hearth, where a large pot was steaming. "I am already boiling the cassina leaves for my son's team," she said. "His wife"—her lips tightened—"is supposed to make the black drink for their opponents. I hope she sees to it soon, or the tea will be too weak to do them any good. Then, when my son's team is victorious, Black Wolf Running will say that his men lost only because their tea did not purge them properly."

Moon of Winter could see for herself that Palm Tree Bending had hung a pot of water over her own hearth and was stirring the potent leaves into it, but she did not argue the point. "You are certain Outina and his men will win the game?" she asked.

"Whenever my son plays, his team wins," Walks Tall Woman said.

"It must be hard for Palm Tree Bending," Moon of Woman ventured, "to have her husband and her brother on opposing sides."

Her aunt merely tossed her head and strode toward the door. "I must speak with Watches for Omens about tonight's ceremony," she said.

When she had gone out, Moon of Winter crossed to Palm Tree Bending's hearth. "Whenever I smell that brew," she said, "I am glad I'm not a man. To prepare it takes the breath away; to drink it must demand more courage than I will ever own!"

"Yet the men vie with one another to see who can consume the most before vomiting," Palm Tree Bending said with a shrug of her narrow shoulders. "It's a good test of their strength of will, and they must be resolute as well as strong if they hope to win the Ball Game. Or a battle."

"Or influence the other Principal Men during a Council meeting," Moon of Winter said. "Nonetheless, I'm still glad women are forbidden to drink it."

Palm Tree Bending smiled a little. "Women need not prove their strength of will to other women, or even to themselves. When we have need of it, it is there."

Moon of Winter considered. "I have never given it much thought, but that's true of most of us, I expect." There were times when her own will had proven woefully weak; as for Palm Tree Bending, her strength of will had never been put to the test until Walks Tall Woman began her campaign to adopt one of Outina's sons. Although her sympathies were all with her cousin's wife, Moon of Winter doubted that quiet resistance would be enough to thwart anyone as resolute as Walks Tall Woman. "Have you spoken with Outina about what his mother wants to do?" she asked impulsively.

Palm Tree Bending shook her head. "My sons belong to my clan," she said. "It is my place to deal with this, not his." She set aside her wooden spoon, swung her pot to the edge of the fire, and looked outside to where the afternoon shadows were lengthening. "We should go and call our children," she said. "The Ball Play Dance will begin soon, and they won't want to miss that."

It was clear that Palm Tree Bending did not wish to pursue a subject her companion had hoped to discuss further, but Moon of Winter, as she followed her out of the house, offered up a silent vow: having been rash enough, and possibly foolish enough, to choose sides in this battle of wills, she would do all that she could to help Palm Tree Bending stand firm against Walks Tall Woman.

Because no other town or chiefdom was involved in this Ball Game, Watches for Omens began the day's activities by calling upon the gods to favor the stronger, more skillful team. And although he blew tobacco smoke in the four sacred directions, as was traditional in the Ball Game prayer, he did not puff a fifth time to bring confusion upon one of the groups of players. It was not for him to name either team *enemy*, not when both sides consisted of warriors who were ordinarily comrades.

The warriors themselves felt no such compunction. Outina's

players, liberally daubed with black paint, scarcely waited for the incantation to be finished before screaming insults into the red-painted faces of Black Wolf Running's team. Black Wolf Running responded by spinning around until the snake's rattles fastened in his topknotted hair warned the Holata that his men could expect no mercy on the playing field. And all the warriors screeched soul-chilling threats as they brandished the pairs of arm-length sticks they would soon be making expert use of.

"My son had Palm Tree Bending tie into his hair both eagle feathers, for keen sight, and a deer's tail, to lend him swiftness," Walks Tall Woman said to Moon of Winter. "They will serve him well. Those silly snake rattles Black Wolf Running is wearing . . . what can they do but make noise?"

The two women stood among the spectators that lined both long sides of the playing field as the grim-faced warriors separated to allow the Shaman to toss onto the middle of the field the plum-sized ball that every eye immediately fastened on.

Outina and Black Wolf Running raced for it simultaneously, but neither succeeded in snatching it up in the webbed loops capping their playing sticks; instead, they collided with an audible thwack. It was Sends a Signal, his red-painted body telling the watchers that he was one of Wolf's men, who ducked around the thrashing pair and caught up the ball, raised his stick, and slung it in the direction of another red-painted warrior. His aim was good, but three warriors from Outina's side, sticks waving wildly, intervened; one of them, leaping high, hooked the ball and sent it hurtling toward the opposite end of the field.

Outina, his ear ringing from a blow delivered by Black Wolf Running, saw it coming. He thrust both sticks into the air, imprisoned the sphere between them, pivoted on one foot, and propelled the ball directly between the two posts that had been planted at the western end of the field.

A resounding cheer went up from those who had kin on Outina's team, or who had wagered that they would be victorious. Walks Tall Woman, usually so self-contained, was shrieking as loudly as anyone, and Outina's sons were jumping up and down as they yelled their father's name over and over again. Additional bets were offered and agreed to. Outina's jubilant teammates hurled new and more creative insults at Black Wolf Running's, who replied in kind and reminded them that this was only the start of the game.

"Have you wagered?" Moon of Winter asked her husband. The ball was back in play, and yelping warriors rushed to scoop it up.

He grinned, then winced in sympathy as one thwarted warrior struck another with both of his playing sticks. His victim retaliated by butting the attacker in the belly. "Only with our sons. Which means that I feel compelled to cheer for both sides; Hawk is certain Outina will win, while Fox is sure that it will be Black Wolf Running."

"Well, Palm Tree Bending is cheering for both, too. How can she do otherwise?"

They both fell silent as one of Wolf's warriors hefted a stick and slammed the ball toward a fellow player. A black-painted warrior intercepted it, but was wrestled to the ground by four opponents before he could send it on. The air was thick with dust; roiling brown clouds of it hampered the spectators' view. All they could see were scores of flailing sticks as warriors vied to capture the ball that had, somehow, been launched once more. Men were kicking one another, trampling upon the fallen, even leaping over their own teammates in their zeal, and more than a few were decorated now with blood as well as paint.

"I'm glad you are not on the field today," Moon of Winter said as one man, limping badly and half blinded from the blood pouring from a gash above his eye, took himself to the sidelines for a moment's rest.

Kwambu, who would have given a great deal to be able to participate, merely grunted. Just watching the game heated his blood and had the muscles in his arms and legs twitching. But this was something his gentle wife would never understand, and the fact that he had seen thirty-seven summers come and go made him a bit too old for such vigorous sport in any event. He let loose with a mighty *"Ho!"* as the battered ball smacked into a pocket of webbing, and felt a little better.

The ball was catapulted over the forest of sticks raised by Outina's men, plucked from the air by Black Wolf Running, and sent skimming between the goal posts he aimed for. The crowd went wild, hailing or bemoaning his achievement with squeals and howls and rhythmically pounding feet.

Kaia, standing in front of her mother, clapped her hands over her ears even as she went up on tiptoe to try and see better. Kwambu bent down, swept her up in his arms and settled her upon his shoulders. "Now you will be able to see everything," he told her, holding firmly to the long bare legs that dangled over his chest.

One of Outina's men had reclaimed the ball and sent it streaking toward the west. Both the Holata and Black Wolf Running sprinted for midfield, their sticks pointed at the sun as they ran. As they neared each other, Outina dropped one stick directly in Wolf's path, roared with exultation when the Paracusi tripped over it, then claimed the ball as it began to descend.

Wolf pressed both hands against the ground, pushed himself into a crouch, threw himself at Outina. The Holata went over backward, but he did not surrender the ball. Instead he popped it into his mouth and swallowed it.

Black Wolf Running gave a great cry of rage, came fully erect, and jumped with both feet upon Outina's chest. Outina merely grinned derisively and twisted himself from side to side to make Wolf lose his balance.

Wolf sprang up, came down again with both feet to force Outina to eject the ball. When no deerhide sphere came spurting out of his mouth, he repeated the maneuver yet again, landing on his opponent's chest with as much force as he could muster.

This time the Holata groaned and regurgitated. Wolf's sticks raked up the bile-covered ball and—shouting to his teammates to block the opposition—he prepared to race down the field with his prize.

He had barely flexed his knees before Outina, still retching, somersaulted up, wrapped both hands around one of his playing sticks and brought it down on the back of Black Wolf Running's head. The ball bounced free as Wolf toppled to the ground. Outina caught it up, dodged a menacing quintet of red-painted players, and zigzagged down the field until he found space enough to raise his stick and chuck the ball in the direction of the goal. He put all his power behind the cast, watched the ball streak between the posts, and was still dancing in celebration when three of Wolf's men tackled him and sent him crashing to the ground. Three of his own men pounced upon those who had brought him down, hitting out with sticks and fists, gouging eyes and squeezing genitals, tearing with their teeth at ears and fingers and toes.

The dust-laden air was further weighted with the stench of fresh blood and vomitus, and laced with curses, moans, coughs, and sneezes. Amidst so much turmoil, no one but

Watches for Omens noticed that Black Wolf Running still lay motionless on the field. No one saw the Shaman hurry to his nephew's side, no one except his youthful acolytes heard him shout for a litter. And no one saw the fear in the old man's face as Black Wolf Running was carried off the field.

Not until the game was finally pronounced over and Outina's team the victors did anyone learn that the leader of the losing side was in such perilous condition that death might even now be sitting on his shoulder.

Chapter 29

Moon of Winter pushed aside her uneaten venison stew, looked across the hall to where Palm Tree Bending sat alone by her own hearth. If Black Wolf Running died, that poor young woman would lose more than a beloved brother; her small clan would be even further diminished, and so far she had been sent no daughters to ensure its survival. No wonder she was weeping. And in the circumstances, it was probably only natural that she should have rebuffed her husband when he tried to comfort her. Would she do the same to her? Moon of Winter wondered. There was only one way to find out.

Murmuring apology for her lack of appetite, she left her aunt's hearth and went to join Palm Tree Bending. "I wish I could do something to relieve your worrying," she said to her.

"Can you arrange for my brother to wake, and stand, and speak? That is the only thing that can ease my worrying." The words were wrapped in bitterness, and Moon of Winter flinched.

"You know I cannot," she said, sitting down next to her cousin's wife. "All I can do is offer sympathy and understanding. It is a terrible thing, to fear that someone you love will die."

"It is beyond terrible, since my own husband will be responsible for his death." Anger coated this statement, and Moon of Winter, whose back was to the others, hoped none had overheard.

"Black Wolf Running was wounded several times during the Ball Game," she said. "You cannot know which injury—"

Palm Tree Bending did not let her finish. "Outina struck him on the head, struck him with such force that Wolf cannot recover from the blow," she said flatly. "All of us saw it happen."

Moon of Winter could not refute this. "Our Ball Game is sometimes called 'the little brother of war,' " she said after a moment. "Men die during wars, Palm Tree Bending. I wish they didn't, but they do."

"And their womenfolk are free to hate their killers," the other woman said. "It must dilute their grieving, to be able to hate."

Moon of Winter thought of the pale-skins who, years before, had ruthlessly slain all the men of Outina's town. Those who came home to mourn the dead had hated the Christian soldiers, but had their hatred done anything to lessen their sorrow? She could not be certain, this long afterward, but she was certain that she did not like what she saw now in Palm Tree Bending's eyes. "Surely you don't hate Outina?" she asked quietly. "Wolf was his oldest and dearest friend; your husband's anguish is as great as yours."

"He has his mother to comfort him, however," Palm Tree Bending said. "I have none, nor father, either. No one is left of my clan except my uncle and my children, and it is for me to comfort them rather than for them to comfort me."

"Perhaps, in giving comfort, you will find it," Moon of Winter said, then wished she hadn't. Platitudes were powerless to take away the anger betrayed by Palm Tree Bending's rigid face, her clenched hands. "Black Wolf Running would be unhappy to see you like this," Moon of Winter said, "and he would not want you to blame Outina for what happened. He—"

Palm Tree Bending leaped to her feet. "My brother would want revenge," she shouted. "That is what Black Wolf Running would want, and that is what I will claim for him." She swung around, looked straight at Walks Tall Woman. "If my brother dies," she said to her, "one of your clan will have murdered one of mine. The law of the Timucua allows me to claim a life for a life. On the day my brother is buried, I mean to do just that."

Ignoring the cries of her frightened children, shaking off the restraining hand of the husband who hurried to her side, the distraught young woman blundered to the door and rushed out of the house as though pursued by demons.

Which, Moon of Winter thought wretchedly, she was.

"He has not opened his eyes, or spoken, or moved so much as a finger," Watches for Omens told Kwambu and Moon of Winter when they went to the small house the Shaman shared with his nephew. "There is swelling around the wound, but what concerns me more is the way all of his flesh has heated. If I could get him to swallow water, it might cool a little. But I cannot." The anxiety that pinched the old man's features had siphoned the saliva from his mouth; his voice was dry as pollen at the end of blooming season.

Moon of Winter glanced at her husband, turned back to Black Wolf Running's uncle. "We are here because Kwambu once heard of a . . . a kind of ritual that might help our Paracusi," she said.

The Shaman's tired eyes focused on the trader. "Please," he said. "I have tried everything I know. If you can recommend *anything* . . ."

Kwambu frowned; if only he had more to go on than hearsay. But Wolf's unnatural sleep warned that it would not be long until his spirit grew weary of being confined within so useless a body. "Years ago," he said slowly, "I had a friend in the south, someone whose people were accustomed to trade with a tribe that lived even farther south and far to the west. He described to me how certain priests in this Mexica tribe deal with injuries similar to your nephew's." He walked over to the bunk on which the unconscious man lay. "Using a thin, sharp knife," he told Watches for Omens, "they peel back a section of the scalp. Then they puncture the flesh above the injury"—his hand indicated the distended area on Wolf's head—"and, rotating the knife as we do our fire-making drills, they penetrate the bone beneath. They do not stop until the blade has gone all the way through the skull, leaving a hole in it."

Moon of Winter swallowed to contain her nausea; it was no easier hearing the procedure outlined a second time.

But Watches for Omens was nodding his head. "Surely boring such a hole would release the demon that is keeping Black Wolf Running from responding to my medicines," he said excitedly.

"It might," Kwambu cautioned. "I was told that sometimes this cures the sickness that often attends head wounds, and sometimes it does not. I have never seen the drilling done, you understand, and there is always the risk that I do not accurately recall what was told to me."

"Your memory has rarely deceived you in the past." It was statement, not question, but the confidence with which the Shaman spoke vanished as he held out his hands. "I am old," he said, "and occasionally my fingers tremble for no reason at all. You must make the passage for the demon to depart from Wolf's head, Kwambu."

The trader stepped away from the Paracusi. "I am no priest, no Shaman. I have no knowledge of healing."

"Thanks to what your friend told you, you have the knowledge needed to bring healing to my nephew," Watches for Omens said. "I will call upon the gods to help you, and Moon of Winter will stand at your side with her crystal. Together, we can offer spirit power to both you and Black Wolf Running. But age has made me feeble, and your wife lacks a man's strength; you are the only one able to cut through the bone."

"What if I fail?" Kwambu asked hoarsely.

The old man smiled again. "My nephew's spirit will forgive you if that happens, trader. As I will. To try and fail will be more honorable than not to try at all." He hesitated. "I have another reason for asking this of you. I would prefer it if no one else discovers what we mean to do. My niece's concern for her brother has filled her with an anger she is ill-equipped to deal with. If Palm Tree Bending learns that I am encouraging you to make a hole in her brother's skull, I cannot predict what her reaction might be. She and Wolf have always been close; if she did not have her sons to care for, she would refuse to leave Black Wolf Running's side. She would not trust even me to tend him." His final words quivered; he understood why his niece felt this way, but it hurt regardless.

Compassion triumphed over Kwambu's reluctance. "I will try," he said. "And I think I must do so soon if we are to have even the slightest hope of succeeding."

The others did not ask what he meant. They could see for themselves that Black Wolf Running's spirit was poised to slip away to the world where his ancestors waited. But given the option, surely even Wolf's spirit kin would prefer to have one so young remain in This World until the fullness of years was upon him.

Moon of Winter's heart thudded in her chest as she walked with her husband through the gentle light of early morning, thudded more violently as the two entered the Shaman's house. Her hand went to the pouch around her neck, felt for her crystal; she must find calmness, for Kwambu's sake. He had slept little the night before, and she knew that the mask of confidence he had put on for the benefit of Watches for Omens only thinly veiled his own trepidation.

The Shaman greeted them quietly, called their attention to the section of roof he had torn away so that Sun's light might fall directly on Black Wolf Running. Not only would this enable Kwambu to see more clearly, but the grandfather-spirit of all the Timucua was being encouraged to lend his strength to the young man who lay unmoving within that shaft of pale gold.

"My niece has taken her sons to the river, as she always does at this hour," Watches for Omens told them. "And I have seen to it that several older matrons, who will be there, also, will ask her assistance in such a way that she is unable to deny them. We need not concern ourselves that she will return beforetime."

Moon of Winter, remembering Palm Tree Bending's vengeful tirade, hoped he was right. She slipped her crystal from its pouch, begged it silently to grant them all the time they might need to revive the life force in Black Wolf Running.

Kwambu took from the sack he carried the specially hafted knife he had honed until it was a keen-edged, glistening sliver of flint. He wrapped around it the cord of a bow drill fashioned from wood and gave an experimental twist to the bar he had set horizontally atop the knife's handle. It was functioning properly.

"I have cut away the hair around the wound," Watches for Omens said, "and said a purification chant over it." He took up position at the foot of the bunk. "My nephew is ready for you, Kwambu."

Moon of Winter held out her hand, let Sun's rays caress the crystal, tilted it so that miniature rainbows of light played upon Black Wolf Running's head. *Please,* she begged silently, *send*

*your power along the trail my husband will blaze, and banish
the demon that has stolen the strength of our Paracusi.*

She watched as Kwambu traced three sides of a rectangle in
the flesh around the wound and gently drew back the flap of
skin he had incised. Nor would she let herself flinch when he
set the point of his knife against the wound, pushed down
firmly, and began to rotate the bow he held perpendicular to
the ugly swelling. Battling the desire to close her eyes, she
continued to watch as the knife's blade slowly ground its way
through turgid flesh and into the bone beneath. Even when its
tip grated against Black Wolf Running's skull and Kwambu,
perspiration sheening his forehead, began to press down harder,
she did not turn away; only a slight tremor in the hand that
held the crystal hinted at her unease.

Kwambu's hands did not shake, even a little, and he thanked
all the gods that were or ever would be for their steadiness. His
sleep had been besieged by visions of failure, he had spent
long hours wrestling with doubt. But he had no time for such
things now; all of his concentration must be on the task he was
pledged to perform.

With frustrating slowness the narrow flint blade ground
through the Great Warrior's skull. The rasping sound it made
underscored the chant Watches for Omens had begun the moment Kwambu picked up his knife, the rustle of Moon of Winter's skirt as she shifted in order to draw more of Sun's light
into the heart of the crystal. Sacred herbs smoldered in pots the
Shaman had set beneath the bed, and scented smoke drifted up
to merge with the sunshine that poured in a heartening stream
over Black Wolf Running.

The muscles of Kwambu's arms knotted as he grasped the
horizontal handle of the shaft more securely and rotated the
bow a trifle faster, yet suddenly there was a rhythm to what
he was doing and he leaned into it gratefully. Soon he no
longer saw the crystal-spawned rainbows caressing the polished flint, no longer heard the Shaman's singsong voice, could
not even smell the incense rising around him. The deepening
hole in Black Wolf Running's skull became his whole world;
nothing else existed for him.

Twice more Moon of Winter altered position to keep her
crystal within the brightening rays of a sun that followed its
destined path across the sky. Watches for Omens's voice
thinned as his throat roughened. The herbs in their pots shriveled and blackened.

But as the last trace of incense sifted into the air, the hypnotic movement of Kwambu's dark hands all at once ceased. With infinite care he withdrew the knife blade from Black Wolf Running's skull. Clinging to its tip was an uneven disk of bone, and as Kwambu lifted this out of the narrow tunnel he had drilled, a slender spate of pale pink fluid gushed in its wake.

Watches for Omens clasped his hands together, bowed his head. "The demon has been set free," he whispered.

Kwambu looked at him. "I have been able to make freedom available to it," he said quietly. "Only time will tell if the demon has chosen to make use of it."

Moon of Winter slipped out of the Shaman's house as soon as she could trust her legs to support her. She needed to be alone for a while, needed solitude to regain the self which had melded with the crystal during her time in Watches for Omens's house. She would go to the women's hut, she decided; nobody was using it at the moment, and if Moon of Winter left her moccasins outside, no one would come in without first announcing herself.

She kindled a small blaze on the hearth inside the hut; her shivering was born of tension mixed with fear, but a fire can comfort as well as warm. And she was frightened still; what if Black Wolf Running should fail to recover, despite Kwambu's heroic efforts? The Shaman had vowed to forgive him if that happened, but who could say how others might feel about it?

She hunkered down, contemplated the dancing flames, unclenched her hands and told herself to relax, to send her fears into the river that ran behind the hut and let its current carry them away.

The tightness across her shoulders eased; her shivering abated; she settled herself more comfortably. The weariness that provides fertile ground for apprehension was dissipating.

"Moon of Winter."

Her eyes, which had almost closed, flew open at the sound of her aunt's voice. She flexed her arms, her legs, pushed back the hair that had fallen over her face. "You may come in," she called, and hoped her annoyance did not reflect in her tone.

But vexation gave way to shock as the Principal Woman entered. For the first time ever, Walks Tall Woman failed to live up to her name. She fairly crept into the hut, and her eyes, when she looked at Moon of Winter, held none of their usual glitter.

Black Wolf Running has died, Moon of Winter thought immediately. And waited numbly for the awful words to be said.

But they were not spoken. "I have come to a decision," Walks Tall Woman said as she seated herself across from her niece, "and I need you to look into your crystal and tell me what will happen if I act upon it."

The relief that washed over Moon of Winter was followed by a rush of surprise. Her aunt had never before shown the slightest interest in the crystal that awed most of the townspeople.

"The Law that Palm Tree Bending has threatened to invoke also decrees that some other member of the manslayer's clan may satisfy the liability," Walks Tall Woman went on. "If Black Wolf Running dies, I have decided to ransom my son's life from the Quail clan by offering them mine."

Moon of Winter was uncertain how to respond. That Walks Tall Woman had the courage to make such an offer, she did not doubt. For all her faults, the woman was no coward, and her love for her son knew no limits. "Outina is agreeable to this?" she asked faintly. Her cousin was no coward, either, and she could not imagine him letting his mother make so great a sacrifice for him.

"He does not know. And since I mean to make the arrangements ahead of time, he will not. Until it is too late."

So. Once again Walks Tall Woman was taking it upon herself to decide what was best for her son. "Do you think it is right for him to go in ignorance of something so important?" Moon of Winter said.

"I am elder of our clan. It is my responsibility to deal with the kind of problem we are likely to be faced with." Her aunt's gaze sharpened. "You understand that you must keep to yourself what we are discussing?"

Moon of Winter nodded reluctantly. What was told in confidence must be kept in confidence. That was also Law.

"I need to know that Palm Tree Bending will agree to what I propose," the older woman said, "and that my dying will accomplish what I hope it will. That is why I am asking you to consult your crystal and make certain that Outina will not be reviled for what I mean to do. If our people should reject him as leader because I voluntarily bartered my life for his . . ."

Fear flared in her eyes; her spirit would never rest if that should happen.

Moon of Winter's head began to ache. "The crystal predicts only when it chooses to," she faltered.

"I accept that," Walks Tall Woman said. "But you must look into the crystal for me, Moon of Winter. You must!" She sprang to her feet and began to pace the hard-packed earth floor. "I am not afraid to die," she said, a little of her innate fierceness reasserting itself. "But what will become of my son if I am no longer here to advise him? That is another question I need an answer for. He is a fine Holata, Moon of Winter, one that people have come to admire. But he has always looked to me for guidance. What will happen when I am no longer here to give it, and to remind him of what a leader can and must be?"

Moon of Winter studied the glowing embers within the neat circle of stones. Was Walks Tall Woman completely unaware that Outina had been thinking for himself for some years now, that he continued to listen to his mother's counsel mostly out of courtesy and affection? "Perhaps," she said cautiously, "you do not give your son sufficient credit. Whether you should offer your life to the Quail clan in exchange for his is something only you can decide, when and if the need arises. But . . . would it be such a terrible thing for Outina to have to think for himself? You have raised him well," she added hastily, for Walks Tall Woman had stopped her pacing and was swinging round belligerently, "and prepared him thoroughly for the status he has come to. You need to have more faith in your own teachings, I think. And in your son."

Walks Tall Woman, hunger for reassurance reclaiming her emotions, seated herself again. "If I could be certain that Outina is the kind of Holata who will become a legend among his people," she said, "then I will go gladly to my death. But I need more than your opinion to prove to me that he is. Please, Moon of Winter, look into your crystal and tell me what you see there."

With a sigh, Moon of Winter tipped the crystal into her palm. If she looked into it and once more saw nothing but reflected light, what could she do? And wasn't it possible that its use during the curing ceremony had drained some of its potency? Yet Walks Tall Woman seemed truly in need; how could she deny her?

"You know that the spirits sometimes withhold answers

from us," Moon of Winter said. "If that happens, there is nothing I can do to force them."

Her aunt nodded soberly, but her gaze was fixed on Moon of Winter's hand, on the glistening facets of the magic stone nestled in her cupped palm.

Moon of Winter closed her eyes, roofed the crystal with her free hand and prayed. Then she let her thoughts roam as she waited for the stone to signal that it was ready to serve the woman who held it. Palm Tree Bending was a good woman, a gentle woman. She had suddenly shown herself to be stronger than anyone would have guessed by demanding blood revenge should her brother die, but would she actually go against her own nature to collect it?

The crystal was no longer cool to Moon of Winter's touch. She opened her eyes and her hands and looked down into it, but the swirl of light and dark that infused it was nothing more than a reflection of the fireglow and shadow filling the hut. Her temples pounded and moisture beaded on her brow. What should she do? Was there no way she could help the woman sitting across from her?

Finally, Moon of Winter surrendered to instinct. Without spirit-guidance, nothing else was available to her. "Outina is a natural and able leader," she said, and her own certainty of this lent confidence to her voice. "In the years to come, he will be revered by his people, and his praises will be sung even by their children, and their children's children."

Her aunt's clenched hands relaxed and her breathing resumed a more normal rhythm. "I thank you," she whispered, and rose to her feet, either not realizing or not caring that Moon of Winter had answered only one of the questions she had asked. "I know now that I have made the right decision, and will rejoice to abide by it."

Then she was gone, and Moon of Winter was left to plague herself with recrimination.

"No!" Outina shouted. "I will not permit you to do such a thing." Stunned by Walks Tall Woman's announcement, he had forgotten both his age and his status; he was simply a son who was horrified by the thought of the mother he adored being slain in his stead. "If blood-payment must be made to my wife's clan," he said hoarsely, "then it is for the manslayer himself to die."

His face was nearly as gaunt as Walks Tall Woman's, and

this owed little to the ribs that had been splintered during the Ball Game or even to the pain that persisted despite the Shaman's efficient binding of his upper torso. He could not, would not, believe that Palm Tree Bending might make good her threat. This woman had lived with him and shared his bed for more than a decade; she had given him two sons; as greatly as she loved Black Wolf Running, surely she would not want to see her husband, the father of those sons, put to death? "I forbid you to do this," he said to his mother, "or even to speak of doing it."

"Palm Tree Bending already knows what I mean to do," Walks Tall Woman said. "As is proper, I have sent an intermediary to tell her of my offer."

Moon of Winter started. She'd had no idea that her aunt would move so quickly! Now she must pray all the harder that Watches for Omens had been able to find ways to keep Palm Tree Bending away from his house until they could know if the skull penetration had been successful. If she should discover what had been done that morning, it would surely inflame her further.

Outina stalked away from his mother's hearth, lowered himself cautiously onto his bed and rested one hand on the embroidered robe Palm Tree Bending had made to cover them when winter came. He had never thought to tell her he considered it beautiful; had never, ever told her that he considered *her* beautiful, come to that! And when was the last time he had said that he loved her? Why, he had not even admitted to her the awful guilt he felt because of what had happened to Black Wolf Running, had not confessed that, if his friend died, to lose his own life would be easier than living beneath a sky-obscuring cloud of self-blame. Perhaps his careless assumption that she understood all these things without him saying them was reason enough for Palm Tree Bending to hate him and want to see him dead. But . . . he did not want to die. Not really. He balled his right hand, brought it down hard on his knee. If only none of this had ever happened . . . !

When footfalls sounded outside, he tensed, and had to force himself to turn around when his wife entered the Principal House. But he let none of his soul-searching show in his face as he stood and greeted her formally.

Palm Tree Bending tilted her head slightly in acknowledgment, then went and stood before Walks Tall Woman. "I was told that you are willing to die in Outina's place," she said. "Is this true?"

Walks Tall Woman came to her feet. "It is."

Outina came out of the shadows, stood between the two women. "Walks Tall Woman made an offer; I am hereby rescinding it."

"You cannot." Walks Tall Woman and Palm Tree Bending spoke almost in unison. And neither of them so much as looked at him.

Moon of Winter went and stood behind her cousin. "This is no time to speak like a Holata," she murmured. "Let your words be those of husband, and son."

Outina reached out, grasped one of Walks Tall Woman's hands and one of Palm Tree Bending's, and would not let them go. "I love my mother too much to see her die for me," he said, gazing intently at Palm Tree Bending. Then, turning to Walks Tall Woman, "And I love my wife too much to deny her the ransom she feels she must claim. If Black Wolf Running dies, let my blood be spilled in atonement."

Both women shook their heads. "Our people need you," Walks Tall Woman said to her son. "My death will make little difference to them. Therefore, I should be the one—"

Palm Tree Bending lifted a hand to interrupt her. "No blood need be spilled," she said wearily. "That is what I came here to say. The offer Walks Tall Woman made was nearly enough to satisfy any debt that might be owing to the Quail clan. If she will agree also to abandon her scheme to adopt one of my sons, then I will consider the debt paid in full." Her mouth trembled, but somehow she kept her voice steady. "Whether my brother recovers or no."

Her husband's eyes narrowed as he turned to his mother. "You have been trying to take one of Palm Tree Bending's children from her?" The incredulity in his voice was buttressed by rage.

"How else can one of your sons serve as Holata after you?" Walks Tall Woman asked, spreading her hands. "Surely you do not want to see the leadership pass eventually to another branch of our clan or—worse yet—to another clan altogether?"

"The leadership will remain with the White Deer clan," Outina said impatiently. He drew Moon of Winter forward. "Have you forgotten that my cousin has two fine sons? Why do you think I delight to work with them whenever I can, to help them become praiseworthy warriors? When I am gone, either Hawk or Fox will become Holata. This is as it should be, and as the Law says that it must be, so long as our people agree to the succession. Which I promise you they will. And even if Moon of Winter were barren, I would not allow my wife to give one of our children to you merely to keep leadership in our clan. How could you ever think that I would approve such a thing?"

Walks Tall Woman opened her mouth to respond, but Outina had already turned his fury on Palm Tree Bending. "You did not think it needful to tell me what my mother was trying to do?" he demanded. "White Tailed Stag and Long Path Follower may belong to the Quail clan, but they are the sons of my flesh. And of my heart. Was I to have no say in the matter at all?" His expression gentled. "For what I did to Black Wolf Running, I am sorrier than you will ever know," he told her, "and my grief will be as great as yours if he does not recover from the wound I gave him." Moon of Winter was gladdened to see tears well in Palm Tree Bending's eyes; the young woman knew her husband spoke sincerely, and this surely meant the beginning of new understanding, for both of them. "However," Outina went on, his voice still quiet, but with authority in it once more, "never again will you keep from me what it is my place to know. I must have your promise on that, Palm Tree Bending."

His wife inclined her head a second time, but there was no stiffness in the gesture this time. "You have it," she said.

Both of them looked toward Walks Tall Woman then, and it was as plain to them as it was to Moon of Winter that the older woman was finding it difficult to find the words she knew she must not only say, but mean. "And I give mine," she said at last, "to never again even mention taking one of your sons into the White Deer clan." To openly apologize to Palm Tree Bending was beyond her, and all of them knew it. Nor would the humility her son had heaped upon her quell her for long; all of them knew that, too.

Exhaustion made Moon of Winter stumble as she moved away from the three, and only the sight of her husband and the Shaman coming into the house kept her on her feet at all. Anxiously, she searched their faces, but their own exhaustion left their expressions indecipherable.

Then Watches for Omens cleared his throat and looked at Palm Tree Bending. "Your brother is asking for you," he said.

Only after his niece, brushing away tears of joy, had rushed out, did the Shaman ask the others to be seated while he told them everything he had been keeping from them. "By midday, Wolf was moving his arms and legs," he finished. "Soon afterward, his eyes opened and he was able to drink a little water. And now he has spoken; spoken rationally." The old man smiled at the trader, who had taken a place beside his wife. "Thanks to Kwambu, Black Wolf Running will recover."

Moon of Winter sat in silence while questions were asked and answered, disbelief coped with, and words of praise heaped upon the man sitting next to her. Now that it was over, now that life could return more or less to normal, what was Kwambu likely to say when he learned that a son of his would one day be a chief among the Timucua? Because she and her husband had always assumed that her marriage to an outlander made her sons ineligible for tribal leadership, they had never spared thought for such an eventuality.

She decided to wait until he had rested before she told him the truth of it.

Chapter 30

❖ ❖

Dancing Egret tipped the last of the steaming liquid into Prowling Panther's conch shell cup, carried the empty jug to the doorway of the Headchief's house and set it outside. By the time the counselors' cups were empty again, Ysabel would have refilled the ceremonial jug and added a few red-hot stones to keep the potion boiling. The Spanish woman would take pains to do so quietly; longstanding rumor insisted that anyone who eavesdropped on Calusa's Council would face certain, and unpleasant, death. Dancing Egret had never known such a thing to happen, but perhaps rumor had always been enough to ensure the Headchief's privacy.

She took her accustomed seat a little apart from the men, began to sew variegated shells onto the sheath she was making to hold Shore Walker's knife. The pattern she'd chosen was a simple one, a half-coiled serpent; she could easily listen as she worked. And she would, as usual, be virtually unnoticed; like the clan plaques that indicated each man's seat in Council, her attendance at these meetings had become an accepted thing.

As Vision Seeker began the ritual chant that preceded Council business, Egret's attention wandered to the ceremonial cloaks worn by the counselors. Why had the graceful feathers and soft-tinted shells that had been prized ornamentation in her father's day fallen into disfavor? Now most cloaks boasted hammered disks of silver and clusters of shining red and green and yellow stones, stuff salvaged from shipwrecks. Her brother's cloak had glittering chains of gold draped over its white feathers, and a large gold clasp held it closed. Did men honestly think they looked more elegant when they imitated the dress of pale-faces?

The priest had taken his seat, and all heads turned toward the young man who sat alone on the upper tier of benches. Calusa bestowed a smile upon each of his counselors in turn, then leaned forward. "It has taken more seasons than we had planned," he told them, "but the rebuilding begun after the hurricane is finally finished. All of my people have sturdy new homes; our seawalls have been shored up in some places, and in others rebuilt; we have extended several of the canals, and even constructed a fine deep reservoir on the northern side of the island, one that will catch and hold an abundance of fresh water whenever it rains." He beamed as congratulations were sent his way; the idea for the cistern had been his, and, despite the enormous amount of work entailed, everyone agreed that something of the sort had long been needed.

Dancing Egret, selecting an auger shell for the tip of the serpent's tail, took appreciative note. The men were right to praise her brother for so clever an innovation.

"We can be proud of our new town," Calusa went on, "and I am sure all of us would like others to see what we have accomplished. Which is why I have arranged that my marriage, so long postponed, will take place at the next round moon."

Twisting River stood up. In old age his face, except for its webbing of fine lines, had resumed its infant cast; all of his features were puckered by his bulbous cheeks and overhanging eyebrow ridges. "I will speak," he announced when he had everyone's attention. "It occurs to me," he said to the Headchief, "that waiting until the next Ceremony of First Harvest would be advisable. Our leaders usually marry at this time so that a single feast serves to celebrate both harvest and wedding."

The elder of the Conch clan was one of the two men remaining from Great Calusa's original Council. Shark Fin, representing the Seagull clan, was the other. *It amuses me to watch two codgers arguing,* Egret's brother had told her, *and occasionally their bickering distracts everyone enough so that I am able to win prompt approval for something I want during the confusion that ensues. Which saves me both time and energy.*

Predictably, Shark Fin rose the moment Twisting River sat down. "You approved our Headchief doing something new when he commanded the reservoir to be made," he said, "yet you disapprove this proposal simply because he means to do something else in a new way." Indignation gave the tip of his beaklike nose particular definition. "You are inconsistent, Twisting River, and therefore your protest has no merit." Pivoting on the stick he used for support when he walked, the lame man glared at his old enemy as he lowered himself carefully onto his seat.

Shore Walker's cousin, Growling Bear of the Cormorant clan, a man whose appreciation for the richness of his native tongue made him an ideal Chief Speaker, came to his feet. He was a bit older than Egret's husband, as well as shorter and stockier, but he resembled Shore Walker enough to prove their kinship. Tactfully avoiding offense to either of the feuding counselors, he intimated that their Headchief's first marriage ought to be cause for separate celebration.

Dancing Egret stitched a half-dozen shells in place while the men who had kept silent until now decided to support Shark Fin and Growling Bear. And she hid a smile as her brother, with deft application of his lavish charm, persuaded Twisting River to withdraw his protest so that the decision could be unanimous.

"Twisting River was right to raise the issue of the extra provisions we will need in order to prepare two enormous feasts within a single season, however," Calusa went on. "I have considered this, also, and have found a solution to the problem. First, I have sent emissaries to demand a more favorable treaty from Holata Mocoso of the Timucua. I had hoped to do this soon after I became Headchief, but the hurricane changed that, as it did so many things; I allowed the treaty made by my father to stand until the men of this town finished its reconstruction and could return to the activities warriors are more properly concerned with. Now I have demanded that Mocoso and his brother-in-law accept a smaller portion of goods as payment for my traders' safe passage through Canegacola's territory."

Egret, carrying the brimming ceremonial jug Ysabel had just refilled, kept her expression neutral as she poured the bubbling brew into Calusa's cup. She had foolishly assumed that her brother had either forgotten this scheme of his or had decided against it. Yet his listeners were nodding their heads; apparently even the seasoned counselors foresaw no problems in inviting Mocoso's wrath, and that of Canegacola as well. Problems her father would have recognized at once.

He would have recognized the inadvisability of his son's next proposal, too. "A new treaty will help considerably," Calusa said as Egret decanted the last of the drink into Growling Bear's cup. "But it has taken until now to accumulate reserves of food, and I have no wish to see our storehouses emptied so that we can feed the many visitors who come to the island for my marriage. Therefore, I will let it be known that the Townchiefs and allies who plan to be our guests must bring more than token gifts with them. Some will be required to contribute meat or grain; others will be encouraged to bring tools or weapons instead."

"That is wise," Shark Fin said. "Rebuilding demanded so much of my time that the number of new weapons I have been able to make is small. And what are warriors without decent weapons?"

Prowling Panther grunted agreement. His own dart thrower needed replacing, and anything he made for himself would only be a sorry imitation of what the weapons maker could produce!

"Shark Fin and the other craftsmen have no excuse for not getting to work now," Twisting River said sharply, "and our hunters are free now to go after more meat." He turned to Calusa. "We ought not be hasty about asking Townchiefs and allies to supply us with food and weapons and tools," he said. "Why risk being named inhospitable when nothing truly prevents our being the generous hosts we have always been?"

"You have such an instinctive aversion to any amendment of the traditional that we waste our time listening to you," Shark Fin retorted. "On so auspicious an occasion, why should visi-

tors object to bringing with them more than just some paltry
marriage gift?"

Before Twisting River could respond, Calusa intervened.
"Let us hear from the others," he suggested.

Dancing Egret, as arrows of argument flew back and forth,
never doubted that once again her brother would have his way.

He did, and rubbed his hands together as he praised his
counselors for their acumen. "All that remains, then," he told
them, "is to bring Oathkaqua's daughter to the island. Her father means to send a small escort of warriors with her, and she
will have her women attendants, of course; but it would be
courteous to meet them halfway. Prowling Panther, I leave it to
you to select a party of warriors to do so. Kwambu the trader
will lead your men into the upper Lake country, and I will send
the two Spanish traders to Oathkaqua to let him know where
the meeting place will be." He stood up, smiled upon his
Council. "I promise you that the marriage celebration will be
a splendid one," he said. "It will make up for the hardships of
the past few years. Let this be known throughout the town,
Growling Bear; the people will be cheered by the news, and
your Headchief delights in seeing his people happy."

"He is the same as he was when he was a child," Dancing
Egret fumed. "No. He is worse. When he was little, my
brother did not like being told he was acting unwisely, but at
least you knew that he had heard what you said. Now, although he continues to look at you, even to smile at you, he
hears only what he wants to hear of what you're saying.
And what he chooses not to hear is that perhaps he is wrong
in what he is thinking or doing!"

Shore Walker scrutinized the raccoon he was carving, decided its expression lacked the mischievousness he was aiming
for, and began to pare thin strips from the underside of the
creature's jaw. "I suppose you have been speaking with Calusa
about something that happened in Council this morning?"

She nodded, flung herself down beside him. "It would probably be better for our people if Crested Heron had been born
ugly," she said. "Or at least with an unpleasant personal-
ity. The counselors are too easily swayed by him, Shore
Walker. They occasionally put forth reasoned arguments—
which is their purpose for being there, after all—but he talks
so persuasively, and dazzles them so with that brilliant smile of
his, that they quickly forget they started out being opposed to

what he suggested. Always, he gets what he wants. And what he wants is not necessarily what is best." She jumped up, went and looked upon a night humming with insect song and sweet with the scent of the grass the women had scythed from between the houses that day. "He is jeopardizing our safe-passage treaty with Mocoso," she said morosely, "the one our father worked so long and hard to arrange. And since he has already sent out couriers demanding what he calls 'more favorable terms' for the Calusa, we can only hope Mocoso takes the time to negotiate instead of simply refusing outright and leaving our traders with no secure route into the country of the northern Timucua."

"Mocoso is older than our Headchief, and age usually tempers a man's rashness," Shore Walker said. "He'll probably initiate negotiations, and Calusa cannot refuse to listen to *him*, Egret."

"True, but when I lived in his town, Holata Mocoso was noted for his arrogance. Even if he does insist on meeting with my brother, it will be a meeting between two arrogant men. How can agreement be reached if each is absolutely convinced that his is the right way, the only way? And you may be sure that Canegacola will be recommending to Mocoso that force be used to persuade Calusa against any treaty changes. Over the years, Mocoso's brother-in-law must have come to depend upon his share of the goods he exacts from us, and he has so many warriors that his entire southern boundary can be patrolled without leaving the rest of his province undefended."

Her husband nodded. "So we have always heard, but we can't know if that continues to be so, can we? Besides, I don't think it will come to war, Egret. Both Mocoso and Canegacola would be denying themselves access to any of our trade goods should they make such a choice, and as you said, each is accustomed to receiving a portion of what our traders carry through Canegacola's territory."

Dancing Egret looked up at the sliver of moon dangling over the Temple mound across the canal. Shore Walker made sense, and perhaps her unease was baseless. She decided not to mention Calusa's plan to require tribute from his wedding guests; perhaps she was wrong, too, in thinking they might be offended by his demands. Her brother truly did want everyone to like him, so his message to Townchief and ally would not lack diplomacy. Most of them would probably end by thinking the contributions were being made freely, she thought wryly.

"What bothers me most," she said, crossing the room to sit on the bed again, "is what he said when I reminded him yet again that Kwambu does not entirely trust Fontaneda and Gomez. My brother is sending them to Oathkaqua, you see, to let the chief know that he is ready for his bride to come to him."

Shore Walker held the raccoon up to the light from the rushes Egret had rigged to burn in a platter of bear grease. Except for painting, it was finished. "And what did he say?" he asked.

She sighed. "He said he was grateful for the reminder. Then he laughed and said that he knows now what he will give to Oathkaqua to thank him for sending his daughter to him. Shore Walker, he means to foist the two Spaniards off on my father's old friend, and with no warning to be wary of them, either!"

Her husband set aside the carving. "There is nothing you can do about it, Egret. But Oathkaqua has been a coastal chief for a very long time, and is not unacquainted with the Spanish; it's unlikely he'll put trust in that pair until he has tested them."

"Which is more than my brother has done," Egret said.

"I know. And he should have, the first time you told him what Kwambu said. But we islanders have had much to cope with since the year of the big storm, Egret; many things we ordinarily would have done have been postponed."

Dancing Egret smiled. "You are charitable, as well as wise," she said. "What would I do without you?"

He put his arms around her, fingered a strand of hair as dark and soft as it had been the day they married. "You will never have to do without me," he murmured, seeking the ear closest to him and teasing at it with his tongue.

She drew breath sharply, let her fingers wander over his broad chest. "I take that as a promise," she said, caressing his hard nipples with butterfly touches, then fluttering her hands over his flat stomach until they found his navel.

He stretched out on the bed, pulling her down beside him. "Don't stop there," he whispered, curving himself around her before lowering his mouth to one upthrusting breast.

She slid her hand down, closed her fingers around his jutting penis, moved them slowly up and down, up and down. His delighted moan was muffled by the breast he was suckling, and with her free hand she pressed his head tighter against it.

Both were moving now, fired by passion to anticipate the

glorious union they were journeying toward. Shore Walker moaned again, and Egret's pulses became an erratic drumbeat that set the rhythm for their expedition into ecstasy. When she could wait no longer to reach their destination, she wrapped her legs around him, guided his throbbing penis into her, molded herself around it.

They slid apart until their combined agony was too much for them to bear, came together again. The next parting was briefer, their agony more intense; flesh fused with flesh, eased away, rushed to joyous reunion. Neither wanted the excitement to end, yet both yearned to achieve the pinnacle. Lungs bursting, bodies straining, they moved faster and faster until they were poised together upon the apex of need. Crying out together, they tumbled over it, each somehow cushioning the other's fall. They came to rest in their own enchanted land, a land they had learned to cherish and were more and more reluctant to leave. Cocooned in peace, and still embraced, they slept.

The grease-saturated rushes in the platter, deprived of further fuel, sputtered in frustration; darkness wrapped itself around the sleeping lovers, and only the plaintive hoot of an owl disturbed the silence that ruled their world.

"Teach us a new song, Dancing Egret," Chattering Squirrel begged. "We haven't learned a new one in a very long time."

For once, her twin brother did not echo her words; Running Rabbit was too busy envying the warriors making ready to go north and meet the woman who would be marrying their Headchief.

Squirrel's eyes, so like Brown Pelican's, reflected her eagerness to sing something different today. Her little sister, Rain Drop, although too young to distinguish between new song and old, nonetheless begged also for a new one.

Shore Walker was one of those who would be escorting Oathkaqua's daughter to the island, and Egret had hoped she could be with him until it was time for the party to set out. But it was plain that he was busy, and would be for some time. She smiled down into her nieces' faces, sent her smile farther, to welcome the children who had ranged themselves behind their spokesmen. "Would all of you like to learn a new song?"

Except for the murmurs of the shyer youngsters, the response was a yes so resounding that heads turned toward the group. One of those who looked their way was Kwambu. The trader would be taking no sledge with him this time, and his bluejay feather–trimmed staff was already in his hand, so Dancing Egret beckoned to him. "The children are clamoring for a new story," she said when he had joined them, "as you heard. I thought I might teach them the tale you repeated to me long ago, the one your mother told you when you were a small boy. Would you like to listen to it with them?"

"The one about the monkeys?"

Egret laughed. "When you heard your mother tell it, it was about monkeys. But if you recall, you had to explain to me what monkeys are, and that wasn't easy! So I've changed the story a little, to make it simpler for Calusan children to understand."

"Then I must certainly hear it," he said. "I have often thought to tell that tale to my daughter, but knew she would be as confused as you once were when I started talking about an animal no one in this land has ever seen. Perhaps I will borrow your version of the Legend to tell to Kaia."

As always when Kwambu spoke of his daughter, or of his wife or sons, his brown eyes took on a warmth that restored boyishness to his entire face. Dancing Egret thought that Moon of Winter and her family were fortunate indeed to be loved so much that merely mentioning their names could subtract years from Kwambu's age. Was that the purpose of love, she wondered as she settled the little ones in a semicircle, to perpetuate youth?

"This Legend comes from across the eastern ocean," she said, raising her voice as a burst of masculine laughter drifted across the squareground. One of the warriors, most likely her clan-cousin, Burrowing Kingfisher, a man noted for his keen wit, must have told a joke to his comrades. "It comes from the land that our trader was born in, for that is where all of this happened." She took Rain Drop onto her lap, cuddled her as she went on. "Long, long ago, an old woman lived with her grandson, who was a great hunter. While he took his weapons and went in search of animal flesh to feed them, Grandmother tended a field of corn so that they could always have bread with their meat. But during the nights, raccoons came so often to steal corn from her field that most days the two had only meat to eat." Egret took from her pouch the miniature raccoon Shore Walker had recently carved; she had been so entranced with its whimsical face that he had given it to her as soon as the paint dried. "The hunter slew as many of the corn stealers as he could," she said, holding the carving up so everyone could see it, "but no man can sit up all night, every night, and still go hunting during the day. And while he was away hunting, the raccoons came also to strip the corn from his grandmother's plants. So when a beautiful maiden came to visit the old woman, the hunter decided to make her his wife."

"Because she was so beautiful?" Chattering Squirrel asked.

"Only partly. And his grandmother tried to persuade him not to marry her, for she did not like this young woman. But the hunter wanted someone to guard the cornfield when he could not be there to do it himself, so he married her anyway. And each time he went out to hunt, he sent her to watch over the corn."

"Did she kill the raccoons, or only chase them away?" The boy who asked this clearly doubted that a woman could handle a weapon well enough to slay the corn thieves.

Egret smiled. "Well, the hunter's wife claimed that she frightened them away by stomping her feet and shouting. But the peculiar thing was that, with her guarding the field, the corn disappeared even faster than before.

"Now, the hunter's grandmother still mistrusted this young woman, so she complained to her grandson and told him to follow his wife next time she was sent to the field. 'Hide yourself,' she said, 'and watch what she does.' "

Rain Drop put her hands over her eyes; it was her way to "hide." The older children grinned as she peeped at them from between spread fingers.

"When he did as his grandmother asked," Egret said, letting suspense creep into her voice, "he heard his wife sing this song:

> "Dungo, dungo, dar-mar-lee
> Co-dingo, dar-mar-lee
> Co-dingo, dungo-dingo
> Co-dingo, dingo
> Dar-mar-lee co-dingo."

Already small mouths were forming the syllables, tasting the strangeness of the sounds.

"When she had finished her song," Egret told them, "the hunter's wife was suddenly transformed into a raccoon, and all at once her brother and sister raccoons waddled onto the field and began to gorge themselves with corn. But as much as they ate, guess who ate the most?"

"The hunter's wife!" the children shouted.

Egret nodded. "The young man ran home and told his grandmother what he had heard and seen, and she told him to remember the song and sing it to his wife the moment she returned home.

"This is what he did. And the young woman—for she had turned herself back into one before leaving the stripped field—began to scream and sob and twist herself this way and that. Then suddenly she was a raccoon again, and made haste to run away before the hunter could pick up his weapon."

"Did she ever return to the cornfield with her kin?" Running Rabbit asked.

Egret set Rain Drop on her feet. "The Legend doesn't say. But I think that probably both she and her brothers and sisters found other fields to destroy after that."

She stood up, stretched. "Tomorrow, I'll begin to teach you to chant that story," she said. "For now, repeat to each other what you can of it, especially the song the hunter's wife sang."

To a ragged chorus of "Dungo-dingo, dar-mar-lee," the children dispersed, the girls running to share the new tale with their mothers, the boys to watch the warriors leave for the north.

"Everything appears to be ready, so I must be going," Kwambu said. "But I am glad I had time to hear the whole story. You've changed little, except for making a raccoon out of my monkey, and I thank you for that."

"I try hard to pass on our Legends exactly the way I learned them," Dancing Egret said, crossing the squareground with him. "Naturally, I did the same with yours." She spoke sincerely, but her eyes were busy searching the group of warriors they were nearing. Where was Shore Walker?

A cluster of men parted and there he was, striding toward her. He took her hands in his, pressed them, smiled. "You know we'll be away only three or four days," he said, "but I hope you will miss me anyway."

Kwambu, ever discreet, went and took his place beside Prowling Panther.

Egret did not see him go. "I miss you whenever you are not with me," she said to her husband, "as you know full well." She returned the pressure of his hands, let her eyes tell him what it would not be proper to say aloud with so many people around.

"I feel the same," he said after a long moment. "And when I come home, I shall rejoice to prove it to you."

Calusa started down the ramp to have a last word with the warriors, and Shore Walker went to join his fellows.

Egret watched after him until the column of men disappeared in the direction of the canoes that would carry them to the mainland. Only a few days, she told herself, and he would return to her. Then she pursed her lips in mock chagrin. Shore Walker had not even left the island yet and already she was anticipating his homecoming. Was that any way for an old married woman to behave?

She considered the matter, nodded her head. It certainly was, so long as the woman in question was Dancing Egret. As Shore Walker would be quick to agree.

Chapter 31

•— —•

"I am heartily sick of the sight of corn," a warrior grumbled as Kwambu led the band of men from the planting fields of the Lake country Calusa into the planting fields of Canegacola's people. The plain spread out behind, ahead, to the right and to the left, and everywhere the ripening plants grew shoulder high. "Except for that strip of border, where nothing grew but stickerweeds and poison ivy, I have looked at enough corn to sour me on the stuff!"

"Then I must remember to tell your wife to never again serve you roasted corn. Or corn bread. Or corn pudding," Burrowing Kingfisher said, a twinkle in his eye. "And once you are fleshless as a possum's tail, I'll have a man I can be certain of besting when we hold our wrestling contests."

Prowling Panther, walking ahead of the pair with Shore

Walker, turned around. "The trader says it's not far now to where we will be meeting the people from Oathkaqua."

"After which," Burrowing Kingfisher said to his companion, "we will turn around and retrace our steps. And you'll have yet more corn to feast your eyes on!"

Shore Walker laughed. "Kwambu could take us a different way," he said, "but from what he tells me, that would mean crossing ground so marshy that we might sink up to our ankles in it."

"My corn-hating friend would probably prefer to have mud up to his waist rather than march through planting fields," Kingfisher said. "But he will have more to look at than corn on our way back to the island, won't he? Our Headchief's soon-to-be-wife is a beautiful maiden, and the women attending her may be pleasing to the eye, as well." He glanced to the rear of the column where his fifteen-year-old son walked with three other new-made warriors. "Swift Eagle and his comrades will doubtless make the most of it if any of her attendants are young and pretty," he said. "As I would have done at their age."

"As you would do this time if your son weren't with us," his companion said, delighted with a chance to retaliate. "Everyone knows you think yourself irresistible to the women, Kingfisher; you've acted the fool often enough in your efforts to prove it."

Kingfisher was unruffled. "I like women, that's all," he said. "So where's the harm in being pleasant to them?"

"There is none," Prowling Panther said. "Unless your wife finds out about it, of course."

"Quiet Lagoon knows I love her best," Burrowing Kingfisher said comfortably. "After all, I've never taken a second wife, have I?"

"Only because you value your manhood," the man at his side said swiftly. Contrary to her name, Quiet Lagoon was prickly natured and quick to find fault with everyone, including her husband. Why Kingfisher put up with her was something no one could understand, but he'd done so without complaint for seventeen long years.

They emerged at last from the monotony of tasseled crops onto a vast meadow checkered with the yellow-green of saw palmettos and the cooler green of ancient hardwood stands, but if Kingfisher's companion was relieved to see the last of the corn, Shore Walker was not. It had heartened him to look upon field after field of sentinel-straight plants, and reminded him that earth was glad to nurture all the people of this land. There was a lesson to be learned from this, he thought, then was diverted as one of the younger warriors eased out of line to cast a small-game dart at a gangly wood turkey he'd spotted.

"One bird will scarcely feed all of us," Burrowing Kingfisher called derisively. "You will have to—"

A mask of disbelief dropped over his amiable features as he crashed to the ground, and the feathered shaft that had pierced his neck was quivering still as he died.

From the trees ahead burst a horde of whooping, topknotted warriors. They rose up like raging bears whose sleep has been disturbed, swooped like carrion crows from the limbs arching overhead, fell upon the Calusa like wolves upon a herd of white-tailed deer. Their battle-axes flashed in the sunlight, their clubs swung in deadly arcs as the Calusa—fitting darts into hurlers and snatching blades from sheaths—broke rank and dove for cover.

Their attackers were many, nearly twice as many as they were, but the islanders would not let that dismay them. "Try and bring down their leader," Prowling Panther said. "If we can do that ..."

Shore Walker nodded grimly. To slay the man who led a war band often demoralized his followers.

Kwambu, clutching in his hand the trader's staff—crowned with the blue feathers that ought to have guaranteed all of them safe passage—slithered up beside the pair. "They are Canegacola's men," he said. "Their leader is the one wearing a medicine bundle and a copper gorget." He did not add that he knew the man, that he had shared both food and jest with the Paracusi of this province whenever he had come this way on trading missions. Such things did not matter now.

Prowling Panther crawled to the nearest tree, raised himself enough to look beyond it, released the arrow he had ready, then flattened himself to give Shore Walker room to send his own missile hurtling toward the Timucua.

Kwambu saw the death-dealers find targets, watched two of Canegacola's men fall before they could reach the oak grove they were running to. Neither was the Paracusi. The hand holding his staff tightened; it would make a weapon of sorts if only he were allowed to fight. . . .

Like shadows, warriors from both sides flitted among the trees. Arrows sped between the bands, thwacked into tree trunks or, with sickening softer thuds, into flesh. The three men sprawled in the knee-high grass took no notice; for them, the battle was over. Taunts that only Kwambu could understand flew over their lifeless bodies, were returned by Prowling Panther and his men in a language the enemy warriors did not know. It was, the trader thought bleakly, a ridiculous waste of breath.

Yet the silence that followed was worse. Canegacola's men would be moving now, creeping through terrain familiar to them, bent on launching an attack from the rear. Prowling Panther signaled, and the word was passed along: turn and make ready for hand-to-hand combat.

A pair of black-and-white-flecked birds seized the moment and scurried from a clump of palmetto. Whistling agitatedly, they flapped their stubby wings and whooshed into the clear blue sky.

Shore Walker slid his knife from its shell-decorated sheath. Hugging the ground, he worked his way through the brush, senses on the alert as he made for the outer edge of the copse of trees. A bone-chilling gurgle breached the silence; another man had died, but whether one of theirs or one of the Timucua, he had no way of knowing. And he could not take the time to find out.

The perspiration coating his flesh seeped into his eyes, and he dashed it away before peering through the interwoven branches of a thorny bush. Directly in front of the shrub were the heels of a pair of moccasins, and those moccasins were made from deerskin, not gator hide. The man wearing them was crouched only an arm's length away, unaware that he had company in this patch of briars. Shore Walker smiled, gripped the haft of his blade more securely.

His arm lifted as he sprang, descended as he threw himself upon the enemy. Jerking back the struggling man's head, he ripped open his throat with a single slash. Burrowing Kingfisher was avenged.

Shore Walker hauled his victim upright, looked for a copper gorget, let him fall again. This was not Canegacola's War Leader.

He winced as pain shot through his arm all the way to his shoulder. He had wrenched his wrist, his unreliable right wrist, when he'd administered the death blow. Thanking the gods that he had been surreptitiously training himself to use both dart thrower and knife with his other hand, he lowered himself to the bloody ground and, using only his left arm and his legs to maneuver, slithered back into the underbrush.

Kwambu sat alone beneath a fragrant wax myrtle. "You are trader, not warrior," Prowling Panther had said before he'd left him there. "Plant your staff beside you and stay put."

He had obeyed to the point of remaining where he was, but he saw no reason to wedge the unadorned end of his staff into the damp earth. The color of his skin was enough to tell Canegacola's warriors who he was, and the jay feathers pinned in his tight-curling hair proclaimed his status. He gritted his teeth as a triumphant howl told of another warrior slain; whoever it had been, Calusan or Timucuan, Kwambu had likely known him.

So far as Kwambu knew, there had been no response from Mocoso since Calusa had sent emissaries to him demanding a more favorable treaty. Was this attack to be taken as his response, or had Canegacola made an independent decision to lay in wait for the party from the island? And how had either of them known the Calusa were coming, or when?

Fontaneda and Gomez. It must have been the Spaniards who alerted either Headchief or Townchief. They would have had ample opportunity to contact Canegacola, at least, on their way to Oathkaqua to name the meeting place his daughter's escort should journey to. Had annoyance at being sent as a gift to Holata Oathkaqua prompted them to it, or had it been simply the same resentment they had felt all along at being made to serve people they felt superior to?

A piercing yell ended his speculating. He swung around and saw young Swift Eagle darting across the clearing, a Timucuan warrior in pursuit. The lad threw himself into the brush beneath Kwambu's tree, rolled behind its broad trunk just in time to avoid the club sent spinning after him. Before he could right himself, Shore Walker materialized on his other side, dart hurler at the ready. He pulled back his left arm and let fly at Eagle's pursuer.

There had not been time enough to aim properly, and the arrow merely pierced the Timucuan's side. Yanking it out, he ducked beneath the ground-reaching branches of the tree nearest him.

The three lurking behind the myrtle heard a startled yelp, the crack of conch shell against bone. A moment later a long-haired warrior showed himself briefly as he tossed the

Timucuan's body into the meadow grass. The corn-hater who had been Burrowing Kingfisher's companion on the march had also avenged his comrade.

Swift Eagle slumped against the tree trunk. "My friends," he gasped. "Two of them are slain, and I have not seen the other since the fighting began."

"And you have been injured," Kwambu said, noticing for the first time the ugly gash in the boy's shoulder.

"Someone threw a knife, and I failed to duck in time," Eagle said. "It is nothing," he added stoically.

Shore Walker examined the wound. "No serious damage, I think," he said. "Take off your loincloth and I'll bind it up for you."

"I will do that," Kwambu said. "You have more important matters to attend to, Shore Walker." Traders were forbidden to wield weapons, but tending the wounded was surely permissible. Anyone may assume the duties of a berdache, he thought bitterly.

Shore Walker nodded, raised himself to reconnoiter, and was gone as silently as he'd come.

Swift Eagle made no sound as Kwambu pressed his torn flesh together and wrapped the shoulder. The youth's eyes were opaque, as though he were looking inward, and the trader realized that only now was he allowing himself to think about his father's dying.

"Burrowing Kingfisher will be remembered with honor," Kwambu said quietly. "More than that, he will be missed because he was a man well-liked by everyone. And although your mother will grieve when she knows what happened, her grief will be eased a little by her pride in you, Swift Eagle. Your first battle came before you could expect it, yet you have conducted yourself admirably."

"I ran," the youth said angrily. "I ran from the man with the club." He looked down at the sharp-edged weapon, thrust out one foot and sent it rolling. "There is nothing admirable in that!"

Kwambu raised his eyebrows. "You had already been wounded; your pursuer was too close behind for you to turn and face him without having that club split your skull. You showed sense by leaping for cover, Eagle; good sense is as important to a warrior—and is as worthy of admiration—as skill and courage are."

Swift Eagle considered this. "I did not run away when my

friends were killed," he said slowly. "Instead, I ran after the Timucua who had slain them. One got away, but"—his eyes cleared, brightened—"one, I knifed in the gut." He sat up straighter. "His comrade, the one who escaped, gave me my wound. He thought I was dead, and left me on the ground beside the man I had—"

A scuffling sound somewhere on the right reminded him that his first battle was not necessarily over. Heedless of Kwambu's careful bandaging, he dropped to all fours, crawled in that direction. The trader, ignoring the command the War Leader had given him, crouched low and followed Swift Eagle.

Dust and leaf mold powdered their faces, ground-hugging bushes impeded their progress, and nettles gouged their flesh, but still they pushed on. The scuffling sounds were more pronounced now, and punctuated with grunts, but they did not discover their source until they reached the mass of brambles edging a small clearing.

Shore Walker and one of Canegacola's warriors, bodies locked in an obscene parody of sexual union, were struggling for control of Shore Walker's knife. From the splintered limb the two came close to tripping over, Kwambu realized that the Timucuan, stripped of his own weapons during the early part of the fighting, must have taken refuge in the tree roofing the clearing and pounced upon an unsuspecting Shore Walker when he passed beneath him.

The blade clutched in Shore Walker's right hand had already been used to advantage; the topknotted warrior's cheek was slit to the bone. Whether this had happened before or after the Timucuan bit off half of Shore Walker's ear and raked the lethal points of his fingernails down the middle of Shore Walker's face could not be guessed; but both combatants were liberally streaked with blood.

Swift Eagle's fingers scrabbled for a good-sized boulder, a chunk of wood, anything that might serve as weapon. Why hadn't he thought to bring the Timucuan warclub with him? And how could he find a way through this blockade of briers?

The slap of sweaty flesh against sweaty flesh echoed as Shore Walker shifted position in an effort to squeeze the breath out of the burly Timucuan. His adversary applied pressure to Shore Walker's right wrist, shook it to make him release the knife. Strain contorted their faces, swelled the muscles in arms and legs.

Abruptly, Shore Walker relaxed, and the tendons in his wrist shrank just enough to make his opponent lose purchase. The Timucuan, fingers clawed, fought to reclaim his prize, but arm and hand slid eellike from his grasp.

The burly man sprang out of the way, but he could not win sufficient distance to avoid the blade that came barreling toward his chest, the blade that found and punctured his heart.

Shore Walker grunted once more as the man dropped, then raised his hands and wiped the blood from his face. Accidentally touching his truncated ear, he grimaced, but his raspy breathing abated as he looked around for the dart thrower he had tossed aside when the Timucuan fell like a log across his shoulders. There was fighting still to be done.

As he searched for the weapon, however, a challenge in an alien tongue rang out. Shore Walker spun around, found himself face-to-face with the man he had been seeking since the moment Burrowing Kingfisher's death marked the beginning of this battle. The copper disk the War Leader wore glinted as midday sun poured into the glade. So did the blade of the axe he held in his hand, a hand already lifting for the toss.

Just as there was no time for a pair of unseen observers to come to his aid, there was no time either for Shore Walker to shift his knife to his left hand. He flung up his right arm, angled his wrist for maximum thrust. And his whole hand went numb. As though no longer a part of him, his fingers spread themselves. The knife slipped between them, began a lazy descent to the ground.

Before it reached its destination, the Timucuan axe flew threw the air and embedded itself in Shore Walker's belly. The stricken warrior's legs flew out from under him; his torso folded itself, clamped down on the protruding haft as though to stem the river of red pouring out around it. The torrent could not be dammed; when Shore Walker hit the ground, he splashed into a pool of his own lifeblood.

Canegacola's War Leader walked without haste to where the Calusan lay, jerked his weapon from a snarl of entrails and started to leave the glade.

In that moment Swift Eagle managed at last to free himself from a tangle of branches snaring his legs. He slid like a snake into the clearing, and his feet made no sound on the blood-soaked ground as he glided to where Shore Walker's knife had buried itself in a patch of purslane.

The oblivious Timucuan's stride did not falter as Swift Eagle, knife in hand, crept up behind him. Only when the long blade penetrated his lung did he make a sound, and it was a bleat of surprise. Before he could turn around, Eagle stabbed him again. And again. When the War Leader fell, it was face forward, and then there was no question of his turning, or of his moving at all.

Kwambu, having made his own frantic escape from a veritable prison of brambles, raced to Shore Walker's side. The warrior's flesh was cooling rapidly, but he opened his eyes when the trader spoke his name. "Please," he managed to gasp. "You will . . . tell Egret?" Weakness took him into blessed unconsciousness; searing pain shoved him back into This World. "Tell her," he said, "that she must not . . . stop Singing." His eyes closed again; his body tensed, convulsed, and then was still. Incredibly still.

Even though young Swift Eagle had come to kneel by his side, the trader felt no shame when his tears blended with the blood of a man who had been his friend for many years. And if Kwambu wept as much for Dancing Egret as he did for her dead husband, and as much again because circumstance had forced him to be passive witness to the slaying, that was something Shore Walker, at least, would have understood. And he would also have forgiven Kwambu for failing to come to his rescue . . . which was more than the trader would ever be able to do for himself.

Dancing Egret left the island before dawn. She had not slept, or even closed her eyes, during the endless night that had followed the warriors' return from the north.

Like the rest of the townspeople, she had been prepared to welcome Prowling Panther's band with celebration, with feasting and dancing and storytelling. The bride and her attendants were to have been feted extravagantly as a prelude to the marriage festivities. And when the merrymaking ended, Egret would have been able to offer her own special welcome to Shore Walker, would have held him close to her and let her heart beat to the rhythm of his, would have traveled with him once more to the land that was theirs alone.

It was a land she would never again visit. Savagely, she dug her paddle into the sullen waters of the bay, sent the canoe zooming toward the mangroves that guarded the mainland, guided it into a tannin-dyed channel winding its cautious way through a labyrinth of reticular roots.

Kwambu had come to her, come with anguish in his eyes, to

tell her what she already knew, had known since the moment the stern-faced warriors moored their dugouts and began their halting progress into the town. Many wore red-stained bandages, all were weary and slump-shouldered; but even those who had needed support from their comrades had been walking, had been alive. And she had seen at a glance that Shore Walker was not one of them, seen with a second despairing glance the litters being borne by those bringing up the rear of the bedraggled procession. Litters whose occupants were shrouded in the motley assortment of threadbare sleeping robes the warriors had taken with them against the possible chill of nights in Timucuan country.

"His last thoughts were of you," Kwambu said unsteadily, "and his final words were a message for you. 'Egret must not stop Singing,' is what he said. And I promised to repeat his words to you, and to make certain you remember them."

He had taken her hand then, wrapped both of his around it, looked with pity into a face that refused to crumple, into eyes that refused to weep. "He died a hero's death," he told her, "and his slaying was avenged by Swift Eagle."

Emotion flooded back into her, but it was not sorrow that replaced the nothingness in her eyes. It was rage. "Do you think that matters to me?" she had demanded. "To be dead is to be dead, no matter how you die. To be dead is to breathe no more, to walk and talk no more, to love no more!" And she had torn her hand from his and fled from him, fled from the dear friend who had wanted only to comfort her.

She shook the hair out of her face and dipped the paddle again. Someday she would ask Kwambu's forgiveness for the way she'd acted, but she was not ready to do so yet. Nor could she endure the consoling murmurs of her kin or Ysabel's solicitous hovering. Her great need now was to be alone.

And alone she was, here in the river glades, following without conscious thought the route she and Shore Walker had taken on the day Egret first realized she loved him. Unlike that day, which had been sun-blessed in every way, this one was painted gray. The clouds sagging over the sawgrass might have been formed from wet pinewood ash; the green had been leached from leaf and blade; dreariness prevailed, a dreariness that accurately reflected the spirit that dwelt within Dancing Egret.

The Pelican-headed God had been generous with rain this season, filling the glades' sloughs and streams until only the tips of the sawgrass showed in many sections. There would be no need, this day, to sing her way through barricades of cutting sedge. Which was as well. With his last breath Shore Walker had said that his wife must go on Singing. With his last breath Shore Walker had asked the impossible of her.

The dugout skimmed over canescent water in which schools of tiny fish surged restlessly back and forth. The weighty air had the pungency of fresh-picked corn, and its odor lingered on the tongue. Listless swarms of mosquitoes waited until she approached before attacking, and even then seemed disinclined to bite. Egret brushed them away with a gesture equally listless, went on following the twisting waterway without thought of destination.

The clouds grayed further, were at last unable to contain the rain that engorged them. Surrendering to pressure, they released a torrent that lashed the river into brown spume, beat against the sharp-edged grass until it bowed submissively, cascaded over the woman in the dugout and left her shivering. Shudder after shudder rippled through her, yet she did not wrap her arms around herself in an effort to restore warmth to her puckered flesh. She sat limp, uncaring, not even bothering to blink the water from her eyes.

It did not occur to her that perhaps she was hoping the deluge would wash away her grief, her heartache; indeed, she was not thinking at all. She merely waited, indifferent to the wind that added sting to the rain, indifferent to the rising level of water in the canoe. It lapped against her ankles, crept slowly to her knees, saturated her skirt, sent the small boat deeper and deeper into the river it had previously been gliding over.

It was then that the clouds paled and thinned to transparency as the sun slowly burned through them. The wind dwindled to a breeze, danced through the reviving sawgrass spears and made them whisper together as they dried. The whispers blended, became a song unique to the glades. From an embryo tree island up ahead, small green frogs offered throaty counterpoint, and a redbird's melodic whistle lent brightness to the anthem. The croaking salute of a great blue heron added depth, and the chittering of a damp-furred squirrel, percussion.

Egret, who ordinarily rejoiced in all of nature's orchestrations, was deaf to this one. But she gradually became aware that the rain had stopped and that she would progress no further unless the dugout were relieved of the water that nearly filled it. While the earth sent up a hymn to the strengthening sun, she bailed mechanically until only a thumb's depth of rainwater remained in the canoe, then picked up her paddle again.

She took no note of the freshness of the air, or of the bow of shimmering colors that stretched itself briefly across the horizon. She simply paddled on. Whenever the way narrowed and the sedge grew taller, she knelt and hunched her bare shoulders to avoid the vicious bite of the grass that leaned into the boat. But it was instinct only that made her do so; she cared not at all if her flesh were scored until the blood ran, might even have welcomed the pain of it. Any feeling is better than no feeling at all.

A pair of dolphins, playing truant from the coastal waters they usually kept to at this time of year, rolled lazily and smiled at her; she turned her head away. Two alligators, submerged to their concave nostrils, measured her strokes with wary eyes and swam off as she neared them; except for steadying the canoe against the waves created by the slap of their huge tails, Egret paid little heed to them. What undid her was the sight of two graceful deer, browsing the shallows adjacent to the slough. As she watched, the stag shortened his stride so as not to leave the obviously pregnant doe behind. Drawing in the paddle and laying it across her lap, Dancing Egret bent her head over it.

Dolphins. Gators. Deer. All creatures went in pairs today, it seemed. She lifted her head, spotted two dragonflies dining on a lushness of water bugs, lowered it again. Even the insects were flaunting their togetherness, taunting her with it, reminding her that this woman no longer had a mate, that all she had ever known of joy, of passion, was ended.

They would have taken Shore Walker to the Place of the Dead by now, to leave him there until his second soul had shrunk enough to disappear from the world of the living. After his bones had been given burial in the mound, Egret would be able to go there and try to commune with the fragment of spirit destined to remain forever in This World. But a spirit has no mouth to smile with, no arms to embrace with, no long, lean body to allow the sort of communion Dancing Egret was aching for. And even if she were able to find a modicum of comfort in purely spiritual communion, she could not spend the rest of her life crouching over her husband's burial place; the third soul was a fragile thing, and could be destroyed by too much contact with the living.

The bow of the canoe bumped gently against a jut of land that extended from a sizable hammock, a hammock rimmed with thorny bushes and canopied with the lustrous green of oak and buttonwood. Startled, Dancing Egret looked up; the paddle dropped from her hands, clattered into the dugout. What malignant god had brought her to a place that could only torment her further with memories she was neither willing nor able to cope with? She fumbled for the paddle; she must backstroke, get herself away, put as much distance as possible between herself and the hammock Shore Walker had brought her to on a day long ago—a day she must not, could not, would not, let herself remember yet.

But her hands refused to obey her. They would not fasten themselves around the paddle, for all that she begged them to, commanded them to. And the river, which before had been arrowed with a lively current, was all at once still; it made no attempt to coax her canoe away from the bit of land it had nosed into. Nor did rocking the narrow boat from side to side dislodge it.

For a long, long moment Dancing Egret sat staring at a mass of trailing vines that cascaded down the low embankment and into the water. Silvery fish flashed beneath their sharply veined leaves, agitating the winged insects that had perched on them. Each time a fish leaped, the insects lifted themselves, hovered in a miniature cloud until danger passed, then settled once more. Occasionally one was too slow and the scaly hunter snapped up his prey, but always the cloud of insects descended again to the leaf. This was the pattern of their existence; to alter it was out of the question.

Dancing Egret rose stiffly, climbed out of the dugout, hauled it halfway out of the water, snugged it with a length of the sturdy vine. She pushed through the bushes, made her way past solution holes brimming with rainwater. The trees she found herself among were blanketed with green-striped snails—their shells identical to the one she carried in her pouch of treasures—and adorned with spiky air plants. And with orchids; orchids yellow as the butterflies that swirled around them, orchids so white they dazzled the eye, orchids as vibrantly purple as the sky in the aftermath of a blazing sunset. A breeze came out of nowhere and aroused them; their frilled throats vibrated as though songs were pouring out of them, but these were songs only the gods could hear.

Egret went on, ducking beneath the loops of moss that

dressed low-hanging limbs, heading unerringly to the glade Shore Walker had once taken her to, the glade centered with the placid pool she had tumbled into. Shore Walker had rescued her from it, pulling her out of the water and into his arms. . . .

She seated herself on the rock they had shared that day, closed her eyes, waited for misery to claim her. Instead, the buzzing-whirring-chirping symphony of the hammock filtered into her ears, trickled down into the awful void she had expected desolation to fill. The breeze revisited the hammock and ruffled the pool; the soothing lap of water, the rustle of leafy branches bending over it, seeped into her soul. This place she had feared to come to, the place she had envisioned as a silent dispenser of painful memories, was anything but silent. It was a celebrator of life, of growth, of perpetual regeneration. The air pulsed with its praise-singing.

Until the shadows lengthened, Dancing Egret sat and listened. It was earth's medicine, that music, and coming here had once more opened her mind and heart to it. This woman may have Sung her last Song, but earth's voice continued strong, strong enough to persuade Egret that the living must go on living. Time cannot stop, cannot reverse itself, because a lover dies.

Her face was somber still when she left the hammock, yet the seeds of acceptance had been sown in her spirit, and with them, resurrection of the strength she would need to take the first faltering steps in her journey through the lonely years ahead.

Chapter 32

⇒ ⇒

Kaia had been pensive since the day her clanswomen gathered in the hut by the river and, verifying her status as maiden, invited her to dance with them in celebration. The sharing of female secrets was as much a part of this rite of passage as sober instruction, and laughter had softened the solemnity of the occasion. Still and all, the onset of monthly bleeding was an appropriate time for reflection, and Moon of Winter was not concerned about her daughter until she realized that she had scarcely seen a smile on the girl's face since the last new moon.

"Will you tell me what troubles you?" she asked her at last. "Was your cramping so bad that you fear your next menses?"

Kaia shook her curly head. "There was little," she said. "Walks Tall Woman had said I might be bent double from pain, but nothing like that happened. I only worry because"— she coaxed an attractive curve into the lip of the pot she was shaping—"Walks Tall Woman also said, when she skirted me that day, that now I must wed and bear children to bring honor to my clan and to my tribe." She set aside her clay-stained paddle and looked up. "Moon of Winter, I am not ready to take a husband!"

Her mother squatted down beside her, hugged her fiercely. "At thirteen? I should hope not. What Walks Tall Woman said was only part of the ceremony, Kaia. You were not expected to come out of the hut, purify yourself, and then ask the first man you stumbled upon to marry you. However long it takes you to find him, your father and I want you to wed a man you can love as much as Kwambu and I love each other, and who will love you as strongly in return." She refrained from saying that Kwambu hoped it would be many seasons before their daughter took a husband. When their sons achieved warrior status, he had rejoiced for and with them; but that his adored little girl should suddenly be grown up was difficult for him to deal with.

Moon of Winter, after a hug that was reciprocated with fervor this time, left her daughter to fire her pottery and returned to the Principal House. Both she and Kwambu had felt suddenly older when the last of their children was child no more—until they visited their place of magnolias. She smiled. Then they became youthful lovers again, as passionate as ever, and as eager to pleasure one another. Just thinking about it made her wish Kwambu would return soon. Sooner than soon.

But only Outina and his mother were in the house when she entered, and their serious faces put abrupt end to her daydreaming. "The scouts have returned?" she asked her cousin.

He nodded. "Saturiba is preparing for war," he said. "Our men have scarcely recovered from their last battle with Potano, yet they will be called upon to arm themselves again. And if all of them join the war parties, who can I send out after meat to sustain us during the winter season? However great our need, how can I ask some of my warriors to pass up a chance for glory and stalk game for the cooking pot instead?" He sighed. At times he felt like the dominant wolf in a pack harassed by hunters: haunted by the demands of leadership and dreading to make an incautious decision.

Moon of Winter had worries of her own. Her sons had returned safely from the battle with Potano, but now she must worry all over again while they followed Black Wolf Running against Saturiba. "Is it true that white-fleshed soldiers will be with Saturiba's men?"

Again Outina nodded. "That is the rumor throughout his territory."

"I told you," Walks Tall Woman said sharply. "I told you when the outlanders came that you should give them the gold they asked for so their people would fight for you. Now they fight for Saturiba instead."

"I have only the little bit of shiny metal that has come to us in trade over the years," Outina said. He held out his tattooed arms to call her attention to the wide gold bracelet he wore above each elbow, ornaments that—like the gold gorget he wore on ceremonial occasions—had come to be symbols of his status. "Should I have given them these, and let our people suspect that I no longer care to be Holata? Kwambu will try and bring more gold when he returns from Calusa country, but that's no help to me now. Saturiba, on the other hand, has a storehouse brimming with stuff he has collected as tribute from his coastal Townchiefs."

"Perhaps the soldiers who call themselves Frenchmen are not even trained fighters," Moon of Winter said. For the men who had arrived unexpectedly in Outina's province less than a month ago had not been Spanish; indeed, they seemed insulted when asked if they were. Fortunately, they had been around Saturiba's people long enough to learn a little Timucuan; even Kwambu, although he had heard of the faraway country these men named as homeland, did not know their language. "And I wasn't sorry to see them leave here. After what happened in this town, how can we bring ourselves to trust any people whose skins are white?"

"Saturiba has seen both his power and his status increase since he made the Frenchmen welcome," Walks Tall Woman said. "I sometimes wonder if my brother did not anger the Spanish by refusing at first to treat with them. Perhaps, if he had offered them hospitality when they requested it, instead of bombarding them with threats, all of those slain would be alive today."

She did not truly believe that, Moon of Winter thought. She couldn't. But she wanted so much for Outina to be a Holata as renowned as Saturiba that nothing else mattered to her. And, according to Outina's scouts, the Frenchmen really did seem uninterested in invasive expeditions; they had built themselves a huge wooden house and—except for bouts of harmless exploration—were reportedly content to remain there. They were not only French, but something called Huguenot, and the men who had spoken with Outina vowed that this meant they respected the rights of all people. Yet if that were so, why were they offering to take any part whatsoever in Timucuan warfare? "Kwambu says we should be watchful of the French," she murmured.

"That's one of the reasons my scouts spy on their fort as well as on Saturiba," Outina said. "They tell me that the pale-fleshes, although they have certainly been here long enough, have cleared no fields for planting. They hunt occasionally, and more rarely fish in the long river that separates Saturiba's province from mine; but all other foodstuffs are given to them by Saturiba." He rubbed a hand over his face to dispel his weariness; ever since Potano's warriors had finally bested Outina's in the Ball Game, there had been skirmishes along the southern border. Saturiba knew this, of course; that was why he was planning to attack some town on Outina's eastern border. And if the French soldiers should swell his forces . . .

"Your husband knows nothing about the French," Walks Tall Woman said to her niece. "He admits as much. And if there is to be war between us and Saturiba, we need to have the white-fleshed fighters helping us rather than them. It only makes sense."

And victory in battle is another way for a Holata to earn widespread praise, Moon of Winter thought.

"My Principal Men have suggested that you consult your crystal," Outina said, turning to his cousin. "If we can know in advance when the omens will be favorable, we'll be better able to deal with our enemies. There are ways to delay confrontation, or speed it up, but we must have foreknowledge to make use of them."

"It's the Shaman's place to interpret the signs when battle is imminent," Moon of Winter said quickly. "For me to do as your advisors suggest would be going against tradition."

Walks Tall Woman, who was pleased to pretend that she had never turned to Moon of Winter and her crystal for help, inadvertently came to her aid. "Moon of Winter may own a crystal, but she is only a woman. What do women know of war? How can any woman decide what signs are auspicious and which are not? Go to Watches for Omens, my son, for that kind of help. As is proper." Outina might have been a seven-year-old still, from the scolding note in her voice.

Moon of Winter saw the Holata wince and knew that only courtesy prevented him from telling his mother that, but she was much relieved when he abandoned the subject. The crystal promoted healing and brought comfort during difficult times, but it stubbornly withheld the future from her.

Perhaps that was as well; to see beyond the moment just might prove more curse than blessing.

Kwambu had been summoned to appear before Calusa's Council and tell them about the strangers in Timucuan country. Dancing Egret, sitting apart from the men as usual, admired the ease with which he answered the questions put to him. When there was something he didn't know, he said so calmly rather than pretending to knowledge he did not have. Egret had been attending these meetings long enough to realize that most men, even ordinarily forthright men, found it difficult to do that.

She ran her fingers through hair that had grown below shoulder length since she had cut it off to mourn Shore Walker. Pushing it back impatiently, she told herself she ought to arrange it so that it was not constantly falling over her face. She was a widow, and would be one to the end of her life; she did not need to be bothered with the constant combing long hair required. Leave that to maidens trying to attract husbands.

Kwambu inclined his head and smiled at her as he went out; he was the only man who ever did that, too. To the rest, she was next to invisible. Except for Growling Bear, she amended, as the Chief Speaker's mellifluous voice rose to sanction some suggestion made by Prowling Panther. Shore Walker's cousin always took courteous leave of her after Council meetings, but his smile was so like Shore Walker's that it wrenched at Egret's heart and she was never able to respond to him. She supposed he understood, and if he didn't, well, that didn't matter any more than it mattered that she continued to attend these meetings. For she no longer sought out her brother afterward to talk over things that had discomforted her. When, after a few unsuccessful retaliatory raids against Canegacola, Calusa had agreed to reinstatement of the original safe-passage treaty with Mocoso, she had accepted that it was useless to try and guide him; Calusa would go his own way no matter what she said, so why expose herself to endless frustration?

Anger had played a part in her decision. "Canegacola's men killed my husband," she had said tightly. "Killed him and Burrowing Kingfisher and two of your youngest warriors. How can you treat with his brother-in-law, who must have sanctioned the attack, as though there were no enmity between you?"

Calusa had looked pained. "Sister, I also suffered loss. The woman who was to have become my wife was abducted, and has since wed Canegacola instead. Which means I suffered shame as well as loss. But I am Headchief; I cannot let personal feeling stand in the way of good sense. You know our traders tested alternate routes to the north, and that none of them were practical. I had hopes that traveling by water to Tocobaga's province and then going overland might be the answer. But you know what happened when Kwambu attempted that."

Not only knew, but had predicted the outcome. Tocobaga had refused even to let Kwambu beach his canoe. He was not the kind of person who sympathized with the plight of another, and never had been. Ever since he had received Kneeling Cypress as a "gift" from Mocoso, accepting her as nonchalantly as other men would accept a bundle of hides or a basket of freshly harvested shellfish, Egret had recognized that Tocobaga's feelings must be shallow as a mud puddle.

What was worse, she had begun to suspect that her brother's ran no deeper. If he had suffered the sense of loss, the shame, that he spoke of, it had certainly been fleeting. There had been a marriage to celebrate regardless, with all the lavishness he had planned for his wedding to Oathkaqua's daughter. Only days after learning of one bride's abduction, he arranged to take another: Brown Pelican's eldest daughter. And his gift to her was the collar of gold beads that had been made for the maiden he'd originally planned to wed.

Demanding tribute of his wedding guests had not caused anyone to reject Calusa's invitation, but at least one allied chief had made no secret of his displeasure. Tequesta and White Gull, although they brought with them the tribute Calusa's emissaries asked for, had not stayed on for the three days of feasting and games; as soon as the rite itself ended, they went home—tacit insult to their host. Now there was ill feeling between Tequesta and Calusa, and an estrangement her brother seemed indifferent to.

A stir among the clan representatives brought Egret out of her reverie. "We can be grateful that these latecomers the trader called Frenchmen have chosen to remain among the Timucua," Calusa was saying to them. Then, with the dazzling smile that was characteristic of him, he dismissed his Council. Yawning, he rose from the ornately carved stool that had been cleverly made to fit over the highest bench in the tier and came to retrieve his cloak.

"You are pleased that I am allowing the trader to take a generous quantity of gold and silver to his friends in the north?" he asked as she passed the garment to him.

Egret merely nodded; if she no longer attempted to make her brother reconsider unwise decisions, neither did she praise him for good ones. Besides, he was not exactly giving away the ornaments he referred to, and of which he had an abundance; Calusa would be receiving goods he wanted in return.

"That Timucuan chief, the one whose province lays alongside the eastern ocean: he may be showing wisdom by establishing friendly relations with the pale-faced men the trader told us about. I am surprised our father, who made a habit of turning potential enemies into allies, did not think of doing that when the Spanish came. If he had, perhaps a great deal of trouble could have been avoided."

Trouble? Was that how Calusa labeled killing and maiming and the destruction of entire towns? Egret thought incredulously. She would never have used so mild a word. "Only time will tell if Holata Saturiba is wise, or not," she said noncommittally, and was all the more thankful that the Frenchmen's ships had not brought them to Calusa country. Their father had known that a stag does not invite wolves to sup with his does and fawns, but he had neglected to teach this to his son.

Ysabel was waiting in Egret's house with a platter of clams, glistening hot in their shells and nestled among disks of crusty zamia bread. The rotund Spanish woman worried that Egret did not eat enough since she lost her husband and Egret herself was aware that a certain amount of flesh had melted from her bones during the past few seasons, that her squarish face had thinned until nose and cheeks were more pronounced than they had been. But her hungers were not the sort that food, even Ysabel's remarkably tasty food, could appease.

Nonetheless, she ate, and Ysabel beamed approval as she took away the empty plate. "I will fatten you up," she said. "You will see, Dona Egret. Then you will have the energy to laugh again, and to entertain the children with your songs."

"I laugh," she protested. "When there is something to laugh about, I laugh."

"Not as you once did," Ysabel said. "And it has been a long time since I have heard you Sing."

This was something Egret would not discuss, not even with the serving woman who had become so close a friend that she was confidante as well these days. The children still begged for stories from time to time, but Dancing Egret would not subject them to a voice that would surely have no more lilt in it than a crow's. For now, she had told them, Chattering Squirrel must take her place; the girl had learned many of the Legends, and had a talent for retelling them. Squirrel had relished being praised and been glad to substitute for her aunt; but the now Egret had mentioned stretched on and on. Lately Squirrel had been asking Egret when she would come and teach them new stories. "The children are bored with hearing the same ones over and over again," she had said earnestly, "and I am as anxious to learn others as they are to hear them."

It had been hard to refuse the child, but songs must come from the heart, and Dancing Egret's heart was a hollow thing with no music in it anymore. "Your mother knows other stories," she had told her gently. "We learned the tales together when we were small. Please, ask Brown Pelican to help you. Truly I cannot. Not yet."

Chattering Squirrel hadn't understood, any more than Ysabel did. Which meant it would be best to distract her serving woman before Egret became embroiled in futile explanation. "I need your help," she said to her. "I cannot cope with my hair as it is. See if you can devise some way of pulling it back, or up, or both."

Ysabel's eyes rounded. "But your hair has much beauty, Dona Egret! And it only needs to grow a little longer before it hangs down your back like a soft, dark cloak, as it did before."

"If I need a cloak, I will wear the one you made for me out of doeskin," Egret said. "I've grown accustomed to having my hair off of my back, and that's how I mean to keep it." She twisted the length of it between her hands, positioned it at her nape in an untidy clump. "Like this, perhaps."

Ysabel snatched up a comb. "That way? No," she muttered, unclasping Dancing Egret's fingers and studying the hair that spilled free of them. "It does not need to be so unpleasing, what you want." She separated the hair, began to plait half of it with nimble fingers. "Other people see you more often than you see yourself," she scolded. "You insult them if you make yourself ugly." She was speaking in her own tongue now, a habit she had fallen into whenever the two were alone together, but Egret had no trouble understanding her.

"I have never been particularly pleasing to the eye," she re-joined, also in Spanish. It was a language well-suited to argument, she reflected; the words took to honing, and could be flung as swiftly as darts. "You cannot make a pumpkin blossom out of a stickerweed, Ysabel, no matter how you arrange my hair."

"It is a dreadful thing that you say," Ysabel said, busily braiding. "You are no more a stickerweed than I am a . . . a long, skinny garfish!" she finished triumphantly. And shook with laughter. "Whatever I am," she said, "you will agree that it is not *long and skinny*."

Dancing Egret laughed also. She hoped Ysabel noticed how quickly she did so, and how wholeheartedly. If she did not laugh as often as she used to, well, surely it was not unnatural for a woman to find less and less to amuse her as she grew older? "Ysabel," she said impulsively, "have you ever heard of a place called France?"

"France?" Ysabel's lips pursed. "I am only a humble peasant woman, Dona, but I have heard of that country. There have been wars between Spain and France, usually because the Franks insist upon harassing merchant ships sent out by my country."

She had used a word Egret did not recognize. "What is 'merchant'?" she asked, and committed the new word to memory when Ysabel told her it meant the same as *trader*. "Soldiers from France have come to the northern part of this country," she went on, wondering how she might tactfully ask if Frenchmen were as cruel and bloodthirsty as the Spanish Christians who had come to Calusa territory. "Are they Christians, like the Spanish?" she ventured, hoping that would bring her the answer she wanted.

"Some are," her serving woman said, winding one of the braids into a circle and using a decorative comb to anchor it above Egret's right ear. "Some, I have heard, claim to be Christian, but"—she shrugged eloquently—"since they forswear Mother Church, I do not see how that can be so." Which led to a halting discourse on the Holy Catholic Church and those misguided souls who in recent years had come to protest its teachings and rebel against its dictates.

Egret followed as best she could, but was left only with the impression that there must be two kinds of Christians, and these always fighting each other. Perhaps it was similar to intertribal battle, she thought, with each side appealing to different gods for protection. And if the Christian gods were anything like those of the Calusa and the Timucua, they doubtless turned their backs and left warring children to fend for themselves.

"How do you know all these things?" she asked Ysabel. "You have been away from your homeland for a very long time."

"Some things, they do not change," Ysabel said. "And shipwreck survivors still come to this island, dona. When they do, I go to the Spanish village and talk with them. It is pleasant, to speak with your own kind from time to time."

"Do you miss your homeland so much?" Egret said, for there had been a wistfulness in Ysabel's voice.

"I miss it, and I do not miss it," she replied. "It has been many years since I left Spain for Havana, dona. I was only a girl when I was taken to Cuba, and a very young woman when the ship in which I was returning to Spain went aground on the reefs south of your island." She smoothed the hair framing Dancing Egret's brow, shaped it to her satisfaction. "Sometimes I do not even feel Spanish anymore. My husband is Calusa; my children, although half Spanish, think and act as though they are wholly Calusa. My son has married one of your maidens, as you know, and since my daughter is finding more and more reason to visit the Arawak community, I expect that a young man from there will soon be talking with my husband about having her for his wife. But"—she stepped back, frowned, made minor adjustment to one of the coiled braids—"I still find it pleasant to talk with those who come from the place where I was born."

Dancing Egret could understand that well enough, and said so. What mystified her was that she should be trying to find out from a woman who was both Spanish and a good and loyal friend if the people who had made themselves at home in Timucuan territory should be feared as much as Ysabel's own countrymen were feared! It seemed a strange thing to be doing, yet she had no other way of satisfying her curiosity. "Are the Frenchmen in the north likely to be peaceful-natured?" she asked after a moment.

Ysabel snorted. "They are soldiers; soldiers are not lovers of peace." She studied the results of her efforts, smiled and took out the mirror her husband had selected as part of his reward when he'd volunteered to dive for salvage from a foundered ship. Never mind that he had also chosen a steel-bladed axe and steel knife for himself; when he had brought home the mirror, and the big metal pot that was so handy for cooking, and the shiny red beads Ysabel had been wearing ever since, she had been passionately grateful. And age had not drained her of passion, Ysabel thought complacently; that night had been blissful, indeed, for both of them. "Look, and admire," she commanded, passing the mirror to Dona Egret.

Obediently, Egret peered into the mirror. She did not shrink from the sight of her remarkably clear image, as she had the first time Shore Walker found one of the shiny reflectors. The child she'd been then had wondered uncomfortably if her life force might not become trapped in it. But time had shown her apprehension to be groundless, as Shore Walker, wise beyond his years, had somehow known it was. How he had teased her for being wary of something that was surely no more danger-ous than the quiet stream the maidens often ran to when they wanted to be sure that they looked their best! She smiled, re-membering, then started; it was the first time she had reveled in a memory of her husband since his death. And she had Ysabel to thank for that.

"Do you like it?" Her serving woman was growing impa-tient.

Reluctantly, Egret let the memory fade, gave all her atten-tion to the plaited spirals that clung to each side of her head, to the hair above them drawn back loosely enough that it lent an alien softness to her brow and drew attention to her eyes. Her neck, which she had always considered too treelike to be attractive, looked almost slender now, with no hair tumbling around it. She turned her head this way and that, found herself smiling again. "I had not expected this," she said. "You are skilled, Ysabel."

Ysabel's round cheeks burgeoned as she grinned. "You look like the noblewoman you are," she said. "This is how the senora I once served wore her hair, but the style suits you better than it did that one. Her face was as sour as her disposition; nothing could have given her beauty."

Dancing Egret handed back the mirror. "Nothing can give me beauty, either," she said cheerfully, "but you have made me look respectable, and that's no small accomplishment."

"I have made you look handsome," Ysabel said firmly. It bothered her that Dona Egret was blind to her unique elegance, an elegance that had come to her gradually as her youth waned. With some women, usually those who had been regarded as plain during the early years, this miracle happened, and it was foolishness not to appreciate it and make the most of it. She fingered her lovely red beads; Dancing Egret's elegance need not go to waste. If Dona Egret could not appreciate what she had, Ysabel was determined that those who looked upon her would.

The man studying his reflection in the looking glass scarcely recognized himself. His dark hair and beard had finally been neatly barbered; his silk shirt was soft against his flesh; once more, silk hose embraced his muscular legs; the green velvet of his doublet had a fine nap to it. But twenty months in prison had pared both face and body, emphasizing the austerity he prided himself on, and fear for his son lurked in his deep-set eyes.

Last year, while the older man was imprisoned in Castile due to the false charges brought by the corrupt Casa de Contracción, Juan had been named admiral of Spain's treasure fleet. He had set out from Havana, and that was the last anyone had seen or heard of the flota he commanded. Or of him. The violent storms that so often erupted in the seas around the New World had most likely claimed the ships. Juan and his men, and all the wealth the *galleones* had been weighted with, might well be at the bottom of the Atlantic now. But even if a hurricane had come roaring down upon the fleet, tossing huge ships about as if they were nothing but bits of straw, breaking them in half and consigning them to the depths, that did not necessarily mean hope should be entirely abandoned. Often, ships were wrecked close enough to the coast of la Florida that some of those sailing in them survived. The aborigines there, people who must be kin to peoples first encountered in the Indies, had more than once rescued crew and passengers from downed Spanish ships. There was a slim chance that this had been Juan's fate also.

He clenched his hands. Was that truly a fate he should wish for Juan? Rumor had it that the poor souls rescued by the heathen Indians only exchanged death by drowning for a more terrible death. The aborigines were said to delight in creative torture, even in human sacrifice. *Madre de Dios!* No sane man would wish such an end for a beloved son.

The only thing that prevented him from despairing altogether was that not all survivors were tortured or killed. He had it on good authority that occasionally some were spared and kept as slaves. If Juan had been one such, then his father could surely search for and find him, remove him from bondage to savages by the sword if necessary, and bring him safe home. King Don Felipe agreed that it would be worthwhile to search for Juan, praise be to God. The king had arranged for the release of the man he had made Captain-General of his flota and of all New World trade, for he knew well the charge of smuggling was baseless. Now he meant to send him to chart the coast of a land earlier explorers had failed to conquer, to rout the French Huguenots who had been audacious enough to attempt a settlement there, and . . . to look for his son.

Just as soon as he could provision his ships, Pedro Menendez de Aviles—a man who revered only God ahead of his king—would be sailing west. West, to *la Florida*.

Chapter 33

◆—— ➡

Kwambu knew before he heard the maidens chanting praise-songs outside the Shaman's house that Outina's warriors had

been to war again. A red-painted pole standing in the center of
the Ball Game field was festooned with drying scalps, yet the
slightly mournful undertone to the women's chant warned him
that it was not unqualified victory that they celebrated, but
only the valor of the warriors who had fought in the battle. No
doubt the enemy—Saturiba? Potano?—was celebrating also,
and also had a collection of scalps to display.

Kaia was probably among the singing maidens, but he did
not pause in his swift progress to the Principal House to feast
his eyes even briefly on his beautiful daughter. Hawk Flying
High and Red Fox Barking would have followed the Great
Warrior into this latest battle, and Kwambu must be certain
that they had returned safely from it. Fear that one or both
might have been severely wounded or even slain made a buzzing in his ears and set his heart to thumping wildly.

"They came home with the others." One glance at her husband's face told Moon of Winter what he urgently needed to
hear. "Hawk was arrow-shot in the thigh, but the point did little more than pierce the flesh. He will limp for a while, that is
all. Fox returned whole, and envies his brother for the attention
he'll be getting from the maidens because of his injury." Heedless of Walks Tall Woman's disapproving shake of the head,
she went to Kwambu and embraced him. "We are all of us
well, husband."

"Unless you consider those men who lost their lives when
they went to drive Saturiba's warriors from our borders,"
Walks Tall Woman said, "and the two taken prisoner. Who can
say what tortures they will suffer? And one of them our
Paracusi!"

"Black Wolf Running was taken?" Kwambu drew back
from his wife, looked to where Outina sat hunched over Palm
Tree Bending's hearth.

The Holata raised his head. "He was. You gave him back
his life once, trader—you, and the Shaman and Moon of
Winter—but you can do nothing for him this time. He will die,
and in a terrible way." Mingled anger and despair skewed
Outina's mouth and painted shadows around his eyes.

"Did the Frenchmen fight alongside Saturiba's warriors?"
Kwambu asked Moon of Winter. Calusa should be told about
it if they had.

Outina, rising slowly and coming to join them, answered the
question. "Our warriors report that they saw no pale-skins
there. Why, I do not know; my scouts are intelligent and reli-

able, and I believe them when they say Saturiba expected the French soldiers to ally themselves with his." Duty denied a Holata the luxury of prolonged grieving, and there were things to be done. "I will send my spies back as soon as it is safe, so I can know if Saturiba plans to raid another of my towns, and when." He looked away briefly. "Also, I must discover the fate of Wolf, and of the young warrior who was seized when he was." In truth, part of him pleaded to be spared the awful details, but ignorance was as crippling to a tribal leader as a poorly strung bow to one of his warriors.

"I have brought you a sack filled with ornaments retrieved from wrecked ships," Kwambu said, deciding that distraction was better for Outina right now than the most sincere sympathy could be. "Calusa would like flint in exchange, and copper, and a supply of the medicinal herbs that are not readily available in the south." He looked questioningly at Moon of Winter.

"I will speak with Watches for Omens after he sends the warriors back to their families," she said. "We have herbs in abundance, but it is for him to say how many can be spared."

"You may take with you as much copper as we have," Outina said absently. "It is of little use, save for decoration. As for the flint, the quantity I can give to Calusa will depend upon how much we estimate will be needed for new arrowheads and spear points."

"You need to let the Frenchmen know that you have gold and silver now," Walks Tall Woman said. "Saturiba was probably niggardly in what he offered them, and if you offer enough, the white men may be willing to help our warriors next time. Then it will be seen that Outina is both wiser and more generous than Saturiba." She smiled. "It will devastate Saturiba if people who have accepted his hospitality turn against him."

Outina, who had opened his mouth to protest, closed it. His mother could be aggravating, but there was no denying her shrewdness. To heap shame upon a man of Saturiba's stature was a more effective way of achieving victory over him than to send a host of warriors against him. Walks Tall Woman's suggestion might well be worth acting upon.

Moon of Winter clung to her husband's hand as they walked back to the town from their place of magnolias. They had been unable to visit it on the day he'd returned from Calusa country, and the chores that invariably came with summer's end had kept them too busy to do so for weeks afterward. Now, new-fallen leaves, softened by an all-too-brief morning shower, were soft beneath their feet, and an autumn sky stretched like an unwrinkled canopy over their heads.

"Whenever we have been together like this," she said quietly, "I find myself wanting to cry for your friend Dancing Egret. She will never again know her husband's touch, never again see love in his eyes or hear it in his voice. How can she survive, having lost someone she loved as much as I love you?"

Kwambu pressed the fingers that were linked with his. "She survives because she must," he said soberly, "but it has not been easy for her. Sorrow is a ghost at her shoulder always, yet she has responsibilities, as all of us do, and does not shirk them. She no longer has the zest for living that once made her unique, but I continue to hope that one day she will recover a little of it. If only she had children, that day might come sooner rather than later. But she does not. Which is all the sadder since she is a woman who truly loves children, and is loved in return by all those she used to Sing Legends to."

"She still does not Sing?"

Kwambu shook his head. "She says that she cannot, that when Shore Walker died, her voice died with him."

"Yet she can talk."

"She talks, yes, although not nearly as much as she once did. But Singing, even ordinary singing, is different from talking." He smiled a little. "I have been talking since I was a toddler, but the simplest chant is beyond my talents."

Moon of Winter giggled. "It is, and I am no better! I have stood next to you often enough during ceremonies; when the thanksgiving prayer is sung, the pair of us sound like two grackles squabbling over a kernel of corn."

They passed through the grove of young pines that marked the limits of the forest and began to cross the stubbled planting fields. Suddenly Kwambu stiffened, released his wife's hand. "Those men standing near the gate," he said, pointing. "They are French soldiers, I think."

Moon of Winter shaded her eyes, studied the group Kwambu had indicated. "Why would the French come again to Outina, when they are said to be allied with Saturiba?" She turned a worried face to her husband. "Have they come to make war on us?"

Kwambu lengthened his stride. "They would hardly be idling in front of an open gate if they had," he said reassuringly. "But I think we should hurry to the Principal House nonetheless and find out what is going on." He managed a smile. "If nothing else, perhaps I will have the opportunity to learn a few words of their language while they are here. I have little faith in interpreters, having served as one myself upon occasion; I know how great the temptation is to condense and modify what is said."

Moon of Winter made valiant effort to keep up with her husband, but ended a few steps behind as they approached the entrance to Outina's town. When she came abreast of them, the pale-fleshed men ceased to jabber in their alien tongue, and she knew instinctively that it was the sight of Moon of Winter that had silenced them. All at once the scarred cheek that she seldom thought of these days began to burn from a rush of blood to her face. Had it not been for Kwambu, who slowed his pace and held himself exceptionally tall while he ushered her through the palisade's narrow entryway, she would have lowered her head or at least turned it aside.

Five more soldiers, accompanied by a shambling, weary-looking Timucuan who was surely one of Saturiba's people, were in the Principal House, but neither Kwambu nor his wife paid more than cursory heed to them at first. All their attention was riveted on two other newcomers who were there also, for these were two men they had never expected to see again in This World. Standing one on either side of Holata Outina, whose mouth was stretched wide in a grin, were Black Wolf Running and the young warrior who had been taken prisoner when the Paracusi was. Palm Tree Bending, her eyes brimming with happy tears, held tight to Wolf's right arm. His left was strapped to his chest, and the youthful warrior had a bandage around his head; but alive they both were, and safe home as well.

Outina put out his arms and embraced the pair. "Go to my wife's hearth now," he told them. "Rest, and eat. Kin and friends will be arriving as soon as they hear the good news, and their welcome will be so warm that you will have little time to savor your food once they are here." He grinned again as they crossed to Palm Tree Bending's hearth, then turned to Kwambu and Moon of Winter. "The French Holata persuaded Saturiba to release the captives he had taken," he said elatedly. "Stay here with me while I try and express my gratitude to his emissaries. In my excitement, I have neglected to do so as yet." He nodded toward the Saturiban. "Ask my guests to seat themselves," he told him, indicating a large mat made from interlaced magnolia and cedar branches, "and offer them my apology for forgetting my duties as host. Tell them the Principal Woman will bring refreshment, and find out if there is some gift I can send to show my appreciation to their Holata."

While the interpreter obliged, Moon of Winter wondered why Walks Tall Woman had laid down for these visitors the ceremonial mat she had made for a Council meeting. But when the young woman examined the soldiers more closely, she understood that her aunt would have deemed at least two of them worthy of it. Unlike the shabbily dressed men outside the gates, the pair wore colorful full-sleeved blouses and ballooning thigh-length breeches, and their feet were shod in relatively shiny boots. On their heads they wore high-crowned, stiff-brimmed hats with plumes fastened to the bands. Both had narrow faces with somewhat pinched features, but the taller—the one Moon of Winter would come to recognize as Lieutenant D'Ottigni—had a thin high-bridged nose as well, with nostrils that flared intermittently, as though assailed by some foul odor.

Kwambu watched the faces of the Frenchmen as they told the interpreter what to say. After a while he thought he could guess at the approximate meaning of some of the French words, but the rest defied his understanding. He would speak later with the interpreter, he decided, and ask the Saturiban to tutor him a little in exchange for some of the trade items remaining in his pack.

Moon of Winter was unobtrusively studying the other men now, men garbed as casually as the soldiers she'd already seen. She found nothing to interest her in a bulky man with a protruding belly or a leaner man whose flesh showed considerable signs of weathering. But the fifth man, who had a face that was nondescript except for expressive, slightly tilted eyes, also had hands with long slender fingers that twitched from time to time as he took in all the details of Outina's hall. Unlike the man with the flaring nostrils, whose flicking gaze had something contemptuous in it, this man appeared fascinated with everything he looked upon, from the smoke-wreathed stone hearths of the women to the pantherskin that hung prominently on the wall. Suddenly his roving glance met Moon of Winter's. He smiled, and she found herself smiling in return before she remembered what was proper and lowered her eyes.

"Lieutenant D'Ottigni," the interpreter was saying to Outina, "is pleased indeed to meet a chief he has heard so many good things about." He paused as Walks Tall Woman brought from her hearth a basket laden with rounds of bread and a platter of chunked venison, waited until the servant who followed in her wake distributed mugs of sassafras tea to all who sat in the center of the hall.

The taller of the French leaders sipped cautiously at his tea, looked surprised, then drank more heartily. A smile hovered briefly around his mouth, and he said a few words to Saturiba's man.

"Lieutenant D'Ottigni asks what the drink is made from," the interpreter said.

"Describe the root, and say that I shall send some to his Holata," Outina replied. "Tell him that this tea, besides being tasty, is a tonic that both soothes and strengthens the body."

Apparently all of the Frenchmen found the tea to their liking, and Walks Tall Woman was kept busy refilling cups as the bread and meat was devoured with equal relish. Nor did she return to her hearth after the last of it had been poured, instead she hunkered down beside her son. If Outina permitted Moon of Winter and the trader to be here, he surely wanted his mother here as well. She would take pains to remind him that he should have seated the Principal Woman first, but that could wait until the strangers had gone on their way.

"A bundle of sassafras root is scarcely sufficient reward for the return of my warriors," Outina said when he was satisfied that his visitors had been amply fed. "Please tell Lieutenant D'Ottigni"—he stumbled a bit over the name—"that I will bring shame upon myself and my clan if I do not send appropriate gift to his Holata. Ask him to name something his chief would like to have. If it is within my power to give it, I will."

Kwambu felt a surge of pleasure as the interpreter obligingly repeated Outina's message. He was certain he could identify now the words for *give* and *like* and *send*, and possibly *him* and *his* as well. It was the beginning, at least, of a new language adventure, and he was more than ever eager to talk privately with the interpreter. The man seemed of amiable disposition, and although he had put on a loincloth for this mission, the trader wondered if woman's garb might not be his normal dress. Many berdaches Kwambu had met owned the keen ear and agile tongue needed to learn a language other than their own.

The nattily dressed Frenchmen were speaking together, and at considerable length. "Instead of a gift," the interpreter said when they signaled him to do so, "the French Holata asks a favor of Outina. He has heard of iron mountains and gold mountains in a country to the north of your territory, and would appreciate your providing guides to lead some of his men to them. He has asked his emissaries also to entreat you to send food to the French fort, for supplies are low there. Naturally, you will receive fine goods in return. Goods such as these."

The man with the long-fingered hands picked up a sack he had placed before him on the fragrant mat, rose, and with a clumsy bow, set it in front of Outina. The Holata opened it, removed a tangle of bright-colored beads, several lengths of a sturdy fabric, and a collection of glass-fronted rectangles with the face of the same bearded man inscribed on each of them. He held up one of these, arched his brows in puzzlement, passed it to Kwambu.

The interpreter cleared his throat. "Those are images of the Holata of all Frenchmen," he said. "He is called Charles, and he rules a land across the eastern sea, the land these men sailed from. It is a great honor to be given these images, and proves that the pale-faces seek only friendship from Holata Outina."

Moon of Winter peeked at the rectangle her husband held. It was like looking into one of the squares of reflecting glass Kwambu had brought from the south, but instead of her own face looking back at her, it was the face of a singularly unpleasant-looking white man. She wondered how the image had been captured beneath the glass. Did it happen when someone gazed too long at his own reflection? If so, this was a kind of magic Moon of Winter wanted nothing to do with.

"I thank you for the honor, then," Outina was saying, nodding toward D'Ottigni. "As for what your Holata wants from me . . ." He paused, frowned. "I, too, have heard of the mountains he has been told about, but none of my people know exactly where they are."

Kwambu signaled for permission to speak. "They are far to the north of here, in a country the Yustega know of," he told Outina. "I heard talk of them when I was there trading. If you wish to help the Frenchmen, I can take them to Yustega and perhaps the Holata will furnish them with guides for the remainder of the journey."

Outina nodded to the interpreter. "Tell them what the trader has offered to do. And say also that I will be glad to send what food we can spare to their fort." He frowned again, turned up his hands. "That will not be much at the moment. Unfortunately, my warriors will not be able to go hunting this month, as they had planned. Just before you arrived, Holata Potano sent a red-painted war club to me. Now all of my men will be needed to fight Potano's."

Moon of Winter and Kwambu exchanged startled glances. The declaration of war must have come after they had left this morning.

The French were clearly dismayed. Outina waited while they whispered agitatedly together, then signed that he would speak again. "I must, of course, confer with my Principal Men before making a firm offer, but if Lieutenant D'Ottigni will leave some of his soldiers with me"—he hesitated, as though not entirely certain that what he was proposing was a sound idea, then continued—"and if the soldiers will use their thunder-weapons against Potano, then perhaps the battle will be quickly won. Quickly enough so that hunting can begin while the forest remains filled with sizable game. With sufficient meat, we will not need to rely so much on what we grow, and I will be able to send additional food to the French Holata."

Walks Tall Woman looked proudly at her son. He had been sensible enough to take her advice, and she had to bite down on her inner cheek to keep from smiling with satisfaction.

Once again the Frenchmen spoke among themselves, gesturing broadly as they did so. Moon of Winter felt suddenly chilled; if they accepted her cousin's offer, would that be a good thing or a bad thing? She fingered the pouch that held her crystal. If only it would communicate with her, she might know the answer to that question in time to avert what she feared might be dire consequences to this parley. But no insight came to her. And even if it had, would Outina pay heed to any warning she might give him? Despite his show of uncertainty, she knew him well enough to know he was eager for the French to agree to his proposal.

Kwambu, who had hoped his volunteering to guide the French to Yustega province would be enough to satisfy them, kept his face expressionless. But he, too, feared that Outina might end by ruing the pact he seemed bent on making with the Frenchmen.

The red banners attached to the sky-reaching trophy pole whipped in the wind as Black Wolf Running spoke to the assembled warriors. "Leave with courage," he told them. "Have strong hearts, walk on your toes, keep your eyes open and never shut your ears. Do not fear the enemy's arrows, and let it be seen that you are peerless warriors. Use all your arrows against the foe, and let your clubs gorge on his blood." He had already spoken of his sorrow that he could not go with them this time, and sung the praises of their Holata, who had insisted on going in his Paracusi's stead.

Now water was brought to Outina. He looked up at the sun, called upon the god to bring strength and perseverance to every man who would be following him into battle. With his hands, he sprinkled water upon the bent heads of the warriors, to signify the scattering of enemy blood, then threw the remainder of it on the fire Watches for Omens had ignited in the moment Sun showed his face. "Death to Potano!" he cried as the circle of flames was extinguished, then accepted the medicine bundle the Shaman held out to him and led the chanting warriors, single file, in the direction of the palisade's gateway. Ten French soldiers, arquebuses slung across their shoulders, ambled after them.

"Do you think the pale-fleshed soldiers will keep their promise to help our warriors during the battle?" Moon of Winter asked as she and her husband walked back to the Principal House.

"I think they will," said Kwambu. "Failing to fight alongside Saturiba's men cost them the provisions they had apparently been depending upon. They must be greatly in need of food to have traveled so far to find some, and they will not dare risk offending Outina as well. Winter is coming soon, and men bent on exploring for gold and iron have no time for growing and hunting their own food. These men seem to feel that tilling fields is beneath them, in any event, according to what I learned from their interpreter."

Moon of Winter was aghast. "How can people live, who will not grow their own food?"

Kwambu's smile was wry. "By getting it from those who do."

She considered this seriously, shook her head. "I would not want to be so dependent on someone else," she said at last.

Kwambu hugged her to him. "That is because you are wise, and they are not."

"I do not like these French soldiers," she confessed. "They

stare at me, Kwambu. At my face. Then they talk among themselves, and I know they are saying how ugly I am."

She spoke in little more than a whisper, and Kwambu knew how much it hurt to say the words, words he had not heard from her in a long, long time. He felt anger rising in him, subdued it; it was not his wife he was angry with. "If it happens again," he said, "remember who you are, Moon of Winter. What was it Outina called you when he presented you to the Frenchmen? 'A true Daughter of the Sun, for the god has made of her both soothsayer and healer.' Remember that, and hold yourself proudly, beloved wife, no matter how the pale-faces stare. As Walks Tall Woman never fails to do," he added with a chuckle.

"It's true that no one would ever dare to stare at her," Moon of Winter agreed. "Or talk about her, except when they are certain she is nowhere around."

He steered her away from the pair of soldiers he would soon be leading to Yustega. "While I am away," he said, "do not let yourself forget the crystal you wear around your neck, and the powers it has helped you to develop."

"What healing I have been able to do is owed to years of studying with Watches for Omens," Moon of Winter said bitterly. "And the crystal you gave me has yet to reveal to this woman even a glimpse of the future."

Kwambu smiled again. "But most people in the town believe otherwise, Moon of Winter; you may be sure the French will hear what a powerful woman you are. And I honestly think you will practice no deception by walking and acting as a Wise Woman should."

She managed to return his smile, yet she had no desire to be a wise woman of any sort. She wanted only to live in peace, to have her husband and children, and eventually her grandchildren, around her, and have all of them blessed with contentment.

She said none of this, however. Kwambu was merely trying to be encouraging, and doubtless his advice was good. "I will do what you suggest," she told him.

But her hand strayed to her cheek, to finger the trio of ridges that was the panther's legacy. And she prayed, ardently, that all of the pale-faces would return to their fort just as soon as Potano had been vanquished.

Outina jerked an arrow from his quiver, sent it flying, then yelped with elation as it thudded into the flesh of a man whose right shoulder was exposed by the mangy shrub he crouched behind. The blood sang in the Holata's veins; it felt extraordinarily good, to be standing where Black Wolf Running usually stood.

The air vibrated with the twang of bowstrings as scores of arrows rained upon the clearing that fronted Potano's town. But where was the gunfire Outina had been listening for since this skirmish began? Why weren't the metal balls the French called ammunition also raining upon Potano's warriors?

The Holata sent three more arrows soaring against the foe, then dropped to the ground and went to find D'Ottigni. Who ought to have been immediately in back of him, but was not.

From the far side of the strip of forest came the smack of club against flesh. It was hand-to-hand combat now in that area, and it never should have come to that. Not with white man's guns to speak for Outina.

He swiped dirt from his sweaty face, was startled to have his hand come away smeared with blood. An arrow must have nicked his forehead, and he had not even noticed. He grinned. It had been a long time since he'd gone to war but—by the gods—he still knew how to be a warrior!

He slid farther through the brambles, wriggled around a clump of palmetto, and happened upon one of his men with an arrow lodged deep in his side. The warrior was young, and the mask of stoicism he had put on was in danger of slipping. The berdache tending him seemed to know what he was doing, however, so Outina merely smiled encouragement at the injured youth before moving on.

But the smell of the warrior's blood lingered in his nostrils, and he was suddenly in a fury. Where were the French gunners? They had not attempted to flee, as Outina had half expected. Someone would have reported it, if they had. Heedless of noise—and with war cries rising on all sides, none would hear him anyway—he raised himself to a crouch and dashed between the trees until a flash of yellow off to one side brought him to a halt. That yellow; it was the color of the breeches D'Ottigni wore.

It did not improve his temper to find all of the French soldiers huddled together within a stand of evergreens. "What are they doing here? Why are their guns silent?" he demanded of the interpreter, who let his own disgust show as he replied. "They say they are waiting for your orders."

"Orders! What need have they for orders? A battle is being

fought all around them, a battle they vowed to help us fight. Do they lack the sense to lift their guns and aim them?"

Lieutenant D'Ottigni did not know what Outina said, but he could guess the reason for his anger. "Tell him," he said stiffly, "that it is his responsibility to position my men."

Outina suppressed a roar of outrage when he heard, used gestures and shooing motions to get the French moving, drove them without pause toward the field. Arrows zinged around them as they neared it, and the soldiers, fear blanching their already pale faces, bent low and shielded their heads with upthrust arms. Outina only gestured more forcefully, then pointed to the meadow where Potano's warriors were darting back and forth like a swarm of crazed bees, releasing arrows on the run and—for the most part—neatly evading the arrows Outina's men were directing at them.

"Tell them to shoot!" he shouted at the interpreter, but D'Ottigni seemed to have come to his senses at last. Already he had signaled his men to do so. Still bent double, they hunted out flat surfaces to set up supports for their weapons or found forked tree limbs to serve as braces and loaded the arquebuses. Finally, just as Holata Outina was about to throw up his hands in despair at the delay, the soldiers applied fire to the powder in the pans.

The multiple explosions were deafening. Never mind that the balls fell short of their intended targets, the noise and the smell of burnt powder were enough to shock Potano's warriors into immobility. And Outina's warriors wasted no time dashing out of the woods to leap upon the stunned foe, knives and clubs at the ready.

"To the rear," Outina shouted, gesturing again. The soldiers looked to their tight-lipped lieutenant, who nodded confirmation, then gingerly retrieved their still-smoking guns and followed the Holata to a bit of even ground where they could set up again. They did so more quickly this time, pointed their weapons toward the tall grass in which the enemy had taken cover, and soon another series of explosions splintered the air. Before the echoes had died, Potano's warriors were scrambling up and pelting toward the trees. Once again Outina's men, screeching exultantly, dashed in their wake, brought down the laggards and slew them on the spot.

Lieutenant D'Ottigni looked toward Outina. Where now? his glance said.

Outina smiled as he beckoned to him the four warriors who

served Black Wolf Running as scouts. He spoke to them rapidly, then signed for the Saturiban to come forward. "Tell him," he said, slanting his head toward D'Ottigni, "that I believe Potano has been routed. I have sent men to verify this, but I am certain that they will find no enemy warriors left anywhere in this forest. If they do come across one or two"—he shrugged—"they will know what to do. The French soldiers may rest now, before we begin our journey home."

The interpreter relayed Holata Outina's message.

Bewilderment lengthened the lieutenant's narrow face. "But the town!" he sputtered. "We have not yet taken the town."

His protests left Holata Outina equally bewildered. "Why would we take the town?" he asked. "There will be only women and children and old people there. We could easily make captives of them, but then we would have to take them home with us. And where would we find the food to feed so many?"

The Saturiban had scarcely repeated this before D'Ottigni was speaking again. The interpreter listened, turned back to Outina. "He says you should make the town yours. It would probably take only half of your warriors to defend it."

Outina could not believe what he was hearing. "Why would I do that? My people have their own towns to live in."

His men were congregating around him now, coming out of the woods in twos and threes. All were grimy and many bloodstained; some were limping, others supported more seriously injured comrades. But several had red-stained scalps attached to their bows, and all were bright-eyed and grinning. It had been a fine battle, and the victory was theirs to boast about! Behind them came the scouts, and one look at their faces told Outina that he had been right—Potano's warriors had fled.

D'Ottigni continued to rant, but Outina paid no attention. They had heaped disgrace upon the enemy, and if the foreigner could not recognize this as victory, then he was a poor excuse for a soldier. Furthermore, not one of his warriors had been slain, so there need be no mourning to sap joy from their homecoming. He signed to the berdaches to bring water for everyone to drink and prepared to head back to his own province. There was excellent reason to celebrate, and Holata Outina meant to make the most of it.

Chapter 34

➡ ➡

Headchief Calusa was at last showing interest in the news Kwambu had brought him. "So the French soldiers followed your wife's cousin into battle," he said, his strong-featured face registering an alertness it had lacked until now. "That is good. Perhaps the pale-fleshes will soon grow wise enough to seek trading treaties with both Timucua and Calusa. I would be pleased to have a reliable source of knives and spear points that are shaped from metal rather than bone, and to be able to have many cloaks as elegant as this one." He stroked the velvety nap of a crimson cape that had been salvaged from a shipwreck, grinned as its color altered subtly. Then he pointed to a blotchy area near the hem. "They would not come to me water-soaked, if I could trade for them," he added.

"If that happens, the white men will want something in return," Kwambu said, "and it may be something you will not want to give."

Calusa was unperturbed. "You are a trader of vast experience," he said. "I will trust you to arrange deals that are favorable to me, as you have always done."

"Trading with white men will not be like trading with Oathkaqua or Tequesta or even Canegacola, where bartering is as much ceremony as anything else. The white men I have known have always wanted considerably better than they give, Calusa."

Calusa waved his hand dismissively. "No man, whatever his skin color, will ever get the best of me, trader. If you do not feel able to deal with them when the time comes, then I will do so myself. With you to interpret for me, of course." He stood up, stepped down from the elaborate stool he favored for even informal interviews. "I wish there were a way to make that time come soon," he said. "There is so little excitement in my life of late. Even the child my wife bore me last season was no cause for excitement; it was another girl." He twirled his new cloak around his shoulders. "It was supposed to be a boy this time," he said fretfully, "and I had planned for a great feast to be made."

"Perhaps your next child will be a son," Kwambu told him.

Calusa's face brightened with the smile he was noted for. "That is true," he said, "and I need not wait long to find out; my wife is already breeding again. And should she disappoint me with yet another daughter, I can always take a second wife. Even a third and a fourth. As my father did." The smile faltered. "But he did not find a woman able to give him a son until he was old, did he?"

"That is true. But when a boy was finally born, it was a son your father could be proud of," Kwambu said diplomatically.

When the smile returned to the Headchief's face, Kwambu asked permission to leave him and was relieved to have it granted. Speaking with Calusa had become an exercise in futility. The young man saw no point of view but his own, was interested in nothing unless it affected him directly. The first thing Kwambu had told him was how the leader of the French expedition had arranged for those traitorous Spaniards, Fontaneda and Gomez, to be transferred from Oathkaqua to his fort. The Headchief had made little of that; he had urged Kwambu to move on to the "important news."

Great Calusa had been so different; he would have wondered at once what Fontaneda and Gomez might be telling the Frenchmen about Calusa country, and how the pale-fleshes were likely to react. And if Kwambu had told Great Calusa about Frenchmen agreeing to fight alongside a Timucuan chief, he would have been answering questions for the remainder of the day. Young Calusa's father would not have been satisfied until he knew all there was to know about the newcomers; he would have probed for reasons why they had made such an agreement, and speculated on all possible ramifications.

Kwambu was so deep in thought that he blundered into a group of children playing tag-me and almost missed seeing Dancing Egret sitting in front of her house. When she called his name, he dodged the laughing boys and girls, loped across the plaza, and hunkered down beside her. "I came here early in the day, before I was summoned by your brother," he said, "but you were nowhere around."

"That must have been when I'd gone to the river to bathe," she said. "But I am here now, Kwambu, and delighted to see you again."

She did not look particularly delighted. Pleased to see him, yes; but he had not seen true delight in Egret's eyes for far too long. Her hair was arranged in a new way, he saw, one that brought an attractive softness to her strong features, but her face was so lacking in animation that it resembled one of those elegant carvings Shore Walker used to make. "And I am happy to be able to visit with you once more," he said. "How do you fare, Egret?"

"My health is good," she replied, "and I keep busy. Other than that"—she shrugged her hunched shoulders—"things are the same with me as they were last time you came."

She did not ask what he had been speaking about with Calusa, but he offered the information anyway. "I am afraid you are right in what you have always said about him," he finished. "He is unlikely ever to be the kind of leader your father was."

"He never even asked what devious reasons the white men might have had for agreeing to fight in a war that has nothing to do with them?" she said, her eyes taking on a hint of their old sparkle. "Or tried to find out from you how many French there are in Timucuan country, and if the ships they came here in ever sail south?"

"You are raising questions your brother should have asked, but did not. Perhaps, if you spoke with him . . ."

Her eyes dulled. "It would do no good," she said. "Calusa has made it plain that he does not want my counsel. And I am weary of wasting my energy—which seems in short supply these days—trying to make him listen to me."

"But what of the promise you gave to your father?" Kwambu said quietly.

"I tried hard to keep that promise," she said. "You know I did, Kwambu. Surely I cannot be blamed because it turned out to be a pledge impossible to honor?"

"Have you stopped attending Council meetings?"

"No. But I go only from habit, I suppose, since my being there accomplishes nothing."

She looked up as a *Ha-ii-ooo* came from the sentry on the causeway. "The men must have returned from hunting," she said absently. "A band of young warriors went over to the river glades three days ago."

A clutch of maidens, hastily smoothing their hair and giggling among themselves, dashed across the compound, slowed to a more sedate pace as they left the town and made for the seawall. Kwambu laughed. "Where there are young warriors, there will always be pretty maidens," he observed. "The girl who passed closest to us . . . she reminds me of Brown Pelican when she was young. Is it one of her daughters, perhaps?"

Egret nodded. "That's Chattering Squirrel. She has gone to welcome home Swift Eagle, I expect. I hope for her sake that he notices her this time and returns her greeting; so far, all of her efforts to attract him have been in vain. He has always looked upon her as his little sister, you see. Not only do they have a great-grandfather in common, but their families were unusually close in the days when all of the children were small."

"They should be well suited. Swift Eagle is a fine young man. And Chattering Squirrel . . . she is the girl you taught to Sing the Legends, I believe?"

"Yes. And she knows them well enough to be able to teach them to those children who have yet to learn them. I can't imagine why she hasn't begun to do so."

"It may be she does not feel confident enough to take the place of her talented aunt," her companion said. "If you offered to tutor her a little more, however . . ."

Egret did not let him finish. "Since I no longer Sing, I'm unable to teach her more."

Kwambu shifted position so that he was face-to-face with her. "So you have not only reneged on a promise given to your father," he said bluntly, "but you have never even tried to live up to what your husband asked of you as he lay dying. I wonder if this lack of energy you complain of is not a forfeit being demanded because you failed to honor the wishes of two men who always had such faith in you, Dancing Egret."

Egret stiffened, made as if to get up. Kwambu put out one hand to restrain her. "Both loved you dearly," he went on relentlessly. "Both of them trusted in you. What would either think if they could see you now, drifting aimlessly through the days, throwing away with both hands the precious gift of life that your father and your husband always made such excellent use of? Just as you once did."

"Much good it did them!" she cried. "They are dead. And

I . . . I no longer have purpose in life, so what good is this 'precious gift' to me?"

The hurt that darkened her eyes made him ache inside, but he reminded himself that any sign of feeling was better than none at all. And if Egret could not be made to feel again, she might as well have died when Shore Walker did. "Calusa lived to a great age," he said, "and was a leader men will forever speak of with reverence and admiration. Shore Walker died a hero's death and will also be long remembered. Only those who spend the substance of their lives carelessly or purposelessly truly die, Dancing Egret, for you may be sure that they are remembered by no one. No one at all."

Egret stared at him, struggled to find words to end a harangue she was shocked to have directed at her by the gentle Kwambu. "You say *people*," she challenged, "but *men* is the word you should have used, isn't it? What can a woman do to earn such honor? Women live on only in the memories of their children and grandchildren." She turned her head away, let an accumulation of bitterness coat her final words. "And where are the children who will remember me when I am dead?"

Kwambu looked around the squareground. The boys and girls playing tag still dominated it, while a scrum of yapping dogs nipped at their heels. From the perimeter, younger children either watched enviously or devoted themselves to games of their own devising. There had been a time when Dancing Egret could not have come out of her house without most of these little ones running to surround her and beg for a story. "In one glance," he said, "I see many children who used to call your name and clap their hands when you appeared, who once followed wherever you went. In the fullness of time, the mothers of these youngsters will have their memories revered by two or six or even ten, depending upon how many of their children outlive them. But consider the scores of children, the hundreds of children, who will remember a beloved Singer of Legends, Dancing Egret." He smiled down at her, and put all of his heartfelt affection into the smile. "Fine storytellers are spoken of generations beyond their own lifetimes. And you, my dear, dear friend, were ever the finest of storytellers."

But Egret would not let herself be swayed. "I can no longer Sing," she muttered. "What talent I once had has abandoned me."

Kwambu looked sorrowfully at the woman whose bent head concealed her expression. "Cannot Sing?" he asked softly. "Or

will not? There is a difference, Egret. And you bring shame to
the spirits of your husband and your father if you refuse to acknowledge this difference, and act upon it."

When she did not respond, he strode away, taking with him
the image of her sitting motionless, head still bowed. Before
he'd reached the far side of the plaza, he was berating himself
for having been so harsh with her. It seemed that the older he
got, the more he indulged his deplorable habit of offering advice where none had been sought. And who was he to tell others what they should or should not do? As a trader, he was
competent to guide people along the trails that crisscrossed this
land; but what made him think he was qualified to guide anyone along the path of life itself?

He sighed. He knew the answer to that question: he had neither the qualifications nor the right to offer such guidance. But
he knew just as certainly that, could circumstances repeat
themselves, he would say all over again what he had said to
Dancing Egret. If she ended by hating him for it, his grief
would be enormous. But the ebullient child she had been, the
lively young woman she had grown into, must still lurk somewhere within the hollow shell Egret had let herself become. It
was to them he had been speaking, and he could only trust that
they had heard him and would understand what he was trying
to do.

Holata Outina, surrounded by the phalanx of Townchiefs he
had summoned to the feast, turned to Lieutenant D'Ottigni,
who—as a courtesy—had been invited to sit on the Holata's
right. "My warriors dance as superbly as they fight," Outina
said, raising his voice to be heard over the piping of flutes and
pounding of drums. He was feeling especially affable; although
he had declined the honor, his warriors had begged him to join
them in the dancing, had made it clear that they felt they owed
the victory over Potano to their chief.

D'Ottigni merely grunted. The so-called music was ear-
splitting; the spectators were talking and laughing all at the
same time; the children, as ill-restrained as usual, were trying
to outdo one another with their shouting. D'Ottigni's head
throbbed from so much noise, and his stomach was queasy besides. How could it not be, after the prodigious quantities of
food the women had cooked and served to the assemblage?
And all to celebrate a triumph that, in D'Ottigni's mind, was
no triumph whatsoever.

Now the women were dancing, too, tossing their long hair as their bare breasts bobbed up and down, up and down. His soldiers were ogling them, and the lieutenant thanked the good God that soon he would be taking the detachment back to the fort. Who could say what sin the fools might not fall into if they remained longer in this accursed place?

On the far side of the squareground, Moon of Winter stood watching proudly as Red Fox Barking danced with the warriors and Kaia with the maidens. They were both so graceful, so pleasing to look upon. She wished Hawk was dancing also, but his wound was healing nicely; he would be doing so next time there was a victory to celebrate.

She frowned. For there to be another victory, there must first be another battle. That was not a pleasant thought.

"You do not enjoy the dancing?" The words came haltingly, and two were mispronounced.

Moon of Winter turned to see the lanky man with the tilted eyes watching her. Kwambu had told her his name; what was it? "I enjoy it very much," she replied courteously. And slowly, so that he would understand her. "My son and daughter dance with the others."

When he asked, she pointed them out to him. Le Moyne, that was the soldier's name. He was the one who had smiled at her on the day the Frenchmen came here.

The man had in one hand a rolled piece of the flat white stuff Kwambu had said was called parchment. In the other he held a narrow bit of charcoal that had been shaved to a point at one end. Now he squatted on the ground, unfurled the parchment, and began to make marks on it with the charcoal. Moon of Winter turned back to the dancing; white men were given to behaving strangely, she thought. The soldier had acted as though he were interested in the dance, yet he had been quick to turn his attention from it.

The warriors and maidens, breathless and perspiring, were acknowledging the praise sent their way by the crowd before Le Moyne spoke again. Then he stood and held out his parchment. "Your son and your daughter," he said, indicating it.

The sun shone so brightly that it was almost summer-warm, but Moon of Winter felt her flesh pucker as she took the parchment from him and looked down at it. Looking back at her were Kaia and Red Fox Barking!

She swallowed hard. It was not really them, of course, but only their images, images similar to those captured in the glass-fronted rectangles the Frenchmen had given to Outina. But how could this be? The parchment had no glass over it, and even if it had, her children had been nowhere near it.

Le Moyne recognized her apprehension and sought for words to allay it. "Your people, they paint symbols on skins," he said. "This is no different." He tapped the parchment with one long finger. "We call it 'picture.' "

"*Pic-ture.*" She tasted the word, studied the parchment on which Red Fox Barking wore the one-sided grin that was rarely absent from his squarish face. And Kaia ... her black curls seemed to be bouncing as she danced, her delicate body flowing with the rhythm of the music she was listening to. "This ... this is magic."

Le Moyne laughed. "No. Not magic; only skill. Like ... like dancing. Or singing." He took from a pack he had fastened to his belt another rolled parchment, spread it open. "Here. Your chief and his wife."

And it was. Outina and Palm Tree Bending stood before the Principal House, his topknotted head angled as though he were listening to her speak. What she was saying must have amused him, for the beginnings of a smile showed on his face.

Now Le Moyne was displaying yet another picture, but this one truly bewildered Moon of Winter. Rank upon rank of warriors, Timucuan warriors, faced each other across an open meadow. Outina was in the picture, his right arm lifted in some sort of signal, and with the second mass of warriors stood another Holata. Many of the warriors had apparently been releasing arrows, for dozens were flying across the space between the two close-knit groups, and the expressions on the men's faces said that each considered the other enemy. Indeed, some arrows must already have found their marks, for here and there a warrior lay wounded or dying.

"This shows war," Le Moyne was saying. "Outina against Potano. We helped Holata Outina fight."

Moon of Winter had never been to war, yet it was impossible to have warriors for sons and not hear all about raids and battles. What the picture showed was quite different from any battle that had ever been described to her, but she smiled politely as she nodded understanding of what the Frenchman said. "You own a wonderful skill," she told him, handing back the perplexing drawing.

He spread his hands. "Others have more skill," he said, "but

Jacques Le Moyne, he alone makes pictures of your people. Someday I show *my* people what your people look like."

The idea of someone beyond the vast eastern sea gazing at the likenesses of her children gave Moon of Winter an eerie feeling, but clearly this man did not hold the people of Outina's town in contempt, as many of his fellow soldiers plainly did. His *pic-tures*, even the one supposedly of the battle between Outina and Potano, told her that. So she returned his smile before moving away from him. With the dancing ended, it was time to help with the cleaning up. Until leftover food had been packed away and pots scoured, no woman would be free to enjoy the final night of this three-day celebration.

Palm Tree Bending and Walks Tall Woman joined her as she walked toward the Principal House. Elation over her son's success in battle had made Moon of Winter's aunt positively amiable for a change, and the two younger women exchanged delighted smiles; perhaps they might be able to persuade Walks Tall Woman to let most of the pot-scrubbing wait until the morning?

Moon of Winter's smile faded quickly, however, as they passed her cousin and Lieutenant D'Ottigni. The Frenchman's expression was far from amiable, and she held back a little to find out why.

"He says you dishonor your promise by refusing to send more food to the fort when he and his men go back," the interpreter was telling Outina.

Outina gestured to the heap of picked-clean bones decorating the center of the circle he and his guests were sitting in, at the crusts of cornbread and remnants of pumpkin shell the dogs were scrapping over. "He can see for himself how much food was used to make such a grand feast," he said. "Tomorrow, I will show him that there is barely enough left in our corncribs to see my people through the winter. Of course, if the men bring back sufficient game from the hunt, then I will send meat to the French fort."

D'Ottigni, hearing, spoke so rapidly that the Saturiban asked him to repeat himself. "He wants to know when that will be," he said to Holata Outina.

"My hunters must travel to the outermost forests of the province," Outina replied. "They will stay there for two months at least, possibly longer."

"Two months!" the lieutenant exclaimed. "What are we to

do meanwhile? Tell him that food must be sent before then, and also that it is a surety we will need more than just meat."

It was Outina's turn to look less than amiable. "We will send what we can, when we can," he said sharply.

But D'Ottigni was seething now, and not inclined to mince words. "Remind him," he said to the interpreter, "that it was a condition of our alliance that he *keep* the fort supplied with food. Anything less will be regarded as an act of treachery."

Moon of Winter started guiltily as Walks Tall Woman, her voice taking on its customary bite, called to her from inside the house. Much as she wanted to linger until the discussion between her cousin and the Frenchman ended, she dared not ignore the summons.

Lieutenant D'Ottigni was shouting still as she went to help her aunt and Palm Tree Bending with the chores.

On the far side of the ocean that separated New World from Old, Pedro Menendez de Aviles put away the epistle he had received the day before, a letter stamped with the royal seal. His Majesty was becoming impatient; it was past time that the heretic French Huguenots were driven back to their homeland, yet Menendez—who had pledged to deal with them—seemed in no hurry to set sail.

Of course, King Don Felipe had not offered to send monies from his own coffers to finance the expedition, and Menendez knew now that he never would. And how can one expect a king to understand that for a man to convert many of his own properties into cash takes considerable time? So far, the transactions had required the better part of a year to effect, and even now he was not fully prepared to undertake the voyage. It was all well and good to be assured that the Spanish already in the Indies would give the Adelantado any assistance he might need to go against the French; ships must still be manned and a decent complement of soldiers, artisans, and priests must be persuaded to emigrate. Barbers, shoemakers, tailors, musicians, farriers, notaries—all of these and more were also needed if Menendez hoped to establish settlements in la Florida. And this he was determined to do. Spain's ownership of that section of the New World could never be disputed again, once the area was properly colonized.

His dark eyes lit with fervor. After the French had been removed from a place they had no right to be, he would concentrate on fulfilling another of the king's dictates: implanting the

Holy Gospel throughout the territories of la Florida. Except for trying to locate the son whose ship had gone down off of that uncharted coast, this was the mission that aroused the most excitement in Menendez. The endless months of waiting, difficult though they had been, had given him opportunity to pray most earnestly that God would permit him to find his son and rescue him, and to pray also that it might be Pedro Menendez de Aviles who brought the Word of God to the natives of la Florida, who carried it to them with such zealousness that one and all would come to recognize and worship the Christian Cross.

He closed the door to his chamber, then knelt before the altar he had set up for his personal use. "Please," he murmured, his hands clasped so tightly that he could feel his life's blood pulsing through his veins, "let me be the one. Holy Mother of God, I beseech You: grant me the power to convert those who have not yet heard of You or of Your Holy Son. Let me bring enlightenment to the ignorant and lead hell-bound souls into the glory of God's heaven!"

He was calm and clearheaded when he rose to his feet, and ready to turn his mind to more practical matters. He must find out who in the Indies could be relied upon to give him accurate directions to the Huguenot fort. No maps available to Menendez offered that information, and certainly His Majesty had made no attempt to discover its exact location. Well, there were many things that a king could not or would not do, but so long as the King of Spain had Pedro Menendez to rely upon, all would be well regardless.

Chapter 35

• ⇒

Walks Tall Woman sifted through the dried beans in the basket. One of her duties was to distribute seed to the women of the town, and they would not be pleased when they saw how little she was giving to each of them. "They will not complain while I can hear them," she said, "but they will complain. And if the rain does not soon begin falling regularly, they will complain all the more. Yet a Principal Woman has no control over such things."

She looked speculatively at her niece, and Moon of Winter averted her eyes. She did not want Walks Tall Woman to even think about asking her to consult her crystal to find out how long the thirsty earth might have to wait for a deep, refreshing drink.

"They understand that you are not responsible for the weather," Palm Tree Bending said to Walks Tall Woman. "They will complain only because they are worried. Just as we are."

Outina, admiring the twisted deerhide his younger son had fashioned into a strong new bowstring, grinned. "With your grandmother supervising the planting," he said to White Tailed Stag, "our crops will not dare refuse to grow. Rain or no!"

His tall son, soon to reach full warrior status, grinned in return. But the three women who overheard did not. Palm Tree Bending and Moon of Winter looked at each other; if only it were so easy, they agreed silently.

"You had better hope our hunters have been successful, so that there will be fresh meat to eat until we have corn and beans and pumpkin to cook again," Walks Tall Woman told her son. "But they have been away overlong as it is, which may mean that the hunting is not going as well as it usually does."

It was true that the warriors had been away for a very long time, Moon of Winter thought. And it bothered her to see only women, old men, and children whenever she went into the compound.

As if in response to a discomfort she confessed only to herself, the pounding of moccasined feet vibrated the ground she was sitting on, and a confusion of voices called for Holata Outina.

At his bidding, a clutter of boys came in, boys smelling ripely of fish, who all started to talk at once. Outina held up his hand. "You," he said to the one nearest him, "will speak for everyone."

"There is a ship," the youth said, "sailing up the river. A French ship."

The Holata frowned. "Doubtless the soldiers have come again to demand food," he said, "even though they know we have none to give. But I thank you for bringing me the news. Ask the Principal Men to come to my house, and when the soldiers reach the town, send them here also. I can offer them hospitality at least."

The boys, puffed with importance to be carrying the Holata's messages, ran into the compound and Outina turned to his mother. "We do have tea we can offer them? And bread?"

"Tea, yes," she said. "But there is only a little bread, barely enough for our own meal." Walks Tall Woman had fought against aging as vigorously as she had resisted anything she had ever regarded as personal weakness, but this was a battle that time was slowly winning. Every now and then she displayed the querulousness common to the elderly.

Oddly, Palm Tree Bending felt a certain fondness for her on such occasions. "We will offer them what there is," she said to her gently. "As you have always told your son, a Holata is expected to be generous, no matter the circumstances."

Walks Tall Woman considered, nodded; this was true. Without further demurral, she went to unroll and inspect the sitting mats.

The seed had been separated into bundles for the town's women, and White Tailed Stag had finished stringing his bow before the sound of footsteps came again. This time they were being made by booted feet, a great number of them.

Those who lived in the Principal House, and the advisors Outina had sent for, ceased their idle chatting. "We shall never be able to feed so many," Walks Tall Woman said. But already she was breaking rounds of cornbread in half and signing to Moon of Winter and Palm Tree Bending to do likewise.

Outina, his son by his side and his Principal Men flanking the both of them, stood courteously as a score of Frenchmen entered. Some he recognized, others he did not. But, as before, Lieutenant D'Ottigni was leading them. "You are come," the Holata said.

D'Ottigni, although he had heard the formal greeting often enough, had never realized that it was one. He thought it a ridiculous thing to say to a visitor. Still, it was not precisely as visitors that he and his men were here. "Tell him," he instructed the Saturiban interpreter, "that I have come on an urgent mission, one I have pledged to carry out with dispatch."

Outina nodded when he heard; did the man think that stressing the importance of his mission would magically fill the town's corncribs with the food he was hoping to take back with him? "Ask them to sit," he said to the Saturiban. "My mother and my wife will bring refreshment. Then we will talk."

But instead of lowering themselves to the woven cane mats, several of the men accompanying D'Ottigni suddenly darted forward, grabbed the Holata's arms and twisted them behind him. Three others seized White Tailed Stag in a similar hold, while their comrades herded Outina's advisors into a tight circle and, making them sit back to back, bound them securely to one another.

Palm Tree Bending screamed. Flinging to the ground the basket of bread she was carrying, she rushed to where her husband and son were being forced to their knees. "No!" she shouted. "You must not!" Walks Tall Woman did more than shout; keening shrilly, she began to pummel the soldiers who had made a captive of her son. Even when one of the Frenchmen backhanded her and sent her sprawling, she continued to screech imprecations at him.

Moon of Winter, as bewildered as the rest and as angry, did not scream. She planted herself in front of the Saturiban. "Why are they doing this?" she demanded, amazed at her own daring even as she hurled the words at him.

But the poor man seemed as perplexed by what was happening as she was. He looked to Lieutenant D'Ottigni for an answer to Moon of Winter's question, forgetting even to translate it for him.

D'Ottigni knew full well what the woman—Outina's cousin, was it?—wanted to know. Raising his voice to be heard above the caterwauling of the females, the cries of protest arising from Outina's Principal Men, the cursing of the soldiers driven to fend off the women, he demanded silence.

It was some time in coming, and even then it was punctuated by Palm Tree Bending's sobbing and Walks Tall Woman's irate mutterings as she picked herself up off the floor. The only calmness in evidence was in Holata Outina's face. On his knees he might be, but he would not give these hospitality abusers reason to look at him with scorn. He murmured to his son, who was struggling still against the hands that held him down, and White Tailed Stag ceased his futile writhing and also put on a mask of impassiveness.

"We are taking your Holata and the boy with us," D'Ottigni said finally, "to the barque in the river. No harm will come to them there, but they will be returned to you only when you have delivered to our ship the foodstuffs Holata Outina vowed to send to us when we agreed to help him in his war against Potano. If you are wise, you will start collecting quantities of food as soon as we have left your town. I will not wait beyond seven days for you to bring to us the supplies we are entitled to, and I will be the judge of how much food is sufficient to win your Holata's freedom. And his son's."

The lieutenant was jubilant. Abducting Chief Outina had been his idea, and Rene Laudonniere, the perpetually ailing commander of the French fort, had needed considerable persuading as to its feasibility. Next, he'd questioned the morality of the plan ... until D'Ottigni reminded him that the ships Laudonniere was having built would require provisioning before the Huguenots could even think of returning home. Which Rene Laudonniere ardently desired to do. Now, with both the Holata and his heir in French hands, the Indians would surely inundate Fort Caroline with food and Laudonniere would see France again sooner than he had expected to. And so, thank the good God, thought D'Ottigni, would he!

He gestured his men toward the door. "Do not think to interfere with us as we return to the river," he said, commanding the interpreter to direct the warning at the trussed-up Principal Men. "I have more soldiers waiting outside, and they will use their guns against anyone who tries such a thing."

Then he, too, was gone, and there came again the sound of footsteps. This time the feet marched away from the Principal House, and the rhythm they made invited terror into the hearts of those who listened to them.

Dancing Egret, true to a habit she had formed during her childhood, awoke before dawn. For a few moments she lay listening to the twittering of birds in the trees and bushes around Calusa's town, then she rose and went to investigate the new day. It would be a pleasant one if the breeze that greeted her meant anything. Egret let it play tag with tendrils of her sleep-mussed hair while she gazed upon the compound. A few children were up beforetime, too, and were tossing balls back and forth or making plans for more demanding activities once the sun had shown its face.

Near the cooking pavilion, a flock of grackles had gathered to prospect for crumbs of zamia bread and corncake. Dancing Egret focused on one of the females, a bird with a single leg, one she had seen there several times before. Whether the grackle had emerged from the shell that way or had lost a leg through some mishap later in life could not be known, but Egret had come to admire the dun-colored bird for its indifference to its handicap. It hopped on one leg as quickly as its kin did on two, which was good; this grackle was a mother, a mother finding it difficult to persuade a youngling to be independent. Whenever the one-legged bird pounced on a bit of food, a daughter who was long past the fledgling stage insisted upon having a share. Each time it did, the long-suffering mother would try to avoid feeding it; and, each time, it would end by plopping a morsel into its squawking offspring's gaping beak. There was something comic in the performance, yet something profoundly touching about it, too.

A ball, ineptly thrown, arced through the dawn-fresh air and bounced into a thicket behind the cooking pavilion, sending the feeding birds into flight. Egret turned her head; it was Brown Pelican's youngest who had thrown it. Rain Drop, all skinny arms and legs, would likely grow into a true beauty eventually. For now, though, her nose was too big, her mouth was too wide, and grace stubbornly eluded her. She blundered into the thorny bushes in search of her errant ball, and Dancing Egret, imagining the scratches that would soon be decorating those scrawny limbs, winced in sympathy. What she did not expect, however, was that Rain Drop would suddenly let out a series of piercing yelps, yelps that a few scrapes would never have spawned.

Egret made a dash for the ladder leading out of her house, scrambled down it and ran to the thicket. On its far side a furious mockingbird was alternately soaring and diving, disappearing into the bushes each time it zoomed down. Whenever the bird dove, Rain Drop would yelp again, and Dancing Egret—forcing her own way into the copse—knew at once what was happening.

"The mockingbird and his mate have built their nest in the tallest bush," she told a sobbing Rain Drop after she had hauled her into the open, "and there must be eggs in it. The bird thought you were after the eggs; that's why it attacked you."

"He kept pecking at me and pecking at me," the girl said between sobs, "and the bush held me captive. I couldn't get away from him." Then her eyes flashed and she stopped crying. "Nasty old bird. I hate him!"

"But that is the same bird whose song is so beautiful,"

Dancing Egret said. "How can you hate a creature who sings so sweetly?"

"I wish he would fly away," Rain Drop said angrily. "I wish they would all fly away and never come back. I don't care how sweetly they sing; birds are mean."

Egret gathered the child into her arms. "You're just upset," she said soothingly. "Birds are not mean. Indeed, birds have been both friends and helpers to us since the Beginning."

"They are not," the child muttered, but Dancing Egret had aroused her curiosity. "How can birds help us? They do nothing but fly around and build nests and sing or honk or squawk. And attack children!"

Egret smiled. "Once upon a time, our ancestors felt that way also, perhaps. But that was before they lost their fire."

"How did that happen?" Rain Drop settled herself more comfortably on her aunt's lap. Dancing Egret had not held her like this for a long, long time, and—even though Rain Drop was far from a baby now—it felt rather good to be cuddled.

"When Man first received the gift of Fire, he honored and protected it, but as years went by he grew careless. Then Owl, who thought he should be the only creature able to see at night, stole Man's fire and hid it in the tallest of hollow trees."

"How awful!" Rain Drop said. "But I told you birds were mean, didn't I?"

"Well, Owl certainly was," Egret conceded with a grin. "But the other birds, you see, had never felt very friendly toward Owl because he so often hunted and ate their young. So when Man cried to see his shivering children gnawing on uncooked meat, the other birds decided to get Fire back for him."

"How did they do that?"

"First they asked Man to have Woman weave baskets small enough for birds to carry," Egret said, speaking a bit more loudly. Several of Rain Drop's playmates had come to find her and were obviously straining to hear what Dancing Egret was telling her. "When they had done so, Gallinule and Stilt, Woodpecker and Blackbird, Tanager, Bunting, and Crested Finch each took one. Even tiny Hummingbird was given one, although he found it difficult to hold since it was as big as he was."

Rain Drop laughed; so did the others.

"Woodpecker was the one who located the tree Owl had hidden Fire in," Egret went on, "and he quickly summoned the others. 'Owl forced Fire through a tiny hole at the very top of that tree,' he told them, 'but I will make the hole bigger so we can lift Fire out and take it back to Man.' He flew up and pecked and pecked with his sharp beak until the small hole became a big hole. But just as he looked down to be certain his basket still hung from the twig he'd put it on, a flame leaped out of the hole and wrapped itself around Woodpecker's head. Woodpecker screeched and flew away, and he has had a red head ever since."

More and more children were congregating, and Egret— suddenly aware of what was happening—felt her throat tighten. But Rain Drop's eyes were fixed on her aunt's face, and it would be cruel to disappoint a child who was in need of comfort. "Blackbird thought it would be easier to reach Fire from above," Egret said, clearing her throat to dispel a sudden hoarseness, "so up he went. But as he hovered atop that hollow tree, his beating wings fanned Fire and sparks rose up and stuck to Blackbird's shoulders. When he smelled his feathers burning, Blackbird flew away, but since that day he has worn red patches on his shoulders.

"Stilt, who had longer legs than his comrades, decided to fly over the tree and reach for Fire with his toes, but Fire bit him, too, and now Stilt's legs are always red. Then Gallinule attempted to use his sharp beak to snatch Fire out of the hole Woodpecker had made. Fire attacked him also, and he has worn a bright red beak ever since. And when Bunting merely flew over the tree, the heat rose up and reddened his underparts. So he gave up as well."

"Couldn't any of them get Fire back for Man?" a little boy asked anxiously.

Egret's voice was all at once strong and lilting. "Wait and see," she said with a smile, and—still smiling—continued with the tale. "Now Tanager and Finch looked at one another. 'The only way to retrieve Fire,' Tanager said, 'is to snatch the very heart of it. Let's work together, and perhaps we can do this.' The pair asked tiny Hummingbird to hold their baskets, and Hummingbird said he would if they would let him carry back at least one coal. 'I want Man to know that I helped, too,' he told them.

"Tanager and Finch flew side by side to the top of the tree and dove together into it. Hummingbird, his wings spinning until they were only a blur, waited and watched and tried hard to hold on to three baskets. Just as he heard a triumphant shout from his friends, one of those baskets slipped from his slender bill and was blown away on the wind. It was a sad Hummingbird who greeted Tanager and Finch when they flew down to where he waited. Not that he recognized either one at first; both were clothed in the Fire they had succeeded in plucking from the hollow tree."

"And they are still red?" Rain Drop asked.

Egret nodded. "You have seen for yourself that Tanager is red, and Finch is the bird we know as Crested Redbird now," she said.

"Poor Hummingbird," another child murmured. "He wanted so much to help."

Dancing Egret looked at her. "Hummingbird got his wish in the end," she said. "Even though he had lost his basket, Finch and Tanager felt so sorry for him that they let him carry a single glowing ember in his mouth as they took Fire back to Man. And we know that is true, for to this day every hummingbird we see has a beautiful red throat."

The children who had gathered to hear the Legend cheered the Singer so lustily that Dancing Egret found herself promising to tell them another tomorrow. "I guess birds really do help people," Rain Drop allowed as, reluctantly, she slid off of Egret's lap. "But"—she grinned—"I do not see any red on Mockingbird!"

Egret laughed as the irrepressible child scampered off with her friends, then started as, behind her, someone else laughed just as heartily. She swung around and saw Chattering Squirrel.

"I will never be able to Sing Legends the way you do," Rain Drop's sister said, sobering abruptly. "You make them so real that even I can believe the impossible when you tell them."

"If you tell yourself that the stories are pure fancy, you will never be able to Sing them as they deserve to be sung," Dancing Egret said just as soberly. "You can't simply learn the words of Legends, you know; you must take them into your soul as the bay absorbs the gold the Sun God pours upon it. Once you can accept that what you call the impossible truly happened, those who hear you Sing will believe also. And who can know what it was like when our ancestors were young? In those days, man was probably in perfect harmony with his world. Because he was, I expect many things happened that we would label magical today."

And that was what was wrong with her brother, she realized suddenly. Calusa was not in harmony with his world, never could be as long as he regarded himself as the center of it. And he could not be blamed for the way he was; from his earliest days everybody had encouraged him to focus on himself, on his own wants and needs, instead of teaching him to recognize the spiritual oneness of all living things and their natural dependence on one another. Which meant that she, as much as anyone, was responsible for the very selfishness and shallowness that made her despair of her brother. And didn't that suggest a certain lack of harmony in her own soul? It was a lack she would take pains to correct, she vowed silently, and soon.

Squirrel had been digesting what Egret had said. "I never looked at Legends that way before," she said finally. "I considered them stories, wonderfully entertaining stories, but that was all." She shook her head at her own obtuseness. "I guess I was not meant to be a Legend Singer, Dancing Egret."

"Are you saying that you can never see them as something other than mere stories?"

Chattering Squirrel shook her head again. "No. Now that you have made me think about it, I'll look at them differently from now on. Eventually I may even learn to Sing them properly." She sent a sideways glance toward her aunt. "It will take time, however. So I'm glad that you are Singing again, Egret. My mother always said that you would, but that you must come to it on your own."

"Brown Pelican obviously had more faith in me than I had in myself," Egret said. And not only Brown Pelican; so had her father, and Shore Walker. Kwambu had been right in what he'd said to her, even if she had been slow to acknowledge the truth of it. She wished he were here now, so she could tell him so, but Calusa had sent him to the eastern coast, and then into the north, to trade. "I do have faith in you, though," she said to her niece. "It will not be long before you are Singing Legends as though you had been born to do so."

Squirrel sighed. "I hope so. Swift Eagle might finally see me as a woman if I become a Singer. Sometimes I worry that he will spend his whole life thinking I am no older than Rain Drop is now."

There was such misery in her expression that Egret ached for her. "You only need to wholly embrace the Legends that you already know," she assured her "and all of the islanders—including Swift Eagle—will recognize you as a Singer." She recalled suddenly a plan she had abandoned when Shore Walker died. "You know, there was a time when I thought about encouraging all of the town's maidens to learn to chant. They are not all destined to be true Legend Singers, of course, but most Calusa women have been blessed with lovely voices, and some versions of our Legends would sound even better if sung by a chorus. Why don't you speak with your friends and see if you can form such a group? You could all sing on ceremonial days, as the children used to."

Squirrel looked anxiously at Egret. "Surely they will be doing so again? If you go on Singing Legends for the children, you'll also teach them how to sing the simpler ones, won't you?"

Dancing Egret laughed and hugged her. "If you will work with the maidens, I will work with the children. I had honestly thought I could never Sing again, but it seems that even a woman as old as I am still has considerable to learn about herself!"

And, oh, but she was fortunate to have a friend willing to teach her what she needed to know. As she would tell Kwambu the moment he returned to Calusa's town.

"You must look into your crystal," Palm Tree Bending said urgently. "How else can we know what to do, Moon of Winter?"

Outina and White Tailed Stag had been imprisoned on the French barque for three days, and not even the Principal Men had been able to think of a way to bring about their release.

"The Frenchmen want food," Moon of Winter said. "My crystal cannot tell us where to find food when there is none to be had." Her voice was sharp with anxiety; because ample provisions had not yet been brought to him, D'Ottigni had declared his intention of trading their Holata to an avowed enemy. If the townspeople would not furnish the French with the food they needed, then Saturiba would be given the opportunity to do so . . . in return for having Outina delivered into his hands.

"And we have nothing left to send except acorn meal and fish," Walks Tall Woman said dolefully. She seemed to have shriveled since her son and grandson were taken captive, and gray had insinuated itself into the hair that swept back from her temples.

But it was the Shaman, pacing agitatedly back and forth, who persuaded Moon of Winter to do as Palm Tree Bending asked. "Our town, and all of the towns that owe allegiance to

Outina, cannot go long without a Holata," he said abruptly. "Our warriors will soon respond to the summons we sent them, and if Outina has not been released by the time they get home, I am afraid we must accept that he never will be. Which means that Hawk Flying High will have to prepare himself at once to assume the status of Holata."

"He is too young for that!" The objection came simultaneously from Walks Tall Woman and Moon of Winter.

Watches for Omens looked sternly at both of them. "He is a man grown," he said, "and Outina himself would recommend this step be taken if he could get word to us."

"That is so," Palm Tree Bending said quietly, and both Outina's mother and Hawk's felt instantly ashamed that she could deal with such a prospect when they could not.

"I will consult the crystal," Moon of Winter said dully, "and ask it how we can meet the French demands." But her stomach churned as she drew her crystal from its pouch. Help me, help all of us, she prayed. My son is good and brave and intelligent, but he still has much to learn before he can be the kind of Holata my people need. Please; show this humble woman, this frightened woman, what we should do.

After a long moment, during which the blood pounded in her ears like a poorly played ceremonial drum, she unfolded her clasped hands and looked down into her crystal.

This time, no meaningless interweaving of light and shadow taunted her; the crystal's shimmer had been erased by a pale mist that, rising like smoke, threatened to surround and obliterate Moon of Winter as well. She shivered, squeezed her eyes shut, told herself that when she looked again the mist would be gone. But fear whispered that it might have thickened instead and trapped her within it, transformed her into a chrysalis with no hope whatsoever of sprouting wings and freeing itself, with no hope . . . no hope . . .

"Moon of Winter!"

The terrified woman sagged with relief. If her friends were speaking to her, then she had not disappeared into the mists!

"The crystal responded?" The moment she opened her eyes, Watches for Omens asked the question she dreaded to hear.

She struggled for composure, struggled even harder to find an answer for him. "Messengers must go to all of Outina's Townchiefs," she said falteringly, wondering as she voiced it where the thought had come from. "Every town must empty its granaries and send the food here. Then we will have enough to satisfy the Frenchmen and they will set free Outina and White Tailed Stag." The three who stood around her looked at one another. Here was the answer they had been seeking! "There is more," Moon of Winter said, moistening dry lips with a tongue only a little less dry. And although she still did not know how or why she knew what to say, she told them everything that must be done.

Chapter 36

⊷ ⊷

Generally, when Kwambu returned to Outina after a lengthy absence, everyone gathered around to hear news from the far-flung provinces of the Timucua and from the southern territories. Today, however, when he had information of considerable import to divulge, they all seemed more interested in talking than in listening.

"I would not be here now," Holata Outina announced as soon as he had welcomed the trader, "were it not for your wife and her crystal."

"Nor would White Tailed Stag," Palm Tree Bending put in, smiling up at her younger son.

"And Hawk and Fox and I helped to drive away the French. We put them to flight without the food they thought to steal from us!" This from Outina's oldest, while Kwambu's two sons vied with each other to convince their father that this was no idle boast.

"Let Kwambu sit and relax," Moon of Winter told them. "He will hear the whole story soon enough." She handed him a dipper of cool water and shushed her daughter, who apparently felt Kwambu would enjoy the tale more if she were the one to tell it.

The trader guided his wife down beside him, invited Kaia to sit on his other side. Moon of Winter's face was a trifle drawn, he noticed, and Walks Tall Woman seemed to have misplaced her customary imperiousness. Whatever had occurred had been of some moment, then; his own news could wait. He looked toward Outina.

"White Tailed Stag and I were taken prisoner by the French soldiers," the Holata told him. "They demanded quantities of food as ransom for us, food we did not have." He shrugged his broad shoulders. "They do not have much sense, these Frenchmen."

"They are deceivers," Walks Tall Woman said harshly. "They came here—to the Principal House!—as guests, and then seized my son and my grandson. And they struck me, struck me so hard I landed on the floor!" She sounded more like her old self, which relieved Kwambu somewhat. Coming home should always mean a return to the familiar.

"But you are here now, you and White Tailed Stag," Kwambu said to Outina. "How did that come about?"

Holata Outina grinned around the handful of dates he was chewing. "That is a question you should ask your wife."

Kwambu looked at Moon of Winter, who only shook her head. "Let others tell it," she murmured.

"We asked her to consult her crystal," Palm Tree Bending said, "Walks Tall Woman, the Shaman, and I. We could think of nothing else to do, nor could the Principal Men."

"The Principal Men did send for us to come home," Long Path Follower said. "A good thing, too; what the crystal said to do could not have been done without our help." He punched his younger brother playfully. "Stag might still be a captive of the French were it not for us, and I do not intend to let him forget it!"

"But your crystal guided you, revealed a plan to you?" Kwambu, not to be diverted, directed the query to his wife.

Moon of Winter hesitated, nodded slowly, then turned her head as the Shaman came into the house.

"I heard you were home, trader," Watches for Omens said, frowning as his joints creaked audibly when the rest made room for him to sit. "They have told you what happened?"

"I know that Moon of Winter's crystal played a part in it," Kwambu said, "but there has not been time enough for me to discover what exactly it was."

The Shaman lifted his veined hands, held up his wrinkled face so that the autumn sunlight, insinuating itself through the thatch, could caress him with warmth. "Like the Sun God, your wife's crystal smiles upon Outina's people," he said solemnly. "By communing with her crystal, Moon of Winter was able to counsel us, trader. She showed us how to outwit the French soldiers and rescue our Holata. Blessed be the day that Moon of Winter was declared a true Daughter of the Sun and granted powers we have not yet fully realized."

"And how did you outwit the French?" Kwambu asked his wife when the Shaman did not go on. But once again she shook her head; it was clear that she did not want to explain.

"She had us dispatch couriers to all nearby towns and villages," Walks Tall Woman said. If her niece would not tell it, somebody must! "They told how Outina was a prisoner, and begged each Townchief to send food to help ransom him."

"More than that," Palm Tree Bending put in. "At Moon of Winter's suggestion, we asked that warriors dressed like berdaches deliver the food to our town. The French are accustomed to seeing berdaches, and no longer pay heed to men who wear their hair hanging down their backs and dress in women's garments."

"When they came," Walks Tall Woman said, thrusting in when her son's wife paused for breath, "they piled the food in the compound and pretended to leave. Actually, they concealed themselves in the forest, put their hair back into topknots and tore off their skirts. Then they waited, with their weapons, for a sign from us."

"By the time the French knew that there was food in the town for them, we hunters had returned." Long Path Follower was quick to pick up the story. "We were met not far from here by a half-dozen young boys who told us not to show ourselves but to stash the animal flesh we had brought back and prepare for a battle." His teeth flashed in his bronze face. "They did not have to ask a second time," he said. "We already knew what the traitorous soldiers had done and were eager for a fight."

Hawk and Fox nodded vigorous agreement. "The waiting wasn't easy, though," Red Fox Barking admitted.

Kwambu hid a smile. Fox had grown to estimable manhood, but he had not left all of his youthful impatience behind.

"Next we sent word to the French ship," Palm Tree Bending said. It seemed strange that the women were doing most of the talking when usually they merely listened to what the men had to say; strange, but rather pleasant. "If the soldiers brought Outina and Stag to the Principal House, we told them, then we would gladly give them many sacks of grain and dried vegetables."

"According to the Saturiban interpreter, the French did not believe the messenger at first," Holata Outina said. "For some reason"—he slapped his angled thigh and guffawed—"they did not trust my people! But they arranged for six soldiers to go back with the messenger and see for themselves if there was food to be had."

"They were amazed to see such a great heap of sacks." At last Kaia found opportunity to speak. "They didn't know that many were stuffed halfway with corncobs and other garbage. We maidens knew," she added smugly. "The warriors that brought them here told us."

Surprise unleashed Moon of Winter's tongue. "You did not tell anyone else," she said.

Her daughter shook her curly head. "We decided not to. That way, nobody but us had to worry that the soldiers would find out too soon they had been tricked."

Kwambu hugged his daughter to him, wished he could embrace all who sat around him. They had known the risks they were taking, and had not let it daunt them. How magnificent they were, and how courageous, every one of them!

"As is usual with the pale-fleshes," Outina said dryly, "greed was their undoing. I understand that they did open a sack or two"—he raised his eyebrows, and the women nodded—"but they were so anxious to have the food, and so certain they had succeeded in what they'd set out to do, that they did not examine them closely before they raced back to the ship and urged the other soldiers to return to the town with them. There was far too much for only six men to carry, you see."

"That was when we warriors, and those who had come here from Outina's other towns, hid ourselves among the huge trees that border the path to the river," Hawk Flying High said. "Moon of Winter's message had said we must not interfere with the soldiers when they marched into the town, and we did not. Although there were some"—he looked sternly at his brother—"who wanted to. Instead, we waited until they had slung the heavy sacks over their shoulders and started back to their ship."

"Surely some of the soldiers acted as guards, however," Kwambu said.

Red Fox Barking laughed. "They did. And carried lighted

fuses so there would be no delay in firing their guns. But that did not stop us. As soon as all the soldiers were on the open path, we pelted them with arrows. Well-aimed arrows they were, too."

"Many soldiers fell before the guards could fire back at us," Long Path Follower confirmed. "But when they did, some proved as skilled at aiming as our warriors were." A shadow fell across his face; one of those slain had been a good friend. "But there were more of us than there were soldiers," he went on after a moment, "and we had had time to plan our strategy. Whenever a soldier prepared to fire, for instance, those he aimed at dropped to the ground and rolled out of the way, then leaped up and directed more arrows at the Frenchmen."

Fox was grinning again. "As they fled, the men dropped the sacks they were toting," he said, "and few soldiers got very far. Warriors were waiting for them farther along the path."

"In the end," Hawk finished, "Black Wolf Running said to let those who had escaped death return to the ship. We knew our Holata was safely home, and the French had been cheated of the food they had stolen, so we agreed with him. And watching the French panic as they made haste to sail away was almost as entertaining as the fighting had been."

"I think the Frenchmen will avoid Outina in the future," the Holata said with a twinkle in his eye.

Kwambu did not smile. "You are right," he said somberly. "There are none left to come here."

Bewilderment spawned silence. Then, "What do you mean?" Outina asked.

"I was in Oathkaqua before I came home," the trader said, "and spoke with a fisherman who had witnessed something I am going to find difficult to describe." He looked around the circle of intent faces. "It seems that the Spanish have decided to visit these shores again," he told them. "Their leader, a man called Menendez, came ashore first in Oathkaqua's principal town. Holata Oathkaqua is an old man now, and wants no trouble with anyone if it can be avoided. So he agreed to meet with the Spaniard. In truth, no ill came of the meeting. Oathkaqua told me that the man wanted only to know the location of the French fort. Once he had that information, Menendez went on his way."

Outina was instantly alert. "Do the Spanish mean to ally with the French?" he asked.

"No. Quite the opposite, as it turns out. They wasted no

time driving the Frenchmen from the fort, after which they set fire to it. A few of the French escaped, I understand, and have probably sailed back to their homeland. But"—his voice harshened as he came to the part of the story it sickened him to tell—"this Menendez rounded up most of the fort's soldiers and had their hands bound behind their backs."

"That is good," Walks Tall Woman said. "It is how the French treated my poor son, and my grandson; I am glad they were made to learn how it feels to be taken prisoner!"

Kwambu turned to her, but his words were meant for everyone. "The French," he said gravely, "did not take Outina and White Tailed Stag to a deserted stretch of ground and slay them. Which was what Menendez did. He spared those who claimed to be musicians, and any who would swear allegiance to the God Menendez worships. And he took into his care two Spaniards who came originally from Calusa territory. But the rest—and there were hundreds—were forced to march to an inlet that lies north of Oathkaqua's territory. Their hands remained tied and they had no weapons, but Menendez ordered his men to fire upon them . . . and to continue doing so until every Frenchman was dead."

"That is good," Walks Tall Woman said again. "And this Spaniard must be good to have been so quick to punish evil men."

"They call it massacre," Outina said heavily, "when defenseless people are slain." His eyes, unlike his mother's, were troubled.

"Yet I am glad that we need not worry about French soldiers coming here again," Palm Tree Bending said softly. She knew what her husband meant by "massacre," but she could not find it in her heart to feel pity for people who had treated him so shamefully.

"We need not worry about the French," Moon of Winter said. "Now we will have to worry about the Spanish."

Hawk Flying High smiled at her. "We dealt with the French soldiers," he said reassuringly. "If it becomes necessary, we can deal with Spanish soldiers also."

"That is what Outina's uncle thought, many years ago," his mother reminded him. "You have heard what happened then."

Kwambu cleared his throat. "The Spanish leader, when he spoke with Oathkaqua, vowed that he wants to be friends with all the people who live in this country, that he wishes to be a 'big brother' to them."

Some of the worry disappeared from the Holata's eyes. "If he means that, and if he truly understands what it means to be any man's brother, then perhaps my mother is right." He sighed. "And if this Menendez can be believed in the first place." He came to his feet, nodded toward Kwambu. "Thank you for bringing me the news," he said. "I will take it to my Principal Men. We must plan now what we will do if the Spanish should come here."

"If they do, it is not likely to be soon," Kwambu said. "I have heard since I left Oathkaqua that the Spaniards are making arrangements to sail south."

A smile slid across Outina's face. "I'll wager my old enemy Saturiba is glad of that. It was bad enough that the French settled in his territory and brought him grief; more pale-fleshes would surely be as welcome to him as a burr in his sleeping robe! And if the Spaniards will soon be heading south, then it is even less likely that we will see them here."

"The couriers I met were not entirely certain that all of the Spanish would be leaving on the ships," Kwambu cautioned.

Outina nodded. "I will tell the Principal Men that also," he said, and went out into the compound.

The others came to their feet and prepared to go on with the day's work. "I suppose that now you and my father will go for a walk," Kaia said to her mother. "And I have scarcely had time to greet him properly." But she smiled, turning complaint into jest. She was a young woman now and wiser than she had been.

Moon of Winter returned the smile. "So we shall," she said serenely. "But you may have him to yourself as soon as we return."

"She will not have me for very long, I am afraid," Kwambu said ruefully as he and his wife made for their place of magnolias. "Calusa must be told of Menendez's plans to sail south, as I am sure you've guessed. And I must go first to Apalachee. Calusa has decided that he does not dress grandly enough for a Headchief, and that he must have pearls to augment the quantities of gold with which he already decorates himself. I dare not return without them, or he will be so angry he will refuse to hear me out when I try to tell him about Menendez." He shook his head in exasperation; Calusa was so unlike his father, who—except for ceremonial occasions—had been content to dress much as everyone around him did. Yet no one, *no one*, ever doubted that he was Headchief.

Moon of Winter fingered the cluster of pearls that dangled from a thong shorter than the one supporting the pouch holding her crystal. Why couldn't Kwambu take these to Calusa? She would gladly give them up if that would let him stay longer with her.

Her husband knew at once what she was considering. "No, my dear. Those pearls are a reminder of your uncle, who loved you very much. And"—a smile lit his whole face—"of the humble trader who, at the time, did not realize why he was so eager for you to have them. Much as I would like to spend the extra time with you, I will go to Apalachee before I hurry back to the island. Fontaneda and Gomez, the Spaniards Menendez found at the French fort, are probably already urging the man to reclaim the 'Spanish treasure' that is stored in Calusa's town. Always it has fretted at them that Calusa keeps, or uses for trade, whatever his people salvage from downed ships."

"But if this Men-en-dez is sincere in what he told Oathkaqua," Moon of Winter said, both glad and sorry that Kwambu had rejected her unvoiced offer, "then perhaps he will ignore them."

"Do you think it possible that Menendez is sincere?"

She pondered the question, shook her head. "I cannot bring myself to trust any white man," she confessed. "I cannot believe that Walks Tall Woman, who surely remembers as well as I do how the man called De Soto murdered my uncle and all of his warriors, can even suggest that one of them might be *good*."

"She is not young anymore," Kwambu said, "and seeing Outina and White Tailed Stag seized by the French aged her even further. I expect she only hopes that Menendez might be a good man because she dares not let herself think otherwise. She knows, as I am sure you do, that what worked this time might not work again." He smiled. "I do not mean that your crystal would fail you," he said, "but only that circumstances might go against you. Yet I must say that I was proud when I heard how cleverly the French were outwitted, and that the plan to do so came from you."

Moon of Winter halted so abruptly that the drifted leaves she was walking through eddied around her ankles. "I do not know where that plan came from," she said miserably. "What I do know is that it did not come from my crystal. When I looked into it, I saw only mist, Kwambu. Nothing more."

"Yet you told your people what to do, and how to do it."

She nodded. "I did. But I only told them what was sensible. Spiritual guidance is not needed for that!"

Her husband chuckled. "You have just spoken words of wisdom, my love. And I am even more proud of you for being the one to see that common sense could provide the answers you were looking for."

Before she could protest that she deserved no praise for acting out of desperation, Kwambu swept her up in his strong arms. Moon of Winter gasped, then realized that they had come upon the glade where the magnolias grew. Although many of the trees that inhabited the forest lifted naked branches to the sky, the canopy of the magnolia retained its glossy green; it would shelter them as efficiently, and as beautifully, as it had done during warmer months. And the ground beneath it was nicely carpeted with leaves shed by its less fortunate brothers. Which, considering the chill in the air, was also something to be thankful for.

Leafy carpet notwithstanding, Moon of Winter was glad when Kwambu removed from her shoulders the cloak she had flung around herself and spread it beneath the magnolia. Suddenly she laughed. "I think perhaps we are growing too old for this sort of thing," she said. "I have been wondering how cold the ground will be, and there was a time I would never have spared thought for the weather when I came here with you."

Kwambu sat, pulled her down beside him, put his arms around her. "We may have grown old enough for our bones to complain when the wind shows its teeth," he told her, "but we will never be too old for this"—he eased her backward, bent his head, and teased at one upthrusting breast with his tongue—"or this"—his hands caressed a delightful curve of hip as he coaxed her skirt away from it—"or this."

Now his fingers were exploring the sensitive folds that surrounded her womanhood, and Moon of Winter was suddenly indifferent to the brisk breezes that sent the leaves above them into a frenzied dance. And the shivers that rippled through her owed nothing to the coldness of the ground.

Sailing south was like traveling through the year, the man on the flagship thought. When they embarked from near the blackened remains of the French fort, it had been all autumn bleakness, with a suggestion of winter in the winds that swelled the sheets. A little farther south, just below the place where his ship had first made landfall—due to stupidity on the part of certain compatriots in Havana, who had proven themselves masters of misdirection—the trees they could see from the ship's deck were crowned with leaves, and the sun shining on the flotilla actually had some warmth to it. And now that they were approaching the elongated tip of the peninsula, the land they looked upon was lushly verdant, endowed with eternal summer, and the wind that continued to bear them to their destination had lost every trace of chill. The men he had left behind to set up camp would have been even more disgruntled could they know what they were being deprived of.

Above the creaking of lines and the keening of the wind as sail was reefed, over the bump-thump-bump of a keg illsecured by a careless seaman, and the slap and swoosh of waves breaking around the bow, came the muted blare of trumpets, the thin wail of a fife, the measured pulse of a softly beaten drum. The French music makers Menendez had generously pardoned for both their national allegiance and their heresy were being instructed by his own excellent musicians. The Adelantado's booted foot tapped in time with the infectious rhythm. It occurred to him that, had his talents not taken him in a different direction, Pedro Menendez might well have become a musician of merit and renown. But the spread of the Gospel was far more important than blowing a horn or beating a drum, and this Headchief Calusa that Fontaneda had told him so much about might well hold the key to dispersing God's word throughout la Florida's lower peninsula.

The Adelantado thought he would be able to win Calusa's friendship without too much difficulty. The native leaders he had met so far had responded favorably to the overtures he had made to them. The one called Saturiba had been wary at first, but once assured that the Spanish fully intended to grow their own food, he had accepted with commendable graciousness the mirrors, knives, scissors, and bells the Adelantado had arranged to be given to him, had even offered gifts in return. This Headchief Calusa would likely be as easily impressed, and as amenable.

Menendez had not been overly interested in tales of Calusa's wealth; he had not been sent here to retrieve treasure looted from sunken Spanish ships. But a wealthy Headchief was certain to rule hundreds upon hundreds of subjects, subjects who would look up to him and follow wherever he led. If this Calusa could be converted to Catholicism, then those he ruled would be quick to embrace it also. Not only would that be an accomplishment to boast of, Christianized Indians would make a fine source of labor for the Spanish colonists who would eventually populate this country. Before anything else, however, Menendez meant to rescue and return to their homeland the many Christian slaves that Fontaneda insisted were being held by Headchief Calusa. Unconsciously, the Adelantado's hands folded themselves into a prayerful position; God grant that his son might be among the Christians Calusa had taken captive. If instead he had been one of those already sacrificed to some heathen deity . . . !

He breathed deep, let salt-laced air fill his lungs and calm him. He would be wise to think of something else, perhaps of those who had explored this land before him. One and all, they had squandered their energies trying to find gems and precious metals, had been blind to the real wealth this part of the New World offered: vast stretches of fertile land, and aborigines who could be taught to use their considerable muscle in the service of God and Spain.

Fortunately, Pedro Menendez de Aviles was not blind. He was a man of vision, and his vision drew him onward like a latter-day Holy Grail.

Chapter 37

⟻ ⟾

"No," Dancing Egret said. "I do not wish to be here when that man comes." She turned in a half circle as she spoke so that her brother would hear every emphatic word. Calusa, clad in bright red breeches, was strutting back and forth to encourage the soft fabric to billow around his muscular legs. A vest, yellow as the sun, hugged his upper torso, and drooping over one eye was what he called a "hat." This was vivid green, and he had fastened to it two gold brooches and three egret plumes. He looked, his sister thought, like an oversized, multiplumaged ibis. "I am not tempted by his promise to bring fine gifts to the women of your family. A multitude of gifts would not change my opinion of the Spanish."

She hadn't spoken so bluntly to her brother in a long time, but he was too absorbed in preening himself to take offense.

"I think you are unwise to let him come here," she went on. "The Spanish are our enemies, and always have been."

Calusa climbed nimbly to his carved bench on the uppermost tier, seating himself with care. "I wonder if he will bring more of those 'biscuits' he served to me on his ship," he said, anticipation lighting his eyes. "When you have tasted them, you will never be satisfied with zamia bread again. The drink the Spanish call 'wine,' however"—he grimaced—"I would advise you to refuse. It is more sour than green plums."

"Since I will not be here during the feasting, that does not matter to me." Anger and frustration combined to sharpen her voice; why wouldn't Calusa accept that she meant what she said?

But he was fingering the gold chains draped around his neck. "If the trader had returned with my pearls," he said, "I might feel that I am properly dressed to receive our visitors. Surely he should have come back by now? If he is lingering in Outina with that woman of his, I shall be most displeased."

"You sent him to trade with Tequesta, and to carry salt into the Lake country," Egret said, stung on Kwambu's behalf. "From there he was to take dates to Oathkaqua and exchange them for ocher and flint. If those things weren't available from Oathkaqua, then he was to go farther into Timucuan country for them." She did not remind her brother that Oathkaqua no longer went out of his way to supply the Calusa with goods. Years before, when his daughter was abducted while being sent as bride to the Headchief, Oathkaqua had been incensed that no ransom was offered for her and little attempt made to claim revenge. Since then, his attitude toward the son of an old friend had been cold and impersonal, and he traded with the Calusa now only when it suited his purposes. "Kwambu might have had to travel to several Timucuan towns before he found ocher and flint," Egret finished. "He is hardly overdue, Calusa."

"Perhaps not, but I must remember to warn him next time that he is not to dawdle. Menendez would be truly impressed if he saw me wearing pearls." He brooded, then brightened suddenly. "But our singers will impress him, in any event. He is a man fond of music, I discovered." He looked directly at Egret for the first time. "You did as I told you and arranged for the maidens to sing for him? And for the children to sing also?"

"Chattering Squirrel has been rehearsing the maidens," Egret said tightly, "and I have taught the youngsters a new song." After a moment, she brightened, too. "I must be with them when they sing," she said, hoping reasonable argument might sway her brother, "so I cannot possibly be with you during the feasting."

But for all his vanity and self-absorption, Calusa was alert to her ploy. "Squirrel can direct both the children and the maidens," he said. "You, Egret, will be here with me to welcome our guest." He turned on her his most enchanting smile. "You will not regret it, I promise you," he said. "I know you think me foolish at times, especially when I seem disinclined to trouble myself with matters you label important, but I know as well as you that the Spanish can be a threat to our people. I chose deliberately to meet with Menendez, even to invite him to my home. For I have a plan, Egret, a marvelous plan. And when it has been fully executed, you will see that we have no need to fear the Spaniards who have come this time." He smiled again. "You may even decide that your brother, far from being foolish, is remarkably clever."

He stood up, smoothed his yellow vest and shook out his scarlet breeches. "Remarkably clever," he repeated, coming down to stand beside her. "But for my plan to be put into effect, I need you with me when Menendez comes. And"—his smile faded and his face assumed a sternness it rarely displayed—"you will be here, Dancing Egret, for I will not have it otherwise."

The brigantine Pedro Menendez had transferred to rode at anchor, the prow of a second brig nosing at its stern. The artillery on both ships had been placed on the landside, with hail shot at the ready. Having Headchief Calusa aboard yesterday, even with twenty fierce-looking warriors attending him, was one thing; the Adelantado had been in control of the situation. But to go ashore this morning and visit the Headchief's island home was a situation altogether different, and he was too experienced a soldier not to take precautions.

He looked beyond the harbor to where the masts of his larger ships were inscribed against a sky incredibly blue. It promised to be a fair day, and Menendez meant to make the most of it. Fontaneda had neglected to mention the Headchief's age, so it had been something of a surprise to find that he was so young; the other native leaders Menendez had met had been older and, possibly, wiser. There could be advantage in dealing with one who was little more than a youth, Menendez reflected. This young chief might be less averse to the changes he would be bringing into his life. The man had certainly enthused enough over the silk breeches and doublet he had been given; the presents planned for his wives would doubtless leave him ecstatic.

His wives. That was a problem Menendez would not attempt to solve as yet, even though one of the two was rumored to be so close a relation to the Headchief that their union must surely be regarded as incest. Once this Calusa had been brought to the worship of the true God, she was the woman he would have to give up.

But that was in the future. For now, Menendez was prepared to compliment extravagantly as many wives and concubines as Calusa introduced to him. He looked down at the square of parchment he had been studying earlier. Before Menendez sailed south, Fontaneda had helped him to write down, phonetically, certain words in the Calusa tongue: *beautiful, elegant, charming, gentle,* and a score of phrases incorporating those words. Menendez planned to distribute them as lavishly as a bee spreads pollen, and for the same purpose: to encourage fruition and growth. Today would mark the germination of civilization among the Indians of the southern peninsula, and that would be no small achievement.

"I am ready to go ashore when you are, Adelantado."

Menendez came out of his introspection, nodded at the short, bandy-legged man who had come up behind him. The brig's captain had agreed to deliver to the ships waiting in deeper water the Christians Calusa held in bondage, for the Headchief had vowed to have them brought to his house after the Spanish dined with him there. He had promised also that he would not prevent their leaving his town. The Adelantado told himself it was unlikely that his son would be one of the group, yet even a practical man is not immune to hope. "You have arranged for our escort?" he asked the skipper.

The short man laughed. "We will be escorted by two hundred arquebusiers," he said. "Everyone wanted to volunteer. Somehow they have heard that the Calusa collected so much treasure from foundered ships that they give emeralds and rubies to their children to play with!"

"Only cretins believe absurd rumor," Menendez snapped. "And there will be no consorting with the natives, and no attempts to relieve them of so-called treasure. I trust you made that clear?"

"I repeated to them your orders: that our purpose is to establish friendly relations with these Indians, and to win them to Christ," the skipper said stiffly. "I was mostly jesting before, Adelantado." What could it matter if savages were relieved of what they considered baubles? The soldiers, whose wages might or might not be given them in the end, could return home with something to show for their travels, and the natives would never know the difference. Still, it was not recommended to cross Menendez. "They will conduct themselves like gentlemen," he said.

"If they do not, you will answer for it," Menendez responded. He watched a hulking man cross the deck. "Captain De Reinoso will be going ashore with us," he said.

"So will a full troop of musicians, countless singers and dancers, and that ridiculous dwarf who is such a favorite of yours," De Reinoso said as he joined them. "Plus servants carrying linens and silver and a table to lay them on, and two friars to set up a cross in what these heathen refer to as a town." Francisco de Reinoso's features were too small for his fleshy face, but his expression was amiable. As it invariably was when he had dealings with those who outranked him.

Menendez smoothed his beard, set his hat more firmly on his head. "Then let us debark," he said. "And let us do our utmost to favorably impress the young Headchief and his people. Where a man can win respect, he is almost certain to receive submission."

Dancing Egret, from a seat a little lower than her brother's, looked out over the town. She watched without expression as soldiers set up a flag in the courtyard and, alongside it, a tall post with a crossbar nailed to it. Inwardly, she shuddered; she had seen such a thing happen before, many years ago, in Ucita's town. At that time, however, there had not been men playing upon some kind of flute, and drummers, and others who coaxed musical sounds from gourd-shaped things with strings stretched across their hollow cores. Nor had there been a host of singers and dancers being directed by the waving arms of a man who surely stood no taller than Calusa's hip. She had taken him for a child until he turned toward the mound and she saw his face. He was agile as any child, nonetheless; now, as he led the Spanish leader up the ramp, he postured and pranced and turned handsprings at every level.

Obedient to her brother's instructions, Egret signaled to Chattering Squirrel, who stood just outside the house with the assembled singing groups. As the heavily bearded man entered, the sweetly pitched voices of the maidens began a Legend, the Legend about the creation of the Calusa. The Spaniard would not understand a word, of course, but Egret hoped her brother would listen to it and be reminded of much that he seemed to have forgotten. And Squirrel had done a magnificent job of teaching her peers; if this Menendez was as fond of music as Calusa thought, he would recognize that the island's singers were superior to those he had brought along. She would be sure to tell Chattering Squirrel that later and give her the praise she deserved. She would tell her, too, how one young warrior, Swift Eagle, had been watching Squirrel with bemusement in his handsome face. Clearly, he no longer looked upon her as a bothersome little sister!

Other Spaniards followed Menendez inside and ranged themselves along two sides of the enormous room. The men and women already there—Calusa's advisors and their families, all of Calusa's kin except his two wives, the War Leader and priest, most of the town's artisans and warriors—studied them covertly as they did so. Dancing Egret, although her eyes appeared to be modestly lowered, focused all her attention on Menendez himself.

He was not a tall man, yet he carried himself as though he were. His features were firmly molded, what she could see of them; dark beard and mustaches virtually concealed his lower face. He did not look like a man inclined to laughter.

He did smile briefly, however, when Calusa rose and—with extravagant gestures—insisted that the Adelantado occupy his bench. Dancing Egret fought down a surge of rage when the Spaniard accepted the offer as though it were his due. How dare he! And now her brother was going down on one knee before him and turning up his hands. No Calusa before him had ever stooped to pay homage; it was unheard of, what he was doing! And he was actually calling upon the clan representatives who made up his Council to do likewise. What was her brother thinking of? Was this part of his "marvelous plan"? If so, more than ever Dancing Egret wanted no part of it.

She watched the counselors as they resumed their seats, and knew she was not alone in her disgust. Twisting River and Shark Fin, those ancients who had all their lives been adversaries, seemed to be in accord for once as they whispered agitatedly together. Prowling Panther, as was his habit, kept his expression unreadable, but Egret did not miss the glance he sent his wife's way, and the tightening of Pelican's lips said how the both of them felt about all of this. Growling Bear's innate tact had patently been put to the test. And poor old Vision Seeker, suspecting that Calusa might order his priest to pay homage also, had stalked to the door, his stiff back and bristling brows announcing more clearly than words that he had no intention of doing so. Ever.

Either Calusa had recognized this or he had never intended to make Vision Seeker defer to a Spanish Christian. In any event, he did not summon the priest. "You will eat now?" he asked Menendez instead, signing to the Spanish slave he had chosen to act as interpreter. The man relayed the question, and Menendez shook his head. "First," he replied through the interpreter, "I have words I wish to say to this lady here."

With a feeling of horror, Egret realized that she was the one the Spaniard referred to. And was looking at. Looking at directly. She lowered her head again; this was not right.

"Come, Egret," called her brother. "The Adelantado wishes to speak with you."

He meant it, and this was neither the time nor the place to argue with him. Woodenly, she rose and went to take the seat Calusa was indicating, the seat between his and the Spaniard's.

Menendez clapped his hands and the spry little man who had come in with him ran forward, clambered to the tier Egret was occupying and laid some sort of green drapery across her lap.

"This gown is for you." To Egret's amazement, the words came not from the interpreter but from Menendez himself. They were spoken falteringly, yet she understood them well enough. "Its beauty fades before the beauty of the woman who will wear it," he went on, stumbling over the longer words. "Your Headchief is a fortunate man, to have a wife of such loveliness."

Dancing Egret did not protest, did not even move. Like a

figure carved from cypress, she sat rigidly, kept her face from registering anything whatsoever.

Calusa, who had been puzzling over Menendez's rendition of his host's language, had finally deciphered his words. He opened his eyes wide and roared with laughter. "Tell the Adelantado that Dancing Egret is my sister, not my wife," he said to the interpreter.

Menendez, when he understood, did not laugh. He should have known, he told himself; smooth-skinned face notwithstanding, this woman was at least thirty-five years old. And she was a long way from being the beauty he had called her. But Menendez had not reached a position of eminence by thinking slowly. Gravely, he spoke one more time. "That does not make you any less lovely," he said to Egret, "nor any less deserving of my gift."

Calusa was grinning now, grinning broadly. Surely no other Headchief had ever devised so clever a plan and so quickly found opportunity to put it into action! "I am pleased that the Adelantado finds my sister so lovely," he said to the interpreter. "Tell him this. And tell him also that the reason I am pleased is because this is the woman I am giving to him for a wife."

She was trapped in a dream, a dream filled with bad omens, but very soon she would awaken and the dream would dissolve into the mists of forgetfulness, as most dreams eventually did. She was not truly eating fish and oysters and Spanish biscuit off a platter made of silver and served from a fabric-covered wooden contraption Menendez had said was a "table." There was not music playing and people dancing as though this were a celebration. And Ysabel was not urging her to come along and put on the dress the Adelantado had given to her. To put it on, and let it serve as her wedding dress.

The night air had enough coolness to warn her that this was no dream, but she followed Ysabel down the ramp and across the compound anyway, somehow managed to ascend the ladder into her own small house. Then, at last, she found herself able to speak.

"Ysabel, I cannot, I will not, do this thing!"

Her serving woman's round face lengthened with pity. "It is wrong, what Calusa did," she muttered. "Just as that Menendez was wrong when he said that all of us in the Spanish village should leave here and go back to Cuba." She snorted. "As though I would abandon my husband, and my children and grandchildren!" She looked into her mistress's angry eyes. "Or you," she said. And meant it.

"I will go away," Dancing Egret said. "Far away. I will not marry that man, that stranger, that . . . that Spaniard." All at once her face softened with contrition. She reached out one hand and touched Ysabel's by way of apology. "Forgive me. I do not mean to insult everyone of Spanish blood. You are dear to me, Ysabel; you know that you are."

Ysabel nodded. "I know. And you are dear to me. That our blood is different is of no consequence. Nor the fact that, over the years, some of my people have slain yours, and some of yours have slain mine." She struggled to explain the unexplainable. "When two people are *simpatico*, nothing else is of importance."

Egret attempted a smile. "I agree. But you do understand why I cannot go through with this marriage my brother has arranged?"

"*Si.* I understand. And I think the Adelantado is no happier about it than you are. I overheard him talking to his companions, Dona Egret; they were trying hard to convince Menendez he would insult Headchief Calusa if he refused to accept you as his wife. Menendez himself, I think he agreed only to be left in peace; apparently he had hoped to find a son of his among Calusa's Christians and was sorely disappointed when he did not." She shook her head. "But no good can come of this. No good."

"My brother thinks that great good will come of it," Egret said bitterly. "He believes he is forging a kinship bond with Menendez, one that will protect our people from harm. And he felt he was strengthening the bond by encouraging everyone to kneel before that post in the compound when those men in robes said they should."

"That post is a cross," Ysabel said soberly, "a symbol of the Christian God. And the men in robes, they are priests."

Priests. That was a word Egret knew, although the Spanish priests with their censorious expressions bore no resemblance to any Calusan priest she had ever seen. Certainly they were nothing like Vision Seeker, who—although he had never hesitated to show disapproval when he thought he should—had too much dignity to wrinkle his nose and suck in his cheeks as though he'd eaten a chunk of unripe fruit. No; she simply could not go and let one of those pursed-lipped men marry her to Pedro Menendez! "Will you help me?" she asked Ysabel. "Help me to leave the island?"

Ysabel sighed. "Dona Egret, there is no place you can go that the Headchief cannot find you."

"I can hide in the river glades," Egret said. "Or I can seek sanctuary with a Timucuan people. I did so once before."

Ysabel chose her words carefully. "If you go to the river glades, warriors will be sent after you. They will know all the places you might hide. And when you sought shelter among the Timucua before, you were only a girl; those who took you in most likely planned to adopt you or expected you to marry into the tribe. Now ..." She shrugged again.

"Now," Egret said harshly, "I am old. No one will want me."

Ysabel made a shushing sound. "You are not old," she said. "But you are no longer young enough to adapt easily to the ways of a different people. A Timucuan chief might even think Calusa sent you to spy upon him." She gestured toward the plaza. "None of this matters, Dona Egret. You will be going nowhere, I fear."

Egret turned, looked over her shoulder. Warriors had congregated in the compound while they were talking, and although they avoided looking toward her house, she realized at once why they were there. "My brother knows me too well," she muttered.

"And he is Headchief of all the Calusa," Ysabel said softly. "I think you will not avoid this marriage, however much you try."

"Unless I take a knife to my marriage bed," Egret said. But both she and Ysabel knew she would not, that to slay Menendez, even to merely threaten him with death, would imperil all of her people.

Ysabel held out the green gown. "Let me help you into it," she said, "and then I will arrange your hair. If you must be forced into taking a husband you do not want, at least do so looking like the queen that you are."

Queen. That was a word her serving woman had often used when referring to her, and Ysabel had long ago explained what it meant. But Egret was no queen, nor did she feel like one despite the care Ysabel took in dressing her. She felt like a victim about to serve as ceremonial sacrifice, and despair went with her when—surrounded by a silent escort of warriors—she returned to the house at the top of the mound.

One of the Spanish priests met her at the entrance, beckoned to Ysabel to follow, and led the way to a spot where he need not shout to make himself heard. "Tell your mistress to kneel," he said to Ysabel, "and translate for her all that I say."

Egret swallowed the resentment his imperious tone spawned, and went down on her knees without protest.

The priest eyed her sternly. "You must become a child of the one true God before you can be the bride of Pedro Menendez," he said. "For that, you will have to acknowledge and accept everything I am going to tell you."

He waited while Ysabel repeated his words, his hands clasping and unclasping the heavy cross that dangled from his belt. "Tell her," he went on when Ysabel had fallen silent, "that she is to say 'yes' whenever I nod my head. After you have interpreted what I shall be asking her, of course," he added quickly.

But Ysabel did not think that he cared much whether Dona Egret understood what she would be agreeing to, and while supposedly translating, admitted her suspicions to her mistress.

Egret shrugged. "We both know I disagree with all that is happening this night," she said. "What can it matter?"

And indeed she scarcely listened as she was introduced to the Christian God and his son Jesus, warned against the horrors of hell and offered conditional entry to a glorious place called heaven. Surreptitiously, she bunched the voluminous silk skirts so they cushioned her knees against the sharp pebbles that littered the ground she knelt on, then she relaxed as best she could while a torrent of words poured over her. "Yes," she said when the signal came, and "yes" again, and again, and again, until at last the priest placed his hands on her head, mumbled words that Egret was fairly certain were not Spanish, and told her she might rise.

"You are Christian now," Ysabel whispered as the two went with him into Calusa's clamorous house, "although you have promised to take further instruction in due course. And . . ." She studied her mistress nervously; she was reasonably certain Dona Egret had understood everything the priest said, but dared not risk her reaction later if one part of the improvised catechism should have escaped her. ". . . your baptismal name will be Antonia."

Dancing Egret made no response. She had not needed Ysabel's obedient interpreting to decipher any of the words spoken by Menendez's priest, and she certainly had not missed his referring to her as Dona Antonia. The name had grated on her ear when he pronounced it, and she had been hard put not to cry out that no one—*no one*—had the right to steal the name her mother had given her on the day she was born.

She clenched her hands, let her fingernails bite into her palms when the priest brought her to the center of the vast room and directed her to stand beside the Adelantado. The people who had been singing and dancing and chattering during her absence fell back to make a great circle around the pair and the black-robed priest. Egret looked at those who would witness this "marriage." There stood Calusa, hands linked behind his back and a gleeful smile lighting his handsome features. The clan leaders flanked him, smiling because the Headchief was smiling but clearly bewildered by the whole affair. Across from them a group of Spanish soldiers were far more interested in the bare-breasted Calusan maidens than in the marriage rite being hastily performed.

Egret ignored the drone of the priest who looked first at her, then at Menendez, as he pontificated on the virtues of Christian union. Her attention was drawn to the women of her family, who had clustered together as though for support. Calusa's mother was there, her eyes dark with compassion; until now, she had been her son's staunchest admirer, but she could not and would not condone what he was doing to Egret. Behind Watchful Doe, Brown Pelican's face glistened with the tears she was quietly shedding; to call this a marriage ceremony was to mock the term and all it stood for.

"Dona Antonia . . ."

Egret started as she realized the priest was addressing her, and nodded her head in response to the querying note in his voice. Then she shifted her attention back to the women, focused on the maid who stood next to Pelican. Chattering Squirrel's weeping was not silent, as her mother's continued to be; now that Swift Eagle looked upon her with new eyes, she grieved mightily to see her aunt forced to wed a man she did not love. Surely, surely, this was the most awful thing that could happen to any woman!

Egret wondered why she was unmoved by Watchful Doe's pity, by Pelican's commiseration, and even by Squirrel's wrenching sobs, why she felt somehow detached from everything and everyone around her. The answer came to her as the priest spoke once more in a language that surely was not Spanish, then announced in ringing tones that this man and this woman were husband and wife.

It is not Dancing Egret who stands here in a green gown streaked with dirt, she told herself, nor has Dancing Egret married Don Pedro Menendez. These things are happening to a stranger called Dona Antonia; to Dancing Egret they mean nothing at all.

And when a bevy of the town's maidens bore her outside to a pavilion set up for the occasion, it was a woman with an alien name who waited alone for her new husband to come to her, who watched dispassionately as the front hanging was pushed aside and suddenly he was standing before her—a man who was no more to her than a darker silhouette against the night's own dark. As she must be to him.

Neither spoke, but only stood staring at what they could not see. Beyond the pavilion, far beyond it, huge fires burned and happy people gathered around them. The soldiers, even many of Egret's own people, were glad enough to pretend that this marriage was reason for merrymaking.

The man stepped nearer, put out a hand and tugged gently at the sleeve of the green silk gown. When there was no reaction, he tugged at it a second time.

Dancing Egret still did not move. It was Dona Antonia who fumbled with the gown's laces, loosened them, and wriggled out of the garment. It was Dona Antonia who listened to the rustle of other garments as Menendez disrobed, and it was Dona Antonia who let him guide her to the bed that nearly filled the small pavilion.

But it was Dancing Egret who, afterward, lay sleepless while her ears were assaulted by the snoring of a man she did not know. It was Dancing Egret who invited rage to siphon away the tears that gathered behind her eyes, and it was Dancing Egret who vowed silently to find a way to rid herself of Pedro Menendez, to send him and all his fellows back to the place they had come from.

Chapter 38

❦ ❧

Dancing Egret hefted the damp skirts that clung unpleasantly to knees and ankles and ignored the stares she knew were being sent her way. What was wrong with these people, that they believed legs must be concealed? And not only legs, but arms and breasts as well. Why should a glimpse of female flesh always prompt coarse—and by now boringly familiar—remarks? Surely Spanish men did not go in ignorance of what a woman's body looked like? Even those who did not have wives and daughters must have mothers and sisters.

She continued to hold the sea-splashed fabric bunched in one hand, while with the other she clutched the rail that was all that came between her and the heaving ocean far below. It seemed to go on forever, that ocean; it met the sky in all directions, and she'd wondered more than once if she would ever see land again. She knew she would, of course; but she knew also that her next sight of it would not be cause for elation. It would not be her beloved island that she looked upon then, but a place called Cuba.

Who could have guessed, just a few days ago, that she would be trying to keep her balance on the deck of a ship with massive winglike sails? Not even her brother had been prepared for Menendez's announcement that his new wife must go to Havana to be instructed in his faith. "She must learn many things," he had said to the Headchief. "True Christians worship one God only, or they cannot go to heaven when they die, and they must worship Him correctly. Your sister was raised to worship a warlike and deceitful god who is called the devil; only Catholic instruction will lead her to forswear the devil, and she cannot be considered truly Christian until she does so."

What he had said must have perplexed her brother as much

as it did her, and Egret had expected Calusa to object, to object strongly, to the Adelantado's plans to send her away. Instead he had agreed, saying that if the Spanish religion was as superior as Spanish music was, then he and all his people wanted to know more about it. When Dancing Egret came home, she would be able to pass on to others what she had learned, which would be a fine way for everyone to come to know Menendez's most excellent God.

Egret grimaced. She could not be sure what had wounded her more in what Calusa—whom Menendez insisted upon calling "Carlos"—had said: his ready acceptance of her leaving the island, or his intimation that the Spanish made more beautiful music than their own singers did. Anyone with two ears knew better than that!

Ysabel came across the deck and positioned herself behind her mistress to thwart the seamen and soldiers whose eyes were fixed greedily on the slender ankles Dancing Egret was exposing, and derisively on the deerskin moccasins that hugged her long feet. Dona Egret had refused to cram her toes into the shoes she was supposed to be wearing, for which Ysabel did not blame her. She herself was no longer comfortable in any part of European dress, but the Adelantado—before he boarded a different ship and sailed off who-knew-where—had charged Ysabel to accustom "Dona Antonia" to proper attire. Indeed, they had not been permitted to set sail for Cuba until Menendez's tailors had fashioned gowns for Dona Egret and Ysabel, and also for the five Calusan women who had been selected to accompany them on this voyage. Still, with floor-sweeping skirts, no one need ever know what Dona Egret wore on her feet. "I have heard that we will reach land before this day is over, Dona Egret," Ysabel said. "You will be glad of that, I expect."

"I will only be glad when I am home again," Egret replied.

"I know. And I appreciate how you feel. I, too, look forward to the day we go back to Calusa's island."

Egret dropped her skirts, gave her whole attention to her serving woman. "I haven't thanked you for coming with me," she said, "which I should have done as soon as you said you would. Parting from your family must have been dreadful for you, Ysabel, but I don't think I could have survived all of this without you."

Ysabel smiled. "From what I know of you, and from things I have heard about your younger days, I am certain you would have survived. You are both strong and resourceful, and that is what makes for survival."

Egret returned the smile. "You must be the same. At least we have not been seasick, like the other women," she said. All five attendants—attendants she neither wanted nor needed, but whom both Menendez and her brother had insisted upon—had been ill since their first day on the ship, and Egret knew she would be glad of landfall if only for their sakes. "What is it like, this Havana we are going to?"

Ysabel hesitated. "It is nothing like your town," she said at last. "There are many, many more houses there, and little space between them. There are many, many people, as well, and they, too, are crammed together. At least, you will think so. They do not, you see, for they have always lived that way." Her brow furrowed. "It is hard to describe," she finished lamely. "You will soon be seeing it for yourself, and then you will understand."

"Tell me again whose house we are going to. I have said the name over and over to myself, but I am not certain I have it right as yet."

"The ship's captain will escort us to the home of the Regidor of Havana," Ysabel told her. "Senor Alonso de Rojas is how he is called. And you will call his wife Senora Rojas, not Dona Rojas. She is the one who is to be godmother to you." Ysabel had already explained what a godmother was, in detail, so she merely repeated the names Dona Egret was trying to memorize.

Egret echoed them, nodded. "It will be odd, to be living with strangers," she said, and for the first time let her sadness show. How she longed for her own little house and the familiar bustle of her town.

Ysabel shared her sadness, but before she could say so, a shout from the upper deck made her swallow words that need not be said to be understood. "They have spied land," she told her mistress. "Soon, very soon, you will be discovering what Havana is like."

Moon of Winter's eyes misted as she watched her daughter scoop half of the watery stew from her own platter onto the one meant for Palm Tree Bending. Without commenting, she added to the plate the small round that was her own portion of bread for the day. A woman who was breeding needed more sustenance than those who were not, and Outina's wife was far too thin for someone who would be delivering a child before another four moons had passed.

"How can it continue so dry?" Walks Tall Woman swallowed a sliver of squash, carefully sopped up the last of the pale gravy with the bread crust she had saved for the purpose. "Dark clouds roll across the sky nearly every day; why don't they send rain upon our fields, and encourage our crops to grow?"

"No one has an answer for that," her son said soberly. "Not even Watches for Omens."

His mention of the Shaman brought silence again to those gathered around the Principal Woman's hearth. Since scarcity of food had gone from a troublesome thing to a problem none could ignore, everyone in the town was thinner than he had been. But Watches for Omens had grown frighteningly gaunt over the last few weeks. And he was an old man, with no reserves of strength to draw upon.

"It demands too much of him, to conduct a rain ceremony every day," Walks Tall Woman said finally, "especially when it is plain that our Rain God is turning a deaf ear to his prayers."

"My brother tells me Watches for Omens insists upon fasting beforehand each time, and that afterward he will allow himself only a bit of cornbread and a dipper of water." Dark smudges ringed Palm Tree Bending's eyes and worry puckered her forehead. She was concerned for all her family, for every person in the town, but she truly feared for her uncle. She took the plate Kaia brought to her, and her abstraction was such that she failed to notice how it held more than it should have. "Black Wolf Running tried refusing to eat unless our uncle did, but that did no good." She smiled a little. "Watches for Omens only scolded him for it, and—old and frail as he is—made Wolf feel like a child who is being foolish."

"My Principal Men, who have heard the same story about the Spaniard that all of us have heard, are beginning to wish the man named Menendez would come here." Outina's face was thoughtful; he had disagreed at first, but now . . .

"I do not believe he made it rain." Moon of Winter spoke flatly, yet somehow this lent emphasis to her protest.

"People who have visited Holata Guale's province swear that it happened," Walks Tall Woman said. "They say the Spanish leader called upon his chief, who lives in a place called Heaven, and that thunder and lightning were sent to Guale. Now corn grows tall there and bean plants flourish in

fields that were once as dry as ours." She turned to Outina.
"Do you think he will come here, my son?"

Outina shrugged. "Who can say? Many of his men remain
in Saturiba's province, but Menendez and the rest have sailed
away again. He is expected to return, but I do not know
when."

"I hope you will never let him come here, even if he wants
to," Moon of Winter said.

Walks Tall Woman began stacking the empty plates. "Perhaps you enjoy starving," she said her niece. "The rest of us
do not. Our Shaman has not been able to bring us rain; you
and your 'wonderful crystal' have certainly done nothing to
help us; if this Menendez will promise to make it rain, then I
say we should have him here and treat him as an honored
guest."

Palm Tree Bending wrestled with her childhood memories
of a town littered with the bodies of warriors, her own father's
among them. Then the babe in her womb moved restlessly.
With her two sons grown now, she had abandoned hope of
ever having a daughter to carry on her clan lineage. Of course,
she could not be sure it was a girl she carried now; even Moon
of Winter said there was no way to be certain of that. But boy
or girl, Palm Tree Bending wanted this unexpected child to be
healthy and strong. "We must have food," she said. "Somehow, we must have food."

"Kwambu will bring us vegetables and dried fish when he
returns from the south," Moon of Winter said. "He said so to
the courier we sent into Apalachee. Then we'll have more to
eat."

Outina shook his head. "He cannot bring enough, Moon of
Winter. I know that, and you know that. Even if every trader
who comes here brought food with him, it would not be
enough. Unless rain comes soon, so that the crops you women
planted grow as they should, and the animals we hunt return to
their feeding grounds, our people will starve." He stood up,
thanked his mother for the meal. "When the Spanish leader
comes back to Timucuan territory, if he wants to visit my
town, I think I must make him welcome."

Dancing Egret wished that the things called candles did not
give off quite so much heat. The light they shed was pretty,
and made it possible to see clearly those who had come to take
a meal with Senor and Senora Rojas. But the room they all sat

in was closed on every side; the openings in two of the walls, the "windows," had shutters fastened across them, and it was not only hot but airless. Egret wondered yet again if a lack of fresh, sweet air might not be aggravating the sorry condition of the Calusan servants who had come here with her. Day after day they huddled together in the room they'd been given, refusing to leave it even though she pleaded with them to do so. The sickness that visited them on the voyage south had never really left them, and—despite Senora Rojas's assurances that the women were more frightened than anything else—Dancing Egret wished that they could be sent home to be tended by those who knew how to deal with the foul spirits that had afflicted the women with illness.

She let none of these worries show in her face. As had become her habit, she remained impassive unless someone thought to address her, then merely nodded or smiled. The wide skirts of a blue gown were spread neatly around the chair she occupied. It had been easy to accustom herself to chairs—they were not so different from benches—but even after two months it still did not seem right to sit around a table to eat. Yet she managed well enough, just as she was able now to swallow spicy foods without gulping water afterward, and to sleep on a bed that was much too soft and was placed in a room as airless as this one.

"Will you have more of the roast pork, Dona Antonia?"

Ysabel, who had become interpreter as well as serving woman for Dancing Egret, repeated what Senora Rojas had said. There was no need, of course; Dona Egret had understood. But Ysabel had pledged to keep secret her mistress's knowledge of Spanish.

"I have had enough," Dancing Egret said quietly. She had been astounded when Ysabel explained that this particular meat came from the beasts that had so intrigued her when she and Shore Walker had gone to spy on the camp of the Spaniard, De Soto. Looking back, she wondered if perhaps she had not fallen in love with Shore Walker that day, while the two of them crawled through prickly underbrush together. Then, later, the alligator had attacked, had clamped its huge jaws around Shore Walker's arm . . .

Surreptitiously, Ysabel touched her hand. Only then did Egret realize her retreat into memory had led her to close her eyes. She forced herself back to the present, concentrated on the babble of voices around her.

Ysabel relaxed and listened, too. Never had she thought to be sitting in so fine a house, and surrounded by people of importance. Noble, some of them were. Yet not a woman present looked as noble as her mistress. She studied Dona Egret; she would never tell her so, but the stylish gowns Dona Egret despised admirably suited both her tallness and the regal bearing Ysabel had seen in her from the first. With her shining dark hair coiled above her ears, and the graceful curve of her neck shown to advantage by the gown's low-cut bodice, she looked positively elegant. And the fact that she refused to wear any ornamentation save the pearl-bedecked wooden combs her husband had carved for her contributed to her elegance.

Egret was unaware of Ysabel's approving gaze. Once again the people around the table were discussing a place called Matanza Inlet and singing the praises of Pedro Menendez. She had paid scant heed last time the subject was mentioned; she'd been busy trying to manipulate the ornate silver implement the Spanish called a knife, but which was unlike any knife Egret had ever held before. This time she was able to give undivided attention.

"My old friend disposed of the Huguenots most effectively." It was her host who spoke. Alonso de Rojas was a big, bluff man with a hearty laugh, but he was not laughing now. "Which is why I am incensed when I hear him condemned for what he did," he went on. "*La Florida* was claimed by Spain long before a single Frenchman set foot there. Our king rightly told Menendez to take back our territory, and left him to decide how best to do so."

"I do not argue with that," another man, one of the guests, said. "I only say that some people—and we know who they are; they delight in criticizing Menendez—are insisting that it was not necessary to massacre the French, that to force them back to their homeland would have served his purpose just as well."

Senora Rojas appeared puzzled. She was a bosomy woman whose gray hair was forever escaping the ivory combs meant to keep it in place; a kindhearted woman who—despite the tongue-lashings she freely administered for any sloth or carelessness she perceived—looked to the welfare of every person in her household. Egret was growing fond of her. "But they were preaching a heathen doctrine to the natives of *la Florida*," she said now. "Surely they should have been punished for that? Which is what Pedro Menendez did. Do his detractors

say the French Protestants should have been left alive to go on
with the devil's work?"

"And because Menendez took them prisoner and disarmed
them before he ordered their execution does not make it a massacre," her husband added, "no matter what is said. Most of
them were not ordinary citizens, but soldiers. Any man who
becomes a soldier accepts that he may one day be slain by an
enemy." He looked around the table, shook his head. "But this
is no conversation to be having with ladies present," he said.
"In truth, talk of war and bloodshed will not aid anyone's di-
gestion. Surely we can find something more pleasant to speak
about?"

His wife smiled graciously, but she was not to be deterred.
"We women are not as squeamish as you gentlemen seem to
believe," she said, "and we are just as interested in what goes
on in our world. We will talk of something else if you wish,
but when Pedro Menendez returns to Havana, I hope you do
not intend to send me away when he tells about where he has
been and what he has been doing."

"But he has already returned, some days ago," the man on
her left told her. "You have not heard from him?"

"*I* have not," Senora Rojas said, looking pointedly at her
husband, "or he would be an honored guest at this dinner."

"He is staying at an inn not far from here," Senor Rojas admitted after a moment. What use to try and keep anything
from his wife? "He has come back to arrange for additional
provisioning of the fort he is building in *la Florida*. The natives there are friendly, he told me, but somewhat wary of any
white men. It seems that the French, when they were in that
part of the country, could not be bothered to grow their own
food; they expected the natives to sustain them. Menendez will
not risk earning their enmity by following in the footsteps of
the Huguenots."

"That is wise," Senora Rojas said, and there were murmurs
of approval all around. "But what you have said does not explain why Don Pedro is not here with us tonight."

Her husband lowered his voice. Dona Antonia, for all that
she had been quick to memorize her catechism, plainly knew
no Spanish, but it made him uncomfortable nonetheless to
speak of her when she was in the room. "He does not yet want
the Indian woman to know he is in the city," he said. "He fears
that if she finds out, she will expect him to come to her, and
stay with her."

"That would scarcely be surprising, in the circumstances," the woman sitting beside him said. And laughed a little.

Senora Rojas bristled; in the time that Antonia had been living in her home, she had come to have great respect for her. The woman was from a country wild and uncivilized, yet her instincts were those of a born lady. Look at the way she sat there, back erect, head held high, feigning polite interest in a conversation that was only gibberish to her. "I hold Pedro Menendez in high esteem," she said carefully, "but this business of his marrying an aborigine"—her face tightened—"it was not right."

"When new territory is being colonized," said the man who had spoken of the massacre, "and the Gospel must be brought to its natives, it is the result that matters, not the means by which it is achieved."

Senora Rojas did not respond to this; who would listen if she did? "Since we seem to be speaking again of subjects ladies cannot comprehend," she said, rising, "this might be a good time to take our leave of the men."

Her female guests trailed her obediently into a small sitting room, and Dancing Egret and Ysabel followed them. On a table beneath the shuttered window sat a silver cage, and those who had not visited recently exclaimed aloud when a trill of melody erupted from it.

"It is a canary," their hostess said, pleased with their reaction. "He greets me with song every time I come into this room." She bent over the cage, cooed at her pet, smiled with delight when he sang a second time.

Sadness clutched at Dancing Egret's heart. Senora Rojas had been certain Egret would take as much delight in the yellow bird as she did, and Egret had sincerely tried to. But that any living creature should be forever confined, that a creature with wings should be denied the opportunity to fly and nest and mate, was to her the worst form of cruelty. Each time she looked upon the canary she was tempted to cry, but Dancing Egret had early learned to resist such temptation.

She turned away from the others, spoke softly to Ysabel. "I should like to go to our room now," she said. Not that she relished exchanging one overwarm and musty place for another, but she had urgent matters to discuss with her serving woman.

Ysabel waited for the right moment, went to Senora Rojas and relayed Dona Egret's request. Then she stood by the door until Egret, as Senora Rojas had taught her to do, smiled upon each woman in turn by way of courteous leave-taking.

"You listened also to everything that was said?" she asked Ysabel as soon as the two were alone. "You heard them speak of massacre? And you heard that Menendez is here in Havana?"

Ysabel nodded. Dona Egret's questions had not been halting; she spoke Spanish now as though born to do so. And Ysabel had been wrong to worry that her mistress might find it impossible to adjust to the unfamiliar; truly, this woman could be at home anywhere.

Egret paced the floor. "From what Kwambu has told me, I'm certain the Timucua are grateful to have the French gone from their provinces," she said. "But the Frenchmen were white-fleshes, just as the Spanish are. If Menendez did not hesitate to slay his own kind because they were in a place where he wanted to be, what will he do to my people, and to the Timucua, if we should stand in the way of his having what he wants?" She whirled around. "Do you suppose he plans to massacre us, as well?"

Ysabel was shaken; she had not considered this. Certainly such things had happened in the past when Spain met resistance to the expansion of its empire. "No one can know what he intends," she said at last. "He has said that he wishes to be friends with all the tribes in *la Florida*," she added hopefully.

"And if we don't choose to be his friends?" Dancing Egret asked. "What then, Ysabel?" She yanked her skirts up, hunkered down on the floor. "Oh, why did my brother allow him to come to the island?" she mourned. "Our town is well-hidden; Menendez would not have known it was there if Calusa hadn't sent emissaries to him."

"He would have eventually come across other of your towns," Ysabel said practically. She sat down beside her mistress. "I think he is more persistent than most, Dona Egret."

"I think he is also a man who plans for what will be," Dancing Egret said. "If only we could know what his plans are for the Calusa, then I could tell them to my brother when we return."

"It may be," Ysabel said slowly, "that he has written them down, those plans."

"*Written?* What is that?"

Ysabel explained what the word meant.

Dancing Egret wrestled with the concept, nodded. "You're

saying that symbols describing what he plans will be captured on what is called parchment." An idea was taking shape in her mind; it was a poor one, perhaps, but at least it was an idea. "Would you recognize these symbols if you saw them?" she asked.

For the first time Ysabel smiled; smiled rather proudly. "*Si*, I would, Dona Egret. In my village, when I was a child, there was a priest. He was a good man, and a good friend to my father. When he taught me my catechism—the same catechism that you have been learning, Dona—I learned so rapidly that he said my mind must be unusually sharp. For that reason, I think, he taught me to read. I cannot read much, you understand," she added hastily, "but perhaps it would be enough." She turned a puzzled face to her mistress. "But what good is that? I cannot see the Adelantado giving me his plans—if even he has them written down—merely because I tell him I want to see them."

Dancing Egret was thinking more furiously than before. "Do you know what an 'inn' is? And where we could find the one Menendez has gone to?"

Ysabel frowned. "There is only one close by here, and it is on the same street as the market the cook goes to. But surely you are not thinking what I am afraid you are thinking?"

"Pedro Menendez does not seem to me the sort who trusts others," Egret said, coming to her feet. "If he has written anything about what he means to do in my country, the parchment he made the marks on will be where he is."

Ysabel scrambled to her feet. "You do not mean to go there!"

Egret nodded grimly. "I do. If you will take me. After all, what could be more natural than a wife going to visit her husband?" The bitterness in her voice was overlaid with satisfaction; she might regret this forced marriage less if it could be used to advance her own schemes. "It has grown late. Menendez will be asleep by now, surely?" It continued to confound Egret that the Spanish slept during several of the sunlit hours, then did not go again to their beds until night was turning toward morning.

Reluctantly, her serving woman agreed that he probably would be. "But we cannot be sure. And if he is, how can you hope to get into his room? There are many rooms in an inn, Dona Egret. We will have to learn which is his, and even then we may not be allowed near it. And should the Adelantado be awake still, what can I say to him to explain our having come there?"

Egret had already crossed to the door to her bedroom, a door that she would never permit to be fully closed. "I'll tell you that while we are on our way," she whispered. Then, signaling for silence, she urged Ysabel ahead of her out of the room.

Dancing Egret had not been favorably impressed with Havana by day; by night, it was a terrible place. The stone houses that huddled close together and leaned toward one another above narrow streets might have been looming, malevolent ghosts out of some ancient Legend. And the stench, that awful mix of alien spices, human sweat, animal dung, and the garbage that overflowed the gutters, seemed intensified by the dark. Once again Egret marveled that the Spanish had not provided for middens when they built their town. This was as hard to believe as was the obvious fact that so many of them went unwashed from one full moon to another.

They scurried past the church Senora Rojas had weekly brought Dancing Egret to, to introduce her to what was called the "Mass," and for her to be instructed by its hawk-faced priest. Egret wondered if the man slept there, or if he had a home to go to. She would certainly not like sleeping in a church, with life-size carvings of anguished-looking people standing all around her. And the church had a suffocating air about it that smoldering incense merely intensified. Each time she went there, Egret had been relieved to return to the fouled streets they were traveling now; malodorous as they were, the streets were not so breath-stealing as the interior of that church.

Luckily, there were not many people about at this hour, only a few men whose lurching gait proclaimed them as drunkards. Dancing Egret had no trouble recognizing them for what they were; since coming to Havana, she'd learned that the "wine" her brother had found so unpalatable had the power to fuddle the brain and make the body unsteady. By darting temporarily around corners or into sheltering doorways, the two women managed to avoid confrontation as they made their way to the inn Menendez had gone to. Still, it was not a pleasant journey, and Dancing Egret was relieved when Ysabel gestured to a lantern hanging outside a building just ahead and said that it marked the place they were looking for.

As they had arranged, Ysabel transformed herself into a

shrew when at last the keeper of the inn responded to her repeated knocking at his door. "You have kept waiting the wife
of Adelantado Menendez," she told him, shaking a finger in
front of his startled face. "He will hear of this, and you will be
sorry when he does. Unless you are quick—quick! quick!—to
direct us to his room."

The man looked beyond her to where another woman,
nearly as old as the dumpy virago, stood in the shadows. "Get
out of here," he rumbled. "Go back to the waterfront where
you belong. There are no customers here for what you are sell-
ing." He laughed scornfully. "If indeed there are anywhere, for
the likes of you two!"

Without backing away from him, Ysabel beckoned her mistress into the light. *"Estupido,"* she hissed at the man. "Are
you so stupid you have not heard that the Adelantado found
himself a wife while he was among the Indians?" She pointed
dramatically at Egret. "How many red-skinned noblewomen do
you think are in Havana? Look at her! She is no whore from
the docks, as you dare to imply. Your own eyes, if they have
not grown too dim from peering through keyholes, should tell
you that."

The innkeeper looked more closely at the second woman,
stroked the mangy beard that jutted from his protruding chin.
It was true that the Captain-General was said to have taken an
Indian woman—some said an Indian princess—to warm his
bed; he had heard also that the woman was here in Cuba, staying at the home of the Regidor. And his eyes—which were
sharp as they'd ever been, despite the bad-tempered one's
baseless accusations—told him that the face he looked upon
was indeed the color of mahogany. More than that, her car-
riage, the way she was dressed, suggested that here stood a
lady. Still . . . "The Adelantado would have told me if he had
expected visitors. Let alone his wife."

Ysabel snorted. "And why should Don Pedro Menendez inform a mere innkeeper of anything?" she charged. "He pays
you to serve him, not to be his confidant! And if you want to
see the money you are doubtless overcharging him for staying
in this pigsty, you had better not delay us longer. I ask you
again: which is his room?"

The innkeeper made up his mind. What a tale he would
have to tell in the *taberna* tomorrow, he thought as he took up
a taper and lit it; it would be worth losing sleep for, to be able
to describe for his fellows the Captain-General's Indian wife.

"I will take you to him," he said, moving toward a hallway leading out of the reception area.

"You will do no such thing," Ysabel said, snatching the candle from him. "My mistress wishes to surprise her husband; that is why we arrive so late. Your huge feet will only announce her coming, and what surprise will there be then, eh?"

Defeated, the innkeeper muttered that Menendez's room was the second one past the corner, then returned to his seat. Never mind; he would still have a story to tell, one that would have his friends supplying him with more rum than he could drink in a month of mornings!

"We had better pray that Menendez is asleep, and that he did not bolt his door," Ysabel whispered as she led Dona Egret to the Adelantado's room. Her hand shook as she tried the latch, but she recovered her wits enough to smile triumphantly when the door opened easily. Pressing an ear to the crack, she smiled again to hear the reassuring sound of a man's rhythmic snoring.

The two women slid into the room, and Ysabel promptly extinguished the candle she was holding. In one corner, before a statue of the Blessed Virgin, stood a cluster of votive candles that gave sufficient light for the intruders to see all they needed to.

Everything had been planned beforetime. Without so much as looking at one another, the women began to search. It was a help to them, Dancing Egret thought as she lifted the lid of a chest, that the room was so sparsely furnished. Had it been like the cluttered rooms in Senora Rojas's home, their task would have been enormous, and dangerously time-consuming.

Ysabel scanned the open shelves of a cupboard, lifted cautiously the helmet and gloves that had been placed upon them, knelt to check behind the ill-fitting doors that concealed additional shelving. She would search diligently, as she had promised, but she was not certain she truly wanted to find what they were looking for. She had not lied when she'd told Dona Egret she could read, but she knew it was unlikely she would be able to make out many of the words on any document the Adelantado might have written. Well, if it came to it, she would read what words she could and confess her ignorance of the others. Perhaps, between them, she and her mistress could puzzle out what the others meant.

Three of the lower shelves were empty; the fourth contained only two shirts and five pair of hose, and there was no rustle of parchment as Ysabel felt around and between them. Closing the doors gently, she turned to the wardrobe.

Egret, having found nothing in the deep chest but spare coverlets and a gun she had been fearful of touching, joined her there. They examined the doublet and breeches hanging on a hook, then reached together for the purse that had been secreted behind them. As they fumbled it down, a handful of coins spilled to the floor, clanked against the tiles, then rolled beneath the bed.

The response to this was another clank, this one the sound of a sword being hastily withdrawn from a sheath tucked between bedpost and mattress.

"You will not move. You will stand where you are and not move so much as a finger!" Pedro Menendez de Aviles said.

Chapter 39

They had planned for this also, Dancing Egret reminded herself grimly. She swung around, stretched her mouth in a wide—and, she hoped, convincing—smile, and flung herself upon the bed, making sure to block Menendez's view of Ysabel as the Spanish woman hastily stuffed the clothing back into the wardrobe. Egret began to chant Calusan words as soon as she hurled herself in the Adelantado's direction; they were nonsense words mostly, but what mattered was not what she said, but that her tone be imploring.

She looked into his eyes and continued to babble, waving her hands as if frustrated that she could not make him understand what she meant. At the last, she lowered her arms, placed both hands over the one Menendez was using to grip the handle of his sword, then closed her eyes and gave a little sob. Now it was up to Ysabel.

Before the astonished Menendez could utter a sound, her

serving woman let loose a torrent of Spanish. "Forgive me, Adelantado," she gasped. "I argued and argued with her, but once Dona Antonia knew her husband had come back to Havana, she would not let me rest until I brought her to you. It was wrong, I know, to sneak into your room, but"—here she somehow contrived to blush—"I, too, am a woman. I understood her desire to be with you, to share your bed as she has not been able to do since your wedding night. You are a great man, a leader of men, and have much to occupy your thinking. But my poor Dona Antonia, she thinks only of you, and longs for you with all the passion that is in her. I . . . I could not refuse when she commanded me to bring her to you."

Menendez had regained his composure. Swinging his legs over the side of the bed, he regarded the serving woman with sternness. "Did you not explain to her that a Christian man who wears the Cross of the Order of Santiago"—he held out for her inspection the gold cross that dangled against his chest—"may not sleep with his wife until they have been together again for eight days?" This peasant woman, a woman so ignorant she had refused to leave her heathen husband and the heathen children she had borne him, would not dare disbelieve him.

Ysabel went down on her knees. "Adelantado, I could have said this to Dona Antonia, had I known of it. But I think it would have done no good. A woman's heart does not listen to reason, Don Pedro." Her expression was contrite, but a wonderful feeling of relief was sweeping through her. Dona Egret had said that whatever happened, she had no intention of actually spending the remainder of the night in Pedro Menendez's bed; now, it seemed that the problem would not arise. She gestured toward her mistress. "I will tell her what you have said."

"Do so," Menendez said curtly, going to the wardrobe and snatching his breeches and doublet from their hook. He pulled them on hastily while the two women were speaking together and felt somewhat better once he was clothed. Combing his hair with his fingers, he made concerted effort to think clearly, calmly. He had spent the last several days importuning, arguing, and—finally—invoking the name of His Majesty Don Felipe, in order to acquire the goods he needed to provide for his men in *la Florida*. In the end he'd had to dig again into his own purse for much of the wherewithal, and he had counted on a good night's slumber to dilute the bitterness and resentment not even earnest prayer had delivered him from. To be awakened so rudely by a pair of hysterical women was more than most men in his circumstances would have been able to deal with. But he was not most men; he was Pedro Menendez de Aviles, and God would give him the strength to cope.

"She understands?" he asked Ysabel when blessed silence reigned once more.

Obedient to Dona Egret's instructions, Ysabel shook her head. *We must not give in too easily,* her mistress had said, *or he might come to wonder if the reasons you gave for our being here were the true ones. He is no fool, and when he is wholly awake he will not think like one.* "She says it is wrong," she told Menendez, "for a husband to sleep apart from his wife, that her brother will never understand your rejection of her. She begs you to let her lie in a corner of your bed, even if the Cross of Santiago does not permit you to touch her, so that she might be able to tell Headchief Calusa that the two of you slept together in Havana. Otherwise, he will think you despise her, and then he will feel no friendship toward any Christians and will certainly refuse to become one."

She had embellished a little what Dona Egret told her to say. Now she held her breath and prayed she had not overdone it. When Menendez, after staring at her for a moment, crossed to the door of his room and yanked it open, her heart leaped in her breast.

But he was only summoning a servant. When the man, rumpled and nightshirted, responded, the Adelantado pointed to a chest that sat parallel to the foot of his bed, a chest Dancing Egret and Ysabel had not had the time to search. "Take out the woman's cloak you will find in there, and a few mirrors and glass beads," he told him, "and pack them up." He turned back to Ysabel. "I am sorry, deeply sorry, that Dona Antonia cannot understand why I am unable to let her stay with me," he said. "Tell her that I am giving her presents to prove to her how sorry I am."

Ysabel hesitated, pretended reluctance to pass on his message. "She is so lonely here, Adelantado," she said. "At first she was busy learning what she needed to know, but now that the priest has said he has nothing further to teach her, she is sure to pine away for love of you."

Menendez smoothed his beard. Senor Rojas had said that the Indian woman had surprised the priest with her ready, and correct, responses to the catechism, which meant that she had memorized the words well enough to teach them to the rest of her people. "Will she be less inclined to pine away, as you put it, if she is taken back to her island?" he asked Ysabel.

Dancing Egret was hard put to suppress a joyous smile. They had failed to find what they had come here for, but if she could go home, and take with her the ailing women she was so concerned about, then the excursion would have accomplished something after all.

She kept her expression inscrutable until Ysabel put Menendez's question to her. Appearing to consider it, she looked mournfully into Menendez's eyes. Finally, she nodded.

Menendez made his tone brisk. "Then tell her to prepare herself to sail in three days' time," he said. "I had planned to go directly to my fort in the north of *la Florida*, but there is no reason I cannot take her first to her brother."

He was conscious of nothing but relief when, moments after he had sent for two of his men to escort them, the women were on their way back to the Regidor's. It was an added complication that Dona Antonia had fallen in love with him, but he had long ago learned how to minimize complications. Or, better yet, turn them to his own advantage.

Menendez winced as one of his trumpeters produced a sour note, a wince that became a scowl as laughter erupted somewhere in the rear. He did not turn around, however; he merely lifted one hand. The laughter subsided abruptly.

No doubt dust had invaded the musician's nose or throat. The tramping of scores of booted feet had raised a cloud that enveloped the whole procession. Obviously, the showers falling daily on the coast were not traveling this far inland. Still, the air was as thick and slow-moving as oil, and thunderheads blossomed on the rim of the sky; perhaps today would bring rain to the trees and bushes that drooped in the stifling summer heat.

The weather, he could do nothing about; unruliness in the ranks was a different matter. He had not been pleased to return to the Fort of Saint Augustine and discover that certain soldiers had so angered the residents of one of Holata Saturiba's towns that its warriors had ambushed and slain most of them. Despite Menendez's relentless questioning, no one admitted to knowing just what the soldiers had done, but he could guess. Gambling, guzzling, and whoring: that was all some of these conscripts ever thought about. And they did not worry that, by their sinning, they consigned their immortal souls to hell. They had claimed to be good Catholics when they joined his expedition, but if the Inquisition could be brought to *la Florida*, it would soon be seen that their Christianity went no deeper than their skin. It might be wise to give his lieutenant more authority, Menendez thought. The man was a strict disciplinarian who would not hesitate to mete out punishment for even minor infractions. God knew, he must have *someone* dependable in this part of the country while he himself was elsewhere.

"We are within one league of Outina, Adelantado."

Menendez studied terrain that to him seemed much the same in all directions, then looked at the man he was employing as guide and interpreter. "You are certain of this, Fontaneda?"

Fontaneda grinned. "I am. When I spoke with the Saturiban berdache who served the Huguenots in the same way as I gladly serve you, Captain-General, I made note of the route he described. These heathen merely count paces between landmarks, but I am able to translate their inefficient method to civilized measurement."

Menendez hoped the young man's confidence was not misplaced. He held up his hand again, and the procession came to a halt. The men did not break rank; they were but lowly foot soldiers, and dared not move until the Captain-General signaled them to do so. Menendez preferred to be accompanied by his cavalry officers, but in this land of swamp and jungle and dense forest, there were many places mounted soldiers simply could not go. One of these days, however, he would inform his cavalrymen that it is possible to travel on two feet as well as four. They would not appreciate the lesson, but Menendez meant them to learn it regardless. "Let us pray that Holata Outina will know of a waterway that connects the eastern and western coasts of this country," he said, as much to himself as to Fontaneda, "one that will carry us directly to the important Indian towns. I have lost count of the number of ramshackle villages we have stopped at, and am weary of receiving only blank stares when I ask their chiefs if such a river exists."

"I have heard that there is one," Fontaneda said, "but these Indians are much given to lying, Adelantado. If there is such a river, I would have come across it during the years I was made to serve Headchief Calusa as courier and trader."

Menendez was not so certain. Calusa's father may once have used Fontaneda to carry messages and goods for him, but the old Headchief was said to have been a shrewd man; he had likely been careful where he sent him and what he let him discover. Fontaneda had long ago made up his mind that all aborigines were stupid; Pedro Menendez knew better.

"You will go with six soldiers into Outina's town," he said to him now. "My treasurer has gifts for you to take to the chief when you advise him I am on my way to visit him. See that you show respect when you offer them. Should he refuse to see me, I will hold you to blame."

Fontaneda swallowed the remark he had been about to make. Menendez was not a man to accept excuses, not even those prepared in advance in case something should go amiss. He would learn, when he had been dealing longer with these savages, that it was impossible to predict their reaction to anything. They were like children; mood rather than reason dictated their responses.

When the seven had gone on ahead, Menendez permitted the rest of the men to take their ease. Most flopped down on the dusty ground and closed their eyes against the glare, but Menendez was made of stronger stuff. He sought the shade of a nearby tree, but held himself straight and tall as he considered what other problems might arise and how best to deal with them.

He wondered how Francisco de Reinoso was faring on Headchief Calusa's island. Now that the Adelantado had come to the belated discovery that the Calusan society was patriarchal, there was still much work to be done there. When Calusa had said he was not yet ready to follow his sister's example and go to Cuba for religious instruction, Menendez had not been overly concerned. At that point he was assuming that, like the Timucua, the ruling clan's lineage descended through its females. Then the Headchief—who delighted to talk, even when conversation was complicated by a need for interpretation—remarked that his latest child was only another daughter, and Menendez was alerted to the truth. *Not that it truly matters,* Calusa had added. *I am a young man, and my seed is as potent as my ardor. One day I shall sire the son who will be Headchief after me.*

The revelation had sent Menendez into immediate action. Through tactful inquiry, he'd learned who the Headchief's successor would be if his boasting should come to naught. For some reason, Dona Antonia had acted strangely when Menendez suggested that this Swift Eagle—who was some sort of cousin to Calusa—should be taken to Havana and indoctrinated, but the Headchief had paid no heed to her protests, and the young man was even now on his way to becoming a Christian. Menendez was a man who always planned ahead, and for every eventuality.

He frowned. Dona Antonia had been docile and obliging all the time she was in Havana, according to the Regidor and his wife. Doubtless her vehement objections when Swift Eagle prepared to take ship had arisen from jealousy, or even from fear. The Calusan servants she had taken with her to Cuba had sickened there; two died just before they would have sailed back to their island, and the other three had not survived the voyage home. Perhaps she feared her young cousin might meet a similar fate? In any event, he hoped Calusa's sister would put aside her unreasonable perturbation and concentrate on persuading the island's people to embrace the Faith. If she failed to do so, well, Calusa's successor—once the priests named him ready—would likely do a more competent job of conversion anyway. Men did not let emotion get in the way of duty.

Menendez scanned the sun's position. Fontaneda should be sending for him soon, and then he would have the opportunity to introduce yet another congregation of pagans to the Catholic faith.

"It was not difficult to build," Kwambu told his wife as she walked twice around the odd contraption on which he had brought huge sacks of grain and squash, zamia flour and dates, dried fish and conch, to Outina. "Calusa's woodcarver showed me how to ream holes in the corners of the sledge I generally use, and how to make tall wooden pegs that would fit into the holes and support a second, lightweight, sledge."

"You stacked them, like shelves," Moon of Winter said, smoothing the cluster of bluebird feathers decorating the upper one. "But how were you able to drag so heavy a load, Kwambu?"

The trader smiled. "I am stronger than I look," he jested. "Truthfully, the double load was no heavier than many ordinary loads. Sacks of food are bulky, but they are much lighter than seashells or pottery, for instance."

"It was good of Headchief Calusa to let us have so much food," Moon of Winter said, smiling at her daughter as Kaia and several friends came out of the town and made for the planting fields. They would find little to do there; even weeds were giving up the struggle to survive without water. "We're in dire need of it, Kwambu."

"There is drought throughout much of the interior," her husband said somberly. "Fortunately, the area around Lake Mayaimi is an exception. Although you are right to say Calusa was generous, some of the provisions came from the Lake country." He hesitated. "I must tell you that Calusa might well have refused to send Outina any food whatsoever. And if he had, I would have been to blame." He returned the salutes of a trio of hunters. The arrows thrust through their topknots were boy-sized; they knew the forest would offer only small game, and not much of that.

"I don't understand." Moon of Winter propped herself against the empty sledge and waited for her husband to explain.

"Calusa was elated when I gave him the pearls I'd traded for in Apalachee," Kwambu said, "so I seized the moment and told him how bad things are here, and asked for his help. He ordered the storehouses opened and said to take with me as much as I could haul. But after I thanked him, I mentioned that I had not seen his sister anywhere about. I spoke somewhat harshly to her last time we met, you see, and wanted to make amends before I headed north." His face hardened. "That was when Calusa told me"—he shook his head; why not call it what it was?—"no, *bragged* to me, that he had cleverly arranged for Dancing Egret to wed the Spaniard, Menendez."

Moon of Winter came erect. "Oh, no," she breathed.

Kwambu nodded. "There is worse," he told her. "Calusa went on to say that the reason I had not seen her in the town was because she had gone with her new husband to Cuba." He looked apologetically at his wife. "That is when I came perilously close to calling him an ignorant fool. In that moment, I cared nothing for what his reaction might be. Only the thought of you, and of how much everyone here needed the food he had agreed to let me have, fettered my tongue."

Moon of Winter went to him, cupped her hands around one of his clenched fists. "If our need weren't so great," she said, "I would wish you'd given in to your anger. That he could do such a thing, and to his own sister . . . !" The hand she was holding uncurled, turned up to clasp hers. "Do you think Dancing Egret will ever return to her home?" she asked hesitantly, for she knew how deep must be his concern for his old friend.

"According to Calusa, she will be home when summer ends," he said, "and Menendez with her. Calusa means to encourage his new brother-in-law to build a house on the island for Egret, and live there with her."

"But Outina's scouts say the Spanish are building a town of their own near the coast, a town sizable enough to alarm Holata Saturiba, from all reports. Surely this Menendez will want to live in his Principal Town, as our chiefs do?" She was distracted briefly as a thin wail arose from the sling carried by one of the women returning to the town with baskets and digging sticks. Her people were becoming gatherers again, as their ancestors had been, yet ground nuts, cane shoots, spatterdock, and pickerelweed would do little to increase the milk new mothers needed to nourish their babies. Moon of Winter thought of Palm Tree Bending's tiny daughter; how long would it be before she, too, cried pitifully from hunger? She sighed, then brought her attention back to her husband.

"Menendez would be more likely to live near his fort than on Calusa's island," Kwambu was saying. "But leaders of Spanish expeditions have rarely stayed in any one place. They go here, there, everywhere, like bees in search of nectar."

Moon of Winter attempted a grin. "Or like traders," she said. But her eyes were sad.

Kwambu hated to make them sadder still, but she must be told the truth. "Because Egret and Menendez are supposed to return to Calusa country at summer's end, the Headchief made me promise I would be back on the island before then. There are others he can send out along the trading routes, he says, but he trusts no one but me to act as interpreter when he speaks with Menendez." He drew a deep breath. "Moon of Winter, I do not know when I will be able to come here again. If Calusa should be right in thinking Menendez will spend most of his days on the island now, then it may be a long, long time before I am permitted to go anywhere at all."

Moon of Winter's face crumpled. To be always hungry, to see those you care for become thin and drawn, was a burden that weighed heavier with each succeeding day. But to have to shoulder that burden without her husband's love to strengthen her, to not even know when she might see him again . . .

"Kwambu," she whispered, "I cannot. . . ."

"You, there! You are Calusa's trader, yes?"

Kwambu had moved forward to take his wife into his arms.

Now he stepped back, turned around to see who, in Timucuan country, was speaking the language of the southern peninsula.

He narrowed his eyes. "I am. And you are Fontaneda. You were also a trader for Calusa, before you gave him cause to mistrust you." His gaze traveled beyond the Spaniard, to the six soldiers who had followed him to the town's gate. "Perhaps your new master will be better able to keep your loyalty." He should have spoken more tactfully, he supposed; but to have this moment with Moon of Winter interrupted, and by a man he had never liked or trusted, fanned the rage that had been smoldering in him ever since the day Calusa told him about Dancing Egret.

But Fontaneda only laughed. "To him it is given freely, for now I serve the Adelantado of *la Florida*. By his orders, I am to be taken at once to Holata Outina, so I may warn him to prepare for a visitor. Don Pedro Menendez de Aviles will arrive in this town before the day is over."

Kwambu watched without expression as Menendez and his escort left Outina's hall. He had not remained here long, the man who called himself Adelantado, the man Dancing Egret—incredibly—now called "husband." Once he had accepted the gifts Outina hastily assemembled in exchange for the colored beads and lengths of fabric Fontaneda had presented in his master's name, and won Outina's permission to erect a cross in the plaza, he had courteously taken his leave. How sincere that courtesy was, Kwambu could not guess; but both the Holata and his mother had been impressed with Menendez's soft voice and gracious manner.

He listened to the drum of rain on the thatched roof and smiled wryly. That was what had impressed them the most, of course, and still had them speechless with awe. For Outina had sent Fontaneda back to tell the waiting Menendez that he would be welcome in his town only if he would make it rain here the way he had in Guale. When the impossible happened—dark clouds racing in from the edges of the sky, Thunder finding his voice at last and commanding Lightning to pucker the air—everyone had run outside to see a veritable deluge begin just as Menendez stepped into the town. Watches for Omens, tottering from his small house, had lifted his arms and, with tears coursing down his wizened face, let the rain beat upon him until he shivered so violently that Palm Tree

Bending hurried to wrap a cloak around him. Even Moon of Winter had been shocked into silence.

She was not silent now. "You're making a mistake by allowing six of Menendez's men to remain here," she said to her cousin. "Please, before he has gone far, send to him and tell him you have changed your mind."

Outina shook his head. "I go in fear of a man whose God can make it rain when our gods cannot," he said. "All of us do, except you, Moon of Winter. And your husband, perhaps." He looked briefly toward Kwambu, who nodded; surely it had been coincidence only, the rain finally coming at just that moment? "Those men are here to teach all of us about Menendez's God, and where is the harm in learning about a god whose power has already been proven to us?"

Palm Tree Bending lifted to her breast the little girl she had despaired of ever being blessed with. It seemed to her she could almost hear the crops in the fields stretching themselves to receive the nurturing rain, and the seeds that had so far refused to sprout sending down roots. Her precious babe would not go hungry after all. "If my husband sends the soldiers away," she said to Moon of Winter, "Menendez will ask his God to take away the rain. He told us so."

Moon of Winter looked at her. "What he said," she reminded her sharply, "was that if his soldiers were not treated well, he will return and cut off Outina's head!"

It was the only time his soft voice had hardened, when he'd said that. But so bemused was everyone by then that Kwambu thought only he and his wife had been listening closely when Fontaneda relayed the threat.

"I did not hear him say that." Walks Tall Woman glared at her niece. "Nor did you, I expect; you are only repeating what the trader—who apparently aspires to a job usually performed by berdaches—told you. And I have often suspected that traders, like berdaches, are merely half-men, and will instigate trouble purely from dissatisfaction with their lot."

Kwambu shook his head at his wife when she turned a furious gaze on the Principal Woman. For Moon of Winter to spring to her husband's defense would only divert the flow of the discussion, and she needed to concentrate on reasoning with the Holata. Like Kwambu, she had noticed how several of the soldiers who were ultimately chosen to stay behind had stared at Kaia when she had done an impromptu dance to celebrate the rain. There had been something other than admiration in those stares, something hot and ugly, and Kwambu and his wife had been much relieved when Kaia's leaps and twirls had taken her beyond them.

But combined fury and desperation suddenly led Moon of Winter astray. "My crystal has warned that disaster will strike if we let the Christian soldiers stay," she said to her cousin. "Surely you will not question what the crystal predicts?"

This time, Walks Tall Woman's vituperation was aimed at her niece. "And just when did you consult your crystal, Moon of Winter?" she challenged. "You and your husband came into the Principal House when the first group of Spaniards did, and you have not left it since."

Kwambu laid a restraining hand on his wife's arm, but she was too upset to pay heed. "I looked into it at the time of the new moon," she said rapidly. "I didn't know then that Menendez would come here, but you will remember how we talked about the possibility of his doing so, and how I was against it. That was why I turned to my crystal, to learn if I was right or wrong in how I felt."

"At the time of the new moon," her aunt said triumphantly, "you were in the women's hut with me, taking care of Palm Tree Bending. And we remained there until the moon was swelling again."

Moon of Winter could not deny this. The birth hadn't been an easy one, and in the end she'd been driven to give Palm Tree Bending an infusion of thorny greenbrier to ease the pains that for nearly three days had wracked her thin body. Only then had her cousin's wife been able to relax enough to let her babe slide into Walks Tall Woman's waiting hands.

She hung her head as Outina looked at her sorrowfully. "I should not have said that I actually consulted my crystal," she whispered. Then her voice strengthened. "But I am sure, surer than I can say, that my crystal is responsible for the bad feelings I have about the Spanish. Please; you must believe me, and send those men away."

It was too late; the damage had been done. Outina came to his feet. "The soldiers will stay," he said.

Chapter 40

— ● —

"I wish I did not have to leave," Kwambu said to his wife. "Like you, I am uneasy about the Spanish soldiers. If I thought he would listen, I would try to persuade your cousin that you are right and he is wrong. But we both know it would do no good."

Moon of Winter added dried animal dung to the corncobs and rotten wood burning in a shallow pit over which she had erected a dome of saplings. "Now that I've lied to him, he will never again believe anything either of us tell him," she said without looking up. "I'm sorry, Kwambu, that I was such a fool." Her pinched voice hinted at the wretchedness he knew must be in her face, and the hands unrolling the deerskin trembled.

"When Outina discovers that your aversion to the soldiers is far from baseless, he will trust you again," Kwambu said gently. "I think you were right, you know, when you said that your crystal warned you to beware of them. By now you must be acutely sensitive to its vibrations." The soldiers Menendez had left behind were doing little to encourage the townspeople to gather daily before the cross in the plaza and pray to the God it represented. They preferred to lounge in the shade and make rude jests about the men and women who happened by. Their targets were rapidly deserting them, however; Outina's people could not understand what the Spaniards were saying, but more and more of them had come to feel uneasy when they were anywhere near the pale-fleshes. "In time," Kwambu told his wife, "Outina will see the soldiers for what they are."

"By then," Moon of Winter said bitterly, "who can say what will have happened? But your staying here, even if you could, won't open my cousin's eyes for him." She produced a strained smile. "I only wish you could take Kaia with you. One of the Spaniards—the man whose nose overshadows his mouth—has more than once tried to separate her from her companions." Their daughter had been told to go nowhere alone, but both feared a day might come when she would be in too great a hurry to be properly cautious.

Frustration gnawed at Kwambu. Even though he had taken his sons aside and asked them to watch over their sister, it was such a passive way, such an unmanly way, for a father to protect his daughter. And Hawk and Fox could not consistently refuse to join the hunting parties that were going out steadily now, not without jeopardizing their status. "I very much wish that I could take Kaia with me," he said to his wife. "But I have already lingered too long; to get back to the island in time, I will have to travel day and night. She would never be able to keep up with me." If he knew that Menendez, before he came north, had taken Dancing Egret back to her brother, he might be tempted to risk Calusa's wrath and make the journey in easy stages. Egret would delight to make his daughter welcome, he was certain. Yet his old friend might still be in Havana, and he would not entrust Kaia to anyone else.

As Kwambu helped Moon of Winter stretch the hide over the dome and peg it down, he silently cursed his circumstances. Why oh why must duty bind him to the whims of Headchief Calusa? A man with a family needed to be his own man, needed to be on hand to shield them from any and all danger. . . .

Moon of Winter guessed what he was thinking. "No harm will come to Kaia," she said. "This, I promise you." And there was such fierceness in her face that her husband dropped his corner of the pelt. Her eyes flashed, her lovely mouth tightened, her delicate jaw thrust itself forward. And her scarred cheek reddened suddenly, as though it were the repository of a rage Kwambu had not thought his woman capable of.

"I believe you," he said. "I feel shame that it is you and not I who will look to her welfare, but I can see that I need not worry about Kaia."

Moon of Winter's expression softened. She stepped closer, lifted her hands and laid them on his shoulders. "We will manage until you can return to us," she said more naturally. "Meanwhile, I'll remember our afternoon in the place of magnolias, and dream of our next time there." She smiled with her eyes. "As I always do. Take care, beloved, until we can be together again."

She did not watch him walk to the gate. Experience had taught that this only intensified her anguish, and today—when months might pile themselves into years before she saw him again—her anguish was already beyond measuring. Crouching beneath the sapling dome, she checked the color of the smoke and estimated when the fire would need feeding again. Her promise to her husband had had a fine ring to it. She had even felt, momentarily, as brave as she sounded. But if and when the time came to test her courage, she could only pray that it would be equal to the task.

Dancing Egret held a sobbing Chattering Squirrel in her arms. "I promised Swift Eagle I would arrange for us to be married as soon as he returns from that . . . that *Cuba*," the young maiden wailed, "and now I find I cannot keep my promise."

Above Squirrel's tumbled hair, Egret's face was testament to her fury. How like her brother to tell Squirrel that since Swift Eagle would be a Christian when he came home, only a Christian priest could grant permission for him to wed. Ysabel had gone with the girl to speak with Father Rogel, the priest who had come to the island on the boat that brought Dancing Egret home. Father Rogel was an improbably shaped man, with spindly arms and legs and a chest so huge that his voice boomed when he talked. Which he seemed to do continuously. Egret had not liked him from the first, and now that he had said Squirrel and Swift Eagle would not be allowed to marry, she heartily detested him.

"Your Ysabel tried and tried to explain that I am not truly Eagle's sister, even though the priest has heard that he calls me that," Squirrel said, struggling to control herself. She sat up, wiped tears from her face with both hands. "It's a jest, you see," she said, offering explanation where none was necessary. "He is a cousin of mine, I suppose, just as he is to you. But"— tears threatened once more—"we were born into different clans, Egret. Why can't the priest understand that?"

Egret looked out across the town, looked beyond it to where Spanish soldiers were erecting both a fort and what Menendez called a "chapel." A chapel was a sort of church, and remembering the one in Havana, the one she had so dreaded entering and had always been grateful to leave, she promised herself that she would never, ever, set foot in this one.

She winced as a misplaced hammer blow spawned a stream of shouted Spanish curses, returned her attention to Chattering Squirrel. "You have been refused permission to marry," she told her, "but don't let that stop you from being with Swift Eagle as often as you can. If he were not ruling clan, it wouldn't matter whether you were formally wed or not. Until he could build a house for you, you'd simply move your belongings to the house he grew up in. Indeed, that's what you ought to do."

Squirrel shook her head. "His mother," she said simply, and Egret nodded. Quiet Lagoon's temper had sharpened, if such a thing were possible, in the years since her husband died. Chattering Squirrel did not need to have her spirit wounded further by the tongue-lashings that would surely be her fate if she lived beneath the same roof as Swift Eagle's mother.

"Our world is changing," Egret said sadly, "and I don't think things will ever again be as they were." There had been no Ceremony of First Harvest this year, for Calusa had bowed to Menendez's insistence that pagan rites would offend his God. Although the Headchief held himself aloof from the cross-worship that was mandatory on the island now, and made mock of the Spanish priest's bombast, he was anxious to prove to Menendez that his was a Christian town. "With so much change, and none of it for the better, all of us need to seize what we can of happiness. So don't deny yourself Swift Eagle's love, and don't cheat him of yours. When he comes home again, you may use my house whenever the two of you wish to be alone together. What Calusa and the Spanish priest don't know, they cannot complain about." She paused, smiled wistfully. "Mine is a house that has sheltered lovers before; it will be happy to do so again."

Squirrel's fervent thanks told Egret she had done the right thing. But as the girl descended into the compound, Dancing Egret found herself wondering what would become of Squirrel and Eagle, of everyone, if things went on as they were. She picked up the winsome raccoon Shore Walker had long ago carved and caressed it as she brooded. To the south, smoke grayed the air above the Temple mound, and Dancing Egret knew that Vision Seeker was once again burning tobacco in an effort to placate the gods. She had never counted herself a particular friend of the elderly priest, but it had grieved her to watch him suddenly shrivel when the Ceremony of First Harvest was cancelled. Now Vision Seeker seemed to shrink a little more each day as he sent up prayer after solitary prayer, beseeched the gods to forgive Headchief Calusa, and begged them to continue to look after Calusa's hapless people. More than once Egret had gone across the canal to visit him, to let him know how much she appreciated his remaining on the island when—in the circumstances—he might be expected to turn his back on it.

"I was priest here when Great Calusa was young," the old man had told her, a small smile tugging at the corners of his thin lips. He'd looked down at his big-knuckled, brown-spotted hands. "I suppose I should say instead: when both of us were young. Your father never forgot to honor the gods of his ancestors," he went on, memory brightening his rheumy eyes, "or to treat with respect the opinions of his priest. I owe it to him to remain here, even though the years weigh heavy on me, and the son of Great Calusa has decided to reject the gods The People have always revered."

"Others left the island when my brother forbade them to celebrate the ripening of the season's crops," Egret reminded him.

That was so. Whole families had packed their belongings and gone to seek asylum with clan-kin who lived elsewhere. Calusa had been indifferent to their leaving until the day his Chief Speaker went to live with a nephew on one of the long islands to the north. Her brother had raged about that: *How can a man I named counselor be so ungrateful?* he had demanded of Dancing Egret. Who had made haste to point out that Calusa had not consulted his counselors before replacing the old gods with the Christian one, and that, since Menendez came, Calusa had not once summoned Growling Bear to speak for him; instead, he used a slave familiar with the Spanish language. She had not told him what Bear said to her before he left: that Calusa no longer needed a Chief Speaker to keep his people informed about what their leader had in store for them. "Whatever the Headchief's plans may be these days," he had said bluntly, "he prefers to keep them to himself."

Then he had stepped down into the long canoe his grandson was steadying against the seawall, and given the signal for his two sons to ply their paddles.

But unlike Growling Bear, Vision Seeker would not be leaving the island. Old he might be, and feeble, but Egret did not doubt for a minute that he would abide by what he'd told her:

"This is where I belong, Daughter of Calusa, and this is where I mean to stay."

Dancing Egret hoped fervently he would not come to regret his decision. Sighing, she set the wooden raccoon back on the shelf, a shelf on which the miniature figure reigned supreme now. On impulse she had entrusted to Growling Bear the other carvings Shore Walker had made, among them the kneeling panther, the alligator, and the doe's head that was her favorite. *It grieves me to part with them,* she had told her husband's kinsman, *but it would grieve me more if the Spanish discovered them and declared them to be symbols of what they call our pagan religion. Should Menendez or his priest order them destroyed, my brother will never hesitate to have it done.*

Bear had exclaimed over their beauty, and sworn they would not fall into the hands of the pale-fleshes, but now Egret had only her flute and this tiny raccoon. Was this how the reshaping of people's lives began, she wondered suddenly, with a severing of all links to the past? She studied the causeway that stretched to the entrance canal. If the Spanish decided they misliked its contours, that the conch shells should be set sideways instead of lengthwise, would they order even the bottommost layers of shell, those that lay beneath the water now, reversed? Very likely. And they would stare open-mouthed when the whole causeway came tumbling down, and never understand why it had happened.

All that was, all that would ever come to be, arose from the past. And although Vision Seeker had been effectively banished to his lonely vigil on the Temple mound, Dancing Egret was still in a position to see to it that her people did not forget their beginnings. Soon the children would be gathering in the compound, as they did every day; soon she would join them there and Sing for them one of the Legends that told how things had been when the world was new.

She returned her gaze to the causeway, and determination stiffened her soul. While she lived, the foundations of the tribe known as Calusa would remain intact.

So absorbed was Dancing Egret in her thoughts, she did not immediately recognize the tall man whose long strides were bringing him from causeway to town. When finally she did, she flew out of her house to intercept him.

"You're back at last!" she cried, holding out her hands to him. "I've missed you, Kwambu."

He clasped her hands with both of his. "Always I come

back," he said gravely, and if there was sorrow underscoring those words, Egret was too excited to hear it. He raised his eyebrows. "But I no longer know how to address you," he told her. "When I was here last, your brother said that you must be called Dona Antonia now."

Egret pulled her hands free. "On this island, I answer to no name but the one given me at my birth," she said harshly. "And before you repeat something else I'm certain my brother told you, I call no man husband but the one death took from me long ago."

Kwambu set down the sack of copper and soapstone he had brought from his canoe. "I am relieved to hear that," he said, "although it is no more than I expected of you, Dancing Egret. I was appalled when I heard that Calusa had forced you to wed a Spaniard, and even more appalled when I learned he had let you sail away to Cuba. Was it very bad for you there?"

"Beyond the fact that all of my Calusan serving women sickened and died because they were made to go with me— which I will forever blame myself for—I managed well enough," she said, and told him briefly of her exploits in Havana.

A smile lit his dark face at the end. "I should have known Dancing Egret can triumph over anything," he said.

Her eyes clouded. "I am no longer so sure of that," she said, nodding toward the far side of the domiciliary mound. "For all that I tried, I couldn't prevent my brother from allowing the Spanish to build a fort and a church on our island."

Kwambu thought of Moon of Winter and her futile efforts to influence Outina. "The Spanish who have come here this time are shrewder than those who came before, and shrewder than the Frenchmen who tried to settle in Timucuan country. So far, they seem to prefer persuasion to invasion." He described for her all that had been happening in the north since the last time they had spoken together.

"I wish you could have brought Kaia to me," she said when he was finished, "but, in truth, I can't honestly say she would be safer here than there. And you need not have hurried back, after all. Calusa has left the island."

"*He* has gone to Havana?" The trader was astounded.

"No, no. But he has sailed away with Menendez. It seems the Spaniard is anxious to find a river that flows from one side of our land to the other, and my brother told him that such a river probably lies in Tocobaga's province." She sighed. "You see, I had told Calusa what I'd heard while I was in Havana, about Menendez massacring the French soldiers who were where he wanted to be in eastern Timucuan country. Because of that, Calusa went to great lengths to convince Menendez that Tocobaga was sure to greet the Spanish soldiers with arrows rather than hospitality. He thought the threat of opposition would make Menendez decide to massacre Tocobaga's warriors before they could even arm themselves, giving my brother belated revenge on a man he has long called enemy."

Kwambu nodded. He remembered how young Calusa had hoped to prove himself cleverer than Mocoso and Canegacola by having his traders reach the northern Timucuan territories by crossing through Tocobaga's province. His rage had been enormous when Tocobaga refused to permit it. As his sister had warned would happen.

"Like Tocobaga, however," Egret went on, "Menendez would not let himself be used by my brother. He insisted Calusa sail with him, both to show him the way and to make peace with Tocobaga. The Spaniard," she added, her lip curling, "claims that he wants all of the peoples in this land to be friends with one another, so that he can be 'big brother' to all of us."

Kwambu slung his sack over his shoulder again, urged Dancing Egret ahead of him across the compound. "Calusa was not happy about that, I am sure," he said.

"He was most unhappy, but in the end he had to go. No excuse he came up with would satisfy Menendez. And I have reason to be glad that he'll visit Tocobaga. Before they left, I went to him and begged him to find Kneeling Cypress while he is there, and to bring her home when they come. I even had Ysabel go to Menendez and tell him I will be distraught if my brother does not do as I asked him to." For a moment, a fleeting moment, moisture glistened in her eyes. "I've never stopped grieving about what happened to Cypress, you know, and would be much relieved to know that she has forgiven me for my part in it."

"I would be surprised if she did not forgive you many years ago," Kwambu said gently. "If, indeed, forgiveness was even called for. But I hope Calusa can speak with Kneeling Cypress and let her know how you feel."

"I think he'll try to, at least. In any event, I expect my brother will return from the journey a wiser man than he was when he set out." She gestured toward the center of the compound. "He orders his people to prostrate themselves before the Christian cross every morning and evening, but you may be sure *he* doesn't do so! He has held himself aloof from the Spaniards and their demands, as though he were god instead of Headchief, but now he will be unable to avoid Menendez. I'll be surprised if Calusa is not—finally—given his own lesson in humiliation."

Kwambu seated himself in the shade cast by Egret's house. "He will not enjoy it. But even with the lesson learned, will he be able to undo what is already happening here? I fear for you, Egret, fear for you as I do for the people in Outina. I worry constantly about my family. Leaving them this time took all the courage I possess. If I had not given my word to Calusa, if I had not pledged lifelong allegiance to your father, I would have stayed in the north to watch over them. As it is, I do not know when I might be able to return to them. Your brother has said that he wants me here indefinitely, to interpret for him when he wishes to speak with Menendez. Of course," he added wryly, "at the time he was confident that Menendez would want to live here on the island. With you."

"Menendez does not want that," Egret said tartly, "and neither do I. He seems as eager to be gone from here as I am to have him gone." She paused to smile at her faithful Ysabel, who—more concerned with a guest's comfort than Egret had remembered to be—was bringing water and food to Kwambu. "As for your concern about your family," she went on when the trader had expressed his own thanks, "I think I will counsel you as bluntly as you counseled me last time we met. You made me realize then that a Singer's talent is a gift from the gods, a gift that cannot, must not, be forsworn. Now I mean to make you see that you ought to go home, Kwambu. To your real home, which is with your wife and children. Never mind what you promised my brother, or what pledge you once made to Great Calusa. This isn't the same world as it was when we were young, nor are we the same anymore. We've permitted an alien people, and an alien God, to come and live among us, and have surely infuriated all the ancient gods by doing so. What can old allegiances matter when everything else has changed so much? And Calusa has no need of an interpreter; he doesn't know it yet, but I'm quite capable of monitoring the slave who has been serving him so far. When he's home again, I'll tell him that I gave you leave to go. I doubt that the whereabouts of Kwambu the trader will even occur to him, however.

Calusa will be in a rage, I expect, but it won't be directed at you, Kwambu. And if the old gods will put aside their anger and listen to one last prayer from me, perhaps that rage can be put to good use."

"You know that you are telling me not only to forsake old vows, but to never come here again?" Kwambu set down the round of bread he had just bitten into. "How can I do that, Egret? I worry about you as much as I do my own family. To never know what is happening here, or how you fare . . . I simply cannot conceive of such a thing."

Once more Egret's eyes misted, proof indeed that their world had been turned upside down. "I would hardly tell the friend I cherish most I never want to see him again. If matters ever take a turn for the better in Outina's town, I hope you'll decide to journey south once more. But I want you to come because you wish to, not because you feel obliged to. Meanwhile, Moon of Winter will have you at her side. Which is not only where you belong, it's where you should have been from the day you married her. Circumstances didn't permit it then, I agree, but you should let *nothing* stand in the way of it now."

"You have always been one to try and manage other people's lives," Kwambu said. Yet his voice was soft, and Egret understood that his words were jest, not accusation. And that he was trying to show his gratitude to her for telling him to do what, in his heart, he wanted to do.

"That won't change," she told him, and managed a laugh. There must be no mournful note in their parting. "I confess to you that, now I've started Singing again, I'm determined to manage things so that the children will not be robbed of their heritage. The Spanish priest, when he sees me with the little ones, is convinced that I am instructing them in the Christian faith. But what I am teaching them are the old Legends, Kwambu, and I will go on doing so. I may not be able to throw down a fort or a church, and I'm sensible enough not to sneak into the compound in the darkest hours and chop down the Spanish cross; yet I can, and will, see that the children of this town do not go in ignorance of what it means to be Calusa."

Her eyes flashed in a way that reminded Kwambu of his wife when she vowed to protect their daughter from harm, and suddenly he knew that he must return to Moon of Winter, whatever the consequences. "I recall saying to you once that you are one of those born with good sense," he said to Dancing Egret. "That is another thing that has not changed. I will take your good advice."

"I wish my brother were as quick to trust my counsel as you are," she said with a sigh. "He has let the Spanish stay here against my advice, has sent Swift Eagle to Havana against my advice, and he ignored me completely when I tried to tell him he should not encourage Menendez to send soldiers and a Spanish priest to Tequesta. Tequesta was furious about that, and sent word that he no longer considers himself an ally of the Calusa. Which probably means that I will never again see my sister, White Gull." She shook her head sadly. "So many people have vanished from my life, Kwambu, people I truly cared for. Each time it's as though a piece of me has been torn away and flung to the winds. How often can that happen before there is nothing left of me?"

She sprang to her feet, made herself smile. "Pay no attention to my complaining," she said. "I'm feeling sorry for myself today, I suppose; I, who have always despised people who wallow in misery! Come; I'll walk with you to the seawall and see you on your way. Then I can be sure you have taken my 'good advice.' "

Hand in hand, as though they were boy and girl again, the two set out. As they approached the canal, Kwambu reached up and removed the bluejay feathers from his tight-curled hair, held them out to her. "Since I will no longer be able to name myself trader, I would like you to have these, Egret."

She took them from him, removed two feathers from the cluster, handed back the rest. "These, I shall keep to remember you by," she said. "But you have earned your jay feathers, old friend. If you never follow another trading path, you are trader still and always will be. Besides"—she laughed aloud for the first time—"you are not yourself without blue feathers in your hair. Would you make me look upon a stranger when I tell you good-bye?"

With one hand, Kwambu replaced the feathers in his hair; with the other, he freed the sturdy mooring cord from the protruding shell he invariably knotted it around. "You must not say good-bye," he said, stepping down into the dugout. "I will not let myself be one of the pieces of you that is ripped away and tossed upon the winds. One day, Kwambu the trader will return to this island, Dancing Egret. You have my promise on that."

* * *

The people in the Principal House knew as soon as Outina came in that something was terribly wrong. He had long since learned to school his expression, but there was a slump to his shoulders and his walk lacked its customary confidence. Also, he went directly to where Moon of Winter stood, and he had not so much as glanced at her since the day the Spanish came to his town.

"I should have believed you," he said to her. "I should have trusted that your crystal has more than one way of communicating with you."

The other women surged forward to hear more clearly what he was saying, and Moon of Winter's sons set aside the arrows they had been fletching and came to join them.

"It pains me more than you know to have to tell you what I must," Outina went on, "That you should be the one to suffer most when all the guilt is mine fills me with shame."

Moon of Winter fought to subdue the shivers of apprehension that made her stomach flutter. "What has happened?" she asked quietly.

Outina bowed his head. "The Spanish soldiers sent that interpreter, Fontaneda, to me this morning. They claim that proper hospitality means more than good food and comfortable lodging. Now they want . . . companionship as well. If I do not provide it within three days, Fontaneda tells me, they will send a message to the Adelantado to return here and punish me for breaking my promise to him."

Walks Tall Woman pushed herself to the forefront of the women. "What does he mean, 'punish'?"

"In this, too," Outina said heavily, "Moon of Winter had the right of it. It seems that Menendez will cut off my head if I do not meet his soldiers' demands."

Palm Tree Bending uttered a cry and flew to her husband's side. "Then you must give them what they ask for," she said. "Whatever that may be."

"So my Principal Men said, when I told them about this. But like them, you do not know exactly what they want." The Holata turned again to Moon of Winter. "They want maidens sent to them," he said, "to serve them as concubines."

Walks Tall Woman snorted. "That should be no problem. I can think of at least a dozen who spend more time slipping away into the forest with warriors than they do at the chores assigned to them. Let them lift their skirts to good purpose for once!"

Outina kept his eyes fixed on Moon of Winter's face. "They do not want just any maidens," he said. "Fontaneda presented to me the names of those they have chosen."

Moon of Winter swayed as apprehension escalated into gut-churning fear. She knew what he would say next. She knew!

She was right. "I am sorry to tell you this," her cousin said, "but your daughter Kaia is one of them."

Moon of Winter's mouth shaped the word *No!* but the sound of it was locked in her throat. As though from a great distance, she heard shocked exclamations rise around her.

None of the exclamations were couched in the deep voices of her sons, however. Silently, Hawk Flying High and Red Fox Barking looked at one another; silently, they went together to the weapons wall and took down their battleaxes; silently, they turned and made for the door.

Their mother watched with expressionless eyes. Then, all at once, reason returned and jabbed her into motion.

"You will not!" she cried, racing across the floor to bar their exit. Like a female bear herding a pair of impetuous cubs away from danger, she flung out her arms, drove them back to the Principal Woman's hearth. "Take the time to think," she said strongly. "If the Spaniard has threatened to slay Outina should his soldiers merely complain of his hospitality, what do you think he'll do if the two of you take the lives of the men he left here?"

It was the Holata who answered her. "He will send more soldiers, to kill everybody who lives in my town."

"If he sends more soldiers, then we will slay them as well," Fox said, his usually cheerful face a mask of hate. "Let us pass, Mother."

"We will not be alone," Hawk said grimly. "When we have spoken to Black Wolf Running, he will urge all the warriors to follow us against the Spanish. And none will refuse him, not when they know why."

"And you believe that the warriors from a single town will be able to defeat all of the Spanish soldiers that have come to this land? For you are speaking of war, my sons, not just of battle." She looked to her cousin. "Tell them, Outina."

"Your mother speaks truly," he said. "I understand and sympathize with what you want to do, but it is not the answer to our problem."

Red Fox continued to rant, but Hawk loosened his grip on

his axe. "Perhaps we could rouse the warriors from other towns also, and even from other provinces," he said hopefully.

"Do you think they will rush here to save one of our maidens from having to sleep with a man who is not her husband?" Outina asked. He shook his head. "As Walks Tall Woman pointed out only moments ago, there is no disgrace in a woman giving herself to any man so long as she is not already wed. Kaia may be your sister, and her situation is considerably different from what my mother was describing, but warriors in other towns do not know Kaia; they will think all of this a great deal of fuss about nothing. As for urging warriors from other provinces to join you, when have we Timucuans ever stood together? Against anything?"

Fox glared at his brother. "Then it is up to us, after all," he said. "Or up to me alone, if you will not come with me."

"Neither of you will be permitted to invite tragedy upon everyone in this town," Moon of Winter said firmly. "I have forbidden it; your Holata has forbidden it; and your father, were he here, would forbid it also."

"And what of Kaia?" Red Fox demanded. "Do you think she will forbid it, Mother, when she knows what's in store for her?"

Moon of Winter sent up a prayer of thanksgiving that her daughter had volunteered to go with Watches for Omens while he gathered herbs and medicinal roots from the forest on the other side of the river. Because of the Shaman's frailness, Outina no longer let him go far from home without being accompanied by at least two young warriors. Kaia was safe. For now. "I will look after Kaia," she told her son. "As I promised Kwambu I would." She breathed deep to calm herself. "Outina, when you came into the hall, you implied that you will never again disbelieve what I tell you, or fail to have trust in me. Did you mean it?"

Her cousin nodded. "I did."

Moon of Winter turned to the others who stood in a circle around her. "And the rest of you, will you follow Outina's lead and trust me to honor the promise I gave to my husband?"

The women murmured assent, and Hawk Flying High, after a long moment, followed suit. There was something in Moon of Winter's face they had never before seen, and it both awed and discomforted them.

Moon of Winter regarded her younger son, the only person who had refused to admit trust in her. "I can do nothing unless

I have your support as well, Fox," she said to him. "If you can't bring yourself to give it freely, will you accept a wager from me?"

His jaw dropped. What could his mother mean by speaking of wagering at such a time? He contented himself with a grunt, which might signify anything.

"I will wager that I can arrange matters so that the Spanish soldiers will no longer want your sister to come to them. If I succeed, you will be obliged to keep your peace with them."

"And if you fail?"

Moon of Winter hesitated, then risked it. "If I fail, I will give my blessing to your taking up whatever weapon you choose and using it against the soldiers."

Chapter 41

Ignoring the open-mouthed stares inspired by her peculiar appearance, Moon of Winter hurried through the town. Once Red Fox had grudgingly accepted her wager, she had set to and transformed herself. After raking fingers through her hair to send it into spikes around her head, she'd smeared red paint over the clutch of scars on her cheek. When she was satisfied that the puckered ridges stood out like fiery brands, Moon of Winter had flung around herself the soiled bed robe Palm Tree Bending spread on the floor for her daughter to crawl on, grabbed a battered basket she'd been meaning to reweave, and left the Principal House before bravado deserted her.

Now she made for the river, and followed it to a place where the ground was low and boggy. As she sloshed through mire, her eyes searched this way and that until they lit upon a lank shrub whose bright green leaves were shafted with crimson. Crouching, she wrapped an edge of the tattered robe around her hand and—pushing aside clusters of creamy berries—broke off several branches, partially crushed their leaves beneath her moccasined feet, and laid them in the basket. Which would certainly have to be burned once this day was over, along with the disreputable robe.

She smeared her hands with mud, the only protection that might not arouse suspicion, then stood up. She had what she needed; there was no sense in postponing what must be done now.

The house the Spanish soldiers occupied sat against the palisade not far from the town's entrance. The men were all outside, sprawled around a fire into which they were tossing kernels of corn. Moon of Winter wondered who had taught them this trick; perhaps they'd seen children do it and noticed how eagerly the boys and girls stuffed themselves with the swollen white kernels that eventually popped out of the flames. It was of no importance; what mattered was that their fire gave additional scope for her "powers" to be displayed.

She let her shoulders sag beneath the robe, hunched her back, and sidled around the corner of their house. One of the soldiers looked up, and she froze. It was the long-nosed man whose lust for Kaia both she and Kwambu had been aware of from the start.

He laughed and said something Moon of Winter could not understand, but which persuaded his companions to look at her also. She fixed her eyes on the interpreter, Fontaneda, and—adopting one of their own deplorable habits—raised her mud-caked right hand and pointed a finger at him. With her left hand she removed a sumac branch from her basket and held that up, too, wafting it from side to side.

"What do you want?" Fontaneda demanded.

She moved closer to the group, using the branch to describe circles and undulating lines in the air, shaking it vigorously from time to time. When two leaves fell off and dropped into the Spaniards' fire, she did not let satisfaction show in the eyes that continued to stare fixedly at the interpreter. "I am here because I was sent," she said in a singsong voice. "Where the spirits send me, I go."

Fontaneda narrowed his eyes. "It is the woman who is a cousin of Holata Outina," he said to his fellows. "Why she is dressed as she is, and why she is brandishing that greenery, I cannot imagine. Or why she should suddenly seem a crone, when I know she is not." He guffawed. "It may be she is one of those shape-changers I have heard savages whisper about!" He flapped his hands at her: *go away.*

Moon of Winter scowled. "No one sends me away but the spirits that brought me here," she chanted. "I am Daughter to the Sun, and must do as he commands."

The interpreter turned his back on her. "She claims to be a daughter of the sun, which is a god of theirs, I believe. Outina said something of the sort about her when first we came here."

The long-nosed man laughed again. "If that is the sun god's daughter, I would hate to see what the god himself looks like!"

Moon of Winter stamped her feet to recapture their attention, began a slow dance around them. "I have been commanded," she said when she was facing Fontaneda once more, "to bring you warning." She shook the sumac branch at him, shook it a second time so that the tips of the leaves brushed against his neck, repeated the words: "To bring you warning."

He swiped at the tickling leaves with one hand, cursed when oozing sap left a sticky residue on his fingers. "I give you warning, woman," he said forcefully. "Be gone from here, or you will be a sorry daughter of the sun."

She swung the branch away from him, trailed it across the upturned face of the long-nosed man, let it come to rest on the bare arm of the soldier next to him. "My father the Sun is displeased with you," she intoned. "If you would avoid his wrath, you will listen to me."

Fontaneda sat up straight, grinned. "We are being threatened," he said to the others. "Shall I ask her why? It might be amusing to hear what she says."

Most of the soldiers returned his grin; they had nothing else to do, and any entertainment was better than none at all. One young man, however, looked more closely at their visitor and a shadow fell upon his face. "Suppose she is *bruja*, witch?" he asked hesitantly. "We ought not sport with her, if so."

He was promptly shouted down. Fontaneda assumed a stern expression. "Only a fool threatens the soldiers of the Adelantado," he said to Moon of Winter. "Think of that before you speak further, witch." He threw the term at her derisively, but to himself he admitted that today this woman did indeed resemble a witch he had once seen on the streets of Havana. Only ignorant peasants believed in witchcraft, however, and Hernando D'Escalante Fontaneda never let himself forget that he had been born into the nobility.

Moon of Winter widened her eyes, told herself she must not

blink. "My father the Sun has many daughters," she said, spacing the words to infuse them with rhythm. For the first time in her life, she regretted that hers was not a voice made for singing, but perhaps her unharmonious drone was more suited to the occasion. "He calls *daughter* any maid born into our tribe, and charges me to protect her." She turned to them the cheek bearing the red-painted scars, lowered her voice to a growl. "I wear his mark; I have his power."

She stamped her feet again, felt the pouch containing her crystal bump against her chest. Was she going too far? Would the Sun God punish her for making claims that were patently false? With an effort, she thrust aside her fears. "I have the power," she said again, "the power to curse those who do not heed the god's commands." She mumbled words that had no meaning, made sweeping motions with the branch she held poised above the heads of the Spanish soldiers. "Any man who thinks to force a daughter of the Sun to submit to him," she said, framing the words precisely now, "will feel that power. His flesh will burn and blister; his belly will heave, and his bowels decay."

Although many dodged instinctively, she touched each man in turn with the crushed sumac leaves as Fontaneda, affecting boredom now, told them what she had said.

The soldier who had first named her witch leaped to his feet. "You may scoff," he said to the interpreter. "Me, I will take no chances that this hag can do as she threatens." And he bolted into the house, undeterred by the insults the others hurled in his wake.

Moon of Winter could not know what the man had said, but his actions told her that he, at least, had been convinced by her performance. Which was enough. By sunset the itching crawl of flesh, the blisters that rose wherever the sumac leaves had rested, should convince most of his comrades that he had been wiser than they. And those still unconvinced? Once she had added the remainder of the crushed leaves to the meal that would be brought to them, their hard-held doubts would evaporate as swiftly as the smoke from their poorly laid fire was doing.

She flung the branch she was carrying into the embers and hoped that the smoke spawned by its burning would creep into the soldiers' eyes. The more they suffered, the better. Then she jabbed her finger one final time in Fontaneda's direction, cackled like a demented she-turkey, and left them to the agony they so richly deserved.

"That husband of yours," Headchief Calusa said, "does not show proper respect to his kinsman. Not only did he refuse to have his soldiers turn their guns on Tocobaga, he would not even permit me to take the warriors I'd brought with me for the purpose and go and set fire to Tocobaga's house." Petulance slitted Calusa's eyes and pulled down the corners of his mouth. "My men and I were going to sneak away from the ship as soon as it anchored and swim to the town. It was a good plan, and would have worked if Menendez had not posted guards to thwart us."

Dancing Egret contented herself with a nod, wondered wearily why it had surprised her brother when Menendez abided by what he'd told him in the first place. It was Kneeling Cypress she wanted to hear about, needed to hear about. But until Calusa vented his discontent, Egret would be wasting words to ask about her.

"When finally he persuaded Tocobaga to meet with him," Calusa went on, "Menendez took the seat of honor beside Tocobaga and I was forced to sit below them both." He flung himself onto his carved stool. "Is that any way for a man to treat his brother-in-law?" he demanded. "And then, to have him insist that Tocobaga and I agree to 'reconcile our differences,' and say that he would go to war against whoever broke the peace he was imposing . . . what right did he have to do that, Egret?"

"None at all," she said quietly. And bit her tongue to keep from saying more.

"He is not to be trusted, that Menendez," Calusa muttered. "Did I tell you what happened on the voyage home?"

He had, but Egret knew she would hear the story again. Her brother had sent away his mother, his wives and daughters, and the clan leaders who had gathered in the house as soon as Calusa returned to it, in order to speak alone with his sister. She told herself she ought to feel complimented, but she was wholly aware that he must want something from her.

"One of the Spanish seamen hit me on the head with a coil of rope," the Headchief was saying. "Hit *me*, Egret! And when I naturally gave him a resounding blow and tried to toss him overboard, Menendez himself wrestled me away from him. Well," he added hastily, "he called for some of his men to help, for he knew I was too strong for him to subdue on his own. And he did not even punish the seaman for what he had done, Dancing Egret. Instead he had his interpreter tell me that I was fortunate, that under Spanish law *I* could be slain for striking a Spanish sailor! Of course, he was already in a sour mood; not only did he fail again to locate the son he's been seeking ever since he came here, but that treacherous Tocobaga swore to him that the only river linking this coast with the eastern one flows through Calusan territories, not Timucuan." He shook his head morosely. "Menendez did not believe me when I said that Tocobaga's words were false, that there is no such river on the southern peninsula. I described how we go from west to east by following constantly changing waterways through the river glades, and that these are sometimes too shallow even for our canoes, yet I saw doubt in his eyes all the time I was talking. As if I would lie to my own sister's husband! That man understands nothing about the bonds of kinship, Egret, nothing at all." He selected a plum from the platter of fruit his First Wife had prepared for him, bit into it.

Egret seized the moment. "While you were in Tocobaga," she asked quickly, "were you able to learn anything about Kneeling Cypress?"

Calusa blinked, as though trying to place the name. "Oh. That girl you were once friendly with. Yes, the interpreter inquired about her, and Tocobaga had her brought to his house." He would not tell his sister that he had forgotten what she'd asked him to do, that it was Menendez who prompted the interpreter to inquire about Cypress. "I was surprised when I saw her," he told Egret. "For some reason, it hadn't occurred to me that she would be even older than you are. But once I'd recovered from the shock of finding myself face-to-face with a woman old enough to be my mother, I told her you were concerned about her, that you wanted us to bring her back to the island when we came." He finished off the plum, picked up a bunch of grapes.

"But you didn't bring her," Egret said. "Why not, Calusa?"

"Because she did not want to come," the Headchief said. "She said she has remembered you all these years, just as you have remembered her. But she has a husband in Tocobaga now, and children, and grandchildren. She said you would understand that she cannot leave them, for any reason."

"Did she seem happy?"

Calusa shrugged. "Who can tell, with a woman? All of you

are given to saying one thing and meaning another. But she looked well. For a woman of her years, that is."

Dancing Egret felt curiously deflated. All that worry and mental flagellation, only to find that Cypress lived surrounded by family she cared for and who surely cared for her. Who would have thought that Egret could end by envying Kneeling Cypress?

"Swift Eagle met me on the causeway this morning and walked with me into town," Calusa said abruptly. "Even though he, too, has a Spanish name now—Don Felipe, is it?—he seems to me no more Christian than you are."

"He knows the words he was taught while he was in Havana," Egret said cautiously. "As I do."

Calusa smiled. "But that does not make either of you Christian," he said softly.

Would this be a good time to beg her brother to sanction Swift Eagle's marriage to Squirrel? Egret wondered. No; better to wait. They were managing well enough to be together frequently. "It's not easy, to turn your back on the gods of your childhood," she said.

Calusa got up, stared out at the steadily rising fort and chapel that were gradually obliterating a view he had always cherished. "Those structures," he said forcefully, "are abominations. We should never have given in to Menendez's pleading that they be built."

We? Egret thought. And there had been no pleading; the Adelantado had said they must be built, and Calusa had pretended delight in the idea! "Ysabel has heard that Menendez means to leave many more soldiers here when he goes away again," she said. "You gave him permission for this?"

"I was not consulted about it," Calusa said tightly. "As I told you, your husband has no conception of the respect due a kinsman." He swung around. "We will soon be overrun with Spanish Christians," he said. "What will become of us then, Egret?"

Egret swallowed hard. How tempted she was to rage at her brother, scream at him, make him admit that he was only repeating what she herself had been saying all along. But angering him would scarcely improve their situation. "Menendez will have more soldiers here than you have warriors," she said. And shivered. "Yet I do not think he will take them away just because you ask him to."

Calusa studied her through half-closed eyes, his long fingers playing idly with the sun-shaped gorget that dangled against his broad chest. Like the chain it was suspended from, it was made of Spanish gold, but the glowing pearls that marked its circumference were a treasure unique to the northern part of this country. When the ornament was new, the Headchief had worn it only on ceremonial occasions, but now that the people were forbidden to go to the Temple mound for the ceremonies that had once highlighted every season, he wore it constantly. And always he caressed the pearls that decorated it as though they, and not the blood that pulsed through his lean body, proved his status. "I had hoped," he murmured, his examination of her finally at an end, "that by now you would be ... fleshier than you are, Egret."

"Fleshier? Why would I—" Suddenly she knew what he meant. "I am not carrying the Spaniard's child, Calusa," she said sharply.

"You disappoint me," he told her. "Ever since I permitted you to go to Havana, I have been waiting for your belly to swell. No wonder Menendez does not take care to treat me properly. What man is satisfied with the gift of an empty vessel? If you could bear even a daughter, it would strengthen the ties between the Adelantado and me. Then I would not be plagued with all these problems. Whenever I made my wishes known, about anything, Menendez would heed them." He opened his eyes fully. "Perhaps, if you tried harder, you could still do this for me, Egret, and for our people. Tell Menendez that you have reconsidered, that you want to live with him in a house on my island. Three days, and I can have one ready for you. Then, if you continue barren, I will find him a second Calusan wife. Brown Pelican's daughter, perhaps, the one called Chattering Squirrel. She is both young and pretty, and shares our blood even though she was born into a different clan. And if she is anything like her mother, she will prove fertile indeed."

Egret vowed silently that she would never let Calusa do to Squirrel what he had done to her. "You think Menendez will remain here for my sake?" she said. "Or because you offer him a younger woman? What purpose would it serve if he did? His soldiers would still be here, and his priest, and his fort and his chapel. If he sired a dozen children here on the island, and every one of them sons, it would not solve our problems, Calusa. No matter what you think."

He sat down again, blew out his breath in an explosive sigh.

"Perhaps you are right," he said. "Perhaps you have been right from the beginning." Which astonished her so that she could not think how to respond. "I doubt Menendez would take Chattering Squirrel for his second wife, even if I offered her," he went on. "He has hinted more than once that, when I become a follower of the Christian God, I will have to put aside one of my own wives." His eyebrows collided as he scowled. "It seems Christian men may have only one woman at a time. Even their chiefs are not permitted more. I cannot imagine why any god would care if a man took a single wife or ten or a hundred, but Menendez says otherwise." Calusa gave a bark of laughter. "He was foolish to do so," he added. "He should have known I will never honor so shortsighted a god!"

He stretched out one hand, pushed away the fruit platter with a gesture that underlined his frustration. "Yet Menendez remains confident that I will become Christian eventually," he said, "which is what disturbs me the most. I am nothing and nobody to that man, Egret. Why, when we were in Tocobaga, Menendez kept calling this island—*my* island—*San Antonio*. Whenever he made reference to it, that is what he said: *San Antonio*. He told the interpreter that this is the name of a saint he is especially devoted to." Briefly, Calusa was diverted. "Egret, what is a saint?"

"Saints are figures carved from wood or stone," Egret replied absently. "Some have very sorrowful faces, and others look as though they are suffering incredible pain."

"Huh!" Calusa said. "Only a pale-flesh would want to name an island for something like that." He brooded further, then leaped to his feet again. "This island is *Calusa*," he said strongly. "It has been Calusa since the day it was built for our ancestors to live upon, and it must never be called anything else." He looked at his sister. All of his arrogance was gone; in his eyes was a blend of anger, determination and—for the first time since he had put on the mantle of Headchief—appeal.

"You and I must find a way to restore this island to the people whose name it bears," he said.

Moon of Winter left the rack of smoking meat she'd been tending and hurried to the Principal House. She glanced toward the rear of the hall, to where Outina's wife and mother were husking a basket of young corn, but—as she'd been told to do by the messenger—she went immediately to a circle that had been formed by the Holata, his Shaman, and his Principal Men.

"We want to give you thanks, formal thanks, for dealing so successfully with the Spanish soldiers," Outina told her. "The Spaniards have decided that their God will be offended if they 'consort with heathen women,' so—whatever magic you worked—it accomplished what we hoped for. You are a Wise Woman in truth, Moon of Winter, and from this day I will heed your pronouncements."

Moon of Winter looked around the circle. Watches for Omens was plainly bursting with pride; every wrinkle in his face turned up as he smiled at her. Many of the rest were smiling also, and warmth coursed through her even as she wondered how to respond to what her cousin had said. She ought to confess that it was trickery and not magic she'd used against the soldiers, but wouldn't that sound ungracious? Perhaps hinting at the truth would be enough. "I am honored by your praise," she said carefully, "but it should go instead to our Shaman. He taught me all I know of plants and their properties. Without that knowledge, I could never have persuaded the soldiers that our women are not for them."

"But the idea was yours. Or your crystal's, which is much the same," the old Shaman said. "You deserve the praise, Moon of Winter."

She returned his smile. "We will share it," she told him. Then, "You do see that you must not relax your vigilance where the Spanish are concerned?" she said urgently to her cousin. For she had lain awake these last few nights, fearful that her scheme might fail, and sleeplessness had encouraged other worries to nibble at the corners of her mind. "So long as the pale-fleshes are anywhere in Timucuan territory, our people are in danger," she continued, trying hard to infect him and all of his advisors with her own sense of foreboding. "Surely you won't let the outwitting of a few gullible soldiers lure you into a complacency that might make you careless?"

Her compulsion to convince had an unfortunate effect: it made her questions sound remarkably like challenges. The assembled counselors retaliated with a silence woven of disapproval, and Moon of Winter made haste to moderate her tone. "On the day the soldiers demanded that they be given choice of our maidens for concubines," she said, looking only at her cousin, "you remarked, despairingly, that we Timucua have never stood together, against anything."

Outina nodded warily. He was not incensed that she had come close to overstepping the bounds of propriety, as some of his counselors obviously were, but neither did he recognize the trail Moon of Winter was leading him onto.

"What you said," she rushed on, "explains why the Spanish, like the French who came before them, easily infiltrated many Timucuan towns. But at the same time it suggests a way to resist both the Spaniards and the God they are trying to foist upon us."

One of the Principal Men spoke up. "If the Christian God can send rain when it is needed, why should the Timucua resist him? We should honor him instead, as we honor our own gods when they smile upon us."

Several of his fellows nodded and murmured among themselves. They not only agreed, they would never be so rash as to disdain the man whose pleas to that God brought an end to drought.

"The rain would have come when it did whether Menendez visited us or no," Moon of Winter said. "It isn't unusual for a long drought to end suddenly and unexpectedly."

"That is true," Watches for Omens confirmed. "Listen to her; this is the Daughter of the Sun, remember, the woman who has recently demonstrated to everyone just how powerful she is."

But his support was not enough, and Moon of Winter knew it. Unless she, too, could bring rain to thirsty fields, many of her own people would insist she only walked in the shadow of a man who could. Nonetheless, she persisted, for she was uncomfortably aware that this would probably be her last chance to speak freely to the decision-makers of this town. "If, for once, the Timucua Holatas could ally themselves with one another," she said, praying earnestly that the skill to persuade might be lent to her, "wouldn't that make us strong enough to drive the Spanish soldiers from our territories? Surely Holata Saturiba must be ready to do almost anything to have them gone. Even though his people and ours have for decades met solely on the battlefield, couldn't you put aside your differences long enough to stand together against a common enemy? And if two powerful Holatas form an alliance, won't lesser leaders be eager to join?" For all her determination to speak calmly, the passion of conviction swelled Moon of Winter's voice.

This time her words were greeted with prompt and vehe-

ment protest. Even Watches for Omens, although he said nothing, looked dismayed. "Should my Principal Men be in favor
of such a thing," Outina said finally, "and it does not seem that
they are, Saturiba would only laugh if I approached him about
an alliance. He would tell everyone that this proves I go in fear
of him."

"You can't be certain of that," Moon of Winter said quickly.
But Outina believed it, which was all that mattered. Although
he'd withheld censure when she had seemed to be questioning
his judgment, now he, too, would brand as nonsense the suggestions she'd been making.

"He is not certain, and never can be. Unless he is brave
enough to send a message to Holata Saturiba."

The Principal Men ceased their agitated muttering; heads
swiveled around as though that strident voice were a cord ex-
erting pressure on seven separate necks. "You have never
lacked courage," Walks Tall Woman said to her son. "What
Moon of Winter suggests calls for something other than
warrior-courage, but it is courage all the same. I think you
should do as she says. Then, perhaps, we will see the last of
the white-skinned beasts that masquerade as men."

The old woman had told no one about it, but when rumor
reached her ears that some of the townspeople felt they were
being mocked by the Spanish soldiers, she had gone to see for
herself what was giving them this surely erroneous impression.
Although she understood the outlanders' language no better
than anyone else, she had always been uncommonly alert to
nuances, and there were certain gestures that must mean much
the same among peoples everywhere. Walls Tall Woman's face
had been hot with more than indignation by the time she
turned around and stalked back to the Principal House. Men
who dared to jeer at her—at her!—were capable of behavior
so vile it did not bear thinking about. Until all pale-fleshes had
departed from this province, Walks Tall Woman knew she
would not be able to rest easy.

All at once Palm Tree Bending came and stood beside
Outina's mother. Her own daughter might be an infant now,
but infants grow into maidens, and Palm Tree Bending never
wanted to see her daughter threatened as young Kaia had been
threatened. "Moon of Winter is right, and Walks Tall Woman
is right," she said to her husband. Her voice lacked the harshness that had made a rasp of her mother-in-law's, but sincerity
gave resonance to every word. "If there is the slightest chance

that Holata Saturiba will ally with you against the Spanish, I think you should take it. And you cannot know one way or the other unless you ask him."

Moon of Winter could scarcely believe what she was seeing and hearing. And if she was astounded, how much more so must Outina be?

Walks Tall Woman had turned her attention to the Principal Men. "If any of you still object to Outina's sending a courier to Saturiba," she said, her eyes spear-point sharp as she focused on each of them in turn, "I would advise you to think carefully before saying so." Wisps of cornsilk clung to her bony forearms, and a single milky kernel decorated one bristling eyebrow, but not a man there saw her as a figure of fun. The Sun God had bestowed power upon Moon of Winter, but by knowing all there was to know about everybody in the town, Walks Tall Woman had amassed considerable power of her own. Everyone in that circle was aware of it, and was equally aware that she would not hesitate to use what she knew for her own purposes.

There were a few grunts of demurral, but they were token only. "I have little confidence that Saturiba will be interested in allying with us," the oldest of the Principal Men said at last, "but I will sanction sending a courier to him." If anyone should learn that this venerable counselor had long ago conceived a fondness for a certain berdache whose female dress suited him better than most people knew, he would be stripped of his status and made an object of ridicule. And Walks Tall Woman's eyes had said that she knew his secret.

His fellows made haste to agree with him. They had secrets of their own they dreaded to have revealed.

Outina nodded. "I will send a message to Holata Saturiba," he said. He had been shocked to have both his mother and his wife show support for Moon of Winter's suggestion, and the prompt capitulation of his Principal Men disconcerted him further. But he had been sincere in his vow to never again mistrust his cousin, so the wisest course seemed to be to ignore his own reservations and make the agreement unanimous.

The sound of voices, voices underscored with affectionate laughter, came from the doorway, and suddenly Kaia ran into the hall. "Mother," she called excitedly, "Kwambu is home again. And this time he is home to stay!"

Here was his courier to Saturiba, Outina thought immediately, and decided to accept the trader's timely arrival as an omen. Perhaps there truly was a chance that his old enemy would respond favorably to his overtures. Or would at least refrain from calling him coward for proposing peace.

As the women had pointed out, he could not know until he had asked him.

Chapter 42

❦ ❦

As the sun's lower edge dipped into the gulf, the shadow of the Spanish cross reached out to touch Dancing Egret and Brown Pelican. They stood at the rear of the crowd in the compound, and had positioned themselves so that none of the townspeople would inadvertently cluster in front of Egret's house and perhaps draw Father Rogel's attention to it. Chattering Squirrel and Swift Eagle had vowed to keep silent while the evening ritual went on, but Egret's memory was long; she knew how easily passion triumphed over common sense. And if the priest—or Menendez—should learn that the young couple had disobeyed the command to gather round the cross at day's end, they would not be pleased. For Squirrel and Eagle to be discovered together in Egret's sleeping place would reveal that they were lovers, too, and Father Rogel at least would be incensed about that. Not only did he persist in regarding the pair as siblings, he frowned on most things that were both right and natural.

The priest's voice swelled as he neared the end of his exhortation. "Those who fail to submit to the one true God," he thundered, forefinger stabbing the air, "will become as spitted deer. They will scream and scream as their souls writhe and sizzle, but it will be too late then for salvation." He was speaking again of hell, a place where fire ran amok as though a cooking hearth had been left untended in the dry season. Earlier, his voice had throbbed persuasively as he told about heaven, about a golden city where the sun shone always and joyful people went around singing. Father Rogel's interpreter, a former slave of Calusa, did his utmost to translate mood as well as content, but few people listened as the priest rambled on and on. They had heard everything before, many times, and were agreed that hell must be a place of sacrifice to the Christian God—which made them wonder why the black-robed man labeled "abominable" the sacrificial rites of the Calusa. As for heaven, it sounded much like this very island, and no one could understand why the Spanish seemed unable to recognize that here was the Paradise they aspired to. Nonetheless, if their own ceremonies had not been curtailed, Calusa's people might have cheerfully added the God of the Spaniards to their pantheon. As it was, they were disinclined to give Him welcome. When the priest raised his skinny arms and blessed those he had just finished threatening with hellfire, not an islander returned his smile.

"Our brother must be blind," Brown Pelican grumbled as the crowd began to disperse, "if he cannot see how he fosters discontent by making the people listen so often to the Spaniard's ranting."

Dancing Egret watched a covey of soldiers stride from the squareground they had briefly been assigned to. Now that the building of blockhouse and chapel was finished, Menendez's men had little to occupy them, and might have been content to wallow in idleness had they not feared the disapproval of Menendez and Father Rogel. Even the biggest and brawniest awarded near-godlike status to Adelantado and priest, a fact that Calusa hoped to make use of in his campaign to rid the island of the intruders. "He has a great deal on his mind these days," Egret said to her sister, and wished she could be more specific. She had been sworn to secrecy about Calusa's nebulous plans, however.

"Well, *he* will not be inconvenienced even if the Spanish priest rains words upon us from sunup to sundown," Pelican snapped. "I have yet to see *his* face in the crowd that gathers in front of that silly thing!" She flung out her hand toward the huge cross, then sighed. "I suppose I shouldn't speak so harshly about someone who is my Headchief as well as my brother, but what I say is true, Egret." Her eyes brooded as she studied those who lingered in the square, but alertness returned to them when she saw that Rain Drop had paused to gossip with several friends. "That girl knows she is to be in the house by full dark," she muttered, and strode purposefully in her daughter's direction. "Come whenever you are ready, Egret," she called over her shoulder.

Her sister grinned. Darkness might be claiming the east, but in the west a narrow wash of residual pink was merely dappled with gray, as though a mischievous child had reached up his hands and smudged the sky with ash. "She will tell you it is not yet night," Dancing Egret called after Pelican. And if that didn't save her from a scolding, Rain Drop—who knew that Egret planned to sleep in their house—would simply wait for her Legend-telling aunt to arrive and intercede for her.

As a few bold stars asserted themselves in the cloud-streaked purple over Egret's head, even the stragglers drifted away. Soon only three people remained in the darkening square: Dancing Egret, the priest . . . and Pedro Menendez.

At what point the Adelantado had come from the fort to join Father Rogel, Egret did not know, but when she spotted him, she stepped into the blacker dark on the eastern side of the cross. The less she had to do with Menendez, the better.

She was considering taking the long way around the squareground when the voices of the two men suddenly crescendoed. They must be moving toward the plaza's center!

". . . agree with you that Antonia should be doing more," Menendez was saying. Egret winced; how she detested that name. Still, she had better find out what the Adelantado was saying about her. "As for Felipe," he went on, "who is better able to set an example for warriors than a Christian who is himself a warrior?"

Dancing Egret pressed herself against the rough wood of the cross, peered cautiously around it.

Father Rogel was nodding vigorously. "I have noticed that Dona Antonia and Don Felipe have more influence over the people than the Headchief. Which is as well. That one will never agree to take religious instruction, or help to propagate the Faith. His promises are empty ones, Captain-General; I hold out no hope for his salvation."

Menendez shrugged. "We must use what is available to us, then," he said. "Calusa, I will deal with when the time is right." His boots aligned themselves neatly as he stopped walking, and Egret sighed with relief; the men had come perilously close to where she stood. "Not everything can wait until I have returned from the north, however," Menendez added, the fingers of his right hand beating a tattoo against his sword sheath.

The priest turned a puzzled face toward his companion.

"There is trouble again in Timucuan country," Menendez explained. "A chief called Saturiba is mustering his warriors. Even though my lieutenant in San Augustin has had the wit to seize the chief's heir, I am uneasy. I trust no one but myself to deal with rebellious savages."

Father Rogel tilted his head like an inquisitive sparrow. Why had the Adelantado sought him out to tell him this?

Egret waited also for enlightenment.

"While I am gone," Menendez said, clasping Rogel's bony shoulder, "I want you to see to it that Dona Antonia and Don Felipe join forces to lead their people to God." Assurance underscored the directive, as though his giving voice to it guaranteed its accomplishment.

Father Rogel made no secret of his skepticism. Waving his hands for emphasis, he launched into impassioned protest. How could he be expected to win cooperation from two people who had, so far, shown little desire to cooperate with him? It was true that Dona Antonia took time every day to teach the town's children, but she ignored utterly his suggestion that she carry God's word to women and elders as well. And Don Felipe—like all the warriors, he continued to come armed to Mass, even though he had been told again and again and *again* to leave his weapons at home. Surely that showed a distressing tendency to do as he pleased regardless of anything the Priest might say to him?

When Father Rogel came to the end of this litany, he clapped his hands together twice to underline his complaints. Egret was tempted to laugh; if the Spanish did not gesticulate so constantly when they conversed, they might be able to walk and talk at one and the same time! She was grateful, though, that their habit confined this pair to one small area, permitting her to eavesdrop with impunity. Behind her a mockingbird offered up a last melodic trill as it roosted among the plaited palm fronds on a nearby house; from beneath the house a pup whined as its mother nudged him away from a late dinner; the long grass edging the square rustled as creatures of the night began to stir. But Dancing Egret heard none of this, so intent was she on what was happening in front of her.

Menendez, tired of being met with resistance or rebellion on every side, unleashed his exasperation. "You will do what you came here to do," he said tightly. "It seems to me altogether possible that these Indians might be more amenable to conversion if they are presented with an example of how God-fearing people live. So before the sun sets tomorrow, you will send for Dona Antonia and Don Felipe and inform them that the cause of the true God can best be served by their marrying each other and establishing a good Catholic household in this town. One that will have all of these heathen eager to emulate them."

Dancing Egret's eyes rounded with shock. Surely Menendez had not said what she thought he'd said?

Father Rogel was equally shocked. "But Antonia and Felipe," he sputtered, "they are cousins of a sort! We might be promoting incest, to encourage them to wed."

Egret's confusion overrode her fury. What did it matter if she and "Felipe" were cousins? What ought to matter to these "good Catholics" was that she was already Pedro Menendez's wife. And the priest, during his interminable preaching, had more than once said that Christian women may not take second husbands any more than Christian men may take additional wives.

"I have always been a devout Catholic." Umbrage basted Menendez's words together. "Anyone who knows me well will confirm this. So you may believe me when I say that Antonia and Felipe are distant cousins only; nothing stands in the way of their marrying. Which I want them to do as soon as you can arrange for a ceremony to take place." Suddenly his tone was knife-edged. "They are certain to be the Headchief's heirs," he said, "and I will see that this happens sooner rather than later if Antonia's brother does not change his ways. With two baptized Christians leading them, this whole prideful breed can be brought to its knees. In the south, at least, I will have succeeded in my mission."

The blood pounded in Dancing Egret's ears; a reddish haze blurred her vision; the taste of bile was in her throat. *What was this man saying?*

Admiration for the Adelantado's strategy remanded Father Rogel's objections. "Both Spain and Mother Church will be in your debt when that happens," he said. "Nor will they consider you ill-advised to take whatever steps may be necessary to protect these heathen from the influence of that heretic, Calusa. But Dona Antonia: she believes herself to be married to you. Surely she will refuse to wed Don Felipe?"

Menendez strode forward, veered to the right, slowed his pace as Rogel, taken off guard, scrambled to keep up with him.

Egret, still reeling from what she had overheard, did not immediately follow. She could not deal with Menendez's greatest villainy, not yet; indeed, he must never suspect that she had been forewarned of his intentions. But dealing with his plans for "Dona Antonia" need not, and would not, be postponed. No man—and in particular no hairy-faced Spaniard—had the right to take Dancing Egret against her will, then, when it suited him, pass her along to another as though she were a blunted hatchet he had no further use for! That she had never considered herself wife to Pedro Menendez made no difference; any man who would treat any woman so ruthlessly was begging to have his rock-hard arrogance hammered into worthless grit. And as soon as she had heard a little more . . .

Ears pricked so she would miss nothing of what they were saying, she eased away from the cross and slid through the night as silently as a panther on the prowl. When she had overtaken the two, she slipped to the left and secreted herself behind one of the uprights supporting the cooking pavilion. A gibbous moon was slowly emerging from a billow of cloud, and Egret watched the pair stroll toward her.

The Adelantado was fingering his neatly clipped beard as he elaborated on his answer to the priest's question. "You will of course use all the diplomacy at your command when you tell Antonia that the ceremony we took part in was no proper marriage ceremony, that I permitted it only to indulge her brother. If she continues to balk, then you must tell her the truth: that I have a wife in Spain. She has been taught that Christians must be monogamous; she will understand." In truth, he did not think she would; the woman's infatuation for him doubtless obsessed her still. That was why he avoided her whenever he visited San Antonio, and why he meant to be well away from here before the priest arranged for her wedding to Don Felipe.

Anger was another of the emotions Egret had for years kept locked away within herself. Now, like a small flame suddenly exposed to air, it burgeoned into a blaze and sheeted through her, obliterating wariness and turning reason to ash. That she was obliged, for the moment, to repress a deeper, more deadly rage only served to feed the conflagration. Arms raised and fingers curved like talons, she sprang from hiding and landed directly in front of Pedro Menendez.

"*Zorrillo!*" she hissed, her face contorted almost beyond recognition. "*Zorrillo!*" Her eyes narrowed. "Yet how can I call you skunk? To do so is to insult a creature who—unlike you—intends no harm. A skunk taints the air only in self-defense; you, Menendez, pollute the world indiscriminately! Like snail slime, foulness slithers in your wake!"

Menendez, astounded to be suddenly face-to-face with what he briefly mistook for a madwoman, had scarcely recovered enough to identify her as Dona Antonia before he was shocked all over again to realize that she was berating him in Spanish. Fluent Spanish. Instinctively, he stepped back from her.

Dancing Egret darted forward until they were nose-to-nose once more. She was not through with him. "Big brother!" she shouted furiously. "Pedro Menendez de Aviles wants only to be 'big brother' to Calusa and his people, to help them all become children of the Christian God. And how does this 'fine Christian gentleman' show his love for his little brothers? By pretending to marry the Headchief's sister even though he already has a wife. A 'fine Christian wife,' no doubt!"

Neatly coiled braids tumbled down to whip about her shoulders; wisps of escaping hair bristled around her face; and in the moonlight her eyes glittered eerily. Had there been a weapon to hand, Menendez thought, Antonia would have raised it against him and been indifferent to the consequences. He set his feet, put out his hands and grasped her wrists. He had seen jealous women before, but this . . . this was unbelievable! "You must calm yourself," he began.

Egret flung back her head, eyed him incredulously. "Calm myself?" she shrieked. She looked to the right, to the left; all around them people were rushing into the squareground to discover what had broached the quiet of the evening. In the doorway of his house atop the mound stood Calusa, wives and daughters flanking him and flare-toting servants huddled behind. Just below them stood Brown Pelican, clutching Rain Drop's hand; and surely that buxom figure hurrying to join the pair could belong to no one but Ysabel. Warriors were ranking themselves along the mound's broad steps, and children peeped out from between knots of anxious matrons. And the bafflement arising from this motley assemblage was so tangible that it jerked Egret to her senses, warned her that she had been shouting insults in a language she was supposedly ignorant of.

Making heroic effort, she stemmed her rage. It was too late to take back the Spanish she had spoken, but it was not too late to monitor what she would say from now on. And she had better watch every word, or Menendez would surely guess that she had overheard more than she'd already admitted to. For her brother's sake, and for the sake of all those who stood watching, he must somehow be made to think otherwise.

"How can I be calm?" she wailed, praying to achieve the misdirection that had been her father's favorite ploy. "Haven't I just learned you do not love me?" As though her plaint were a Legend she was Singing, she squeezed anguish into her voice. "You have two hearts, Pedro Menendez," she moaned, "one for yourself, and one for the enemies of the Calusa. But"—her keening transformed itself into a caterwaul—"you have no heart for me and my poor people, no heart at all!"

"You are wrong, Antonia," Menendez said soothingly, easing his grip on her now that she seemed less inclined to physically attack him. "Naturally you are upset from hearing that our marriage was ... not precisely a marriage, but it is unseemly, all this ranting and whining. And it will change nothing." He should have known that this woman would be given to hysteria; promiscuous emotion symbolized the disorder her people thrived on. The homes that perched on their truncated pyramid leaned to left or right, and no one seemed concerned if the roofs leaked thatch. Menendez envisioned the garrison that stood foursquare against the sky on the far side of the mound, its solid walls running straight and true and its roof sealed tight against wind and rain. *There* was order. And emotions must be as rigidly disciplined or they would overrule the intelligence. As Antonia's were doing now.

For the woman had bowed her head and was sobbing despairingly. The hands he had finally released were clasped in front of her, and she was wringing them in the way that sinful Eve most likely did on the day she and Adam were expelled from Eden. "You do not love me," she cried. "You have never loved me!" Between sobs, she was saying it over and over again.

Yet the Headchief's sister surely owned more intelligence than either females or savages generally did; she must, to have mastered the language of Spain. When there was time, Menendez thought he would question her serving woman about that. Meanwhile, as he clumsily patted Antonia's shaking shoulders, he rapidly reviewed all that he and Father Rogel had discussed. Although Menendez made a habit of speaking quietly, as a gentleman should, the priest was inclined to declamation even in ordinary conversation. Had Rogel said anything that Antonia should not be privy to? Much as he yearned to detach himself from the spectacle Dona Antonia had become,

Menendez needed first to find out if the woman could possibly know more than it was wise for her to know.

"Be at ease," he said, raising his voice to be heard above the racket she was making. "I mislike seeing you so distressed, Antonia," he told her when she quieted somewhat. "It is true that I did not actually wed you, that I could not wed you if I wished to, but I have"—he fumbled for a word that would impress her—"great esteem for you," he finished. "You are a fine woman, Antonia, and a credit to your people." She had ceased to cry, had even lifted her head slightly, which told him that his compliments must have won her attention. "Calusa," he said, introducing the name deliberately, "should be proud that his family has produced so elegant a flower of womanhood."

Egret raised her hands and wiped imaginary tears from her cheeks. "My brother was proud when he thought you had taken me for your wife," she said, making her mouth quiver as she looked into Menendez's eyes, "but I shall be no more than a stickerweed in his path once he learns the truth of the matter." She sighed deeply, rested one hand upon her breast. "He will be *angry* with me," she whispered hoarsely, and let her head droop again. If Menendez had no more originality than to compare her to a flower, then let him see her as a blossom clinging forlornly to a broken stalk.

The Adelantado permitted himself to relax a trifle. Antonia's body had not tensed when he mentioned Calusa, nor had she shown the least inclination to flinch. And he was a man accustomed to probing the depths of other men; he was satisfied that such betraying signs would never have escaped his notice.

He took her hands between his and she looked up once more. "I will speak with Calusa," he told her. "Then he will be angry with me, and not with you." He let animosity roughen his voice, and fine-tuned his alertness so he might accurately gauge her response to what he said next: "In truth, your brother has no right to feel anger toward either of us. Not when it was he who insisted upon our marrying." He made certain she noticed the scowl he put on. "The right to be angry about what happened is not Calusa's," he said grimly. "It is yours. And mine!"

Egret's nose threatened to twitch; Menendez's vigilance was so marked that he gave off the same odor as warriors do who have just danced in a pre-hunting ritual. She invited a pitiful smile to tremble upon her lips. "If you can deflect Calusa's anger from me," she told Menendez, infusing the words with pathetic eagerness, "then I will be grateful beyond measure. I have too often served as target for his rage. I . . . I do not think I can survive it another time."

Menendez stepped back, inclined his head and slowly returned Antonia's smile. Her obvious distress, the slump of her shoulders as she admitted to dissatisfaction with her lot, reminded him that she was, after all, merely an older woman who had no man to provide for and protect her. Even among civilized people, that position was not exactly enviable. Here, where God's work did not yet occupy the minds and hands of such women, their lives must be miserable indeed. Which meant that even if Antonia *had* overheard what he did not wish her to know—which seemed unlikely—he need not worry. When the time came that, through his offices, she ascended to a seat of eminence, the poor woman's gratitude would be so enormous that she would not concern herself with the reason for her elevation.

He smiled again. "The only thanks I ask is that you help me in my efforts to convert your people to Christianity," he said, and turned Antonia toward the priest, whose head had been swiveling back and forth, back and forth, as he tried to absorb every aspect of a most peculiar conversation. "Let Father Rogel be your guide in that, as in all things," the Adelantado finished, "and God will be pleased with you."

Dancing Egret did not trust herself to do more than nod. Nor did she say a word when—with the briefest of salutes—the Adelantado turned his back on her and disappeared into the night.

Could he have known what she was thinking, however, or where those thoughts would eventually lead her, Pedro Menendez's confident stride would have faltered just a little.

Kwambu took his wife's free hand, pressed it reassuringly. "Menendez is not like the pale-fleshes who came here before," he said. "He seems to have enormous faith in his powers of persuasion. For him, fighting will be a last resort." He believed what he said, but that did nothing to allay his particular fears. Hawk and Fox were warriors, and were where they should be: with their Holata and the Paracusi. Kwambu, if he was not a warrior, was at least a man, and a man capable of helping Saturiba's berdache interpret during the parley. But for Moon of Winter to be here, with the guns from a Spanish brigantine pointed directly at her, was madness! Kwambu had understood

Saturiba's wanting to meet her, and been proud to realize that his wife's reputation had spread so far; yet had he realized she would not be remaining safely in Saturiba's town, he would have somehow convinced Outina that, despite Holata Saturiba's request, Moon of Winter should not go east with them.

The Spanish ship dropped anchor; a small boat was lowered and three soldiers began to row ashore. With them was a Timucuan clad in a woman's skirt. Kwambu and Moon of Winter exchanged glances as the keel of the dinghy scraped against sand. The berdache was the one who had come to Outina's town with the Frenchmen. "If the opportunity arises," Kwambu murmured, "I will speak with him and find out if he has overheard anything that might be useful to Outina and Saturiba."

Moon of Winter nodded as her husband slipped away and walked to where Saturiba's Shaman was burning tobacco to purify the meeting place of the Holatas and Menendez's representatives. She still could not believe that she was standing in the midst of a sizable war party, looking out upon the incredible vastness of the ocean. But she had been included when Saturiba, a silver-haired man whose body looked as though it had been carved from a tree trunk, responded to Outina's suggestion of a truce with an invitation to visit him.

"I am an old man," he had said when the delegation from Outina arrived in his town, "and should be able to feel secure about what will happen after I go to join my ancestors. Until recently, I did; my sister's son, Emoloa, was ready to step into my moccasins, and he is a fine man, a born leader. Now"—he had grimaced—"the strangers I foolishly welcomed to my province have seized him, seized both Emoloa and his young son. And all because I permitted my Townchiefs to slay the pale-fleshes who stole food from Timucuan granaries, and attempted to steal some of our women as well!" He'd spread his hands. "The Spaniards who drove away the cursed French are proving to be as great a problem as the Frenchmen were. Once I have ransomed Emoloa and the boy, I want them gone from here!"

Moon of Winter watched now as the old chief's mouth tightened when the berdache finally finished relaying the soldiers' words to the two Holatas. Saturiba folded his arms and, scowling, made curt response. One of the soldiers scowled in return, spoke a second time, then signaled his companions to return to the small boat and row back to the brigantine.

Moon of Winter looked around her. The warriors who had quietly formed a huge semicircle behind Outina and Saturiba stood impassively. Only someone near to them would notice how the muscles in their tattooed arms twitched from time to time, or identify the hatred in their eyes as they stared out at the tall sailing ship. Like her, they blinked as sunlight glared upon the metal helmets protecting Spanish heads; like her, they hoped that the sun's increasing warmth would prove an irritant to bodies sheathed in armor; like her, they waited, waited, waited, for what would happen next.

Chapter 43

◆—— ⟹

Dancing Egret frowned to see how Vision Seeker's hands trembled as he allocated masks to those who had been chosen to take part in the ceremonial Dance, and was all the more distressed to realize that excitement, not anxiety, was responsible for his tremors. "He should not be going with the warriors," she repeated in a whisper as the elderly priest eased a pelican mask over the face of a slender youth and fastened it securely behind his head.

Calusa, fiddling with the white plumes his wives had pinned in his long hair, sighed. "So I told him," he said irritably. "When you asked me to, Egret. And you heard Vision Seeker say that it is his place to challenge Father Rogel."

"But he doesn't understand," Egret persisted. "He looks upon this as a . . . a spiritual battle, a sort of war between our gods and the Christian one. Why don't you explain to him that you're sending Prowling Panther and his warriors to seize the Spanish priest in order to demoralize the soldiers? That your intention is to keep Father Rogel prisoner until every last soldier has fled to the winged ship that waits in the harbor?"

Her brother had the grace to look ashamed, an emotion new

to him. "He was so pleased with me when I went to the Temple mound and told him I will no longer endorse the honoring of an alien god that I couldn't bring myself to bother him with the details of my plan," he said. "Besides, what he is thinking is close enough to the truth. When I have Father Rogel groveling at my feet, won't that be symbolic of the Christian God surrendering to our gods? For I mean for him to grovel, Egret, make no mistake about that! And the soldiers, before they are permitted to flee my island, will be made to tear down both fort and chapel. Only when they have restored the small mound to what it was, only when 'San Antonio' truly is no more, will I have them escorted to their ship. And only when they are within moments of sailing away will I deliver Father Rogel to them." He nodded vigorously. "Oh, yes, Egret. Vision Seeker will have ample opportunity to show Menendez's priest that the gods of the Calusa are more powerful than the God the Christians worship."

Egret watched Vision Seeker put on his own mask, one carved in the likeness of a buzzard's face, and settle a red cloak upon his stooped shoulders. She suspected that the word "spiritual" meant different things to Calusa and to his priest, but she knew she would be wasting her time trying to point that out. Perhaps if she put forth a different argument? "I still think stealth would serve you better than confrontation," she told her brother. "To approach the fort in daylight is asking for trouble, Calusa."

Her brother waved aside the warning. Ever since Dancing Egret had told him what Menendez and his priest planned for the Calusa, the Headchief had been working toward this moment. Smoldering resentment had escalated into full-blown fury when he learned that the Adelantado—who was not, after all, his brother-in-law—looked upon Calusa as nothing more than a counter in some game, one that could be broken in half and discarded should such a move be considered expedient. If Menendez had not abruptly taken ship for the north, Calusa would have more quickly reinstated the ceremonies of his ancestors, and the deceitful Spaniard would have served as first sacrifice of the season. Calusa would have seen to it that his dying was slow and painful, too; the Eater of Eyes would have delighted in the offering.

"I will be using stealth, to a degree," he said to his sister. "Since Vision Seeker and the Dancers insist upon going along, I have told Prowling Panther to let them be the first to ap-

proach the stockade. Then, when Father Rogel comes out to
rant at them, the warriors will leap from hiding and take him
prisoner." He borrowed a moment to savor his own cleverness.
"You know as well as I do, Egret, that as soon as Menendez's
priest hears the chanting and sees the masked Dancers, he will
burst out of the fort to call upon his God to punish me. For I
shall be there, too, naturally; I want him to know from the start
that I have had enough of his *do nots* and *must nots*! And I
want the Spanish soldiers to see me there, to recognize that
Headchief Calusa is more powerful than that black-robed
spewer of Christian pap!" He pulled his eyebrows together and
turned down the corners of his mouth in excellent imitation of
Father Rogel, raised one hand and shook his finger admonish-
ingly in Egret's face.

Despite her reservations about the plan Calusa was so proud
of, Egret could not help but laugh. Since Menendez had sailed
away, his priest had found more and more to complain about
and preach against. To the maidens he said that to lay with any
man outside of marriage would damn their souls forever, and
he had told the warriors that merely to look upon a woman's
naked breasts would bring the Christian God's wrath upon
them. A few children had grown fond enough of the Spanish
cornmeal Father Rogel doled out to begin to parrot the Credo;
when they lost interest in the exercise, he had named them
cursed as well. Mothers of infants opened themselves to sin by
suckling their babes where the soldiers could see them, according to Rogel, and men who occasionally scratched beneath
their breechclouts showed themselves to be filled with unholy
lust. Even the totems that designated the town's different clans
were regarded with suspicion by the Spanish priest; he was
convinced that the plaques depicted heathen gods, and flew
into a rage when Calusa refused to have them burned.

"I can't dispute your reasoning," she said, her mouth still
twitching a little. "Father Rogel will certainly be incensed to
see Vision Seeker and the Dancers. But how can you be sure
that soldiers, soldiers with guns and swords, will not come out
of the fort when the priest does? If they do, they may be able
to drive off the warriors who are supposed to be taking Father
Rogel prisoner." And, she added silently, if fighting should
erupt, what if it spills over into the town? What will happen to
the women and children and elders if our plaza becomes a bat-
tleground? Why had her brother failed to make arrangements
for such a contingency? But she did not voice these fears; in-

stinct told her that Calusa would only laugh indulgently and name her foolish if she did.

The Headchief gestured to the east, where the fledgling sun was preparing to climb into the pink-washed sky above the mangroves. "The Christian priest will be busy with what he calls his morning devotions," he said, "but the soldiers? We have all seen how most of them are growing fat and lazy. When they are not eating and drinking, they do nothing more strenuous than gaming, or ogling our women. Few of them will even be awake as yet, I promise you."

Until all the commotion starts, that is. But this thought, too, Egret kept to herself. Her brother's mind was made up, and his attention had already wandered away from her. Shrugging into his feathered ceremonial cape and positioning the gold medallion that dangled from his ceremonial headband, he was at the same time examining the litter he meant to ride in, checking the fur robe that lined it for softness and the palm fronds that roofed it for stowaway insects.

"Surely you do not intend to go to the Spanish fort with us."

Egret swung around to see young Swift Eagle, his forehead and cheeks daubed with red and black, eyeing her with consternation. But she could not bring herself to confide how she had so little faith in Calusa's plan that she'd come here hoping to persuade him, even at the last moment, to alter it. "No," she said quickly. "I am here only . . . only . . ." She flapped her hands. "In truth, I'm not sure why I'm here," she finished. "Except that, knowing what is to happen this morning, I could not sleep. So I came here instead."

Eagle, in addition to seeming much relieved, offered her a look of such shrewd understanding that Egret wondered if he had somehow deciphered her thoughts, and knew that if he had, he was in sympathy with them. He was indeed handsome, this man Chattering Squirrel adored, with a look of Great Calusa in the cut of his jaw and the set of his eyes. And he had been sincerely concerned that Dancing Egret might be planning to go where danger threatened. "It is good that you mean to stay behind," he said. "Prowling Panther pretends that it will be a simple matter to seize the Spanish priest, and—compared to forays into Timucuan border towns or the raiding of their coastal villages—it should be. But I think he wonders—as I do, and some of the other warriors—if it is wise for so many to be going to the fort: the priest, the Dancers, all of our clan leaders ... this is bound to spawn confusion, and who can say what might happen in the midst of confusion?"

Dancing Egret had not realized the counselors were accompanying Calusa, but when she turned to look in the direction Swift Eagle indicated, there they all were, clad in their finest cloaks and holding the plaques that proclaimed clan identity, those elegantly carved totems that Father Rogel had wanted to destroy. Like everyone else who had crowded into the huge room, they were laughing and talking among themselves. In one corner, the musicians would be playing for the Dancers were testing their drums and pipes; in another, the servants assigned to Calusa's litter were attaching fox and raccoon tails to their breechclouts. Other servants were dashing about offering dippers of water to the thirsty and bread and fruit to the hungry. And in the midst of the hullabaloo stood Calusa, patting the rounded buttocks of a pretty female servant, then waving his hands to illustrate something he was saying to a trio of warriors and roaring with laughter when one of them responded with a sly jest. Egret sighed; in a number of ways her brother had never grown up, and never would.

Her uneasiness sent down roots and sprouted into apprehension. It might have been a celebration everyone was preparing for, rather than a raid of sorts. Where was the tension that dictated caution, the commonsense fear that mandated alertness? Swift Eagle had admitted to a healthy trepidation, and studying the War Leader's face, Egret thought Eagle had been right in thinking that Prowling Panther was not entirely sanguine about the way this affair was going. But the rest seemed to be following the example set by their Headchief, and his confidence was not far removed from juvenile brashness.

The sun had almost cleared the mangroves now, and its warmth was beginning to seep into the house at the top of the mound. But Dancing Egret shivered as she watched the warriors being sent on ahead to conceal themselves around the low mound upon which the Spanish had built their fort. By the time Vision Seeker and the masked Dancers followed in their wake, and four sinewy servants had hoisted her brother's litter and moved out onto the ramp after them, the cold that had been born in the pit of her stomach was numbing her fingers and toes. And she was suddenly afraid that not even the sun of midday, when it came, would be enough to warm her.

* * *

"Keep the cannon loaded with small shot," Pedro Menendez said to his lieutenant. His eyes itched from exposure to salt and sun, and sweat glistened even in his beard. "And warn the soldiers to increase their vigilance." The Adelantado was well aware that laxness can creep into any action that is repeated and repeated, and the more hostages his men carted back and forth, the more likely they were to grow careless.

"I have already given the cannoneers orders to keep the demiculverins ready to fire," the lieutenant said stiffly. Menendez professed to have much faith in the commander of San Augustin, but it was plain that, in truth, he trusted no one but himself to do things right. This so-called rebellion he had hastened north to put a stop to, for instance; the lieutenant had had the situation well in hand. He had taken captive the savages that huddled in the bow of this ship right now, and—left to his own devices—he could have dealt competently with a wrathful Saturiba, too. And there would have been none of this nonsense about meeting Saturiba on "neutral ground," to swelter while they "parleyed." For two hours the dinghy had been ferrying between brig and shore; for two hours the translators had been relaying demands and counterdemands; for two hours they had, in effect, been sitting on their hands!

Menendez was once again studying the hostages. Saturiba's heir, like the Holata himself, was a man broad of shoulder and square of torso. Despite the chains that shackled ankles and wrists, he sat erect, not allowing himself to lean against a convenient bulkhead. His son, sitting beside him, was thin in the way that boys so often were, with rapidly expanding bones pushing hard against the meager layer of flesh that contained them. The other captives ranged from middle-aged to elderly, and were said to be Emoloa's advisors. From the sparseness of conversation since they had been brought on board the brigantine, it would seem that they had little advice to offer at the moment.

He watched as the Captain of the Guard prodded two of the older Principal Men to their feet, oversaw the removal of their manacles, and herded them over the ship's side and into the waiting dinghy. Saturiba kept insisting upon talking with his nephew, but Menendez had no intention of sending him ashore while so many painted warriors were gathered around the Holata. Gathered around the *two* Holatas, he amended silently. Cupping his hands around his eyes, he peered again toward the beach. He had not been mistaken; the man standing next to

Saturiba was indeed Holata Outina. And the woman who stood a little behind him was that cousin of his who was said by the aborigines to have otherworldly powers. He frowned; the soldiers who had recently returned from Outina's town had intimated that they, too, believed this woman to be extraordinary. That was ridiculous, of course, but ... why was she here, where no woman ought to be? And the blackamoor who was helping with the interpreting ... the blue feathers he wore told Menendez, who made it a point to learn such things, that he was a trader. But the blackamoor, too, had been in Outina's town when Menendez was there, and he was here now when the trading to be done was far from being the sort he should have a hand in.

Menendez had first heard mention of a black-skinned trader while he was in the south, and since there surely could not be more than one of them walking the trading trails of *la Florida*, then the man obviously moved freely throughout all territories. Could he be a spy, perhaps? He was well situated for it. If so, he might have been carrying messages back and forth between Saturiba and Outina for a long, long time. And if he had been, why hadn't the Adelantado heard about it?

A flurry of seagulls swooped down to squabble over a crust of bread some seaman had tossed into the water, but Menendez did not notice them. When this business was finished, he told himself, he would see to it that Indian leaders throughout this land bound themselves more securely to the man they had sworn to accept as their older brother. And they would be made to understand that an older brother should be kept fully informed about everything that goes on among his subordinate siblings!

He looked shoreward one last time, saw old Saturiba lean close to Outina and say something he did not want Menendez's interpreter to hear. "Those two *have* made alliance," the Adelantado said. "I am certain of it now."

"What two, Captain-General?"

Menendez stepped back from the rail, turned to his lieutenant. "The two Timucuan chiefs, Saturiba and Outina," he said. "Which I had not expected. Saturiba referred so disparagingly to Outina when I spoke of visiting his town during my trek inland that I took them to be avowed enemies, a suspicion that was later confirmed. Or so I thought. Yet there they stand, the pair of them, and more like brothers than friends, let alone enemies. I do not like it."

The lieutenant contented himself with a sympathetic murmur. Since Menendez was so fond of preaching the importance of accord among all aborigines, then his displeasure must arise from the fact that these two chiefs had achieved it without his intervention. Wiping sweat from his high forehead, he looked enviously at the Adelantado; was the man immune to this accursed heat? "The Indians who have just been taken ashore," he said hopefully, "look to be tribal elders. Perhaps they are the ones to influence the chiefs to do as you want them to do. Perhaps, before much longer, Saturiba and the one you call Outina will have agreed to your conditions for the release of our prisoners."

Menendez gave a short bark of laughter. "They are elders, yes, and therefore will be courteously listened to. But even if they pleaded for the warriors to be sent away—which they will not—the only thing those chiefs are interested in doing is stealing back the prisoners. Then, when I have nothing to bargain with, they will send their warriors swooping upon our fort."

The lieutenant shrugged. "They have no guns," he said. "We would very soon repel them, should they be fools enough to try."

Menendez sighed; he had expected this man to be more astute. "The aborigines have their faults, but their tenaciousness must never be underrated," he said. "The fort could turn into a prison if they decided upon a prolonged siege and we found ourselves without food and water." That would never happen, of course; from all he had heard, the Indians were not given to the sort of warfare he had described, and even if they were, Pedro Menendez would still find a way to outwit them. But the lieutenant would be no use to him if he did not learn to prepare for any and all eventualities, even the most obscure.

The brig's captain materialized at Menendez's elbow. "One of Emoloa's Principal Men is being rowed back to the ship," he reported. "Will you hear what he has to say, Adelantado?"

Menendez followed the skipper to where an elderly man was being hauled unceremoniously over the rail. Ignoring the Indian, the Adelantado turned to the red-faced soldier who swung himself onto the deck after him. "What news?" he demanded.

"The interpreter says that Saturiba still refuses to come aboard and speak with you until he has seen for himself that his sister's son is unharmed, and the young boy also." The heavyset man hesitated before telling the rest, but it was, after all, his duty to do so. "He told the interpreter to say that if you refuse to send the two ashore, it can only be because you and all of your soldiers are hens dressed as cocks." He looked away. "From his tone," he said carefully, "I believe the savage meant that as insult, Captain-General."

"He did, and will be sorry for it," Menendez said grimly. "He was told yet again that I want to be his friend, his big brother, just as I have said from the beginning?"

The beefy man nodded. "The Indian turned his head and spat on the ground when the interpreter said 'big brother,' " he told him. "As he did the last time those words were spoken. I think he does not trust you, Adelantado."

Menendez's right hand caressed the hilt of his sword. Above his head, the rigging sang as a cooling gust of wind buffeted the furled sails; the brigantine bucked as though it were a spirited steed in need of exercising. By the Virgin, he had been patient too long. He had gone to great lengths, some would say extreme lengths, to win over these heathen, but not even a saint would continue to extend the hand of Christian fellowship only to have it contaminated with spittle! And he was a strategist of considerable skill: he knew he could not afford to let Saturiba, and Outina as well, boast that Pedro Menendez de Aviles had been made to back down.

"If the Holata does not choose to avail himself of the parley I have been courteous enough to offer him," he said quietly, "then he has no one but himself to blame for what will come." He swung around to face his lieutenant. "The dinghy must make one more trip to shore," he told him. "I have decided to return Emoloa and most of his Principal Men to Saturiba."

The lieutenant could not conceal his shock. "You are giving in to him?" he gasped.

Menendez's mouth arranged itself in a thin smile. "So Saturiba will think when he sees him," he said. "But Emoloa shall take with him this message from me: Emoloa's son and two of his Principal Men will not only be held as permanent hostages, I mean to take them to Spain when I go there again. And if Saturiba or Emoloa—or Outina, or any other Timucuan Holata—makes a show of force in objection to this, I will have the boy's head, and those of the elders, chopped off. After which I shall issue orders that the head of the chief who defied me is also forfeit." He looked toward the shore; the stubby shadows of midday reinforced his conviction that his efforts to achieve peaceful compromise had gone on long enough.

"Saturiba has made it clear that he wants war," he said. "It is time to show him that I am prepared to give him what he asks for."

Dancing Egret never knew what made her follow in the footsteps of those who had set out for the Spanish fort. Perhaps the lost and lonely spirit that had infected her with bone-rattling chill decided on a whim to prod her in the direction the others had taken. She knew only that she did not run out the door and down the ramp by choice, that she had no desire whatsoever to circle the huge mound and push through the brambles at the rear of it until she stood at the foot of the rise upon which the Spanish had built fort and chapel. A narrow, curving ramp led up to the blockhouse's entrance, and already Vision Seeker and a score of Dancers were weaving along it, moving to the rhythm of pipe and drum and stamping their feet vigorously as they ascended. There were no signs of the warriors who had surely arrived here before them, but Egret had not expected that there would be. One and all would have concealed themselves where the brush was taller and more dense, or positioned themselves on the far side of the fort where the wall was unbroken save for a few slitlike openings set well above head height.

The scene she gazed upon was impressive. The new-risen sun pointed up the reds and yellows, blues and blacks, of fresh-painted masks, brought out the almost hurtful whiteness of the strings of spiny shells embracing necks, wrists, and ankles; a white that in its turn enhanced the ruddiness of flesh liberally anointed with fish oil. The priest's crimson cloak was banner-bright at the head of the procession, and Egret fancied she could hear his quavery voice dominating a chant that ebbed and swelled like the waters of the sea, a chant which—like the sea—had been born at the world's Beginning.

The sun's light strengthened, spilled upon the lower half of the blockhouse and the chapel that stood to its right. It flooded the area on the far side of the meandering ramp and called into bold relief the canopied litter upon which Headchief Calusa sat. The servants who held him aloft, and the counselors who had lined up nearby, were hidden from view by the swaying Dancers. The Headchief, resplendent in the feathers and shells that had always adorned leaders of the Calusa, but wearing as well the gold and pearls and colored gems he had come to admire, appeared to have levitated himself so that he hovered above all the lesser beings of earth. It was illusion only, Dancing Egret knew, but she was reminded of the day her brother had first put on their father's sun-shaped badge of status, and of how she had thought then that the Sun God himself, could he take human form, would not look more magnificent.

Vision Seeker and the first of the Dancers had reached the gateway now, and their chanting grew louder and more impassioned. Despite the thickness of its walls, those within the fort must surely be able to hear it. Dancing Egret fixed her eyes on the joined planks that sealed shut the blockhouse, curled her hands into fists as the door on the left was thrust open and a spindly legged, barrel-chested figure burst out to confront Calusa's priest.

If Father Rogel did not feel like a dull-plumaged grackle surrounded by woodpeckers and tanagers, buntings and jays, then the man had no imagination, Egret thought. But if he did, he did not let that daunt him. Already one black-sleeved arm was lifting, already the boom of his voice was assaulting the ears of those near enough to make out what he said. And suddenly Egret was moved to hysterical laughter. What did it matter who heard what he said, or what Vision Seeker might say to Father Rogel? Save for a few words each priest might somehow have gleaned along the way, neither would have the least idea what the other was saying! Calusa had arranged for many people to gather at the Spanish fort this morning, but an interpreter was not among them.

So much for confrontation, then. The pair would go on talking, of course, for each man believed fervently in the God or gods he served, and used words as a warrior would use weapons. But even though they talked themselves hoarse, neither would ever understand the other.

Dancing Egret turned her gaze from the gesticulating pair, looked toward her brother. Why was he letting this foolishness continue? Why wasn't he signaling for the warriors to rush out of hiding and seize Father Rogel? As if her thoughts wore wings and flew to where he sat, Calusa swiveled his head and looked directly at her. He offered her a dazzling smile, raised his right hand and detached one of the fronds that roofed the litter. He waved it to and fro, as though fanning himself, then let it drop.

Warriors rose up from the ground like shadows suddenly granted substance and raced up the serpentine path, while those who had been concealed behind the blockhouse hurtled down it. It was a maneuver that should have been smooth, effective, and would have been if both groups had not needed to dodge Dancers whose masks prevented their seeing anything clearly. As it was, there was time and to spare for Father Rogel to give a mighty shout, for the other side of the mammoth gate to be shoved wide, and for Captain De Reinoso and his soldiers to come to the aid of their priest.

The hulking Francisco de Reinoso shoved Father Rogel behind him, swung his clubbed lance and sent Vision Seeker sprawling. The soldiers flung themselves into what was now a melee of furious warriors and dazed ceremonial Dancers, wielding sword and lance and club indiscriminately. Metal grated on stone as a thrust went wild, but too many were better aimed. Calusan blood began to soak into the hard-packed sand of the ramp and stain the grass that marked its verges. Egret saw two Dancers, masks askew, slip and slide as they zigzagged to where the unconscious Vision Seeker lay, but they succeeded in grasping the old man's arms and hauling his limp body out of the way of the fighting. For Calusa's warriors were returning blow for blow; flint-head spears rejoiced to skewer generous Spanish flesh, and cudgels smacked so fiercely against helmeted heads that ringing echoes announced each soldier's fall. But this battle was being fought on an incline, and the Christians held the advantageous position. Slowly but surely, and in spite of Headchief Calusa's encouraging shouts, his warriors were being driven back.

At least, most of them were. Prowling Wolf and a small band of warriors, Swift Eagle among them, refused to give way. Decorated with wounds though they were, and smeared with blood and sweat, they stood elbow-to-elbow on the outer edge of the ramp, made a living wall between their Headchief and the Spanish soldiers. Swinging their conch shell-crowned clubs to the right, to the left, slashing with long-bladed knives and thrusting with shorter ones, they held the soldiers at bay while Calusa's terrified servants, prodded into action by the clan leaders, bore his litter down the ungraded side of the mound.

Why don't you jump out and run? Dancing Egret wondered if her brother would hear her if she screeched the words, knew that over the clang of steel, the thwack and slam of clubs, the groans of wounded men and the shrieks and grunts of those locked in hand-to-hand combat, he could not. And would probably ignore her if he could. For he continued to sit tall, her brother, to keep his shoulders squared and his head high despite the jolts that threatened to unseat him. Regal was his attitude, as befitted the Headchief of the Calusa, and although Egret considered it ludicrous in the circumstances, she found herself admiring him for it.

But his unassailable pride was his undoing. From the entrance to the Spanish fort, Captain De Reinoso had an excellent overview of the ongoing battle. He spotted Calusa's litter mere seconds after its bearers began their downhill flight. Reaching for his crossbow, he thrust his left foot through its stirrup, forced back the cord and hooked it. He did not hurry; the uneven ground Calusa's servants were maneuvering over did not permit rapid descent, and the captain knew it. Straightening, he set an arrow against the taut string, squinted and aimed, smiled as he applied pressure to the trigger.

In the moment that arrow spurted from bow, Dancing Egret looked up. Horror fastened clammy hands around her throat as her eyes, glazing with shock, traced the arc of the missile's flight. Only when it reached the limit of its trajectory, only when its lethal point met and pierced the target it was destined for, was power of movement restored to her.

That was when she screamed and raced to where Calusa, half tumbled from his elegant transport, the white plumes in his hair spotted now with red, coughed up his life around the arrow lodged in his throat.

As she wrapped shaking arms around him to help ease him from the hastily downed litter, she spoke his name. "Heron," she said, and again, "Heron!"

For it was not the Headchief of all the Calusa who died in her arms that morning. It was the boy whose engaging smile had brightened the lives of everyone around him; the child who had listened wide-eyed to his big sister's tales; the little brother Dancing Egret had loved so very much.

Chapter 44

⇒ — ⇒

Kwambu wished he dared leave the tree he was perched in long enough to run to the river he had drunk from early in the day, the wide, crystal-clear river that—to the north—flowed past both Menendez's fort and Saturiba's Principal Town. But it was imperative that he maintain surveillance of two unpalisaded villages, one of which would likely be the Spanish soldiers' next target.

He fumbled a strip of dried venison from his pouch, chewed it in an effort to invite saliva into his dry mouth, retied the pouch without even glancing at the blue feathers he'd tucked inside when Outina appointed him courier-sentry for the War Leader. *I cannot go so far as to let you exchange those feathers for weapons,* he had said, *or Moon of Winter will probably lay a curse on me!* He had laughed when he said it, but both men were aware that this was not the reason for Kwambu's being given so undistinguished a role. Despite the warrior's blood that ran in Kwambu's veins, he was only a trader. And unless trained to weaponry from childhood, so that being unarmed left him feeling incomplete, a man with bow or spear was no asset to any war party. More than ever, Kwambu yearned to prove himself a true son of the brave man who had fathered him, but it was not to be; thanks to a decision made long ago by Headchief Calusa, Kwambu simply did not qualify as warrior.

Kwambu told himself that dwelling on old injustices was not only fruitless, it was distracting. And at the moment he could not afford distraction. He scanned the forest bordering the first Saturiban village, then turned his head to the south to survey the tree-studded hillock upon which the second one sat. Nowhere did he see sunlight glinting off metal armor, and no thump of booted foot or clink of Spanish steel visited his ears. But were his senses still sharp enough to catch subtleties? he wondered. He had not been among those who ambushed Christian soldiers whenever they ventured from Menendez's fort; he had taken no part in wrapping arrowheads in flaming moss and aiming them at the army's powderhouse; he had done nothing more strenuous than track the movements of the Spaniards, so that the warriors eventually sent to raze the fort knew in advance where the heaviest resistance was apt to come from. But Kwambu was not immune to dawn-to-dusk tension and restless nights; after six long weeks, he was as weary as anyone else. And, being no warrior, he was not served the Black Drink periodically to rekindle his strength and enthusiasm.

If only the soldiers did not so greatly outnumber the warriors. It should not have been that way. Soon after Emoloa delivered to Saturiba the Adelantado's declaration of war, Kwambu had carried throughout eastern Timucua an invitation for all leaders to rally in Saturiba's province. But some of the deputies Menendez left in village and town to plead the cause of Christianity had been dedicated to their task; even where they had not yet been wholly successful, they had cleverly built upon the rumors that told of Menendez bringing rain to parched planting fields. Fearful of angering a man who owned such awesome power, many chiefs—even those not otherwise impressed with the white-skinned outlander—were reluctant to go against him. And certain Holatas who had long been enemies of Saturiba or Outina refused even to listen to Kwambu once they learned why he had come. In the end, no one had united with Saturiba and Outina. Now a dwindling and exhausted band of men was trying to deflect the Spaniards' retaliatory raids on towns like the two Kwambu was watching, undefended towns occupied solely by artisans, women, children, and old people.

On the outskirts of the forest a mockingbird had been sweetly serenading its mate. When a fresh spill of song was all at once aborted, Kwambu pointed his face toward the west, narrowed his eyes and examined with care the town's forested approaches. When he found what he expected to find, he cupped his hands around his mouth and the *ah-whoo-whoo-whoo-whoo* of a barred owl filled the silence left by the mockingbird's abbreviated trill. Three times he hooted, then he eased out of his tree and, melting into the denser woods that spread away from the river, loped swiftly toward the village the Christian soldiers were on the verge of attacking.

The warriors, alerted by his signal, arrived before Kwambu did, for they had concealed themselves at a point that gave easily onto either of the towns. Their howls warmed Kwambu's heart as they sprang from the tall grass they had crawled through, and he silently cheered to see their arrows rain upon the Spaniards just emerging from the forest. The warriors, during these chaotic weeks, had become skilled at slaying men who dressed themselves in metal. No longer did knapped points bounce harmlessly off gleaming plate; now they flew to where sheets of metal met one another, found and pierced vulnerable flesh, even drove between bones to penetrate heart or spleen.

A soldier screamed; as he tumbled to the ground, his hands scrabbled for the shaft of the arrow protruding from his segmented knee piece. Kwambu, leaping over him on his way to hustle the villagers into the safety of the forest, refused even to glance into his bearded face. He felt no sympathy for him; on the day of the parley, when Menendez had ordered his cannoneers to fire upon the Timucua—to send their deadly shot so fearfully close to the place where Moon of Winter stood that it still sickened Kwambu to think about it—the trader had seen Saturiba's Paracusi and three younger warriors go down beneath the treacherous volley. As they died, his heart had swelled with such desire for vengeance there was no room left in it for pity.

He scrunched down as he zigzagged from house to house. Not all of the Spanish marksmen had been distracted by the screeching warriors. Keeping to the rear and sheltering from a hail of arrows, one contingent was concentrating on the destruction of the village and its inhabitants. Their guns spoke loud as Kwambu thrust wailing infants into the arms of frightened matrons, ordered maidens to take the hands of older children or guide trembling elders, made sure everyone understood that they must exit through the rear and keep low as they headed for the trees.

The guns spoke again as Kwambu darted into the last of the seven houses, and the smoke hanging over the minuscule squareground thickened enough to tarnish the gold of the afternoon sun. The house was empty, and Kwambu hoped fervently that its occupants had escaped on their own, that fear had not driven them into the arms of murderers. It bothered him that a hatchet, new-made, lay beside the stone hearth as though dropped by someone in a hurry. If the people who lived here had been thinking sensibly, surely the weapon-maker would have taken the hatchet with him?

Closing his ears to the war cries and soldiers' curses that were making their own peculiar assault upon the village, he looked to the rear wall. The door hanging had been jerked aside so roughly that half of it was torn loose from its fastenings. As he started toward it, another arquebus boomed, and this time the sound was deafening. Kwambu threw himself flat just as the gun spat its death-bringing ball into the house. Not only had the trader been spotted, he had been followed into the now-deserted town.

Heart drubbing in his chest, Kwambu crawled across the dirt floor and, sliding beneath the skewed door hanging, rolled swiftly sideways to put the house's rear wall between himself and his pursuer. But instead of coming up against the hardness of seasoned wattle and daub, Kwambu's back met something soft at the end of his roll, a pulpy mass that yielded to contact. Cautiously, he turned his head.

Bile flooded into his throat. Had the body been that of a grown man, perhaps uncomplicated fury would have neutralized his nausea. But it was a child who lay next to what had been her home, a plump little girl whose round face was the sort made for laughter. She would never laugh again, this daughter of the woman whose own sprawled body was separated from the child's by only a hand's width. An arquebus ball had shattered her sturdy chest; slivers of bone gleamed white within the congealing blood that painted her tender flesh with monstrous decoration.

Retching, Kwambu came to his hands and knees, looked beyond the woman, who even in death kept her arms outstretched toward her daughter. Not far from them lay an older woman, a man, and a boy of about twelve. Like the girl and her mother, they were newly—and horribly—dead.

Kwambu swallowed hard, flexed his fingers, and looked down in surprise to see that he still held the hatchet he had found by the hearth . . . the hatchet the dead man might have used against the Spanish had he remembered to bring it with him.

A gun spoke again, and the rear wall trembled as an iron ball careened into it. Kwambu turned away from the carnage, went into a crouch, and began to circle the small dwelling.

Having spent most of his life among the tribes of this country, he appreciated the importance of war in their lives. War gave a man a chance to test himself; it sharpened his hunting skills, keeping him agile and alert; and excelling on the battlefield brought a man the finest trophy of all, the respect of his fellows. War was many things, but it was not designed for the slaughter of innocents.

Although shot still fell sporadically upon the town, Kwambu called upon his trader's discipline to shroud himself with silence as he started toward the squareground. Which is why the flies buzzing around a heap of dog dung were able to call his attention to the toe of a Spanish boot extending past the corner he was making for.

That boot could belong only to the soldier who continued to seek an elusive quarry—a quarry named Kwambu. Yet the image of a cruelly slaughtered child and her family lingered behind Kwambu's eyes, and suddenly he rejected the passivity that the word "quarry" implied. That—in truth—the word "trader" implied. All traces of nausea disappeared as rage built a fire in his chest and the metallic taste of hatred filled his mouth. He tested the weight of the hatchet in his hand, and let the cutting edge of that grisly image slash at the restraints that had so long held him back from his proper destiny.

It was too late now for Kwambu to become truly adept with a warrior's weapons, to have reflexes as finely honed as those of a properly trained fighting man. But the desire that fueled such a man, the spiritual thirst that only the shedding of enemy blood can quench—these were not beyond his reach. And they would be enough to let him exercise his patrimony.

Exultation rode on the next breath he took in, was tempered only a little by the regret he felt because he had not claimed his birthright years before. If, on the day Shore Walker died, he had been brave enough to shed the confining skin that traders are forced to wear . . .

Well, he could not alter the past. The future, however, was a different matter. Approaching the corner of the house, he came erect, raised the hand that held the hatchet, poised himself to simultaneously swing around the side of the house and challenge the man with the gun. Kwambu's long-repressed warrior instincts were fully aroused; he lusted for confrontation.

All at once, the toe of the boot he was staring at pressed itself more firmly into the ground. In the next heartbeat the rest of the armed Spaniard would come into view.

Kwambu's eyes narrowed to slits; his foot went flying out and collided with the angled leg in the instant that it appeared. The astonished soldier, thrown off balance, teetered, hovered briefly over the heap of dog dung, tumbled to the ground.

Kwambu dove, and landed squarely on the astonished man's protuberant belly. Breath whooshed out of the Spaniard, and his white-rimmed eyes rounded farther when he spied the weapon in Kwambu's right hand. Kwambu leaned forward, flipped up the strap that held the soldier's metal helmet in place, knocked the protective covering from his head. He looked down into the Spaniard's face, gloried in the sight of the sweat that greased forehead, cheeks, and chin. For it was the cold perspiration of fear that trickled into the Spaniard's ears and overflowed the creases in his neck, and Kwambu had inspired that fear!

His fingers gripped the hatchet almost lovingly as he prepared to hoist it, as he visualized its downward stroke and the wave of blood it would send up to wash away that unnatural perspiration. Awareness would desert eyes bulging now with terror, and the soldier's agitated breathing would be silenced forever. And in that moment Kwambu the trader would be transformed into Kwambu the warrior.

Yet something stayed his hand. Powerful as the urge was to avenge the little girl's slaying, there was within him something even stronger. And it owned a voice, a voice that gradually took on compelling rhythm, a voice that said the warrior's way was not the only way, that—for certain people—it was not even the right way.

A Spanish trumpeter sent up a brilliance of brassy notes; as if to mock him, a Timucuan warrior made the air vibrate with full-throated shrieking. Kwambu, cloistered in suspended time, heard nothing but the hypnotic chanting of an unseen taleteller. He found himself listening to the story of his own life as though it were something he had been ignorant of until now. He wept with the child who was seized by slavers; suffered the beatings inflicted on that boy by his Spanish master; felt the salt water's stinging embrace when he leaped from the deck of a ship sailing along *la Florida*'s coast. He rediscovered the admiration Headchief Calusa had aroused in a grateful refugee, and pride stiffened his back all over again when he understood that he had earned Calusa's trust. Warmth coursed through him as he stood once more with a laughing Dancing Egret and realized that a friendship whose roots were sunk so deep would never cease to flourish. He relished anew the companionship of such stalwarts as Shore Walker and Black Wolf Running—and was reminded that Wolf, too, would have long since deserted This World were it not for Kwambu the trader. And the love he shared with his wife and children was everywhere woven into the song, making it a tale so enthralling he could not, would not, close his ears to it.

It seemed to Kwambu that his story went on and on, but he had been admitted to some fugitive fragment of time; in reality, the whole of it could have been narrated while a single bolt of lightning flashed across the sky. And like a lightning flash, the tale was illuminating. It helped Kwambu to see clearly that decades of conditioning were only part of the reason this man had dedicated himself to building trust rather than promoting fear, to proffering the hand of friendship instead of the red baton of war. To have done otherwise would have put him at odds with his own nature.

Yet being made to recognize and acknowledge that nature did nothing to bridle Kwambu's fury. When the inner voice at last fell silent, he found that the fingers he'd wrapped around the axe handle had not relaxed their grip; his need to make the Spaniard he was still straddling atone for the vicious killing of a helpless child continued to be an ache in his gut.

A growl erupted from his throat. He raised the hatchet as high as he could, then brought it down with all his might—and thumped its blade deep into the ground next to the soldier's left ear.

The man sent up a soaring scream that broke as it descended into a froth of senseless babble.

Kwambu thrilled to the sound even as his nose wrinkled in response to an overwhelming stench of dog shit. The Spaniard had squashed the dung when he landed in it, and now it was seeping into the fabric of his breeches. Nor was that the only stink fouling the air; Kwambu swung his head around and confirmed his suspicion that fear had punctured the man's bladder as well.

He turned back and studied the face of his captive. The man's eyes were squeezed shut, as though he hoped that what he could not see did not exist. Kwambu grasped a beefy shoulder, shook it until the soldier's eyes flew open. Then, with mesmerizing deliberation, he reached out and snatched a clump of the man's matted hair. While the Spaniard squealed and blubbered, Kwambu used the virgin axe blade a second time—to sever the hair at the roots.

Waving this unimpressive trophy, he lifted himself off the soldier, picked up the man's gun and smashed it against a rock, then stood staring down at him. If anything, the stink of feces and urine was stronger now, and the man was sobbing as though he were a child trapped in nightmare. Kwambu was glad he had not been able to kill him; to see him wallowing in filth and shame was somehow more satisfying than his dying could have been. And if Kwambu thought this only because he was who he was, well, that did nothing to invalidate the feeling.

With a grimace, he tossed aside the hank of hair, then looked at the hatchet; despite the opportunities offered to both its maker and Kwambu, no blood had stained it after all. Perhaps the spirit of the stone that formed its blade, like the spirit that had given life to Kwambu, had been one of creation rather than destruction. Kwambu tucked the small axe into his belt. When they returned to Saturiba's village, he would give it to his wife to use for household chores. He would tell her where he happened upon it, and describe how her husband had at last been given the chance to be a warrior. And confess that he had wasted that chance.

Maybe they would laugh together about it.

Meanwhile, it appeared that the Timucua had managed to lure Menendez's men away from the town. From the sounds, the fighting was thickest near the river, and it was time that he sought out Black Wolf Running. Outina's Paracusi might want a message delivered or—had the casualties been many—he might be needed to help carry litters back to the camp.

He pivoted, checked to be certain no stray Spaniards lingered anywhere around the village, then made for the riverbank. His mind was clearer than it had been, and his body not so weighted with weariness, which was good. Menendez himself had been leading the soldiers who were waging this particular battle, which meant there would be no quarter given on either side. The fighting might very well go on until full dark.

His friends in the south, he thought suddenly, owed the Timucua a debt of gratitude. While the Adelantado was so busy in the north, there surely ought to be peace of a sort on Calusa's island.

The four women in Dancing Egret's small house kept their voices low even though none of the Spaniards in the compound seemed particularly interested in them. Soldiers patrolled at the foot of the domiciliary mound, of course, and a sentry was posted permanently now to guard the house that topped it. The new Headchief Calusa could not even go outside to relieve himself without Captain De Reinoso and Father Rogel being advised of the fact.

"The Spanish priest goes to Swift Eagle every morning and demands that he take you for his wife," Chattering Squirrel said to Egret. "Eagle tells him again and again that he will marry me and no other, but"—anger and sadness competed for her expression—"we have not been alone together since . . . since . . ." She lowered her head; she hadn't intended to remind Egret of the day her brother died. Not that anyone would ever forget it. Because of that day, the Spanish would allow nobody, not even fishermen, to leave the island; because of that day, their dead Headchief, and the men who died with him, had been denied proper burial; and because of that day, the island's surviving warriors were confined to their individual houses. Indeed, if the Spanish did not lack respect for the intelligence of women, she and her mother would be restrained from visiting Dancing Egret because of that day.

"You must accustom yourself to calling your husband 'Calusa.' " Brown Pelican smiled when Squirrel looked startled. "He is your husband already, according to the laws of the Ancients," she said, "and has been since you realized that you carry his child."

"Which is something Eagle—I mean, Calusa—doesn't even know!" her daughter wailed. Then her lovely eyes narrowed. "We must do something, we women, and we must do it soon. We cannot go on living like prisoners in our own town."

"I agree," Egret told her, pleased to see anger claim precedence over Squirrel's misery. "Because the Spaniards constantly monitor the warriors, and have stripped the town of every weapon they could find, they consider us powerless. Well, I say they are wrong."

"They did not get every weapon," Brown Pelican said quietly. Hadn't she herself hidden her husband's dart thrower beneath the pelt that lined the hammock their youngest grandchild was sleeping in? And Prowling Panther had thrust his best knife into the dirt beneath the floor mats and stomped on it until even its hilt was out of sight. With him being War

Leader, theirs was the first home the soldiers had come to when they set out to confiscate weapons, but there had been time to do that much at least. "The Christian soldiers are fools to think we are ignorant of what they plan," she went on, and smiled at Egret's serving woman. "So long as your Ysabel dares to help us, we can learn whatever we need to know."

Ysabel went and scanned the plaza yet again, then—satisfied—rejoined the others. It felt strange to sit with them like this, instead of waiting upon Dona Egret and her guests, but that was what she had been invited to do. "I cannot possibly overhear everything," she warned. "The soldiers, they have grown used to me coming around the fort and"—she grinned—"many look forward to the good food I often take to them. But the *capitán* does not trust me, I think. As for the priest"—she shrugged—"he is suspicious of everyone, that man, but fortunately I have seen little of him."

"He spends most of his time railing at our new Headchief," said Egret. "I feel sorry for Eagle, but while Father Rogel focuses on him, he hasn't the time or the energy to harass anyone else. He still doesn't realize how often Ysabel goes to the fort, nor does he know how the soldiers there are considerably less constrained without him around. The maidens who are suddenly finding reason to walk in that direction have certainly discovered this, however!"

Chattering Squirrel shook her head in dismay. "Many of the Christians are young, and some are not unattractive. To those foolish girls, one man's admiration is much the same as another's, I'm afraid."

Brown Pelican laughed. "You sound as though you were a gray-haired grandmother," she said to her daughter, "yet only two seasons ago you, too, were young and foolish. As I was once, and Egret, and Ysabel. To be a little foolish is part of growing up."

"I never smiled at any man but Swift Eagle," Chattering Squirrel protested, then sighed. "It wasn't my fault that he ignored my smiles for so long," she added, "or that he went on calling me 'little sister' when I didn't feel at all like a sister to him!"

Egret, her eyes twinkling, turned to Pelican. "We can't argue the truth of that, can we? Everyone saw how this daughter of yours trailed after Swift Eagle until finally she convinced him that she was the woman for him."

"With men," Ysàbel put in placidly, "it is the only way.

How can any of them know what they want unless we show them?"

All four laughed then until their sides ached, and for a moment their very real worries ceased to loom. It occurred to Egret that in this ability to focus on the ordinary lay the unique strength of women. It offered respite from the overwhelming, and in the process sometimes transformed intimidating oceans into manageable rivers.

As it might have done this time. "Those friends of yours who toss their hair and waggle their hips to attract the Christian soldiers," she said to Squirrel, "do they understand what a dreadful threat those soldiers are to all of us?"

Squirrel's brow wrinkled. "They do, and they don't," she said. "They realize that the Spanish being here on our island is not a good thing, but they don't regard as harmful the smiles sent their way by this young soldier or that. Quite the contrary! Especially since, like everyone else, the maidens resent being told by the Spanish leaders what to do and what not to do. Because the Christian priest says they are to stay away from the soldiers, they are all the more determined to go to the fort to tease and distract them. But, given the choice, they would rather have our world the way it was before the pale-fleshes came. As we all would."

"Just how strongly do they feel about it, I wonder?" Egret said. "Strongly enough to help us deal with the outlanders? And are they courageous enough to put themselves at risk so that we can be rid of those who have stolen our freedom?" She came to her feet, began to pace. The time for jests, for laughter, was over. "For you spoke truth, Squirrel, when you said that something must be done, and soon. Bad as matters are now, they will worsen when Menendez returns. And with the soldiers keeping such close watch on the warriors, who is there left to act but the women?"

She came to a halt, looked at her companions, was tempted to offer them apology. She was chanting fine-sounding sentiments—sentiments she knew they shared—but more than forceful words would be needed if what they yearned for was to become reality. Suddenly Dancing Egret felt not only inadequate, but downright ridiculous. Why should the other three women, friends though they were, take seriously anything she suggested?

Yet the expressions on their faces said they did. "You do not exaggerate when you say 'close watch,' " Pelican said. "The

Christian soldier that watches our house during the day—or a different one; in truth, I cannot always tell them apart—also walks back and forth in front of our house all through the night." Suddenly she buried her face in her hands. "It is horrible," she whispered, "*horrible*, to be watched like that!"

Chattering Squirrel put her arms around her mother. "And I am afraid, terribly afraid, that they will do more than just watch Swift Eagle," she said wretchedly. "If he doesn't soon agree to do as the priest demands, they are likely to kill him. Just as they killed Calusa."

No one made light of her fears. Everyone knew that Captain De Reinoso had called Calusa's death an "execution long overdue." Still patting Pelican's hunched shoulders, Squirrel dammed her own tears and looked back at Dancing Egret. "I know all of the maidens well," she said. "Even though we've had little opportunity to sing since the Spanish came, we still get together regularly to practice the ceremonial songs, or just to gossip. The foolishness I accused them of is the sort my mother described; the girls are not truly light-minded, and I expect that every one of them would be willing to do whatever you ask of her." She smiled at her aunt. "Most of them, when they were small, were taught our Legends by you, and you have never lost their respect and devotion."

Brown Pelican was sitting up straight again and listening intently. "I have no idea what you want from the maidens," she said to her sister, "but please remember that there are others in our town who are able to go more or less where they please. The Spanish think that elders, like women, cannot possibly pose any threat to them. That's why they pay no heed to Vision Seeker, so long as he stays in the Temple. He may be priest, but because he is old the soldiers think he is of no account."

This was true. Vision Seeker, tended assiduously by the island's berdaches, and with the town's matrons taking it in turn to cook him nourishing soups, had recovered from the blow given him by Captain De Reinoso. Whether he would also recover from the blow his spirit had received that day, no one could tell. But he had grown strong enough to return to the Temple and his prayers, and was largely ignored by the Christian soldiers and Father Rogel.

Dancing Egret hesitated. Was the plan that had been gestating in her mind worth revealing? Could she bear to speak the words that would breathe life into it? She looked at Pelican, at

Squirrel, at Ysabel; what would be their reaction if she did? Then she recognized her questions as the delaying tactics they were, and reminded herself firmly that if anything were to be done, it must be done now. Before Menendez came back.

All at once, Dancing Egret wished she might be more like the Wise Woman who was Kwambu's wife. Not only did Moon of Winter know all about plants and herbs, she owned a crystal that told her what the future held. And Egret knew she would feel a great deal more confident if she could be given at least faint promise of her scheme's succeeding.

Chapter 45

Smoke from the ship's cannon fouled the air in Saturiba's Principal Town, but Moon of Winter no longer jumped every time one of the big-mouthed guns roared. Like everyone else, she had learned that, even though the town paralleled the river, it was beyond range of the iron balls that left fearsome holes wherever they touched down.

She pushed hair back from her throbbing temples, shook a palmetto frond to disperse the ubiquitous flies, and saturated the moss covering her son's torn shoulder. "The mangrove-bark distillation will make your wound heal cleaner and faster," she told Red Fox Barking.

"When can I return to the fighting?" he asked. As he always did.

"It's too soon to say," she said. And was unsurprised to see him frown: Fox had little liking for the idleness that was a necessary companion to recuperation. She looked around her at the injured warriors crowding the huge pavilion the berdaches had erected. In a far corner lay her older son, nearly asleep from the potion she had given him to ease his pain. A ball, smaller but no less dangerous than a cannonball, had lodged in

Hawk's buttocks, and she still shuddered inwardly when she recalled how deep the Shaman had dug before he was able to remove it. It was never easy for a mother when her children suffered, not even when those children were grown men. But what heaped guilt upon Moon of Winter was her relief that, injured though they were, both of her sons were alive and safe. At least for now. And perhaps, before they were fully recovered, this war with the Spanish would have ended. She knew better than to express that hope to them, of course, yet she embraced it with near desperation.

A groan brought her spinning around, but berdaches were already doing what they could for a youth whose multiple wounds had left him vulnerable to assault by fever demons. Saturiba's Shaman had performed a ceremony to drive them away, but they seemed to be as firmly entrenched in the young man's body as the Christians were in Timucuan territories. From the ship patrolling the river, another cannon bellowed and more black smoke swirled into the town. Moon of Winter wrinkled her nose, then told herself she should be grateful to have the persistent stench of pus and blood briefly overlaid. She bent to examine an older warrior who had lost his left ear to a Spanish sword. As she used the rust-colored liquid to moisten the dressing she had earlier wound around his head, the scar on her cheek began to throb, something it hadn't done in many years. Weariness might account for the phenomenon, she supposed; after all, her legs ached, and her arms, and—straightening, she massaged her lower back—virtually every part of her hurt to one degree or another. Nonetheless, she felt strongly that her scar ached in sympathy with the wounded men she was helping to care for.

Saturiba's sister came in, followed by two slaves carrying between them a big kettle of broth. The stuff would be somewhat shy of meat, but it would be rich in vegetables from the early crop the women had harvested only days before war began. What was hardest to come by was the water needed to cook soups and stews; water for everything, come to that! Boys too young to have earned warrior status crept out at night and hauled what they could from the river, but how long dare they go on doing so? Someday soon the Spanish would surely guess how the besieged townspeople were managing to avoid dying of thirst. Would Moon of Winter be binding up the wounds of children then? Would Saturiba's sister be spoon-feeding broth to some twelve-year-old, as she was doing now to a warrior whose crushed spine had made useless things of his arms and legs? And when she did, would she weep because the child reminded her of her grandson, the poor boy Menendez still refused to set free?

Moon of Winter's own eyes misted. Well, doubtless the urge to weep was another thing to be charged to fatigue. If only Kwambu were also back from the war, if only she could see for herself that he was well and whole, perhaps all of her aches and pains, the tears that periodically threatened, the illusion that she had lived eighty-six years rather than forty-six, would disappear the way the smaller stars do whenever a round moon rules the night. Meanwhile, she shouldn't be taking the time to brood, and it was a dangerous exercise in any event. Suppose she allowed herself to think that the wounded she was caring for were the fortunate ones, that the longer the fighting went on, the more warriors would be brought back here only to be mourned and buried, that—

She turned abruptly and moved stiffly, jerkily, out of the pavilion. Although there was some sort of commotion at the palisade's gate, the cannon were quiet now and the smoke that had belched from their muzzles was dissipating. The sun poured unscreened light upon Moon of Winter and caressed her with golden fingers. She did not feel them. She felt nothing but coldness, a numbing coldness that began in the pit of her stomach and crept relentlessly outward. It was strangely seductive, that coldness; it seemed to promise rest, and respite from worry. She could not resist it, even if she wanted to. And she was not at all sure that she wanted to . . .

. . . until all at once there were human hands grasping her slender shoulders, hands big and dark-skinned, hands strong enough to infuse her with the wonderful healing warmth the sun had been incapable of providing.

"Kwambu," she whispered, and let herself sag against his broad chest, let herself feel as well as hear that beloved voice when it spoke her name softly, yearningly. "Thank the gods you are back," she told him, tilting her head to look into his face. Seeing its haggardness, she was assailed by new guilt because she had been ready to surrender to a tiredness that could not possibly be as awful as Kwambu's.

He was probably hungry as well; trail rations were poor substitute for real food. "The day's soup is hot," she told him, smiling to see his face brighten, "and I know there is cornbread to go with it, for I smelled it baking this morning."

Then, recovering fully from her lapse into depression: "Outina returned with you? And Saturiba?"

Kwambu nodded. "They went directly to the Principal House," he said, and anticipating her next question, "Like me, they are unharmed." He looked down at himself and grinned. "Filthy and sweaty, and smeared with blood from minor scrapes, but unharmed." He looked toward the pavilion. "Hawk?" he asked. "And Fox?"

"Both are healing well," she assured him, then noticed the hatchet thrust through his belt. Her whole body went rigid. "Why does a man who is not a warrior carry a weapon?" she cried.

He lifted the small axe, held it out to her. "It is a gift for you," he said. "This hatchet wants only to chop wood for the building of drying racks." He smiled broadly enough to coax an answering if perplexed smile from his wife. "Truly, it has no desire to be a weapon," he said, and without elaboration or apology, recited its history.

She was neither shamed nor amused to hear how he had been put to the test and failed. "In the midst of war," she said slowly, "it must take more courage not to kill than to kill. I'm proud of you, Kwambu, and will treasure the hatchet you have brought to me."

Tired as he was, Kwambu was all at once aware of a wonderful lightness of heart. Moon of Winter's words had been reassuring, but it was the glow in her eyes, a glow he recognized as undiluted pride in the man she had married, that dissolved the last of Kwambu's uncertainty about the choice he had made during the battle. For he knew instinctively that she could never have been even half so proud of him had it been a Spanish scalp he'd presented her with. He understood also that this woman of his knew him better than he knew himself, and he was grateful beyond measure that he had not foolishly destroyed the man she knew and loved, and sent a stranger back to her.

For several moments they stood in silence, just looking at one another. Then Kwambu snapped his fingers. "I have brought you a second gift," he said, opening his pouch and taking from it something wrapped in damp moss, "but I am not sure it is still in one piece."

Carefully, he lifted away the moss, but even before Moon of Winter saw the delicate white petals it had been protecting, the aroma told her what this gift was. "A magnolia," she said, and tears glistened in her eyes as he presented the battered blossom to her. "Kwambu, I—"

"I picked it on our way back," he said when the sob in her voice thanked him more poignantly than words could have done. He waved a hand to indicate a town thrown into turmoil by weeks and weeks of war. "No one knows how long we must go on battling the Spanish," he told her, "or can guess how it all will end. Which means that it may be a long while before you and I will see our place of magnolias again. I wanted you to have this flower to remind you of our special place, and to remind you of how much I love you, and need you, and want you."

As he had pointed out, his whole body was liberally streaked with dirt and sweat. Twigs and truant leaves studded his tight-curled hair, and his fingernails were jagged and grimy. A long blood-encrusted scratch ran down his right arm, its twin decorated his left leg. And he was decidedly pungent; even the odor of dog dung could still be detected if someone sniffed hard enough. But to Moon of Winter, Kwambu was more beautiful than anyone or anything she had ever looked upon. Holding the magnolia so that its satiny petals rested against her cheek, she told him so. And he did not doubt at all that she meant it.

Together they went into the pavilion so he could visit with his sons and pay his respects to Saturiba's Principal Woman. But when Moon of Winter went to take reluctant leave of him so that he might go to the sweathouse, he shook his head. "I should have told you at once," he said, "that I am supposed to take you to your cousin and Saturiba. But I was selfish; I wanted you to myself for a short time first."

She smiled; it was good to know that their moments together were as important to him as they were to her. "What do they want with me?" she asked as they headed for the Principal House.

He shook his head. "I think I will let them tell you that," he said.

"This war path we are following has more twists and turns than a devious stag's spoor," Outina said ruefully as he made a small ceremony of seating his cousin across from Holata Saturiba. His deeply shadowed eyes were heavy-lidded and his black hair had become threaded with silver. It was as though the weeks since they arrived in this town had changed shape and swelled into years.

"And there are so few of us walking it," Saturiba said. He, who had been old at the start of the war, looked ancient now. Wrinkled flesh sagged from jowls that had not been apparent before, and the veins in his gnarled hands crawled like bruise-colored, bloated worms from wrist to fingers. "The Spanish offer Christianity to our people and—as though it were a new and delectable brew of sassafras tea—too many are lapping it up." He spat into his sister's cooking fire. "When the time comes for them to belch, they will discover that it is not so tasty as it seemed on the way down. Those of us who have already discovered its bitterness tried to warn them, but they would not listen. So there are only Outina's warriors and mine to send against the Spaniards, and I fear we are not enough to overturn the kettle in which the Christian tea is boiled."

His broad shoulders slumped, his chin rested on his chest, his whole attitude was one of dejection. His nephew, Emoloa, had been the first warrior brought to the berdaches' pavilion, and only the young man's mother refused to see that he was unlikely to leave it until death carried him away. And surely not a moment went by without Saturiba thinking of Emoloa's son, the boy whose head Menendez had threatened to cut off if Saturiba defied him. To ignore that threat must have been the hardest thing Saturiba had done in all of his long life, and it must have cost him as dear to see the pain in his sister's eyes when he explained that he must fight regardless, that to give in would rob their people of the freedom of choice they had enjoyed since the day their ancestors were created. How could Moon of Winter add to the poor man's misery by refusing to do what she knew he would soon be asking her to do?

But it was Outina, not Saturiba, who made the request. "Please understand, Moon of Winter," he said, "that both Saturiba and I are committed to what we are doing. But if you will look into your crystal, perhaps we can learn whether or not the final victory will be ours. If we can be assured that the omens are favorable, then we shall have something with which to repel discouragement." He smiled again, but his eyes were bleak. "Discouragement has lost more battles than cowardice," he said, "and is far more difficult to deal with."

Moon of Winter lowered her own eyes and wished she had never urged Outina to join forces with Saturiba, wondered almost angrily what had persuaded the pair to seek help from someone whose advice so far had been worthless. Yet she knew the answer to that: neither Outina nor Saturiba had any-one else they could turn to in order to find out what-would-be.

Oh, why had she ever been so foolish as to let people be-lieve she could glimpse the future? Her crystal, which had never, ever revealed anything to her, would do no better this time. And she had had enough of practicing deception.

"Moon of Winter." Kwambu's voice infiltrated her thoughts and she turned to look at him. "They do not lightly ask this fa-vor of you," he said gently. "They seek confirmation of the faith they have in themselves and in the men they lead into battle."

"But if my crystal shows nothing? Or if it cannot show me what they want me to find there?"

It was Saturiba who answered her. "We will understand," he said heavily. "We ask only that you try."

She could not bring herself to disappoint him, this former enemy of Outina, this legendary bear of a man whose teeth and claws were worn to nubs. She set the magnolia blossom on the mat in front of her, took her crystal from its pantherskin pouch, cupped her palms around it, closed her eyes and waited for the stone to come alive.

When her fingers began to tingle, she opened her eyes, un-covered the crystal, and focused both her eyes and her mind upon it. Noises from the compound—the piping of young voices, the birdlike sounds of matrons gossiping, the yip of a dog trying to dislodge a pesky flea—faded into silence, a si-lence that gradually filled with a muted hum. It was a sound unlike any Moon of Winter had ever before heard, a sound that shaped itself to the vibrations emanating from the faceted stone she held and drew her into a world where nothing existed ex-cept the crystal and Moon of Winter.

She saw nothing but that translucent stone, not even the hand it rested upon, for she was as distanced from the familiar as though a yawning abyss separated her from it. And it was not so much that she had retreated from the ordinary world, but that she had somehow been transported from the world she knew into the world of the crystal. The stone enfolded her, ab-sorbed her, until woman and crystal became a single entity.

When clouds began to form around her, she was not afraid. She let her heart's rhythm adapt to the hum that was the pulse of the crystal, and waited. The embryo clouds mushroomed, they billowed and surged restlessly, and still she waited—without fear—for what would come.

Her patience brought her reward. Slowly the clouds thinned, became fog, gossamer mist, disappeared altogether. Moon of Winter gazed upon a sky of sparkling summer blue, a sky from which a radiant sun smiled. Her heart, like the crystal's, basked in its warmth, and the hum was suddenly a song of praise, a hymn born of unbridled joy.

Then a ripple of white disturbed the blue at the outermost edge of the sky. It slithered across the horizon and wound itself into a coil, a coil from which a triangular head protruded. When unblinking eyes focused malevolently on the golden sun, the heart that was shared now by Moon of Winter and her crystal began to pound; the hum that was their voice became a scream.

But the vision was not over. The white serpent extended its sinewy length once more and—yellow eyes fixed on yellow sun—glided through a sky it did not belong in, could never belong in. And while those yellow eyes took the measure of the glowing sun, the life-perpetuating sun, the serpent's hinged jaws spread themselves wide, impossibly wide, menacingly wide.

Then, without haste, while its white scales glittered obscenely against the sky's healthy blue, the alien reptile thrust out its gaping jaws and swallowed the sun, swallowed it whole, stole all the light from the world.

Moon of Winter did not know she'd flung down her crystal, did not realize she had lifted her hands to shield her eyes. She was unaware of the fact that she had begun to tremble violently, uncontrollably. Only when Kwambu's arms went around her, only when he had three times shouted her name, did she awaken to reality.

"You had a vision, a true vision," Kwambu said soothingly as, gradually, her tremors ceased.

Unable to speak, she nodded, and wondered distractedly why her husband's voice was so thin and high-pitched.

The trader looked at the two Holatas. "She will tell you what she has seen when she can," he said.

And this time his voice sounded to Moon of Winter as it should, deep and musical. She uncurled her clenched hands, inhaled slowly and exhaled much of her lingering tension, then sat up straight. When Kwambu looked anxiously at her, she managed a smile, a small smile that promised him she was almost herself again, that soon she would be able to speak.

But . . . how to describe her vision? What to say to Outina

and Saturiba, who were struggling to contain their eagerness to know what the crystal had revealed to her?

The crystal. Confused, she looked around her, raised up enough to check beneath her. Kwambu reached out, plucked the stone from under the fringe of the mat Saturiba sat on, put it into her hand. "Can you tell us now what you saw?"

Outina leaned toward her, and Saturiba's age-dulled eyes were all at once shining with expectation.

"So long as each of you stands by the other," Moon of Winter said hoarsely, "the gods will smile upon your efforts." She cleared her throat, strove to put assurance into her voice. "In the end, the gods we have always trusted in will prove stronger than the God the white men brought here." She looked at each Holata in turn, saw how Outina's relieved smile restored youth to him, watched Saturiba's fierceness of spirit reassert itself. "Our gods are more powerful than their God," she repeated, "so our warriors must surely triumph over theirs."

She unfolded her legs, picked up her pale-petaled magnolia and came to her feet. Kwambu stood up also and spoke for the both of them. "My wife needs fresh air to revive her," he said, and led her outside to a spot where they could be alone.

"There is much you have not said, I think," he told her, studying her face. "Will you speak of it to me, Moon of Winter?"

If she were a truly strong woman, she thought, she would not share that horrifying vision even with Kwambu. She would keep it to herself, let her own hopes be the only ones to be destroyed. But she urgently needed to describe what she had seen, to have someone besides herself interpret it. After all, she was no wiser than she was strong; perhaps her interpretation was flawed.

"I lied," she said finally. "For the first time ever I was granted a vision, and I lied when I told Saturiba and Outina what it meant." In a voice so expressionless that it shrieked of tamped-down emotion, she told Kwambu everything the crystal had shown to her. "What I saw," she finished, "was a dark, dark end to the trail my people have been walking since the Beginning of Time."

Kwambu would not insult his courageous wife by trying to persuade her that the vision might have meant something different. Instead, "You did right to tell Saturiba and Outina what you did," he said soberly. "Since they have already decided to go on with this war, it was what they needed to hear. It would be cruel to take away their hope when hope is all they have left. And you could not be cruel if you tried, Moon of Winter."

She looked down at the blossom she held. Its petals were browning at the edges but its perfume was as sweet as ever. "What will become of us?" she asked unsteadily. "What should we do, Kwambu?"

He laid one arm across her narrow shoulders. "We cannot know the answer to that first question," he said after a moment. "Despite your vision, we cannot know exactly how long either of us will live, or what will happen to us, to our children, to the world we grew up in, during the years that are left to us. As for what we should do"—he hugged her to him—"I expect we shall do as we have been doing all along: live each day as it comes. In truth, there is no other way to live, vision or no vision."

Moon of Winter thought of the darkness, the featureless, fathomless darkness that had descended upon her crystal when the sun was swallowed up. Then she lifted the magnolia, breathed in its fragrance, touched her lips to its cool petals. She was no stronger than she had been when they came out of Saturiba's Principal House, but one thing she knew: she was strong enough to face the endless night that lay ahead so long as the man she loved was by her side. She did not need a vision to teach her that.

She looked into Kwambu's face and squared her narrow shoulders. And her smile, though tremulous, was radiant.

Chapter 46

Dancing Egret checked the position of the moon. More than half the night had passed since yesterday's sun dove into the restless waters of the gulf, and there was much to do before a new sun climbed into the eastern sky. For the third time she tested the fastenings of the bulky pack that rested against her back, and fingered the familiar pouch she wore at her waist to be certain her old wooden flute and the tiny carving of a raccoon were nestled inside. Crossing the room to where the upper rails of the ladder rested against the raised floor, she waited until her breathing slowed and quieted, then concentrated on the sounds drifting up from the plaza and down from the domiciliary mound.

The soldiers guarding the homes of the island's warriors continued to pace back and forth, but where their steps had been firm and rhythmic at first dark, most of them shuffled now. Studying the shadowy form of the Spaniard at the top of the mound, Egret noticed how he paused to rest every so often. From within the Headchief's house Swift Eagle would have noticed that also, and be preparing to take advantage of his guard's weariness. Eagle's mother, when she took him his meals, had kept him informed about the plan that was to be put into action tonight. The Spanish leaders had decreed that no one, not even his counselors, could visit the new Calusa, but there wasn't a force anywhere strong enough to stand against Quiet Lagoon. The priest and the captain understood little when she raged at them for thinking they could keep a mother from her son, yet when her angry words buzzed around their heads like a swarm of persistent wasps, they deemed it prudent to allow her entry.

A tatter of cloud wiped the moon's face, and Egret skimmed down the ladder and slid into the pool of shadow beneath her house.

"I thought you would never come." The words were breathed rather than whispered.

"I waited for the right moment," Dancing Egret said, her own voice no more substantial than a sigh.

Which Chattering Squirrel knew well enough. Just as she knew that, like her, Egret had been on the alert ever since sunset. Both had watched the flitting silhouettes of the maidens who had volunteered to go to the fort and empty the pouches they'd been given into the soldiers' wine kegs. Squirrel hoped earnestly that the men had sickened before the blatant seductiveness that gained the young women admittance reached its natural conclusion, but she was sensible enough to know that several of her friends were quite prepared for matters to turn out otherwise. However it had been, at least all of them had returned from their sojourn; an anxious Squirrel had kept count of their homecoming figures to be sure of that. As Egret had surely done also.

The darkness stirred, eddied, stilled, as a third person crept beneath Egret's house. Ysabel, of course. Squirrel smiled. She'd known it would do no good for Dancing Egret to tell Ysabel she ought to stay with her family tonight. The Spanish woman wouldn't hear of such a thing. *They will manage without me,* she had said. *My place is with you, Dona Egret.* She had reason of her own for wanting to have a hand in all of this: although many soldiers had laughed and joked with her when she delivered food to the blockhouse, others had pelted her with vulgarities because she had taken a Calusan man as husband. *As if he is not worth twice any one of them!* she'd said furiously. And her help had been invaluable. Who else would have realized that a disabling emetic could be produced by boiling excessive quantities of the same leaves that were used to brew ceremonial tea for Council meetings? Egret had thought of incapacitating most of the Christian soldiers by feeding them something to make them ill, but she hadn't been clever enough to know what plant or herb would serve her purpose. And it was no use asking Vision Seeker; these days, he was coherent only when he chanted his pleas to the gods.

Dancing Egret was thinking about the priest, also. Except for the smallest children, he was the only one not told in advance what would happen tonight. At first, she and her cohorts had fretted over how to spread the word to the rest of the townspeople without arousing the suspicions of the Spanish, but Brown Pelican had been right: to the soldiers, old people were not worthy of note. Elders of every clan had been approached with ease by Egret or Squirrel or Pelican and been entrusted with disseminating the news.

Even Vision Seeker must know by now, Dancing Egret thought, looking toward a Temple mound haloed by moonlight. The two oldest members of Calusa's Council had been friends of the priest since boyhood. Setting aside their lifelong rivalry, they had joined forces to fetch Vision Seeker tonight, and had been confident that they could persuade him to leave the island when everyone else did. *If not,* Twisting River had said, *Shark Fin can knock him unconscious with his walking stick, and I will sling him over my shoulder and tote him to a canoe.*

Leave the island. How that phrase echoed and reechoed in Egret's head, and how dreadful it made her feel. Yet, contrary to what she'd expected, no one had seemed unduly shocked when they learned that this was her plan. Even those who'd protested at first had come to see that it was the only way possible to thwart the Spanish. *It may be,* Dancing Egret had said when she'd first outlined her scheme, *that the Christians will leave after we have gone away. Why would they want to remain, in those circumstances? Perhaps we will be able to return someday, and rebuild.*

For there would be nothing left after the islanders fled the bit of land that had been made by Dolphin for their ancestors to live upon, nothing but causeways and mounds. This thought, more than any other, knotted Egret's stomach and assailed her with doubts. Was it really necessary to . . . ? She closed her eyes, told herself to stand tall and accept what must be, started when Squirrel suddenly tapped her on the shoulder.

What had alerted her niece, Dancing Egret would never know; some sharing of thought with her lover, perhaps. But just as Egret opened her eyes, Swift Eagle eased out of his house, leaped upon his yawning guard, throttled him, and sent him tumbling down the ramp.

The soldiers patrolling elsewhere on the mound, alarmed by the thudding of their comrade's lifeless body, looked toward the ramp and were promptly set upon by the warriors to whom they had been assigned. Knives flashed and clubs descended, and so synchronized were the blows that not a single Spaniard cried out before he died. Then, brandishing the few illicit weapons they had been able to conceal from the Spaniards, the new Headchief and his warriors descended into the square-ground and, as the eastern sky began to pale, crept toward the rear of the domiciliary mound.

The hand with which Squirrel had grasped Egret's shoulder tightened once, twice. "I am going," she whispered, and before Dancing Egret could stop her, she had slipped away to follow in the path of the warriors.

Egret dared not shatter the predawn silence that was their ally by calling out, and there was no time to go after her. The first faint lifting of the night brought the villagers, old and young, from their homes. Like wraiths, they drifted toward the outermost section of the causeway where the fishermen, under cover of full dark, had moored the canoes. Each family took with it no more than the adults and older children could fit on their backs, and in every case this included food and seed. Hordes of mosquitoes, come to feast now that the nighttime smudge fires had dwindled to ash, were stoically endured. No hand swatted the insects, no mouth uttered so much as a grunt of vexation; the people scratched the swellings that blossomed on exposed flesh and kept on walking. Even those youngsters most irrepressible during storytellings preserved silence.

So did the toddlers, although they had been roused so early from sleep that their steps were faltering. Egret put aside her futile worrying about Squirrel and the warriors, ceased to strain her ears for the first sounds of altercation from the Spanish fort. Bless Brown Pelican, she thought. It had been her idea to give dried plums to all children too young to understand what was going on. *The babies will have their mothers' teats to suckle,* she'd said practically. *If their older brothers and sisters have something sweet to fill their mouths, they will be quiet, too.* It was plain that Pelican had not raised ten children without learning from the experience.

Ysabel moved close enough to her mistress to murmur into her ear. "The boys, they are here."

Egret turned to see a score of youngsters, all of them carrying the long torches used to illumine the night during Celebrations. It was near enough day now for her to confirm that the torches' moss-wrapped heads were glistening with oil. Four of the boys, the oldest and tallest, held dart throwers besides, and the tips of the arrows clustered in the quivers on their belts were also wrapped in oil-soaked moss.

Ysabel hurried to the cooking pavilion, uncovered the hearth, and knelt to blow on the embers. When her right hand fumbled for the stack of kindling she'd cut the day before, Egret nodded, and the boys made a circle around the ripening fire.

Once again Dancing Egret concentrated on listening. The world was filled with birdsong as dawn's heralds greeted the rising sun, but no other sound came from the area around the Spanish blockhouse. And it was not birdsong she should be hearing from that direction if the warriors had succeeded in luring outside any soldiers not prostrated by the tainted wine. Could Ysabel's decoction have been potent enough to be fatal? Had it been drunk by every one of the soldiers, and by Father Rogel as well? This did not seem likely, and Egret dared not let the boys do their part if there was any chance that the warriors had found reason to deliberately postpone the battle they meant to instigate.

Ysabel, having resurrected the fire, was also looking uneasy, and Egret came to a decision. "Be vigilant," she said to her, "and as soon as you hear anything at all from the direction of the fort, see that the boys ignite their torches." She looked at the quartet armed with dart throwers. "Yours will be lit before the others," she told them. "As soon as they are, come after me and take up the positions you decided upon beforehand." She managed a smile. "The rest is up to you."

They were no more than thirteen, the chosen four, yet the faces turned toward her were suddenly not the faces of boys. In their narrowed eyes, in the firming of their jaws, they were men, men with a mission they meant to carry out regardless of cost.

Dancing Egret prayed that the cost would not be their lives. Even if the boys' parents could bring themselves to forgive her for such a thing, she would never, ever, be able to forgive herself. Then she set her own jaw and moved out onto a squareground that had lain deserted for some time. Most of the townspeople would have sorted themselves into various canoes; some would be well into the bay and making for the mainland river that would, if everything went as planned, serve as meeting place for the emigrants.

She was halfway across a plaza ringed with houses that were already taking on an air of abandonment when the early morning stillness was ripped apart by an uneven volley of gunshot. As her heart catapulted into her throat, the ululating shrieks of Calusa's warriors finished tearing the embryo day to shreds. Egret began to run, to run as she hadn't done since she was a girl. Behind her she heard Ysabel speak sharply, but what she said was drowned out by the chaos of sound she was running toward.

She swiveled her head, glanced over her shoulder. Four boys were bearing down on her, their faces decorated with purposeful grins, unsettling grins, and just before Egret faced forward once more she saw Ysabel snatch a blazing torch from one of the other youngsters and thrust it against the timbers that floored Egret's house. *Yours will be the first to burn,* she had promised her, *the first to send the message that the Calusa will sacrifice all they have to live free.*

Loyal Ysabel had kept her promise, but even had there been time, Egret could not have borne to watch flames gorge themselves on the house Shore Walker had built for her. She reminded herself of the hurricane that long ago razed the town. "What has been built once can be built again," she muttered; but she knew that, for her, this was no longer true. So she went on running, running, running, as much to escape the smell of burning wood and thatch as to reach the far side of the mound. The four boys drew abreast of her, sped by her, and now she followed them and their sputtering torches, leaped the small bushes they leaped, skirted the same clump of sea grape that they went around, plowed through and over brambles and stickerweed, plunged into brush so overgrown that the snaking branches of one shrub wound themselves around the multiple stalks of another. When she had come this way before, surely it had not taken so long. Was it the ominous cough and boom of arquebus, the distinctive clang of steel against stone and shell, the earth-shivering pound of booted feet and moccasined, that made her think she would never emerge on the far side, that she would never come upon the mayhem her imagination was so vividly depicting?

But all at once the domiciliary mound was behind her and, lungs bursting, she was fighting her way to a stretch of higher ground, to a place where Chattering Squirrel, both hands pressed against her mouth and eyes bulging with horror, was standing. And at last the whole ugly scene spread itself before Dancing Egret, making her think for a moment that the wind of memory had blown her back to the day her brother died. Once again soldiers and warriors faced one another, grappled with one another, all along the curving ramp; once again blood reddened grass the dew had not yet dried on; once again Captain Francisco de Reinoso, Calusa's slayer, stood near the top of the ramp, his expression gloating as he reveled in a plethora of new executions.

What had gone wrong? Ysabel had been so certain her potion would leave most of the soldiers weak as newborns. How had they recovered quickly enough to thwart the warriors' stealthy approach to the fortress? Spaniards with primed arquebuses erupted from the blockhouse, fired upon a group of warriors forging uphill toward the gates. As though a giant hand had picked them up and tossed them into the air, two warriors hurtled backward and landed in a heap at the foot of the small mound. The warriors' leaders, Prowling Panther and Swift Eagle, sprinted forward before the gunners could retreat into the fort, seized the nearest pair, hauled back their helmeted heads and slit their throats.

In that moment, four flaming arrows, sent arching from four different directions, struck the roof of the blockhouse. The planks that shaped it, tindery as all wood was before the rainy season could undo the damage wrought by the dry, welcomed the fire, embraced it, and four pillars of smoke ascended into the sunlit sky to merge with the spark-laden billows rising from the town. Egret pounded her thighs with fisted hands; another part of the plan had gone awry. There were no ailing soldiers to be driven from the protection of the fort, and had its burning been postponed, the boys need never have been put in danger. To think she had been so arrogant as to accuse her brother of inefficient planning. This was a terrible way, a soul-searing way, to learn that she was no strategist, either.

But if nothing else, the warriors were holding their own, and keeping the soldiers so busy that none could be spared to douse the fire that was diligently devouring the building's upper half, or to save from burning the chapel that was the dart throwers' next target. By the time Father Rogel fled the smaller structure, his booming voice preceding him as he demanded armed escort, its destruction was well under way. And the people who had gone to the canoes at first light were surely approaching the mainland by now; even Ysabel and the youngsters selected to fire the town would have reached the canal and be waiting for the older boys to join them. We have come so far, Egret thought. We have no choice but to go on.

She looked to where one of the thirteen-year-olds, head thrown back and hands on hips, had lingered to admire the results of his skill with a man's weapon, and she waved her arm to catch his eye and send him to the causeway. But he did not see her signal soon enough; a knife with haft and blade of Spanish steel flashed through the air and buried itself in his side.

Egret stifled a scream, sought frantically for the quickest and safest way to go to him. Before she could map it out, his three friends converged on him, lifted him from the ground and carried him away. Egret forced her cramped hands to unclench. Ysabel would remove the blade, stanch the blood, wash the wound with salt water, and bind it up. The boy would survive; he *must*.

A scream cleft the air, soared until it rang above the shouts and groans and shrieks of the men doing battle. But it was Squirrel's throat, not Egret's, that the scream had erupted from. Dancing Egret looked toward the fort, saw Swift Eagle locked in chest-to-chest combat with a burly Spaniard. The ground upon which the two fought was slippery with blood spilled from the slashed throats of the arquebusiers Eagle and Panther had slain, and even from this distance she could see that leather boots were affording better purchase than alligator-hide moccasins. Swift Eagle's right leg had shot out from under him, was bending at an impossible angle as his opponent transformed his considerable weight into weapon. Both women were watching when the bones in Eagle's leg snapped beneath the awful pressure; both women were watching when the beefy soldier wrapped both hands around the hilt of his sword and pinned the fallen Eagle to the ground.

Squirrel screamed a second time, a vibrating *"No-oo-ooo!"* that was both protest and lamentation. Then she tensed to move, to rush to where Swift Eagle lay. Dancing Egret grabbed her, refused to release her even though Squirrel was screaming repeatedly now, screaming that she would go to Eagle, she would, she *would*!

Egret shifted position and slapped Squirrel's face, slapped it hard. "They have killed your husband," she shouted when the girl's screaming stopped abruptly. "Will you invite them to kill your child as well?" Then, without allowing either Squirrel or herself to reconsider, she started to half drag, half carry her niece back the way they had come.

But Squirrel's screaming had reached the ears of a Christian soldier and drawn his attention. He eyed the departing women speculatively, calculated range, and sent his lance spinning after them.

The weapon fell a trifle short; instead of embedding itself in flesh, it struck a nearby boulder, sent chips and chunks of rock flying. The soldier shrugged, turned back to the real fighting.

He did not see Dancing Egret slump sideways as a wickedly pointed sliver of rock penetrated her left heel, did not see the shock on her face as she understood that she might not make it to the canal. And if she could not walk, what would happen to Squirrel?

That unvoiced question was quickly answered. The last of Chattering Squirrel's hysteria vanished when she realized Egret had been hurt. Biting down on her lower lip, she hauled her aunt upright. Now it was she who supported the older woman as they clambered through spiny underbrush and pushed their way between shrubs that seemed determined to bar their passage.

"I can walk, I think," Egret gasped as they staggered past a domiciliary mound wreathed in sullen smoke. "Let me try."

Squirrel kept a firm hand on Egret's arm as she stood upright and put pressure on her injured foot. "I can't think whether we should stop here and pull out that rock splinter or leave it where it is for now," the girl said anxiously.

Egret summoned up a smile of sorts. "I know no more about such things than you do," she told her. "But since I can walk, or at least hobble, let's leave things as they are until we reach the canal."

They moved on, Egret's senses so focused on ignoring her pain that she almost failed to notice the tears trickling down Squirrel's face. When she did, she paused and put her arms around her niece, wished they could be beyond earshot of the battle that still raged near the Spanish fort. How much longer would it go on? The plan had been for the warriors to engage those soldiers who had not been enfeebled by the purgative, but they were to fight only long enough to give the rest of the islanders time to disappear into the river glades. Then the men, having slain or thrown into confusion the Spaniards still left standing, were supposed to retreat to the canoes and take themselves to the glades, to the one place that would forever remain an enigma to people not born in this country. But now . . . Egret swallowed hard; who could say what would happen now?

"He did . . . die quickly. Didn't he?" Chattering Squirrel was making valiant effort to stop crying, but sobs punctuated her plea.

This at least was a question Egret could answer. "He did," she said quietly. "As both of us saw. And you will be able to tell your son that his father died a hero's death. That will be a good thing for our future Headchief to know."

It seemed poor consolation to offer, but to be reminded of the babe in her womb helped Squirrel shift her focus, made her move faster toward the place where the canoes were moored.

The pace she set became too much for the limping Egret. "I need to rest a little," she said when the throbbing pain in her heel had spread throughout her foot and sent tentacles creeping up her leg. "Go on ahead," she urged her niece, lowering herself to the first section of seawall they came to. "You know where the fishermen hid the dugouts. If you'll bring a small one back here and pick me up, we'll save time in the end. As it is, I can only slow down both of us." She was careful not to mention that there would be several long canoes moored alongside the small one, canoes reserved for the warriors. Why encourage Squirrel to wonder, as Egret was doing, if those dugouts would wait in vain for the men they were supposed to carry across the bay?

After Squirrel hurried off, Dancing Egret closed her eyes and let her shoulders sag. Prowling Panther had been fighting still when they'd left their vantage point. Would he make his way eventually to one of the long canoes? Or would Brown Pelican be a widow before this day ended? And Squirrel—must her niece mourn father as well as husband because Dancing Egret had somehow persuaded everyone that she knew what was best for them?

A seagull mewed as it glided over the water, and instinctively Egret opened her eyes and looked for it. But smoke made a noxious brown veil between her and the white bird with its black-tipped wings, smoke that taunted her, tormented her. A manatee and its calf rolled through the canal, surfaced long enough to let the sun nuzzle their wrinkled faces; Dancing Egret, who had never outgrown her fascination with the creatures, did not even notice. She only sat there and castigated herself, berated herself, and suffered a remorse that hadn't the power to change a single thing.

It was then that her dull and listless gaze happened upon a small pile of white feathers. Egret blinked, looked again, crawled to where the body of one of her namesake birds lay wedged between two chunks of coral. An arrow, a metal-tipped Spanish arrow, had brought the beautiful thing out of the sky, and it had been left to die here where black ants could crawl with impunity through its glorious plumage and invade its sightless eyes. It was Law that egrets were slain only by members of the ruling clan, and never without a priest conducting proper ritual beforehand. This poor thing had not been killed for its plumes or even—although the thought sickened her—to eat. The Spaniard had taken its life merely for the sport of it.

She hunched over the dead egret and all at once knew that, despite the mishaps that plagued it, the plan she had offered her people was their only hope of salvation. The Calusa could never share their world with men who, for no sensible reason, would destroy the loveliness that was a bird in flight. She laid her right hand, fingers spread, upon the matted down that clothed the egret's breast, murmured apology to its spirit, then gently removed two of its elegant plumes so that its death might not have been in vain. One she would give to Squirrel's child when he was born, to remind him of his heritage. The other? It had bothered her from the start that Kwambu, if ever he returned here, would have no way of knowing where the islanders had gone. Here was her means of leaving a message for him to find.

Opening the pouch at her waist, she took out the jay feathers the trader had given her as a parting gift and the snail shell she had brought back from the hammock on the day Shore Walker first spoke of love to her. That was the place she had suggested the islanders make for when they reached the river glades. Some of them would remain there and make it their home; the rest would eventually move on to other hammocks and be joined, perhaps, by people from the many Calusan towns and villages that dotted the southern peninsula and its islets. White Gull might even persuade the Tequesta to seek refuge with them. And from the depths of the river glades, warriors could fan out and harass the Spanish on both coasts, then melt back into that vastness of tree islands and sawgrass, jungle and swamp.

She leaned over the edge of the wall and worked loose one of the conch shells that faced it, a shell situated immediately above the one Kwambu always used to tether his trader's canoe. Then she broke off a length of thin vine and carefully tied together the egret plume and the snail shell. When Kwambu came back and found what she was leaving for him, he would know that his old friend had gone to the hammock where snails live in green-striped shells.

Dancing Egret fitted the busycon back into the wall and fastened the bluejay feathers to its protruding end. Then she smiled; Kwambu would never miss seeing those, and he would know at once to look behind the shell that wore them.

Would he follow Dancing Egret and her people into the glades? Even if he did, he would not stay there. Not when Moon of Winter and their children waited for him in Timucuan country.

Dimly, she heard Chattering Squirrel call her name, but she was suddenly so overwhelmed with grief that she could not respond, could not even lift her hand to show the girl where she was sitting. Not only had Dancing Egret seen the last of her home, of all that was left of her father and the husband she had adored, of everything dear and familiar, it was possible that—despite the blue feathers and the white feathers and the snail shell she had so painstakingly arranged—it was possible she would never again see the one person whose friendship had enriched all the years of her life.

Her throat tightened. A hot rush of tears pressed against her closed eyelids. Bowing her head, she let them cascade over her cheeks and fall like bitter rain upon the dry sand that lay atop the wall. Dancing Egret, the woman who had always scorned to weep, who had thought herself too strong to weep, made no effort to stem the flood. Only when she had no more tears to shed did she come shakily to her feet and signal to the girl in the small canoe—the canoe that would take them both to a place where their people would be free to live the way they wanted to live, free to keep their beliefs and their Legends undefiled. Which was all that mattered; towns can be lost and new towns built elsewhere, but if a people loses its identity, its uniqueness, they can never regain it. For the proud Calusa, that would be worse, infinitely worse, than annihilation.

Egret let Chattering Squirrel help her into the canoe, then picked up a paddle and pointed the little boat toward the future.

Epilogue

◆—◆

A detachment of foot soldiers, sweltering in metal helmets and breastplates, stumbled through reddish water reeking of decay, tripped over a welter of humped roots on which sharp-shelled oysters clustered. Surely it was a fool's errand they had been sent on; what civilized man could hope to track down the savages who had fled Calusa's island? That they must have crossed to the mainland was obvious; but where their canoes had taken them after that, who could say?

"The Adelantado, he was furious, yes?" asked a beefy man as he swiped at his face with a sweat-stained kerchief.

The Captain of Infantry who had been given charge of the detail grunted assent. Merciful God, but it was hot in this jungle. And summer was still some weeks away! "If his orders had been obeyed, the Indians could not have revolted," he said, using the tip of his sword to demolish a huge spiderweb. "Menendez is not a man who appreciates insubordination at any time; when it leads to so many of our people being slain . . ." He shook his head; tramping through a denseness of mangroves on such a day was no stroll through Paradise, but it was better than being assigned to bury the maggot-infested bodies of soldiers, or to pile up and burn the redskins who had also been found dead near Fort San Antonio.

And at least the trees were thinning out a little. Now the men could see mangrove seedlings gestating on the muck-coated rock that gave onto a vastness of yellowing sedge. But despite intermittent patches of sun-baked mud, despite the dryness that caused the mica-edged grass to rustle when drag-onflies lighted on a nearby clump, the persistent glint of water told the soldiers that it was ocean, not prairie, they had come to.

539

A young soldier shaded his eyes against the glare of the high-standing sun. "What *is* this place?" he asked.

The captain did not ridicule the awe he heard in the infantryman's voice and saw in the faces of his companions. "The natives call it the river glades," he said. "From what I have heard, this sea of grass stretches from here to the eastern coast, and for many, many leagues both north and south. No!" he added sharply as his second in command began to take a long stride forward. "That grass bites, amigo, bites worse than any mad dog ever did. Not only will it rip to shreds your clothing and your flesh, but you will find also that your feet are stuck fast in the foulest, blackest mud it has ever been your misfortune to encounter."

His friend stepped back hastily. "You speak as though these glades were alive," he jested, hoping his abrupt retreat had not been interpreted as cowardice by men of inferior rank.

A mosquito whined a warning before piercing the skin behind the captain's left ear. He swatted at it, listened to it complain as it zoomed away to rejoin a hovering swarm of the bloodsuckers. "You must have heard, as everyone has, of mountains that belch fire," he said when he had sorted out his thoughts.

His comrade nodded.

"Volcanoes," volunteered the heavyset soldier.

The older man scratched his mosquito bite. "They have life of a sort, those volcanoes," he said, "and the river glades, they are alive in the way that volcanoes are." He pointed to where a troop of mangy pines marked the existence of a hammock. Dirty-looking clouds cast eerie shadows upon them, monstrous blotches of purplish-brown that lay like funerary palls upon the hammock, the incredible expanse of grass, and the nearly invisible river that flowed from horizon to horizon. "The people we have been sent after might have hidden themselves among those trees," he said to his men. "Or they may be on any one of the hundreds of other small islands that I am told are out there somewhere. But even if we had a dugout such as the savages use, we might never be able to make our way even to the hammock we can see so plainly. Some will say that this is because—unlike those who were born here—we can never know where the channels lie in this sawgrass sea. Me, I think the river glades themselves decide who will be allowed to pass through them, and who will not. And I think that they would deny us passage."

"That is nonsense," his second in command said after a moment. And as the youngest soldier hastily crossed himself, "*Superstitious* nonsense."

The older man shrugged. "Perhaps. But even if we had a canoe, even if we could elude the serpents and alligators that lurk within the sawgrass, even if we reached that hammock and found there the fugitives from Calusa's town, what then? They have been named rebels, and we all know the penalty for rebellion. But I have no stomach for the slaying of women and children and old people. And I will not invite their ghosts to chase me through"—he gestured sweepingly—"a place where I have no business being."

His comrades, some of whom had looked around uneasily at the mention of dangerous reptiles, were slowly beginning to sense what their captain had felt since his own introduction to the glades some months earlier. Here, even the heat was an entity. The late afternoon sun decanted it upon the grass; the grass digested it, then fed it back into air made so heavy by the infusion that its lethargic ebb and flow was visible. Nor was the heat-impregnated air content merely to form a pulsating blanket above the sawgrass; it reached out sluglike fingers and wrapped them around human flesh, squeezed vital moisture from human bodies, turned the simple act of breathing into a demanding physical exercise.

"His Excellency will not be pleased if we fail in our mission," the second in command said hesitantly.

The infantry captain shrugged again. "I doubt that he expects us to succeed."

"The Indian woman he *married* is with the fugitives," the overweight soldier snickered. "Perhaps Menendez only wanted us to make sure he is truly rid of the shrew!"

"She has no place in his plans, regardless," said the captain. "Once the settlements he speaks of have spread throughout this land, once the Indian villages have all been replaced by Spanish towns, the savages will have importance only for the priests."

"I was in the north with Menendez," said his friend quietly. "If he has his way, the Indians will be forced to build the towns we Spanish shall live in and grow the food we eat. Perhaps that is the reason he wants those who escaped from Calusa's island to be found: as a lesson to their compatriots that the Adelantado's word is law."

The captain sighed. "I have yet to see a town—or anything

else—that has been built by men in their dotage and women and children. Besides"—he slapped at another mosquito, squashed this one flat—"Menendez's dreams of colonization might come true in the northern part of this country, but who in his right mind will ever want to live where we are standing now?"

The men looked again at the sawgrass sea that spread itself in front of them. As they watched, a ripple slithered through it, the trail of some errant breeze that none of them was fortunate enough to feel. Above the pine-capped hammock, a vulture drew monotonous circles in a sky from which the light was slowly fading; the clouds that, before, had seemed disinclined to bestir themselves, were beginning to swell and darken. What had been an uninviting vista at the start had now become subtly menacing.

Suddenly there came a sound that iced the blood of those who stood in a tight little group on the edge of the river glades, a screech that had no identifiable source but simply erupted from anywhere and everywhere all at once.

"*Madre de Dios!*" the fat man exclaimed, swinging his head from side to side. "Where is that poor woman? What terrible thing is happening to her?"

Most of his companions, also looking frantically to left and right, were as shocked and bewildered as he was.

"There is no woman," the leader of the detachment told them, turning on his heel as the sound came again. "That scream came from a panther's throat. And unless one of you wishes to prove his courage by tangling with the beast, I suggest we make for our boat and return to the island."

A flock of black-crested herons, squawking indignantly, flapped from their roosting place as he guided his men into the mangroves that stood between them and the shore. He muttered a curse as his foot slipped on a tangle of roots splattered with fresh, and odorous, guano. Not to anyone would he say that the Adelantado lacked the vision he was reputed to have; nonetheless, the idea of white men living in this accursed place was not dream, but nightmare!

Behind him thunder grumbled faint-heartedly. As if in response, the panther yowled a third time.

There was, perhaps, a hint of triumph in the sound.

Author's Notes

◆━ ━◆

The historical plot elements in this book were taken from chronicles written by, or about, the Spanish and French who explored the peninsula that later became the state of Florida. There is little need for an author to call upon her imagination when events that actually took place include Panfilo de Narvaez's cruelty toward Chief Ucita and his aged mother; Juan Ortiz's capture and subsequent adaptation to the Indian way of life; the battle between De Soto's soldiers and the warriors of Outina; the French abduction of Holata Outina and his son; the seizing of Calusa's promised bride by a Timucuan chief; the massacre of French Huguenots by Pedro Menendez, and his "marriage" to Headchief Calusa's sister. Even the "rain story" that convinced some of Florida's aborigines that Menendez's God must be all-powerful was described in one of the chronicles, all of which offered such a wealth of detail that I had only to order the events (telescoping occasionally to make a smoother narrative), then consider their possible effect on the natives of sixteenth-century Florida.

Hernando D'Escalante Fontaneda was also a real person, one who did not enjoy his fifteen-year sojourn among the Calusa and Timucua. In his *Memoirs* he says of them: ". . . They will never be at peace and less will they become Christians. . . . Let the Indians be taken in hand gently, inviting them to peace; then putting them under deck, husbands and wives together, sell them among the Islands. . . . In this way, there could be management of them, and their number become diminished." Fontaneda was not the only one to advocate such a thing. Pedro Menendez de Aviles, who founded the city of San Augustin (St. Augustine), recommended the enslavement of "recalcitrant" Florida Indians and their transportation to Cuba or other West Indian islands.

But what really happened to the aborigines in the years following the close of this book? Although by the early seventeenth century Jesuits had established forty thriving missions in Florida and Georgia, the two missions begun in south Florida (one on Calusa's island and another on the Miami River in Tequesta territory) were abandoned after the Indians took refuge in the Everglades. In the end, it was disease that vanquished many of the Timucua and virtually all of the Calusa, disease introduced into their world by those who came here from Europe and Africa.

And what happened to the explorers and would-be conquerors who brought those deadly germs across the ocean? Among those slain in the New World were Ponce de León and his men, Panfilo de Narvaez and nearly four hundred men, Hernando de Soto and more than seven hundred men (including Juan Ortiz). Of the twelve priests who accompanied De Soto, eleven did not survive the expedition. After 1549, clerics who came here—including Father Juan Rogel, who was brought to Calusa's island by Menendez—either died here or gave up and returned to Havana. And Don Pedro Menendez never did find the son he had hoped to locate in the land known as *la Florida*.

Apparently all of those who contribute to the making of legends must pay dearly for the privilege.

Kate Cameron
Florida, 1994

P.S. An interesting sidelight that residents of extreme South Florida will appreciate: In August 1992, when Hurricane Andrew struck with a vengeance we had not witnessed in twenty-eight years, I was working on chapters twenty-six and twenty-seven of *The Legend Makers*. Although my home is situated some twenty miles north of the truly devastated area, this is not the sort of firsthand experience I would recommend to other writers.

118
92
___
26

54A
318
___
806

By Kate Cameron
Published by Ballantine Books:

AS IF THEY WERE GODS
ORENDA: A Novel of the Iroquois Nation
THE LEGEND MAKERS